DAWN OF WONDER

Book 1 of
The Wakening

By Jonathan Renshaw

Cover art by Animmate
Scene sketches by Richard Allen

4th edition

Contents

Illustrations

Spoiler alert!
This table is intended as a reference, not a door for sneak previews.

Pronunciations

of the less obvious names and places.

Allisian—a-LIS-ian
Aedan—AY-din
Castath—CASS-tith
Clauman—CLAW-min
DinEilan—din-EE-lin
Dresbourn—DREZ-born
Kalry—KAL-ree
Kultûhm—kull-TOOM (kull as in full)
Lekrau—LEK-rouw (rouw as in now)
Liru—LEE-roo
Malik—MAL-ik
Mardrae—MAR-dray
Mardraél—MAR-dray-EL
Merter—MER-ta
Nymliss—NIM-liss
Orunea—a-ROO-nia
Osric—OZ-ric
Pellamine—PEL-a-meen
Torval—TOR-vil
Ulnoi—ULL-noy (ULL as in FULL)
Vallendal—va-LEN-dil
Wildemar—WILL-dim-ah
Yulla—YOO-la

The North-West Mainland

100 miles

N W E S

Lekrau

Orunea

Nymliss

Mt. Lorfen

The Mistyvales

Glenting
Crossroads

Tullenroe
Falls Harbour
Rinwold
Stills

Din Ellian

Stonehill

Lake Vallendal

Kultûhm

Thirna

Fennlor

Drumly

Verma

Mts

Castath
Port Breklee
Wenwood
Morren
Eastridge

Nueric Ocean

Pellamine

Eymnoeri

Vinterus

Alorem

Murkintel Sea

Gechlu Mts

Torburesh

Mardraél

Sulea

Krunvar

Chapter 1

Even the wind now held its breath.

A hush of anticipation swept through the trees, causing forest creatures to hesitate in their scratchings and birds to falter in their songs. The woods grew still as everything was pressed under a deep, vast silence.

It came from the east, from the mountain wilderness of DinEilan. It was like a swelling of the air, a flexing of the ground, as if some enormous power had been hurled into the earth hundreds of miles away sending tremors throughout the land.

Directly over a country lane, a young squirrel was clamped to the limb of an ancient walnut tree. Tawny hair all over its body now rose and quivered as moss began to prickle underfoot.

The deep, shuddering stillness flowed through the woods. In and amongst the trees, fur and feather trembled in a vice-grip. The squirrel may have lacked the words for what stole into its mind, but in the same way that it knew the terror of jackal teeth and the lure of high branches, a vague yet frightening awareness was taking shape. Somewhere, many miles distant, something was stirring, changing … wakening.

Then the feeling passed as swiftly as it had arrived and the squirrel released its breath and looked around. It lifted a paw and examined the mossy bark, sniffed, and turned quick eyes to the ground, to the leaves, to the sky – all in vain. As before, there were no answers to be found. It was the second time since winter that this alarming thrill had surged through the air, departing without a trace.

But something else now caused little eyes to dart and ears to twitch, something quite different. The leaves strewn across the forest lane were beginning to quake and shiver. Several pigeons that had been huddling on the ground burst away in all directions with a wild clapping of wings. For the squirrel, this was warning enough. It fled across the branch, disappearing up the walnut trunk and into a knot hole as if drawn by a string.

Before it had a chance to push its head out, a horse and rider hurtled around the bend, apparently unaware of the recent quieting of their surrounds. Hooves slipped on the moist surface, flinging up dark clods, but there was no slowing of pace – wide eyes and foamy flecks suggested that the pace had not slackened for many miles. The tall rider's green military coat whipped and snapped around him as he leaned forward in the stirrups, head close to the horse's plunging neck. In his fist, crushed against the reins, was a rolled sheet of paper. The speed, the foam, the clutched paper ... Anyone he passed by would have instantly read the look on his face: Please, let me not be too late!

———

A few miles up the road was the farm of Badgerfields. It held tumbling meadows working their way upwards in the early sun, sheep and cattle working away at the meadows, and an assortment of labourers who were engaged in something that did not resemble work at all.

Ploughmen whose harrows lay discarded in the fresh new earth were balancing on a fence for a clearer view. They were placing bets, grinning. On the far side of the river, a cart loaded with dead wood creaked to a halt. The driver scrambled onto the heap of timber where he peered out over a lush green pastureland, chuckled to himself, and dug his boots into the wood pile until he had a steady footing. This was something he was not going to miss.

All around, farmhands dropped their tools, and even the long grass, silvered and heavy with dew, caught the mood and leaned forward.

Everyone's eyes were fixed on an old stone bridge over the Brockle River. The walkway was narrow, the stones doubtful, the wall slippery, and there was a lot of air underneath. To the farm's adventure hunter who would give his name as Aedan and his age as almost thirteen – though he had only recently turned twelve – it was irresistible. It wasn't just the lure of danger, but something it afforded that was far closer to his heart – friendship.

Under a scruffy head and smudged face, there was no missing the eager young eyes that were bright with hope for the morning's project. Adventures, he had discovered, became cold and lonely things if he couldn't, at some stage, get friends to share them. And friends, even old friends, were never quite on the level of companions until they shared his adventures.

Whether or not the friends actually *wanted* to share them tended to have little effect on the outcome. Aedan had become an expert in coaxing and nudging – and perhaps one or two of those nudges might have been misunderstood as shoves, but they had been given with the best intentions. Everyone was always glad afterwards. Mostly.

It had taken much work and perhaps one or two improvements on the facts about the landing, but Aedan had finally convinced Thomas to attempt the dreaded jump. The images he had painted with his words were irresistible – the thrill of the leap, the wonders of soaring flight, the softness of dropping into water. Deep, icy, emerald water that clinked and rattled in the chasm below.

Thomas, after explaining to Aedan once again that he did not want to do this, and being assured in the most ardent terms that he did, finally conceded and lifted his shaking hands from the lichen-coated wall. He raised himself by unsteady inches until he stood wobbling on the cold stones a dizzy height above the river. The soft, pink skin on his back was alive with shudders.

Many eyes watched from various points along the sheer banks but only one other person was on the bridge. Kalry, a year older and half a head taller than Aedan, bit her lip as she glanced at Thomas and then peered beyond him, over the wall. It was a long, long way down.

"W – what if I land on a fish?" Thomas was staring past his toes into the hungry river. "These trout have got spines on their fins. If they are pointing up and I'm going down, it could be like the time I …" He turned a glorious ruby red and glanced over at Kalry.

When she smiled encouragingly at him, he attempted a careless chuckle, swung his arms, and almost lost his balance.

"Oh tripe!" he gasped, regaining control of his shivering limbs only just in time.

Aedan was getting worried. He had to help his friend past this remarkably creative pessimism. How did Thomas manage to think of trout fins?

"Fish always keep one eye looking up," Aedan said. "They think falling people are eagles, so they get out the way." He had a strong suspicion that this might not be entirely true, but it should be, which was almost as good.

Kalry's wrinkled nose told him what she thought of it, but he shrugged off the uncomfortable feeling. Disarming encouragement radiated from this short, scruffy boy.

Mischief lurked.

He tried again, "Once you're in the air it feels just like flying. The only frightening part is before you jump," he said.

Kalry frowned at Aedan and opened her mouth to speak, but he fixed her with a stare and shook his head. She narrowed her eyes, but held her tongue.

He was about to try the angle of "If you don't do this now you'll hate yourself forever" when he was distracted by a sound that drifted over from the main farm buildings.

The faraway pounding of hooves that had been steadily growing erupted into a harsh cobblestone clatter. He looked just in time to glimpse something pale and green flashing across the gaps between dairy, stables and feed barns. The last opening was broader and revealed a large grey horse and a uniformed rider. They dashed between labourers at a reckless pace. Instead of halting before the main courtyard rail, the horse actually jumped it and pounded up the fine lawn to the very doorstep of the manor house. Then the timber shed blocked the view.

Aedan's curiosity caught alight, but he stamped the flames down. Nothing could be allowed to distract him now. The interruption, however, gave him an idea, a spark of inspiration that matched Thomas for creativity.

"The rumours of lowland bandits or slave traders could be true this time, Thomas. This might be your last chance before you are made a slave for the rest of your life. Or beheaded. Or … or … locked in your room while our soldiers fight them for years and years until you are too old to make the jump without getting killed."

Thomas flinched. "You mean people can actually die from this jump?"

"Of course not. Even Kalry's done it."

"But you just said it would kill me if I was too old."

Aedan frowned and kicked the stone paving. "I didn't mean that part. It sort of sneaked in there without me actually wanting it." He glared at Kalry with an unspoken demand for help, but the girl's hazel eyes were now full of laughter. She shook her head and buried her amusement behind a tousled mass of sun-and-barley hair. Aedan had to soldier on alone.

"Think of it, Thomas. Once you jump you'll be one of us, one of the Badgerfields Elites. And … and you can have my second sling."

"Didn't you break it yesterday?"

"It could be fixed."

Kalry, the smile still lingering, held her hands up with a look that was really a soundless groan. Aedan was equally unimpressed with the strength of his arguments, but he was grasping now. The golden moment of decision was passing by, and it would not come again.

Just then a cloud drifted in front of the sun. Thomas shuddered as an inquisitive breeze explored his soft skin.

"I – I think I'll wait for it to warm up a bit first," he said. "Anyway, I want to know what's going on at the manor house. I can see lots of people running."

Aedan's and Kalry's eyes met, and something flickered between them. As Thomas bent over – the first of several careful manoeuvres in getting down from the wall – two pairs of hands reached up and provided the "encouragement" that they would later claim he had as good as requested.

The howl of terror that split the morning and echoed down the chasm would live on in Aedan's dreams for years to come, always bringing a sigh and a smile. The falling boy actually ran out of breath before he hit the icy river, allowing a theatrical pause before the sharp smack of belly and limbs. It was the loudest landing they had ever heard.

"Aedan, I think we might have killed him," Kalry said, her eyes on the frothy impact point far below.

Without a word, Aedan was over the edge and in the air, plummeting towards his friend. Kalry was not far behind. She was airborne by the time Aedan hit the water.

The river crashed up around him. He always said that cold water felt less wet, more like liquid stones. It certainly felt that way now as the brisk current jostled him downstream. His feet throbbed from the impact, and he'd forgotten to block his nose resulting in a stinging shot to the brain, but there was no time to worry over such things. The moment he surfaced, he spun around looking for Thomas.

Kalry landed about six inches away and gave him the best fright of his young life. By the time he could see again, she had taken the lead in the rescue of their friend.

"Kalry, you wind-brain!" he spluttered. "You – you could have made me shorter!"

Kalry laughed as she swam away with the current towards the disturbance in the water that was Thomas. He was gasping in snatches. Eyebrows raised almost to his hairline indicated that he was still experiencing the full force of the shock and the cold – the Brockle was a river born of snowmelt and hidden by forest until it rushed into the sun only a mile upstream. The two rescuers caught up and guided their friend out of the current onto a sandy bank. He crawled from the water in a series of desperate jerking movements.

"I'm going to kill you Aedan," he gasped.

"Kalry helped."

"Then I'll kill you twice." He panted and coughed up an impressive quantity of river. "I'm going to hang you and after that I'll skin you alive."

"You mean 'skin me dead'. That's what people are after you hang them."

If Thomas was impressed by Aedan's expertise in the area, he did not show it.

Aedan had made a solemn promise to his parents that he would stay away from the execution at Crossroads gallows a year ago, and had spent a year wishing he'd kept his promise. Finding himself where he did not belong was apparently a habit he had been born with. The memory of that day still made him feel like gagging, but he never let on. Instead, he wore it like a badge. It gained him a kind of morbid respect amongst his peers.

Thomas whimpered as he touched his belly. It was blushing like sunrise, as if he'd spent the day sprawled out on the sand and been scorched to a crimson perfection. Even Aedan winced at the sight, but he recovered quickly and leaned forward.

"So did you catch a fish?" he whispered.

"Aedan!" Kalry said.

Thomas glared, assembled his still-wobbly legs beneath him, and clumped away. He seemed to have forgotten that he was a mild boy and stopped after a few yards to cast a very dangerous look back at the guilty pair.

Aedan tried to look apologetic but then realised he didn't feel apologetic. He knew Thomas would thank him one day. Well, perhaps not quite thank him, but at least join in the laughter.

Or at least not scowl at the memory.

Though it hadn't gone exactly as planned, Thomas had finally shared the adventure.

When they were alone, he turned to Kalry, "Another successful mission for the Elites. Thomas is a member at last."

"I feel horrible," she said.

"It was good for him. He'll be happy about it one day."

"I think I'm going to feel horrible until then."

"Nonsense. Make him a pearlnut pie and he'll forget everything after the first bite."

"Will you help me search for the nuts then? They aren't easy to find this time of year."

"As long as it's quick – I want to see what all the fuss is at the house – and as long as you don't expect me to bake."

"We have to give him something nicer than the fall, so you won't be baking."

"Wind brain."

"Frog nose."

They let the bright spring sun dry them as they jogged over the hayfields towards the mysterious pearlnut tree. This tree, a curiosity known to the whole midlands, was unnaturally big – several hundred feet high, its smooth leathery trunk almost as wide as the hay barn. Every autumn it produced large nut-like seeds with a translucent milky flesh that Kalry described as a mixture of pecan nuts, honey and snow.

But there was more that intrigued them than the size and the magical taste of the kernels. In the last year something strange had happened. It was Kalry who discovered it by putting her ear to the trunk and listening as she often did. With a startled cry, she'd leapt away. But fright dwindled before curiosity. When she pressed her ear to the smooth bark again, her expression slowly melted into quiet wonder.

"It's sighing," she explained, "not in a sad way, but big and full with thoughts of delicious soil and warm sun and crisp, clean air that drifts high up where pearlnut leaves can tickle the feet of cheeky low clouds."

Aedan argued at first that it was just the sound of wind passing down the trunk the same way those hollow, eerie sounds pass down a chimney when the sky is restless and the house is empty. But then he too put his ear to the tree. It was quiet for a long time, and he was almost out of patience when he heard a deep rumbling breath that didn't sound much like wind and that made him think of soil and sun and air. Still, determined to prove his point, he stepped back to indicate the wind in the boughs.

There hadn't been any.

Since then he had always felt a slight quiver in his bones when approaching the tree, and he felt it again now.

But before he and Kalry had covered half the distance across the east field, their attention was drawn by William, the elderly but still-strong farm manager, who was engaged in a lively discussion with Thomas. William pointed to the manor house and the boy raced away. Then William spotted Aedan and Kalry and started running towards them.

"Now we're in for it," said Aedan.

Kalry was watching William. "I don't think he's coming to talk about the bridge," she said. "He's running. He never runs."

Aedan stopped. Kalry drew up alongside him.

"There's Emroy," Aedan said, pointing at a red-headed youth, "going like he's got a wasp in his rods. Hope he has. Isn't that Thomas's father over there by the sheep pens? He's running too."

Old Dougal was surging up the hill, limp forgotten, hands flailing about him as if attempting to gain some additional purchase from the air.

"Aedan," said Kalry, taking his arm. "Something has happened. Aedan, I'm scared."

"You!" It was William, bellowing as he came within range. Though his words were aimed at them, his eyes cast frantically about the perimeter of the farm. "Get to the house now! Keep in the open and move quickly!"

"What is it?" Kalry asked, but William was already bounding away and turned only to yell,

"Run!"

He was not a timid man, but the worry beneath his words was thicker than flies in a pig pen.

They ran.

William threw his voice out across the fields. From all directions labourers began hurrying towards the manor house, shaken from their stations like overripe apples in a wind grown unsteady – the first gusts of a storm.

Chapter

When Aedan and Kalry reached the courtyard outside the main buildings, they found a small crowd of farm workers gathered in fluttering nervousness. Dresbourn, the farm owner who was also Kalry's father, stood at the front of the crowd in earnest conversation with the stranger in the bright green military coat.

Half-a-dozen men were posted as lookouts, standing on the nearby roofs of hay barn, dairy and timber shed. The uniformed stranger paced before Dresbourn and called regularly to the lookouts.

Aedan was balancing on an empty wheelbarrow, peering over the heads that towered in front of him.

"Can you see what's happening?" Kalry asked.

"I think he's waiting for everyone to get here." Aedan said. He jumped down and they headed over to a cart that had just been loaded with hay. After some scrambling, interrupted by a series of sneezes, they were balanced at the front edge overlooking the restless gathering.

There was some reassurance to be found in the backdrop of the grand manor house. It was three storeys high with solid walls, heavy doors, and thick oak shutters on the windows. It could certainly be made secure, but in truth, it was no fortress. The peaceful midlands did not call for battlements or turrets.

Aedan fixed his eyes on the stranger who had most people's attention. He was an impressive man – tall, powerfully built, even intimidating, as could be seen from the fawning of those near him. Though his words did not carry to the back, his posture and manners told of great authority, an impression cemented when he turned from the lookouts to the swelling crowd with bold, intelligent eyes, eyes that caused most to find sudden interest in their shoes. This, Aedan thought, was no mere soldier. This was the kind of man the great histories were filled with, and he was here in the rural Mistyvales!

Aedan and Kalry leaned forward, trying to catch the spillage of several dozen conversations beneath them, but it was clear that nobody had the slightest clue as to why they had been wrenched from their labours – not that anyone minded. The two friends listened all the same, wild speculation being no less exciting than actual facts, and as there was nothing they could do to hurry things along, this seemed the best way to endure the waiting.

They made an unusual pair. Both were without siblings and had, by all appearances, adopted each other. Aedan was a short boy whose brown skin owed as much to sun as soil, whose clothes were constantly sprouting new rips and stains and never lost the smell of wood smoke, and whose eyes were either brimming with adventure or lost in deep musings that, when spoken, seemed strangely misplaced in a boy so small and grubby. The workings of his young mind were in fact so extraordinary that he was sometimes referred to as the Brain. Dorothy, who ran the kitchen and was forever pursuing his muddy steps with a mop, quickly amended this to the Drain.

What proceeded from Aedan's thoughts was a combination of boyish mischief and deductive genius. In superstitious circles, some whispered that he was unnaturally gifted – or tainted. The menfolk, especially the old soldiers with whom Aedan was forever discussing the wars, were repeatedly astounded by his knack for thinking like a seasoned military strategist. The women were appalled. Their efforts to direct his thoughts to milder, more age-appropriate interests and to steer his feet along cleaner paths met with absolute failure. He remained stubbornly battle minded and mud brushed.

Kalry, on the other hand, was able to share most of Aedan's adventures and yet remain surprisingly neat and clean, which in Aedan's estimation was more or less to miss the point. There was one part of Kalry's appearance, however, that was never neat. It was her hair. Aedan had once said that she could conceal herself anytime by leaping feet first into a hayrick. Unfortunately the implied comparison was a little too good, and after seeing the look on her face, he had never mentioned it again. The problem was that Kalry's hair was not that easy to tell apart from hay – it was a stubbornly untameable, straw-like mass that hung long and wild down her back. It fell in an assortment of braids, stalk-like shafts and rebellious curls. The whole effect of the wind-blown tangle was something that drew concerned pats from grandmothers and barbed teasing from children. Aedan secretly adored it, though he couldn't bring himself to say so. As he saw it, Kalry's wild hair was to her what coppery leaves were to autumn.

He spotted Thomas on the far side of the yard and was trying to gauge how angry his friend was when Kalry interrupted his thoughts.

"What's that mark on your neck?"

He stiffened. "Nothing."

"Was it Emroy? Does your father know?"

"I don't want to talk about it." After a while he glanced at her and recognised the soft frown he hated seeing.

But he couldn't tell her. Not about this. When a tree was being ruined from inside, the bark would hide its shame, at least for a time. Aedan had kept his bark wrapped tight. He wanted none to know, least of all Kalry.

But there was another reason he could not speak of it. When he had confided in Brice, the news had reached the boy's parents, and Aedan had been asked to stay away from their farm. He wasn't going to lose Kalry too. The silence strained between them and he began to feel very lonely.

"It's not that I don't trust you," he said. "The thing is ... well, Brice and I aren't friends anymore *because* I told him."

Kalry looked at him and at the bruise on his neck again. Her voice was gentle when she leaned over and whispered in his ear.

Aedan caught his breath.

She leaned back. "It's him isn't it? He did this."

Aedan was silent, his jaw grinding.

Kalry put her arm through his. "See, I'm still your friend, and I won't tell."

His throat bunched up tight and he felt pools forming in his eyes. It took all his concentration to keep them from spilling, to keep the pain inside. But Kalry would know anyway; she mostly did. And she held his arm fast.

The last group of labourers arrived, breathing heavily, eyes casting frantically around them. The stranger appeared to be concluding his discussion with Dresbourn and making ready to address the crowd.

"First to guess his origin?" Kalry offered.

"If you are prepared to lose," Aedan said, glad of the diversion.

"I won the last three, remember."

"Well I wasn't really trying my best."

"Who says I was? Let's both try our best this time, then there are no excuses."

"Deal." Aedan spat in his hand and offered it to Kalry who grimaced and brushed the glistening palm with a handful of hay.

"Boys are such barbarians," she muttered.

The stranger raised his hands for silence and the courtyard fell into a deathly hush.

"I am glad that you were able to get here so quickly," he said as he paced before them, his agitation all too obvious. "Your manager is to be commended for his promptness and efficiency" – he indicated William who acknowledged the compliment.

"I am Lieutenant Quin of the Midland Council of Guards. I have been assigned to the Mistyvales, to sound the warning that will soon be ringing through every corner of the midlands, and to assist in protecting our people. I am here to oversee and strengthen whatever defences are in existence. Sir Dresbourn of Badger's Hall has examined my commission."

In spite of his surging curiosity, Aedan felt himself shrink away at the mention of Dresbourn's noble title. He hated being reminded that Kalry was of noble blood. In the rural Mistyvales, social distinctions were not given much weight, but the potential for separation still haunted him. Dresbourn, however, did not appear displeased at this reminder of rank. He took a deep breath and puffed up – an unflattering effect for an already puffy-looking man – before closing his eyes and inclining his head, indicating that the lieutenant should continue. The man turned back to the crowd, shook his arms and straightened the green coat of his uniform.

"For the past thirty years, the central midlands has been unthreatened by Lekran slave hunting, especially the wind-flung areas like this. Rumours and warnings of slave traders have always turned out to be as empty as cargo holds in the wake of pirates. The consequence is that these areas have been softened by ease. We fear that this has now been discovered.

"Recently, one of our parties, while scouting south of here, sighted a Lekran slave convoy from a distance. Our men were outnumbered and could take no action, so they rode to the nearest town, Glenting, where they discovered that dozens of townsfolk had been taken. One here and one there as they became isolated. The slavers were swift, not one was seen, and not one captive escaped. We suspect that Glenting is only the beginning, that all isolated midland areas will now be seen as lagoons full of trapped fish."

"We should move to the town centre!" Dougal shouted in a thin, wheezing voice. "Keep the women and children in the middle. Reinforce the walls. Let them try take us there. We'll show these filthy Lekrans something they'll carry to their island graves!"

There was an outburst of agreement, disagreement, and a general din of nervous commentary. The lieutenant raised his hands for silence. When the last conversations had died away, he shook his arms and straightened his coat again, a shadow of annoyance or perhaps discomfort crossing his face.

"I am glad you made that suggestion. It is a good one, but in this case I think we are too late for that."

He paused to let his meaning sink home. The eyes that stared back at him were growing large and white. Men edged to the outside of the circle, grasping pitch forks and shovels.

"Yes," Quin said, nodding at them, "I believe they are already here, and unless I'm sorely mistaken, this farm will be the first target. It is the ideal size, and sufficiently isolated. If I am right, then travellers attempting to reach the town, even large groups of us, would make easy targets. On the road, the advantage is theirs. They are well-armed and highly trained. We would stand no chance.

"Sir Dresbourn agrees with me that the wiser move at this stage is to fortify the manor house until it looks like a sea urchin. My orders are to ensure that you do not make yourselves vulnerable, so I must insist that you remain here until guard reinforcements arrive tomorrow. Sir Dresbourn has already agreed to this. Do I have your cooperation?"

There was a murmur of agreement. After a brief conference with Dresbourn and William, Quin began issuing instructions.

Riders were dispatched to the farm's homesteads. Everyone was to be brought to the manor house. Livestock in distant fields was to be left for the evening; only the nearby fields could be cleared. Nobody was to move alone or unarmed.

Among the older listeners with longer memories, there were deeply worried faces, and some of the younger children were crying.

Aedan frowned and turned to Kalry. "Think it's real this time?" he asked.

"Never been real before," she said, "at least not in our time."

"Well, even if it's not another snot-in-the-wind story, I think we're safe here with everyone around."

Kalry sighed. "You with your snot and spit. It's no wonder you can't write poetry when your brain is full of ideas like that."

Aedan was about to say that he thought poetry the only repulsive one of the three, but Kalry pre-empted him. "Want to finish the game? I'm ready to beat you again." She grinned.

"Alright bigmouth," he said. "You go first."

"Only if you promise not to use my ideas."

"Promise."

"Don't! ... spit in your hand again."

Aedan lowered his hand and blew out his cheeks at this girlish silliness, then folded his arms with an almost-concealed smirk and settled back to listen.

For years, the two of them had been sharpening their uncommonly acute minds with games like this that intrigued yet baffled their friends – and even some of the adults. Aedan enjoyed the challenges almost as much as he enjoyed winning them, but it had been a while since he had tasted the sweetness of victory.

Kalry took a breath, glanced over at the lieutenant, and began. "I think his uniform is from either Rinwold or Stills. They are the only towns that would have such ugly fashions like the hideous pointed collar and the swallow-tail jacket. He struts like a rooster when he walks and he looks at us like those snobby south-midlanders who only pretend to like other people. And ... what was the other thing?" She narrowed her eyes. "Oh yes – and his accent is high. He says each word really carefully, like a man who has studied how to make speeches. None of that seems like backward Stills, so I say he's from Rinwold. What's your guess?"

Aedan was silent for some time. "I'm just confused," he said at length. "Every time I tried to settle on an idea he did something to squash it."

"You still need to put your origin down before we ask him."

Aedan thought again. "My first idea, and the only one that seems to work, is that he must live near the sea because he kept making boat and fish comparisons. I don't know what sea urchins are, but I'm sure you don't find them in the midlands. I'll choose something coastal and not too far north, like Falls Harbour."

"The sea comparisons ... Good point," she conceded. "I remember that now. We might both be right though. He could have grown up at the coast and moved away later, but if he did, he must have worked very hard to lose the western accent. Let's go find out."

They clambered and slid down the hay and dropped off the back of the cart under a small shower of straw and dust. Dougal had pulled the lieutenant aside and was whispering questions, nodding rapidly at the brief answers and then attacking with further questions. The lieutenant was giving all the signals – tapping hands, stamping feet and wandering eyes. He finally tired of the business, and while making a last reply, he spun on his heel and strode away, directly towards Aedan and Kalry.

The annoyed cast of his features changed as he saw the slender young girl with the warm eyes. He smiled.

It was only a flash, but Aedan had a sudden impulse to push him away.

"Lieutenant Quin," she said in her bellish voice, "can we ask you where you come from?"

The smile slipped and he narrowed his eyes. "What do you mean by that?"

Aedan was liking this lieutenant less and less. That was no way to talk to Kalry.

"We have this game," she explained. "We try to guess where people are from by using clues. I guessed Rinwold, and Aedan guessed a coastal town like Falls Harbour. Did we come close?"

Understanding eased his features, but he remained aloof when he replied. "Rinwold it is. I congratulate you. You are as discerning as your father. It is always a pleasure dealing with others of noble blood." He kept his eyes on her.

Aedan flinched. He had wanted to ask further details, but was only too happy when the man turned and strode away. He wondered why a soldier had bothered to find out who was related to whom.

"I don't like him," Aedan said.

"That's because he made you lose your fourth in a row," Kalry laughed. "And wasn't I right about his snobbishness? Wanted us to know about his noble blood too."

Aedan was frowning, lost in thought. "Kalry," he said, "if he hadn't been wearing that uniform, would you still have thought he was from Rinwold?"

"Well that's the point, isn't it? We're supposed to use all the clues that we have to lead us to a conclusion."

"I don't know. Maybe he got a good promotion through a friend, and he's actually spent most of his life doing something shady in one of the seaports. That would explain his bad manners. And there's something else about him. Something I can't put into words. Something that worries me. If this slave business actually turns out to be real, I don't think I want him in charge."

Kalry looked at Aedan. Her eyes had grown a lot more serious. "He did make a lot of sea comparisons, didn't he?"

Chapter 3

"Kal-ree!"

The courtyard was still emptying when Dorothy's voice rang through the commotion. She was, without doubt, grandmother to the whole farm, but the greying of her hair had not been accompanied by the slightest flagging of energy. There was enough wit and zest in her veins to match any of the young troublemakers. "Over here, my girl. Vegetables to be washed. We need all hands in the kitchen, even little ones. Aedan, you too, you mangy mud-vole – though you do look surprisingly clean this morning ..."

She stepped in front of him, hands on hips, a half-smile tugging the dimple in one cheek. "Been in the river, haven't you?"

Aedan nodded.

"A sad day for everyone downstream," she said, giving his ear a tweak as he darted past. She followed him, still talking. "Well at least you won't be able to leave my ingredients dirtier than you find them. Now don't just stand there looking at what has to be done. Hop to it before I give you something to hop about!"

By late afternoon, labourers armed with rusty swords and frail spears returned from the nearby fields. In the manor house, belongings and weapons cluttered the floor in every room. Fireplaces were set to work against the air that had turned cold. Salted pork, preserved figs, and bowls of nuts were brought out from the larder to ease the waiting while a thick mutton-and-vegetable stew began to weave heady aromas through the house.

Dorothy's cooking was legendary. It had once been said that she could turn soil to cake. William, her husband, had remarked

24

that he could achieve the reverse, earning himself a sharp smack with the rolling pin.

The men had gathered in the main hall and were now discussing shifts of three groups that would be rotated through the night. Aedan, eager to know how the defences would be arranged, was listening intently to the scraps of talk that carried through to the kitchen where he was still imprisoned. He heard the outer door open and William's voice, usually so bold, was deferential as he explained the new idea to whoever had entered. Aedan guessed that it had to be Lieutenant Quin.

"I appreciate that you have been so proactive" – it was definitely Quin – "while I have been scouting the surrounds. But from what I see, the manor house is strong and well situated. Such precautions as you suggest would be excessive. Remember that these are slavers who rely on speed and stealth, not force of numbers, so the gathering of this many people would, by itself, ensure safety. When weathering a storm with all sails down, the greatest enemy is panic. We can all relax, trust me. Situations like these are my daily occupation."

From the responses, it was clear that everyone approved. It eased the tension considerably. Soon the house began to fill with talk and laughter as bellies were filled with an ample supper.

Dorothy found out about the morning's business at the river and punished the two miscreants by sending them back to the kitchen to clean the dishes. Aedan was hopeless. He started by washing and handing the crockery to Kalry to dry, but what she received was a stream of wet, dirty plates.

"Aedan! You wash dishes like you're worried about getting infected by them."

"Washing dishes is disgusting." Aedan was trailing the cloth over a plate, clearly trying to keep his fingers dry.

"You play with slugs and dung beetles, use horse droppings for target practice, and spit in your hand."

"So do you."

"I don't spit in my hand."

"Washing dishes is still disgusting," Aedan grumbled. "All those things are clean dirt. This job is just revolting. Anyway, *you* hate it just as much as me. I've heard Dorothy moaning at you and calling you back to clean properly lots of times."

"Well at least I do my washing quickly, even if it isn't perfect. Here, let me wash. You can dry."

"Fine."

The new arrangement worked far better and it wasn't long before they were finished, leaving a pile of almost clean, completely wet dishes on the counter. Aedan draped the cloth over the top to reduce the chance of someone noticing and calling him back to dry them properly. If Kalry had noticed, she was saying nothing. She had never cared much for these mundane chores. Storybooks, sketchpads and fireside conversations had far too strong a grip on her affections and drew her away more than Dorothy thought acceptable. But the old lady was not here now and Kalry wasted no time heading for the door.

Aedan lingered, hovering at the gap between the heavy shutters that looked out towards the forest. He willed his eyes to travel into the foggy darkness gathering behind the boles of elm, sycamore, oak and hornbeam.

Nymliss was a forbidding forest even in daylight, a dim world of ancient things and terrible secrets preserved only in folklore. At least that was what the folklore said. But the stories were not without effect. Few dared enter the forest, and those that did were mostly shunned, the superstitious folk marking them as tainted by the feared darkness within. Aedan had never bothered himself with such ideas, and as the son of a forester, had been quite at home tracking, exploring, hunting, and wandering freely under the leafy roofs.

What he had found in there had not entirely convinced him that the folklore was wind and smoke. There was something about the forest that demanded his respect, though what it was he could never decide. And ever since that peculiar storm, he had felt as if there was something whispery about Nymliss, almost awake, not in a haunting way but as if it were more alive than before.

Now, however, what he imagined in the deep shadows had a much clearer shape and intent.

"What is it?" Kalry asked.

"None of this is making sense. Something is wrong."

"Wrong with what?"

"The way everyone is acting. It seems like a party. Look at the forest, Kalry. You could hide an army there, fifty yards from this house, and nobody would know. The lieutenant worked so hard to convince us that the slavers are real. He made sure we went to all the hassle of staying here for the night, but now he seems more worried about the hassle of too many sentries than about slavers.

He doesn't realise that with us all here at the edge of the forest we could be in even more danger. I know how easy it is to hide behind the trees."

Kalry smiled. "You always look at things differently, like you're climbing onto the roof to get a better angle while everyone else looks from the ground. Let's get William in here. You should tell him what you just told me." She waved her arms from the doorway until she caught the manager's eye and beckoned him with a smile full of honest affection. A moment later, William walked in. Aedan had never grown used to how tall and impressive the man was up close. Most in his position would have retired a dozen years earlier complaining of exhaustion, but even into his seventies William's strength was formidable and he seemed to have little interest in setting any of it aside. A smile drew the wrinkles of many good years into their best arrangement.

"Yes, you young miscreants? What mischief are you brewing now?"

Kalry told him that Aedan had something he needed to hear. The man turned a patient look towards Aedan who unloaded his worries.

William smiled when the explaining was done. "Ah, the imagination of youth. In some ways I envy you, Aedan. Leave this matter with me. I promise you I will keep my eyes wide open, but I don't think you need to be worried. I know you have a way of understanding military matters, but remember that I've actually served in the field – and this lieutenant, he impresses me. The labourers I sent into town earlier saw him on the road this morning, said he rode like a tiger was after him. A less responsible man might have spared himself and his horse. There is no question that he has our best interests at heart and I believe he has made the right decision under the circumstances – nobody is going to attack a sturdy building like this when it's full of armed men."

Aedan scrunched his mouth in thought. William had a point, and William was no stranger to battle.

"Set your mind at rest, Aedan. We are safe here. If your wild thoughts persist, all I ask is that you don't spread them. It is very important that everyone stays calm. We don't need the madness of fear in these closed quarters. I've seen what that can do." He put a finger to his lips, looked at the children, and held their eyes until he was sure they understood him. Then he ruffled their heads with grandfatherly gentleness and left.

Aedan wasn't quite sure what he felt. At least part of it was relief. But there was something in his mind that wasn't quite settled, like dry leaves shifting with the careful movements of a little unseen creature.

He and Kalry left the kitchen and slipped into a crush of bodies that filled the central hall. The rich teak and red-oak furniture had been moved against polished stone walls. Fine paintings, a dozen pairs of antlers and as many bearskins hung all the way up to the high vaulted ceiling. Kalry had always thought the room too big. "It's so un-cosy you may as well be outdoors," she had once told Aedan. Everyone else considered it a magnificent hall, the pride of one of the midland's finest homes.

Because they were unable to see over the crowd, they did not notice Emroy until it was too late. As they lurched out into the clear, there was no chance of pretending not to recognise him and ducking the other way.

"Stink!" Aedan grumbled loudly enough for Kalry to hear.

Emroy had cornered Thomas in what was clearly an unpleasant conversation. Both boys looked up as the two arrivals stumbled out from the press of bodies.

"And here he is," Emroy called. "Ha! Aedan, you really have a way of rubbing people's noses in it, don't you? I would simply have named Thomas a coward, but you had to go and demonstrate it."

The boy was three years older than Aedan and much bigger. He stood a good foot taller and looked down at a steep angle. But apparently this was not intimidation enough and he stepped so close that he was almost looking directly down through the half-dozen wiry hairs that had recently sprung up on his chin.

"Are you planning to kiss me?" Aedan asked.

"No." Emroy wrinkled a pimply nose.

"Then why are you standing so close?" Aedan's tone was perfect innocence. Emroy bristled and stepped back while Kalry hid her grin with a hand.

"Who told you Thomas was a coward?" Aedan asked.

"I don't need ten-year-old children to tell me what's obvious. I can read people, Aedan. I can tell that you are a fool."

"Well, you can't tell that I'm almost thirteen, and a moment ago it looked like you couldn't tell I was a boy, so I'm not too worried."

Emroy's spotty cheeks flushed and he raised the head of a fine ivory cane in dramatic warning. Nobody paid it much attention because he wearied everyone so by constantly drawing their eyes to this mark of rank.

"What makes you think I demonstrated that he's a coward?" Aedan asked.

"The bridge, fool. Or have you forgotten? He couldn't make the jump. You had to shove him. Everyone's talking about it." He ended with a flourish of his cane and settled down to stroking his chin hairs and smiling a condescending smile.

"How many times have you made that jump?"

Emroy looked aside as if distracted by something on the other end of the room. "Hundreds," he mumbled.

"Has anyone ever seen you do it?"

"Of course."

"Who?"

"What does that have to do with it? I wasn't looking for spectators."

"You're a stinking liar and you know it," Aedan said, shaking his head.

"How dare you accuse me!"

"You just accused Thomas of being a coward and you called me a fool. That makes us even. But remember that Thomas got up on the wall on his own. That is the worst part, and the most difficult. We all know that you never got that far. He's not the coward. You are. You're embarrassed that he has more nerve than you."

"You're lucky we're in Dresbourn's house, else I'd teach you all a good lesson," Emroy growled. He began counting them off, pointing the head of the cane at each of them in turn. When he included Kalry, Aedan slapped it aside and stepped in front of her. Something in his eyes had changed. Even Emroy drew back a fraction, though he recovered well, obviously remembering that he was a good deal bigger.

"Emroy, please don't be like this," Kalry pleaded.

Aedan's way of dealing with these confrontations she so hated was quite different. Where she would try to douse the flames, Aedan would catch alight and fight fire with a hotter fire.

"I know the lesson you mean," he said, glaring at Emroy. "The bigger you are, the more rubbish you're allowed to talk, and if anyone says you are wrong, you'll prove that you're actually right by hitting them. That's what rubbish-talkers mean by proof."

Emroy's jaw clamped and he moved towards Aedan, but he couldn't demonstrate his "proof" here, and he had already been accused once of preparing for a kiss, so he turned and stamped away, shoving an inconsiderate path through the crowd.

When he was gone, Aedan wondered aloud if the slavers would take requests. Kalry smacked him over his scruffy head and Thomas pulled a wry grin.

"We intended to make you a pearlnut pie," Aedan said to him. "It was all this business about slavers that spoiled our plan."

"Was that going to be your way of saying sorry?" Thomas asked.

"It was meant to be congratulations. We are still impressed that you got as far as you did. Nobody else ever stood on the wall and swung their arms before."

Thomas smiled. There was no anger left there. He was never much good at being angry – his soft features looked uncomfortable and drawn out of shape by hard expressions. Even when something did rouse his ire, he lacked the stamina for holding resentments.

"Pity," he said, "I could have done with some pearlnut pie. As long as Kalry was going to make it and not you."

Aedan laughed. "I feel exactly the same."

As he glanced around he noticed the Lieutenant in the far corner. Something irked him about the way the man's eyes were moving over the people in the room. Kalry was right about one thing – he certainly considered these people beneath him.

Finding the hall stifling, they climbed the stairs to Kalry's room. It was colder on the upper floor, but there was a fire going in the hearth. It revealed a spacious and relatively messy room – cushions and books and sketchpads and flowers collected from the fields were scattered liberally.

"Where's Dara?" Kalry asked.

"I'm sure she's tucked herself away in the quietest corner," Thomas said. "Think like a mouse and you'll find her."

Kalry disappeared and returned a short while later with the mouse-mannered, doe-eyed girl in tow. She was the youngest of them, only nine, but her small frame and timid appearance made her look six. It was deceptive though. She was not as timid as she looked. Aedan braced himself when he noticed that there was still something smouldering there. She fixed her eyes on him and stood stiffly against the doorpost. In the way of anger and resentment, she was Thomas's perfect opposite.

Thomas looked up at her. "I forgave them," he said. "They wanted to make me a pie to apologise, but they did a good job of chasing Emroy away instead."

"Ooh, I hate that boy!" she said, and then blushed at the fierceness of her outburst.

"Come sit," said Kalry, as she settled on the large rug before the fireplace that was humming with bright flame. The rug was where they always sat. As Aedan had put it, chairs made them feel like they were still half standing. Dara dropped down beside her friend and began braiding the rug's long woollen tufts, while the boys took turns with a pair of fire irons, balancing chestnuts over the coals for roasting.

A sound drifted through the window from the dimness of a wet and early dusk. It was the song of a rainbird, clear against the silence of all the other forest birds that would be tucking themselves into their feathers and hunching up under dripping leaves. Aedan listened and heard the soft pattering of rain. One thing he shared with the singing bird was a love of rain and especially of storms. He always felt a deep thrill of awe when the pale sapphire cloaks of sky were flung aside and dark raging heavens roared and plunged and cast fire and water and ice upon the earth.

Something landed on Kalry's shoulder and nuzzled against her neck.

"Hello Skrill," Dara called. She reached for the young forest squirrel, plucked it from its roost and nestled it in her arms where the fluffy creature settled and began to clean itself. Dara made a little tent over it with her long brown hair. "I hope you've learned some manners," she said. "If you poop on my frock again I'm going to shave your tail."

Aedan grinned. He had found the little animal, weak and abandoned, after a violent storm. Since he was already looking after a fledgling woodpecker at the time, Kalry had kept the squirrel.

The fire was the only light in the room and it threw out a dancing radiance charged with the magic of stories beautiful and terrifying. Appropriately, Thomas had found Kalry's book of original stories on the rug and was struggling his way through the letters now.

"Is that a new story?" Dara asked him.

"Yes. I think you'll like this one."

"Oh, please read it aloud."

Thomas handed it to Kalry. If he were to read, it would be one laborious word at a time.

Aedan had half wanted to air his concerns again – at least they would make for an exciting discussion. But he wasn't so sure about them now, and William's warnings were never given idly. What finally made him drop the idea was his co-author's pride when his eyes fell on the book. Dara shifted a little closer to the fire as Kalry placed the book in the warm light.

"It's just the first bit," Kalry said. "We decided to turn our old quest for the silver dwarf's hideouts into a proper story, so we made a start on it yesterday. This is how it begins …

In the most secretish and magical places, the silver dwarf makes his home. But he never stays there for long and that's because he is always looking for the one he lost long, long years ago. It all began many hundreds of years before.

He was only a little dwarf boy when he accidently cornered a young moon-scaled river maiden. She was terrified that he would drive her to the shore and knock out her teeth (because everybody knows that the teeth of these river maidens are the most perfect pearls) but the dwarf stepped aside instead. She was so surprised at his kindness that she stayed and talked with him. They soon became very good friends and met whenever pure starlight fell on the shivering crystal waters of the Brockle.

But one day a vile and ugly serpent slid through the river behind her while they talked. The dwarf saw it but he didn't have time to warn her so he leapt towards her with his knife raised so he could strike the serpent but she never saw the serpent and both of them (the river maiden and the serpent) dived away and vanished into the darkness of the water never to be seen again.

From then and forever onwards he spent his days searching for her so he could explain what really happened, and also to avenge himself on the serpent by challenging him to mortal combat and hacking him into tiny little bits and feeding them to the crows.

Aedan glowed with pleasure at his relatively obvious contribution. Still, he thought, there wasn't nearly enough blood and glory there. He would have to put in a lot more monsters and battles as they continued with the tale. That was what any decent story needed.

"Where is the silver dwarf now?" Dara asked.

"The last signs we found," said Kalry, "were on the west bank of the Brockle under a hidden patch of shady ferns where the light is dim and mystical."

Dara's eyes grew large. "Will you take me there tomorrow?"

"Of course."

"It's going to be so much fun. I can hardly – Oh Skrill! Not again! Yuck. Here Kalry, you take him."

When the little crisis was over, the girls continued discussing plans for the expedition and the pursuit of the little magical being.

Aedan and Kalry had invented the legend of the silver dwarf when they were five and six. Over the years, they had explored every corner of Badgerfields and all the shadowy valleys, wind-buffeted hills, dreamy woodlands and secret forests they could reach, hunting for enchanted places marked with tiny boot prints and dwarf-sized shelters.

Aedan had never felt embarrassed about his imagination. Without it there was no magic. Whether or not they actually found the silver dwarf wasn't important. The magic was in searching their whole world, lost in the wonder of it all. Without imagination, things were only as they appeared – and that was blindness. Things were more than they appeared, so much more. When he considered an oak tree, it was not just a tree. To someone small, like an ant, it was a whole landscape of rugged barky cliffs and big green leaf-plains that quaked when the sky was restless, a place of many strange creatures where fearsome winged beasts could pluck and devour someone in a blink.

And it wasn't just about magic. Without imagination, one could not think very far into things, like that Lieutenant. Without imagination, he was no more than he said he was. But there was more to him …

It brought Aedan back and he decided, warning or not, he was going to pour out his doubts. Before he could begin, though, Thomas asked if they had played their origins game.

"We did," said Kalry.

"And?"

"He says he's from Rinwold."

"So who won?"

"She did," said Aedan. "Again."

Kalry frowned. "I'm not convinced I did. Aedan said some things about him that kept me thinking all day. Thomas, have you noticed anything odd about him?"

"He's very impressive, almost frightening. But he's a strange kind of man, that's for sure. Not one with a lot of sense neither. I saw him take his coat off as soon as he was done with talking, even though the wind blew winter back for the day. Said he didn't feel the cold, but there was gooseflesh running all over his neck and arms."

The silence lasted only a few heartbeats before Aedan gasped and leapt to his feet.

"Kalry! Kalry, we need to speak to your father. Now!"

Chapter 4

The chill wind that had been rising through the early evening had brought a thick, soupy mist. Aedan slipped back past the lone sentry into the house, teeth chattering.

"He's not in the courtyard. Could he be in his study?"

"If he is, it would definitely be a bad idea to go looking for him," said Kalry. "He doesn't like to be disturbed when he's there."

"Can we afford to wait?"

Kalry bit a fingernail. Aedan had told her in a torrent of thoughts what he feared, and the dread was clearly growing in her mind. "No," she said. "I don't think we should. But this might not go well."

They had to step carefully now as they passed back through the hall, over and around makeshift beds on which some of the children had already fallen asleep. The passage leading to the study was dark, but they felt their way easily enough with a hand brushing each wall – though Aedan could not quite reach both at the same time. There was a section of the passage where the floorboards were loose; they clattered like falling tiles under even the stealthiest tread. Light poured out from beneath the closed door at the far end of the passage. Dresbourn would be within. Aedan felt his stomach shrink and the blood begin to rush in his ears. He hated these meetings.

Kalry knocked.

"Who is it?" The voice was terse.

"It's me, Father," Kalry replied.

"Come in."

She opened the door into a large room, richly carpeted and lit with several lamps. The walls were lined with shelves that held more bronze and silver bookends than books. As in the hall, expensive paintings and large sculptures stood proudly, displaying their owner's financial success and social status. There was a large teak desk on the far side of the room where Dresbourn, swollen even larger than normal in a rich fur coat, sat opposite Lieutenant Quin.

Not for the first time, Aedan wondered how such a man with his puffy cheeks flanking a self-important little chin, haughty brow, and turned-back arrogant nose could be Kalry's father. Her mother must have been a princess. Not wanting to stare, lest his thoughts be revealed, he dropped his eyes and noticed a long scroll that lay unrolled between the two men. He had a feeling he was trespassing there and he looked up again, uncertain, from Dresbourn to Quin. There was no welcome in either face. Dresbourn's raised eyebrows had grown distinctly colder on noticing Aedan.

"This is the same boy I saw with your daughter earlier," said Quin. "Is he noble too?"

"Aedan?" Dresbourn said, with a short humourless laugh. He regarded the scruffy boy as he would a porker on display at the farmer's market. "Not as we understand it. He's a notch above the local commoners thanks to his mother's line and the education she's given him, but his father more or less nullifies that."

Aedan stood silent, too intimidated to be offended.

"Well, Kalry," her father continued. "What do you want?"

She cleared her voice and tried to clear the look of distress from her face as she pulled her eyes away from Aedan. "We wondered if we could speak to you," she said. "It's really important."

"Make it quick."

Kalry looked at the lieutenant and then at Aedan, unsure.

"Actually," stammered Aedan, "we need to talk to you alone."

"Children," said Dresbourn, standing so suddenly that the desk lurched and a quill toppled from the ink jar, "I do not have time for your games now, and I am embarrassed that you would insult a guest, a man of rank and breeding. Kalry, I have raised you better than this."

"It's perfectly alright," the lieutenant interjected. "We can resume the discussion later. It so happens that this would be a good time to check on a few things." He left, closing the door behind him. Dresbourn did not sit immediately. When he did, he leaned back in his chair and levelled his gaze at Aedan. It was that heavy, withering look that demanded an explanation while making it clear that anything said would be considered an impertinence; it was a look that, if cast about the farm, would cause young shoots to turn around and dive back into the earth.

Whenever Aedan explained his thoughts to Kalry, her unfeigned enthusiasm was like summer's rain and shine – his ideas burst into life, growing surer with the telling. But her father's wintry intolerance never failed to shrivel the words on Aedan's tongue. Dresbourn's look did more than expect disappointment, it demanded disappointment, and reaped it every time.

Aedan tried to swallow but his mouth was too dry. Eventually he found his voice hiding somewhere back in his throat and hoped, as a hundred times before, that he might sound convincing.

"We think he's lying," he said. It came out like an apology. He saw Dresbourn's jaw clench, but decided to press ahead while he still could. "His jacket doesn't fit him, that's what gave him away. It's why he didn't wear it even though it was cold. Probably pinches under his arms. It's not his jacket. I think he stole it from the real Lieutenant Quin on the way here. If what he says is true – about slavers being in the area – then I think he's one of them."

The room fell silent.

The awful words hung in the air.

Dresbourn tilted his head back and released a tired breath, disinterested eyes looking down at Aedan. He said nothing. Aedan knew that tilt all too well; it had always made him feel like a liar even when telling the truth. He would not be endured much longer. He tried again, his voice sounding thinner,

"The lieutenant's plan doesn't make sense. He's only one man. It took him almost the whole day to prepare us, but there are forty farmsteads that he has to get to, so it would take him a month to reach everyone. I think he has a band in the forest. It's really easy to hide lots of people in there. I think he's leading them from one farm to the next, gathering us like chickens. I'll bet he's planning to take sentry duty at midnight and open the door wide."

"Is that it?" Dresbourn said, shaking his head with exaggerated slowness. "Because his jacket doesn't fit, you think he's a spy? He came to this farm first because he deemed it to be the first at risk. He will coordinate matters from the village tomorrow. We have just been discussing it. Do you honestly think I would not have discovered by now if he were false?"

"There's more than the jacket," Aedan said, snatching the chance to get in a few more words. "There were things in his story that didn't make sense. He said that the slavers were well armed, but he also said that nobody saw them except at a distance, even when they raided the previous village. So how does he know that they are well armed? He said they only attacked people who got isolated, but when Thomas's father suggested moving as a big group, he said they would attack us. Then earlier this evening he said that they would not attack us in the house and stopped us putting lots of sentries on duty. I think he's just making things up so we'll do what he wants and we'll be easy for slavers to catch."

Dresbourn's eyes were hard. "Kalry, are you part of this nonsense?"

"We aren't looking for trouble, Father. It started when we tried to guess his origin, but there was so much that didn't make sense. He said he's from Rinwold, but lots of his words sounded like a sailor's talk. I think Quin has been acting since he galloped in. Apart from his coat and that letter that could both have been stolen, how do we know he is who he says? Aedan and I think he's a Lekran who has prepared himself for this act."

Aedan had been thinking. Something bothered him and suddenly he realised what it was. He had not heard the floorboards. The lieutenant, or whatever he was, had not left.

"I can prove it!" he said, and ran to the door, yanking it open. The light of the lamps fell on the man's surprised face.

"See. He's been listening the whole time!"

"Not at all, my young friend," said the tall man, stepping inside and putting his hand on Aedan's shoulder. The grip tightened like a horse's bite, but nothing was betrayed in the man's face or the smooth voice in which he continued. "I returned from my rounds and decided to wait until you were done talking. I simply wanted to avoid interrupting."

"But the floorboards –" Aedan began.

"Aedan, that is enough!" Dresbourn's voice struck like a bullwhip. "You have insulted my guest along with my judgement. I forbid you to spread these disrespectful ideas any further. Due to the present crisis I will tolerate you here tonight, but at first light I want you out of my house. Now leave!"

After beating a miserable retreat through the hall and back to the upstairs room, Aedan closed the door behind him and dropped onto the floor. He nursed the shoulder Quin had gripped, while Kalry recounted the ordeal to the others.

"Maybe he's right," said Thomas after they had sat in silence awhile. "How could children have spotted what everyone else couldn't?"

"Because we haven't killed off our imaginations," Aedan mumbled behind a wrapping of arms and knees.

"I don't think you are wrong just because you are young," said Dara. "Anyway, Dorothy always says you and Kalry are too clever by half. What's the word she always uses?"

"Prodigies," Kalry mumbled, "but I'm sure it's more Aedan she means."

"Maybe your dad just got embarrassed 'cos you two thought out something he didn't."

Aedan finished off for her, "And I made him hate me forever."

"Not if we are right about this," said Kalry.

"If we are right," Aedan retorted, "then we will be marching in a line with ropes around our necks by morning. How is that better?"

"Isn't there something we can do?" asked Dara. Her voice was small.

"Don't be frightened." Kalry put an arm around her. "Maybe we are wrong."

"I don't like him!" the little girl said with characteristic fire. "I saw him looking at Tulia like he wanted to eat her. Tulia had her back to him and when he saw me walk into the kitchen he smiled in a way that made me want to run. I don't think he is a good person at all."

Everyone was quiet. They had all climbed onto Aedan's roof now, his vantage on the situation, and what they saw terrified them.

"Kalry," Aedan finally said, "do you still have that rope?"

She pulled it out from under the bed and tossed it to him. "What are you planning?"

"Something that will either save everyone or put us in enough trouble to last a year. You don't have to join me if you don't want. I'm going to the town for help." He stood up.

"But it's too far," said Thomas. "In this mist it would take all night. By the time you get back with help, that's if anyone believes you enough to come out, it will be morning. If there really are slavers around, that might be too late."

Aedan sat down again with a dejected thud. He plucked at the coarse fibres in the coils of rope and let his eyes drift upward and across the thatch for a while.

"We're going to have to split up," he said. "Two will need to stay here and watch, but without being seen, and two will need to go for help. The two who stay will need to count how many slavers and say which way they went, because rain might spoil the tracks. The ones who go will need to take horses, so I think that means Kalry and me."

Everyone nodded.

"But how will we watch without being seen?" Thomas asked.

"At the front there is the timber-shed roof – it's flat and one of you could lie there and not get spotted. At the back there's the tree house. Just remember to pull up the rope ladder. We don't know which way they'll come, so you should split up."

Aedan looked at Dara. Her chin was trembling. This was asking a lot of anyone, but for a nine-year-old girl, waiting alone in the dark for a band of thugs to abduct everyone she cared about was too much. He realised this could not work.

Kalry had seen it too. "Shouldn't we at least try to tell some of the adults? At least warn them?" she asked.

"Even after we were told not to?" Aedan put his ear to the door. "Your father is down there now. He'll be watching and he'll put a stop to anything we start. Anyway, I don't think a single adult will believe us."

"Then who do you think will believe us in the town?"

"Nulty."

Kalry nodded. "Yes, I suppose he would. But can he help?"

"I don't know, but it's the best I can think of."

"Aedan," she said, looking at the little girl beside her, "we can't ask Dara to wait alone outside. She'll be terrified."

"I know. I was thinking that maybe you should stay with her and I'll go alone."

"I'm the better rider," she replied. "And I know the horse trails better. If one of us goes it should be me."

"You can't go alone. You hardly know Nulty. If I let you go and your father finds out, he'll hang me."

"Wait," said Dara. "I'll do it. I'm scared, but I'll be brave for my mum and dad."

They all looked at her with proud eyes.

"You *are* brave," said Kalry, hugging her tight. The little girl leaned in, trying to control her shivers.

"We need to pretend to be asleep," said Aedan, "so we'd better put cushions under our blankets in case anyone peeks inside."

Once they had set the room up, he pushed the shutters open, tied the rope to the central beam of the window and turned back to give some final advice.

"Dress warmly and paint your faces with soot. Don't come down from your hide-outs until we get back, and whatever you do, don't shout out or they will find you and take you too."

Thomas and Dara both nodded, though she was shaking visibly. Then Aedan and Kalry climbed down the rope and stole away through the darkness.

A half-moon was drifting somewhere up in the heavens, but the mist was thick enough to engulf almost all the light. They felt their way along the stone walls to the corner, then followed the next wall until the courtyard was before them. They crossed this swiftly and headed in the direction of the tack room, feeling their way along the wall again until stone gave way to the familiar touch of wooden panels.

Hinges screeched at them as they edged the door open. They waited. Nobody raised the alarm. Inside the dank little room the smells of waxed leather and saddle soap were almost strong enough to see by, but Aedan was no mole and he groped through the utter blackness of the room, bumbling this way and that until something poked him in the eye. Fortunately Kalry knew the room well enough to locate what she needed by feel, and soon she dumped a saddle and bridle in Aedan's arms.

Saddling the ponies proved to be more complicated. Aedan had to quietly upend a water pail to make up the height he lacked. He hoped Kalry wouldn't see from the adjacent stall. Bluster, his pony, was quick to mimic the nervous manner. Aedan had to dodge stamping hooves while feeling about in the darkness for the girth strap. Finally the saddle was on, at least it felt like it was, and it looked to be facing the right way too.

The bridle presented a new problem. Bluster was swinging his head and shaking his mane with obvious anticipation. Aedan had no idea how to bridle something that was whipping through the air like a storm-tossed branch. Suddenly Bluster pricked his ears at a scuttling noise outside. Aedan recognised his chance. He slipped the bridle on and over the focussed ears, securing the buckle while his pony stared out into the darkness.

"Are you ready?" he whispered over the divider into the adjacent stall, feeling a good measure of pride at having tacked up first.

"Almost," Kalry replied. "Just setting the stirrup length."

Aedan cringed. He had forgotten about that. Saying nothing, he pulled the stirrups down from the saddle and estimated that his feet would swing freely above them with a few inches to spare. He tore at the leather buckle, yanking in a good foot of the strap and secured it again at the highest possible notch.

"I'm ready," she said.

Aedan darted recklessly under the pony's belly and repeated the procedure, wishing the leather would not creak so.

"Aedan?"

"Yes," he replied, leaping against the saddle and scrambling up until his foot could reach the stirrup that was now some height above the ground. "I'm ready." He looked at the dark shape of the stable door blocking his exit, muttered something and slid down again, the saddle pulling his shirt up and grazing his belly. He eased the door open. Kalry was already on her way out. He repeated the scrambling mounting operation, but this time Bluster had no reason to stay put, and walked out of the stable with Aedan still clawing his way up.

When he finally seated himself he couldn't reach the reins – they had slid down the pony's lowered neck. Fortunately, Kalry's pony stepped in front causing Bluster to raise his head just enough for Aedan to strain forward until his joints were popping, grip the leather with the tips of his fingers, and draw it back with a gasp. He tried to stifle his ragged breathing.

"Now we reach the difficult part," Kalry whispered.

Aedan said nothing, mostly because he didn't want to betray his exhaustion.

"It will be best if I lead. Stay close so we don't get separated in the mist. Are you alright? You seem quiet."

"I'm trying to listen." It was sort of true.

They walked the ponies with as much stealth as the clip-clop of hoof on stone would allow. Soon they left the paved farmyard and the horses' tread dropped to near silence on the damp earth. It was an eerie sensation, floating through the mist with the ground barely visible, the only sign of movement the drift of pale eddies. Any sounds that reached them were wrapped in a thick dreamy blanket.

"I think we are getting to the gate," Kalry whispered. "I don't want to dismount here, so I'll try to open it from above."

They drew to a stop. After a few clinks of the chain and a metallic groan, the heavy wooden beams of the gate loomed out of the fog and swung past. Aedan hoped she wouldn't ask him to close it. Perched up in the air as he was, his short arms would never reach the top beam. He dug his heels into the pony's side and Bluster surged past.

"Let's take the juniper track," Kalry said, ignoring the gate. "It's slower than the road, but less than half the distance, and we can't do any more than walk in this mist anyway. The track lets us drop more quickly and the mist might clear up as we get lower."

Aedan grunted. He hated the track. When the horse aimed uphill, all was well – holding on presented little difficulty. When the horse aimed downhill, it was like sitting on the side of a perilously steep roof, always at that desperate point of sliding off. And this was a roof that bounced and lurched and made unexpected grabs at succulent shoots of grass and reeds. Once, not too long ago, he had lost his grip and gradually advanced down the horse's neck in a smooth buttery slide until he ran out of horse and dropped off the end. He would make sure that did not happen again.

He saw Kalry swaying easily with the pony's motion as they walked away down the path. He braced himself, gripping the pommel of the saddle with both hands and let the reins hang slack. This pony would have to steer itself. As Bluster's hooves reached the drop, his withers sank and Aedan felt himself slipping down the lurching slope. He made a quick grab at the cantle behind him and clung on, rigid with desperation that seemed to be making up for the deficiency of leg length and technique.

"How are you managing back there?" Her voice was annoyingly calm.

"Fine," he said through gritted teeth.

He was wearing his warm deerskin jacket, but now little waterfalls of sweat were running off his nose and eyebrows as he fought the pony's every movement. They walked in silence for what felt like hours, descending rapidly.

As Kalry had hoped, the mist was a low cloud that thinned with their descent, revealing a long grassy slope levelling out ahead and, beyond that, the dim outlines of a sleeping village. The whole central valley began to open up around them. It was curiously bigger in the dark. Though the basin was only a few miles across, the wooded slopes on the far side, now murky and black, looked to be a half-day's journey away.

"We can make up some time here. Are you able to trot?"

"Of course," Aedan said, already wincing, and hating the fickle mist for abandoning him to such a fate. What followed was every bit as unpleasant as he had feared. Whenever he was about to settle into the rhythm of the stride, he got bounced a little too high and dropped on a saddle rushing up to meet him, a collision that loosened every tooth. Eventually, after he had been hammered to a tender perfection, the ground levelled out and Kalry broke into a canter.

"At last!" he sighed, grasping the pommel and sinking into the saddle.

The village wall was a ten-foot-high ring of stakes and planks. It was a relatively flimsy construction by war standards, but it would be more than enough to keep them out if they could not rouse the sentry and persuade him to open the gate. Aedan had to hammer at the planks for some time before there was a response. The sentry's curses were vigorous and they arrived at the peephole before he did, so that he was more than a little embarrassed when he recognised Kalry, daughter of the most important landowner in the Mistyvales.

"Begging your pardon, Miss," he stammered as he applied himself to sliding the bolts. "I was thinking only that you would be a – that is, somebody of the other – er – other sort, and not a lady, if you take my meaning. No offense I hope?"

"Don't worry yourself, Beagan," she said with a smile as she rode through. "I'm not going to tell, and I don't think I understood half of it anyway."

"Thank you, Miss," he said, the relief obvious in his voice. "You always been treating us rough folks good." Beagan, obviously flustered by the trouble his ill manners might cause him, had completely neglected to ask the reason for the peculiar arrival, an omission that could have landed him in even more trouble.

Aedan had never seen the village at night. The houses with their domed thatch roofs resembled lines of squat ogres with round haircuts. But then his angle changed and a few chimneys and a wind vane pushed the strange likeness from his mind. The road led past the town hall with its high bell tower that rose over the surrounding roofs, silhouetted against the shrouded moon. A cat's hiss interrupted the dull tread of hooves, but nothing else stirred. It was now late and all would be asleep.

They took the next turn to the right, passed three silent houses, and stopped outside a large building. Here they dismounted and tied the ponies to a rail.

Aedan's legs were trembling. With every step they threatened to collapse and pitch him forward onto the ground. He willed his way to the door and knocked, softly. Then, after several attempts, he knocked loudly. Finally he slipped a small knife from his belt, set to work at the gaping edge of the door and, bit by bit, slid the bolt free.

"We're not going to be thrown in prison are we?" Kalry whispered.

"Of course not ... I think."

Chapter

Aedan stalked into the darkness of the room. He placed his foot on something that rolled, throwing his balance off to the side. It caused him to stumble and stamp on the edge of an object that flipped over with an almost musical clang.

"What are you doing?" Kalry hissed, stepping into the room and promptly falling. She landed with a thump and a dull crunch of something that didn't sound like it would be repairable.

"You have to watch your footing in here," Aedan said, completely unnecessarily, as he stooped to help her up. "It's very cluttered."

"Why don't we light a lamp?"

"It would take us hours to find one, even during daylight. I'm just going to nip over to wake him. He'll know where his lamps are. Can you wait for a moment?"

"Happily," she said, nursing her shin.

Aedan slipped away. Not only did he slip, he tottered, fell, stumbled, sprawled and collided into all manner of interesting-sounding things. A gang armed with clubs would have been hard pressed to make more noise. He had covered about half the distance when a door opened at the top of a stairway ahead of him and light streamed into the large space, revealing, in silhouette, a jungle of items covering every possible description and size.

Aedan looked back to see Kalry gaping at the strange clutter that filled the aisles between overflowing shelves. At least she would now understand what he had just endured. Her father had never brought her here – such a place was beneath his more refined tastes. On the shelves beside Aedan were urns, branding

46

irons, chipped flower pots, a millstone, rolls of dressmakers' linen, and a weird green suit of armour underneath a stack of frayed parchments and a rat trap. Then, over most items was a soft sheet of dust, as though the shelves had been tucked away to rest for several years.

"Who is the foul wretch? I'll have your skin and I'll have it slowly!" The voice was chilling – thin and menacing.

"It's me – Aedan. Don't be angry. We need your help."

"Aedan? Oh, hmm, yes, it is you." The voice had changed completely and now gave the distinct impression of dreamy afternoons and the lazy humming of beetles. "I thought I should try to be a touch sinister considering that you sounded like a burglar. Perfectly useless one, I might add."

"Nulty, we need to speak to you. It's urgent. This is Kalry."

The light and its bearer advanced from the doorway onto a wooden platform that overlooked the maze of shelves and aisles. He was a portly little man wearing an oversized nightgown, one woollen slipper and one sock. He had small bright eyes in a round face with side whiskers which made it even rounder.

"Ah, young Miss Kalry of Badger's Hall. What an unexpected honour. Are you also a burglar?" He smiled and chuckled and turned red at his little joke. "No, no of course you're not. Well come along the both of you. I'll get some tea brewing and you can start talking."

"Actually we are in a terrible rush –"

"Yes, yes, it's what they all say, but my ears work just as well whether the kettle is over the fire or not. The parlour is this way. Hurry along before I take the light."

Nulty was balanced on the edge of a threadbare couch, absorbing the last details as the kettle began to purr.

"Yes, I think you two are quite right. Yes, I most certainly do. Odd that all the adults missed it and only children saw it ... but maybe it's not that odd. We adults are often blind to what children see. And then you two possess the sharpest young minds in the midlands." His gaze was distant and he drummed his fingers together.

"What are we going to do?" Kalry asked.

"Hmm? Ah, yes, what to do ... Hmm. You and Aedan are going to put some hot tea, fresh bread and honey into your bellies.

I am going to assemble a little army. By the time you are full, I shall be back." With that he marched out of the building.

Aedan lost no time carving two colossal hunks of bread and lathering them with deep coats of honey while Kalry poured the tea. Outside, they could hear the growing sounds of shouting and banging on doors. Despite the tightness in his stomach, Aedan finished his tea and bread in far less time than was entirely healthy, then fell into an exhausted reverie. He lost all sense of where he was and he looked up with a start as Kalry called his name slightly louder than was necessary.

"Yes?" he said.

"Why didn't you answer me the first time?"

"Oh. Sorry. Didn't hear you."

"Something's worrying you, isn't it?" she said. "You had such a horrible look on your face." '

"I realised something. What if Quin notices that we are missing? He knows we suspect him. He's bound to check on us and he's not someone who's going to be fooled by lumps of clothes and pillows under the blankets. I've been a fool."

"How are you the fool? You saw what nobody else did."

"I only made one plan. Remember the stories we read about the border wars and the young General Osric who became so famous?"

Kalry nodded.

"Well, what made him so difficult to beat was that he always had a heap of plans which he could choose from, like different tools. The plan I made won't work if Quin finds out that we left. He could change his strategy."

"I'm sure he won't. He wouldn't be able to convince everyone to stay in the house for another night. This is his chance. Anyway, there's nothing we can do about it now. We just need to hope. Don't be upset with yourself Aedan, you're doing better than any of us."

Aedan ruffled his hair with honey-coated fingers, producing a startling imitation of an upended tree, and walked to a large rack of shelves where hundreds of little copper vials were arranged, all neatly labelled. He began to run his fingers along them, searching.

"So he's an apothecary too. What are you looking for?" Kalry asked.

"Found it," he said, snatching one, checking the label and dropping it in his pocket.

"Hadn't you better ask first?"

"I'll ask, just not first."

"Well what is it?"

"Something I might need for another plan if Quin is still there by breakfast time. Better that you don't know. Don't want you to have to lie to your father if he gets suspicious."

Kalry looked upset. "I'm going to wait outside seeing as you obviously don't need me here." She lit a second lamp and took herself, with her barely nibbled bread, back through the maze and out onto the porch.

Aedan drifted down between the aisles. A cacophony of banging and clattering suggested that he was searching for something. He emerged into the open a little later with a small crossbow and a quiver of short bolts draped over his shoulder. His little frame made them look like a giant's weapons. They swung awkwardly as he walked, bouncing off his thighs and jabbing him in the neck.

Kalry was not in sight. Aedan felt a rush of fear and darted around the corner into a narrow alley. There, crouched in the shadows, she sat beside the young village beggar-boy who was wolfing down the last of her bread with sticky gulps. The thought jumped into Aedan's mind that the boy had stolen her meal, but then he saw the soft look on her face. It wasn't the first time he'd seen her do this. He had once argued with her and justified eating his whole sandwich while she had called him a greedy pig and shared hers with the beggar-woman's son. Aedan's sandwich hadn't tasted as good as he'd expected – nothing ever did under those circumstances.

The growing sound of hooves roused them and they walked back to the road where dozens of hastily armed men were gathering. Some wore uniforms. Among these was the local sheriff, Lanor, who was clearly taking charge. The group swelled as more riders cantered up from the dark streets.

Nulty returned and called to Aedan. "Listen, my boy, there's something that I wanted to be clear about. You happened to mention an odd detail – that Dresbourn was showing Quin his ancestral scroll when you walked into his office. Are you sure about that?"

"I think so. I've seen it once before when Kalry showed me."

"Listen to me," Nulty said, leaning forward. "If what you suspect and what I suspect line up ..." the little man gripped his whiskers and his face turned bright red. "Try not to leave her alone, Aedan. Make sure she stays safe."

"Who? Kalry?"

"Yes, of course Kalry! Who else?"

"But –"

"No time now. Just stay with her, Aedan."

With that he dashed into his store and, after a tremendous commotion, re-emerged, armed with a representative of almost every conceivable weapon strapped somewhere to his rotund form. He clinked with chain-mail, blades, clubs, a bow, and even a great oval shield that hung on his back, making him look like a large tottering tortoise. He had managed to find a pair of boots but he still wore his night gown under the many belts and straps.

There were one or two smiles as he approached, jingling with every step, and heaved himself onto his horse. It took some of the attention off Aedan who had been hovering, waiting for a moment when he could scramble onto his pony's back unobserved. He saw his chance, leapt at the saddle, and clawed his way up.

Sheriff Lanor began to speak. He was a hard-looking man with a loud voice that commanded instant silence. "Thank you all for joining us. There is little more to be said than what you have already been told. The slaver threat appears to be real this time, and the ploy is a devilishly cunning one. If we are not quick, Badgerfields may be empty by the time we arrive, every single person there bound for Lekran slave ports. Keep your weapons at the ready; these are not principled men. If you intend to show mercy, stay at home."

He rose in his stirrups and cast a fierce stare over the gathered men. He meant what he said. Only Kalry looked away. Lanor finished his inspection, satisfied. "If anyone lacks a weapon," he concluded, "speak to Nulty."

Most of the men laughed as they moved off. The party, now numbering about fifty, thundered through the gates that Beagan swung open while staring with wide eyes. They left the town and began devouring the miles to Badgerfields. The mist had risen slightly, so Lanor chose to keep to the main road where he could set a bold pace.

Aedan rode at the back with Kalry and Nulty. In spite of the painful thumping of the crossbow, his thoughts were elsewhere, turning on possibilities as he tried to imagine various situations.

The hasty meal had done him much good and he felt stronger, yet there was an uncomfortable nagging at the back of his thoughts.

What if he was wrong? Could he be wrong? Nulty had obviously repeated the tale to the sheriff with a lot more certainty than was due mere suspicions. The little man had taken a big risk trusting Aedan's conclusion. So had Kalry. Even Thomas and Dara would be headed for trouble if it all turned out to be empty imaginings. *Was* he too young to interfere with such matters? Should he rather have just silenced his "disrespectful" thoughts?

Looking at the large party of men roused from their homes, galloping towards Badgerfields all because of his suspicion, made him realise just how far he had taken his ideas this time, how high up onto his roof he had climbed.

And how long the fall.

Gradually, one or two of the horses less accustomed to such sustained exertion dropped behind. Only a few miles remained. Night began to fade and a dull grey morning drifted in on a brisk wind.

They rounded the last bend. Badgerfields came into view.

Aedan tried to control his runaway breathing and gripped the pommel to stop his hands shaking. The sheriff motioned for silence. They approached the farmyard through the gate which had not been shut.

Nothing stirred.

By this time there would usually have been much activity. First light was more than light enough for farm work. But now everything was silent. The farmyard was completely deserted.

With Lanor taking the lead, the group walked their horses towards the main house. Some of the men loosened their weapons; a few held spears at the ready. They had advanced only a little way when they saw movement at the manor house and everyone drew to a halt.

Dresbourn and Lieutenant Quin stepped out into the courtyard and approached.

Aedan felt his heart slip into his shoes.

"Dresbourn!" said the sheriff. "We expected to find you in a more desperate plight."

"I have no immediate complaint besides the threat of slavers. But we were amply warned and have taken due precaution as you can see." He motioned to the house from which people began to emerge.

Though the sight should have relieved him, all that Aedan could feel now was an empty humiliation and a surge of dread. He knew what was coming.

"We were certain that you had been betrayed by your messenger, and that last night you would all have been rounded up. But it appears we were wrong."

Dresbourn's eyes narrowed. "How, pray, did you come to such a conclusion?"

"Why, young Aedan, Clauman's son, and your daughter arrived in town a little after midnight. We assumed you had sent them."

Dresbourn's face changed colour and when he next spoke his voice was edged with steel. "Are they among you now?"

The two children were ushered to the front where they dismounted.

"Kalry," Dresbourn said, his voice shaking with anger, "stable your pony and get into the house. I'll deal with you later." As she moved away, he turned to Aedan and lifted his voice so that it carried well beyond the two of them. "Was disgracing me and insulting my guest last night insufficient amusement for you?" His voice rose. "Did you need to bring the whole town to my doorstep to embarrass us further? Where is your imagined treachery, Aedan?" he roared. "Answer me!"

Aedan tried to speak but no sound escaped his throat.

"Is anyone else involved in this?"

A noise drew their attention from the timber-shed roof where a sooty-faced Thomas stood and clambered to the ground. He approached with his eyes fixed on his shoes, dragging a blanket.

"Who else?"

"D – Dara is in the tree house," Aedan stammered.

"What! You put a nine-year-old girl out in a tree house during a slaver threat!" Dresbourn was shouting for the entire farmyard to hear.

"I didn't really send her, she –"

"Silence! You have done more than enough talking." He turned to the swelling crowd, "Someone go and find her." When he turned back to Aedan, whatever restraint he had been exercising broke. "You insolent cur!" he shouted, mouth twisted with rage as he raised his hand and strode forward.

But something changed in Aedan's face. There was a flash of recognition and then his features went slack with vacant terror. He uttered an almost animal moan and sank to the ground, cringing, arms clutched over his head, body shaking as a dark stain spread through his trousers.

"What is this! A coward? There's enough talk of your hair-brained adventures, but you can't even stand up and take a beating. You little fraud. Revealed at last for all to see!"

The crowd began to murmur. It was an unexpected sight – a boy widely known for his pluck now cowering and whimpering in his own mess like a beaten dog. This was not the way for a boy of the Mistyvales to behave when disciplined. Men frowned, women talked, Emroy smiled.

The one person at the farm who would have understood what was really happening in Aedan's traumatized thoughts was in the stable, out of sight. Only Kalry had glimpsed the damage and decay taking place under the tough layer of bark; only she would have known that this was not fear of her father, and it was certainly not cowardice, but a brokenness that ran far deeper. She and Aedan had once seen Dougal – a brave man and a veteran of many wars – freeze at an unexpected clash of steel. He had shrunk against the wall, slack-jawed and trembling, unable to take command of himself. Aedan had been in no war, but he had known what no child should know, and the damage was much the same.

"That's enough, Dresbourn." Nulty had managed to work his way through the riders and stepped in front of the incensed nobleman. "If there is fault here then I am as much to blame. What he did, he did in good conscience to aid you not to harm you. Surely you can see that."

Dresbourn ignored him as if he weren't there. "Sheriff Lanor, I do apologise and I assure you that this delinquent will be punished most severely. His reins have clearly been too loose. His behaviour has put our whole town at risk."

"I can see it was no fault of yours," the sheriff replied. "But what of this threat? I have never known you to house the entire labour force in your house after similar warnings."

"That was at my bidding," the lieutenant said, stepping forward. "I am Lieutenant Quin from the Midland Council of Guards. I had it on very good authority that this farmstead was under direct and immediate risk. It was my first priority to secure the farm and arrange defences. I had planned to be in the village today when I will gladly discuss the matter further with you."

"I look forward to it," said Lanor. "Dresbourn, I apologise for the intrusion." With that he gave the signal. The group of riders wheeled and left the farmyard.

Dresbourn lowered his gaze to where Aedan crouched in the mud. "Get my horse into its stable," he said, hovering over each word, "and remove yourself from my land. You will not speak to my daughter again. If I ever find you back here you will regret it for the rest of your life."

"Dresbourn," Nulty said, "can I just mention that –"

Dresbourn turned his back on them and walked away. "See that this ridiculous man leaves before he injures someone," he said as he passed William.

Aedan's hands were shaking so much he couldn't undo the straps. He fetched the bucket to give himself more height, not caring anymore who saw. Still, he yanked and twisted to no effect, and finally gave up. Putting his head against the pony's flank, he let the sobs take him. What did it matter who saw? He flinched as he felt a hand on his shoulder, but it was gentle, and he turned to see Kalry's tear-lined face.

"Let me help you," she said. She unclipped the straps and soon had the tack neatly stored.

Aedan choked back his misery and stood in silence.

"I'm sorry, Aedan," she said. "It's not fair. You were trying to save everyone and you get this ..."

Aedan couldn't speak. He dropped his eyes, unable to look at her.

"We'll find a way to fix it," she said. "I'll talk to my father when he is in a better mood."

But Aedan knew there was no fixing what had been done to him this morning. He had kept the nightmare locked away, and at Badgerfields he had been able to live free of its horror. But now it had found him. Now it would haunt him here too, even if he were allowed back – and he would not be allowed back.

"Kalry!" her father's summons boomed across the courtyard. She took Aedan's hand in both of her own. "We'll fix it," she said again, and ran back to the house.

Aedan stared through the doorway. The courtyard was clear. Everyone had returned to the house. Never had this place seemed so empty to him. He lived with his parents, but this was his home.

Had been his home. The welcome was over. He trudged between the buildings with an ache that threatened to tear him asunder.

It was like pushing his way through a dead dream.

Numb.

The walking took forever. The feelings of irrational nightmarish fear and shame drained away, leaving him empty, hollow, and tired. So tired.

The scene played over and over, the words etching themselves into his memories. Coward. Fraud. He would never be rid of them. But what did it matter anymore? What did he care? There was no return from this. Finding a trough of water, he rinsed himself. It would go poorly if his father were to find out.

But matters were not about to improve. As he rounded the last building, Emroy appeared from the other side, walking in the same direction, away from the manor house.

"What are you doing here?" Aedan asked in a frail voice, tensing, trying to hide the catch in his throat.

"I live this way, remember."

"But everyone else is still inside."

"I have no interest in taking any more orders. It's well enough for you commoners to be bossed around, but I won't stand for that treatment any longer." He swung his cane at the long grass. "The lieutenant said he wanted good visibility before anyone left. This is good enough for me. I told him so and walked out. Say, that was quite a show you put on. Fancy raising a whole town to fight off non-existent bandits, or did you tell them it was a dragon?"

Aedan put his head down and walked.

Emroy's laugh oozed smugness. "It was really interesting to see you crumple in the mud like that. You should have heard the people talking about it, especially about how you wet yourself. We expected more. Well they did. I always knew."

Aedan had no fight in him. He kept silent.

They had covered about half a mile when they heard the first screams.

Chapter 6

Nulty hung back from the others. After being shoved and shooed from the farm, it was no surprise that he wanted to keep to himself.

The road cut a gentle curve through the deep hillside grass. It was so quiet, so peaceful. But Nulty huffed and pulled his whiskers and finally began to speak his thoughts to the dappled mare.

"There was more at work there than the fear of a beating, Pebble. Something is damaged in that boy, and something is unsettled in me. Am I embarrassed? No, that's not it. Perhaps angry with Dresbourn? That's not it either. No, it was something else. It's something about the lieutenant, that look he gave Aedan at the end. It was such a strange look. What do you think, Pebble? Am I imagining monsters?"

He reached a bend in the road. Beyond this point he would be unable to see the farm gate which had already grown tiny with distance. He stopped, hesitated, and then appeared to make his mind up, dismounting and settling down on a rock while Lanor and his men walked their tired horses round the bend and out of sight.

The two boys spun around and stared at the manor house. The screams rose. Morning had not yet broken through and the air was still hung with frail mist so that only hints of movement could be seen. They ran back along the path until the shapes became clearer. There appeared to be far more people than they had left behind at the house, as if the townsmen had returned. But the people were not fighting a fire or securing animals; they looked as though they were struggling with each other while a growing number fell to the ground. And suddenly Aedan realised what he was looking at.

"No!" he whispered.

Emroy let out a wordless whimper and dropped, trembling into the grass. "Get down, Aedan! They'll see you and come after us too."

Aedan's thoughts were a jumbled confusion of fears and disbelief. It was actually happening. Earlier, when thinking about the possibility of slavers and what he could do about it, it had been easy to clear his head and arrange his thoughts. As he stared, he felt tricked by his senses. This was either not quite real or it was too real.

"Aedan! Get down, you idiot!"

Emroy's voice was close and unmistakably real. Aedan's fuzzy thoughts, still sluggish from the earlier emotional battering, were beginning to clear.

He dropped. The grass, thick and long, hid him completely, but he knew he had been too slow. A glance confirmed this. Someone was running towards them.

There were hundreds of places to hide on the farm – tall pastures, hidden gullies, tangles of bush, dense forest, interlinking barns and lofts. Aedan tried to think. If this had been one of the war games they had played so often, he would already have made half-a-dozen plans and selected the best. But here he crouched, shivering like a cornered rabbit.

Then he remembered the man approaching them. The distance would be closing. He turned to look and in so doing jabbed his neck with the crossbow. The crossbow! He still had it.

He tore it off his back, shoved his foot in the stirrup and began to pull the string back to the catch. He felt as if his arms would be wrenched from their sockets though he could only pull it half way. He heard the sound of footfall. Time was up – he would have to bluff. Slipping a bolt into the groove he stood and pointed the bow at the man. Only thirty feet separated them, but Aedan hoped the darkness of the morning would hide the fact that the bow was not bent.

The man stopped and shouted in a language Aedan had never heard, then took a step forward. He was tall, rangy and sunburned, and his features were exaggerated by a thick, oily beard platted into something resembling black seaweed. His strong hands were not empty. One held loops of cord and the other gripped a light club.

None of Dresbourn's haughty looks had ever made Aedan feel as he did under this man's glare. The lack of respect for the two boys' humanity was absolute, the capacity for cruelty limitless. Aedan shuddered. He almost dropped the crossbow and fled, but then he realised that his bluff was working. After a few more foreign words, the man turned and ran back to the manor house, shouting at the top of his voice.

"He'll be back," Emroy wailed.

Aedan's mind was starting to orientate itself in this strange reality. He was beginning to feel the touch of details that so often formed the building blocks of his strategies. Position, enemy intention, misdirection, surprise, reinforcements ... He had been taught such details and used them in threats that were imagined and games that were real. Could he not put together a plan for a real threat? With a shuddering effort he hauled himself from the water of his internal floundering, and stood.

He looked at Emroy – quaking, whimpering. Instinct told him to abandon someone so clearly unfit for anything, but that was thinking like a rabbit again. With only one, there would be no chance of coordinating anything.

"Follow me," Aedan said. He slung the crossbow over his shoulder, turned off the path and pushed through the long grass. It was so heavy with dew that he was drenched after a few yards. He turned to check that Emroy was following. The older boy's face was slack with terror, but he was moving. They climbed a small ridge and skidded down the far side, directly above a cattle pen. Aedan looked back. The tell-tale path of disturbed dew was as obvious as a paved road. He remembered something he had once used in a war game played with Thomas and some of the other boys.

"Run to the back of the tool shed. Wait for me there," Aedan called as he scrambled down the bank towards the pen.

"Where are you going?" Emroy asked, clearly unwilling to be left alone.

"I need to set a false trail. Go!"

Emroy hurried away through the grass, leaving a clear trail behind him.

Once Aedan had the gate open, one or two flicks of the whip sent the cows on their way and scattered them through the pasture. There were enough trails now to confuse anyone. Aedan sprinted after several of the cows that were heading towards Emroy. They took fright and sped from him at loping gallops, carving a spiderweb of dewy tracks in the grass. There would be no immediate suspicion cast on Emroy's trail now.

Aedan could no longer see over the ridge, but he was sure the slavers would be approaching it at speed. He ran as fast as the heavy waist-high grass and waterlogged trousers would allow. When he reached the buildings, he spotted Emroy crouching against a woodpile between two logs, each with a long axe buried in it, chips of wood scattered around. It didn't take much imagination to see the axes put to another purpose.

"They will search here," Aedan said, gasping for breath. "We need to circle round to the forest on the other side of the manor house."

Emroy remained where he was. Aedan knew that waiting here would destroy any chance of sending for help. There was no time for argument.

"Stay if you want," he said, "but I'm leaving." With that he ran out along the track that led down, away from the manor house and towards the homesteads. It wasn't long before he heard Emroy's heavy clumping behind him. The ground was hard-packed here and took little impression. It was the perfect place to depart from the track.

As soon as the houses came into view, Aedan stopped and turned to the deep strip of plane trees that edged this side of the farm. Keeping his feet together, he sprang as far as he could into the grass, then repeated the procedure in a zigzag, haphazard fashion until he reached the dry forest floor.

"What are you playing at?" Emroy said. "This is no time for games."

"Something my father taught me. These marks don't look like people walking. If they follow us, they will ignore this and think we went down to the houses. Do you think you can land where I did without touching anything in between?"

Emroy snorted but did as Aedan suggested, surprise showing in his face at how much ground the smaller boy had covered with each bound. He looked more than a little pleased with himself when he was able to match the effort.

"Keep off the soft ground," Aedan said, picking a path that threaded over as much rock as he could find. By the time they had walked a few hundred feet, the track they had left was hidden by a screen of undergrowth and tree trunks. Aedan changed his direction and headed towards the farm gate, picking up the pace to a brisk jog, but he had to slow down again because of Emroy's blundering tread. The boy crashed his way over the ground like a blindfolded colt on jittery legs. In his defence though, plane trees made for a noisy floor with big flakes of bark and dry twigs aplenty. Moving in silence required quick eyes and quicker feet.

After a few hundred yards, Aedan heard shouts in the direction of the track they had left. He stopped and waited for their pursuers to move out of earshot – it was not worth giving Emroy the opportunity to plant one of his hooves on a nice thick branch and announce his presence. Overhead, a starling raised a raucous alarm. Aedan hoped these men were not attuned to such clues. The shouts dwindled away towards the homesteads and the two boys moved on, picking up the pace.

They jogged now as the trees began to thin and the gate came into view. Dropping down, they crawled over the road – a double groove carved by a thousand cart journeys – and slipped into the forest on the other side. The cover here was far thicker. Dark oak leaves still held night's shadows under heavy boughs.

Emroy was peering into the dimness with undisguised fear.

"Wait here," Aedan said. "I'm going to get a better look. I need to see where they are being taken." Emroy did not object and showed no desire to move an inch further into the forest. This was Nymliss. His big eyes made it clear that he believed all the stories.

Aedan thought of saying something to reassure him, but then remembered how Emroy had treated him earlier and decided against it. He slipped into the shadows, quickly found a deer track and padded away. He knew this particular track. It branched ahead. The left branch ran close to the forest edge and at one point gave a view of the manor house. When he reached the spot, he crawled forward until he could see between the leaves of a dense bush. Earlier, the details had been hidden by distance. Now he saw the blood, the torn and soiled clothes, the looks of disbelief, pain, and horror, the way in which people had been turned to animals. By animals.

Many were crying. Tulia began to wail and a heavyset man walked over to her, made her look at him and placed his fingers on his lips. When she wailed again he whipped her like Aedan had never seen any beast whipped. She screamed and the man repeated the gesture. This time she was silent.

Aedan felt his composure crumbling. He drew his attention away from her and passed his eyes over the bodies strewn across the grass. They were all there. From Dresbourn in his fine coat to little Dara, they lay on the ground, roped hand and foot. Some like Tulia were even being gagged.

William, Dorothy, Thomas … he counted them off as he recognised their forms. His breath caught and his vision blurred as he found the tangle of straw-like hair. "Kalry," he whispered.

One of the foreigners ran up to Quin who was clearly in charge, and gave a brief report. Quin hit him hard and yelled in a way that made his feelings clear though the language was foreign. He walked through the litter of writhing bodies, kicking and stamping until he reached Dresbourn.

"Where are they?" he yelled at him.

Dresbourn's white eyes were as blank with fear as confusion.

"Aedan and that snobby brat who left early. Where are they? How could they disappear? You must know where they would go."

"I – I don't know." Dresbourn stammered.

Quin walked over to Kalry, grabbed her by the hair and lifted her off the ground. She shrieked with pain, and Aedan almost charged out of his hiding. Quin stood her in front of her father and drew a knife.

"No, please!" Dresbourn cried. "I'll tell you everything I know."

"I'm listening." Quin pressed the tip of the knife against her neck.

Aedan's fists were clenched so hard that some of the nails drew blood. It was only by the greatest force of will that he managed to stay where he was. Showing himself now would aid nobody. He had to wait.

"Aedan lives three miles to the west, but if he saw he would probably head for the town. It is possible to cut straight down the slope. Emroy will be hiding somewhere. Eventually he will go home. His father owns the mansion near the south-west boundary."

Quin considered this. "Yes, Dresbourn," he said at length. "That sounds like an honest answer. I would not have expected you to show any loyalty to the boys. Your assessment sounds correct, but even if the meddlesome one does run off to town as you say, I don't think anyone will listen to him a second time. The other boy has the look of a coward and he will sit tight until it is too late to do anything that might aid you."

Kalry cried as Quin lifted her off her feet again. With a swift stroke, he sliced through the mass of hair beneath his fist. She dropped to the ground and he flung the thick handful onto her. "How am I going to sell you with hair like this? It belongs on a deck-mop! I'll have to have your head shaved." He smiled as he walked away.

Aedan was breathing heavily. The tears that ran down his cheeks were liquid fire. His now-bloody fingers itched for Quin's neck. The man's mask was finally gone and the slaver was revealed. It was not a face of obvious cruelty – twisted and sneering – but rather one of utter indifference to the anguish of others, an airy comfort with his work, his destruction of lives.

Kalry was not far from Aedan. If he ran and cut her bonds, the two of them could probably make it into the forest. Quin was looking away and only one of his men was with him. Aedan pushed the branch aside and measured the distance. But then he realised that he was not thinking far ahead. If he risked freeing her now, there was good chance he would fail and be caught, and then there would be no hope. Emroy would sit tight just as Quin had foreseen and no warning would reach the sheriff in time.

The logic tore him. It was cold and heartless, yet what it demanded was the better choice. He looked at Kalry. She trembled with sobs, her shorn locks scattered over her like refuse. All his morning's agonies were forgotten as his heart broke for her.

He would not fail. He *could* not fail.

Quin's men returned in groups. They were given terse orders and began to get the captives to their feet, roping them by the necks and untying the bonds on their ankles. Quin kept barking orders, clearly eager to be gone with his catch. When they were ready, he spoke,

"You will march. We move at speed and in silence. Anyone who attempts to slow us or makes any kind of noise, even a question, will be executed immediately – man, woman or child."

He gave a string of orders and three men moved to the front of the line of captives. One of them took the rope and yanked. Dresbourn's head jerked and he staggered forward, pulling the line behind him. Aedan began to count. Forty-seven captives, twenty-seven slavers. He sat tight. Another three arrived. The line disappeared into the forest and Quin's men set to work covering the trail that had been left. They were thorough. Aedan was glad that he was watching – even his father might have missed such a carefully hidden trail. If they continued to show this kind of caution he would need to keep them in sight, but if he followed now he would be alone, and what could he do alone?

He looked around the farmyard and an idea struck him. It was an outrageous plan. No sane person would consider something like this, but it was perfect.

He crept back onto the hidden deer track and sprinted to where he had left Emroy. The older boy was still there, sweat-soaked and pasty. As quickly as he was able, Aedan explained what he had seen. Every word was putting him another yard behind the slavers. When he had finished with his observations, he explained his plan and Emroy's jaw dropped.

"You want me to do what?" he gasped. "If anyone finds out it will be all over for me!"

"If you don't do this it will be over for everyone at Badgerfields. Emroy, I can't be in two places at once. I need your help. If you do this it will be like a thousand bridge jumps. Everyone will think of you as a hero."

Emroy considered. He reached for his chin hairs with shaking fingers. "Fine," he said. "I'll do it. But remember that it's your idea – and just so you know, I think it's terrible."

Aedan had a sudden urge to kick Emroy, but he pushed it aside. "Wait until you can no longer see or hear the slavers. If they are too close they will come back. But don't wait long or it will be too late."

Emroy blinked and nodded.

Aedan led him back to his vantage point and left him with the crossbow and a whispered reminder of the plan. Then he slipped under a leafy branch and was gone.

Emroy's mumbled words drifted after him, "Idiotic plan. Utterly idiotic!"

Chapter

Nulty scratched his head as he cast one final look out towards the distant farm.

"Well, Pebble, if we wait any longer we'll be marked as spies. It's time we –"

That was as far as he got. His little blue eyes grew as round as his gaping mouth. "Oh, oh, oh my whiskers … Lanor! *Lanor!*"

He sprang into the saddle as if the ground were on fire and set off at a gallop that pulled the whiskers flat against his cheeks.

The party had been walking for some time, but Nulty caught them after a few miles.

"Lanor!" he yelled as he came careening round the bend at perilous speed. The men drew to a stop and Nulty burst into their midst.

"The farm – it's on fire!" he gasped.

"On fire?" Lanor said.

"There's a huge tower of smoke growing thicker and darker by the moment. The only time I've seen fire like that is when houses burn down."

The sheriff levelled his eyes at him. "If this turns out to be another wind chase then you are spending a day in the stocks."

"I accept. And if it's not, will you spend a day's wages in my store?"

Lanor grunted something, then raised his voice and gave the order to head back to the farm. There was more than one complaint, and two or three of the men ignored him. They were not soldiers and did not need to obey. The rest of the party cantered back to the bend and there they saw what Nulty had described, only now it was twice the size – a swirling pillar of grey and black that flung shards of fire from its turbulent innards. Nothing could have sent a bolder message of tragedy.

Without a word, Lanor kicked his horse and galloped forward. There was no hesitation this time as the rest followed.

The first impression they had on entering the farmyard was bewildering. They rode into a snowfall of stringy ash and blinding smoke. Even so, the glare and roar of the flames cut through the haze. At a good two hundred feet, the men at the front cried out and held their hands before their faces as the wind backed and the heat struck them.

It was not the house but the hay shed that was burning, and not a soul was to be seen looking on or dousing the flames, though by this stage nobody could have carried or even thrown a bucket anywhere near the inferno.

A pallid red-headed boy emerged from behind a bush and shouted over the din to Lanor. They drew back until they could speak.

"Emroy?" Lanor asked. "Son of Mennox?" Everyone knew the district's titled men and their kin.

The boy nodded. He looked sick with worry. "They have all been carried into the forest," he said, pointing with rattling fingers. "They covered their tracks, but Aedan is following and will leave marks on the trees."

Lanor looked as if he were about to strike someone.

Emroy backed away a step.

"Who were they?" Lanor asked.

"That pompous lieutenant's men, whatever his name is. Big, ugly-looking brutes, all well-armed. They spoke some filthy-sounding language I couldn't understand."

"How many were they?"

"Thirty."

Lanor glanced at his men, at the collapsing barn, then back at Emroy. The boy looked as if he were about to justify himself.

"You've done well," Lanor said, pre-empting Emroy. "No soldier could have done better with only two men. This was all your idea?"

Emroy hesitated, but only for an instant. "Yes," he said.

Lanor gripped the boy's shoulder and turned to address those who had not heard.

"It seems we have a young general in our midst," he announced, then explained what had been done and what lay before them. Many of the men nodded their approval at Emroy who accepted it with a tired grace.

"We all know the stories about Nymliss. Now we have no choice but to forget them. Any man who turns away, knowing what has befallen our friends, will be denounced as a coward to the town. If these criminals who abduct even women and children can enter Nymliss, then by the giants' wrath so can we!"

There was a loud cheer, though several faces had turned very white.

Horses would not be able to pass through the tangled undergrowth so they were left in Emroy's care, despite the noticeable squirming in his manner. He seemed eager to be off at speed, his back to the scene.

Men readied their weapons, and after Emroy showed them where the slavers had entered the forest, they soon found the first of Aedan's cuts on a branch where the bark had been sliced and peeled back, leaving a pale scar.

After he had taken a few steps, Lanor stopped and shouted to Emroy, "How good a lead do they have?"

Emroy considered. "It was still grey when they left."

The sheriff looked at the sun that was now clearing the smaller trees. He cursed, then turned and plunged into the riot of dense undergrowth.

Aedan held his breath and tried to squeeze deeper into the soil under the fallen log, hoping his deerskin jacket would help him melt away. It was a poor hiding place, but it had been a desperate scramble to elude an unexpected glance. One of the three trail-sweepers had grown suspicious as Aedan had grown bold and followed too closely.

The man was creeping past him now in a half crouch, dagger raised. Not much concealed Aedan – only a few branches and the log under which he had wormed himself. The log was in that crumbling stage of rot, and Aedan had a tough time keeping still as he felt things drop onto his back and neck and begin to crawl around. A sharp pain on his arm showed him what he should have expected. Ants. The little red ones with tempers to match their colour. His arm had dug right through their nest and a sizable army was swarming over the offending limb. If he so much as flinched, he would be discovered and caught, or worse. He grimaced as the bites multiplied.

The crouching man paused. He listened and swept his gaze slowly around. Aedan shut his eyes as the man's search passed over him. In games, he'd found that eyes often gave someone away – they were frequently to blame for that treacherous reflection or flicker of movement. Finally the man straightened up and returned to the others. They spoke loudly and disappeared around a bend.

Aedan wasn't fooled. He'd also used this trick. He rubbed the ants off his arm, edged a little ways forward to where he could see over the roots, and waited. When they should have covered a half mile, he heard the faintest crack. It was enough. He remained where he was. A little while later he saw a branch shudder. The three men slid out from their ambush, peering round the corner and back up the empty track before moving off. This time their withdrawal appeared genuine, but there was no telling if they would wait again further along. He considered his options.

If he stayed where he was, he could join up with Lanor and his men. Together they could track and fall on the slavers at their camp, wherever that would be. Many would die, perhaps even some of the captives from Badgerfields. The idea sickened him.

He remembered something and checked his pocket – the vial was still there. He had taken it on impulse, imagining a situation that had not materialised, but another plan began to take shape.

About ten miles ahead was a cave that opened into a clearing beside a spring. It would be irresistible. Surely that was where the slavers were headed. Apart from two or three splits that circled through the bush and got lost in hog burrows, the faint track they were using would take them directly there. Hopefully Lanor and his crew would be able follow the trail from here onward.

Aedan would have to take another route and reach the cave ahead of Quin. He placed a few branches on the ground, making an arrow, then crept into a vine-strewn thicket and pressed deeper into the forest. Once he was far enough in, he began to move in a way that showed he was no stranger here.

Since his fifth birthday, his father had encouraged him to explore, to grow familiar with the language of the forest, and learn to move through it quickly and silently.

To say he ran would be misleading. He flowed, leaping over gullies, skimming under branches and bending around tree trunks at a speed that never dipped. What was most remarkable was the sound – apart from the brushing of trousers he was nearly silent. This was his secret place where he had found adventures beyond counting and mostly beyond telling, for it was unwise to talk of entering Nymliss.

The pace took a toll though, and after a few miles he was scratched from the rank thorns and grazed from tumbles where fallen leaves concealed slippery rocks. It was a reckless pace, but he had to win back the time or it would be for nothing.

He was ragged when he eventually topped a crest and looked out. This was one of the few places he had found where he could sweep his gaze over the canopy and see the slow folds of the great forest rooftop. Before him was a long and steep valley. Beyond it, thickly wooded hills emerged through the mist – a hazy first breath of the damp forest awakened by a swelling sun. The river tumbling down below was as noisy as the birds. It almost drowned out the stream that gurgled past the clearing.

Aedan did no more than glance to find his bearings. He crept towards a short drop of crumbling soil and tried to work his way down. The ground began to slide from under his shoes. A quick look ahead revealed a monkey vine just out of reach. More earth started to crumble around him. It was closer to a reaction than a decision – he leapt out into the air and snatched the vine with both hands, just ahead of the rumble and hiss of falling rock and debris. The vine, fortunately, reached all the way to the ground. Aedan clambered down and dropped into the thicket at the edge of the clearing.

He took a few steps forward and then stopped, calling himself a fool. His boots were leaving clear tracks. He took them off and tried walking barefoot, but this wasn't good enough either. An experienced tracker would see. After a moment of uncertainty, he came up with a way to puzzle any tracker. He tied his jacket to one foot and his shirt to the other and arranged them until he was walking on cushions that left no recognisable print on the bare ground.

The clearing was generous, but the massive branches hung thick and full over the space, leaving only a central gap where sunlight poured through. Here, standing proudly in the light, a tall, dried-out oak retained its old ground. Dead roots still reached into the earth and held up the massive trunk, a statue that honoured the once-majestic life. A creeper that had once thrived in its branches clung stiff and stark. It looked like an impossibly big spiderweb that had become knotted and tangled during a gale. Some of the threads hung down not too far from a fireplace ringed with stones. It gave Aedan an idea, but as he peered up at the smooth branches, he realised how dangerous the climb would be. The first part of the climb did not even seem humanly possible. He looked around, but all the other plans he could assemble were pitiful in comparison or would require a large team of labourers to set up.

He walked to the base of the tree and noted the prints of many boots, the ashy powder not yet dislodged from the exposed surfaces around the fireplace, and the edges of blackened cinders that were still sharp. This was definitely their camp, no more than a day or two old.

His eyes drifted back to the oak tree. *Could* it be climbed? It would have taken half-a-dozen men to ring the trunk with their arms, so hugging and edging upwards would not work here. He spotted a series of finger-sized pockets that had been left by some wood-boring creature. A little above that was a woodpecker's hole, and above that, a horribly thick and smooth branch that he might just be able to scramble onto. From there he could see a way up, but it would be slippery, and high. He looked to where the creeper hung and his stomach twisted. Experience told him that looking down would double the distance. The bark-stripped, smooth surfaces would double that again.

He almost walked away, but then he thought of Kalry and of Quin, and the knife that had torn through her hair.

He kicked off his cloth shoes, plugged his fingers in the holes in the aged trunk, and hauled himself off the ground. For once, his lightness was to his advantage. Nevertheless, tendons screamed and arms shook as his bare feet searched in vain for some purchase on the slippery wood. Groaning and shaking with the effort, he lifted himself as high as he could and raised one foot until he could work his large toe into a small pocket in the wood. It was an uncomfortable position but he held it only long enough to catch his breath. Then, with his chin and chest sliding against the surface, he pushed off the already-aching toe and hauled on his numb fingers until he could snatch up with his left hand and jab two fingers into the next pocket. He tottered for an instant, his weight almost carrying him over backwards, but there was just enough grip to keep his fingers from slipping out. Finding a second toe-hold, he managed to work his way up to larger pockets that admitted three fingers. It was becoming easier, but this was still the most difficult and treacherous tree he had ever attempted.

Getting onto the first branch was terrifying. After he finally wrestled himself around it, he began to move up with chameleon hesitation. He hadn't thought dead branches could sway, but he felt movement as he edged out, higher and higher. Beads of sweat that slid down and dropped from his nose seemed to take half a day to reach the ground. At least if he fell he would have time to think matters over.

He reached the ropey arm of the creeper and began to edge it along the branch with him as he moved further out. It was completely rigid, retaining the curve of the oak branch where it had rested at its death. Pushing it along by giddy inches, Aedan finally reached what he hoped was a position directly above the fireplace. He tested it by breaking off a withered chunk of the creeper's bark and dropping it. It fell a yard short. He advanced a yard, tried again and was rewarded with a dead-centre hit.

The creeper dangled a good fifteen feet above the ground, too high for anyone to reach or, he hoped, notice. He secured it over a knot in the branch and edged his way back down again. Reversing the climb was a little less terrifying though far more awkward. By the time he reached the ground, Aedan was grazed from chin to toes as thoroughly as if he'd been caught under a wagon and dragged.

He strapped his makeshift shoes back on. Supplies needed to fuel seventy people on a sustained march would have been hidden somewhere. The cave was the obvious place. It was more of an overhang than a cave, but deep enough that the interior was dim. Aedan had thumped his head on the roof here before, so he walked carefully, hand outstretched, as his eyes acquainted themselves with the darkness.

A pile of flat rocks caught his attention. He lifted them and found the sacks of food. At first he worried he would not find what he was looking for, but eventually he came across a metal container that looked about right. He pried the lid off, tasted the contents, and smiled. The vial from his pocket was promptly emptied into the container and the powder mixed in. Then he packed everything back as before.

Not far off, a branch cracked. An instant later, men entered the clearing – the advance scouts. They looked around for a moment, then dropped their light rucksacks and began collecting firewood.

Aedan crouched in the shadow. He would never be able to slip out of the cave now, so he crept into a dark hollow behind a large boulder. He was only just in time. One of the men entered the cave and made for the food store. A projection on the roof caught him just above the eye, unleashing a string of poisonous-sounding words. He sat on Aedan's boulder to nurse his wound, and remained there until Aedan, unable to move, was so cramped he wanted to scream. The Lekran was close enough to smell, and smell he did, carrying the unmistakeable odour of one who had not washed for weeks.

While the afternoon slipped into darkness, Aedan worried and hoped that nobody would discover his shoes. He had left them behind a bush, intending to recover them after making his preparations, but there was nothing he could do about it now. Then he realised he had not cleared his tracks from those first few steps either. He gritted his teeth and inwardly named himself a royal idiot.

He began to think about Lanor and the men following the trail through the forest. There were no trackers among them; they were village folk and would probably be lost by now. He silently lashed himself again, wishing he had thought more carefully. He should have waited and led them here. His plan had tried to accomplish too much, and it had made no allowance for the people involved. Hadn't he just read the words of one of the great generals – Osric or Vellian – saying that a battle plan unable to bend would shatter? He had made just such a plan. A slight deviation would bring failure.

Yet, there was one frail chance.

Crunching footfall preceded the arrival of the rest of the party. The injured man made his way out into the open, still holding his forehead.

Aedan let his breath out and stretched his aching limbs. Unwrapping his shirt and jacket from his feet, he pulled them over his cold skin and edged forward to see where the captives were dumped on the far side of the clearing. Two men stood guard. The rest settled themselves around the fire that had just begun to crackle. Aedan slipped back as four of the Lekrans collected pots and food bags. Though the men were clearly relaxed, there was little in the way of joviality – they were stern to the point of sourness.

The guards began shouting at one of the prisoners. Quin approached and stooped down. Aedan could not determine what he was doing, but caught his breath as he saw him stand up again, dragging Kalry past the fire to the cave. Aedan crawled back into his hiding. Quin shouted and a man brought a burning branch that cast a light into the cave. They dropped Kalry against the wall and tied her ankles. She was only feet away from Aedan. If the light had been better, they would have seen him. He shut his eyes to hide reflections.

"You want to talk? Fine," Quin snarled. "Here you can talk all you want. Next time I'll cut out your tongue." They disappeared with the light, bar a few glowing flakes that had dropped on the ground and were turning black with a soft crinkling sound. Kalry was whimpering in a voice that shook with fear.

"Kalry," Aedan whispered.

She gasped. "Aedan?"

He crawled over and untied her shaking hands. As soon as the ropes came loose she flung her arms around him and buried her head in his neck, sobbing. Aedan wasn't too sure what to do; this was not his area of experience. He put his arms clumsily around her shoulders and held her until she was breathing easily. She let go and sat back against the rock.

"They killed Dorothy." Her voice quivered as if her own words had cut her. "She couldn't keep up so they slit her throat and left her like an animal."

Aedan almost choked. He heard the agony as she continued.

"The way William screamed … I never knew a man could scream like that. I don't think I'll ever get those sounds from my head. He screamed and screamed until they clubbed him down, and then they kept on clubbing him until he was as still as her." She gave way again to deep, silent sobbing.

Aedan was shaking. He couldn't speak for a long time. It was the sheer impossibility of what he had just been told that stunned him. He had heard of cruel deaths when cities were sacked or when murderous gangs did their work, but such things only happened in grim histories and tales gone wrong. They happened in other times, other places, to other people; they were not … real.

But finally it took hold, and he tasted the bitter ache. It hardly seemed possible, but Dorothy, gentle, playful Dorothy, and her straight and true William were gone.

When her sobs had settled, Kalry spoke again in a voice that was heavy and tired. "These Lekrans are cruel in a way we cannot understand, Aedan. They didn't feel anything. They didn't even look angry. They murder like they're pulling out weeds."

Aedan shook his head to clear it and took a deep breath. "They might get what they deserve tonight," he said.

"What do you mean?" she asked.

"I got Emroy to set the hay shed alight so the sheriff and his men would come back. I marked the trail for them. They should be nearby in the forest now, if they haven't got lost." He decided not to tell her that he had left them to find the second part of the trail on their own.

"It will be a bloodbath."

"Maybe not." Aedan explained the rest of his preparations and what he hoped would happen. It sounded good in theory.

"You know, Aedan," she said, looking at him. "Sometimes I think you must be the cleverest person in the Mistyvales."

He smiled, embarrassed, slightly guilty, and she continued.

"You were right all along. I heard about what my father said to you. I'm so sorry. I know what he did was wrong, but I don't want you to hate him. Can you forgive him?"

Aedan nodded. For her sake he would try.

"You're not a coward," she said. "Not to me, not to anyone who knows you."

In the rush of preparations he had managed to escape that awful thought, but her words brought it back, in spite of her kind intentions. "I know … I know you don't think I am. But everyone who saw … me … saw what happened … they will."

"I think they will see you as a hero when they discover what you have been doing." She took his arm in hers and they looked out into the fire-lit clearing.

When the broth was cooked up, the slavers served themselves using wooden bowls. Each captive was given half a potato and a sip from a waterskin passed down the line. The slavers began to sprawl out on the ground as others removed the cooking pots and built up the fire.

Aedan and Kalry watched.

For some time nothing happened, but gradually the thicker logs succumbed to the heat and added to the blaze. The vine dangled idly in the air currents, but Aedan knew from experience how hot it would be up there. The flames did not reach, but the heat did. It happened quickly.

First there was a bright glow that popped into a young flame, and then the flame began to climb. The more it climbed the hotter it grew and the faster it moved. Someone shouted and men stood to their feet, pointing. Suddenly Quin appeared and began bellowing orders. Clubs and stones were thrown, but to no avail. Several men, with much confusion, formed themselves into a hasty tower and hoisted one of their comrades as high as the lower branch where he scrambled, slipped, and fell to the ground, landing on his back with a jarring thud. He remained where he fell.

It was too late. The mass of knotted creepers had begun to burn with a bright yellow glare. Leaping spears of fire lunged upwards and branches caught the blaze. The flames climbed steadily through the boughs until half of the tree was crackling and humming in a fire that pierced the forest roof and lit the ground like daylight.

"That should draw them," Aedan said with satisfaction. It was working far better than he had expected.

The slavers, in spite of the tragedy, appeared exhausted and flopped to the ground, contemplating the blaze from wherever they lay.

"It looks like the sedative is working too," said Kalry. "I think Nulty has some dangerously strong potions. Or maybe these Lekrans use a lot of salt."

"I don't think the smaller pot was salted though," said Aedan. "Quin and his two officers don't seem to be affected."

One of the branches, as broad as an ox, cracked and fell with a swelling whoosh. Men rolled to their feet and tottered out of the way before the impact. The branch struck the ground with a booming crack and burst with a shower of sparks, throwing several men onto their faces where some remained, apparently asleep. One had been too slow to react and joined the ancient tree in its long awaited cremation.

The captives began screaming. Quin, who appeared to be quite lucid, advanced on them with his knife drawn.

A deep bellow called his attention away. He turned to see Lanor storm into the clearing, followed by his enraged men. Some of the slavers reached for weapons, but they were too slow. One managed to get a crossbow loaded and shot at Nulty whose clattering arms drew the most attention. The Lekran could not have chosen more poorly though, as this was the one man wearing chain mail. The mail took most of the force. Nulty rushed at his assailant, blocked the desperate swing of the crossbow with his ample shield and heaved a great agricultural stroke at the man's leg with an axe. Dark blood spurted and the Lekran dropped. Nulty tripped and fell on top of him with a tremendous crash. Only the storekeeper got to his feet again.

The rest of the slavers attempted to fight, but their feeble blows were easily deflected. They were hacked and bashed to the ground with increasing swiftness as the sheriff's men began to sense their superiority.

"Ah," Kalry gasped, shutting her eyes, "I can't watch this."

It was over soon. A few of the Lekrans had slipped into the darkness of the surrounding forest. Those that had been unable to escape lay dead.

"Let's get out of here," Aedan said. He led Kalry, who limped slightly, out into the open.

The yellow blaze of the oak was gradually fading to an orange glow while shadows crept back to claim their ground. Around the edges of the flames, women and children wept in each other's arms. Thomas stared ahead of him with vacant eyes – Aedan could only guess what horrible sight still lingered. Dara was cradled in her mother's lap, crying, rocking. Dresbourn sat rubbing his wrists while surly grimaces pulled down the corners of his mouth.

Kalry moved towards her father but Aedan held back. She stopped and turned to him, raising her eyebrows.

"I need to get my shoes," Aedan said. "All those cinders ..."

"I feel safer with you next to me."

Aedan smiled. "I'll be right back. I promise."

"Wait," she said, biting her lip as if unsure about what she was about to say. "Aedan, it's been bothering me that I didn't tell you everything I was thinking earlier. I forgot while they were fighting but it's come back now and I need to say it before the people get in the way." She paused again and then pushed on. "This thing inside you that made you collapse today and that other time at your house when I saw and I left again without saying anything because nobody noticed me – this thing is not you, and you are going to find a way to beat it."

Aedan was shaken to the roots by the revelation that she had seen him crumple once before, but the embarrassment was swept away as she came forward and took both his hands in hers. Her brows were pinched in earnestness as she continued.

"When I was younger I was scared of so many things, especially Nymliss. You were the one who taught me to be brave. No matter what anyone says about today, you need to remember that I have met a lot of brave people, and you are the bravest person I've ever known. Please don't let anyone take that from you … or from me. You are going to beat it, even if it takes a very long time. Tulia always says that big forests are cleared the same way as small forests, but it just takes longer. I know this thing inside you is a big forest, but it's going to come down eventually. I know it."

Her words filled him with a courage and hope he hadn't known for a long time. "Thank you, Kalry," he answered, very softly, knowing that what she had said would stay with him forever.

She smiled, lingering. Friendship, loyalty, devotion, and love. They poured from her eyes, all the more striking for the harshness of the setting.

It was a moment Aedan would never forget.

Her face was still hovering in his mind as he reached the edge of the forest, now in shadow. He began sweeping with his bare feet.

Nothing. That was strange.

He got down on his hands and knees and advanced along the ground, deeper under the bush.

There was a soft rustle of branches and something struck him on the back of the head, knocking him to the soil. A powerful hand clamped over his mouth and another wrapped around his frame, almost crushing him. The man held him from behind so that they both faced the clearing.

"We lucky, find shoes." The slaver's broken speech was a whisper. "Captain tell me wait here, catch you, revenge. Take you, take girl."

Aedan, unable to move or shout, could do nothing but stare. Kalry was nursing her father who, being a largely inactive man, must have been pushed to the bitter end of his reserves. He drained the mug of water she had brought him and handed it back with what looked like a request for more. She moved away towards the skins, and that was when it happened.

The shadows all but hid the stealthy form that darted out, grabbed her from behind, clamped her mouth, and carried her back into the darkness. Aedan thrashed, but he may as well have fought against the beams of a cattle crush. Dresbourn had not seen, and nobody else had noticed.

The Lekran grunted his satisfaction and shifted his grip as he began to turn back into the forest. Aedan felt a finger pressing against his teeth; it was all the invitation that was needed. He opened his mouth, the finger slipped inside, and he bit down like a mole. With a yell the man snatched his hand away and Aedan shot into the clearing, screaming, "He took Kalry, he took Kalry! After him!"

A few puzzled expressions and bewildered glances were all he received. He ran over to where Dresbourn reclined and pointed desperately into the shadows, still shouting.

"Everyone is fine," Lanor said, misunderstanding him and gripping his arm. "But where have you been? Emroy gave you the simple task of marking trees and you only did half the job."

Aedan ignored him. "In here, we must go now or we'll lose her."

"She's with us, you impertinent little fool!" Dresbourn snapped. "She just went to fetch water. I would have seen if –"

"Where Dresbourn? I don't see her," said Nulty as he came trotting up. "I think it would be wise to listen to Aedan this time."

"Will someone remove this annoying man before I –" Dresbourn began.

"Listen to him!" Nulty roared. A shocked silence settled over the scene. Even Dresbourn stared open-mouthed.

"He's right," Lanor said, looking around him. "Kalry is not here." Several voices called her name and when there was no response, Lanor's voice was hard.

"Aedan, you are the only one who saw. Point the way. Five with us. Murron, you remain and take charge. Set up a perimeter for the evening and return to Badgerfields at first light. Stay together."

Lanor, Nulty and another four men followed as Aedan led the way into the shadows. Dresbourn came after them, demanding forcefully that Aedan be sent back before he could ruin their chances.

Lanor's words were swift and sharp. "Sir Dresbourn," he said. "Fall in silently or return to camp. But if you raise your voice again I will have you bound and gagged."

Dresbourn did not reply. He attempted to follow, but he was barely able to walk and did not last long.

Aedan pressed forward into the shadows. After about fifty paces Lanor whispered, "How do you know where you are going?"

"I don't," Aedan replied, whispering. "I'm getting us away from the noise of the people so we can listen."

He was worried Lanor might want to take the lead after this admission, so he moved quickly ahead. In spite of his age, he was the only one who had been trained by a forester, and this was a forest he knew well. From the snapping and crunching behind, it was clear that none of the men even knew how to walk when on the hunt. After the camp noises had dwindled to nothing, Aedan stopped and whispered.

"There are at least two of them. We need to listen until we know how many and where." Then he repeated something his father had often told him. "Don't talk when you hear something. Keep listening. Be patient and very quiet."

Aedan caught the look on the sheriff's face. The man was clearly surprised at what he was hearing; it appeared to be causing some shift in his thoughts.

They waited.

There were many forest noises. A fruit bat pinged, crickets creaked, frogs belched, a forest owl hooted. Nearby, a shrew that had been waiting in fearful silence began to gnaw.

As he drank in the noises, immersing himself in the surroundings and filtering out the distractions, a part of Aedan's thoughts turned back to what Sheriff Lanor had said earlier. Emroy must have seen the opportunity to win a name for himself and taken it. The thought was dismissed as swiftly as it took shape. It was a gnat compared to what he now faced.

Crack. Some distance off to the right.

Lanor tapped his shoulder, but Aedan shook his head. The direction was wrong. He guessed that it was the second man trying to join up with Quin.

A heavy crunch sounded from the same direction.

They waited.

It was so quiet that Aedan wasn't sure at first, but then it repeated – the sharp growl, like the teeth of brambles as they pull from clothing.

Aedan spoke quickly in a whisper, "Quin is about a hundred yards ahead, to the left. One of his men is joining him from the right. I think they are heading west."

"Lead the way," Lanor said. "You seem to know what you're doing."

Lanor's respect was not easily earned and Aedan felt a strange warmth in his chest. His eyes had recovered from the glare of the fire and now welcomed the sparse needles of moonlight. He threaded a course between the trees, keeping away from brambles and the skeletons of dry branches that would defeat any attempt at stealth. They moved at a good pace with little noise. Even Nulty had contrived to hold his weapons close and tame the metallic cacophony.

The ground began to slope downhill. Aedan realised with a sudden rush of panic where they were heading and increased the pace. One of the men at the back tripped over some unseen object and fell onto the man in front of him. They came to ground heavily. The thump and snap of twigs would be unmistakable. Aedan stopped. They listened. Apart from the forest sounds there was no noise. Then branches cracked and rapid steps echoed through the night.

"They are making a dash for the river," Aedan said. "Hurry!"

Stealth was abandoned and they charged forward, tearing through thorns and creepers in a headlong plunge down the slope. This time Lanor could not keep up. Aedan flew over the ground at a speed that would have been reckless even in daylight. Several times he tripped and once he caught a branch across the neck, but he rolled to his feet and pushed on. He knew he was leaving the rest behind, but they would find him again at the river bank. He had a desperate fear that boats were already being launched.

Stark moonlight poured down into the valley and revealed his small form as he leapt out between clusters of ferns onto boulders. The river bent away upstream and he could see nothing but rocks. Downstream, all was still. But then the shapes of two canoes emerged from cover a hundred yards from him. He bounded over the tops of boulders, but by the time he reached the spot, the canoes were well into the river and sliding away.

"They would have needed more than two," he said to himself, and raced up to the trees where he found several more canoes. They were light, the kind that could be borne along trails between men, so he was able to drag one to the river. He launched it, but dark water welled up from a splintered gash in the hull. Dismay welled up too, threatening to choke him. He ran back to the other canoes and searched. They had all been staved in.

"Aedan," Lanor called, scrambling over the boulders, his gasping men in hot pursuit. "Where are they?"

Aedan pointed, unable to speak.

The sheriff looked at the fast-flowing river and then his eyes dropped to the ruined hulls that ended the pursuit. "You did well," he said, putting his hand on Aedan's shoulder.

But Aedan was not listening. "We can cross," he managed. "We can use clothes to plug the holes. We just need to get to the other side. The ground is open there and we can outrun them if we go over the spur."

Lanor followed the direction of Aedan's arm, and turned back to look over the canoes.

"Maybe, just maybe," he said. Then he straightened up. "Each man find a boat that will get you across. If you can't swim I suggest you remain here and wait for us."

They dragged canoes to the water, but after testing them, all except Lanor and Nulty drew back. Aedan had stuffed his jacket into a punctured hull and was already paddling. Lanor and Nulty followed. The current was swift and carried them downstream faster than they had expected. Aedan made it most of the way before he had to jump into the shallows and wade. Lanor was heavier, but he rowed more powerfully and made a similar landing. Nulty was as heavy as he looked, and though he made a courageous effort, thrashing about him with the oar, he was in the middle of the current when forced to abandon the sinking canoe and swim for his life. Fortunately he had remembered to throw off the chain mail and heavier weapons, so he was not dragged straight down to a watery death. Aedan and Lanor jogged along with the current until the storekeeper was able to reach the ground and fight his way to the shore.

"Are you able to run?" Lanor asked, his voice betraying a touch of annoyance.

"Quite," Nulty spluttered, "Yes, quite able." He shook off the excess water and pushed in front of the sheriff at a jog.

The hill was murderous, partly due to the steepness and mostly due to the urgency. Lanor, who had perhaps expected to be cracking a whip at Nulty, found himself wheezing and straining at the back. That a small boy and a man so round and mild could leave the sheriff behind was not something anyone would have expected. Lanor was a fearsome man, but the rage in Aedan's face and the dogged resolve in Nulty's made the sheriff seem the mild one.

They crested the hill and were faced with another. Lanor groaned as the others pushed on. All three were blowing hard. But the burning in Aedan's chest and the agony in his thighs were nothing compared to the panic in his heart.

What had Nulty said? Stay with her, Aedan. There had been a deep worry in the storekeeper's eyes back then, and as Aedan turned now, he caught a look of stark dread. He began to whine under every expelled breath and tore at the ground beneath him with hands and feet, surging upwards.

He scrambled over the shoulder of the hill where the ground levelled. Without a word, Aedan broke into a steady run, Nulty and Lanor following close behind. The dark forest was behind them now and only isolated stands of small trees speckled the hilltop. Long grass was all they had to contend with as their feet drummed towards the far end of the spur where the river turned back.

A shriek sounded in the night and a herd of forest gazelle bounded away in high, hanging leaps. Gradually the slope began to drop as Aedan passed the watershed. He lengthened his stride, approaching the second valley.

Something warned him that the drop ahead was more than a slope, and it was fortunate for him that he slowed down, for his last stride carried him to the edge, not of a bank, but of a cliff. He peered over the lip as the sheriff drew up beside him.

Deep craggy lines scarred a face that plummeted a hideous distance to the churning current beneath. The cliff extended up the river, to the left. But to the right, where the river bent away, the cliff did not bend; it continued towards the forest, effectively cutting off any descent. They could go no further. The only way to reach the river was to head back all the miles they had just run.

Nulty arrived, his boots thudding against the rocks. He collapsed and crawled to the edge where he stared with round eyes and open mouth at the horrible drop. All were wheezing. Aedan coughed and something salty and sticky filled his mouth.

"Even if possible, it would take us till morning to climb down there," said Lanor, when he was able to speak, "and the chance of surviving a jump like this has got to be very small."

"It ... cannot ...," Nulty gasped, in snatches, "cannot ... cannot be ..."

Aedan stared in disbelief at the empty river churning far below. Lanor was looking at him. Once the desperation had left his breathing, the sheriff spoke.

"It was all your plan, Aedan, wasn't it? Burning the barn, marking the trail, setting the tree alight to guide us?"

Aedan nodded but he was still looking at the river.

"Why did you leave us to get lost?"

"To drug their food, so they wouldn't be able to fight."

Realisation flooded Lanor's face and he stared anew at the young boy before him.

"They always said you had a commander's brain in a boy's head. I just took it for farm stories, but I see now that there was no exaggeration. The town will learn of this, and Emroy will learn the price of lying to the sheriff, regardless of who his father thinks he is."

Aedan stiffened, eyes locked on a small shape that drifted from the shadow of the cliff.

"Kalry!" he bellowed with all the force of his young voice.

"Aedan! Aedan!" Her cry echoed up the rocks and they saw the young girl stand in the front of the canoe. Quin was fast with his oar and struck her across the back, dropping her to her knees. Aedan screamed.

Then he went very still.

He looked around, grabbed a fist-sized rock, and tossed it gently over the edge. It fell and fell, hanging in the air far too long. When it struck the water, it barely cleared the boulders. He watched the movement of the canoe and counted out the same time the rock had taken to drop. He had done this often over the Brockle when the targets had been drifting leaves. He knew now how far the canoe would move during the fall, and using that distance, he marked a point upstream from him.

"Can I use this?" he asked, pointing to a small war hammer that Nulty still carried on his belt."

Nulty unhooked the weapon and handed it over.

"From this height, you have as much chance of hitting her as him," Lanor objected.

"I'm not going to throw it from here." Aedan's voice was shaking now.

Both men looked at him, confused.

"You just told us our chance would be small," he said to Lanor, "but what about her? I promised not to abandon her, and I won't." He looked at the river. The canoe was approaching the mark.

"No Aedan," Lanor said, stepping forward and reaching out with a big hand. "You won't make it. I won't let you –"

But Aedan was too quick for him. With a deep breath, he clenched his jaw, slipped around Lanor and sprinted at the edge. Moonlight made it difficult to be sure-footed over the broken ground. A mistake now would rob him of the speed he needed to carry him over the rocks. Instinct dug its claws in and willed him to stop. He felt sick. He didn't want to do this. But he drove himself on. Fear surged as the edge rushed forward. He placed his final step. His stomach twisted.

Then he leapt.

The chasm opened its jaws beneath him. Every muscle locked and his throat clamped shut. Wind began to thrum and then scream in his ears as he fell. He glimpsed features in the rock face rushing up past him – deep, craggy lines and hard shapes – but his eyes were fixed on the canoe. It was as though everything slowed down and he saw in strangely vivid detail. Though his mind was operating on the most primitive level, the impressions were being etched with the weight and depth of runes on an ancient lintel.

Kalry was in the front of the canoe, crouched on her knees, staring up at him. There was no relief in her eyes, only fear – no, horror at what he was doing. He knew she would never have wanted rescue at this price, just as surely as he could not have withheld it. They had never actually spoken of what they meant to each other, but they spoke it now, with an eloquence beyond the reach of words.

Then Aedan fixed his eyes on Quin. The man was staring open-mouthed at the impossible spectacle. Aedan raised the hammer above his head. At first he thought he had misjudged, but realised now that he would land close to the canoe, almost in it.

Another rush of fear almost caused him to abandon the throw and prepare for impact, but he pushed it aside, took aim, and hurled the hammer with all the strength remaining in his body. The throw caused him to turn. He would not land well. He forgot about Quin, even Kalry, as he shrank into a ball and tensed.

An explosion of pain shook him. Water as hard as rock. Then he felt no more as all was swallowed in dark silence.

Chapter

The dreams were confusing, a distorted jumble of nightmarish pain, tender words, and familiar voices. Sometimes it was his parents, Clauman and Nessa, that he sensed, sometimes others. Sometimes night, sometimes day. Thomas's voice was there too at the edge of his tangled musings as he wandered, lost within his own mind. Once he recognised Dresbourn's voice and then his father's raised in anger – even in his dream world he crimped up and braced himself. Sometimes the dreams seemed to be reality, and the taste of food passed through his thoughts more than once.

He began to drift back and relive the events of those days – the danger, the hope, the falseness and the loyalty. Then that final scene played out before him again, and as he hit the water he sat up in his bed with sweat beading his forehead.

Searing lances shot through his body. Arms, legs, back – they all felt wrong. He collapsed into the mattress with a shudder of agony.

His mother was beside him in an instant. She cried, clutching his hand as if trying to keep him from escaping again, but his vision dimmed and he drifted off.

When he awoke, she was ready with soup which he was made to drink before she would listen to a word. When he had swallowed all he could, he asked in a cracked whisper, "Kalry?"

"Rest, Aedan," she said and looked away.

Aedan wanted to press but did not have the strength. He tried to ask again the following day but was met with the same response.

As consciousness returned, so the pain increased and his slumber became fitful. When he was able to lift his head, he discovered that one arm and both his legs were bound and splinted. They looked thinner than they should have been. The angle of the sun from his window told him that spring was gone. Weeks, even months must have passed.

He awoke one morning to see his father sitting on the end of the bed.

"Where is Kalry?" Aedan asked.

"That's not why I am here," his father replied. His face was expressionless, apart from its native cast of stern dissatisfaction. "Dresbourn received a letter two days ago and what it contains could destroy us. He had copies made, posted them all over the town, and I took one. I need you to listen and then answer some questions." He began to read.

Dresbourn

As you are by now aware, I am a Lekran slave trader. Though that makes us enemies, there is a certain respect that is possible even between enemies. I write this partly from that respect and partly from anger, an anger that you will understand shortly. It appears that we have both been betrayed and I believe it would give us both comfort to have the treachery punished.

You may have wondered how I obtained such good information on the lay of the farm and the approach my men used. Two months before our invasion I was able to bribe a young boy into divulging every detail of the farm and its occupants. He was to keep clear of the place during a specified time – the time of our arrival.

Have you not wondered how Aedan was able to work things out from those ridiculous clues? The little turncoat was only pretending to work out what he already knew. It is to your credit that you were not taken in by his invented stories.

I paid him well to keep his mouth shut, paid him very well. First he betrayed you, then he betrayed me. I leave it to you to decide what to do with him. In my land, however, the punishment for this kind of treachery is most severe.

It is true I acted deceptively while with you, but I hope that you can see I have nothing to gain from being deceptive now.

Aedan had barely listened to the words. "Did he say anything about Kalry?" he asked when his father was finished.

"First answer my questions," Clauman said. "Did you accept money in exchange for that information?"

"No."

"Did you ever see Quin before he arrived at Badgerfields?"

"No."

"Is anything in the letter about you true?"

"I – I don't think so … No."

Clauman's eyes were hard. "Then tell me what happened, and mind you don't stretch or bend it. I want straight answers. Don't think that your injuries will keep me from getting them."

Nessa stepped into the room. "Clauman," she pleaded, "you can't do this now. He's barely able to draw breath."

"This is a matter that could spell our doom, woman! Have you forgotten that Lanor is dead? Do you know who the acting sheriff is? Dresbourn himself!"

She opened her mouth to speak, but the deep intelligence of her eyes withered to a girlish timidity as her husband pointed at the door. With a last look at Aedan, she shrank from the room.

"How is Lanor dead?" Aedan asked his father.

"It is currently under inquest. Now tell me what happened to you."

Aedan, discomposed even further, tried to collect himself and see the events again as they had unfolded. Beginning with the supposed Lieutenant Quin, he pieced those two days together as best he could. It was disjointed, and some parts he covered without detail, like his humiliation before Dresbourn. His father's sharp eyes bored into him at that point and Aedan moved on quickly. When he finished, Clauman looked at him with judge-like detachment. There had been no emotion in his face, not even when Aedan told of the cliff and the jump.

"Yes," he said, "I think that is the truth. You have not the wits about you to put together such a complex lie, and it agrees in many details with that ramshackle storekeeper's account. Quin wrote this to avenge himself on you."

Aedan should have known there would be no word of approval, of fatherly pride. Clauman was a man who never praised anyone directly. Sometimes he would use glowing words about someone, but never in front of them. Though Aedan was familiar with this cold reserve, the emptiness of his father's response still cut him. Clauman continued, partly talking to Aedan, partly airing his own thoughts,

"Dresbourn then, was blinded by Quin's flattery on the day of his arrival. He declared you a fool in front of his entire staff and a few dozen townsmen, and while his words were still drifting to ground, *he* was shown to be the fool. He is rightly shamed. But he can salvage his reputation if he shows that you were in with Quin from the beginning.

"Emroy, that pimple-ravaged, insolent upstart has claimed full credit for the plan you put together, saying the reason he sent you ahead was because he knew you were familiar with the forest. It was a cleverly calculated detail and this is where the next problem comes in. The men you outran have now begun to tell stories, saying that you moved through Nymliss like something unnatural, that twigs don't break under your feet and thorns don't cut you." He cast his eye over the web of scratches covering Aedan's arms and face and the torn feet still grooved with scabbed wounds.

"Some in this town are almost religiously superstitious of that forest. They say your trespassings there brought this tragedy on us, that we are being punished for your crime of entering forbidden regions. As a former king's forester, I care nothing for such idiocy, but people are beginning to talk of a purge. With Lanor around, no such nonsense would have spread. But the sheriff is gone and the town now looks to the high houses for order, leaving Dresbourn in a very powerful position. He is deliberately letting the talk grow wild. He even started a rumour of his own, suggesting the sheriff discovered your treachery and you killed him for it, pushed him off the cliff."

"But Nulty was there. Why didn't he say what happened?"

"He did. He said he made part of the jump, barely escaping with his life as his injuries show, and fished you and the sheriff out of the water. I was there at the hearing. When he was finished, Dresbourn said that such a story would require either a powerful swimmer or a powerful liar and that the fat storekeeper did not look like much of a swimmer. Nobody listened to your witness after that. It is starting to look like charges of treason and murder could be laid. I think you are too young for the gibbet, but I can't be sure that Dresbourn feels the same, and he is now the law. I fear we will soon be in great danger."

"But I did nothing wrong!" Aedan cried.

"I don't think Dresbourn cares. He loves his pride more than his own daughter. You took that pride from him and he wants it back. Wants it at any cost."

"Will you tell me about Kalry now?" Aedan asked.

His father snapped out of his thoughtful manner. "The storekeeper said he would be here later. He will be able to tell you. There are pressing matters that need my attention if I'm to keep our house from burning around our ears. He walked to the door, but then paused and turned, looking at his son lying broken on the straw pallet. His eyes softened just a little and he opened his mouth as if to speak. Aedan looked at him, hopeful. They held each other's gaze, his father tottering on an edge, but then his jaw clamped and he turned and strode from the room, while Aedan remained with heaving chest, staring at the empty doorway.

The window-shaped frame of sunlight had travelled across his floor and was climbing the dried-clay wall, reflecting, washing the little room with a deep red ochre. His father had left the house after their conversation, and his mother, despite her constant hovering about him, would answer none of his questions. When he heard Nulty arrive, he almost shouted for him. The portly man barrelled into his room and his eyes shone.

"Oh bless me, boy! I never thought to see you awake again."

Aedan smiled. Nulty carried his arm in a sling and walked with a heavy limp.

"What happened, Nulty?" he asked. "The last thing I can remember is throwing the hammer. Nobody will tell me anything except that I've been named a traitor and a lot more."

"Yes. I'm very much afraid this is true. We must hope, though, that the madness passes and reason prevails. But don't you worry about that now," Nulty said, settling himself onto a low stool and stretching the injured leg before him. He looked at Aedan and began,

"Quin managed to dive away from the hammer, but the wave from your landing almost toppled the canoe. I think you must have landed closer than you intended – I actually thought you clipped the edge. We saw him lose his balance and fall into the river. If it had been only him, it would have worked. But there was a second canoe. The second man pulled Quin out of the water and they caught up with Kalry before she could untie herself."

Aedan's colour drained.

"When we saw the second canoe, Lanor followed you off the cliff. Whether it was the water or a rock, I don't know, but he did not survive. I think you survived by sheer luck. With the two of you either unconscious or dead I thought it would be unwise to try the same, so I slipped and bumped my way along the crag until I found an overhang about half way down. It was still the most awful jump. I pulled you both out of the water. Lanor was dead. I thought you were dead too, but once the water drained from your lungs, you coughed and I began to hope, and here you are now." Nulty's soft eyes shimmered.

"You carried me back?"

"Only until the first river where the others had built a raft. Two men returned for Lanor's body. A sheriff should be buried in his town."

"I owe you my life," Aedan said.

"Nonsense. You and Lanor both offered your lives for Kalry, and *you* seem to have been given yours back again. You need to spend it wisely."

"I'll find her, Nulty. I will."

Nulty was quiet, apparently considering whether or not to give voice to what was in his mind. "Aedan," he said at length, "there's something you need to know about the slave trade." He paused, collecting himself. "The highest prices of all are paid on Ulnoi, the northernmost of the Lekran Isles, for young girls of noble descent – easily a hundred times more than for any other strong, young slave. To Quin, Kalry was worth more than the rest of the farm put together. She was probably the reason for the attack. Dresbourn was never quiet about his noble line and it seems that the knowledge reached the ears of an informant who probably takes a cut."

Nulty shuffled in his seat. His eyes lifted to Aedan's and darted away again, dropping to the floor, before he continued. "On Ulnoi, every year, one family is required to sacrifice a daughter to the gods of the island. Substitute slaves are permitted if they are of high blood. A few weeks back, Dresbourn stormed into my shop demanding to know if I had anything to do with the disappearance of his prized ancestral scroll. When I asked him if what you had noticed was true, that Quin had read the document, he admitted that the slaver had shown a strong interest in it. Quin must have taken it to get his price. Last week ..." Nulty closed his eyes and pressed them tight.

"Tell me!" Aedan blurted, raising himself up in spite of the pain, peering into Nulty's face for just a glimmer of hope.

Nulty dropped his head and spoke at the floor. "Last week a parcel arrived. It contained a note. Quin said the sacrifice and burial would take place on the middle day of summer, and in order to give closure, he had sent a pouch containing her hair which he shaved off before setting sail. According to the Lekran calendar, the first of Horth was a week ago, the middle day of summer. I checked my compendium of foreign cultures, and it seems that for once Quin was telling the truth – that is the day when the rituals are known to take place. The ship would have made it to Ulnoi by then with weeks to spare. Of what followed there can be no doubt. This morning the pouch was buried in a grave beside her mother's. I am sorry, Aedan. I am so sorry."

Aedan could say no more. He turned his head away and sobbed, deaf to Nulty's quiet departure.

When his eyes were dry, the sorrow deepened into a hollow, voiceless pain beside which his physical wounds were pale things. The night brought no sleep. Exhaustion finally overwhelmed him at daybreak.

During the afternoon, Thomas and Dara came to visit. He had to clear the gunge from his eyes before he could make them out. Dara burst into tears when she saw how his withered frame was trussed to splints and cut to shreds. Thomas was clearly struggling with a lump that interfered with his voice. Wordlessly, he placed a small leather case in Aedan's free hand. Aedan held it up and looked at the design on the cover – a little oak sapling growing beside a large toadstool. He realised what it was and his eyes grew large.

"Thomas!" he gasped. "How did you get this?"

"Don't you worry about that. You just hold onto it."

There was no need for this last suggestion – Aedan was clutching it so that his nails were white. When he was able to peel his eyes away, he held it against his chest, his fingers as tight as the knots on a barge rope.

When Thomas was able to speak more easily, he said, "We knew it was all lies, all that filth about you working with Quin and killing the sheriff. We heard Nulty's side of the story, and though Dresbourn told us not to spread it at the farm, me and Dara know it's the truth."

"I knew you would," Aedan said quietly.

"Nulty says you ran with bare feet till they were a bloody pulp and then you jumped off a cliff seven times higher than our bridge to try save her."

"None of that matters. I never should have left her alone at the clearing. Nulty told me to stay with her and I didn't. If I hadn't gone to fetch my shoes, she'd still be here. Shoes! I put my shoes ahead of her. I failed her."

"You did not!" Dara snapped. She fixed Aedan with a look of such fire that it quelled all argument. "Her father was the one that failed her and failed all of us just because he didn't want people thinking you are cleverer than him. You gave everything you could for her. Kalry always loved you, and now she knows how much you loved her back. We all know." She dropped onto the stool and covered her face.

"Dara's right," Thomas said, massaging his throat. "You couldn't have given more to save her. What you tried was so terrifying that almost nobody believes it."

"But *we* do," said the little girl, lifting her head, big dark eyes blinking. "And we are going to tell all the people we can, no matter what Dresbourn says."

Aedan offered a grateful smile, but he knew the weight of the nobleman's word. Facts would not be determined by truth but by power. Without the sheriff, Dresbourn had more of that than children could hope to oppose.

There was something that Thomas wasn't saying though. Aedan knew the way his friend looked when holding something back.

"What are you not telling me?" he asked.

Thomas glanced at Dara. He sighed and looked out the window. "There's a lot of bad talk, talk of burning your home and banishing your family, even talk of hanging. Tulia and our parents are getting worried for you. We've seen people snooping around here like crows. They talk about law and justice, but they are all the ones that used to slip around the corner when the sheriff came their way, like one-eye Kennan and his two friends that were always in the stocks for thieving."

"Does my father know?"

"Yes. It's because of him that we heard about it. He came to Badgerfields to tell Dresbourn what was happening, and ask for men to help keep the law. Dresbourn said ..." Thomas trailed off.

"What did he say?" Aedan asked.

"I – I don't want to repeat it."

"I want to know."

Thomas looked out the window again before speaking. "He said he would let nature do its worst – or something like that – to this low-blood and his coward-fool of a son. Your father looked like he was going to hit him and Dresbourn looked like Emroy that time he teased William's dog and then realised its rope was untied. But your father didn't hit. He just walked up to him and said something that was loud enough for us all to hear. Dara liked it so much she wrote it down. Tulia helped us remember some of the difficult bits. Thomas didn't bother trying to read it and simply handed Aedan the page, but Aedan's free arm was too weak to hold it up for long enough.

"Dara," he asked. "Would you read it to me?"

The little girl rubbed her face and took the page with a shy smile. Her voice was small, but it trembled with strong emotion as she read:

"I'll respect that you were man enough to accuse me to my face, but if you think my son either a coward or a fool then your wits are beyond the reach of the thrashing you deserve. The only man in this town to match my son for courage was Lanor, and the only folly Aedan knew was to love your daughter more than his own life."

She handed the note back to Aedan and added, "People on the farm have been talking about it ever since."

Long after they had gone, Aedan pressed the note to his chest, remembering his father's words. When it came to honouring or complimenting, Clauman was usually silent while his wife spoke. Anything that even approached sentimentality usually locked his jaw like a trap. Aedan had begun to suspect that his father was simply embarrassed by such things.

He also suspected that if he had been there, his father would not have spoken as he had, but there was no doubt in his mind that all of it had been sincere. The words had come indirectly, but they were his to treasure.

Chapter 10

Aedan awoke to a strange sensation. It was almost as if he were floating, or rather, as if his bed were floating. He opened sleepy eyes and looked around. The dim, candle-lit walls were drifting past him. There seemed to be someone walking in front of his bed and he could hear breathing from behind him. As he glided into the chill darkness of the night his head cleared. A sudden fear seized him and he tensed.

"Easy, Aedan," his mother's voice soothed. "You just lie still."

He relaxed, recognising the tall, nimble form of his father carrying the other end, walking with the long, steady strides of a forester. They lifted him up onto the fully loaded wagon and tied his pallet down.

"That's everything." It was his father's voice. "Open the doors to the goose and chicken houses. I'll untether the cow and mules. Let's not have them dying in their pens when the water runs out." Rough as he could be with his own, Clauman often demonstrated the most peculiar tenderness with animals.

In the darkness, Aedan waited, listening to the stamp of hooves, the creak of gates, the rustling of wind through the poplars.

He thought back over the past days, how the jeering had grown louder, how the idlers had gathered. Emroy – who was apparently now hailed as a hero – was in the crowd always. There had been stones, and thieving, and then a spear wrapped in a burning cloth that sank into the thatch, angling down over Aedan's bed. Clauman had doused the flames and done all he could to protect his property, but the following day there had been three burning spears.

This was it then. They were leaving. It would probably be seen as flight, an admission of guilt, but what choice was left to them?

His parents returned and he felt the wagon tip slightly one way, then the other as they climbed onto the driver's bench. There was a gentle slap of reigns and the wagon lurched.

"You still haven't told us where we are going," he heard his mother say.

"Quite true," his father replied.

There was a short silence. She tried again, "I know you've been looking at the maps of DinEilan. Please tell me you aren't –"

"I looked at many maps and the only thing I'm going to tell you is to hold your tongue. Homesteads are approaching. Be quiet now."

DinEilan. The name echoed in Aedan's mind like a warning. Once it had been sparsely inhabited, but no longer. Bold travellers attempted to pass through it from time to time and most of them disappeared. The few that returned told of creatures attacking their horses in the night, of trees that moved without wind, of hair-raising calls echoing down the ravines – deep, earth-shaking calls, hollow and savage that had caused them to huddle round their fires and pray for daylight.

DinEilan was an untamed place with a murky history.

The only part of it that was charted was the wild hinterland west of the mountain spine. Beyond the mountains was a region said to be a turmoil of rocky crests and deep ravines choked with impenetrable forest.

Aedan ran his thoughts back over the rumours that had been peppering country talk. There was always bad talk of DinEilan, but it had been growing worse, and strange. Many travellers had seen things over the mountains – unusual storms, weird and sometimes impossible shapes in the heavy clouds. It was always from a great distance, so nobody was certain unless deep into the ale. Many scoffed at the stories, but Aedan was unable to dismiss them after what he had once seen.

Though he had never told the adults, the descriptions matched the storm he had witnessed earlier in the year over Nymliss. Nobody had paid it much attention for rough weather was common in the north, but he had watched, and for just an instant, he had glimpsed the impossible.

The forest had been different since then. Though he was never able to say exactly what, something had changed, something that thrilled and frightened him at once. That was after only one of these storms. DinEilan had seen many.

But whether or not anyone believed the new rumours, the fact remained that those who travelled or explored near those mountains seldom returned. The sensible explanations involved wolves, bears and the wildness of the land itself. But Aedan wondered if there was more.

While he could understand his mother's alarm, he knew his father was no fool. Clauman would never take that road, but like any wise traveller or tracker, he was carrying in his mind a far bigger map than the actual journey required. Keeping his plans from everyone else was just his way.

As Aedan stared up into the fields of stars above him, he began for the first time in weeks to turn his thoughts forward. As children they had talked often of journeying and exploring the outer reaches of Thirna and beyond. They had imagined and drawn pictures of the places they most wanted to see – the great fortress of Tullenroe, Castath and its famous academy, treacherous Kultûhm lost in mystery, Mount Lorfen – Kalry had always wanted … The thought fell to ground like a swallow dying in mid-flight. The stars blurred and wouldn't clear again.

Could she see him?

For a long time he stared up. Remembering. Aching.

The track wound down the hill, skirted the palisaded town centre and joined the main road. Though it hurt, Aedan propped himself on his elbows to catch a last look at the village. It slept quietly in the pre-dawn, wrapped in blankets of mist that drifted continuously down the valley – peaceful, perfect.

How could a place so good, with people so neighbourly have turned on him so unfairly? Not long ago these same people had ridden with him through the night to defend Badgerfields, had followed his trail through the dreaded forest to rescue their neighbours. Some had even run with him in pursuit of Quin.

As betrayed and angry as he felt, he knew the feelings were short-sighted – he had often seen sheep turned, panicked, and led around by one bleating troublemaker – and Dresbourn knew how to bleat. He would have been convincing in the meetings; the town hall would have seethed in response to his speeches.

As Aedan looked back at the familiar shapes of thatch roofs rising above the outer wall, his feelings were confused. But one wish stood out, a wish that things had been different, that Quin had never found them, that life could have remained unchanged, and that they might have gone on living here all their years.

He had often pondered death – tragic accidents, illness and sometimes outlaws had occasionally meant loss of the deepest kind to someone in the town – but he had never before felt the stab of grief in his own heart. He had not thought its blade could sink so deep or sting so fiercely. Yet he chose not to hide from the memories that appeared before him.

His eyes drifted to the side of the road and he began to notice things. There was a young maple tree they had climbed, where Thomas had got stuck and where they had spent the whole summer day coaxing him back down. A little ways on from that was a thick hedge concealing a muddy brook perfect for mud pies which had been launched at a passing wagon, where little Dara had yelled that Aedan was standing in her new-made pies. Her shrill voice had carried to the road, and as there was only one Aedan in town, punishment had found them swiftly.

A little wooded nook was just coming into view. It was a favourite spot where chestnut trees abounded. They had often made little fires to roast the nuts and, once, the little fire got away and burned down most of the hill. This time it was the smoky clothes and singed eyebrows that gave them away, for they had fought bravely to beat out the flames.

Aedan smiled at the memory, and it was like fresh water, the first drops just beginning to wash away some of the salt. And it felt good, it felt right, for nothing grows in salt.

The wagon arrived at Crossroads just after daybreak. It was a large town built around the famous compass-point junction in the middle. The town owed its affluence to the fact that it was the first Thirnish settlement reached by all Orunean trade caravans. The result was a large and very busy market visited from all the surrounding countryside. It was here that Aedan and Kalry had learned the manners and accents of various towns and regions.

The wheels rocked to a standstill outside a general supply store where Clauman bought a few bags of grain and vegetables as well as fresh loaves and cheese for breakfast.

Once the purchases were done, he set the wagon rolling again, but to Aedan's surprise, took the south-midland road.

"Tullenroe is west," he heard his mother say. "Why aren't we taking the west road?"

"Because, my Nessa, we are not going to Tullenroe."

"But – but where then? Surely you can tell me now."

Clauman was silent for some time. "Castath," he said at last.

"Castath! Nobody travels that road alone, and even if we did link up with a caravan, the journey would take six weeks!"

"Ten weeks. We are going to take the inland track that passes between Lake Vallendal and the DinEilan Mountains."

Aedan's breath caught.

"Between …" Nessa bolted upright. "But … DinEilan! … And that will lead us right past Kultûhm!"

"I can read a map." It was partly true, and it was a tender point. Clauman could interpret the lines and shapes, and he knew the names of places by memory, but he could not read the text.

"Clauman, please – we can't go there! It's the one place in all Thirna that nobody dares approach anymore. It's not just tavern tales – you know I have no ear for those – it was historians. One party after another disappeared. I would know. It was one of my father's chief interests and I read all the reports."

Nessa was a scholarly woman from a scholarly family, something for which Clauman never revealed a hint of respect. Aedan knew well what would happen now. Whenever his mother used any kind of intellectual background to win an argument, his father would do precisely the opposite of what she advised. He did just that, in the worst way. Instead of cutting her down with some retort, he laughed. Whether it was forced or not, Aedan could never tell. He'd heard it so often. His father would now be as set on his course as if his pride depended on it – and perhaps it did.

Aedan raised himself on his elbows and looked out to the south-west, though Kultûhm would still be hundreds of miles distant. For a long time he held himself up. Everyone had heard of the place. It was to DinEilan what fangs were to a viper. His heart began to pound. What was in his father's mind? How could he set a course in that direction?

"Wouldn't it be safer to join a caravan and go south?" Aedan ventured. "I'm not going to be much use in an emergency."

His father turned and regarded him in silence before replying. "Anyone who follows us would look on the west road first and then on the south. If we take the inland track, nobody would follow us even if they knew where we had gone."

Nessa was silent for a time before voicing the obvious question. "Why would they want to follow us?" she asked. "There were no formal charges. Legally we are not fugitives." Aedan sensed the caution in her voice.

Clauman laughed. "My, but you are naïve, dear. The law in the Mistyvales now lives in Badger's Hall where it nurses a hatred for us that you wouldn't have read about in your books. Innocence and guilt don't come into it. In spite of what you think, we will probably be condemned for fleeing so-called justice, and there's a good chance the law will come after us. But I'm more concerned about thieves smelling easy pickings." He tapped his velvet money-pouch. After a while he began humming to himself, and Aedan craned his neck around to see the bulging pouch that clinked as Clauman patted it from time to time.

Aedan had been wondering about the unusual brightness of his father's mood – no angry outbursts, no blaming, not even the silent brooding. Clauman almost seemed positive about their flight, as if he were looking forward to a future that overshadowed all they had left behind. That swollen money bag, no doubt, contributed much to this optimism. Neither Aedan nor his mother would have guessed that they were so wealthy. It was a blessing to know they would not be tempted to steal to feed themselves along the way.

During the afternoon, they reached a junction. To the left was an overgrown suggestion of a track that led to DinEilan. Undisturbed dust, a mat of settled leaves, and the giant networks of orb spiders showed how long the road had rested unused. Clauman, after inspecting the ground, grumbled to himself and climbed back into the wagon. He continued along the well-travelled road. After two miles he turned off to the left and ploughed through long grass for some time before stopping and walking back.

When he returned, Nessa asked where he had gone.

"Wasn't it obvious?" He threw a look of haughty surprise at her, one of those so-you-don't-know-everything? looks. "I went to cover the tracks. I don't expect they would follow us this far after seeing we were headed south, but if they do, I don't want them seeing where we turned off. If we had taken the DinEilan split through all those webs and leaves and dust, it would have been clear as writing a note."

Aedan was surprised. His father really was serious about pursuit. Clauman drove them through the grass and under some large leafy boughs until they broke out onto the disused inland track.

They camped in the open for five nights before they reached a burned-out stone house. From here the track became very wild. It had clearly remained unused for many years. In sections, Clauman was obliged to take detours to negotiate obstructions and, more than once, to use his axe on trees fallen across the way.

As the distance lessened, the mountains lost their purple veil. They began to reveal green slopes that would turn gold in the afternoons, and dark rocky faces higher and sterner than Aedan's imagination had ever painted them.

For a little over two weeks they travelled in complete isolation. Aedan's back and limbs began to heal somewhat. He could now sit up, but he could not walk; his legs simply refused to bear the weight.

At one of the camps, Clauman cut some branches from an elderberry tree and began shaping crutches while Nessa boiled the little dark berries into a jam. Aedan sat and watched, too weak to be of any help. His attention was drawn by the bright chinking call of a tiny wagtail that strutted fearlessly through the camp, hunting for disturbed insects. He envied the little bird's independence.

When the crutches were shaped and the armpit rests padded with cloth, Aedan was able to take his full weight on them, swing his legs forward, and stand with his feet together while planting the crutches ahead for another stride. It was a painful process – armpits, back, legs, they all ached. When he fell, which happened often, there was no laughter. He practiced for a few days, but it was hardly worth the effort. He spent most of his time near the campfire, miserable, lost within himself.

It was Clauman who spotted the smoke – a thin blue, wispy trail that pointed down into a birch grove a few miles away. When they came near, he stopped the wagon.

"Wait here," he said, gripping a heavy staff and heading into the trees. A little while later he returned wearing an amused expression. "Now this," he said, "I did not expect."

Chapter

They stopped the wagon outside what Aedan first took for an enormous log-and-panel cottage, only that it appeared to have been built more like an inn. Just outside the front door stood a middle-aged couple. The man was tall and broad of shoulder with workmanlike hands, an ox's head and a mouse's expression. It was the woman who dominated the porch. Her short but solid frame was crowned with a wild eruption of yellow, curling hair pulled back from eyebrows that looked to have been raised all her life, demanding from the world just what it thought it was doing. Not even the smile could conceal that this was a woman who knew how to take charge.

"Welcome, welcome!" she cried, clapping her hands in front of her. "You are our first guests these past four years. Oh this is so exciting! I am Harriet and this is Borr. We have so much to ask and so much to tell. This is going to be wonderful! Oh look at your wagon, packed to bursting. You must have been on the road a long time. Oh my! What is this? What happened to you?"

Aedan had managed to slide himself out of the wagon and was making his way over on his crutches.

"A long story," Clauman answered for him.

"Well there will be plenty of time for stories later, but I think now we should get you settled in. Yes?"

Clauman nodded.

After a silent handshake, Borr hefted the two large sacks that Clauman handed down to him. He led the group through the parlour and down a passage where he opened a door and led them in.

He frowned.

His wife shrieked.

The guests stared around in astonishment.

Cockroaches rushed from them like a receding tide, flowing over a few dead rats and frogs. Grey drapes that had once been spiderwebs were now transformed by dust into useless sagging folds that caught nothing more than lizard droppings and expired moths. The floorboards were caked in a fungus so well established that it might have been mistaken for moss were it not for the overpowering smell of rot – it was as if they had stepped into the bowels of a giant mushroom.

"Oh dear," Harriet said, "Oh doubly dear. Oh mother of a … Sorry, pardon me, it's just that, oh, oh my …"

It turned out that the rooms had been left in perfect order three years back and Harriet had expected, somewhat foolishly, to find them a little dusty perhaps, but no worse than that. A hole in the roof explained much of the destruction.

Harriet showered her guests with apologies, and found two rooms that were in a less shocking condition. She spent the remainder of the afternoon apologising and scrubbing beside Nessa who would not be kept from sharing the burden of cleaning. The men unloaded in silence while Aedan got the kitchen fire going and was given a chicken to pluck. By the time he was finished, it looked like he had made a fairly complete transfer of feathers from the chicken to himself. Leaving Harriet to finish the scrubbing, Nessa chopped carrots, celery and potatoes, and tipped them with a sprinkling of salt and a sprig of rosemary into the pot to keep the chicken company. The result was a simple yet toothsome pot-roast. Borr nodded in surprise and appreciation when the meal was served that evening. Harriet mumbled something about the meat being underdone.

After the meal that was never without the buzz of conversation – for the women had become fast friends – Clauman accepted Harriet's invitation to remain a few weeks, at least until Aedan's injuries had healed. He offered to pay for accommodation, but she reminded him that money had no value this far from town, so it was agreed that everything would be shared, both labour and food.

"Is the rooster going to sleep in the house?" Clauman asked, as everyone retired for the night.

"Oh, don't you worry about him," Harriet laughed. "If there's one thing I know, it's how to manage my livestock. He's no early riser that one. Laziest chicken in Thirna. We call him Snore."

Snore angled his head and gave Clauman a challenging stare, then, clucking confidently, made his way with great dignity to the parlour window where he hopped up onto the backrest of a deeply scratched chair and buried himself in his feathers for the evening. Clauman looked sceptical.

Morning had not even begun to intrude on the night's reign when there was a feathery disturbance at the same window. A soft whooshing of wings and scraping of claws suggested a few stretches. Then the starry silhouette revealed the shape of a beak and crown as the king of the morning threw his head back – and roared.

Barely stifled curses poured from under the door to Clauman and Nessa's room as the panelled building shook with the thunder of "Cock-a-doodle-dooo!"

Borr and Harriet, powerful sleepers both, awoke well after sunrise and were surprised by their guests' subdued and somewhat grumpy manner at breakfast. Clauman made his feelings for Snore quite plain. Harriet insisted that he was exaggerating and that it could not be that bad and that, if he chose to, he could ignore whatever clucking had woken him.

Clauman dropped his spoon and looked at her without expression, and then said that either his family or the rooster would be leaving immediately. Snore was given a hock on the far side of the buildings.

That day the men worked well together setting traps and making repairs to goat pens, chicken coops, and the long-neglected roof of the inn. Their language was the silent understanding of getting the job done. When words were used, they were few and to the point, like "Mallet", "Next beam", or "Let me have a go". Aedan found this quiet camaraderie both surprising and amusing.

Borr was an experienced carpenter with an impressive tool shed, though it was no tidier than the house. He had cut many of the inn's logs and panels himself. When Aedan remarked on the enormity of the task, Borr merely shrugged his heavy shoulders. To follow orders and plod through chores appeared to be his complete expectation of life.

At dinner, Aedan fully understood why Harriet had called the previous night's meal undercooked. A charred crust lined almost everything on his plate. Borr's look of delighted surprise was gone and Harriet wore one of satisfaction. This, apparently, was how it was done. It made no difference what herbs were used – all her meals tasted like soot. Nobody dared comment. Aedan learned to pinch his eyes shut and swallow hard. He'd always thought that when people said someone could burn water, it was just an expression. Harriet, however, had apparently mastered that dark art; she could burn anything from water to wooden spoons and whatever else that came in contact with her pots.

On the second morning, Harriet bustled out onto the porch where Aedan was sitting at a small table, writing.

"What are you writing?" she asked, without preamble. "Here, let me see that." She pulled the page out from under his hand.

Aedan was surprised at her abrupt approach, but was not entirely upset. After all, what was a writer without a readership?

"The adventures of the mountain warrior," she read. She was silent for a while, letting her eyes rove over the lines. When she finished, she put the page on the table and sat down. Aedan waited, breathless.

"Just as I feared," she said. "All empty boyish silliness. You have obviously let your imagination go wild with weeds like a garden full of … weeds. Imagination is not good for you, just like weeds aren't. So I am going to help you dig out the weeds and put yourself in order."

Aedan frowned, not sure that he liked where this was going.

"I happen to know," she resumed, "that someone your age has no understanding of such notions." She pointed at the page. "Love, tragedy and revenge," she said, shaking her head. "These are exactly the kinds of ideas that I will not allow in your sweet little head, my boy. What could you possibly know of such things?"

Aedan gathered himself to answer, but she was too quick for him.

"You see – nothing. One thing you'll soon discover is that I know how to read people. I'm glad that you are writing – it shows some refinement, but I cannot allow you to ruin yourself with such empty ideas – and violent! Really Aedan, this is too horrible for someone so young and delicate. I can tell by your injuries that you are made soft. It's time for you to accept that. I'd like to see you writing valuable thoughts from now on – recipes, garden arrangements, even plans for my new shed."

"But I … I don't want to."

Harriet wasn't listening – something she had apparently developed to a fine art. She was on her feet pacing, her finger tapping against her pursed lips like someone planning a large-scale renovation – which was exactly what she was doing – and Aedan was the object of this renovation.

"We'll begin by putting you in charge of household chores. Sewing was the thing that gave the finishing touches to *my* refinement – but needles can be dangerous. Maybe we'll keep that back until I've taught you responsibility and foresight."

Aedan looked out onto the empty road and wondered how those qualities had contributed when Harriet and her husband had built an inn on a dying route. Back down that road were Aedan's friends who knew him for what he was, who wouldn't try to change him into something else. He reached up and felt the little leather case that now hung from a cord around his neck. Though its touch gave him comfort, it had been a mistake to draw attention to it.

"What's that?" Harriet said.

Something changed in Aedan's face. With both hands he gripped the little case and pressed it to him.

Harriet narrowed her eyes, but stayed where she was. Her glare dropped to the treasure Aedan held, and he clasped it tighter.

"This is a bad start for you. A very bad start. I can see there is a lot we are going to have to mend here. I may not be a mother, but if there's one thing I know, it's how to make even the worst person into someone decent. I've done so for my husband and I can do so with any boy." She threw her head back and glowed with defiant pride.

Aedan recognised the ambition in her eyes. She was not a mother but she certainly wanted the job. Though he dreaded what was coming, he did not have the strength to oppose it, and Harriet was strutting like a boxer.

As soon as he was alone, he hobbled off the porch down the stairs, dug a few handfuls of soil from beneath them, slipped the leather case into the hole and covered it again. He had a suspicion that Harriet just might root through his things when he took a bath. If she found that case, if she looked inside …

That night he spoke to his father about Harriet's threat to reform him, but Clauman merely laughed and did nothing, perhaps thinking of his dinner and hoping Aedan would be made to cook. Then Aedan spoke to his mother. She listened attentively, promised to stand up for him ... and quailed under Harriet's domineering presence.

From the next morning, Harriet took charge of Aedan as a personal project, mending him with constant criticism and ensuring that he was never without some self-improving duty. He was given vegetables to cut, drapes to clean, furniture to polish, and floors to scrub. He couldn't help but notice that the dirt he removed was thick and old.

Harriet was only ever satisfied with Aedan when she had just corrected him. Anything that came of his own initiative, or for which he showed any kind of eagerness, was a threat that had to be weeded out. He was not allowed to be one of the men. He was constantly pulled from their company and sent elsewhere on some domestic errand.

His opinions on anything were found to be wrong. Harriet pointed this out and generously supplied her opinions for replacement. It quickly became evident that she knew all there was to know of anything worth knowing. Whenever she received new information she would secretly digest it with a bored expression that said "old news". On some topics the breadth of her opinions made up for the scarcity of detail. Sailing, for example, was dealt with in one grand sweep: "All sailors are fools, because what happens when their boats sink? If we were meant to breathe in water we would have fins." This was followed by a patient smile and a lift of the chin that signified, "Bet you hadn't thought of that."

Laughter would have been dangerous, and Aedan just didn't care enough to argue. Yet, silly as the woman could be, it was clear that she was proving herself a good companion for his timid mother. So he withdrew into a little shell and let the tide roll him around. But the waters were only just beginning to stir.

No matter what he was doing, Harriet found the time to supervise him, to point out the spots he had missed or scoop out carrots that had been sliced too thickly. She monitored everything he did. Evaluated him constantly. The worst was her encouragement.

"Well, Aedan," she would say. "You worked well today and showed a much better attitude. I was really pleased to see you pulled yourself together and did a better job of sweeping the porch. I think we are improving you well. Tomorrow I want to see you doing even better than today, and I want to see you smiling as you work. It's not just the results, but the attitude too. Smiling is the key. Sometimes humming a song. I'll be watching and listening for those tomorrow. But you are doing very well, very well indeed."

This was harder to bear than her anger. She was really just exulting in her domination, securing her rule over him. Hours began to feel like months.

Aedan came very close several times to smashing the broom across the table. This house was turning into a jail. Within a matter of days, he found himself pressed under a new social order that had all the weight of the law. If he hobbled out for a walk, he would be confronted on his return with a tapping foot and a demand to know what he had been doing.

But he had to depend on Harriet too for the medicinal herbs her garden provided, the massaging of his stiff and shrunken legs – in which she showed more skill than his mother – his food, his bed and, at times, the arm that helped to steady his tottering steps. She was an attentive nurse. Having to lean on her arm undermined his right to complain, or rather, his urge to scream. He wished he did not have to depend on her so, but what choice did he have? Gratitude and suffocation held each other in place, but by the end of the first week, it was the latter that was dominating.

Harriet told everyone with obvious triumph that her efforts were turning this delinquent into a more polished and respectable boy. Aedan was convinced she was trying to turn him into a girl. She seemed to have done the same with her husband who, big as he was, quailed under her stare and took orders as meekly as a chambermaid.

Aedan found some comfort in being able to slice a few earthworms into the stew on occasion, any spiders he found got dangled on Harriet's chair, and where else to put that smelly dead frog than in one of her spare boots?

By listening to Harriet's instructions and then disregarding them and doing whatever he felt like, he actually learned to cook quite well. Harriet generally shook her head in disapproval when she tasted his dishes. "Underdone" was the usual judgement, along with "not enough salt" and "badly sliced". Then she would down her portion and help herself to more.

During the second week, Aedan arrived late at the dinner table and a fairly typical scene played out.

"What did I tell you about being late?" Harriet snapped.

"I was getting my boots on. Couldn't find the one."

"Well you should have put it where it could be found, now shouldn't you?"

Aedan grumbled something about putting them on the sill to dry and one falling out, but he said it too softly. He didn't really want to be explaining himself to her.

"Excuse me! Don't you mumble at me, my boy."

Nessa and Borr cringed. Clauman picked up his bowl and headed out to the porch, something he had taken to doing in such moments. When his temper was roused, he could be terrifying, but walking out on conversations was another thing he was practiced at. He showed particular contempt for these petty squabbles. Harriet followed his back with her eyes before returning to Aedan. He was staring at his bowl, trying to hide within himself, to find some quiet corner where his presence would not be offensive. He just wanted to be left in peace.

"Are you sulking?" Harriet demanded.

"No."

"Look at me when you speak to me."

Aedan looked at her and sighed.

"Did you sigh? Ha! So you are sulking. Gave yourself away, didn't you? Don't you turn your head away." She waited for Aedan to turn back. "Sighing is the first mark of sulking, and if there's one thing I know, it's how to put an end to sulking. Now you snap out of this and fix a smile on your face this instant or you'll be scrubbing floors till midnight."

He could no sooner have smiled than sprouted feathers and begun laying eggs. So he scrubbed.

He began doing things poorly. Why, he was not entirely sure. Perhaps it was a desperate attempt to keep part of himself from Harriet's conquest of him.

It was this very imprisonment that sparked something in Aedan. In a dusty part of his mind he began to remember that he was not a mule – a drudge without mind or soul. He began to realise that he missed the freedom of wandering through the trees, of racing the wind and laughing in the exhilaration of a rabbit-chase, of searching the hills for mysteries and listening to the forest for secrets, of climbing so high that he was afraid and then casting his eye over a world far wider than it had appeared from the ground, of wondering what lay in a direction and setting out to discover — of pursuing a course that was his own.

So one afternoon, while Harriet was burning something for supper, he slipped out and asked his father if he could join the men, then hobbled out into the yard where he worked beside them on the jobs that his crutches permitted, getting himself as dirty as he knew how. When Harriet found him, she threw a mighty tantrum and ordered him to clean himself and get back into the house where he belonged. Aedan's reply was strategic: "My father said I could work with him."

Harriet glared at Clauman who looked back without expression. Neither said anything and she stormed back into the house. Aedan released a small sigh, wondering how long the respite would last. When he turned, he saw his father was looking at him with a hint of amusement.

As soon as the work was done, Aedan limped out into the trees, in search of the solitude he had so desperately craved. It was difficult going. His left leg had healed enough to take weight, but his right was considerably weaker.

He moved through the woods and his thoughts soon began to tug in other directions. After covering a very painful mile, he found an isolated spot where the birch trees grew thickly and he could sit and let his mind loose without fear of interruption. He had kept his feelings deep, guarding them well from Harriet's prying. Now they tumbled out.

Sadness over the events in the Mistyvales, the invasion and destruction of peaceful lives, had gradually been giving way to anger, a white hot anger that rose in him now and caused his breath to come quickly.

For mere profit, men had brought death to the gentlest and kindest person he had ever known.

He would repay Quin with a fitting violence, a fitting justice. And not just Quin.

Lekrau, the nation that had been no more than a rumoured threat had entered his life and torn half his heart from him. Lekrau had become his personal enemy.

He realised how much he hated tyrants, the strong who stood on the weak. If he had only been stronger … It was a thought that had returned to him often in the past weeks. He needed to learn to face up to men. He needed to grow strong, stronger than the tyrants that marched over his life – Quin, Dresbourn, and even the one man who had begun it all …

Then, once he was able to keep his feet before even the strongest of men, he would avenge her. After that he would avenge every person that had fallen to that hateful nation. Before he died, Lekrau would know the sting of its own whips, its slave ships would find the bottom of the sea, and chains would be turned on their masters. If no army was bound that way, he would raise it. There was no solace to be found in hoping these traders would avoid him, that they would pick another place, another town. That was no better than wishing tragedy on others. There was a time when the hunter had to be hunted.

One day.

Suddenly the thoughts were no longer idle ideas. The images seared, fixed themselves in his mind. It was not the purpose he had expected to hold, perhaps not the purpose his parents or even Kalry would have wanted, but as he pictured burning ships and slavers hurled into their own dungeons, there was a fierce stirring in him, a hunger that demanded action. No, she probably wouldn't have wanted this, but every time he thought of her – and he knew it would happen often in the years to come, for how could he ever forget her – every time, he would see those flames, and he would let them grow.

It had to start now.

Fighting against the pain, he got to his feet and worked his way up to the top of a knoll that faced west, that faced Lekrau. He dropped both crutches and grimaced as he took weight on the shrunken right leg. Then, throwing his fist in the air, he let out a scream of defiance that tumbled through the valley and echoed between the rugged crags. It might have seemed a small thing – the raging of a mere boy – perhaps even something a man might have laughed at, yet there was flint behind it, flint that could one day set whole nations alight.

The echoes faded, but in Aedan's head they seemed to grow louder, building, growling, sparking. When he returned to the house, his step was firmer, his face grimmer, and something flashed in his glance.

He did not work in the house again and instead remained with his father and Borr. Harriet voiced her growing concerns – that he was losing all the ground he had gained, that he had slipped down the ladder again into reckless, filthy and shameful ways. Aedan began to realise that there were some people whose good opinion he actually didn't want.

From then on, things changed quickly. He brushed from his mind the dull passivity that had gathered there. He ate well and started to exercise his legs, overdoing it at first and causing enough pain to rob himself of sleep for two nights. But when he found a bearable routine of flexing, stretching and slow walking, he began to build the muscles without damaging them. His right leg still hurt, but he was at least able to walk again. He took full advantage of this. By the end of his first month at this lost inn, he was disappearing for hours at a time into the woods.

There had always been a wildness to him, but it was like it had been uncaged and now grew by the day, despite Harriet's frantic efforts to tame him. Eventually she abandoned her project and regarded him with surly disappointment.

As his evenings were freed, Aedan found he had the time to resume his lessons with his mother. They read to each other from the store of books Nessa had managed to slip in between her belongings while packing. When the others retired, the two of them would translate stories and jokes into Orunean, talking and laughing late into the night. Instead of making him tired, Aedan found these times reviving his mind in the same way exercise was reviving his body.

As Aedan's strength increased, so did his father's restlessness. One afternoon, Aedan spotted a column of grey smoke a few days journey back along the trail they had taken. When he reported it, Clauman dashed from the house and ran to the nearest vantage point. He returned pale and tense.

"Time is up," he said. "We leave at first light tomorrow."

The women were seated at the table when Clauman, followed by
Borr and Aedan, rushed into the house. Clauman told his wife in
clipped terms what he had seen, and informed her that they were
to begin packing immediately.

"But who is it?" Nessa asked.

"No way to tell at this distance, and we are not waiting to find
out."

"It's been half a year since that slaver tragedy, and our faces
haven't been seen in the Mistyvales for at least two months. Do
you think they still are after Aedan?"

Clauman's expression shifted and his eyes turned back to her
as if he had been thinking something very different. "Aedan? Yes
… of course. Who else?"

Aedan felt his skin turn cold at the idea of being dragged
before a court with Dresbourn as judge.

"Is it more of that hullabaloo from the Mistyvales?" Harriet
asked in the way a nanny speaks to a tale-spinning child.

Clauman raised an eyebrow at her tone. He replied without
expression, "It seems they aren't satisfied with our exile."

There was a heavy silence in the room.

"Castath, you say?" asked Harriet.

Clauman nodded.

"Borr and I have been talking. We've had enough of being
marooned out here on our own. This was supposed to become a
busy road. Instead it's been forgotten. So we would like to come
along and start over at Castath too."

Aedan muttered something rude under his breath.

"We will take the DinEilan road, east of Vallendal," said Clauman. "Through the territory of Kultûhm."

Nessa paled and Aedan shuddered as they now remembered the original plan.

"Then we cannot join you," said Borr, whose eyes were large with disbelief. "How could you even consider that route? Haven't you heard what –"

"Oh hush!" said Harriet. "The quantity of stories only proves that they are all nonsense. That's always the way it works. The more stories there are about something the more certain you can be that none of them are true, or haven't you learned that yet?" It was the nanny tone.

Borr dropped his head. Everyone else shifted uncomfortably.

"Anyway," Harriet continued, "that is the shortest route from here, and I don't want to be travelling when the baby gets bigger." She patted her belly and winked. Realisation didn't come immediately, but when it struck, Nessa leapt off her chair and threw her arms around her friend.

The men exchanged a silent handshake.

Aedan slipped away and, after checking that nobody was watching, retrieved the little leather case from under the stairs, hung it around his neck and tucked it under his shirt.

Borr and Harriet had a large wagon drawn by a ponderous carthorse. They had to pack and unpack several times through the night before they were satisfied. Finally, Borr strapped a few chicken coops on top and tied a dozen goats to the back while the rest were freed. Clauman groaned as Snore flapped his way up the luggage and settled himself bravely beside the hens.

Borr and Harriet lingered a while as the other wagon moved off. When they joined the trail, their faces reflected the thoughtfulness of leaving home.

Clauman doubled back to cover the tracks and to pin a note to the door. Aedan had watched over his mother's shoulder as she wrote what her husband dictated. The note invited visitors to make themselves at home until the owners returned from a two week long gold-scouting trail. Aedan hoped that one of the visitors would be literate. Anyone would wait a long time for news of gold.

For ten days they travelled east, Clauman pushing for speed, seething at every obstruction, peering back from the top of every rise. The terrain grew more rugged and the land wilder by the league. Often in the night, Aedan woke to the noises of nearby sniffing and the leafy crunch of padded feet. Once, the camp erupted in a furious squawking and flapping. The yells of the men and screams of the women were enough to frighten away whatever had applied its very sharp teeth to the hutches, as deep grooves told in the morning light.

The next evening there was another attack. This time the growls were deeper and the wagon shook with some violence, but by the time the men approached with flaming branches there was no predator to be seen. It was only when the sun rose that they discovered some of the goats were missing. Clauman looked for a long time at the wide, three-toed prints in the sand without being able to recognise them. After that they kept the fire burning high all night. Whoever was on watch had the responsibility of adding wood whenever the flames dipped. They lost another four goats when Harriet dozed off.

Near the end of the second week they reached a split. Left led to a pass in the mountains and eventually to Rasmun. It was the old Orunean road, forgotten and overgrown. They turned right, onto what was little more than a vague suggestion of wagon ruts.

Mostly they were not sure if what they had was the road or a deer track. Times beyond count they had to double back and find detours around gullies or thickets the wagons could not cross. Twice they came upon stone bridges spanning deep ravines. Clauman walked up onto the first of them alone while the others watched in tense silence. Aedan could see his father stepping across holes where rocks had lost their grip and plunged into the churning river below. When Clauman came back, he shook his head and opted for a long detour. The second bridge was in better condition, though it spanned a far more terrifying gorge. This time the detour would have been too long. They led the wagons over one at a time, and all released deep sighs of relief when the last wheels rattled off the stones onto the grassy earth.

At the foot of the bridge, Aedan found a stone pillar engraved with symbols he had never seen. He scraped away some of the lichen and peered at this remnant from a distant time. The edges of the script were weather-scarred in a way that told of great age, but the symbols themselves told nothing until he began to look more carefully. Some of the shapes were almost like pictures – waves, fire, the moon, a bird – and he began to wonder if it might actually be possible to understand something of the meaning. He pored over it, full of imaginings, until voices called him back to the present and to the receding wagons.

More and more regularly, Clauman sent Aedan ahead to scout and find where the dwindling marks reappeared. When Harriet objected to a child being given that responsibility, Clauman's reply was terse: "I taught him. He can manage." Then he turned to Aedan and whispered, "If there's one thing she knows, it's not to be found out here."

Aedan laughed and his heart swelled. It was a sudden togetherness, a sharing, and he knew how much he had missed working beside his father. Clauman was often distant, even when near. But in that little shared secret, that moment of understanding, the magic of a father-and-son bond was rekindled. From then on, Aedan scouted with a will, cutting across any terrain to reach a vantage point from where he could discover the best route. He was now able to walk without pain and could even jog for short stretches.

Hills grew around them as they approached the constantly rising DinEilan Mountains. When they reached the foothills, the colossal peaks filled a great portion of the eastern sky. Mornings were now cloaked in a dreamy shade, and dew remained long on the grass until the sun was able to clear the spine of the range.

The trail rose and fell steeply over the many valleys and sometimes wound along the contours of great mountain slopes that pushed out between the hills. Aedan often found his eyes drifting from the road, drawn up the grassy banks that rose higher and steeper until at last, when it looked as if they would fall back on themselves, they gave way to sheer walls of grey rock. The precipices were stern in aspect and bewildering in size – when they could be seen – for they were lost more often than not in mist and cloud. It was the first time he had been at the foot of one of the great mountains, and he knew now why there were so many poems about them. He also knew, without bothering to attempt it, that it would never be possible to squeeze them into words.

The shapes of the peaks, oddly enough, were more obscure from close. They hardly resembled the names they must have been given from a distance – the Red Fist, the Bullhorns, the Chariot, the Three Sisters. The horns looked as blunt as the fist from here and the sisters were nothing alike. This, however, did not take away from their impressiveness, as each day they soared higher and higher over the approaching travellers.

The wagons splashed and clattered over rocky beds of young, shallow rivers and creaked up the ridges where the tough stalks of dense tussock grass sighed in the wind.

From here they were finally able to look out over the great expanse of Lake Vallendal, a body of water so vast as to be more of an inland sea. Aedan had often heard of the great lake. Many myths and adventures surrounded it, some of which played out in his imagination as his eyes took in the great reaches, like the fleet of fishing boats that sank in a storm and were said to now sail beneath the water, searching for the harbour. When the lake was still, it was a giant mirror cracked only by the occasional breaching fish or a busy fleet of ducks, but when the wind was restless, the choppy water looked dark and deep and full of mysteries.

The mood of the party grew heavier as they progressed. Clauman's eyes cast about in all directions, not just behind. They were now in the heart of DinEilan – the territory of bears and wolves said to be unusually bold and vicious, and soon they would enter the lost realm of Kultûhm.

Travelling so near to the peaks, they often woke in thick mist that would slip off the rim of the mountains and glide down through the valleys during the night, swallowing the slopes and woods in a murk of quiet secrecy. It made travel far more dangerous. Aedan never ventured far ahead in these conditions for fear of getting lost in the vastness of dim, shrouded hills.

The day was just beginning to clear when Nessa exclaimed and pointed to a stand of trees a few miles up the valley they were crossing.

"Look! They are as big as the pearlnut tree."

Even at a distance it was clear that the trees were giants, swaying with ponderous gravity in the wind that caused lesser trees to shake and shiver. It was not just the trees that were oversized – even the surrounding scrub and wildflowers stood as thick and tall as reeds. The island of strange growth reminded Aedan of the way grass springs up near a seep or over a patch of rich soil, but he had never known water and compost to produce such growth.

Aedan wanted to explore, but Clauman kept him back, eager to push on and leave the area by nightfall.

Aedan slept fitfully that night. It was a little before dawn when something drew him from sleep. He sat up and listened. A chattering river leapt down its rocky bed nearby, a few crickets creaked, there was a muffled pop from the sleeping coals in the fireplace – somebody, probably Harriet, had let it die out again.

That was not good. He listened now with a sense of alarm. It had been something else, something that had not belonged ...

A huge sound filled the air. He jumped to his feet. The distant reverberations of something between a bellow and a howl shook in his chest. The tone was floating and mournful, but full-throated, deep and resonant.

Clauman had his head cocked. He was listening too. Nessa's eyes were wide open.

"What is it?" Aedan whispered.

It boomed again. Far away, yet loud enough to rouse any sleeper. Borr and Harriet, however, slumbered on.

"The pattern of the call reminds me of a woodland fox," Clauman said, not whispering, "but it's obviously too deep, too big. It must be something like a bear, though I don't know any that call in this way. It is probably an animal that we don't see further west, and it's definitely something with a big throat."

"It sounds lonely," said Aedan.

Though it was dark, the embers illuminated Clauman well enough to reveal a hard look.

"Don't you get any ideas about going out there. It's probably a lonely stomach and you'll fill it nicely. This is not the Mistyvales. We don't know this area and some of the stories just might ... You stay put."

With that, Clauman got up and began to rouse the fire and boil water, stamping his feet and cracking branches as loudly as he could. Sleeping on the watch was something he was not prepared to accommodate. Aedan knew there would be no point lying down again, so he rolled up his blanket and sat on it in front of the reviving flames as a grey dawn crept in. But that did nothing for his restlessness, so he climbed a tree, hoping to see through the holes that were torn in the mist from time to time. All he could make out were leaves and a few tree tops. When he was slick with an icy film of gathered mist, he dropped down through the branches and tucked into a breakfast of boiled maize crush – a simple porridge, but delicious.

The deep hooting call ceased, but Aedan could not shake a feeling that made him want to constantly check behind him. As soon as his bowl was cleaned and his blanket packed, he scuttled up the tree again in the hope of glimpsing the strange animal. But as he hung in the mist, another thought crept towards him – the fortress of Kultûhm could not be far ahead.

This was the part of the journey that had been hanging in all their minds like a great sleeping bat nobody wanted to rouse. He climbed down as wheels began to creak and roll out of the camp, jumped onto the back of his father's wagon and climbed to the top of the baggage, the highest point. His eyes were busier than usual.

It was later that morning as the hills were just emerging from their misty blanket when he spotted a dark round tower standing well over the distant hills, cruel fang-like spires cutting into the sky.

It brought an end to conversation. They travelled with their eyes fixed ahead. The beast with the strange call was forgotten.

The land was such that they were not able to give the fortress a wide berth, for on the left the mountain pressed its flanks out, and on the right the lake crept in and stole the low ground. It was with a feeling of some inevitable advancing fate that Aedan watched the tower loom higher with every advancing mile. Most of the day had gone when they emerged from a thick glade to a sight that caused even the horses to stop and raise their heads. Both wagons shuddered to a halt. The whole party gaped.

The ancient mountain fortress of Kultûhm was something that few claimed to have seen, but there were none who had not heard of it, and for good reason. It had been the home of the Gellerac people – the most powerful and, without a doubt, the cruellest empire ever to dominate the western mainland. Their navy had ruled Lake Vallendal, using it to reach far out into the surrounding areas. Fleets would swoop down on lakeside towns and armies would march inland. They would take what they pleased and none could oppose them. Taxes were harvested with a brutality that was almost inconceivable – villagers were simply burned alive until the coffers were full.

There had been many uprisings. Coalitions of rulers had more than once laid siege to their oppressors, but the great fortress had never been taken. Rebel armies broke against the walls like waves bursting on a rocky peninsula.

Yet at the height of Gellerac power, the oppression abruptly ceased. A wrecked fleet of ships was found washed up after a storm, and this was the last that was seen of Kultûhm's population. The fortress lay open, in deathly silence.

Plague was the word, mostly, but stranger theories abounded. Explorers and researchers, once they ventured behind the great walls, were never seen again. The emptiness of Kultûhm was a question that had lured many into its shadows, and released none.

While Aedan was not free from curiosity's tug, he knew too much about those doomed ventures. Looking from this distance was more than enough.

The fortress was colossal on a scale he had never imagined. He had heard stories, even read an account of the dimensions and architecture, but to actually see it now where it crouched on its mountain throne, to fall under the spell of its silent watchful power that seemed to hush even the songs of birds ... He shivered. It was as if he had stumbled across some giant predator.

The fortress rose over a hill with sheer quarried sides, dominating the surrounding land. Only the nearby mountains stood above it. The hundred-foot-high walls were of dark stone turned black in places where centuries of trickling water had stained the surfaces and fed cloaks of moss. Trees fought for light at the base while ferns draped, spilling from narrow slits and cracks. An enormous creeper clung from the great round tower and reached its thick arms out over the surrounding buildings like tentacles.

Despite the invasion of plants, a few cracks and some crumbled stone, there was little structural damage that could be seen. Most of the towers and turrets stood firmly among the city that rose within. The place would have been impenetrable even now if it were not for the lowered drawbridge and the heavy wooden gates standing ajar.

Though the castle itself was impressive, there was something else that made it significantly more intimidating. In front of the walls was a plain where about a dozen statues ringed the buildings, facing out as if on guard. But these were statues the likes of which none of the travellers had ever seen. From a distance it was clear that they stood nearly as high as the walls themselves.

Some of these stone giants took the shapes of fully armoured soldiers, one with a sword many times the height of the surrounding firs, one with a poleaxe the size of a small ship. Beyond the giant soldiers were mythical beasts with features so life-like that they appeared only to be holding their breaths while under scrutiny.

The party found it as uncomfortable to take their eyes off them as to stare. Clauman was the first to snap out of the trance and urge the horses on.

They chose a course to the right and hurried around the outside edge of the plain. Nobody spoke as they rattled past, though their eyes turned constantly to the left.

From the shadows in the high windows, Aedan found it easy to imagine the much-rumoured darkness looking down at them. Amid all the speculation, the one thing unanimously agreed on was that those who attempted to explore Kultûhm never returned. It was clear that none in the party wanted to know why.

"Probably a hive for bandits," Borr said. "Foolish to linger."

That was about as many words as Aedan had heard from the man in a week. It was also complete nonsense – there would be no bandits in such a forgotten corner of the world. But nobody argued. Not even Harriet raised her opinions on "those empty stories". Aedan looked back at the hollow eyes of statues and the dark slits in the turrets. There was something watchful about the emptiness of Kultûhm, and he was very happy to be travelling away from it.

They had covered about a mile when a high keening howl floated over the air and turned it to ice.

It was Harriet who shrieked the word that leapt into everyone's minds. "Wolves!"

Chapter 13

Both wagons stopped and all eyes scanned the hills.

"There!" said Clauman.

They looked in time to see the grey shapes surging down the distant slope, racing towards them. It was a big pack, very big. The fold of the land soon hid them, but everyone knew what was coming.

Aedan looked around. There were no trees nearby, no refuge, except …

"The fortress," Clauman shouted. He turned the horses and lashed them to a gallop, causing the wagon to leap over the ground. The other wagon, drawn by the ponderous carthorse, fell behind.

"Take the reins Aedan," his father shouted, handing them over and reaching back for a bow that he tried to string.

The fortress grew larger and they turned off the track and bounced over the plain. They headed for the stone road that cut a long, twisting way up a steep slope, edged on the left side by a sheer drop into a rocky chasm, and leading eventually to the giant gate.

"Don't slow down," Clauman yelled over the clattering wheels, as Aedan allowed the horses to ease the pace through the first corner.

"But the wagon might tip."

"Don't you question me!" Clauman found the whip and applied it to the animals.

Aedan braced himself for the next corner. The wheels skidded and kicked up a shower of chips from the cobbled surface. He felt the inside wheel lift slightly, and caught a glimpse of the drop beyond the outer wall. The next corner was worse.

Clauman looked behind him and spun round, his face pale. He lashed the horses furiously and did not hold himself back as they approached the last corner.

"We're going too fast," Aedan screamed, pulling on the reins. His father wrenched the reins away.

The corner was on them. The horses had veered off their line in the confusion and now made a jagged turn. The wagon lurched, its inside wheels lifted and struck the inner wall, thrusting the wagon over onto its side. It slid over the road with a grinding of stone and rending of beams until it crashed into the outer wall which collapsed and fell into the chasm. The three people had been thrown to the ground, but the horses were dragged after the wagon. It looked as if they would be pulled over the edge until the strain became too much and the leather snapped. The animals surged up from the ground, stamping and rearing, while the wagon, with all the family's worldly belongings, hurtled downward to be smashed and lost among the rocks far below.

Aedan pushed himself off the ground. A heavy rattling drew his attention and he turned to see the other wagon taking the first corner at the bottom of the hill. More than a dozen wolves were closing in, coats rippling, ears flattened, long legs reaching for more ground with each stride.

"Run!" Clauman yelled, grabbing his wife's elbow and heading for the gate. Aedan was half a stride behind.

It was perhaps fifty paces. Before he reached the gates, Aedan saw what looked like a drawbridge lowered to the ground. As he approached it, he understood its purpose. The final sixty feet of road was simply missing. With the drawbridge raised, there would be a barrier of air over two hundred feet deep. Aedan tried not to look to the side as he ran after his parents onto the bridge, their feet causing the ancient beams to shudder beneath them. They had to bend their course around two large holes where rotten timbers had fallen into the chasm.

The walls, imposing from a distance, were mountainous now – ancient buttresses that reared overhead and blotted out half the sky. A hideous turret-like figurehead stood over them, directly above the gate, leering down through hollows that Aedan half expected to disgorge burning oil.

They reached the end of the drawbridge and sprinted between the colossal wood-and-iron gates, at least three feet thick, into a long stone passage with an elevated ceiling. A gridwork of heavy iron bars loomed ahead. It was a portcullis that could have held back any army, but fortunately it was half-raised and probably rusted into position for good. They sprinted underneath the iron spikes and burst out into daylight. Aedan staggered to a halt, casting his eyes around him. Horror locked his feet in place.

It was not the height of the walls, or the weight of the iron and stone, or the vastness of the courtyard in which he now stood that froze him.

Kultûhm was not empty, not as Aedan had understood the word.

Skeletons were strewn everywhere. Some were the bones of animals, but many were not. The eye sockets of countless skulls fixed him with dark, haunting stares.

Beyond the acres of dead remains, the courtyard was enclosed by heavy walls of stone. Against them, standing as if on ceaseless guard, were lines of twenty-foot statues – soldiers with the heads of snarling tigers, bears, wolves and lions. Lips drawn, they glared at the intruders from green jewelled eyes set in black stone.

Clauman seemed less affected than his son by the deathly spectacle. He only hesitated for an instant before turning to the side and rushing them all into a guard room. Once within, he put his shoulder against the door of iron bars, and with feet skidding on the dusty floor, heaved it closed, drawing screams from the neglected hinges. He kicked the bolt until it broke free of its rust and scraped home.

As had become his habit, his hand went to the velvet pouch on his belt, but it was not there. He had left it with the baggage.

Aedan began to tremble as he saw his father staring into the courtyard, fists and jaw clenching. He knew those signs. He knew what was coming. The fragile closeness they had built over the past weeks, no more than twigs and thread, was about to be met with steel.

Clauman turned around, his whole body rigid.

Nessa was standing between them. "Please Clauman, don't." She may as well have spoken Orunean. There would be no more reasoning with him until the rage had been given its way.

He thrust her aside and strode at Aedan.

"That was everything, you wretched, disobedient fool of a boy!" he roared, his face twisted and contorted by the violent emotions, almost unrecognisable. "Everything we own!" He lunged forward and struck Aedan on the head, threw him to the floor and proceeded to kick him while shouting profanities, setting his fury loose to take its accustomed course.

When Clauman turned away, gripping Nessa by the arm to keep her from comforting her son, Aedan crept into the corner and scowled. Gradually the paralysing fear drained away and what took its place was a cold, whispery anger. He glared at his father's back. His fists shook as he imagined driving forward, hitting, screaming and settling the debt.

Yet for all the flames of retaliation that grew inside him and swirled around until his vision was seared, this was his prison. He knew from hard experience that the anger would not liberate him. It would only torment him with images of snarling revenge that tasted so sweet and would later turn to a dead weight of depression and guilt. But he did not care, and gritted his teeth all the more until his head shook with the violence of his thoughts. These feelings were his secret, his to guard. It was his right to nurture them and to indulge the glowing hate, shivering before its cold fire, drawing it into his bones.

Clauman was staring out through the bars at something, or nothing. For some men it was drink that moved them to this kind of utter destructiveness. Clauman needed no such aid. When it flared, his anger carried him past all restraints of reason. It carried him to a place where the treasured bonds with his wife and son – even if they were treasured in secret – were forgotten, where all he could see was the inferno of his passion. And every time it was getting worse. Aedan knew his father's eyes would be hooded with shame for many weeks, but it would be a bristling, angry shame, as though the fault lay with the one carrying the bruises.

The two horses galloped out from the passage into the courtyard and did not stop. One threaded its way between the heaps of bones until it found itself in a far corner. The other disappeared beneath a colossal arch at the far end of the courtyard, and the echoes of its hooves were lost within the unstirring city.

The second wagon boomed through the passage and clattered under the portcullis into the open, surrounded by the leaping, snarling pack of grey wolves. The big carthorse screamed and snorted, kicking and stamping as the wolves darted in and out.

The goats were gone. Harriet was bleeding from a cut on her face and Borr from gashes on both arms. It looked as if they were about to be torn apart and devoured only a few yards from safety.

But then something strange happened. A few of the wolves raised their noses to the air and their tails dropped as they began to whine and glance around them. Unease spread quickly. The pack lost interest in their prey; their heads spun in all directions.

Borr took the opportunity to crack his whip on their backs. Several yelped and fled, opening a path to the guard room where Clauman stood and called.

Wolves began to shrink from the courtyard and slip out the gates. Borr said something to Harriet. They jumped from the wagon and ran to the door that was held open for them. Two wolves moved forward, more out of habit than intention, but they quickly turned away, looking around with wide eyes and twitching heads.

A sound like a heavy pouring of coarse sand grew and filled the courtyard. All looked in vain to find its source. It seemed to be coming from everywhere, but there was no movement on the ground or on the walls. Aedan was on his feet now, tears brushed away, the experience pushed back into a festering vault. Something was happening.

He looked at the wolves and tried to determine where their ears pointed. Some were as bewildered as the people, but a few on the opposite end seemed to have agreed on a direction. He followed the angle of their heads. Not far from the wagon, there was a wide ramp that descended into the ground. A thick wooden trapdoor had once covered it, but this was now splintered and crumbled. It was completely dark beneath the fragments of wood, but Aedan was sure this was the source of the rough pouring sound.

He had heard of sand being used as a timer – shifting ballast for large traps. He also knew that Kultûhm had been home to the most advanced engineers of many ages. Tales of castle explorations rushed through his thoughts – arrows whistling out through cracks in the walls, floors collapsing over spear-filled pits, falling rocks, channelled floods … He had never thought he would actually face any of these. But what happened next was unlike any of the stories he had read.

The trapdoor snapped open and a sound rent the air, like the explosion of steam from a cauldron overturned on a bed of coals.

Aedan covered his ears and fell to the ground as a cloud of black vapour burst over the wagon. From within the cloud something enormous moved. Everyone fell back from the door. There was a deep fleshy thud that Aedan felt in his chest and a violent clatter of wagon wheels.

Wolves yelped and cried, scattering in all directions, some even vanishing into the city. Those that remained in the courtyard shrank into corners with their tails tucked and every hair raised.

The sandy sound returned, just audible under the squealing and whining, but this time it died away quickly. The air cleared, revealing nothing but a wagon dripping with sooty slime, and a scattering of frightened wolves.

The carthorse was gone.

Tattered ends of the harness lay on the ground.

"Did anyone see what it was?" asked Clauman, his voice thin.

Nobody spoke. Nessa whimpered. They waited for a long time, but nothing else happened.

"We need to get out of here!" Harriet gasped.

"Yes," said Clauman, "but if we run without the wagon we will not last. I'll fetch my horses. Borr, try to make something of the broken harness. The rest of you, stay in here."

The wolves paid scant attention as the men left their refuge, but Clauman and Borr each took a heavy bush knife from the wagon. Nessa continued to whimper as she saw her husband striding through the mounds of bones to the far corner where one of the horses turned and pranced about, held in place by its fear. It reared several times when Clauman tried to take its bridle, hooves whistling through the air at head height, but eventually the forester was able to snatch a broken rein and gain control.

It was an even slower process coaxing the animal back through the maze of skeletons towards the wagon. Clauman held it in place while Borr repeatedly fumbled the harness straps. At last, the knots were secure. They drove the wagon around to the entrance of the guard room, away from the trapdoor.

"One will not be enough," Clauman said, looking at how the horse strained before the huge wagon. He left them again and weaved his way towards the distant arch – one of three entrances to the city – where the second horse had disappeared. A dark forest of towers and spires and hulking buildings rose up beyond the walls of the courtyard, daring, challenging. As Clauman walked on he grew smaller and smaller against the backdrop. It almost seemed that Kultûhm was swelling over him.

Aedan watched him walk away and tried to get a hold on his emotions. He wanted to lash out – his anger still lingered. But as he thought of his father meeting his end, something began to wail inside, growing louder with each breath.

"I'm going with," he said, and slipped out the gate before anyone could stop him.

He was half way down the courtyard when the buttresses and towers rang with a horse's scream, a wild scream of fear that was suddenly cut short. Three wolves dashed out through the archway ahead and bolted past, paying him no heed. Then Clauman emerged, running hard.

"Everyone in the wagon *now!*" he yelled.

Aedan's face flushed with relief that his father lived. His father's flushed with anger.

"I told you to stay inside!" he shouted. "Do you need another lesson?"

Aedan turned and ran.

He followed the women, climbing up on top of the luggage as the wagon began to move. Clauman took the reins. He gave the trapdoor a wide berth as the wheels turned and rolled out of the courtyard, through the passage and over the drawbridge.

"String it," Clauman said, picking up Borr's very crooked bow and handing it to Aedan. It was not easily done – the ridges were poorly carved and the string was as weathered and dried as the lizard he once put in a box and forgot about. It would not suffer many shots. Once it was strung he handed it back. He hoped his father would tell him to put it to use, but instead he handed it to Borr who made it immediately clear, by the clumsy way he attempted to nock an arrow, that he had little skill with the weapon.

They moved down the stone road as fast as they dared – all knew what had happened to the other wagon – but when they reached the plain beneath, Clauman drove the horse to its limit which was little more than a fast trot. They passed the five goat carcasses that were leaping and jerking between tugging jaws as if still alive. Not until they had covered several miles did Clauman slow the pace.

Borr's arrows never landed within ten yards of a wolf – he would have done better to throw his tools – but the pack always withdrew after smelling the black coating that clung to the wagon. Though it looked and reeked like the slippery gunge from some untended drain, the foul substance seemed to be ensuring their safe passage. The wolves did not come near them. Aedan had no illusions about what would have happened otherwise. Those carcasses continued to jump around in his mind.

At the first rise, Clauman's horse showed itself no match for the lost carthorse, so several heavy bags and crates had to be discarded. While they were unloading, Harriet asked in a shaky voice what Clauman had seen.

"Streets were very dark," he said. "Saw no more than old bones, but I heard enough to know that my horse was gone. That is one place I will *never* set foot in again."

Little more was said about their experience as the travellers put ground between themselves and the fortress. Nessa remained traumatised for several days and even Harriet lost her tongue for a while.

The adults stood guard every night, but there was little sleep to be found within the turmoil of their dreams. When Aedan offered to take a shift, his father refused without offering a reason. So Aedan took a shift every night in secret from his bed, coaxing his ears out into the night. Sometimes he fell asleep, but he quickly learned to keep himself uncomfortable with roots and branches. It only failed once and he awoke with a neck as gnarled as one of his roots. He found it best to double Harriet's watch, and it was well that he did, for DinEilan was not yet finished with them.

It was the ninth day from Kultûhm. Harriet was going through her routine. She started by sighing and pacing, proceeded to sitting, then leaning, then leaning a little deeper, collapsing, and finally snoring.

Aedan got up and tossed a few branches into the dimming fire. He took the bow and a quiver of arrows, climbed onto the wagon, and wrapped himself in his blanket. He found a comfortable position, settling into a nook between bags of luggage. The gentle growling of the fire lulled him. His thoughts drifted, slowed, deepened.

A soft crack of a twig and a snort from the horse brought him to the surface with a start. He looked out into the darkness but saw nothing. Quietly nocking an arrow, he aimed out into the trees where he thought he had heard the sound. But the horse, ears pricked, was facing the other way. His father had always said to watch an animal's ears for direction. Deciding to trust the horse, he turned around and looked back towards the fire and the four sleeping bodies.

On the far side of the camp something shimmered. It was like liquid darkness that oozed out from the grass. Some of the black edges revealed themselves as it stalked into the firelight on powerful coiled limbs. It was lower than a wolf, but longer, and much heavier. Aedan had only looked at drawings of panthers; he had never seen one in the flesh. He could barely see it now. But the outline that betrayed frightening speed and power was unmistakable. It was heading for his mother.

There was no time for careful aiming. He drew and loosed the arrow in one motion. It was a wild shot, plugging into the ground well short. The panther stopped, but did not turn away. It looked at him, then looked at Nessa and crouched deeper, hindquarters bunching.

"No!" Aedan screamed, throwing his blanket aside and vaulting off the wagon. "Get away! Get away!"

He ran towards the fire and, instead of digging around for a burning branch, simply kicked at a section of red-hot coals. The fiery embers showered the huge snarling cat. And Harriet.

The panther was gone in a blink without making a sound. Harriet made many sounds and continued to make them for some time.

She called Aedan a lying, vengeful, mean-spirited, ungrateful, disrespectful, uncivilised, immature, irresponsible, untrustworthy delinquent. She bawled for the benefit of any creature that happened to be within half a mile.

"Where, Aedan? Where?" she shouted. "I don't see any panther. Do you Borr? No. What do you take me for? A fool? Do you think I don't see through your little schemes? I think it's clear to everyone that Aedan has had enough time to ruin his character and it's time I took him under my charge again, beginning with an admission of what he was trying to do here – and fitting punishment."

She began to simmer down when Clauman found the prints, clear as writing.

"Who had the watch?" he asked. "Wasn't it you, Harriet?"

"Yes, and there was no panther. The prints must have been from before we got here."

"I would have seen them. These prints are fresh. But what I want to know, now that I look at where the coals fell, is how they could have stung you unless you were in your bed."

"I was not sleeping, if that's what you imply. I was simply resting an injured leg."

"And snoring," Aedan mumbled.

She turned to him with eyes more threatening than the panther's.

Nobody slept again. They built the fire high and waited for daylight. It was only after travelling a few more days that they began to rest. Then something got the chickens – crushed the cages and took all of them except Snore who flapped down into the campsite and sheltered among the people. They heard a bear the following night, but it did not approach.

After that, the land grew less wild, and things settled down. Nessa slowly regained control of her nerves, enough to allow her to resume lessons with Aedan. They took up their reading again, though the only book remaining to them was one Nessa had been carrying in a small shoulder bag when their wagon was lost. It was among Aedan's favourites, a history of some of Thirna's greatest warriors – beginning with the legendary Krawm. Aedan read and re-read it, occasionally asking for explanations of wordy passages. His interest in war now had a keen edge that he did not attempt to disguise. Though his mother showed little enthusiasm for the descriptions of battles, even she was impressed by the feats of bravery, especially those of Krawm.

"He reminds me of William," she once said with a catch in her throat, "fearlessly loyal."

"Except twice as big," Aedan reminded her. "Remember the time Krawm picked up a coal stove and flung it through the door when the rebels inside refused to open up."

"I'm sure it's exaggeration," Nessa said with a smile as she ruffled Aedan's hair. But he didn't believe her – wouldn't believe her. In the company of these great men that strode through the worn pages, he was liberated. He wanted to believe in the impossible, the chance of a life that rose above what he had known. These men told him that it could be done, that even the strongest oppressor could be overthrown.

Sometimes in the evenings Aedan would move a little ways from the others and sit with his back to a tree, looking out at the great wall of mountains that stood silent and majestic in the moonlight. No one to bind them, nothing to press them down.

He felt the bruises that still marked his arms. Something was becoming clear – hoping to grow strong under his father's rule would be like trying to grow a tree under a rock. But even if his father did not constantly crush him, Aedan needed to learn more than his father could teach. Men like Quin were not only strong; they were trained, well-studied, and cunning. He would need to be more so.

An idea sprang up like a bright yellow flame in dry tinder.

At Castath there would be an army – he would join it. He would learn to fight, and he would enrol for officers' training where he could study the art of war, perhaps even under the great leaders like the generals Osric, Vellian or Eranath. He was old enough now to be an apprentice; even his father would understand that. He would have to be careful how he asked, though, and would need to pick the time well.

Over the next weeks Aedan worked hard to develop his hunting skills, bringing in birds, rabbits and occasionally a small deer. The meat was no mere luxury – their supplies were dangerously low. When he brought his kills in, there was a part of him that tried to forget the past and that hoped for a nod or word of praise from his father, but those grey eyes seldom met his.

This was how it had happened before. It was Clauman's sudden anger that moved him to break the relationship but it was lingering shame that kept him from mending it. It would be a long time before the freshly painted incident would fade, a long time before they would laugh again.

Nessa was quick to praise Aedan's hunting which she said was remarkable for someone of his age. Though he appreciated her compliments, they only made his father's silence louder. At times like this, he mulled over the words Thomas and Dara had brought him, the words his father had spoken, and he wondered if he would ever hear such words himself.

Harriet, however, was not so backward in making her feelings known. She shook her head with exaggerated disapproval every time she saw Aedan return to camp, dirty, scratched and flushed with returning health; though she ate her share of the meat without difficulty. In spite of her constant dissatisfaction that hung like a low grumbling cloud, the storm did not burst again. Perhaps it was that they were no longer under her roof. Whatever the explanation, Aedan was thoroughly happy with the change.

But there was one storm that he longed to see again. Every day he looked towards the mountains, hoping to glimpse those cloud formations, the spectacle that had recently become legend. A few storms did cross their way, but only the usual wet and angry kind.

He did, however, see several more of the giant trees. Unlike the first, though, almost all of them were dead.

A few more weeks of travel brought them to the end of autumn and the beginning of the southern settlements. The track became a road, and for the first time in months, they were found in the company of other people. The landscape had changed. Gone were the tumbling hills and valleys of their northern home where grass and forest grew as thick as wool. Southern Thirna looked to be an area of great open spaces.

As they reached the top of a gentle rise, the wide Castath basin rolled out beneath them. Colossal plains covered in fine grass reached away into a hazy distance. Standing like sentinels over the low-lying bowls of land were hills clothed in dark green trees and topped with rocky faces. Between them, farmers ploughed and sheep grazed, the animals speckling the fields with tiny puffs of white. The sky, however, held not a single cloud, and the warm afternoon breeze drifted up to them carrying the distant lowing of cattle and the murmur of water. A lazy silver river snaked across the plain, and a few miles ahead, on its banks, were the walls of the great southern city, Castath.

This was the first inhabited city Aedan had seen. Where Kultûhm had awed him with its towering walls and a sense of fearful power, Castath bewildered him by sheer sprawling size. He had never even imagined the possibility of so many houses. They gathered with increasing density along the roads nearer to the city walls. He could only wonder how they would be packed against each other within. Travellers poured towards and from the city gates like ants.

On the south side of the river, much of the land was covered in a large forest, and that gave him some comfort. Beyond it, to the west, was an unusual range of mountains that stood straight up from the ground like a knife pressed into the earth along its length. He had read about the Pellamines. They were not high, but even from here the sheer face was impressive.

After questioning several travellers, Borr and Harriet decided to look for work in one of the many inns that lay outside the city. Clauman kept a tight silence and said only that he would head into the city itself. Borr offered to pay double for the horse, because without it his wagon would have remained at the fortress. Clauman would accept only the regular price. When Harriet insisted, Clauman became firm, almost harsh, as if he had been offended.

The women embraced and promised to make contact as soon as they were settled. The men, apparently seeing no need to break from tradition, exchanged a silent handshake.

Aedan had chosen to walk much of the recent journey to build his strength, but the walking now was unlike any he had yet done. Traffic began to fill the roads, and he learned quickly that the road itself belonged to those on hoof or wheel, while those on foot kept well to the side.

He had heard stories of Castath, but because it was said to be smaller than the northern stronghold, Tullenroe, he had naturally assumed it to be small, a kind of overgrown village. There was nothing village-like about what he now approached. The number of people was overwhelming, dizzying. But what surprised him more than the number was the diversity.

Nobles glided past in varnished carriages drawn by horses that were groomed to dazzling perfection, while filthy ragged children shouted and ran abreast, holding out their hands until the driver's whip chased them off. A farmer in a dirty woollen tunic trundled along, pushing a cart of turnips and cabbages and singing a light ditty. Then he flung the handles down and thrust his arms in the air to call down pestilence after being splashed by the chaise of a wealthy silk merchant. The merchant's clothes proclaimed him a man of great class while his shouted reply revealed him a man of none. An open wagon humming with flies and drawn by mangy oxen sloshed past, headed towards a dump near the river. The smell of the wagon struck like a hammer. Aedan pulled a face as he guessed what it contained. A little further along was a stall filled with sweetmeats, and beyond that a gallows where raven-pecked criminals performed their parting service to the city by delivering a warning to all.

The heavily defended gates of the city grew sterner as the distance shrank. Soldiers of the guard were everywhere. Above the gates, the battlements were lined with more soldiers, all fully armed and threatening in their bold uniforms of yellow and red. Aedan was glancing from side to side and he noticed more than one guard looking at him. More guards stood at the gates. Their faces spoke no pleasant welcome and their eyes drilled through the stream of people that flowed in. Some they stopped and questioned. Of these, they sent a few back in the direction they had come from with harsh words and sometimes blows. This was nothing like the oversized cattle-gate at the Mistyvales where Beagan exchanged cheery greetings and quiet jokes that brought loud laughter.

Aedan felt his pulse racing. The overwhelming crush of people. The closeness of the air. The approaching hostility – he could not even pretend to belong here. The soldiers would stop them …

The soldiers did stop them.

Chapter 4

The senior guard looked from Aedan to Nessa to Clauman.

"Name and business?" he said in a strange, flattened accent.

"Halbert son of Cian," Clauman replied. "Tired of the north. Hoping to start over. Our wagon was lost on the way."

Aedan and Nessa had both glanced up at the use of false names and an untrue story, but the guard failed to notice their expressions.

"Northern accent, northern ignorance," he said. "Castath won't be an easy landing for the likes of you." His face softened as he glanced at Nessa's frightened eyes. "Go to South Lane by Miller's Court. Cleanest lodging you'll get for copper. If you can pay with silver, there's some fine places in the north-east quarter."

Clauman thanked him and they turned to leave.

Aedan had been so lost in dread, struggling with wild fears of being sent away or being jailed for the breach of some strange law, that the sudden relief was like the lifting of a physical weight. He felt an immediate liking for this senior guard with the greying hair and grandfatherly authority. He wanted to reach out and establish a form of kinship, especially as he intended to be a soldier himself.

"May I ask your name?" he said.

The guard smiled. "In twenty years, there's nobody ever asked me that. You must be small-town folk." He smiled at the adults and dropped to a knee before Aedan. "Cameron is my name. What's yours?"

"Aedan."

"A good name, a brave name which looks to fit you well. I hope you are able to settle down here, Aedan. As our south-side mayor likes to say, may the winds of bounty reward your labour."

"Thank you," Aedan said, attempting to shake Cameron's hand.

"Ah," said Cameron, stopping him. "In the south we greet men by grasping the forearm, like this." He gripped Aedan behind his wrist and gave a firm squeeze. "Else you'll be getting some strange looks. You can take a woman's hand, but the men won't like it. Remember that."

"I will. Thank you again."

Cameron smiled, nodded to all three of them, and returned to his post.

Aedan felt his heart swell. His face glowed.

Nessa smiled.

Clauman glared. As they walked away, he pinched his son's ear and muttered, "Next time you speak past me to a soldier I'll nail your tongue to the wall."

"But ... but I only meant to be friendly."

"You meant to be noticed, and that is something that could destroy us here."

Aedan was not sure what his father meant. Surely Dresbourn would not attempt to find them here. But it was clear that now was not the time for questions.

As they walked through the gates, they passed a building on their left that had soldiers all around it – obviously a small guard barracks. Aedan assumed the main barracks and military headquarters would be further in, probably near the keep.

He followed his parents into a broad cobbled street marked as King's Lane, which appeared to serve as the central artery for the city. The road was lined with stalls and booths of every description – cutlers, tailors, shoemakers, carpenters, fishmongers and many more. Scattered here and there were stands where farmers displayed the produce of their soil. All around, chickens clucked from their cages, girls trilled as they moved through the crowd with trays of delicacies, buyers haggled, and children shouted and jostled, pursuing their games. The town crier, backed by a trio of jolly musicians, cast his voice over the din with the day's news including royal decrees, notorious criminals' sentences, and the weather prophets' lies.

Though much of the arrangement was haphazard, it became clear as they continued that the buildings were growing larger and the clientele better-dressed – feathers, capes, furs, and rare cloth of blue and purple. Eventually they came to the emporium of the ill-mannered silk merchant.

Aedan saw his mother looking across the road with a hint of nostalgia at the office of a scrivener. He remembered that her father had owned three such enterprises and had taught her the skills that she had since passed on to him.

Clauman stopped to ask an elderly man of respectable appearance for directions. The man frowned at the mention of Miller's Court. He pointed across the road without a word, turned, and walked away.

They pursued the road indicated, stopping and asking for directions several more times. Streets became narrower, and dirtier. Here people moved more quickly. Few lingered where the shadows fell heavily and the smells rose thick as soup – a soup gone horribly wrong.

It was in one of these alleyways that Clauman asked a group of older, very seedy boys for directions. Their cocksure disrespect was barely concealed behind a thin coating of servility. They would be trouble. Aedan could sense it. One came up and started to explain. Two others approached and tousled behind the first boy, knocking him onto Clauman. Aedan caught just a glimpse of a hand slipping from his father's pocket, grasping the little pouch of coins that Borr had counted out. He was about to yell to his father when he noticed everyone had stopped moving. The first boy was frozen where he stood and his hand slowly found its way back to the pocket, returning the pouch. It was then that Aedan saw the dagger that his father held under the boy's chin. He must have had it ready before asking assistance. Clauman whispered something and the boy nodded as much as the dagger would allow.

"We have a guide," Clauman said, allowing his prisoner to step away.

"This way, sir," the boy said, as he walked past his companions, shaking his head at them.

Aedan's desire to be out of this tightening, hostile place was growing to a panic. He shrank from the glares of the boys, now undisguised, as he hurried between them. The only thing that kept him from running was the narrowness of the alley that was clogged ahead of him.

Miller's Court might once have had space for a court, but it was hardly possible to imagine a more densely populated spot of land. Houses pushed up like weeds competing for any shaft of light. South Lane breathed a little more, being opposite the southern wall of the city.

Before dismissing him with a coin, Clauman took the boy aside and spoke to him. Aedan saw the youngster nod with more than a trace of deference before he spun and slipped away into his warren of shadowy lanes.

After speaking to a few landlords, Clauman began to haggle with a thin, oily-looking man who was clearly more interested in Nessa than in him. Clauman appeared not to notice this and complained about the price which shifted downward with each glance the landlord made over Clauman's shoulder. Finally they struck an agreement and the family was led up four storeys to an apartment that consisted of a single room and a window. Nothing else. It was dry, in places, and the mildew had not quite completed its conquest of the floor. Other than that, it was acceptable to a man of low means and perfectly horrible to a woman of any means. Aedan knew his mother's childhood had been a comfortable one. He saw her wince, but she voiced no complaint.

The landlord scurried to the window and pushed it open. It made a crunching sound and he couldn't get it closed again, so he pretended to be setting the right angle and left it.

"There," he said, with a weaselly smile. "Best view in South Lane." His eyes wandered to Nessa.

"It will do," said Clauman, who held the door for the landlord and closed it after him. He walked to the window, busy with his own thoughts, while his wife and son looked on.

"Borrow some rags and a bucket and have it clean before I get back," he said, stepping out the door and closing it behind him with a thud.

Nessa's expression was as bleak as the room; she stood in shock. It took her some time before she was able to process the experiences of the day sufficiently to break down and cry. But after a little while, she brushed her tears aside, buried her embarrassment and summoned the courage to request what she needed from the eager landlord. Then she got scrubbing. Aedan decided he would not add to her misery, so he put his back into the labour.

Clauman returned with blankets, candles, and a loaf of hard, dark bread that had not recently emerged from the oven. They ate their first meal by candlelight on the floor. Little was said; nobody had the energy to talk, though Clauman's eyes held a flicker of something like keenness. Before lying down for the night, he said something that kept Aedan awake as effectively as one of his roots,

"Your time of idling has come to an end. For once your small size makes you useful. The forest is gone, but I have a new forest to teach you, new eggs for you to fetch."

The words unsettled him more than the thin drizzle slanting in from the open window. When he finally slept, the dreams were dark. That velvet pouch bulging with coins began to take on a new meaning, an impossible meaning, but one that would not be banished. He remembered having once seen such a pouch on Dresbourn's desk and could imagine no context in which Dresbourn would have willingly handed it across. Then he remembered his father's panic when he had seen smoke near Borr and Harriet's home, and constant watching behind them on the trail, the false name given at the gate. Confusion grew into an awful suspicion. What kind of man was his father? Did he know him at all?

Aedan awoke with his throat on fire and the drizzle still running out his nose. When Clauman heard him cough that morning, he swore and made him stand at the window facing out.

"Don't you splutter over me before tonight! Would you ruin our fortunes again?" With that, he dressed and stormed from the room. He did not return for the next two days.

They were not comfortable days. In spite of the lateness of the year, the room sizzled and steamed during waking hours, the heat unlocking rotten vapours in the soggy boards; and the evening rain continued to spit through the window, replenishing the damp. The landlord knocked several times a day, calling through the flimsy boards to check if they needed anything and if Aedan wanted to go and explore some exciting places he could recommend. Nessa froze at such moments and the look in her eye caused Aedan to grip the handle of his knife and to keep the door bolted, though the bolt would have popped off the frame with the slightest shove. By the end of the first day they were worried. By the second night Nessa was pacing.

"Do you think we can send a message to Borr and Harriet tomorrow?" she asked.

Aedan was gratified that she should ask him. He pointed out the difficulty of finding a messenger when they had no money. They could not both go, because one had to remain in case Clauman returned. She proposed, weakly, that she should go, but even Aedan knew that a foreign woman alone was more likely to draw attention than a boy.

So a little before first light on the following day, he traced his way through the maze of buildings, getting lost and nosing his way back on track. It was unlike pushing through the dense confusion of a forest, but he was soon depending on the same feel for direction he had always used, mostly without thinking – sun, slope of the ground, sounds, smells, temperature, movement of the air, and the general character of spaces. The detours helped him place a few more landmarks on his internal map and he was sure he could find a better way back to South Lane than the one they had first taken.

As soon as he was through the gates, he began to worry about his mother. He had left quietly, but the landlord had a sharp eye. The mounting worry urged him on. Soon he was running. It was early morning when he reached the area where their company had parted. It was Snore's crowing that put him on the right path, and with a few questions, he was able to locate the deep-slumbering couple. Harriet's sleepy face grew distraught and Borr's grim as they listened. Soon they were bustling out the door and headed for Miller's Court.

Aedan made only one wrong turn on the way back and recovered quickly. They could hear raised voices by the time they were half way up the stairs. Aedan heard his mother scream and raced ahead. He threw the door open and ran into the room. His mother crouched against the wall and his father stood over her, his hand raised. He spun on Aedan.

"Where have you been?"

"I – I ... We thought that it was dangerous here ... I went to ..."

"*I* chose this place," Clauman said. "Is your judgement now better than mine? It seems you also need another lesson in respect and obedience." Aedan cringed as his father advanced on him, anger rippling his face. But the blow never fell.

After an extended silence, Aedan opened his eyes and looked up to see Borr and Harriet standing in the doorway across the room. There was no friendly recognition.

"So this is how you manage your family," Harriet said. "When your anger boils up, you tip it out on them. I thought I glimpsed fear in their eyes before. Thought I saw them flinching when you made sudden moves."

"You dare question me under my own roof? The man of the house is to be respected, not like your neutered oaf with a cabbage leaf for a tongue and milk for blood."

Borr swallowed, but said nothing. It was clear the insult had struck hard.

Harriet coloured. "You call this respect," she said, pointing at the cowering wife and son. "She flinches every time you turn to her. You like that? Those bruises Aedan had after we escaped the wolves. That was you, wasn't it? Lost your temper after losing the wagon, didn't you? That's why you couldn't look him in the eye for weeks afterwards when he tried to impress you with all that silly hunting of his. I would guess the only time you truly give him recognition is when you're too angry to hold it back. Isn't that so?"

Aedan cringed. For once Harriet had struck the mark. Even he felt his father's shame and couldn't bring himself to look at him. He wished, though, that Harriet had understood a little more, enough to know that her tirade would only serve to provoke. Instead she carried on.

"Clauman, it's time I put you in your place. If there's one thing I know, it's how to –"

"Enough!" Clauman bellowed. The look he turned on her was pure hatred. "Get out of my house you foolish woman before I give *you* something to flinch at."

Suddenly, whatever ran in Borr's veins began to boil. He stepped in front of his wife and fixed Clauman with a look that had no milkiness to it. "You … you speak to her like that again … I'll … I'll …" His arms were pushed out, fingers twitching. Words, as usual did not serve him well, but he made his meaning clear enough when he smacked a heavy fist into his palm.

Even Clauman flinched at that. Borr let his eyes linger awhile and then turned to leave, but Nessa called him back.

"Wait!" she shouted. She got to her feet and spoke in a voice that trembled as though her very soul were quaking. "If it were just me, I could take it. But I cannot stand by and see my son beaten like a dog anymore. Harriet, you have finally said what has died on my tongue for years, and if I don't speak now, I'll never find the courage again. Clauman, it cannot carry on."

Aedan wished someone would say something. The silence that now filled the room was more threatening than any of the preceding words. His father's lips twitched and his eyes grew as hard as frost.

"You have chosen poorly," he said to her with deathly composure. "From now on you would be wise to count me among your enemies."

With that, he strode from the room and slammed the door behind him, striking them harder with his leaving than he had ever done with fists or boots. Nessa disintegrated into a flood of tears, and Harriet rushed to her while Borr stood silently by.

Despite Harriet's insistence, Nessa decided to wait a week, in case Clauman changed his mind. Both Borr and Harriet looked worried as they left. Aedan had never expected to want their company, but as their footsteps faded down the stairwell, the fear that crept up in him was sharp. When he and his mother were alone again in the empty little room, he felt the weight of the city begin to swell and press from all around. Not even in DinEilan had he felt so trapped, so vulnerable. There were enemies here he would not even recognise, enemies against which he could take no precautions.

The day was interminable. Heat and worry exhausted him. That night he remained awake as long as he was able, but finally a deep sleep fell on him like a thick and heavy blanket, shutting in fatigue, shutting out everything else.

Chapter

When the town bells pealed out through the darkness, Aedan thought it might be some midnight celebration. But then other sounds filtered into his dreamy half-thoughts – crashing timbers, panicked voices and a deep roar that sounded at first like a rushing wind. He opened his eyes. A ruddy glow from the gap beneath the door revealed twisting billows of thick smoke.

"Mother!" he yelled, and burst into a fit of coughing. Smoke was filling the room at an alarming rate, drifting up through the floorboards. His bare feet told him that the boards were dry, for once – and hot.

He reached his mother and began shaking her. She surfaced slowly, dulled by the thick air, and looked around in a stupor.

"Is it day already?"

"Fire!" Aedan shouted. "We need to get out."

She staggered to her feet, taking in the scene and grasping its meaning. Flames began to leap up through the gaps in the floorboards as they staggered to the door. They opened it and immediately fell backwards from the heat of flames that surged into the room. Aedan slammed the door closed. It felt as if the skin on his face and hands was bubbling.

For a moment he was overwhelmed with the pain in his temporarily blinded eyes. When he was able to look around, he saw his mother biting her fingers, eyes travelling the walls helplessly. It was clear she had no idea what to do. Neither did Aedan. A puff of clearer air disturbing the smoke reminded him of the permanently open window.

He rushed across, leaned out and looked beneath him. The walls were panelled and sheer. He might be able to climb down, but his mother would have no chance. He looked up. Long beams projected just over the window. It looked as if it would be possible to step from there onto the roof and then move along the row to a building that was not on fire.

Nessa was still biting her fingers, staring.

"Mother," Aedan shouted over the growing rumble. "We need to get onto the roof."

His mother looked at him with something between disbelief and horror.

"Look," Aedan said, drawing her to the window. "We can't go down. The only way out is up."

She stared for a long time at the people running and screaming in wild confusion. Aedan looked back at the flames growing through the floorboards, and the smoke streaming under the door. At last she agreed.

Aedan went first. Trying not to think of the fall, he put his left leg over the windowsill and gripped the inside of the frame with his right hand while reaching out with his left for the outer beam. Once he had a firm hold, he released his grip on the frame, leaned out and reached for the next beam. With his hands secure, he stood on the base of the sill, jumped into the air between the beams he was holding – at which his mother gasped – and straightened his elbows, taking all his weight on his arms by pressing down with his hands. This allowed him to swing his feet onto the same surfaces. For a light-bodied tree climber it was nothing much. A step would take him to the roof.

He shouted encouragement down to his mother over the rumble of the fire and the screams of those fleeing it. But something was wrong. Even over the past days he had noticed a vacancy and slowness in her eyes, an aimless shuffling within some deep internal labyrinths. Now the shuffling had slowed to a halt.

"Mother!" he yelled. "You have to move or the fire will catch us. I can't carry you."

She gazed at him with semi-lucid recognition, then with no apparent awareness of the danger, repeated the motions Aedan had just demonstrated. She might have lacked his agility, but her greater height made the manoeuvre far less demanding. He grasped her arm and helped her onto the roof. It was built of slippery wooden shingles and it was steep. Barefoot, they were able to creep up to the spine. One shingle leapt out from under Aedan and almost took him with as it spun off the roof into the waiting void.

When their heads rose over the apex, they reeled, taking in the full force of their enemy.

The fire that they had seen in the stairwell was but a hatchling. The surging beast that towered before them, its feet planted in Miller's Court, was a monster, a swelling fiend with blood-red limbs that curled and thrashed overhead. It roared with enough force to shake the ground as it ate its way forward. They stared and blinked, dumbstruck, their eyes dazzled by the glare. The whole city seemed to be lit up, bright as day.

Once he had recovered his wits, Aedan looked around for some escape. To the right, shingles burst and caught fire ahead of a second blaze as flames surged up from below. He could feel that the roof beneath him was warming quickly. To the left, there was no fire, only a little smoke, but neither was there a way down or a crossing to another roof. It ended in a sheer drop of four storeys. But if they could get into one of the rooms at the end of the wing, Aedan thought, they might be able to find a different stairway.

"This way," he called, tugging his mother's sleeve. When they reached the end of the roof, he leaned over the edge and saw that the shutters of the room beneath were closed, blocking that entry. He decided that this might not be a bad thing as he didn't want to trust his mother with that climb again.

Making sure of his footing, he began to work a shingle loose, careful not to drop it on the crowded street below. Once the first was out, he found it easier to remove more. The beams under the shingles were close together but they were weak and old. A few good kicks produced a hole big enough to climb though. The ceiling boards were soft with rot and broke easily, allowing him to see into the room. It was dark. He helped his mother, lowering her down into the room, and followed after her.

With a pang of fear, he realised that there was smoke in this room too. He ran to the door and pulled it open. Small flames and acrid clouds filled the stairway, billowing into the room, but the heat was bearable. It would not be that way for long.

He grabbed his mother's hand and pulled her out onto the landing and down the stairs. At the second floor, the flames had spread across the stairway but were still small enough to be crossed. It was when they reached the first floor that their good fortune ended. Two furiously burning trusses had fallen on the stairs, blocking them. There was no way to squeeze past without being set alight.

As Aedan looked, he heard the growing roar through the wall partitions.

It was close, he could feel the floor shaking as the monster rumbled forward. This was no time for careful thinking and thorough planning.

Covering his face as well as he was able, he ran up to the first truss and kicked it, then dived back from the heat. It still stood. He tried again. This time he heard a crack. On the third attempt the truss split and collapsed, but as it fell, it brought down a section of red-hot planking that struck Aedan across the side of his head and pinned him to the ground. The hiss and stink of burning flesh were accompanied by a pain so acute that even his mother's screams were dreamlike and distant. He was vaguely aware of being dragged through the opening he had created, down the last stairs and into the cool air of the street.

"Water! Water!" he heard her shouting, but there was no water to be spared for burns.

As he lay on the ground, he caught a glimpse of a man running wildly down the road. There was something wrong with him because he was glowing as brightly as the fire. Someone doused him with a bucket and Aedan recognised the landlord. All his oily skin was burned away. He stood shuddering for a moment, looking at his red hands, before uttering a single sob and dropping forward onto the ground. Aedan could think no more ill of him, and only wished he would get to his feet.

Then the pain found him again and he cried out. It felt as if there were glowing embers still clinging to the side of his head. He was on fire himself! He reached up to brush the coals away, but all he felt was a soft ooze, and the sudden agony kept him from touching it again. The street grew brighter and his mother dragged him away from the heat to the city's outer wall. She crouched down as the whole wing erupted in angry fire. The great beast now towered over all of South Lane.

Aedan looked around at the people leaping from windows, perched on collapsing roofs, and fleeing between buildings that rained fiery projectiles among them. It felt unreal. The bells had grown distant. Even the screams were muted, lost somewhere in the foggy glare. His mother sat beside him with her arms clasped about her, staring vacantly, rocking in a childlike trance.

It was morning by the time the blaze had lost its fury and retreated into the blackened ruins. Smoke hung in the air, darkening the sun's light. When Borr and Harriet appeared, they were clearly exhausted from searching. It was as if Aedan had been waiting to hand over the watch, for in the moment he recognised their voices, his head fell.

——

The chatter of birds and the touch of a cool breeze caused him to stir. It was the second time he had awoken in bandages. The first time, he had lost spring and part of summer. This time, judging by the soot he had to blink out of his eyes, he had only slept through a day and a night. He looked around, taking in the small loft, its single window and a closed trapdoor. He reached for his head which still felt as if it were on fire, but his fingers met with only bandages. The gentle pressure hurt, even through the dressing.

He climbed from the bed and waited until the pounding in his head subsided enough to be bearable. It left him giddy; he had to be careful while raising the trapdoor and descending the ladder into the room beneath. Nessa sat in a chair, staring out the window.

"Mother," he said.

She didn't move. "No sign of your father," she said, her voice soft, eyes unfocussed.

Aedan had expected as much, yet the words struck a hollowness inside him. It rang with a note near to loneliness, but with intruding overtones of anger like the buzz of a string or the rattle of a gong.

Then Nessa's look cleared somewhat and she turned to Aedan. "What kind of mother have I been? I never stood up to him, never asked for help to protect you. Even during the fire, what good was I to you? If it hadn't been for me, you might not have been burned."

"Don't talk like that," Aedan said, sitting beside her on the couch and taking her hand. "I didn't want to tell anyone about him beating us either. Anyway, you *did* ask for help, and it was *you* who pulled me out of the fire in the end and got burned doing it.

Don't try to hide the bandage on your other hand. I saw it when I walked in."

She smiled and ruffled his hair. "In some things, you always were older than your age, if that makes sense. You always wanted to be as old as Kalry ... Oh, I miss her ..."

Aedan had to look away until the blurriness left his vision. After a long silence, he decided it was time to be open, to share the plan he had been nurturing. "I'm going to make sure that what happened to her is brought to a stop," he said. "So I've decided I want to become a soldier, like the great generals."

Nessa looked at him with her quiet eyes. "A soldier ... So that's why we read all those war books on the way here?"

Aedan nodded and waited.

"You no longer want to be a forester? Do none of the other trades interest you?"

"No."

"Have you thought this through properly? Are you sure?"

"I'm sure, very sure."

Nessa sighed. "No mother would have the military as her first choice," she said, "but I suppose if all mothers kept their sons from the army, we would all fall victim to those like Quin." She looked at him again. "I know it would not have been your father's first choice either, but he would not be displeased. *My* father would have been proud."

"So ... you don't mind?"

"I would rather you become a scrivener or a clerk in some high tower where you'd be safe, but I think you'd just die slowly – your veins are filled with as much fire as blood." She eyed his bandage. "Wait until your injuries have healed, and then perhaps Borr can take you to the barracks. You will need money, and I'm afraid I have none, but I'm sure Harriet will help. She has been a good friend to us."

"But she's such a ..." He was about to name the four-legged beast well known to dairy farmers when Harriet, as if drawn by the mention of her name, bustled into the room and began scolding Aedan loudly enough to make his tender head ring. "Off with you," she said. "Stop disturbing your mother. She needs time to rest, and so do you." She took him by the arm and returned him to the ladder.

Later, Aedan climbed down again, but his mother had been moved to another room. He tried the doors that were not locked but all he found was Harriet busy at the sink. He closed the door quietly and retreated to his loft.

For several days he rested until he could stand without feeling as if his head was about to burst like a squeezed grape. He crept downstairs regularly, and when he was able to find his mother, they shared quiet conversations until Harriet intruded and separated them. With Clauman out the way, she was riding high in the saddle.

Nessa implored Aedan to stay on good terms with Harriet. Her frequent appeals for him to be accommodating revealed that she saw the discord well enough, but tried to mend it on Aedan's side rather than where it originated. Without realising it, she was repeating the fault she had so recently lamented. Too fearful to intervene and hold back the tormenter, she was pleading instead with the victim to be more submissive. It was a solution that would resolve the conflict while entrenching the problem. Aedan didn't have the words to understand, but he could feel the wrongness of it.

One morning Harriet called Aedan down to the kitchen where she was seated with Borr. Aedan took the place indicated.

"Your mother is weak," she said. "Weak in body and in mind. She was a prisoner to fear and guilt for too long."

"What guilt?" Aedan asked, annoyed. "She never hurt anyone."

"Guilt for not defending you like she should have. Do you think *I* would have stood by and watched?"

Aedan bristled. Harriet was treading very freely on ground that was private.

"We need to discuss your future, Aedan," she said. "Due to your mother's weakness, it is necessary for someone more capable to take charge of you. It is time to start again with your lessons where they were cut off. There will be no more hiding behind your father. I am going to set you on a decent path and Borr will see to it that I am obeyed."

Aedan looked at her, unsure how to begin. For the duration of their travels he had avoided speaking of his plans because Harriet had shown a readiness to listen in and then peck at him. He had found that the best way to survive was to keep distant, and when that was not possible, silent. But silence would not aid him now. He needed money in order to enter any trade, even soldiering, and who else could he ask in a city of strangers?

But before he could frame his words, Harriet continued. "You have spent more than enough time dabbling with bows and slings, poking around in forests. These kinds of things are for dirty, reckless boys and trappers, and you will be neither. We have discussed it and have agreed that you are to enter a trade. The best course for you would be something very different to whatever your father tried to teach you. You must be scrubbed of his influence. So we have decided to apprentice you to a chef at the inn nearby. You will start today. During the evenings I will resume the task of improving your character. It is clear to me that your mother's influence has spoiled you, indulging your irresponsible notions. That will also come to an end."

Aedan tried to calm his pulse – the throbbing felt like hammers against his temples. "I want to become a soldier," he said.

"Oh don't be ridiculous, Aedan! Look at you. You've been in bandages half the time I've known you. Your frame is not sturdy enough for soldiering."

"But my mother –"

"I have spoken to your mother and cleared up that foolishness already."

Aedan wasn't sure if she was lying or telling the truth. It worried him that both were possible.

"You, my boy, do not have the makings of a soldier. All of us can see it."

Aedan knew his face was turning red. He knew his next words would be red too, but he made no attempt to hold them back. "The things that put me in bandages killed grown men! Ask my mother if you don't believe me. Do you think soldiers don't get burned, or that they fall from cliffs without getting hurt? What do you know about the army anyway?"

Harriet's lips were bunching as her eyes narrowed, but Aedan was not finished.

"And you talk about getting rid of my father's influence, but how many times did his trapping or my hunting fill your belly? *He* taught me. It was *his* skills that kept us alive on that journey, or have you forgotten all this now that you're comfortable?"

Borr placed his hands on the table and rose to his feet. He looked at Aedan, shaking his head. This man they had assumed to be a plodding ox was turning out to be more of a guard dog, silent and watchful until roused.

Aedan drew back. He knew he had taken the wrong tone. He considered explaining his reasons for wanting to take up arms, but that would mean baring the deepest part of his soul, and he would not do that here.

"I want to become a soldier," he said again, more quietly this time.

"You will do no such thing!" Harriet snapped. "If there's one thing I know how to correct, it is stubbornness. Now get to your room, pack your clothes, and clean yourself up. Then come down here with a better attitude. The chef expects you before mid-morning." She tapped her knuckles on the table with a look that declared the conversation to be over.

Aedan dropped his head, turned and left the room.

He had no choice.

He did as he was told – went up the ladder to his room, packed his little bag, and cleaned himself up.

Then he climbed out the window and headed for the city.

Harriet could tap that table all she wanted. She had been accommodating and kind to his mother, but her kindness did not grant her ownership of him. He was no chef's assistant, and he was not going to be bullied into this woman's choices. He covered ground quickly. The last thing he wanted was for Harriet to send Borr after him.

How he would get into army training without being able to pay fees was a problem that rose tall and stern. But for now his biggest worry was escaping the prison Harriet had built.

At the gate, Aedan's bandaged head drew some attention, but the guards did not appear to bother much with children and they let him pass. Cameron was not on duty, so Aedan approached the most friendly looking of the guards.

"Hello," he said. "I want to become a soldier. Where should I go?"

The guard's surprised face broke into a grin.

"Oi, fellas, lookee here. We've a young one what wants to start soldiering." A few of the guards looked across and smirked.

"Looks like he's had some experience with violence," one said. The others laughed.

"Order!" The guard who shouted was clearly the ranking officer. He walked up.

"Don't mind them," he said to Aedan. "Only difference between you and them is that you aren't pretending to be grown up." There was some grumbling behind him. "The barracks are in the middle of the north-west quarter. You could go through the Seeps but I wouldn't recommend it. Rather follow King's Lane all the way up. You'll pass the regent's office on your left and the city market on your right. The road branches at the keep. Don't stare at the guards. Take the left branch and follow it west until it brings you to a big courtyard and the gates of the barracks. The marshals' headquarters are nearby. They have an office that faces the same courtyard. Don't mistake them for the army."

"What are the marshals?" Aedan asked, intrigued. "I think I once read something about them, but it was only a mention."

"You don't know about the grey marshals?" The soldier was almost shocked. "Ah, I suppose I should have guessed from your accent. You are new here?"

"Yes, sir."

"Well, then I'd best warn you that the marshals are not men you want to be mingling with. They are a strange breed, only ever seen where trouble is worst, normally at night. They are wolves in their grey cloaks, sent in to deal with things the rest of us would rather not know about."

"Are they soldiers too?"

"Certainly not! There is a divide between us that not even a common cause would be able to bridge. They skulk about in secret. We deal in the open. A regiment of our men came across a pair of them in the Seeps last week. Tried to question them. When they refused to answer, the soldiers tried to escort them to the barracks. Ten men they were. Spent the next week in the infirmary."

"Two marshals!" Aedan exclaimed.

"Wolves, I tell you. Unnatural and uncivil. Best keep your distance. Soldiers are the ones you want."

In Aedan's mind, the information was having a different effect. If ten soldiers could have the stuffing beaten out of them by two marshals, then how far would a soldier's skills get him? He needed to grow strong, not jolly and chummy.

Aedan glanced past the old guard at something that had caught his eye. The young guards were questioning a group of pretty young girls while a heavy-looking cart trundled by unnoticed. He saw one of the girls glance nervously at the cart and realised she was connected somehow. The girls were a decoy.

"Thank you," Aedan said. "In return for you kindness, can I point out the cart that has just slipped past your guards. I think you'll find something in there that doesn't belong in the city."

The old guard knew to act on tips. His orders were crisp and loud, and the big man trundling the cart was apprehended. It cut Aedan when he heard one of the girls screaming for her father.

As he watched, he caught sight of someone riding a horse through the crowd. Through the clutter, he couldn't tell if it was Borr, but decided it would be best to avoid finding out. Aedan ducked into the first alley and began weaving his way north-west. It wasn't the path the soldier had recommended, but it was now necessary to avoid open roads. He pulled his jacket from the pack and wound it round his head to hide the bandage lest he leave a trail of observers who could point after him through the entire city.

The girl's wails kept echoing in his thoughts. It reminded him again of that hanging he had watched. For some reason the man's wife had been present. He could still hear her scream. Sometimes he still felt angry at the hangman.

Was the law just another tyrant? Was it better to let all people go their own way and not interfere? He wondered if his father might have said yes.

He paid little attention to the surroundings while he busied himself with his thoughts. He didn't notice how the lanes grew narrower, darker, and the idlers more watchful.

Part of what eased his thoughts was a presence of another boy a few years older than him, fifteen or sixteen he thought. They had been walking a few yards apart for several blocks now. Though they shared no words, they exchanged a look or two, found each other unthreatening, and established a kind of neighbourliness, the peculiar bond often felt by travellers on uncertain roads.

Though taller, the other boy was slight and shrew-like in his movements, almost timid, but he seemed familiar with the area. When a split in the alley offered a broader road to the right, he hesitated. Aedan, eager to show some initiative and pluck, walked on, but quickly wondered if it had been a good decision. A large group of older boys was gathered here. It looked as if they were doing some kind of dance.

They stood on either side of the road, eyes fixed on each other. One at a time they would leave their line and walk up to the other side with jaunty steps and cold, challenging stares. The stares were returned with such vehemence that it seemed the prelude to a fight, but it never went further than these threatening gestures. Apparently the boys were gaining some enjoyment from the performance.

Encouraged by this, Aedan decided to walk on and slip past. He assumed it was just another unusual aspect to this city's culture. But instead of continuing, unaware of him, this strange dance immediately re-formed around him, placing him at the centre.

He smiled and tried to excuse himself, but there were no smiles in return. Everywhere he stepped, a glaring face appeared, blocking his way. He was sure the looks of hatred were given in jest and would soon be cast off.

Then he was not so sure.

But how could they possibly be in earnest? He had given no cause for offense.

It was when the first shove threw him off balance that he knew he had made a mistake.

Chapter 16

The blow that took him from behind almost split his head apart. He dropped to his knees, and even before he hit the ground, a quick hand snatched the bandage and ripped it away.

Cries of disgust filled the alley and several boys spat at him.

"This here is my ground, Ooze-head. Who gave you permission to enter, especially with a filthy pus-drenched head like yours?"

Aedan's thoughts were clearing.

The words drifted past unheard. Deep, wild instincts were taking over.

"Oi! When I am talking –"

No rabbit ever bolted from a circle of hounds the way Aedan took off now.

He darted between a pair of legs before anyone could reach him, felt the whoosh of something through the space he had just occupied, and put on a wild burst of speed. A big hand lunged towards him but he struck it away, veered, and almost had his teeth knocked out by a swinging stick.

He dived beneath it and tumbled to the ground where he slipped and sprawled through rotten vegetables and filth that was even more evil-smelling. Before he had stopped sliding, he pushed himself up, filling his hands with the mush as he did so. He was almost quick enough.

The gang was behind, but one of their number had been loitering near the far end of the alley and now pounded to a stop in front of the slime pond. He gripped Aedan by the neck with steel hands.

"I've got the little –"

That was all he managed, because he suddenly got something he had not expected when Aedan lunged up and slapped both handfuls of muck into his eyes. The steel hands released instantly, accompanied by a howl of pain. Aedan slipped past, leapt over a broken crate just ahead of stretching fingers, and hared away down the alley. He didn't stop until the pain in his bad leg was strong enough to taste.

This alley was darker, but it was quiet. He could hear the shouts behind him. Apparently the boys had given up the chase. The voices were receding, but were also getting louder and more excited. Like the yapping of dogs on a trail.

Suddenly Aedan remembered his young travelling companion. On cat feet, he stalked back to the last corner and peered around. It was as he had feared. The young boy had watched for too long. They had him now. Blows and kicks were raining down on him until he was too stunned to defend himself.

"Answer me!" It was the same voice that had spoken to Aedan. He couldn't make out the speaker, but between the gang's legs he could see his friend.

"I –" the boy tried before a boot dug into his back.

"Did I say you could talk?"

Laughter. The speaker's voice reminded Aedan of Emroy.

"This is my ground. You'll be respecting me. You'll be looking up when I talk to you."

The boy tried to look up but someone swung a baton against his head with a sharp *tonk* that brought a cry of pain.

"Did I say you could move?"

More laughter, mean laughter. When it was quiet the first boy spoke again.

"I am the Anvil. You remember that, you little cockroach. Next time I find you or that Ooze-head friend of yours here, I crush you. For now, well I'll just be cleaning you up a bit."

There was a sound of shuffling and coarse laughter. Aedan guessed what was happening before he saw the filthy splashing stream. The laughter continued.

"Much better," the Anvil shouted when he was done. "Now send him off."

The boy was hauled to his bare feet and relieved of his jacket and shoes. They kicked him away and pursued him with a hail of stones, rubble, and an assortment of rotten vegetables. The taunts and threats that pursued him were no less vile.

Aedan felt sick. He had stood there and done nothing, just watched. He knew there was little he could have done, but that didn't make him feel better. He saw the boys pulling open a bag and tossing out the contents – a shirt, a wad of paper, a book, a sling. Wondering why it all looked so familiar, Aedan realised that it was his bag. His shoes were there too. Obviously he'd lost them in the first wild dash. There was no going back for anything now. With a start, he slapped his hand against his chest.

It was still there.

The little leather case was hanging around his neck and he pressed it to him. If any of the boys had reached for it he would have fought to the death.

He hurried away from the scene, uncertain where he was going, only that he needed to be well away. The numbness of flight was receding and the injuries began to seep into his thoughts. He realised the skin was gone from a heel, several toes, his knees and elbows; and his head ached like it had been struck by an anvil, as in fact it had.

At first he was confused by the suddenness of it all, but as he hobbled on through the alleys, the treatment he had felt and witnessed began to soak itself past the skin, and such a torrent of anguish swept through him that he found his eyes moist, his teeth clenching. The gang had only managed to get in a few shoves and cuffs, but after all that Aedan had recently been through, the force of each blow was multiplied a hundredfold.

Anger started to burn in him. He wanted to go back and find the Anvil – or Dilbert or Zuffy or whatever his real name was – and beat him to a pulp, restore his own identity, his sense of being someone who deserved respect.

But he couldn't, so instead he grabbed a plank from a broken crate and assaulted the nearest wall, feasting on images of a gory revenge. He battered away until the wood was in fragments and his fingers raw with splinters.

But when the fury subsided, the heat gave way to something cold – aloneness. He began to realise just how small he was in a city that was as cruel as it was strange. The people that walked past looked at him without the recognition he had been accustomed to in the Mistyvales, and in its place was a constant wariness, almost suspicion. As an unaccompanied, penniless, barefoot and dirty boy, what hope did he really have of walking off the street into military training? And if this failed, where would he go? He scraped the shreds of his confidence together and pushed on.

Aedan was exhausted when he stumbled out of the maze of alleys into a surprisingly spacious courtyard. The military offices and barracks were clearly marked on one side. On the other side was a colossal high-walled enclosure. The sign over the main entrance arch proclaimed it to be *The Castath Royal Academy of Security and Foreign Associations*. The wordy name baffled him for a moment until he realised that this must be the great academy that was famous across the whole of Thirna. Nearby, an office set in the wall was marked *Castath Marshals, Public Office*. He hadn't realised that it was at the academy where the grey marshals were trained. Suddenly he wanted to enter marshal training in a way he had seldom wanted anything before.

He found a small pool of rainwater where he washed the blood and filth off as best he could, neatened himself up, and approached the entrance to the marshals' head office.

As he drew near, his hands began to fidget. The guard at the door raised his eyes. The look he wore was not inviting. Aedan's step faltered and he stubbed his already-skinned toe. When the shudders had passed, he looked up again. The guard was watching him and shook his head; his face was as hard as the offending brick. What remained of Aedan's bruised courage collapsed and he turned aside and found himself hobbling away towards a nearby library.

It appealed to him on a few levels – solitude, his love of reading, and most importantly, opportunity. All the buildings in this area clearly belonged to the military, and this would have to be the famous library Aedan had read so much about where Castath's great tacticians drew their books on histories and cultures. Respectable members of the public were allowed to browse during the day when they would occasionally find themselves alongside the military's renowned strategists and leaders.

The guard here was not paying attention, but just to be safe, Aedan walked beside a middle-aged couple as they climbed the stairs. Once within the building, he kept them between himself and the librarian's desk until he could slip down one of the aisles.

The library at the Mistyvales had consisted of a few dozen books and scrolls on topics ranging from soil management to trade law to tales of sea-monsters, intermittently lost and found on Nulty's shelves. Nulty had his own personal collection, but Aedan had never seen it. Dresbourn's shelves held some stuffy volumes of lineage, and Nessa had kept two shelves of histories.

What surrounded him now was nothing short of staggering. Had he not seen it, he would never have believed that this many books and scrolls existed. The racks were so high that movable ladders stood against them at intervals, allowing access to the upper shelves. He walked down the aisle, his bare feet hardly whispering on the thick carpet. Cool, leathery air seemed to swallow all sound. It reminded him of walking through the forest paths of Nymliss – a place for remembering, forgetting, sorting things out. There was a similar kind of space to think here.

He took a few turns, moving towards the back of the building, and found a place well away from anyone else. Then he let his eyes start drifting over the spines. Some had the titles written on them, others only an arrangement of numbers which he assumed to be the library's code. A title caught his eye and he drew out a squat volume – *The Five Generals of the Elgan Epoch.* If he were to meet one of the great military leaders in this place, it would do well to be found with such a book.

Sitting down on the carpet, he opened the cover and began to pore over details with a young tactician's eye. If questioned, he wanted to be able to deliver an answer that would impress.

The scribe's hand was elegant but still clear. Aedan was less familiar with the southern variations on some of the letters but his mother had taught him the differences. Soon he was lost in a scrutiny of events. At first, he was enthralled, but then he grew confused, and finally dismayed. This book was not what he had hoped. He was on the verge of abandoning it when the aisle darkened.

"This is no place for boys." The voice had a depth and command the likes of which Aedan had never heard before.

He gasped and leapt to his feet, leaving the book on the floor. The man was enormous, filling the space between shelves, and so tall that he would have no need of the ladder. Iron grey hair and weather-worn skin suggested age; powerful limbs and lithe movement decried it. He looked strong enough to walk through walls of stone with only minor inconvenience. His face was hard, not mean, but stern as flint and with just as much promise of fiery sparks.

But then it all went wrong. This was no military man. The hair was not just combed but groomed like a nobleman's, the suit was cleaned and pressed to fastidious perfection, and the shoes were so carefully polished that they glistened like beetles in the sun. This was someone who belonged in glittering halls on velvet couches. He was no campaigner. He'd probably never handled anything dirtier than silver cutlery.

Aedan turned and scurried off before being sent on his way with more than words. But before he reached the end of the aisle, the big voice rang out with paralysing authority, "Stop!"

His feet stuck fast, as if gripped by the deep carpet. He swallowed and turned around, fearing that he had damaged something. The man was holding the book.

Aedan prepared to run.

"You were reading this?"

"Yes, sir."

The man regarded him. "This is not likely reading material for someone your age. Did you understand it? Was it instructive?"

"No, not really," Aedan admitted. He could have said more, but all he wanted was to get away.

"I thought not," the man said, returning the book to the shelf and lining the spine against its neighbours with absolute precision. "As I said, this is no place for boys. Don't let me find you meddling here again."

Something about the injustice of the man's conclusion bit Aedan. He had endured enough injustice for one day and drew himself up.

"I didn't understand it because it makes no sense. How could catapults have sunk Lekran ships anchored near Verma? I knew an old sailor and he used to tell us about how shallow the water is there because of the reefs. The ships would have been half a mile out. Even our big thumper catapults don't have a range like that. I think the ships were sunk in some other way – like maybe they got blown onto the reef – and someone is trying to make it look like we pounded them.

"I also can't see how seven hundred soldiers could march twenty miles through a dense forest during the night to defend a town by morning. Even during the day, with a bright sun, it's difficult to go fast and to keep going in the right direction through forest. I think the soldiers set off a day or two before the beacons were lit. Must have been some commander's lucky guess. Now this historian wants to make it look more solid-like, as if our defences don't need luck. This is supposed to be a book about facts and it seems to be loaded with fairy tales written to make us look invincible."

The big man's face did not look like it was accustomed to showing surprise, but it was getting some practice now. "How old are you?" he asked, walking up with giant strides.

"Almost thirteen."

The man studied him. "For a twelve-year old boy, you have quite a mind for detail. I'll grant you that. Not many have uncovered the problems with this book so quickly. How did you learn of such things? Who taught you?"

The unexpected interest the man was showing caused his face to seem less severe. It revealed a deep sincerity that made Aedan want to talk, to share some of the weight he carried.

"I used to speak with the old soldiers a lot, and I read a lot. My mother taught me and my friend ..." – Aedan couldn't bring himself to say her name, not today – "taught us to read. We read many stories and histories. I agreed to discuss the stories with her if she discussed the battles with me. So we knew all the great battles in detail, all the great generals."

"I would like to meet this friend of yours –" The man stopped short at the look on Aedan's face.

Aedan coughed to clear his throat and swallowed a few times. "I tried to save her, but I couldn't." The man waited, so Aedan continued. "They were Lekran slavers. They took her as a sacrificial substitute because she had noble blood." He pressed his eyes shut. "When I'm grown, I am going to tear that trade to pieces and sink what doesn't burn. Every one of those murdering priests is going to meet his filthy god. She was the kindest, gentlest person I've ever known. As soon as I am strong enough I'm going to bring them justice and make sure they can't take anyone else the way they took her."

The man dropped to his haunches and looked Aedan in the eyes. "Revenge is a selfish pursuit full of empty promise – I would know," he said. "But you speak of justice, of defending the innocent by felling their oppressor. I see that anger is still fierce in you, but I believe you'll learn to temper it with wisdom." He stood to his full height. "How will you reach this strength you need? Who will train you?"

"I wanted to become a marshal …" He stopped speaking. The man was eying him critically.

"How sturdy are you? The selection process is extreme and the training is even more so. You don't look to be in the best of health."

"I'll recover. I just need a little time."

"You won't have time unless you are prepared to wait a year."

There were two things that shot through Aedan's mind. One was a bellow from his heart saying that it would not stand idly by for an entire year. The other had an even keener edge – a vision of yellow curls and raised eyebrows demanding that he get back to where he belonged this instant. "No," Aedan said quickly. "I'm ready now." He wished it were true.

The man nodded. "Very well. Let's get you enrolled."

"I tried already. The guard warned me off. He won't let me in."

"Only one guard, you say?"

"Yes. But he was big."

"There are meant to be three. Come along. If you are going to be part of the military, it's time you learned something about discipline."

Aedan had to run to keep up with the long strides. Librarians stared as the unlikely pair passed the front desk and left the building. They marched down the courtyard towards the academy entrance with its solitary guard, passed it, and turned into a little recess. Two more guards were crouched in the shade over a board, gambling chips piled on each side.

Without breaking stride, the big man kicked the board over, causing the soldiers to leap to their feet with angry yells and blazing eyes. But their eyes grew with fright as they stared up at the towering intruder. He said nothing. In two swift, effortless motions, he flat-handed both surprised faces with enough force to send the helmets flying. His hands were as big and heavy as coal shovels and must have been just as hard. The soldiers skidded across the bricks and slumped against the wall.

Aedan glanced around. He could not afford to be seen in the company of a man assaulting the city guard. But he was too frightened now of his guide to say anything. This strange man adjusted his suit and led Aedan back to the entrance where the solitary guard turned rigid, saluted with a trembling hand, and backed against the wall.

"You should have reported them," the man said, his eyes sparking.

"Yes, yes, sir. Sorry, sir. It was just that –"

"I am going in to sign a register. By the time I leave the building, you will be back here with two new guards and two more will be chaining the post-deserters."

The guard saluted and took off, sprinting towards the barracks on the far side of the courtyard, yelling at the sentries long before he reached them.

Aedan and his companion turned away and entered an airy chamber ornamented with brass hangings and large paintings. A clerk sat behind a wide marble desk, talking to a man and a boy who looked to be about Aedan's age. He was saying something about fees and enrolment times. The big man walked past the line of people, snatched a register off the desk, asked Aedan his and his father's name, and wrote them in. The clerk noticed, but made no attempt to interfere.

Aedan's curiosity was gnawing at him. What kind of person had such authority? Royal blood might have explained it, but nobody with royal blood would act with such directness. Perhaps he was rich – rich men tended to have social power. Dresbourn had been similarly respected. But nothing like this man.

"Now we need to make a visit to the infirmary," the apparently wealthy patron said as he led the way out again, past three rigid guards, "and you are going to tell me how you arrived here."

While Aedan was being re-bandaged by a middle-aged nurse, he told the man about all that had befallen him, leaving out details that might cast too dark a shadow on his father.

"So your mother's friends have become your slave-lords, and to boot, you are friendless, homeless and penniless. Well, I think I can solve a part of that. Follow me." He strode, Aedan jogging at his side, to a row of closely built apartments, and ducked under the doorway on the ground-level. It was hardly the lodging of a wealthy man, and Aedan was left wondering again. Furnishings were simple, but the uniformity, the symmetry and the intimidating spotlessness of the place pointed to an owner who tolerated no deviation from perfect order.

Something began to ring in the back of Aedan's thoughts. He had read of a military man – one of the greatest – who had been described as unreasonably neat. Aedan had overlooked that piece of information because it conflicted so sharply with his own convictions.

Seating himself at the heavy oak table, chair protesting furiously, the man motioned for Aedan to do likewise.

"Your trials will begin on the first day of winter, when you will find a bunk with the apprentices. Until then you may remain here, pending your mother's permission. Fees are dealt with. I'll have clothes delivered by evening. All I ask is that you keep the place tidy and help with the cooking if you have any skill, for I certainly lack it. Most of my meals turn out like that greasy sludge we boil and throw from the battlements. It's even been suggested that my stew might be a more effective deterrent for attackers ..."

Aedan was crying now. The man's kindness had knocked down his walls. The accumulated strain and injuries poured from him in deep sobs.

"You don't have to eat it."

The sobs gave way to laughter and the jumbled flood of emotions carried on for some time. "I don't know how to thank you," Aedan said at last. "I don't even know your name."

"Cook something I can swallow without effort and I'll be thanked enough. My name is Osric."

Aedan stared, mouth agape. "Osric? General Osric? *The* General Osric?

"To you I am just Osric. Understand?"

Aedan nodded, trying not to stare, failing.

"Supper will level your opinion of me."

It was true. There was plenty of stew to be had and Aedan went to bed hungry. Osric never cooked again. And Aedan began apprenticing to his childhood hero, the most famed of all Thirnish generals, as a chef after all.

Chapter 17

Any warmth now brought by the sun fled early, and when the night sky was clear, shallow pools that lay in the open reflected icy stars for only a brief spell before they froze into opaque tiles. But strollers who happened to tread too freely on one of these tiles would be given the chance to see stars of their own. Though light blankets of snow settled occasionally, the frail coating seldom lasted the day, unlike the deep northern drifts.

Aedan stepped carefully through the darkness along streets that were now familiar to him. He had not intended to be up so early, but Corey, an old friend of Osric's and owner of a bakery known to the whole city, had a way of charming sleep from the clutches of the sleeper. Aedan's morning began an hour earlier when the wind drifted down from the south-east, from where Corey filled the air with maddening vapours. Dreams of roasting barley bread, golden oat cakes, and his special blended-grain breakfast loaves that crunched as if singing to the belly, were enough to wrench anyone from slumber.

It wasn't long before Aedan was at the service door marked in the darkness by a frame of golden light. The main entrance had not been unbolted for sales, but as the general's apprentice, many back doors were now open to him. He slipped inside and, before long, re-emerged, satchel bulging with breakfast loaves, and one, of course, in his hand.

On the way back, something caught his eye and he slipped into an archway against a door.

Shapes were moving further down the road, darkly clad men whose movements were furtive and stealthy. They were busy with a window, expertly removing the shutters. Two of them climbed inside while the rest kept watch.

Suddenly the door of Aedan's alcove was shoved open, knocking him into the road. The light of a lantern fell directly on him as a man in his nightgown emptied a basket of refuse at his feet and told him to push off. The door slammed. The gang was looking at him. They knew.

"Tripe!" he said, and ran.

He glanced over his shoulder – three of them were in pursuit. On an inspiration, he ducked into a broad lane that ended with a sharp bend. It was the worst place he had found for running at night; he still had the bruises. Nearing the end of the road, he slowed gradually, carefully, until he was walking. The men appeared at the top of the road at a run. Aedan put his hands in his pockets, smiled at them and sauntered around the corner. He heard the pounding of angry tread, the gritty crunch of boots on stone, then of boots on something far less gritty, and then the horrified screams as three pairs of boots took to the air and three bodies skidded along the ice and slammed into the wall. One lay groaning, but two scrambled to their feet and hobbled after the little shadow that darted around another corner.

Aedan took several more turns in quick succession and tunnelled into the darker alleys. He was sure he had lost them, but decided it would be best not to show himself in any of the broader roads. It meant a detour through the squalid part of town where he had met the Anvil and his gang. The Heaps was the official name of the area, but everyone knew it as the Seeps.

Most of the illegal trade and shady dealings in the city happened here. No signs marked businesses – at least, not accurately. The barber could produce a few combs and a rusty razor on inspection, but no client ever emerged from his rooms with shortened hair. There was a cloth merchant who couldn't tell the difference between wool and silk but who was able to supply, to those who earned his trust, second hand jewellery at impossible prices. The innocent purveyor of pipe tobacco had patrons who seemed to have been leached of health. They would often enter his store in a frantic itch of paranoia, then, a little while later, float out with distant eyes and bleary smiles. The taverns here were dirty and loud, and the attached inns served a number of other purposes. Soldiers regularly swept the areas and made some arrests, but a business that needs no signboard simply dissolves away at the slightest hint of trouble.

Aedan was making his way through a section where only the most desperate pursuer would follow. No one but a drunk or a fool walks through the darkness at the back of a sleazy tavern, and he was just that fool. At least he would be left alone. Rancid air spoke forcefully of the night's party – the inland celebration known as Harvesters' Toast. There would be many sore heads today. He feared that his would be one of them. His throat tightened; he felt dangerously close to retching. The vapours were particularly ripe this morning. One of his shoes sank into something soft; in the darkness, there was no telling what it was. He blocked his imagination, forcing himself to walk without thinking.

The next street was hardly any better. This part of town needed a rainstorm with a temper. A few shadowy forms darted ahead of him through the narrow walkways, no doubt on shadowy pursuits. The streets opened up a little and he quickened his pace. Just ahead were the academy and military courtyard. He raced over the open ground and reached the door to Osric's apartment as a clerk ducked out.

"Good luck," the man said, wiping his brow. "You're late. The general is waiting for you and it looks like he ate a thunderstorm for breakfast."

"But I'm still early."

"Not early enough for him. It's the opening assembly this morning, remember."

Aedan hadn't forgotten, but the detour through the back alleys had taken longer than expected. The sky was growing light. He took a deep breath and stepped inside.

"Aedan!" Osric spoke in a shattering tone of raw command. Even after seeing the gentler side of the man, Aedan still found it easy to preserve a healthy respect. Sometimes the general could be truly frightening. It had become clear that the first impression had been more or less correct – Osric was in fact built from a combination of metal, flint and fire, a solid monolith of a man that towered around seven feet off the ground.

The steely frown he now directed at the boy would have withered a number of veteran soldiers in their shoes, but Aedan recognised this as the general's frustrated look, one that held no personal threat. Most of the officers, in fact most who knew the general, were cautious. Aedan was one of few who had learned to interpret "Where in the name of blackest torment have you been?" as "I've been worried about you."

"It is the morning of the assembly!" Osric barked. "Do you want to be late?"

"I got spotted by a gang working Baker's Lane. Had to run."

The frown relaxed slightly, then deepened into a familiar look of pained exasperation. Aedan wondered what he had done wrong, but suddenly guessed it and sighed as Osric began,

"Could you not have given just half a thought to your appearance before leaving the house? It looks like you mopped the floor with your head, you are wearing your sleeping shirt, and there are bread crumbs all over your face! You would agree that I don't put much stock in appearances, but responsibility demands complete respectability."

Aedan did not agree with the first statement at all, and wasn't too sure about the second, but he held his tongue. There were very few days when Osric didn't make some complaint about his appearance, especially his shoes. Even now he saw the general's eyes fixing themselves with growing ire on that area.

"What, in all the rotting wastes, did you walk through?"

"I was keeping off the main roads. I had to take a detour."

"So you managed to find a route through a swamp?"

Aedan considered explaining, and then realised that Osric's swamp was several degrees better than the reality. If only it had been a beautiful swamp…

In the end he abandoned his defence and said, "I brought you breakfast. Got the oven fire going before I left so you can melt cheese on some of Corey's breakfast loaves."

Osric eyed him, clearly not ready to be mollified. Finally he turned and finished with, "Clean habits are the first guard against disease. A single desperate campaign will teach you that. One day you will accept it. Now where is this breakfast?"

The courtyard hummed with excitement. Three hundred boys had gathered from the city and the surrounding villages. Positions within the Castath marshals, or grey marshals as they were often known, were coveted for reasons noble and otherwise. The marshals carried great authority and were trained in ways that were a matter of enduring mystery to those outside their ranks.

Curiosity, therefore, was a strong lure. Others felt the temptations of power. It was understandable for a family to want one of their sons to be a grey marshal. But the ambitions of most were headed for disappointment as the majority of applicants would be filtered out and referred to the regular army. Many fathers who stood around, loud with such eager praise for the institution, would soon be its most bitter critics.

Aedan had not wanted his mother walking through the city for the sake of a ceremony, so he and Osric had visited her the day before. Aedan had laughed when she hung wordless at the sight of the towering general.

"Told you they didn't exaggerate," Aedan said.

She had been full of encouragement over the trials. Remembering her words gave him an added layer against the cold.

Boys from the same villages chattered nervously, shoving and stamping in the chilly dawn, waiting for the mayor's opening speech.

Aedan felt a sharp sting behind his good ear – the other side of his head was still dressed with some light bandages. He spun around in time to see a small boy with bright red hair turning away and almost managing to conceal a peashooter against his wrist. Aedan watched. Slowly the head pivoted and the young eyes met his. They stared with such a grotesque parody of innocence, defying accusation – a look that was almost hostile. Aedan felt his skin grow hot. He was tempted to walk over and even the score, but at that point there was a general stirring and hushing as people began turning to the front.

Three men approached the steps of a wooden podium. Aedan recognised those on the outside as two of the masters of studies whom he had met briefly at Osric's house. They were both short and grey, and their lined faces appeared to be etched with the letters and runes that had been so many years before them, but apart from this, they could not have been more dissimilar. Giddard, who crabbed his way up the stairs on the left, was withered like a man who had missed too many meals, and Rodwell, stumping heavily and filling the space on the right, appeared to have eaten them. The man in the middle, who by his splendid robes and chains would have to be Balfore, mayor of the city south, was tall and strong, and strode with confidence. He was a striking leader displaying golden hair, golden rings, and a golden voice with which he now greeted the assembly.

"Blessings of the dawn to you," he said, his words ringing across the courtyard.

Aedan wrinkled his nose at the man's lofty expression. It would have been pompous even for a gathering of kings.

"It is a fine day to embark on a noble course such as you have chosen, and well have you chosen. The Castath marshals are our pillars of strength, our shields of honour, and our ambassadors who carry themselves not with pride, but with the humility of service to our people."

There was a warm buzz of agreement and loud cheers. Aedan wondered if the rest of the speech would continue along these lines – fine words chosen to hide facts behind a pretty glow. He wondered if "spies" was hiding behind the word "ambassadors". Recently, he had learned that the marshals were not only trained in the ways of war, but were taught to speak several languages and that much of their time was spent in places where foreign relations were complicated. But this was of minor interest. What mattered to him was that of all positions associated with the military, the mention of marshals was the one to draw instant attention, even fear. Whatever their training was, he wanted it, needed it.

"As you all know there are only a few places made available each year."

Silence fell over the courtyard.

"For the next two months, tests will be held until the selection of twenty is made known and training begins in earnest. I would speak to those of you who do not find a place in the final number. Be bigger than the petty lure of jealousy. Remember that the selection process is not about choosing the best boys, but choosing those who are most suited to this particular form of service to our great city."

A few grunts and calls of agreement sounded from various points in the crowd.

"It is important that we do not have marshals in whose ears other callings sing more sweetly. The next two months will enable us to know who belongs here. Today I ask of you two things: Commit to giving more than you have ever done; and have the bigness of heart to embrace either continuation or redirection with equal ardour." Balfore pressed his gaze masterfully over them.

"We are glad to have you all here this morning. May you advance with honour." He bowed his head and stepped back as the crowd applauded.

Something zipped through the crowd and Aedan felt another stinging bite behind his ear. The impressive accuracy only made him angrier.

Clerks made their voices heard. They divided the assembly of boys into fifteen groups of twenty and directed them to bunks in the army barracks. Only those who made it through the selections would see the inside of the academy and the marshals' training grounds.

Aedan gritted his teeth as he spied the red-headed pea-shooting tormentor at the back of his group. Peashot – that would be an appropriate name. Debtors had to have names and there was a debt to settle. It was appropriate that this heckler had the same red hair as Emroy.

An army sergeant was assigned to their group and led the way through the heavy iron gates of the barracks, across a large courtyard, down an airy corridor and past many doors with numbered brass plates above them – sixteen, seventeen, eighteen. They stopped outside number nineteen. Inside was a long room lined with beds, upper and lower. The boys waited while two clerks conferred. Aedan drifted to the back of the line where Peashot idled and looked about with cocky self-assurance. His arrogant slouch and mean little eyes were enough to light Aedan's fires. The rage stored away from fantasies he had cradled of revenge on his father, on Emroy, on the Anvil, surged up in him until he almost choked.

It was time to change things. He had been weak under his father, but today was the beginning of a new part of his life. He would no longer sit passively and be a soft target for every malicious boot. If scores were not settled, who would ever learn to respect him? They needed to know that he was not afraid to take revenge, and it would begin now.

With no introduction, he grabbed the smaller boy's ear and twisted it until he saw the look of pain.

"If you want to keep your ear, midget, then aim elsewhere. Understand?"

The little boy tried to grab for Aedan's face and kick at his shins, but the pain Aedan was causing took the strength from those efforts. The little foxy eyes, though, were defiant, even mocking.

Aedan's anger leapt in him and he made no attempt to tame it. He hit the boy in the stomach and shoved him against the wall, thumping his head hard against the bricks. The defiance fell away like a shattered screen and revealed someone very young and small. Aedan saw his advantage and twisted the ear further. "Understand?" he repeated.

"Yes," the boy said, coughing and gasping.

Aedan was filled with a strange elation. Power, control. At last he was taking charge of matters. Instead of cowering in corners, he was dealing with those who needed to be put in their place.

He grinned to himself as he walked away. He felt good. At least he expected to feel good.

Instead he became aware of a strange creeping discomfort. He tried the smirk again, but it reminded him of the way the Anvil had leered. He straightened his face out and began explaining to some inner judge why it had been necessary, how the debt was now settled.

But he knew he had done more than settle a debt. It had not been about justice at all. He had let his anger out to satisfy itself, and the aftertaste was not sweet. He tried to pass it off as a small thing, but small as it was, it carried the odour of his father's "lessons" as if poured out from the same jar.

And then he imagined what he would see in Kalry's face if she had been watching – and perhaps she had. He felt a deep revulsion with himself that drowned out the next set of instructions.

Boys were rushing into the room, leaping onto the hard boards. Aedan was left with the bed at the entrance. He noticed that Peashot had no choice but the one above his. The boy tried to hide his face. Aedan guessed the reason when he saw a sleeve dabbing downturned eyes, and he could not smirk now.

The soldier was speaking, "Your first assignment is to collect bedding straw from the army farm on the south road. You are all injured. Five of you have a useless leg, five a useless arm, and the rest are blind." He handed out white bandages and allocated afflictions to the disappointed boys. "If we see anyone using an injured limb or a blindfolded boy using his sight, he will be going home before supper."

On that first day there was a lot of laughter and names were learned quickly. Nobody from Aedan's group went home, but it was rumoured that three from another group had cheated and been sent away in disgrace.

Though he joined in as was required, the day was poisoned for Aedan. He could not help but notice that Peashot neither laughed nor smiled all day. He resolved to make amends as soon as possible, so that evening he took his dinner plate and sat opposite the small boy who had found an empty table.

"Listen, Peashot, I'm sorry for being an ass earlier. I was just angry. If I can help you ..."

The boy stood up and left the table without a word.

Aedan felt as foolish as he looked, sitting alone.

The next day they ran around the city twice, seven miles that had them gasping for breath. Aedan managed the first lap easily, but during the second his leg began to weaken. Since recovering the ability to walk he had not attempted such sustained exercise. He was one of the last ones back. On his return he was directed to the stables where he found the rest of the boys. The first job was to take out the old straw, which had them trying not to breathe, and the next was to empty the barrack latrines, during which, ten of the better-dressed boys staggered out and simply went home.

At the evening meal – an uninviting colourless stew that tasted vaguely of lentils and smelled, like everything else, of latrines – Aedan tried again to apologise and met with the same result. It was no less embarrassing.

He realised that he was feeling constantly awkward. When there were activities under way, he, like everyone, was slotted into some kind of social grouping by duties or by the officials. He belonged. But in the idle time, little clusters or pairs of friends drew together and he was left standing alone. Peashot had joined in with another group.

As a small-town boy, Aedan had never really made friends; he had simply grown up with them. He wasn't sure what to do or how to do it, and began to feel increasingly out of place. At times, when he took his bowl to a table by himself, too uncertain to impose on anyone, the loneliness and embarrassment of his isolation became so strong he started to consider just walking out on the whole thing.

One evening, approaching his empty table again, he decided it was time to put timidity aside, time to cross some barriers. He recognised a rowdy group from his dorm and sat at the end of one of their benches. Since leaving the Mistyvales he had still to share a decent conversation with anyone his age, so he was more than a little uneasy. As he sat, the talk died. All eyes turned on him.

"You're the northerner, aren't you?" asked a strong, dark-haired boy with handsome features and the most unusually bold, piercing eyes. Aedan had seen him often. Malik was his name. He was popular, definitely someone who would be good to have as a friend.

Aedan smiled. "Yes, I got here before the winter."

Malik frowned. "Why would I care when you got here?"

There was a ripple of partly withheld laughter. Aedan felt a sudden prick of doubt. Had he aimed too high with this group? They seemed to be speaking a language of their own to which he was not privy. Their eyes were full of it.

"Tell us something interesting about where you're from, North-boy," Malik said.

"What do you mean?"

"Anything – something that we wouldn't know."

The boys gave him their full attention, but not in a considerate way. Their fascination reminded him of how jackals or vultures behave around a stumbling fawn. He tried to string his thoughts together, stumbling.

"Well, uh, something, that maybe, I don't know if you've heard, but the snow there can easy get to three feet on the fields. In a bad winter, that is, sometimes."

Blank eyes regarded him.

"Sorry, North-boy, but was that it? The interesting thing. Deep snow?"

"Well, it was always very exciting, uh, that is for us at least." Aedan was thrashing about in his memory for anything that could rescue the situation. "Once we lost a sheep and we had to burrow around for half a day to find it. Thomas actually – Thomas was my friend there – he got lost himself even though he was only twenty yards from the pen." Aedan laughed to cover his discomfort. He laughed alone.

Their eyes were lances. Then, when he fell silent, the whole table erupted in hard, barking hilarity. He had never known laughter could be so unfriendly. His appetite was gone, but he dropped his eyes and ate simply to disguise his humiliation and confusion.

He did not belong here. They did not want him.

"Hey North-boy, sing us a song. They say that you northern lads have voices like milkmaids." The laughter broke out again. This time the table alongside had caught on. More than one reference was made to his pretty bonnet bandage that covered most of his head. "Silence everyone! A song, a song!" They stared at him, hungry.

Though nothing showed on his face, Aedan was drowning in a maelstrom of anger and tears. He dropped his spoon in the bowl, stood, turned, and headed for the gate. A wave of boos and jeering rose up and struck him from behind. It only helped to carry him forward.

When he reached the gate, it was shut. The guard had slipped away. There was another boy waiting, tall and skinny as a winter tree.

"You also wanting to leave?" the other asked.

Aedan nodded. Then he looked up. "Your accent is different," he said.

"I'm from Verma."

"Don't fit in?"

"Not with this crowd," the tall boy said. "Anyone from outside Castath gets treated like gutter scum. Not all of them are bad, if I'm honest, but there's enough of the bad ones to turn everyone else rotten."

"Oi!"

Both boys looked out through the gate and Aedan took two rapid steps back. The Anvil stood just within the light cast by the barrack torches, his gang assembling around him. He strode forward, dipping and hoisting his shoulders, thrusting his chin, jerking from side to side. This time there was no mistaking it. The half-dancing gait was a studied and perfected expression of raw hostility – threat, challenge, defiance all combined and embodied. It was almost as if belligerence had been turned to art and then made to walk.

For the first time, Aedan got a proper look at the Anvil. He was not the biggest member of his gang by height or breadth, but he was certainly the biggest by presence. He swaggered and jinked with an expansiveness and intrusiveness that dominated the space around him. Quick hands twitched and quicker eyes constantly thrust here and there like accusing fingers. He did not wear rags. His clothes looked surprisingly good, but nobody would have taken him for a young man of class. The way he carried himself bespoke his character all too clearly.

"Look at the little army men! Nice and safe behind their little gate," he shouted. With a sudden lunge, he reached through the bars and swung a thick club, catching the tall boy on the cheek and knocking him to the ground. There was a roar of applause from the gang.

"Oi, would you be looking at that one," said the Anvil, pointing his club at Aedan. "I think we remember you, and I think we know your name. What's his name, lads?"

"Ooze-head!" they roared.

"Come out here Ooze-head. I think you'll be needing some attentions from us. Last time you left early. But I heard you stayed to watch your friend. Isn't that so?"

The boy from Verma was on his feet again, tottering slightly. "What does he mean?" he asked Aedan, his voice shaking.

"Don't know. Never seen him before," Aedan lied, immediately wishing he hadn't when he saw that the boy believed him without question. It felt like the time he had tricked a lamb into taking a mouthful of feathers and glue. At first Aedan had thought it would be funny, but by the end he was laughing only to conceal a growing misery at betraying the simple animal's trust.

And this open-faced boy had not deserved a lie, even a little one.

Aedan's thoughts were interrupted as something struck his shoulder hard. He saw the club skittering past into the shadows. He turned and walked away from the gate.

"Thief! Thief!" he heard from behind him. "You stole my club! You'll be coming out here and handing it back from your knees or I'll hunt you down, you duck-livered coward!"

Aedan kept walking. He saw the guard hurry back to his post and heard him shout at the gang, but the Anvil was not to be put out by a soldier behind a fence. He shouted right back and the jeers rose from the rest of the gang too.

"Come into our world, soldier man. Let's see how long you last. We've marked you now. We'll know you. We'll learn where you live, who your family is. You fetch us that little thieving coward and toss him out here or you'll be sorry."

It was the last Aedan heard. He hurried out of sight, behind the buildings and found an empty fire pit. By the time he was able to think clearly, the surge of self-pity that had almost borne him out the gate had passed. The boy from Verma settled on the other side of the fire pit. There was blood on his cheek, and it looked like he was trying not to cry.

"What's your name?" Aedan asked.

"Lorrimer."

Lorrimer was as awkward as he looked, but there didn't seem to be a mean bone in his gangly frame, and Aedan discovered that it only takes a single friend to put loneliness to flight. He would be able to face the next day. They both would.

The rest of the month continued in a medley of exercise – running, hauling, climbing, even icy swimming, and a good deal more menial labour. Aedan and Lorrimer remained, but some boys found, as Balfore put it, that other callings sang more sweetly in their ears.

Near the end of the month, everyone was told to gather in the courtyard. The chief supervisor announced that they would have one day to rest, and recommended that they make good use of it. "More than two hundred of you will be going home," he said. "The first round of eliminations takes place the day after tomorrow."

Acdan bit on a knucklc. He knew he was not ready.

Chapter 18

"This elimination is one that tests agility, strength and stamina."

It was ironic that Rodwell, the soft, rotund master who embodied none of these qualities, should be explaining the rules.

For two nights Aedan had fretted over the need to sleep, and more or less kept himself awake with the fretting. But there was no lethargy now. He fixed his attention on Rodwell, not missing a detail. The crisp morning caused puffs of steam to dance around the man's mouth as he continued in a surprisingly thin voice for one of such generous girth.

"You will run from here to the army farm where you will complete a series of obstacles, return along a trail to this square, and finish between the two orange poles. Orange flags have been set out to mark the entire course.

"The rules are simple. First: You must complete the whole circuit including every obstacle. Anyone who is unable to complete an obstacle will be punished – carrying rocks, crawling through mud, that sort of thing. In every case the punishment will take longer than the obstacle, so skill and agility will be rewarded. The second rule: No interfering with your opponents. Foul play will result in disqualification. The first eighty to complete the course will progress to the second month and the final eliminations."

Aedan took his place at the start, trembling partly with excitement but mostly with worry. He had recovered well from his injuries in the Mistyvales, but he had not yet reached his full strength, not even close, and the fire had set him back further. Looking at the crowding boys, he wondered if he would be able to beat enough of them. Most were bigger than him and many looked strong, as if they had been training for years. His worry deepened. What would Osric say if he failed at the first trial?

Race officials approached.

The babble of nervous voices died down. Aedan found he was breathing fast. The churning in his gut made him feel suddenly light-headed and weak.

Two officials raised their flags.

Silence. Every head was raised, every muscle tensed.

The flags dropped.

Aedan felt only partly conscious. The roar of voices, the shoves from all sides, and the working of his own legs were dream-like, as if his senses had overloaded. Then it all burst on him and he found himself in the centre of the surging mass. Some were sprinting ahead, others jogged, husbanding their strength, some broke off to the sides and filtered into the back roads, but most kept together and tramped up through the main streets towards the city gate, temporarily disrupting the morning's business. He recognised Lorrimer, the tall boy from Verma, loping away near the front on his long spider-legs. The boy could certainly run.

It was as they were passing through the gate that a tight group drew up alongside Aedan. The large boy nearest him growled, "Go home, North-boy," and gave him a sudden shove to the side. Aedan lurched and just managed to get a foot underneath his weight, but the shove had carried him off the road and he trod on an apple-sized stone that turned beneath him. In one horrible instant he felt and almost heard the rending of ligaments as his ankle twisted. Immediately, he took the weight off the foot and tumbled into the rocks. The bruises were nothing in comparison to the pain that had shot through him, that still thrummed in his ankle. He sat up and looked around. There were no officials here, nobody who could make a case for him.

He got to his feet carefully and tried a few steps. It wasn't as bad as he had feared. As long as he avoided uneven ground it was a pain that could be endured. Another twist would finish him off though. Making sure he kept away from other runners, he set out, grimacing at the first strides until he became used to the little stabs of pain. He was sure he would not be the only one to sustain some injury, and it was going to take a lot more than a mild sprain to hold him back.

Once he had found his pace again, Aedan kept slightly behind the middle of the field, preserving his strength. He knew the day would drain him of every last drop. The route was familiar, but somehow it was different today. He wondered why he was breathing so hard. Then he realised that even the moderate pace of the midfield was faster than any pace they had set before. But if he slowed down he would never make the first eighty. He tried not to think about the distance, and kept his eyes on the ground, setting targets of fifty yards at a time.

When they arrived at the farm, orange flags guided them to the first of the obstacles – a series of a dozen ropes that had to be scaled, traversed and descended. Falls meant starting again. Aedan decided to catch his breath before beginning. He knew it had been the right decision when he watched a group of panting boys run past him and attempt the climbs. They all slowed, began trembling, and slid down, burning their hands.

Once he was breathing normally, Aedan took hold of a rope and scaled it with little difficulty. From there he traversed another that was fastened between beams, climbing underneath, using hands and heels. He descended and ascended the next two ropes and traversed again. For one who had spent much of his time clambering through high branches, this section was a breeze. He was a lot nearer the front of the field when he descended the final rope and set off for the next obstacle.

The track wound over a steep hill coated in a wintery fur of long dry grass. On all the north- and west-facing slopes, the grass was frosted white, awaiting the sun's touch. Aedan looked out from the crest over a series of hills dotted with orange flags. The distance was intimidating, but it was less worrisome than the spectacle immediately beneath him. Sunk partly in the shadow of the slope was a muddy dam, and its surface was alive with struggling, splashing bodies. He cringed. That water would be freezing today. The swim, however, was only about three hundred yards and there were rescue boats at various points – they would probably mean both life and penalties for those who clung to them. A few boys crawling around the edge of the dam let him know what the penalty would be in this case.

He ran down slope and sat on the bank to remove his shoes, but the nearby official shouted to him that the dam was to be swum fully dressed. Aedan groaned. That would turn the three hundred yards into a lot more. He ran into the water, gasping with every deepening step. The water was so cold it stung. When he was deep enough he began paddling. At first he tried to kick, but his encased feet seemed to pull him backwards. He found the best was to bend his knees and let the shoes drag in his wake, while pulling with his arms. It was like paddling a mostly sunken coracle. The going was very slow, but fortunately he had no lingering injuries on his arms and they felt strong enough. He began to drift past a few swimmers who bobbed and splashed around him.

From all sides, he could hear rapid breathing, and by the time he reached the middle, his breath was beginning to whine. The water was bitterly cold here, sapping his strength further. He saw several boys clinging to boats. Aedan turned on his back and propelled himself just enough to keep his feet from sinking, but without the use of his legs, it proved hardly worth the effort. He was growing worried. The water here was dark, cold and deep. Would it not be wiser to head over to a boat and rather do the mud crawl?

"Two laps around the dam if you touch a boat," the nearest official called.

Two laps! He would never make up that loss. The shore was not far away. He decided to push on. Breathing fast and paddling with short, almost desperate strokes, he turned away. There was no concealing the urgency in his panting now. The shore hardly seemed to come any closer. He was sinking deeper in the water than he had at first, obviously slowing.

The scream for help was on his lips when he sensed a change. It was growing warmer. Sudden hope gave him a burst of strength. He clawed at the water with doubled efforts until he paddled into a sun-warmed, muddy swirl and decided to test the depth. His feet touched the bottom. He waded the last forty paces and stumbled up the bank, water cascading from his clothes and sloshing in his shoes. It was high time for a rest, but another swimmer crawled out of the water behind him and set off for the next obstacle. Aedan stumbled after him.

The next sections involved climbing over nets and walls, filling a leaking bucket from a nearby river using a cup – sprinters required fewer trips and finished in a fraction of the time taken by joggers – crawling through muddy trenches, carrying containers of rocks up a hill and, finally, running the homeward trail.

It was the rock-haul that finished Aedan. He had been able to nurse his ankle over the other obstacles, but doing so in this one had put too much weight on his bad leg. It ached in a way that worried him. He knew his reserves were running out. Though he had gained much ground on the agility sections, he began to lose it again as he started the trail. Runners passed him – ten, twenty, forty. Eventually he stopped counting. A glance behind showed lots of empty land and little else.

He imagined the disappointment on Osric's face, and decided that he had more to give. Blisters ate into his feet as he clumped along the trail. He had to walk the hills, but flew down the declines with long runaway strides. He passed several boys on the last downhill, the achievement spurring him on. But when he reached the level at the foot of the slope, the feeling of weightlessness died under the crush of exhaustion.

He stumbled to a halt. His shoes felt like millstones. Hands on knees, he doubled over, groaning as bones and muscles made desperate complaints. He was too tired even to swat the flies that settled and began crawling over his face. He needed a moment.

There was a sharp sound of something flicking through the air. A wasp-like sting brought him up and he slapped a hand against his injured neck.

Peashot glared and ran. Aedan forgot everything in the surge of indignation. This was one injury, one foul more than he was prepared to take. He had no hope of catching the nimble-footed fox, at least not with heavy plodding strides, so he tore at his laces, hurled the shoes away, and set off in pursuit. Immediately, he wondered why he hadn't done this earlier. Peashot glanced over his shoulder just in time to see Aedan flying towards him.

Wrath and fear urged them to a speed that should have been impossible at this stage of the day. Aedan had to slow somewhat, and Peashot, ever aware, slowed as much as he could afford while still preserving a safe distance. The trail led them back to the road and they ran on, the walls of Castath rising in the distance. Aedan's feet were taking a hammering on the stony road, but freedom from the waterlogged shoes had given him wings. A large crowd of boys was passing through the city gates about a mile ahead – it looked like a good hundred of them – so the hope of making the first eighty was gone. He paid no attention to the runners he was passing, and fixed his eyes on the little darting menace.

Peashot was showing himself to be fleeter of foot than Aedan had expected. They ran on, weaving through slower groups, and began swerving between carts and pedestrians as the road intersected others and traffic increased. Finally the walls were before them. They sped through the city gates, blind to the guards and deaf to the cheers and laughter of the people.

Instead of taking the main road, which was now heavily congested, Peashot slipped down a narrow alley. It enabled him to streak away from the crowds, but not from his pursuer. Over the past weeks this had become Aedan's ground too. The gap between the boys closed as they threaded the dim corridors, moving swiftly through the city towards the barracks. Aedan could hear his tormentor's breathing now. Another few turns and he would have him. Finally they burst into the open. Peashot stumbled for the first time and it was all Aedan needed. He shoved from behind, throwing the smaller boy down, and then pinned him on his stomach, a knee in his back.

But now that he had Peashot at his mercy, he hesitated.

He remembered the last time he had taken personal revenge, letting his temper and hatred have their way. It had not felt good. It had not made him feel strong – threatening yes, but not strong. Nor had it done anything to mend the hollowness his father had left in him. As he looked at his fist, he understood for the first time that using it this way could never be strength. It was the opposite of strength, a spineless yielding to low urges.

He took the weight off his knee and sat down against a sun-bathed wall, giving himself over to the ragged pursuit of air and the throbbing in his bad leg. Peashot turned over and sat up, surprise and relief blending on his face between the red and white splotches of exhaustion.

Noises reached them from the far end of the courtyard as two boys crossed the space and were greeted with, "Seventy-five, seventy-six."

It only took a heartbeat for realisation burst on Aedan and Peashot. They leapt from the ground and sprinted over the cobbles just as a large group of runners emerged at the other end, also at a full sprint. The distance closed; it would be tight. Peashot was ahead, but Aedan's bare feet moved in a blur and he caught up. The other boys were taller, fierce-looking contestants that pounded the earth with big strides.

Wind hummed in Aedan's ears as he leaned forward and threw every last ounce of strength into his legs. He passed the smaller boy and they shot between the finish markers to the sound of, "Seventy-seven, seventy-eight!"

His bad leg buckled and he plunged forward, skidding and tumbling until he came to rest in a panting heap. He was only dimly conscious of a growing riot of voices behind him. Something about barefoot and rules. A horrible thought began to grow as one of the race officials approached him.

"What happened to your shoes?" the official asked.

"I took them off on the last section of the trail."

"You were told to keep them on. It was one of the rules."

"We were only told that for the swim. Nobody said anything about the run."

The official shook his head. "You should have known. You were meant to keep your shoes and will have to be disqualified. It means that —"

"Silence!"

The voice was enormous, and quite familiar. The courtyard hushed instantly. Osric was not shouting, just making himself heard. Those near him backed away.

"Rules are presented before they are to be obeyed, not after. Agreed?"

Everyone agreed except the boy who had apparently raised the objection. Osric fixed his eyes on him. The boy nodded quickly.

"No rule against running barefoot was made known. Does anyone contest that?"

Nobody contested it. Osric walked away and conversation resumed.

Aedan hobbled over towards Peashot. There were several things he wanted to say, many of them barbed. The small boy's defiant screen was up, but Aedan had no desire to break it again. Finally, putting his hand to the tender spot on his neck, Aedan grinned.

"Good shot," he said, and lurched off to the barracks.

Chapter 19

The nurse removed the last of the bandages and Aedan stared at the polished brass plate, shocked by his reflection.

"The top of your ear will not regrow I'm afraid. The hair on the side of your head may, in time. But I doubt it. I think the best would be to keep your hair a little longer to cover the damaged area."

Aedan barely heard. He had not expected this. There were scars that gave a kind of respectability, but this did the exact reverse. A heaviness descended on him. How could he present himself in daylight? He looked like a chicken half-plucked and part-mutilated. One of the younger nurses walked into the room. He turned his head away in embarrassment, keeping the ruined side hidden from her. The older nurse saw what was happening and gestured for her young assistant to leave.

"This may be a difficult time for you, Aedan, but you will be your own worst critic. Nobody will pay it as much attention as you, and eventually not even you will notice. Besides, you are strong and healthy. You have much that others don't."

On the way back to his dorm, words fluttered around and behind him – singed, branded, scorched, roasted. Then there was the innocent question of a child come to visit his father at the barracks: "Daddy, what happened to that boy's head? He looks so ugly." The embarrassment of the parents was almost more stinging than the curiosity of their child. The nurse, Aedan was beginning to realise, had not really told him the truth.

The first eighty were back, following a two-day rest. Aedan had spent most of the time sleeping and reading at Osric's house –

his leg and ankle were so stiff and sore that he could not walk the day after the race. He had been looking forward to the company of the others. Now he dreaded it.

The groups had been rearranged and the only face he recognised from his original dorm was Peashot's. The reception from the others was as bad as he'd feared.

"Wow! What happened to him?"

"You should have kept the bandage."

"There's a barber out there who needs to be tried in court."

"You forgot to toast the other side."

"If I had a hog with a face like yours, I'd doc its tail and – Ouch! Which snivelling son of a ..."

Aedan stared in surprise. Peashot faced the big boy down, his little tube still poised. It was Jemro, a beefy young giant said to be as mean as he was strong.

For someone of his size, he covered the distance at an impressive speed. Peashot ducked the first blow and landed one of his own in a muscle-bound neck before the momentum of the charge carried him to ground. He received only one stunning punch to the eye. The next stopped short when Aedan grabbed a handful of blonde hair and tugged.

Jemro bellowed and leapt to his feet, catching Aedan with a wild backhand that sent him reeling. Aedan's bad right leg collapsed under him, but he scrambled to his feet again. He was not afraid of boys like this.

"If you had a hog," he shouted, "your manners would make your mother unsure which one to feed on the floor."

Jemro looked like he did not know exactly what Aedan meant, but he understood the tone clearly enough. "Nobody insults *me*!" he yelled, and charged.

Aedan backed away quickly, taking his weight on his good leg and keeping his eyes locked on Jemro's until he felt the wall behind him. As the charge commenced, he narrowed his eyelids to slits and let his features contort with the anticipation of pain. Jemro would crush him against the wall – the eagerness in the big boy's face was plain to see.

Then, when the distance between them was little over a body's length, Aedan dropped under the charge and felt the wall shudder with a meaty thud and a clonk that had the percussive quality of a skull.

Jemro moaned. His trembling knees appeared unable to reach a decision. Aedan assisted them with a good kick, dropping the bully in a solid heap. He stepped back and waited, but the oversized boy only cradled his head and whimpered.

Aedan hadn't exactly thumped him; it hadn't been a fight in the traditional sense, but he didn't think Jemro would be too eager to start with him again. The chatter resumed as he walked back. Boys retold their favourite moments of the encounter in excited voices. Aedan found his bunk. It was the same one, and Peashot had his too.

"You don't have to fight my battles," Peashot said. "I didn't ask for your help."

"I didn't ask for yours. Why did you shoot him?"

Peashot thought about it. "He just needed tenderising. When he started speaking like that I had no choice."

"Why did you think I needed tenderising?" Aedan asked.

"You reminded me of someone I knew, someone I owed."

"And now?"

"No. You're alright now."

"Good," Aedan said feeling his bruised jaw. "I'm feeling tender enough."

The next month was one of study. At the end of the month they would be examined on the knowledge they had acquired. Their characters would then be reviewed and the final list of twenty names compiled.

The bombardment of information began on the first day and covered history, law, navigation and cartography, foreign relations, and war strategy. Giddard drew a few chuckles when he pointed out that the last two subjects were not intended as a sequence.

Those who could not write sweated with the effort of retaining information that now streamed from the masters. Giddard and Rodwell took the classes of history and law respectively, and both proved to be thoroughly impressive teachers, particularly Giddard. He could hold the whole lecture hall in silence, retelling ancient chronicles in a way that brought dead kings to life and stirred the dust of forgotten battles until they raged again in the minds of his students.

Law was far more interesting than any had expected. Rodwell, in his piping voice, presented the subject by making people the focus rather than policies. He was careful to maintain a flow of interesting examples illustrating how laws were applied to individual situations. Unfortunately he also maintained a flow of frothy missiles, as those near the front quickly discovered. It was a curious thing to see boys stampeding into his class only to fill up from the back.

Aedan began to itch again with a returning hunger for knowledge, a hunger that he had known back in the Mistyvales when his mother had been able to teach him without interference. His father had exploded at them one afternoon, accusing her of turning Aedan against him with her lessons. By then, Aedan had reached the stage where he was conversant in two languages. Kalry had also been taught Orunean, and the three of them had often shared long conversations in the foreign tongue. Clauman, who had always sneered at the idea of being taught anything by his wife, had seen these gatherings as a personal attack, as if he were being shown up for his illiteracy, excluded and mocked. It was during the last of these confrontations when Aedan had stepped in to defend his mother, and learned to fear his father's hands. After that, Nessa had stopped teaching her son during the day and only risked short lessons at night.

Now, without the looming dread of his father's wrath, Aedan's mind stirred, looked about, and found itself eager. He scribbled notes as fast as his hand would allow. Once, when the boys reading over his shoulder began to distract him, he switched to Orunean, and was rewarded with their frustration and eventual loss of interest.

Classes would end at mid-afternoon, and the boys could spend the evenings as they chose. Most gathered to discuss and refresh themselves on what they had been taught during the day, cudgelling their brains to retain the growing mountain of material. Few could read or write. Some of the literate ones kept to themselves, revising their notes in private. Others, like Aedan, would read them out to the groups that quickly formed around them. It was no labour to him – at last his company was widely sought, even if it was only for the sake of what he could offer.

Peashot was seldom absent from these groups. Aedan often noticed him repeating extracts to himself, and imagined his ears to have the same foxy sharpness as his eyes.

Though they were not quite friends, there was a growing understanding between them, a growing respect. There were friendlier, politer boys, but there was something dependable about Peashot that ran deeper than his manners – which were appalling at all times. Aedan realised it when he imagined being in another fight. Though he wasn't sure how, he knew that Peashot would be the one to stand with him.

Not many in the dormitory could read, so Aedan was regularly prevailed upon. Jemro objected on the first night, saying he would smash the mouth of the next person who opened it, because he wanted to sleep. There was a short lull and then an eruption of voices, individual boys finding courage in the anonymity of the mass. Jemro was told, among other things, to go sleep at the farm with the other lazy beasts, to go have a rematch with the wall, and to go stuff his head into a compost heap and moan there. The upshot was that he pretended to sleep while Aedan read, repeating sections that some struggled with and adding a few bits of relevant information gathered from his own reading.

Some proved to be adept learners, in spite of the inability to use letters. One boy, Vayle, understood foreign relations in such depth – his father being a sea merchant – that he was able to explain some aspects in even more detail than the lecturer. He also seemed to be possessed of a near-perfect memory, recalling any facts that had been too quick for the pen. They assumed he was illiterate until he snatched one of Aedan's more poorly recorded pages and filled in the blanks. Vayle simply did not need to write in order to remember.

When it was discovered that Aedan was apprenticed to the great general himself, he was harried for inside information concerning the exams, but Osric had foreseen this and forbidden Aedan to contact him until the exams were over.

The weeks passed and the day approached. A stony-faced clerk explained how things would proceed. All the exams would be oral. There would be six rooms, one per exam. The boys would enter each of the rooms individually where they would be asked a set of questions and their answers would be evaluated.

The announcement caused an immediate outcry and panic. What was the sixth topic?

The clerk would tell them nothing more.

Aedan was kept up late the night before the exams with questions and requests to revise sections. Nobody minded. Even Jemro was seen to be mouthing a few of the passages.

The big day arrived. It was a dark, icy morning, an iron sliver of midwinter's heart. The courtyard was buried under frozen sleet. Boots stamped constantly. The same clerk instructed the group to line up according to height. Peashot mumbled something and scraped his way to the front; Aedan was only a few places behind. Once a boy was called, the rest would not see him again until they had finished their examinations and were taken to a hall where they were to wait.

Aedan watched as Peashot was called and led towards the first exam. The shivering, stamping line watched in silence, but things got noisy when they realised conversation was not forbidden. Aedan's turn came sooner than he had expected. He tried to calm himself as he was led along a one-walled, open air passage to the first room. An official stopped him and made him wait several paces short of a closed door. When the door creaked open, the boy who had stood ahead of him emerged wearing a look of abject shock.

"Next!"

A dart could not have given him a sharper jolt. Aedan scurried into the room where he was confronted by a large desk, behind which sat Giddard, his lined face as hard as the morning's ice, and two clerks who were dipping quills and preparing to score the new candidate. Aedan suddenly realised that Giddard was speaking – no – had finished speaking, and was looking at him, apparently awaiting a response.

"I – I'm sorry, I wasn't listening properly."

"Not listening properly? That's a poor start when our purpose is to determine if you listened properly for the past month. I asked your name."

"My name is uh ..." His name. What was it?

Giddard furrowed his brow.

The scribes frowned.

Thoughts scattered like rabbits under a hawk's shadow. There would be no chance of recalling anything now, not even a name. What a way to leave. He would be known as Aedan the nameless.

Ah!

"Aedan, sir. Yes. Aedan. That's my name. Aedan."

The clerks frowned again and shook their heads as they wrote.

"Very well Aedan, I have four questions for you. Try to answer promptly." He directed a meaningful look.

"Yes, sir."

The clerks dipped their pens and held them ready to pronounce judgement on the attempt.

"First: Name the kings who mark the seven epochs in Thirna's history."

Aedan relaxed. This would be easy. "Vendun, Tana, Merr, Athgrim, Eilif, Broknerra, and Elgar who still holds the throne at Tullenroe. Do you want me to say that Tana was a queen and not a king?"

"Noted," Giddard said, without looking up. "What is the origin of our city and its name?"

"It was started by prospectors who discovered a large silver deposit and while they were here they found that the soil was much more fertile than at the coast. After a few years they were making more from crops than from mining. The name of the city is an abbreviation. It was the castle of Athgrim, shortened to Castath. Originally it was much smaller and only the keep –"

"That will do. Next: Why did Thirna lose the southern reach of its sea border?"

This was something that had been covered at the end of one of the first days when many pairs of eyes had glazed over. Aedan had taken notes – he could see the words in front of him, but there was a problem. A big problem. He began tentatively,

"It was during the ... uh ... the floods of the ... the ... era of Merr ... when the ... the ... soil ..."

"What is the matter boy? At this rate your answer will span the morning."

"I'm sorry, sir. It's just that I made that section of notes in Orunean and –"

"Cleu Orunä a menim en lerrias tor."

Aedan should probably have expected to find that he was not the only one in the room who knew the language. He had not spoken it in a long time, but was able to recite his notes with something far nearer to fluency than he had achieved by translation.

One of the clerks smiled slightly and made a note; the other looked at Giddard, blank, waiting for enlightenment.

"It was correct," Giddard said to him, with a touch of amusement. "Final question: What do you feel was the biggest mistake made by any of the kings during the epoch of Athgrim?"

Aedan considered. He knew what the wizened master wanted to hear, but he had a different view on this – one he was eager to present. "Banning of the midwinter jubilee in the reign of Leod."

Giddard frowned, clearly disappointed. "How could that be worse than doubling taxes and wasting the money on royal finery, or starting a war in a desert where troops would be defeated by lack of water?"

"Well in my hometown –"

"Which is?"

"The Mistyvales."

Giddard nodded.

"Every year we held a fair. But one year we had a new sheriff, and he decided that the fair was wasting money and slowing production because it took people away from their work. Instead of working harder, labourers just stood in the fields and complained for months. It was the worst yield ever. They still grumble about it as though something had been stolen from them. The sheriff lost more support from that than from his fancy clothes and the big carriage that our taxes paid for. We replaced him before the year was up.

"I think that banning the midwinter jubilee was the thing that got people to hate King Leod. It was only two months later that the coup began, leading up to the crimson summer. I think people are used to putting up with wars and taxes, but this would have felt like the king was attacking their happiness. I think it was the decision that made Leod an enemy to his people."

"That's a new perspective," Giddard said, rubbing his chin in contemplation, "and not without merit." He nodded at the clerks who made their entries.

"One more question," he said. The clerks looked up in surprise. "I understand that you have perused *The Five Generals of the Elgan Epoch*. As a young historian, how would you describe the nature of recording?"

Aedan shuffled. Was it a trap? Had Giddard been one of the contributors? Obviously the man had spoken to Osric, so there was no backing down from his original criticism of the book.

"Very ... creative," he said at last.

Giddard nodded, a hint of mischief in his eyes. "You may proceed to the next exam."

Law proved a less enjoyable examination. It seemed that Rodwell was in the clutches of a bad breakfast because his face twitched and contorted during Aedan's answers, making concentration difficult and confidence impossible. Aedan knew the answer to the first question which involved levels of crime and punishment. He was less convincing with the next one dealing with means of assessing witness integrity. But it was the last question that he found nearly impossible to answer with the corpulent man wincing and shuddering at random, causing his chins to wobble and drop little beads of sweat. Aedan was asked to give an example of how mercy might be allowed a voice at the court of justice.

The memory of the girl crying for her father at the city gate was still vivid in Aedan's mind, and he explained how sentences might be mitigated for the sake of dependents. Rodwell did not seem impressed with the answer, saying that such mitigation would then encourage large, unsustainable families. Aedan left feeling thoroughly deflated.

Navigation and cartography presented no difficulties, the names of towns, rivers and mountains being long known to him. The calculation of distances and directions, and drawing according to scale he explained easily.

The examiner for foreign relations was a young man named Kollis. He had an apparent love for questionable cultures, and bristled visibly at any hint of intolerance. "There is no such thing as a bad culture," he would say, "just as there is no such thing as a bad spice. It's all about being able to appreciate and understand from an unprejudiced perspective."

Kollis looked bright and eager. "Well Aedan, due to the imminence of the Lekran threat, I've decided to focus my questions on their fascinating culture. First: Name the three most important celebrations on the islands of Lekrau."

Aedan's jaw locked. He fixed his eyes on the oak floorboards, trying to contain his disgust. He had ignored every word said about Lekrau, and had more than once been tempted to walk out when Kollis had played for affections with Lekran folk stories and even jokes. As he considered his experience of Lekrau, his feelings became words and barrelled out.

"Their entire economy runs on slavery and murder! And you want me to talk about their celebrations?"

Kollis drew himself up and glared with the wrath of injured pride. "Your prejudice is due to ignorance boy. Sheer ignorance.

The proceedings require that I put the question to you again. Name the –"

"The only celebration of theirs I want to know about is where every one of their ships burns, every slaver with blood on his hands hangs, and the rest are locked in their own cages."

"Thank you for your candour. You have made it clear that you are not fit to be a marshal."

"If being a marshal means I have to be chummy with murderers, then I agree."

Aedan had seldom been so angry. He stormed from the room. That anyone could sympathise with the beasts that Quin represented was incredible to him. He had half a mind to go back and suggest that Kollis try an interesting new spice on his next meal, one that a world of fools had not yet learned to appreciate, that ignorant and prejudiced people knew as arsenic.

"Name?" The voice broke in on his vengeful thoughts. It was Skeet, the petulant retired commander who clearly resented the fact that he was stuck teaching boys, not out on the field hurting people with sharp and heavy objects.

Aedan gave his name crisply, fire flashing in his eyes. He was in the mood for a brawl; he was going to be failed anyway.

"First question: You have a force of a hundred archers at the top of the Narill valley which provides excellent cover. A division of four hundred heavily armoured infantry enters the bottom of the valley. You must defeat them, even at the cost of your men. What is your first order?"

"Run away."

"What!" Skeet slammed his fist on the desk. Though he was a relatively small man, his aura of sparks and smoke gave him a colossal presence. A partly shrivelled left arm proclaimed the reason for his recall from the field, and the rest of him proclaimed his frustration. Explosively so. At first Aedan had thought this master to be similar to Osric, but he had learned that while Osric was a deep cavern of hidden thought and carefully directed power, Skeet was all immediacy and reaction. With him, annoyance felt was annoyance expressed.

Aedan glared back. "I saw that valley not so long ago. It is a death trap for archers. It is filled with low branches and vines that would make a clear shot impossible even from ten yards. The high ground means nothing because the slopes are so thickly overgrown the infantry would be invisible while they moved uphill. Even if arrows were somehow shot on target they would get caught in the tangle of branches. You said it has excellent cover, but it's the kind of cover infantry dreams about."

Skeet's fist hovered, seeming a lot less sure of itself. "Your next order?"

"Retreat to the plain with the archers and wait until the whole force of infantry has taken up the chase, shoot a few crooked and broken arrows to make it seem like arrows are out, and then lead them far enough onto the plain to make their retreat impossible. After that, unload on them. If they charge, run away again. Their armour will make them slower and they'll get tired quicker. If they flee, chase them. They won't survive long under falling arrows. Only fools or people who've got no knowledge of terrain would attack in the valley. Loss of sight, loss of command, loss of advantage, and no knowledge of the outcome until the last survivors trickle in."

Skeet took a deep breath as if to say something, then let it out again, this time scowling at the notes in front of him. He looked up at Aedan. "Blood and fire! You're right." Then he turned to the clerks and spoke in a dangerously quiet voice, "Which of you halfwits set this question?"

Both shrank into their seats. Each pointed at the other. Skeet ignored them.

"Good work, Aedan. You are the first to impress me and I fully expect that you will be the last."

The next two questions were simple explanations of standard tactical procedures.

In the sixth room, there were only two men. Aedan started as he saw the tall grey-haired examiner wearing the long blue robes of the academy's high seat. This could only be the great Culver, the man before whom everyone in the academy quailed, the most learned scholar in the city if not the land.

Beside him sat a voluminous scribe with a wild black bush of hair and another of beard. The hair covered all but a large round nose that glowed slightly from the cold, and sharp eyes that twinkled as if he'd played some terrific prank on the world that morning.

"Aedan, son of Clauman, why do you wish to be a Castath marshal?" Culver asked without any preamble.

Aedan, despite his lingering anger, was intimidated, but he squared his shoulders and tried to sound confident. "I want to bring justice to Lekrau," he said.

"Is that all? Have you no other ambitions?"

"I hate tyrants. I hate bullies. All of them. If I could bring war to the whole lot I would, but I intend to start with Lekrau."

"You want to start a war with Lekrau?" Culver lifted his brows. The weight of his eyes was imposing, but his incredulous tone felt to Aedan like mockery, and it raised his temperature despite the warning at the back of his mind. Unconsciously he clenched his fists as he replied.

"Lekrau has already started a war with us. We sit and cower, hoping that they will choose the village next door. That is not avoiding war. It's just fighting it badly." His voice had been too loud. He knew it.

Culver regarded him in silence for an uncomfortably long time. "Have you any more to say?" he asked.

"No, sir."

"Then you may leave."

The bushy scribe was writing and did not glance up. Aedan was taken through to a hall in which a large fireplace, several yards across, was hard at work against the chill of the day. Here he found Peashot and the others who had been ahead in the line, slowly baking themselves in front of the coals.

"Ever seen anyone with less personality than that last dried up stick of a man?" Peashot asked.

"You mean the chancellor?"

Peashot fell silent with his mouth open, then bit his lip.

"What did you say to him?"

"Nothing."

The other boys joined them and bombarded Aedan with questions, comparing answers, but even their nervousness couldn't shake him from the bitter experience of foreign relations and of Kollis the Clown. When the questions had run dry, he dragged himself away from the group and the fire to a gloomy corner where he kicked at the floor, waiting for the hall to fill and fates to be announced.

Eventually, the last of the hopefuls arrived, and then the examiners walked through and entered a room that opened off to the side. Before the doors closed, the aromas of hot tea and oats-and-honey cakes drifted out, taunting the cold and hungry boys.

They didn't have long to wait before matters became interesting. It sounded like several men were speaking together, loudly. Kollis's moralising tones took over and then a voice that could only have been Skeet's cut through all conversation, "By my sword-arm you shall not! You take your ideals too far, sir!" Culver's voice intervened and restored calm. It was midday, though still cold as dawn by the time the examiners emerged and walked to the stage. Giddard approached the lectern with a sheet of paper.

"There are twenty names on this list," he said. "But before I read it, I must congratulate every one of you. We have never been privileged to examine such a competent group. Those of you who are not named now will be shortlisted for potential military promotions should you choose to enrol there. Every one of you would be a valuable asset to our permanent garrison."

With that, he read the list. Peashot, or Bede as he was officially known, was the first named. Several followed until Aedan realised these were all boys who had gone after him.

He felt sick. His head dropped forward. How would he explain this to Osric? What kind of fool loses his temper in an examination? He wondered if he even had the right to go back to Osric after this. But to face Harriet again …

Giddard folded up the page. Some boys were ecstatic and grouped in little victors' circles. The others began to drift away.

"And Aedan son of Clauman."

He glanced up at the mention of his name. Giddard held his eye with a stern face. It was all the reprimand that was needed. Aedan dropped his eyes, relief flooding through him, and in spite of his effort to remain grave, smiled.

Chapter 20

The boys were given a week to spend with their families. Aedan went to visit his mother every day and stayed as long as Harriet would allow. There was no news of Clauman, but mother and son constantly reminded each other that in a city so large it might take him some time to find them. For all his abusiveness, he was still husband and father, and they missed him.

Nessa was delighted to hear that Aedan had made it into the academy. Harriet was not. She wanted to know what he thought he would learn there that she could not have taught him. It was an answer so colossal that Aedan didn't know how to begin. Harriet interpreted the hesitation differently. She shook her yellow curls with a look of infinite wisdom and noble pity.

"The academy is a place for fools," she said, "a place where loud-mouths sit around in soft couches and talk about things they've never seen."

"Oh," said Nessa, with sincere enthusiasm, "have you seen it?"

Harriet pulled a sour face. "Of course not. After everything I've just explained, why would I care to?"

After their break, the twenty boys gathered at the main entrance. Some had arrived early in the afternoon, bursting with curiosity. The sentry made it clear, however, that they would not be allowed in before the day's end – when a clerk would officially escort them through the gates. None had ever been inside, and they were all eagerness and impatience as they gnawed through the hours. Finally, the long awaited clerk arrived, took charge of them at the outer gate and led the way past the guards, along a passage and through a second gate. Then the Royal Academy opened up, as did every mouth.

Wide wintery lawns lined with ancient trees were surrounded by the most unusual and fascinating stone buildings, unlike anything else in the city. Apart from the central meeting hall, each of four main wings was between three and five storeys high. Pillars were fronted with statues of exquisite beauty and separated from each other by gargoyles of startling hideousness, all of them quite life like. There were noble arches, airy corridors, plentiful windows and high balconies. The intricately featured walls and columns were all faced with limestone and marble that glowed a deep imperial rose in the lingering sunset. Even the stables beyond several acres of fenced paddocks exuded noble condescension.

"Academics are split into four sections," the clerk said, indicating with a hand as he listed them. "Marshals, military officers, legal administrators, and physicians. Beyond are the residences where the masters and some seniors are housed. There are also a few other buildings that not even I can identify. Best keep clear of them. The Royal Academy is very old. There are more than a few secrets within these walls."

"Why are there physicians here?" someone asked in a reverent whisper.

"A level of medical knowledge is required for marshals and officers, so it is convenient for them to be housed on the premises. Where better for a medical school to locate itself, where better to find open wounds on which to practice, than where military and legal men are brought together?"

A few boys whispered to each other. Most were still staring around in awe.

"Rules will be explained tomorrow. For now, keep to the marshals' wing. The lawns and stables belong to everyone, but some of the law students can get territorial. They tend not to like marshals and will make trouble with the hatchlings – that would be you. The two giant crindo boards – you'll all want to have a go at shifting stone pieces as big as yourselves, but if hatchlings are caught there they spend the rest of the day doing chores for whichever senior finds them. Keep well clear of the central meeting hall and the surrounding lawn within the ring of statues.

That place is almost sacred here. You don't want to learn the penalty for trespassing."

The boys paid him scant attention as they gaped, some shaking their heads. Aedan was laughing. He was awash in amazement. That such a place could exist in the middle of a city … and right alongside the Seeps!

The clerk snapped his fingers and led the way into the marshals' wing. Their footsteps clattered down long stone corridors as they took one turn after another, eventually stopping outside a set of dormitories. Each room was split into five partial divisions, each section having a bed, a desk and a set of shelves. A range of equipment was piled on each bed – hooded cloaks, shirts, trousers and sturdy boots, a small hunting knife, a leather satchel, and an oil lantern Aedan recognised as a kind of dark lantern. It had panels that could be flapped closed, directing or shutting off the light – perfect for studying after the others had turned in. Also perfect for secret explorations after dark.

The furnishings were rough, like what might be expected in a logger's cabin, imparting a rugged charm that was almost homely. Names had been assigned and Aedan found himself nearest to the door again, sharing a room with Peashot, Vayle, Lorrimer and one other he had not met.

"You may explore if you wish," the clerk said, "but I would recommend a very good night's sleep before tomorrow. If you don't take my advice you will be sorrier than you can imagine."

Once he left them, the unanimous decision was to be sorrier than they could imagine.

In Aedan's dorm, the air was charged with excitement. "You think the rumours are true?" asked Lorrimer. Everyone looked at the tall boy with the big hands, big feet, enormous ears, and little but sinew linking everything, as if he had been clamped at those points and stretched. His quivering voice underscored a general impression of frailty. Aedan wondered how he had made it through the obstacles of the first elimination. "The ones about the building going down underground, I mean," Lorrimer added, his big ears blushing at the attention he had drawn to himself.

"I'm for finding out," said Aedan, with a tentative glance at the others. "How about we start with that?"

"I doubt they would want us to discover such secrets. That would be looking for trouble." It was Vayle, slouched lazily on his bed with a detached look in his eyes, a look that only faintly betrayed constant, calculating thought. Aedan was glad, but not in the least surprised to see he had made it through.

The mention of trouble sat Lorrimer down on his bed as firmly as if he had been pushed. Peashot, however, popped off his.

"Fine by me," he said, slipping a tube up his sleeve.

"Um … Hadley?" Aedan ventured, glancing at the name tag above the far bed.

The large boy at the far end was going through his equipment. He had the look of a supreme athlete, and no fool either. He raised his head. "So you're in charge?"

Aedan's mouth dropped open and he was about to say that he had no such ideas, but Peashot's tongue was quicker.

"Yeah, he's in charge. You want to start trouble?"

"Maybe," Hadley said, standing up and advancing on them with an easy smile. He was big. He looked older than the rest of them by at least a year.

Peashot stepped forward too, and for the first time Aedan guessed why the little boy's nose had such an odd, flattened shape, like he'd spent the past dozen years using it to hammer nails or ram billy goats. He raised his fists.

Aedan groaned. This was the worst way to begin.

The distance closed with Hadley's long strides. "But unlike you," he said, pushing past and dropping a big hand on Peashot's head, "I need a decent reason to fight. Maybe we'll find one later. Come along lads. There's nothing I hate like dawdling." He stood at the door and motioned them through.

Nobody argued with him, nobody resisted, though Lorrimer slipped past very quickly and Peashot's dark glare retained all its menace. Aedan had been desperately hoping that he would make real friends in his dorm. This Hadley worried him, made him nervous. The boy's confidence was almost unnatural.

It was an uneasy group that filed out into the corridor.

As they passed the other dorms, another boy flew out from one of them and barged into their midst, glancing repeatedly behind him.

"Hey!" he said, his voice shaking strangely. "You going axporing?"

"What?" said Hadley.

"Think he means exploring," Vayle suggested.

"Yes, sorry," said the boy. "Thirnish are not my main language. Saying things through the river."

"You're Orunean, aren't you?" Aedan asked. He had heard that there was a kind of military exchange between the sister nations of Orunea and Thirna.

"Yes, how you know?"

"Only Orunean foreigners would be allowed to be soldiers or marshals here. Also, through the river – in Orunean it means mixed up. Unfortunately it doesn't work like that in Thirnish. But, yes, we are going exploring. Want to come along?"

"Yes, thank you. There is a belly on my dorm, he more older and also bigger, and making us to clean his things. When I don't have a cloth for the cleaning of shoes he tell me to lack them."

"I think it's a bully who wants his shoes licked," said Vayle.

It was obvious that the new boy was recovering from the verge of tears. The edges of his mouth trembled, and the forced smile looked as though it was about to collapse.

Something had been building in Aedan as he listened, and now it erupted. Without waiting for another word, he spun around, flung the nearby door open and marched into the dorm. A thickset, heavy-limbed boy was standing over three of his roommates who were busy brushing and polishing various items. Aedan's fury grew. He would get a sure beating if he picked a fight with someone this size, but he was too angry to care. As he stepped forward a big hand dropped on his shoulder. He turned to see Hadley looking down at him.

"Me first," Hadley said, knocking Aedan off his stride and shoving past. The scrubbers and polishers on the floor looked up at the heavy steps. "Out!" Hadley shouted.

They jumped to their feet and scurried from the room. Aedan heard the rest of his dorm gather in the doorway behind him.

"Busy?" Hadley asked the remaining boy.

"As if you can't see for yourself."

"Yes, I can see, and I'm not sorry for interrupting. I'm Hadley. You are?"

The big-limbed boy looked like he wanted to avoid an answer, but Hadley's eyes bored into him. "Warton," he said.

"Warton, is this the kind of marshal you are going to be?"

"This is my dorm, fat-head. Who do you think you are to come in here and lecture me?"

"Lecture? I'm here to knock your teeth out, that is, if you're going to carry on like this. What's it going to be? You choose.

Teeth or no teeth?" Hadley's knuckles clicked as his heavy fists rose in front of him.

"You're a coward. You threaten me two on one."

"Three," said Peashot, sounding annoyed at having been overlooked.

"Four," said Vayle, stepping beside Peashot, narrowing his eyes and looking equally dangerous.

Lorrimer hovered at the back and said nothing, only trembled a little.

Aedan felt a sudden respect for these grim-faced roommates of his. He turned back to Warton. "We're all here because we're angry, not scared. Anyway, do you really think Hadley needs help?"

Warton glanced back at Hadley who did not look like he needed help, and Warton did not appear quite so threatening anymore. He swallowed and took a step back.

"Well?" Hadley advanced two steps, closing the distance to something uncomfortable.

"Fine," Warton said, turning and walking away. "Now leave me alone."

As they left the room, Hadley punched the door – a solid thud. It flew away from his fist and slammed with a crash. The other boys edged away.

Aedan summoned the courage and asked, "Would you have hit him?"

"Was planning to. He spoiled it by backing down."

"I – I'm glad you stopped me – I was too angry to talk. I would have just swung at him without talking. Probably would have got caned for it later."

Hadley glanced across and smiled. "My father always tells me I'm as pushy as an avalanche, but it looks like you're a bit of an avalanche yourself when your blood hots up. I think we'll get on." This was followed by a heavy back clap.

Aedan grinned and hoped it would be so.

The corridors were high and broad, lavishly decorated with paintings and artefacts that looked as old as the walls themselves. The little group bumbled their way through the passages and rooms of the ground floor, the stairs being locked. They discovered several interesting nooks, a kitchen, mess halls, the dorms of older apprentices, classes, and a large number of offices. All in all, it turned out to be a slightly disappointing tour.

There was only one room that had aroused curiosity. It was a large space in the centre of the building, filled with statues of past governors, mayors and chief marshals. In the middle was an open area, like an indoor courtyard, with a large stone feature that stood about twelve feet high and measured as much across each of its six finely engraved faces. Aedan thought it might be a good idea to climb on top, but there was no hold to be found on the surfaces. When sighs and huffs of boredom began to fill the room, they drifted back to the dorm, annoyed at having been unable to reach another level, above or below. The boys from the other dorms had mostly retired for the evening.

"Now that was exciting," Peashot grumbled. "I don't know how I'll sleep."

"It was educational," offered Vayle, "I'd always wondered if the original mayor of Castath looked as foreign as the histories suggest. Did any of you notice the clearly Orunean nose?"

"Oh yes," said Peashot. "It was my lifelong dream to study the snout of a long-dead fat man. What's with this place? Statues, paintings, pretty hallways ... Marshals seem to have bog-rotten taste in design."

"Don't seem to have much sense in architecture either," added Aedan. "Who puts a stupid feature like that in a perfectly good room? The thing wastes so much space." Suddenly he stopped. The others turned and looked at him. "It's not a feature," he said. "Come on!"

In a riot of confusion and curiosity, they raced after him into the large room. Aedan ran up to the central structure and began tapping the surfaces. They were solid. His expression fell slightly.

"What are you doing?" Peashot asked.

"I think it conceals an entrance," Aedan said. He stepped back and looked up. "There must be something here that we are just not seeing."

The boys began pacing around, inspecting everything – floor, statues, furniture, and a mouse that found its retreat blocked and darted between shoes until it reached a drape that it scaled without any apparent loss of speed.

Lorrimer's attention soon drifted and he lounged against a statue. It was a large bronze head wearing an expression so fierce that the contrast between the lounger and his support could not have been greater. The statue seemed about to spark into life and raise a storm at the insolent boy.

"How's that going to help?" Peashot demanded, stopping in front of Lorrimer who was pulling abstractedly on one of his large ears.

"Huh?"

"Wake up and make yourself useful. How about you just reach up for the top of that thing and we'll climb you. Lorrimer the Ladderboy. We could call you Lads for short."

"How about we throw you up with a rope. You're about the right size for a grappling hook."

Peashot had already slipped the tube from his sleeve when Aedan's voice rang out.

"Here! Come help."

Aedan was standing in front of a coiled mass of stringy draping.

"What are you doing?" asked Peashot, running up.

"Getting us into trouble, that's for sure," said Vayle, more to himself than anyone in particular.

"I think these are ropes, not drapes. See the long panels of wooden slats holding the paintings – I think these ropes lower the slats down so they form a ramp from here to the top of that feature." The boys measured the distance with their eyes and slowly all nodded.

"Won't the paintings fall off?" asked Hadley

"Not if they are meant to be lowered."

"So what do we do?"

"Well, I think it could be heavy. If it's just me holding the end I might shoot up to the roof while the panel comes crashing down. Once I unhook it, it's best that we are all holding on."

"Probably won't make much difference what *you* do," Lorrimer mumbled to Peashot.

"I'm sorry. I didn't get that. My ears aren't big enough for super-human hearing."

Lorrimer turned red. He looked like he was about to stamp on a mouse.

"Everyone take hold." Aedan released the catch and sure enough the drapes lurched up from the heap of coils on the ground. They held tight and released an arm's length at a time. One of the long, ladder-like panels that had looked to be part of the room's furnishings leaned inwards. It began to descend towards the central feature where it finally touched and came to rest. They let go. It was a perfect wooden ramp leading to the top of the centrepiece.

There was no order in the wild dash up the slope, curiosity driving them. When they reached the top they encountered a flat wooden surface. It was a stage. Nothing more.

"To think that we almost missed this," said Peashot. "The others will never believe us. It actually has a wooden top. Good job Aedan. We unlocked the marshals' great secret."

Nobody was listening. They were watching Aedan who was moving about, stamping.

"These boards are hollow. We need to lift them."

"But they are bolted down," said Vayle.

"I'll bet they are bolted into something that lifts, just holding them together. I don't suppose anyone has any tools here."

"Maybe me." It was the new boy from the other dorm. He began digging in his pockets and drew out a chisel and a few sturdy nails. "I was helping with my pa today and was forgetting to empty out. He is going to be mad as spit."

"I think you mean spitting mad," said Vayle.

"Oh. Thank you Vayle."

"How did you know his name?"

"I am knowing of all your names, Aedan. I am listening the whole time."

"Impressive. We don't know yours, though."

"Kian."

"Well, Kian, if you're as good with tools as you are with your ears, perhaps you can work out how to lift this."

Kian dropped to his hands and knees, shoved the tip of a nail and the chisel into the gaps at the end of the boards, and managed to lever the edge high enough for the others to get their hands underneath and lift. The boards were indeed secured to a beam that held them together. The whole panel was hoisted and placed to the side, revealing what Aedan had hoped to find, a stairway that led down into blackness.

"Lanterns," he said.

They rushed back to the dorms, snatched their lanterns and returned at a sprint. The lanterns were empty so they went to the perimeter of the room which was ringed with oil-burning torches, the kind with a large iron reservoir and a stout wick. They doused two of them and tipped the oil into their lanterns, then lit their own wicks from the torches that remained burning.

With Aedan and Hadley in the lead, they stampeded back up the ramp and began to descend the stairs. The lanterns were bright but the stairway itself was made of a very dark stone that reflected little.

"Hold a moment," Aedan said as they approached a set of marble pillars. Something shouted a warning in his mind, something he had once read in a story of a castle siege. He placed his lantern on the ground and looked at the surfaces of the steps. The step that lay between the marble pillars was different to the others. It showed no signs of wear and was covered in an undisturbed layer of dust, as if it had never been used.

"Don't stand on this step," he said.

"Why not?" asked Peashot. "Aren't steps for standing on?"

"I think it's the trigger for some kind of trap." That produced a respectful silence. They were all careful to avoid the step and the next two that Aedan pointed out.

The air grew colder as they descended and now held a touch of dampness.

When they reached the bottom they stepped onto a wide landing from which two corridors led. The one was broad, the other narrow and closed off with a heavy chain. Both were dark. Aedan moved a few yards into the open corridor and lit a torch mounted on the wall.

It was immediately clear in the growing light that this was architecture from another time. Large blocks of pale stone were fitted with unerring precision, forming a smooth, arching passage that led into darkness, a darkness that must have stretched away a bewildering distance judging by the deep echoes that whispered back at them. The torch that Aedan had lit was no simple device like the ones in the room above. It was cast from a clean silvery metal and engraved with intricate details of vines threading between unfamiliar creatures. Aedan led the way down the wide passage. Above him, the light of his lantern revealed a ceiling where scores of warriors were engaged in great battles and mythical beasts fought and frolicked in curious settings. The very air in here tingled with mystery.

They passed several doors on each side, but stopped when a massive, arched entrance appeared out of the darkness on their right. The tall and impressively heavy doors were slightly ajar.

Aedan threw his weight against the dark wood. Nothing happened. The others drew alongside. They pushed together, and with a groan that rattled their joints, the door swung back on bucket-sized hinges. They stepped into a vestibule with equally large doors leading right and left, but they barely noticed these.

Before them, recessed into a high, arching alcove was a stone dais on which stood four marble statues. Three huge men and a young woman, hardly more than a girl, faced them. The first man held a sword, the second a spear, the third a hammer, and the young woman a bow. The first two men were large and strong, but the third was enormous – well over seven feet tall, with arms and legs broader than a boy's torso.

"Wonder why they made him so big," said Peashot. "He looks wrong."

Aedan laughed. "You never heard of Krawm? The sculptor didn't do any enlarging. This is the size he was. That war hammer probably weighed more than you. And he wasn't just big; he was fast. Used to run through infantry like a bull. His armour was so thick that arrows bounced off and even spears broke. There are lots of stories about him. The one I'll never forget is the one about his last battle. Heard it?"

The others shook their heads and waited.

"It was when his hometown was attacked. The gate was torn down quickly and he didn't have time to put on his armour, so he rushed to the gate with only his hammer. He stood between the posts of the gate and smashed everything that tried to come in – horses, spearmen, swordsmen. The sight of him gave such courage to the townsmen that every one of them was transformed into a warrior, and that night they turned back a force much bigger than their own.

"By the time the raiders fled, Krawm was surrounded by piles and piles of bodies. Killed more than half the raiders himself. He had about thirty arrows and spears sticking out of him, but he still stood. As the attackers drew together, the bandit-leader rose up in his saddle and shouted that he would return and take personal vengeance on Krawm's family – his nephew and niece.

"It was a mistake. In spite of the wounds that painted him red with his own blood, Krawm leapt over the bodies and sprinted towards the tight band of raiders. They say the ground shook under each giant stride and that he moved faster than any of them had ever seen a man run. The leader spun his horse, but the other horses interfered with his escape. Krawm covered the two hundred yards like a mad thing. He was at a full sprint when he swung his hammer at the man. The blow crushed his chest, killed him instantly and hurled him off his horse and into the ranks of men who scattered in all directions. They say Krawm smiled as he turned and looked at home for the last time. Then he dropped his hammer, sank to the ground and died."

The boys all looked up at the towering statue with a respect too deep to express. Lorrimer finally broke the spell.

"Imagine if there were living men like this."

"I think," said Hadley, "this General Osric is not far off."

"Direct descendant of the nephew," said Aedan. "Saw it on his ancestral scroll."

"Ah. That explains a lot."

"Do you know who the other statues are?" Vayle asked.

"Ulmar on the left, and Hanroc next to him were the two champions who defended King Athgrim, his queen and daughter against a squad of assassins. By the time the alarm was raised and reinforcements arrived, they had killed almost the entire squad of fifteen. Hanroc died of his wounds, but Ulmar lived and married the princess."

"And the woman? Is she the princess?"

"That's Queen Tana, I think. Must be."

"Why's she got a bow?"

"Don't you know the story? These are the stories I grew up with. Tana was princess when her father, a widower, decided to journey to Port Breklee – it was called something else in those days. The royal procession was attacked just west of the Pellamines where the cover is good. The king was struck by an arrow and died. There were only about two dozen royal guards and it looked as if they would be overwhelmed. But Tana took her father's bow and began loosing arrows around her. It turned the battle. Later they found that more of the enemy had been felled by her bow than by the sword. She was only fourteen at the time, but everyone agreed that her courage more than made up for her age, so she was made queen."

Though the rest of them stared, entranced, Hadley was showing symptoms of impatience. He walked to the left door and pushed it open. What he saw brought him to a standstill. The others gathered around.

Their lanterns lit the space revealing a wide and lofty chamber whose walls were stacked with every conceivable weapon – lances, spears, pikes, maces, flails, war axes and hammers, longbows, crossbows, swords, knives and shields. There was a whole wall lined with statues of men and horses in the full armour of every order. The finely curved and ornamented plate armour of Orunea stood first, the jagged and spiked encasings of Fennlor next, and as the line stretched away, the shapes grew unfamiliar, many of them cruder, and more fearsome. It looked as if the weaponry of every known empire was present.

For a long time they could do no more than stare, drinking in the sights that had only existed in their imaginations. Each husk of armour was as good as an army of its warriors, each weapon a legacy of courage and heroism. Here the screams of the dying and the stench of death were only a distant rumour, a sometime price to be paid for the honour of defending their own.

With a sense of awe, almost of reverence, they began to drift to various racks and stands, touching and lifting weapons, replacing them delicately.

All was going well until Lorrimer's big eyes settled on a colossal mace. It was clear that he was in the grip of a hopelessly enchanting vision: a tall hero – himself – on the field of battle, whirling the terrible weapon over his head.

It was too sweet to pass by.

He lifted the mace from the rack, walked a little distance away until he was clear of the others, and placed his lantern on the floor. He gripped the mighty weapon with both hands, heaved it over his shoulders and held it aloft. He stood tall, and he stood proud. He filled his big lungs with the brave air of his nation, twirled the heavy mace above his head with big hands, and gracefully compensated for the momentum with a big step. The whole spectacle changed in an instant as he tripped over one of his big feet and fell in a long, ponderous arc that ended on the stone floor, driving the brave air from his lungs and sending the mace clanging and skidding across the ground.

Two other weapons were dropped out of sheer fright.

Nobody spoke. All were listening, fearing that the noise – utterly shocking in the deep silence – had been overheard.

A door creaked open and light poured into the room, revealing the outline of a broad cloaked man with a spreading tent of untamed hair. Instantly, six flames were extinguished, sinking the great hall into darkness. Something about the bushy outline looked familiar to Aedan.

"Names?" a voice boomed.

Silence.

"I was not addressing the statues. It would be better that you give your names than I find them out."

The silence was spoiled by shuffling which ended with, "Hadley."

"Aedan."

"Bede."

"Huh? Don't try lie now. His name is Peashot and mine is Lorrimer. Ouch, you little vermin!"

"My name's Bede. I just don't like it. Haven't you ever heard of a nickname, Ladderboy?"

"Enough! Next."

"Vayle."

"Kian."

"Kian? You're from a different dorm. How did you find your way into this little band?"

"One of the boys on my dorm was bellying – sorry, bullying of me. Hadley and the others are making him to stop."

"That would be Warton?"

"Yes, sir." It was Hadley's voice.

"You met him then, Hadley. Good. Did you hit him?"

There was a thoughtful silence. "Not yet, sir."

A slight tremor in the outline of the robe suggested quiet amusement. "Candid. I had hoped as much. Well, I should inform you all that, according to the rules, you have reached greater heights of trouble than have ever been attained by new arrivals. Nobody has ever found their own way down here before. Some might think it necessary to flog you. Fortunately for you, I have a different view. Who, may I ask, worked it out?"

"Aedan, sir." It was Hadley's voice.

"Hmm, yes. That lines up. Aedan, try not to discover anything more until the administrators are ready. The rest of you, put on a good show of astonishment as the entrance is revealed, again, tomorrow morning. I enjoin you to hold your tongues as tightly as you would hold struggling fish, or you will prove my suspicion about the flogging. Boys, it is always a pleasure to meet the young and enterprising. Now as you seem to prefer the dark, I leave you to feel your way back. Aedan, don't forget the steps. They work just as well on the way out."

The door closed and all was darkness and silence. The sound of a funnelled gust preceded a sharp cry.

"Ouch! That was my ear, you stinking rat. Where are you?"

"Wasn't really aiming. Not my fault your ears fill half the room."

"I think we need to thump him together," said Lorrimer. "Aren't any of you going to help me?"

"You *were* trying to be selling the rat on him, remember?" It was Kian.

"We say 'Sell him out', or 'rat on him'," came Vayle's quiet voice.

"Oh, thanks again."

"Lorrimer," it was Hadley, "I think you were asking for it, and you have to admit that in the dark it was a ripper of a shot."

"Actually, considering the size of his ..."

"Oh shut up, Peashot! Don't you know when to drop your weapons?"

"Lorrimer does. Let's get out of here before he gets bored and drops something on one of us."

"So who do you think he was?" Hadley asked as they heaved on the drape and drew the ramp back up against the wall where it settled, looking once again like a panel of decorative slats.

"Probably some kind of caretaker," said Vayle. "I bet he lives down there."

"Don't know lots of caretakers what can do writing," said Kian.

"How do you know he can write?"

"He was holding of a quill in his hand and I'm thinking that there was ink dripping off his hand also. Maybe he was dipping of the quill when he got the scare from Lorrimer. Probably made him to be wrecking all of his parchment."

"He cooled off pretty quick if that's the case," said Aedan. "My father would have skinned the lot of us."

"Also mine."

"I reckon he is important here," said Vayle. "I think a less important man would have been more worried. He sounded amused."

"Maybe he's a magician pretending to be a caretaker," said Lorrimer, his eyes growing big.

"I must have missed something," Peashot piped up. "Did someone here ask for a bedtime story?"

Hadley turned to Aedan, "Is Peashot always angling for a fight?"

"No," Aedan laughed. "You'll see. It doesn't happen nearly as much when he's sleeping."

Hadley's eyes crinkled as he laughed and clapped Peashot on the back, ignoring the smouldering glare.

Late into the night they stared at the dark ceiling and talked of swords and axes and secret tunnels and legendary warriors. Then they got onto the topic of Warton and they all said what they would have done to him if he hadn't backed down, and each boy told of the other fights he had been in and how he'd won them. Nobody remembered any he'd lost.

Aedan told of his brawl with Emroy and his snobby friend from town when they had been rude to Kalry. He made most of it up because the real one hadn't turned out so well – and in the context of the glorious battles being narrated he felt some adjustments were necessary.

So as the stars travelled the skies unseen, the boys leapt and tackled and kicked and swung and conquered until the golden haze of victory shimmered and settled down upon a room of quiet smiles and eager dreams.

Chapter 21

"What you think you're waiting for? Daylight?"

The voice reminded Aedan of Skeet, only with a little more of that abrasive insistence, that special nuance attained by expertly combining the rude notes of clanging kitchenware with the blare of an iron bugle.

The apprentices leapt from their beds, dressed by lamplight, and stumbled into a dizzy line in the passage.

"From now on this is the time you rise. Follow me."

The stocky man led them through to a dining hall filled with long tables and benches, and billowing with the steam of oatmeal porridge. There were several other sections in the hall filling up with older boys that Aedan assumed to be the more senior apprentices. The looks weren't threatening, but there was a definite territorial air.

"I don't care if you are not hungry," the man said. "You empty your bowl. I promise that you'll need it. Think of the past two months as rest." There were a few smiles from the adjacent gathering of senior apprentices.

The new recruits lined up, collected their bowls of oats mixed with cream, and settled at the long tables. Lorrimer looked disappointed when his was finished. Peashot's expression began to reveal mild panic as he forced down a mouthful and looked at a bowl still half full.

"Swap?" asked Lorrimer.

Peashot nodded. It looked like the beginning of a mutually satisfying arrangement.

When the bowls were emptied, the man stood and called for silence.

"I am Commander Dun. This is Matron Rosalie. She will do the nannying; I'll do the whipping. Got that?"

Twenty heads bobbed. Twenty pairs of eyes looked hopefully towards the middle-aged, soft-featured matron who regarded them with a pitying smile.

Dun was wearing a different kind of smile. Aedan had never seen a shark, but he imagined they would show their teeth in the same way while circling unfortunates, and Commander Dun was just as muscled and eager as some restless carnivore. His eyes were sharp and his hands ready. He had no need to swing a cane against his boots and glare, showing just how dangerous he could be. Something about his open manner – hands on hips, easy grin – almost welcomed trouble. There was no bluff or bluster here. The boys knew it. Even Peashot sat rigid.

"Now, those of you whose fathers did not explain matters before you enrolled, there is something you need to know. For the rest of the students at the academy, expulsion is a danger. Within the marshals' quarter we have two levels of discipline – punishment and prison. Misconduct will not lead to expulsion because the things that are revealed over your years in training cannot be put out on the street. From this day on, behaviour that renders you unsuitable as marshals will send you to jail. Behaviour that can be corrected with punishment will be punished. If anyone feels he is not prepared for this, I ask you to remain behind in this room and you will be dismissed from the academy."

He picked up a sheet of paper and scanned the details on the page before resuming.

"You have already been introduced to history, law, navigation and cartography, foreign relations, and war strategy. To this we will now add combat and weaponry, woodcraft, languages, and field surgery. Some of your classes will overlap with the ladies of the medical quadrant, and we expect nothing less than impeccably honourable behaviour. We will happily punish anything less. These fine girls are being trained as queen's envoys. Their training is even more guarded than yours and I heartily recommend that you do not ask many questions of them or about them."

Several faces around the tables had shown an interest at the mention of ladies. Some of the smaller boys pulled faces.

"You will have eleven classes a day, beginning and ending with combat and weaponry. The learning is fast, faster than you could imagine. If you want to pass your end-of-year exams and proceed to the next year, you will need to apply yourselves like never before. In eight years you may just have a grey cloak of your own. Now, follow me."

He led them through the passages to the large room with the central feature. Aedan's group exchanged nervous glances.

"I'm sure that all of you tried exploring the place last night and found the building to be a complete disappointment."

Heads nodded. Aedan nodded. He threw a sharp look at the others who quickly followed his example.

"Can anyone see something strange about this room?"

Peashot looked like he was about to burst. Aedan glared at him. The rest of the boys shrugged and made suggestions about the statues and the designs on the central feature.

"No, none of you have it. No one has ever worked it out though it's such a simple trick. What I am about to show you is never to be discussed with anyone who is not a master or student within this quadrant." He proceeded to give instructions for lowering the ramp and lifting the panelled floor on top of the central feature, for which he had a special tool. Aedan's little band ooh'd and ah'd with the rest of them as the opening was revealed and Dun gestured with a grand sweep of his arm like a conjurer making an object appear out of nothing. Peashot was fiddling with something in his sleeve. Hadley stepped in front of him and shook his head.

"Our facilities extend beneath ground level," Dun said. "There are several entrances. This one is yours and will remain yours for the duration of your studies. I would not call this a terribly great secret; there are other secrets far more closely guarded. This is really just a bit of fun. The entrance remains open during the day, so it is possible that trespassers could discover it. But there is another surprise in store for them. Watch very carefully where you tread. The steps beside the marble pillars are the triggers of traps. They won't kill you, not the way we have things set these days, but you will have a long fall and a cold swim."

He led the way down and waited for them to assemble on the landing where the passage split. "That direction," he said, pointing to the dark and barred way, "is forbidden to you, to seniors, and even to most of the masters. Head that way and you are simply heading to prison. Understood?"

When he was satisfied that the warning had been heard by all, he led them along the other passage that now looked regal and imposing in the glow of dozens of the ornate wall-mounted torches. Dun stopped before the heavy doors and heaved them open without assistance – drawing a few furtive glances of respect – and led the way into the weapons hall. Aedan's group did not need to affect amazement here; the sight was every bit as awe-inspiring as it had been during the night.

"Take a good look, and be sure you take nothing more. If I catch anyone so much as touching a weapon until I say so, I'll set your bones a-rattling."

Lorrimer gulped.

"In these classes you will learn combat, from fighting with your hands tied behind your back, to managing an assault tower. By the time you are done here, every one of these weapons will be a personal friend. You will each specialise as your skills develop."

The boys' eyes danced through the racks that lined the walls, singling out weapons that called to them.

"Perhaps one of you will choose a miniature crossbow or blow-dart." He looked at Peashot, who dropped his eyes and tucked the tube back into his sleeve.

Aedan decided it would be unwise to underestimate this man.

Dun had them sit down on the cold stone floor, and paced as he spoke.

"Unlike soldiers, marshals are not sent out with the direct purpose of fighting, but the reality is that you will often be opposed in your duties by violence. It is never for you to pick a fight, but if one is unavoidable, you are to win it because the knowledge that marshals carry during their duties is the kind of knowledge to save entire cities. You will be trained by many marshals over the years, each an expert in his weapon. When I say weapon, I expect you are all looking at the sharp and shiny tools around you. What is the biggest problem with all of these?"

"They can rust?" a large boy offered.

"A small problem."

"Many of them are heavy?"

"Another small problem."

"They can be dropped?"

"Ah. A big problem. A thundering big problem. Complete dependence on these tools is potential disaster. What then is the solution?"

"Learn to run really fast," said Hadley.

Everyone laughed.

"Why are you laughing?" Dun demanded. The noise died down. "There is most certainly a good time to run, just as there is a bad time. When the nation has more to gain by your getting away and living than by your standing proud and dying, then you run. Any argument?"

The boys shook their heads.

"Good. So, what weapons cannot be dropped?"

"Fists."

"Yes, though not my first choice."

"Elbows, knees and feet."

"Good. We carry many weapons around with us." He began to indicate shoulder, elbow, palm, fist, knee, and so on. "But I have left something out. It is the one weapon each of you carries that can defeat anything in this room."

Aedan touched his head.

Dun nodded and motioned to the stacked walls. "We will train you to use all these with perfect standard forms and combinations. But we will never allow you to fall into that lazy confidence in which your mind shuts down and you apply set motions like a donkey circling the mill. You will be taught to think beyond the conventions. Constantly. Everything around you can be used as a weapon to your advantage, even your opponents themselves. As marshals, your first weapon is your mind, and this you will exercise every time you enter these halls. A basic example: Let's say that one of you is armed with only a staff and is attacked by two soldiers in heavy armour. The unthinking approach would be to stand and hack it out, applying perfect technique, hoping that the staff holds together and that you are fast enough to parry blows from two sides. Now what might a thinking man do?"

"Run," Kian reminded him.

"Fine, but let's assume you had to defeat them."

There was a brief silence. The whirring of thought was almost audible.

"Men in heavy armour move slowly," Aedan said. "They are protected, but they are also clumsy and they get tired quickly. I've seen a badger kill a snake by dancing around, always just out of range of the strike, waiting for an opportunity."

"Good. How could you dodge two at the same time?"

"Maybe circle them in a way where one always shields you from the other? You'd have to move quickly though."

"That is an excellent suggestion, and it happens to be one of the exercises you will be given during the week. There are dozens of possibilities to each encounter, and circling might not always be the best solution given additional factors such as treacherous ground. What is important, though, is that during any encounter your mind is as active as a mouse in the larder. That's enough talk. Everyone on your feet and follow me."

They filed into another large hall that was like the first, only that all the weapons here were wooden or strapped with protective leather, and the floor was covered in an assortment of beams, blocks, sand bags, and wooden constructions of unknown purpose. Ropes and ladders rose to platforms and walkways just under the frighteningly high roof. Mounds of straw made potential drops less than fatal.

"Break into pairs about the same height," Dun said, his voice rising to a new level, "and one from each pair collect a sand bag."

Aedan and Vayle were roughly the same height. Kian chose Peashot, Lorrimer found another tall boy who was still a head beneath him, and Hadley stepped up to Warton with an easy smile. Warton had no choice.

"I don't encourage you to punch freely," Dun began, when they were all paired up. "The bones in our hands can break more easily than we would like. There are better ways to strike an opponent, but a punch is still the most natural reflex, so you may as well learn to do it right."

He demonstrated in slow movements how to begin with stance and to throw not just from the shoulder but from the feet. He paused at various stages in the movement to point out the line of force from ground to target. He showed how to strike with the thumb folded away, fist lined straight, and the wrist tensed to avoid the all-too-easy buckling.

"Think of the motion as a spear being driven home."

Once they had all practiced the movement slowly under his scrutiny and correction, they were told to put some weight and speed into it. It wasn't long before a few knuckles were skinned. The sandbags had rough surfaces.

He then showed them the palm punch which he recommended over knuckles, and something he called the thunderslap – a movement that looked like someone throwing a stone and ended with the base of the hand striking the target at numbing speed. Last for the day were the elbow strikes – forward and backward.

While Dun's execution was smooth and powerful, the results on the floor were a motley misery. Knuckles and elbows bled owing to poorly aimed, skidding impacts. Every now and then, a boy holding a bag would totter and drop to the ground clutching an arm after his partner had showed more enthusiasm than accuracy. Some demonstrated surprising skill. Hadley and Warton were in equal possession of sturdy limbs, though Hadley's fluid grace and easy confidence were not to be matched. But even he was breathing hard by the end and showed more than one pink knuckle.

"Enough. Bags down."

The exhausted boys dropped the bags with trembling hands, only too happy to be sent to the safety of their books. "Three laps of the blue course: balance beams, ropes, jump, sandbag-haul, climbing wall, crawl and sprint."

They groaned.

Dun smiled and picked up a short whip. "Anyone need encouragement?"

The first lap was enough to make them realise that this was a different world to the army course. The beam was round, the ropes smooth, the drop from the platform high and the straw shallow, the wall had grips that all sloped the wrong way, and the sandbags were heavy. Aedan was the last to finish. Resting his leg over the past weeks had eaten away at his fitness. It was obvious he was the weakest in the class.

As they collapsed onto chairs in the first classroom, they wore a general expression of shock.

"Ah," said Giddard, walking in. "I see you've had your opening class with Dun. Enjoy the introductory pace while it lasts. In a few weeks you'll be laughing over these easy days."

He seemed unaware of the mute, staring disbelief.

"You have each been issued with books that you will find in your shelves when you return to your dorms," he continued. "During the classes, I expect you to take notes. The seven of you who are not yet literate will attend an additional class every night in order to catch up. You will need to work very hard indeed if you wish to progress to second year with your companions. For now, I recommend that you listen and file things away in your minds as best you can."

The lesson covered the discovery of gold in the north and the founding of the first village, later to grow into the great city of Tullenroe. Giddard explored the formation of society, how the freedom from homeland administration was reined in by the need for a perceived cultural stability. Several interesting questions were put to the class, but apart from some soft whimpering, they had little to say.

Law followed. Rodwell gave a second introduction to the subject, stressing that the detail would never reach that of the full-time legal administrators on the far side of the campus, and recommending deference to them in any legal matter – local, regional or foreign. He then launched into the lesson with passion, spit flying and pelting the first two rows. But neither his shrill voice nor dancing chins were able to draw much response.

In navigation and cartography the boys were given a demonstration of perspective error when the class was split in half, taken to the tops of two opposing buildings and told to map the ground ahead of them. When they returned to the class, the crude maps were lined up in two rows. In almost every case, the drawings from opposite sides disagreed significantly. Understanding the problem was crucial to the reading of potentially faulty maps, and the drawing of accurate ones.

Kollis's love of foreign relations stood in bold contrast to his feelings for domestic ones. He spent a good deal of the lecture glaring at Aedan, challenging him to just open his mouth and provide cause for a whipping. Aedan ignored him. With his skinless knuckles and elbows, he was simply too uncomfortable to bother with the silly man.

They broke for lunch and this time Peashot came very close to finishing his bowl – a beef-and-lentil stew. He even made it more than halfway through his small barley loaf. Lorrimer was on hand to assist. Little was said at the table as hunger towered supreme. It resulted in unrestrained, squelchy chewing and desperate gulping. Aedan noticed the matron looking around, writing down a few names, no doubt for some remedial classes in table manners. Marshals, as ambassadors, were apparently not permitted to eat like farmyard animals.

They were given an hour to relax on the central lawns where hundreds of students stretched themselves out in the sun or pursued games across the broad space. They found a shady spot, and before Aedan knew it, someone was kicking him awake. "You'll be late if you don't stir." It was Peashot. The others had already gone. Aedan wobbled to his feet and was barely able to walk. His mind was awake, mostly, but his limbs were still drifting in some gentle dream and wouldn't respond properly.

The next class was war strategy. It proved the most interesting of the day and woke him up quickly. Skeet explored the details of the sea attack on Stonehill, the abandoned coastal fortress. The fortress was one that was soaked to its spires in mystery; there were aspects of the defences that still eluded understanding. Speculation, of course, held far more interest than fact, so the boys were altogether caught up in the wondrous strangeness of it all.

Woodcraft was a new topic for some, but Aedan had to keep from rolling his eyes at the simplicity of the information. His father had taught him well and had him building shelters and rigging snares by age four, tracking by five, and able to navigate and fend for himself comfortably by six. Nevertheless, he found Wildemar to be one of the more fascinating of the masters. He looked rather like a mongoose or a squirrel with his bristling hair, sharp eyes, and movements so fast and unexpected that conversation behind his back was discovered every time.

Languages surprised them with a re-appearance of Giddard.

"In this class we will cover the introductions to six new languages that you will all learn with fluency acceptable to ambassadorial conversation. I see by your faces that you consider this to be a lot, and indeed it is far too much for a single class, which is why, after a few months, many classes will be presented in foreign languages. Every master can speak all six proficiently and at least three with native fluency. There is one at the academy – though you are not likely to meet him – who speaks thirty-seven with proficiency and fifteen with native fluency."

Mouths gaped.

"In time you will be allocated days of the week on which only a certain language may be used. Breaching this will result in punishment. We will arrange for you to begin spending dinners with foreign families who are connected to our headquarters. There you will learn not just the language but the manners and finer points of behaviour. As marshals you are to look and sound at home in the courts of any of the six major peoples connected to us by trade or threat.

"Understand," said Giddard, clasping his hands before him and leaning back against his desk, "this is not like archery where a slight drift from the centre of the target is expected and compensated for on the second attempt. On foreign soil you cannot afford or correct a slip like 'I would like to eet your family'. Only one letter is missing, yet an ambassador who makes errors like that is likely to go missing himself."

The class was beginning to like Giddard. He had the look of a peach that had spent winter on the tree, but there was a young and ready humour that ran just under the aged surface.

"Unfortunately, it gets more complicated than just being correct. There are different levels of society and while doing any, shall we say, infiltration work, you will need to understand those levels in order to get the language wrong in the right way."

The faces that had lit up at the mention of infiltration now grew puzzled.

"Let me explain. Think of our own city. Compare 'Might I trouble you for a draft of water?' with 'Could you be swingin' a chug maybe o' tha' there wa'er for us?' We recognise immediately the different classes. The second request is full of errors from structure to unpronounced consonants, but they are the right kinds of errors, errors a native speaker of that class would make. No native speaker, regardless of class, would have made that first mistake I gave you. That is the kind of error – and there are limitless possibilities of them – to betray a foreigner. Understand?"

The puzzled expressions faded.

"Just like a weapon, a language is used in many ways, and you must be comfortable with the basic forms. So pay attention during the social outings. They could one day save your life.

"Culture, too, is treacherous, from subtle tell-tales like approaching someone across a class divide in Lekrau to the mortal offense of moving a hand behind your back during a conversation in Vinterus. In Orunea, people greet with a kiss on the cheek. Try that in Sulea and you'll have your lips removed. Look one of their married women in the eye and you'll have your eyes removed too. I'm sure you can understand how diplomatic overtures between those two nations have never met with great success. Neither nation cares much for the ways of the other so negotiations are normally doomed from the outset.

"The academy exists in part to prevent such disasters. Castath's walls are not the highest, but we have used knowledge to secure many years of peace. So, with that in mind, let us begin with your first additional language."

Giddard launched into the basics of Orunean, the language Aedan's mother had taught him, the most common second language in Thirna. There were three others who knew the language in the class. Kian, as Aedan had earlier discovered, was a native speaker, having lived most of his life in Rasmun. For them it was like being taught how to crawl.

The final class of the day was field surgery. The boys' eyes opened wide as they trickled into a large room filled with medical diagrams, weird models that looked like they belonged inside bodies, strange tools that made the young apprentices uncomfortable, and girls wearing hooded expressions that made them even more so.

Mistress Gilda, a short, plump woman with a lively, dimpled face bounced to the front of the class and called for attention.

"Ah, boys, we are so pleased to have you here! Rumours of the dashing new apprentices have been drifting through our section, distracting us horribly. It is so nice to finally meet you. Seeing as you will be spending a lot of time here, I suggest that you all introduce yourselves while I prepare the specimen."

The boys' discomfort soared to alarming levels. They had individually encountered girls before this, but never twenty of them at once; and those strange, amused looks did not help. Aedan eyed them with open suspicion. Something was afoot. He could feel it.

Hadley was the first to break ranks and approach the enemy. He bowed with polished gallantry as he gave his name and asked theirs, even managing to say a few idle nothings that produced tinkling laughter.

Other boys began to shove and show off and laugh loudly to demonstrate they were not insecure or self-conscious, and that they didn't care what anyone thought of them. They glanced repeatedly at the girls just to make sure that the message was being received.

Aedan kept very quiet. He was suddenly ashamed. Even though none of the boys had made any more comments about his melted ear and singed temple, he dreaded the attention of the girls. He knew their eyes would wander across to that side of his face with morbid fascination; he knew that many of the other boys would be forgotten by the end of the day, but he would be remembered by all as the burned lizard. He drifted behind his classmates to the back wall where he found Lorrimer trying to shrink away, his great ears burning.

"Hope they leave us alone," the tall boy whispered.

Aedan nodded.

Many of the others appeared to be having a jolly enough time, some of them drawing together into talkative groups, Hadley's being the largest. Aedan and Lorrimer looked as uncomfortable as they felt.

"You two at the back there!" It was Mistress Gilda. Aedan's gut turned. "I'll have no one hiding. Oh, oh, you must be Aedan."

She bustled forward, caught Aedan by the elbow and dragged him to the front of the crowd.

"Here girls, this is the one I was telling you about, the one that Sister Edith treated."

She turned Aedan so his bad side faced them and lifted the hair. There were a few sharp intakes of breath among the girls.

"Now do you remember how we discussed the scarring process and how the skin that forms is different to what was there before? This is an excellent example. Can you see how the new skin has a thin and shiny appearance and how there's been no hair regrowth in this area?"

She carried on talking about the merits of the right burn ointments and how the results might have been better had he come to them earlier. It was all Aedan could do to hold back the scream of mortification.

"Relax, my boy," Gilda chided, shaking his tense shoulders. "Nobody here is going to think less of you."

Aedan wondered, as he saw the girls whispering to each other, how a grown woman could be such a wool-head. He was somewhat comforted, though, to notice that some of his friends looked angry enough to have lost interest in the girls.

The mistress drifted back to her preparations, and the murmur of conversation resumed. Aedan slunk away to the back where Lorrimer and Peashot joined him.

"My father keeps pigs with better manners," Lorrimer grumbled.

"If it weren't for all the girls standing around us, I would have tenderised her," the little boy said, twirling his peashooter. "Before our classes with her are over I'm going to give her a few scars of her own. She seems to like them enough on other people."

A young nurse wheeled in a trolley bearing something covered in a sheet. Mistress Gilda rushed over and took charge, moving the trolley to the middle of the class where there was an open area.

"I would like you all gathered around here. Boys to the front please." She waited for them to gather and settle down. "In this class you will cover a number of aspects of basic medical treatment. The girls will be fully qualified as physicians and surgeons, but you will only cover the most essential aspects. We begin with field surgery and for this it is important that you are able to control yourselves around some of the things you are likely to see. That means practice. As surgeons, there is only one way we get to practice, and I think you can guess what that means."

All eyes dropped to the sheet, feet began to shuffle back where they bumped into the girls' toes and had to shuffle forward again.

"So," Gilda announced with a smile, "this is the kind of thing you will need to get used to."

She flipped the sheet up to reveal the body of a man who had been dead for some time. Maggots had made significant inroads and students had worked on parts of his torso and arms, so that what remained was disturbing in the extreme.

The reactions were varied. Hadley's easy confidence fled. Peashot wrinkled his stub nose and scrunched his face till it was as puckered as a prune. Lorrimer went for the tougher look. He wore a nonchalant smile, tilted his head back and sank his hands into his pockets. Then he spun around, doubled over and vomited uncontrollably. Warton laughed with open derision until the air from the corpse hit him. The laugh turned to a choke, and before he could recover himself, he joined Lorrimer. Another three added their sentiments to the floor. None of the boys looked pleased and several wearing urgent expressions asked if they might be excused. Gilda sent them all out into the sunlight and the open air where they found quiet corners to resolve inner turmoils.

Apart from cleaning up the deposits of beef and lentils, nothing more was accomplished during the class.

"That was the most disgusting lesson I've ever heard of," said Lorrimer, still spitting, as they crossed the courtyard and headed back to the marshals' block and the training hall.

"Maybe it gets better with time," said Vayle. "The girls were all used to it."

"Then these girls are sick. It's not right."

"If she puts me on display like that again," said Aedan, "I'm walking out."

"I think we'll join you if she does," said Lorrimer. Peashot and Vayle voiced their agreement.

Dun awaited them in the training hall with a cheerful smile. If he noticed the shuffling gait or the tinge of green on sagging faces, he gave it no thought.

"Right lads," he said brightly, "I hope you have a good lunch in you because this session will burn it all up."

They attacked the bags using their knees, shins and feet. Most of them tried to go easy until Dun lost his temper with "all the fairying about" and promised them that if he did not see the bags getting their gizzards crunched he would double the laps on blue.

It was a very quiet group that left the hall and hobbled back up the steps, wincing at the effort required to skip the traps. After lifting the ramp, they shuffled into the dinner hall, collected their plates of chicken, potato and cabbage, and dropped wordlessly onto the benches. Peashot managed a few mouthfuls, then rested his head on the table while chewing and fell asleep.

They had hoped to drop straight into bed, but another surprise awaited them at the dorms. Dun again.

"As part of your training in refinements, you are going to get into the habit of keeping yourselves clean," he announced. "There is soap, a vat of water, and a large pitcher in the little drained cubicle at the end of each dorm. Three pitchers each – that's a minimum. Winter is no exception. You wash yourselves properly. Matron Rosalie has a nose like a shrew and she'll let me know if any one of you shirks this duty. Don't forget the last class of the day for the illiterate ones."

A few boys looked like they were about to cry as they remembered.

"The rest of you are to put in at least an hour of revision. Books are in your shelves, writing material on your desks. Don't let me catch anyone sleeping."

The words "sorrier than you can imagine" were dancing in the air, weaving through the stunned silence.

"Well, get to it! I want you as clean as mountain rain by the time I return, and that won't be long."

Hadley was the least put out by this most recent barrage of surprises. He sat on his bed, leaning against the wall, and folded his hands behind him with a faint smile.

"I'm sure you'll agree with me," he said, "that the time spent with the ladies was the best part of the day. After Aedan showed his scar, they had so much to say. You should have heard all questions about the fire and ... Ouch!" He slapped a hand to his neck. "You little blighter!" Hadley sprang off his bed and stormed down the room.

To everyone's surprise, Lorrimer pushed himself up onto his spidery limbs and stepped in the way.

"What do you think you are doing, Ladderboy? My quarrel is with Peashot."

"I ... I think it's with all of us."

"What! Have you lost your mind?" Hadley looked around in mocking appeal.

"Think," said Vayle, leaning back on his chair and looking out somewhere beyond the ceiling. "Try to hear what you just said, and imagine how it sounded to Aedan. You might have had a great time today, but if you can't see that it was torture for him then you really are a self-absorbed ass."

Hadley's confusion appeared to be restraining him physically, but slowly the redness passed from his face as realisation worked its way home.

"You're right," he said. "I am an ass. Sorry, Aedan. I'll never speak to any of those girls again." He turned away and trailed off to the washroom, a spectacle of self-loathing.

By the time Peashot and Lorrimer returned from their introductory class on letters, Aedan had read the first line on the page about two hundred times and still couldn't get the words to surrender their meaning. The three who had remained in the dorm had agreed to wake anyone who dropped off. Shoes had accordingly been thrown across the room times beyond counting.

Dun was happy to see them all awake when the others returned. He wished them a good night's rest, promising that they would need it.

Chapter 22

When the silence of night was defiled by Dun's cheery rousting, a few strong whispers rose in response. Aedan was convinced he'd only just fallen asleep. Every muscle ached.

Appetites had not yet stirred, but the boys knew how valuable that porridge would be. Lorrimer and Peashot kept to their arrangement and all plates were cleaned.

In the training hall, bandages were made available to those whose knuckles, elbows or knees were skinless. They revised the techniques from the previous day, and Dun began to introduce them to sequences.

"Don't think of this as learning to fight, but learning to knock a man down as quickly as possible. Your duties will place you in situations where you will often be outnumbered, so you won't have the luxury of softening your opponent and wearing him down. You need to execute these patterns as though there are men approaching from behind."

The sequences were direct and brutal, hardly appropriate for a good old tavern brawl. Dun then gave them an overview of the grappling and wrestling techniques they would learn, and how to use their feet to defend when thrown on their backs. "Though you want to avoid going to ground," he said, "many evenly matched fights do. I won't have any of you becoming turtles, helpless when toppled."

Dun got them back onto their feet and drilled them in four different sequences until they could link the movements naturally, then sentenced them to three laps of the green circuit. Though it was less exhausting, this circuit required more balance and cool-

headedness, especially on the high rope-traverse and balance bar –
a rounded, slightly wobbly beam that linked two platforms thirty
feet above the straw. This one suited Aedan far better. Though he
was slow on the basic obstacles, only he and Hadley made it
across the balance bar on their first attempts.

When he had finished his laps, he re-tied his bandages and
went through to the weapons hall to wait. The two boys that
followed him had caught his attention on the previous day, eyeing
him as if hoping to speak with him alone. They approached now,
looking none too friendly. He recognised one – Malik – the
popular boy who had almost caused him to walk out of the trials
once.

"We need to give you a warning," Malik said without
introduction. Aedan looked up and found him a lot more
intimidating from close. He was tall and athletic, but it was his
face that set him apart. His pale features, made to seem even paler
by his dark hair, were as hard and angled as if he had been
constructed from blocks of marble, and little time had been
wasted on smoothing the result. The eyes were sharp and
intelligent and there was an air of high breeding and perfect
manners about him that only made him seem more imposing.

Hadley entered the room and strode up to them.

"Another time," Malik said with undisguised annoyance as he
walked away, leaving Aedan to puzzle over the strange words.

"What do you know about him?" Aedan asked, pointing.

"He giving you trouble?"

"Not sure. Maybe. Said he had a warning for me but cut it off
when you arrived. So? Do you know anything about him?"

"More than he would like. My father knows their family.
Malik's father is rich, a nice man, but he's as timid as a mouse.
His wife married him for the money and now controls everything
in the home. My dad calls her the iron queen, says she's the most
powerful woman in Castath and probably the cruellest too – had
three servants whipped so badly last year that two of them died
and nothing happened to her. If Malik wants anything he goes to
her, but he doesn't like people knowing, so he pretends it's his
father doing things for him. In my opinion, his mother found a
way to push him through the final selection." Hadley paused,
glancing at Aedan. "Malik is strong in all the wrong ways –
cunning and mean as a rat. The less you have to do with him the
better."

"He's popular."

"Only because everyone's too scared to be on his bad side. Nobody really likes him. Big old Cayde hangs around him like a bodyguard – not that Malik needs one – but I think Cayde's like the rest. Only thing they like about Malik is that he's got lots of influence because of his father's money."

"So what you think he wants with me?"

"Let's go find out," Hadley said, turning and striding away.

Hadley, as Aedan was learning, was all confidence and momentum. He seemed to be incapable of hesitation.

"No, wait!" Aedan rushed up, but Hadley had already covered most of the ground and drew up in front of Malik.

"You wanted to say something to my friend?" Hadley asked. "I don't mind if you want to talk now."

Malik scowled. "The matter does not concern you," he said.

Hadley's look grew hard. "You're not trying to cause trouble are you?"

Malik laughed. "Go and shove your nose in someone else's face," he said, then turned his back and strolled off.

"Thought so," said Hadley with a smile. "Definitely nothing good."

The episode bothered Aedan for the next few classes. He had a dim awareness of being watched through the morning. It was only during field surgery that he was distracted enough to forget Malik and his strange words. The boys walked over to the medical wing and entered their classroom with something akin to dread. Aedan kept his eyes on the floor, trying not to catch anyone's attention. Nevertheless, he could feel eyes settling on his scarred left side and he unconsciously tugged on the hair around the burn, trying to cover his half ear.

"Pairs, please," Mistress Gilda trilled. "Gentlemen, find a lady to help you through this class. No loners."

With a lot of awkward shuffling and blushing, the class paired up. Aedan thought that the numbers were uneven and that he had been left out until he spotted the small dark-skinned, raven-haired girl on the opposite side of the room. He had learned first-hand that foreigners did not always receive the warmest welcome in Castath. With her ebony skin proclaiming what must be Mardrae or Krunish blood, she would have felt her isolation every day. It was no surprise when she did not approach, but instead kept her eyes down and stood where she was.

He was struck by the same feeling that had moved him to adopt a dozen grounded fledglings, an injured fawn, an almost-drowned rat, and even an abandoned fox cub. The dung beetles, frogs and lizards had really been abducted.

"Would you like to work with me?" he asked as he approached.

"Thank you," she said, and accompanied him to the remaining table.

"I'm Aedan."

"I am Lee'runda, but I prefer to be known as Liru." She did not look at his scar and made no comment on the previous day's humiliation – it didn't even appear to be in her thoughts – and he made no comment on her foreign ancestry. If he was not paying attention to her skin, her large dark eyes and bold, rounded features, he could almost forget that she was not Thirnish, for her speech had only the slightest whisper of an accent. There was a deliberate precision to her words, though, a hint of woodenness that suggested hard study rather than childhood familiarity with the language.

Mistress Gilda explained the process of making a balm suitable for light cuts, burns and grazes. She pointed to diagrams of the three most effective leaves – copperlip, frabe and elfweed – and explained briefly where each of them might be found in various terrains. Then she handed out ingredients – copperlip leaves, tallow boiled from mutton, flaxseed oil, and honey. The girls already had some experience with salves and were able to demonstrate the use of pestle and mortar.

"Don't just flatten. Crush!" Gilda instructed. "If the leaves remain uncrushed the potency remains locked inside."

The mistress made her presence felt at every desk. When she reached Aedan's she remarked on her recovering burn victim. She was not observant enough to notice Aedan's reddening face. Liru said nothing when the mistress left, though the fact that she no longer explained what she was doing suggested she was far more conscious of Aedan's discomfort than she let on.

Each pair was then told to apply the salve to a bandage and to wrap a wound, imaginary or otherwise, on their partner's arm. The girls had little need for imagination. Skinless knuckles and elbows abounded, many of them oozing under sticky sleeves.

"Lee'runda," the mistress said as she approached. "Why don't you wrap the burn wound on Aedan's head pretending it's fresh. These placements are quite a challenge for bandaging."

"If it is possible," the quiet girl said, "I would prefer to work on his elbow. He has hurt it badly." Liru spoke respectfully, but there was something in her voice that suggested she was prepared to meet firmness with the same.

"As you wish." Gilda whisked away.

"Thank you," said Aedan.

Liru glanced at him. "You saved me embarrassment earlier when you did not leave me alone."

"That doesn't prove I was being kind or anything – we were the only two left."

"You still asked without waiting to be told."

"You looked alone. I know what that feels like."

She regarded him now with a direct gaze. "I think you are kind. I am glad to be working with you. I was very worried."

"I'm glad to be working with you too. I don't think I need to dread this class anym-aaaaahhh!"

The salve stung more than he had expected. Liru patted his arm, a dark amusement lurking at the corner of her mouth, until his face relaxed. Then she wrapped the bandage with a level of skill that could not have been gained in two months.

"Your hands move too fast for someone who just learned this," he said.

"My father is a doctor. I assisted him for many years before I came here." She glanced around, put a finger to her lips, and repeated the procedure on the other elbow before any of the other girls had finished their first bandage. "There, that should feel more comfortable. Change them in two days. I'll help you if I get a chance."

Aedan then attempted to apply a bandage on Liru's forearm, and the only good thing about it was that the wound was imaginary. He had Liru guide him through the wraps and knots again and did a better job on the second attempt.

"So why is it that we only meet with the twenty of you and none of the other nurses in your year?"

"You are disappointed?" she asked with a frown.

"No, not at all. I'm just curious. Are you separate from the rest?"

"We are not permitted to speak of it to anyone."

Aedan was not put off and persisted, in spite of Dun's warning. "We were told that you are being trained as queen's envoys, but from what I can see, it looks like that just means some kind of travelling nurse. Why so much secrecy around nursing?"

"I thought young marshals were expected to be more observant than that."

Aedan looked up. He had been considering her as a kind of little sister trailing and looking up at him with barely concealed awe. Suddenly it felt as if he was the one trailing and being smiled down on. What did she mean by being observant? He thought back over the conversation, the bandaging, and remembered now that he *had* noticed something incongruent with the idea of nursing – two of Liru's knuckles had slight callouses. He was sure there would be more on her elbows.

"How long did you wear the bandages?" he asked.

"That's better," she replied with just a hint of a smile. "You have restored my confidence in you. But not a word to anyone. Promise?"

"I promise. I'll only tell all the boys in my dorm." He grinned.

"Not if you want the antidote to the poison I worked into your salve."

Aedan laughed, but there was no hint of humour in her face as she rose and left the class with the other girls. He felt a twinge of discomfort as he began to wonder if it really had been a joke. Then he began to wonder exactly what sort of doctor her father had been. The girl certainly was a riddle herself. He was beginning to suspect that behind her soft voice, soft dark hair, and soft puppy eyes was a mind as sharp as pike teeth. He redoubled his resolution to say nothing.

Hadley, due to circumstances, had been unable to keep his vow of silence and, after being compelled to speak to the first girl, had abandoned the whole thing and mingled with several after the class.

The second session with Dun introduced them to the first level of body armour. Pads made of reeds stitched against leather and backed by straw-filled pouches were strapped to limbs and torso. They provided a fair degree of protection, though a heavy blow would still lay the recipient flat. It enabled the young apprentices to work through the moves learned earlier at greater speed, without having to worry about injuries.

"Faster, Hadley!" Dun yelled. "You have the grace of a dancer, but that won't make up for sluggishness. Yes, better. Follow through, Bede. You must reach past the target or the blow will feel like a butterfly's landing. Step closer before you swing. No! Hang it all, no! Not like you're floating in water. Step as fast as you can – feet apart and on the diagonal, weight on toes, then step like you're getting out of the way of a falling rock. Yes, that's it. Hands up, Lorrimer. Once you have engaged, the deception is over, no use dangling your arms as if you're deciding whether or not to fight. You too, Aedan. Protect yourself. No, Cayde, a palm punch is not a tap. Remember, thrust from the floor through your body and slam your palm into your opponent like a spear. Vayle, didn't I warn you that knuckles don't last. No, you can repair yourself later. Let's see you swallow the pain and improvise. Oh, are you alright there? Hold! No more elbows to the face until you have helms. Try to restrain yourselves until next week. Alright, carry on ..."

Despite the bruises and exhaustion, there was a glimmer of enjoyment on the sweat-and-straw-caked faces. Some things had begun to fall into place.

On the way back from the dinner hall, Aedan felt a tap on his shoulder. He turned around to see Malik indicating with his head that he should step into a little study cove. He was curious to know what this was all about, so he obliged.

"What is it?" he asked.

Malik looked at him, pale, colourless eyes made more vivid by their hawk-like hoods of steeply angled, dark eyebrows. He said nothing until the noise of footsteps had dwindled. Cayde stood at the opening to the passage and turned towards them, nodding as he crossed his arms.

Aedan began to feel uncomfortable. "Well?" he prompted.

"I don't need to be reminded that I called you here, North-boy." Aedan felt his skin frosting in Malik's breath. "My purpose is to inform you that your life may be in danger."

"Who would have any reason to hurt me?" Aedan asked.

"The boy you displaced by cheating when –"

"I broke no rule! Osric himself said so."

"I don't take kindly to being interrupted, especially not with information that I already have. I was there when your pet general interfered. But as I was going to say, the boy who finished eighty-first, who would have made the cut if you had been disqualified like you should have been for cheating, he has friends that want to see him put into marshals' training where he belongs. They are not afraid to be violent."

"The selections are over. Even if I withdrew, nobody could get in."

"Maybe for you. But there are ways when you know important people. There are also ways of seeing that you get maimed. Perhaps even crippled for life."

"Seeing me … What do you mean? Are you threatening me?"

"I won't pretend that I like you, but it's not me you need to worry about. I am trying to prevent an injury. Face it – you have some skills, but you will never be a marshal. What foreign monarch would want a face like yours in his courts? You belong in the barracks, and maybe you could go far there – I could even get someone to put in a good word for you – but this isn't where you belong. Didn't you notice that the only girl who wanted anything to do with you was the one we all avoided – and for a good reason. Those Mardrae are foul. Trust them and you're always sorry."

"She's not like that –"

"You are interrupting me again. My partner at the field surgery class was quite open about how revolted the rest of the girls are by your shiny scalp and half ear. I don't enjoy saying this – it's not like you asked to be turned into a monster – but you do need to hear the truth from someone who won't try pretty it. I'm not biased like your friends would be, but I'm also not your enemy. I'm just putting it out the way it is."

Aedan looked back in silence, confused, reeling. He would have known what to do with bare threats, but this had knocked him completely off balance.

"Consider it," Malik continued. "If you remain here you will have enemies for life, powerful enemies, justly angry that you cheated your way past them. What's it all for? A false dream. The fact is that you are standing where someone else would do a whole lot better."

Malik turned and walked away with Cayde, but Aedan lingered to sort out his thoughts, making himself late enough to provoke a tongue-lashing by Dun. Sleep did not come quickly and it did not soothe his doubts. The next day he felt worse. He decided to put the matter before someone who could give him perspective, and if Malik was right, then he would be faced with an awful decision …

Giddard leaned back on his desk and listened patiently while Aedan offloaded.

"It's not the threat that I'm worried about," he said after presenting the situation as Malik had put it. "I'm sure it's just tough talk because if anyone did anything we'd all suspect Malik and this other boy. If they really did have plans, Malik wouldn't have told me. What I'm worried about is that I don't belong here and I'm in someone else's position. Did I really make it in, or am I here because I got nudged through or something?"

The aged master pursed his craggy lips as he gathered his thoughts. "Osric," he said, "would probably have defended anyone he saw being injured by an abuse of rules. He has a personal hatred for that sort of thing. As to nudging, no, there was no nudging or charity involved in your placement here. Osric was not even present for the second stage of eliminations or the final selections. There was some division in your case, but it was decided solely on merit. Master Skeet made it plain – quite forcefully I might add – that he had never encountered such mature strategic reasoning in anyone your age. I don't mind telling you that your temper was considered a problem" – Aedan felt his face colour with embarrassment, or was it a faint glow of anger? – "while your unusual perspective on situations was thought by the majority to hold great value. You look at things in a unique way, unlike anyone I've ever taught. That is very valuable here."

This, Aedan found surprising. He had never really thought of it as something good, just something that made him different – often to the annoyance of others. He never tried to take strange angles when considering a matter; he simply didn't know how to think any other way.

Giddard continued, "I hope I am not breaching a confidence when I say that you have a strong supporter here with the authority to overrule any of the masters or even Osric. This patron sees in you a potential he sees in none of the others. Malik is exaggerating the effect of a scar on a diplomat. The more warlike monarchs might even consider it favourable. It might result in fewer swooning ladies at court, but I would not consider this an obstacle to your duties. Don't be concerned that you are a dragging anchor to this institution. This is exactly where you belong and I'll have words with anyone who plants other ideas in your head."

Aedan's relief was visible. He had come here unsure if he belonged in the academy, but Giddard had set things in perspective – and given him something to ponder. Who could this patron be? Surely not Culver. There had been no warmth or support there.

"Thank you," he said. "But can I ask that you rather let *me* speak to Malik?"

"Certainly. I'm glad you want it so. As a marshal you will often have no one but yourself to back you up."

He caught up with Malik while walking across the courtyard of the medical buildings and summarised his discussion with Giddard. Malik listened with a pained expression, blending pity with contempt. When he finally spoke, it was as a disappointed older brother.

"Listen to the people around you," he said. "Don't you notice the stares? Don't you hear the whispers? Don't you understand what they mean? Do you think Giddard with his face of wrinkled cowhide actually understands any of this? Of course he would try to make that thing on the side of your face seem like it doesn't matter. Become a soldier, Aedan. As a soldier, the helmet will hide the damage and put you on an equal footing."

Aedan felt his confidence slipping again. He did not like Malik, and he suspected there was some more personal motive behind this, but he was struggling against the cold logic in the boy's words.

Liru stepped up to them. Neither of the boys had noticed her approach. She addressed Malik in a voice that was clear and even.

"You know little of the southern cultures if you think yourself better off. You have obviously never heard the saying, 'skin pale as sickness and eyes weak as rainwater.' This is a very common saying. It describes such as you. In the south, scars are carried with honour. They speak of strength to those who bother to think on it."

"What do I care of such barbaric ideas?" Malik snarled.

"Do you mean that? You are a student of these cultures. Does this hope to achieve ignorance extend to other areas of your studies?"

Malik's lip twitched. He glared with cold fury before turning to Aedan and saying, "Stay at this academy and you will regret it! This I promise you."

Aedan's brows rose.

Suddenly Malik did not look so impartial – it was clear that his involvement was deeply personal. All that talk about wanting to prevent an injury by others was beginning to seem a little thin, like a performance that's compromised when a prop topples over somewhere backstage. Anger had lunged forward and caused a rip in the curtain, and it was no mild anger that lurked back there. He walked away at such a pace that Cayde had to jog at his elbow.

Aedan turned to Liru. "I worry that you made an enemy," he said.

"My father told me I could not be a true friend without sharing some of my friend's enemies."

"You would want to be my friend at a price like this?"

"Yes. You are kind and I have not always known kindness here. There are many tongues that have injured me in this place, but yours I do not fear."

"Do I need to fear your poison?" he asked, holding up his bandage.

"My father also said he pitied my friends for the poisonous wit they would have to survive." She offered no smile, simply turned and walked into the class.

Aedan laughed to himself and followed.

By the afternoon session with Dun, Aedan was feeling better. Some of what Malik had said was truth, he couldn't deny it; some was exaggeration, he was beginning to recognise that now; and some had been collected from the south side of a horse.

He would carry this burn scar through life and it was time to start accepting it. There were, doubtless, people who would see it as Malik did, but then, should he really care what people like Malik thought?

That was how the reasoning went, but later when the lights were out, the images returned to mock and haunt – images that Malik had spawned – frowns of disgust, shaking heads, hands clamped to laughing mouths and the ever curious stares. They danced before Aedan's eyes though he squeezed them shut and crushed them with his fists.

"Why? Why? Why must I be such a ... such a freak?" he silently screamed into the darkness. "Why can't I just be like everyone else?" He pounded the mattress, pulled at his hair and tore the skin until exhaustion left him in a hollow silence that finally, mercifully, became sleep.

Chapter 23

"In two weeks we will hold the first challenge, and it will go poorly with anyone who fails."

Dun's words brought immediate silence to the dining hall.

"These challenges will take place regularly. Every challenge is different and always a surprise, so I'll tell you nothing except that anything you have covered in your classes may be of use, and that you would do well to get some good rest before the day."

Aedan stopped chewing, even forgot to swallow. He was still too weak for any kind of physical test.

The next day – the last day of the week – was theirs to do with as they pleased, as long as they remained within the academy. Aedan spent it worrying.

Three months would pass before they would be allowed out. The academy, however, was large enough and peopled enough to provide distraction. But with the panic surrounding this challenge, there was no thought spared for anything outside their training.

Following two weeks of dread and preparation, classes were suspended for a day, and the boys began a series of tests.

First was Skeet who had them critique a flawed attack plan using maps and logistical data. Aedan impressed the stern master again by picking up on a detail nobody else had considered – the direction of the small stream that had its source in the enemy camp. It rendered the entire siege useless no matter what was done with troops and catapults, because the besieged force could simply dam up the stream at its source or use filth and rotting carcasses to defile the water as it left their camp, defeating the attackers by thirst or disease.

For the other tests, they had to exchange basic greetings and obtain directions in Orunean, mark the points of the compass using sun and stars, and apply their knowledge of law and foreign relations to a complex case involving an important trade dispute – in which Peashot got in trouble when he recommended Skeet's battle plan.

After completing the theory aspects, they were sent to Dun. Several older marshal apprentices, kitted out in pads, waited in the training hall, tensing their fists and looking hostile. Dun called the first-years out one at a time to face an older boy and demonstrate his unarmed combat skills. Aedan stood at the back of the line. He was relieved to see that none fared too well. Peashot, like most of them, abandoned technique in the excitement and brawled like a tomcat. Dun yelled and called them all an embarrassment to his training, then demanded basic sequences that he could evaluate.

At last it was Aedan's turn. He had hoped that those who were finished would leave, but the crowd remained. He could not be shown to be the weakest, anything but the weakest, especially with Malik's group looking at him like he was something that needed to be cleaned off the floor. He walked to the middle of the hall, a hall full of eyes and whispers. His desperation was rising. It scrambled everything in his thoughts, even Dun's last instruction.

When the signal was given, he charged at his opponent, unleashing a wild flurry of swinging punches, airy kicks and skidding contacts. A shove from the older boy tipped him backwards while his legs were going forward and he landed with a smack. There he lay, staring up at the ceiling and gaping, cod-like, for air that wouldn't come.

The laughter was worse than Dun's shouts. Aedan didn't want to know what the master wrote down, and he vowed to himself that no matter how desperate, he would never again fight without thinking.

The winning dorm – Malik's – was rewarded with an apple pastry which was presented to them after dinner. The other boys retired, Peashot seeming to take forever. Aedan was partway down the passage when exclamations of dismay floated after him. He looked back to see Peashot wearing a deeply satisfied expression.

"You know what's happening in there?" Aedan asked.

Peashot shrugged, but Aedan held the stare.

"Maybe," said Peashot at last. "Maybe the dustpan could have got emptied into the mix. Would have been difficult to spot the chunks of charcoal and sand between all those little raisins. But I'm just guessing."

This was too good to keep. Aedan told the dorm of Peashot's "suspicion" as soon as they got back. The laughter continued for a long time and the little fiery-haired boy received a good deal of congratulation. Nobody was going to tongue-wag on him.

And in that moment Aedan realised something. For the first time since leaving the Mistyvales, he had found real friends – and understood how much they meant. They had not swept his troubles away nor he theirs, but somehow it was easier on those heavy days to stand under the load when standing shoulder to shoulder. He found their company often helped him to see bright rifts in leaden skies. On other days the clouds would melt under a cheerful sun, and the cheer was multiplied a hundredfold when shared.

Previously, he had considered himself a loner because he was comfortable on his own out in the forests. But even in the north, he had secretly enjoyed turning his steps back home after a solitary day. When friends and family had been taken from him, he had felt like the man who says he prefers winter until his coat and shelter are lost.

The growing friendships were warming him again, restoring his confidence. It was clear that the same was true for Peashot, though he was taking a lot longer to thaw. Daily, the loyalty and comradeship were growing.

Then over the next few weeks, there were some other things that started to emerge.

Lorrimer was messy in a way that defied comprehension. And dirty. Socks, heavy with foot grease, would stick and slither over furniture wherever they happened to be flung, and large, stained boots regularly tripped anyone who had to walk past his area on nightly errands to the privy.

Vayle was lazy, preferring to recline in aloof majesty, offering philosophic advice rather than assistance. His tendency to improve others' stories, beginning with "No, that's not what happened ..." was brought to an end when Peashot exploded and told him that if he couldn't listen to a story without correcting it he should move across to the college of legal administrators where he would fit right in.

Peashot had a habit of "collecting" things that had not previously belonged to him, and that nobody had seen him buy. When Hadley once pressed the issue, identifying a gold-tipped letter opener that had formerly belonged to Rodwell, Peashot insisted that it was borrowed. Things grew lively when Hadley's knife disappeared the following day. He marched right over and shoved out an accusing finger. Peashot said something stinging. The extended finger became a hand that grasped for the smaller boy's neck, but the movement was too slow. Peashot slipped underneath and landed a mean little kick. Hadley, hopping on his remaining good knee, managed to wrestle the "thieving weasel" into a corner. It took everyone else in the dorm to separate the combatants.

The dorm was tense for a few days. Then, one evening, Kian arrived to return the knife and thank Hadley for the loan. There was a deep, thoughtful silence. Hadley ended it with a laugh. He walked over to Peashot, apologised, and held out his arm. Peashot clasped the extended forearm reluctantly and mumbled something that Aedan was not convinced was entirely polite.

In this and any number of his interactions, Hadley never showed hesitation. He was nothing if not recklessly headlong. This impulsive tilt was born of supreme confidence, and often revealed itself – true to his father's description – as pushiness. Hadley had no need for space and no awareness of anyone else's need for it. He would invite himself into, and then dominate, all manner of private conversations and solitary reveries.

With Aedan, the first objection was always directed to an appetite for adventure so extreme that Vayle considered it pathological. By the time the three month confinement to the academy was over, Aedan's fitness and confidence had begun to return. He wasted no time before charging back into the ways he had known in the north. Not even Hadley tried to get in front of him now when he bolted off to climb the highest trees during storms, dared the rapids on rafts that were smashed apart more often than not, rigged and tested swings that launched from branches sixty feet above the ground, and prowled at night through wild regions considered hazardous even by the rangers. If there were snakes to be caught, bush pigs to be tracked, or unpredictable horses to be handled, he would be there.

The most problematic aspect was that he found something irresistible behind every sign that ordered caution or forbade entry. Often, the whole worried group had to work together to talk him out of some dubious exploration. Mostly, their efforts failed, and the group was torn between standing watch for officials, and fleeing the scene.

But, with Aedan, there was another problem, and it was of an entirely different sort. It was his breath. He considered the complaints utter nonsense. He couldn't smell anything. In this, the halitosis was like every character flaw in the dorm, for none of the boys recognised their supposed faults, or if they did, considered them harmless.

But Aedan's was not a problem destined to be ignored. One day, Liru handed him a bag containing a large vial of powdered charcoal, mint, and several other ingredients, a reel of silken thread and some kind of brush that looked like a coarse, hairy root.

"What's this for?"

"I do not cry easily, but your breath, it makes my eyes water."

"Are you trying to say –"

"You stink, Aedan. Sort this thing out or I will wear a mask when you speak to me."

Liru, then, could perhaps have been charged with a lack of subtlety, but she would have taken it as a compliment. In any case, the point was made. Aedan slunk away and began sorting himself out.

In the dormitory, Hadley was the natural leader, not because of any real ambition to be so, but because he was usually already on the move before anyone else had finished considering the options. The only time this changed was when Aedan had one of his adventurous or tactical ideas, something that happened often enough for the two of them to trade roles almost constantly.

Winter began to slip away. Aedan turned thirteen at last and promptly began to think of himself as almost fourteen. It was close to a year since Quin had stormed into his life and set in motion the changes that had brought him here. Castath was just beginning to feel like home.

For two months, the routine remained roughly the same, and after the initial shock, the apprentices found ways of adapting. The near-reverence with which they regarded the masters soon melted under the influence of familiarity. They discovered that there were certain classes in which the back row was good for short naps, and that some of the junior instructors failed to notice if a desk was empty, allowing one or two to skip a class. Aedan would have skipped every class on foreign relations, but *his* absence would never have gone unnoticed. Kollis continued to teach as though arguing against Aedan's unspoken opposition.

Peashot was almost removed from training when Dun, who happened to be standing at the door, caught him in the act of tenderising Rodwell. He was allowed to return after a one-week detention, a sincere apology, and a promise to never use a peashooter in the academy again. He insisted to his friends that it had all been worth it for the sweet memory of Rodwell squealing and trying to work his short, pink arms around his girth to dislodge the imagined wasp.

For a while, Peashot made do without his weapon. He compensated for his loss by planting trouble wherever he saw fertile ground. Once, he asked Aedan if it would be possible to move the marble pillars marking the stair traps. Aedan's look had ended the discussion.

But Peashot soon found something else to distract him in the form of a large dead yellow-banded viper. After ensuring that he was late enough to be the last one entering class, he pinned it up on the outside of Mistress Gilda's closed door and then slipped inside. The hinges here all turned inward, so when she opened the door at the end of the lesson, the large scaly form swung into the room and wrapped gently round her.

It was not one scream, but several. The stocky little woman emptied and refilled her lungs with impressive speed. Even Peashot seemed to be in awe of the sonic onslaught. A number of the girls took up the alarm and one or two of the city-bred boys backed away from the swinging viper, falling over chairs and adding to the general air of panic. It was a performance that would be forever etched into the memoirs of the noble institution.

On the way out, Peashot told Aedan how he felt he had benefitted from having his peashooter confiscated. "I've grasped the importance of diversifying. Like Dun said, we mustn't get fixed on one weapon, but must be ready to snatch weapons and opportunities as they appear. He would be happy, don't you think, to see how I've learned my lesson?"

Aedan wondered for an instant if Peashot had actually gone mad, but then he saw the sliding eye and the malicious little grin.

"Weren't you even slightly sorry about shooting Rodwell in the back?" he asked.

"Well if you put it that way – yes, a little."

"That's good to hear."

"I was aiming for his neck. Still bothers me that I had to go out on a shot like that."

Chapter 24

Aedan awoke to a patch of grey light at the window. Dun had never allowed them to sleep this late. He listened for the familiar sounds of kitchen operations drifting down the passage, but all was silent. Careful not to disturb the others, he climbed from bed and dressed. It was early spring, still cold, but he elected to forego the shoes, firstly because he hated shoes and secondly because he wanted to move in silence. The dorm remained blanketed in deep slumber as he crept out and began padding his way down the corridor.

As he entered the kitchen, the light scuff of his feet echoed in a silence usually filled with the clatter of pots and the gossip of cooks. A deep worry began to grow in his empty belly as he retreated through the dining hall. He turned down another passage and began running. Every office was empty, every corridor silent. Even the central display room was vacant and dark, torches having long since expired.

He considered running back to the dorms, but the light from the windows beckoned. He needed to get out of this disturbingly lifeless building. He found his way to one of the exits, unbolted the door and slipped out. The morning was colder than he had expected and he shivered at the touch of mist. A graveyard silence hung in the air.

Something was wrong, very wrong. Never had he seen this place without some hint of life.

He turned back to the open door, but the darkness within the building was even less inviting now. Underfoot, gravel crunched as he traversed the walkway to the lawn, stepping from cold stones onto colder dew.

A movement in the fog caught his eye. He glanced up just in time to see a cloaked figure pass behind a statue and into the central hall. It was all the clue he needed. He sped away across the lawns, slipped behind a line of regal plane trees, and approached the low boundary wall with its perimeter display of oversized bronze statues – the founders of the academy. The ground and building beyond this point were strictly off limits to any student without special permission.

Aedan crept up behind the fifteen foot effigy of Krale-o-Mandus and peered around his side.

There were two guards on each corner. Here in the middle of the wall, Aedan decided, the mist was almost thick enough to conceal him. It was worth a chance. He hopped over into the forbidden precinct and marched across the lawn with his head down, a posture that he hoped would look confident and slightly bored. It failed, perhaps because he was about half the size of any of those who had a right to be within the perimeter.

Shouting voices called him to stop and he heard the tramp of heavy boots. He kept his head down and pretended not to notice, heading for a hedge-lined corridor that approached one of the side doors. The shouts were getting louder now. He dared not look around. The high, opposing walls of the hedges concealed him momentarily as he entered the walkway. He broke into a sprint and dived through the first gap he spotted in the leaves. There was actually a surprising amount of space within the leafy wall which was easily eight feet across.

He crawled out the other side as the guards began searching for him, and darted under the branches of a stout conifer that stood just outside a window of the central hall. Climbing such a tree was a test of will against sticky gum, prickly leaves and sharp seeds, so Aedan was far from comfortable when he settled opposite the window in the darkness of his fragrant tent. He listened to the soldiers prod and scratch a while longer before giving up the search and retreating to their posts. Finally he could turn his attention to the hall. By the rumble of talk, he judged that somewhere in the region of two hundred people were assembled within. Presently a voice called for silence. After a little more shuffling and coughing, things settled down and the voice spoke again.

"Thank you for attending on such short notice. I am sure you will appreciate that the gravity of what you are about to hear justifies the disruption to the morning's schedules."

The voice sounded like Culver's – it cut with the precision of clear thought and the weight of undisputed authority. There was a brief pause during which Aedan realised that he was about to overhear something that could possibly get him into more trouble than trespassing on the sacred lawn. But there was nothing he could do about that now.

"The marshals and rangers that were commissioned last autumn under the Fennlor threat-assessment directive have returned, and I am afraid the news is disturbing. The iron mines that were sighted have grown significantly. Most of the ore is being taken to the smithies in Greel where the marshals found a marked increase in weapons production. There is little work taking place at the shipyards, but there seem to be more stables than houses. If the Fenn are preparing for a land war then they have only three possible targets – Orunea, Vinterus, and Thirna. Fortifications in Orunea and Vinterus have been recently strengthened. As Southern Thirna is now the least fortified neighbour by some margin, we must consider ourselves the most likely focus of their interest."

There was a murmur of discussion that subsided as a question was raised from another point in the hall,

"What does Thirna have that could justify the cost of such a war? Our silver mines are almost depleted."

"It is a point well made. However, it would be unwise to assume that they could have no motive, and so be lulled into complacency. The mere possession of land can be sufficient motive for some."

A general murmur of agreement followed.

"The situation is complicated by news that has been reaching us from the other side of the realm. Reports of escalating Lekran forays are proving upon investigation to be accurate. It seems that as Thirna has relaxed the coastal patrols, slave traders have grown bolder, making regular pickings along our sea border, sometimes sending parties far inland. With our small hold on the oceans, we can offer no retaliation. It has been suggested that the Lekran parties have been testing us, sampling us. If so, they would have found our bellies soft and our spears blunt. While it is not likely that they would attempt to match Thirna's full strength, a Fenn invasion that turns our attention to the east would present Lekrau with an irresistible opportunity. The slavers may be scavengers by tradition, but let us not imagine that they would turn down the opportunity for a full invasion if we were crippled. Even vultures will kill given the right circumstances."

A tense silence was followed by a surge of voices that subsided after a moment, obviously in response to some gesture.

"Let's begin with questions."

A thin voice – Aedan assumed it was made thinner by worry – asked, "How long do we have before the Fenn can reach us?"

"Marshals estimate that their army is still in its early stages of preparation. They will not be able to mount a large-scale assault within the next three years, though powerful skirmishing parties could breach our borders this summer. If they are planning a full conquest of Southern Thirna, it could be as much as six or seven years from now."

The next voice was nasal and vaguely superior, almost cynical in tone. It sounded like Kollis. "Is there anything more definitive than a growing army and an interest in horses? Perhaps their concerns are self-defence and equestrian sports."

"Yes, there is more. In fact, it is all but certainty that the Fenn will cross our borders soon."

"This goes back to their motive, doesn't it? The Fenn have discovered something in our land and you intend to keep it from us?"

"In this, I have no choice. It is by Prince Burkhart's explicit orders."

There was a burst of stamping and shouted protests. What had been found that was enough to start a war? Aedan thought that even the bronze Krale-o-Mandus would leap forth from centuries of silence and raise a harsh yell of dismay at being kept out of such a secret. But Culver could be made to say nothing further on the topic. Finally order was restored and he continued.

"The next matter is of a vastly different nature. By sheer coincidence the returning rangers happened to witness one of the much-rumoured storms over the DinEilan range. Three of them journeyed some distance through DinEilan to investigate. They did not return. All that was found of them was a single boot and some disturbed ground – and yes, a tree that looked to have been pushed over. I tell you this, not to fuel the outlandish talk of DinEilan, but to give you the facts as we have them before wyrm scales, griffin feathers and cyclops prints are added to the report. I must implore you to turn your minds to sensible explanations and not retreat into the kinds of ideas that settle and nest in empty heads."

Culver's last words caught Aedan imagining some frightening creatures in DinEilan – a DinEilan that was obviously growing wilder. He did not want to be guilty of the empty-headedness just condemned, so he pushed the thoughts back and tried to listen.

"While I care nothing for the doomsday notions that natural anomalies always provoke, there was something about this storm that we would be foolish to overlook. The surviving rangers gave a clear and, I must confess, startling description of what they witnessed, and aspects of their description struck a chord with something in the all-but-forgotten Gellerac archives. This history does not propose an explanation, but records a sequence of events that is worrying. It suggests that, should the storms move towards us, we may be faced with a greater threat than war-mongering neighbours. For those of you, which I believe to be most of you, who do not speak Gellerac, I shall translate the first –"

Aedan's concentration had been absolute and his focus so narrow that he had failed to see the parting of leaves or hear the soft crunch of boots. A vice-like hand snapped shut over his foot and dragged him through the gummy branches and out of the tree. The guard gripped him behind the neck, smiled, and nodded to someone waiting at the statues. Aedan could not turn his head to see, but as the guard marched him off, he caught a glimpse of a boy taller than him with dark hair and fair skin – though the phrase that now felt appropriate was "skin pale as sickness and eyes weak as rainwater".

"Seems your friends don't like you much," said the guard. "After a day and a night in the rat cells I don't think you'll like yourself much either. Trespassing in the founders' quadrangle carries a standard penalty. After that they will decide what to do with you."

The cells were tiny stone cubicles in the wall of a dark and airless room. Aedan crawled into the cavity ahead of the guard's eager boot. The iron grill that swung shut pushed his feet in until his knees were not far beneath his chin. There was no way to stretch out, neither was there sufficient space to sit. By the time the guard had left the room, Aedan was already uncomfortable. He lay curled on his side. When his hip and shoulder could take no more, he tried to turn over, bashing head and knees through the wiggling, jerking process. By the time he had managed to wrestle over onto his other side, he was in greater distress than he had been before, due in no small part to the rising claustrophobia. By midday his limbs were in such agony he was not even conscious of his hunger or thirst. The little snatches of sleep that toyed with him through the night were chased off by the cold and the bite of relentless cramps.

But even if he had been draped over cushions, sleep would have eluded him. What had been discovered in the Gellerac archives? – whatever those were. What was this possible threat that was more worrying than open war? His frustrated curiosity added as much to his discomfort as the physical aches.

Heavy boots tramped along the passage the next morning and stopped outside his cell.

"Out with you!" the guard said as he swung the gate open.

Aedan slowly extended his legs against the cramps. It was taking too long. The guard grabbed one of his ankles and dragged him out.

"On your feet! Time for your hearing."

Uncoiling and stretching out was a slow process. The guard was stamping with impatience by the time Aedan was able to stand and shuffle along behind him. They took a few turns and entered a small, bare room where two men waited – Dun and Wildemar. The guard left and closed the door.

"What have you to say for yourself?" Dun asked, rising to his feet and filling the room with his annoyance.

"I'm sorry," Aedan stammered. "There was nobody in the buildings. I was afraid something terrible had happened –"

"Yes, yes, we know that," Wildemar interrupted. His squirrelly eyes snapped at Aedan and then darted around the room while busy fingers worked as they always did when he spoke. He swung back to Aedan and the words began to tumble out like discarded acorn shells. "We would have done the same thing in your place. We are more disappointed with the others for sleeping in. The rule is a silly tradition made by tame men in puffy robes who wouldn't be able to find east an hour after sunrise. Your punishment is over. The thing that bothers us is how it escaped your notice that you were being tailed. You have some remarkable abilities, and it is frankly disappointing to see that you were so easily followed. What can you say to that?"

Aedan was trying to stir his mind but it resisted his efforts like porridge gone cold. He had not been able to follow the speed of Wildemar's tirade, but the part about being easily followed had stuck. "I was concentrating on hiding from the guards ahead of me," he said.

"And you didn't look behind you once!"

"No, I suppose I didn't."

Wildemar's head twitched with feral vigour and he muttered something potent under his breath, clearly disgusted.

Dun was grinning. "Will you make that mistake again?"

"No. Never." Aedan spoke on behalf of every ache that racked his body.

"Good. Then I think this has been a worthwhile experience. As to the matter of what you overheard – the birds were making such a racket in the tree that you were barely able to determine the language being spoken, let alone the words. If we hear otherwise, you will be moving back into your little cell for a very long time. Understood?"

Aedan burned to ask about the archives, but the look in Dun's eye was not one to be trifled with. "Yes, sir," he said, dousing his curiosity and almost choking in the steam of internal protest.

"You had better get to the kitchen and put some food in you. I want you down in the training hall by the time we begin. Run!"

The session was undiluted suffering. Aedan stumbled through the exercises, accumulating a wide selection of bruises and giving none. He fell off every obstacle and collapsed under every load. The classes were worse. The wooden chairs were featherbeds and the lessons lullabies. His name was spoken in sharp tones by every subject master.

Liru looked worried when she saw him – the story had obviously spread the day before. Mistress Gilda was still in a dangerous mood after her encounter with Peashot's snake, so Liru kept pinching Aedan when she noticed him drifting off. During a lull in the class, she turned to Aedan.

"You know what's happening?" she whispered. "All the disturbance – you managed to overhear?"

"I was told that I only heard birds chirping and couldn't understand a thing that was said."

She looked at him with a frown that receded as she caught his meaning. "It is a great pity then that you have not yet been taught to speak bird," she said, and dropped the topic.

For the rest of the week, furious whispering ran like an infection through the academy. Everybody knew something – drought, flood, plague, war, wild beasts and increased taxes – but it soon became clear that nobody knew anything.

At the end of the week, when it seemed they could take no more, the marshals' quadrant was informed. Dun addressed the first-year boys in the dining hall and explained the situation of the border threats.

"Diplomacy, it appears, has failed us. Prince Burkhart has been in consultation with the generals and senior marshals this past week and issued a series of steps we will be taking to fortify our defences. It has been deemed a good exercise that all apprentices should contribute to the proposed designs and strategies. As a result, the next few weeks will see you spending far longer with Master Skeet. Other classes will be reduced."

Dun left the hall, saying nothing about the rangers, the storm, or the Gellerac history and what it implied. Aedan clenched his teeth in frustration.

Glancing across the room, he noticed Malik and Cayde smiling at him as though he were the punch-line of some joke. He had seen it constantly through the week. They had been smearing him with every drop of humiliation they could squeeze from his stint in the rat cell. Between them, they had spread the word as far as they could, making him seem ridiculous to anyone who would listen – which was almost everyone Aedan knew.

He had tried to ignore it, but the lingering exhaustion was making him snappish. Dropping his spoon, he straightened up and glared. They threw their heads back and laughed, along with several boys at their table.

Malik stood, pulled the hair back on the side of his head and held his ear out as if listening for something, then he folded the ear down on itself, mimicking Aedan's, and pulled a face of mock misery as if the half ear had made him deaf. The boys around him shouted with merriment.

Aedan's temper flared. He grabbed his bowl and took aim at Malik's head. Just as he was about to release it, he felt a strong hand grip his wrist. He spun around and scowled at Hadley.

"You won't win like that Aedan. Remember what Dun taught us – fear and rage can both make a man stupid. Malik wants you to –"

The sound of jeering laughter grew and it pushed Aedan over the edge. He broke free of Hadley's arm and flung the bowl with all his might. It only brushed Malik's head, but sprayed several boys with porridge, reaping a storm of angry protests and three strokes of the cane, which did a lot better than brush him.

That night, after Dun had called an end to the study session, Aedan was easing himself into bed when Hadley walked over.

"You are playing his game Aedan," he said. "And you are going to lose."

"Shut up," Aedan said. He had no desire to be counselled or comforted. He just wanted to be left alone. Where was the value in misery when nobody would respect it? He wanted them to recognise the consuming bitterness of his young life, not festoon him with a string of cheap suggestions for brightening the scene.

"Don't be a cur. Just hear what I have to say." Hadley was never easily put out.

Aedan made no response, so Hadley continued.

"Malik is going to carry on doing everything he can to make you hate yourself and this place. It's really obvious that he wants you out, and at this rate he is going to succeed."

"Are you trying to help him?" Aedan asked, annoyed.

"No. I'm trying to help you, and you would see that if you just let me speak."

Aedan grunted.

"My suggestion is that you start thinking. When you lose your temper – which you certainly know how to do – you lose your head as well. You have to find his weaknesses if you want to take him on, instead of just steaming up and exploding."

"What weaknesses has he got?"

"The way he hates you. He would risk a lot to see you leave. 'Over-eager opponents always over-extend.' Don't you remember?"

Long after Hadley had retired, Aedan stared into the darkness, considering his friend's advice. Something did need to change. He was being baited like a dumb carp and beached every time he bit. Yet when he considered putting some vengeful plan into action, he felt no enthusiasm. He wanted to live for bigger things than that. More importantly, he did not want a war here, did not need an enduring enemy among his companions.

He had known enough enemies in his life.

If he succeeded in humiliating Malik, things would only step up a notch. He'd seen that happen with Emroy.

And Malik was too cunning. He was never caught. The taunts were always too small to be considered a problem by any of the masters, but his own reactions were explosions. They would not go unpunished.

That was when he began to understand. Malik's cunning was not the problem; it was his own stupidity. He was taking the bait while it was still insignificant. But if he ignored it, the bait would have to be increased in size, perhaps enough to draw a master's attention …

Yes, Aedan thought. That might work. Why get into a tangle with a tomcat if there is a dog nearby?

Chapter 25

When news of the border threat spilled across the other quadrants, the whole academy was set abuzz. Students skipped classes, ignored assignments, and gathered in clusters that hummed with a mixture of fear and excitement. Strict discipline was applied to restore a semblance of order, but the thrill of far-off danger had taken root.

The first-year marshal apprentices had spent three weeks under a shower of information on defence and one week attempting to apply it. Building for defence was far more involved than they had expected. The detail was staggering – down to things like unsmoothed outer stone being preferable to smooth, because, for some reason that none of them had understood, it suffered less when being punished by catapults. They had submitted their first proposals for Castath's defence and were awaiting Skeet's feedback. The master marched into the class, slammed his books down on the desk and snatched up a page of notes.

"Group one," he barked, "you killed our whole city within a week because you walled us in from all water. Group two, most of us die outside the city because your barbican is so intricate and awkward that the crush of people and livestock creates a killing ground for more than half the population as they try to enter their own refuge. Group three, your huge unmanned outer wall provides the enemy with complete protection from the catapults on your inner wall. Group four, I told you that the maximum amount of sandstone that could be mined, shaped and placed in five years was no more than a million tons. Granite gives you less than a quarter of that because mining and working it is so much slower. Even if I were to replace your granite with sandstone, you have designed a system of defences that would take two hundred years to construct."

Skeet dropped his page on the desk and glared. "Think boys, think. You need to consider the whole population and all its demands, its resources and limitations. Then you need to become the enemy and work out any possible way to get past your own walls, and re-design accordingly.

"The greatest minds in Castath are working on this now. Try to consider what they may have overlooked. It would not be the first time a young mind has seen what an older one has not."

The boys shuffled into their groups to lick their wounds and mend their plans.

"I told you the outer wall was going to be a problem with the catapults if it's that far away," Aedan said to the four from his dorm. "Let's start again."

Hadley made the first suggestion. "I say we dig a well this time. If we don't try to stretch the outer wall down to the river we can broaden it and give it an allure."

"I thought walls were meant to repel," said Peashot.

"It means a walkway on top. How did you manage to doze in *that* class? Skeet was at his most dangerous."

"Commitment."

"If we are going to make the walls broader," said Lorrimer, "I want a talus – that's the lower part of the wall that slopes outwards, Peashot. Makes walls harder to dismantle, upsets siege weapons and deflects whatever we drop – shoots it out into the enemy."

The small boy might have reacted to Lorrimer's tone, but there was an inwardness about his eyes that suggested he had just learned something.

"Here's an idea," said Aedan. "How about a moat on the inside? It would encourage the Fenn soldiers to spend weeks tunnelling only to get flooded at the end of their efforts. We could also use it to water livestock grazing between the walls. It would be like a long dam. Could put some fish in there too. Might be useful in a siege."

The others nodded.

"Sorry Peashot," Lorrimer said with a smirk, "Livestock are the –"

"Oh, go shove a gizzard down your throat!"

The others grinned.

"An internal moat sounds good," said Hadley, "though I'm not sure if keeping it a secret is practical."

"Even if they have spies to tell them, it would keep them from tunnelling," said Aedan.

"Tunnelling all the way through to our side yes, but sappers only need to get the tunnel under the wall before they fire their supporting timbers and collapse everything, wall included."

"Alright, so it won't stop sappers, but neither will an external moat, at least not for long – they would just fill in the section where they need to work. No! Wait. We *can* stop sappers. Wherever we see them digging, we could wall off and dry out a section of our internal moat, then dig a few tunnels of our own under the walls – and we could start right at the walls, not way back like they would have to. We could listen for where they are working, dig into their tunnel, release our moat and flood them before they can set anything alight. Flooded tunnels would be useless if we kept them flooded. Then we push loads of sand and cement into the tunnels to make them solid again."

"Might be difficult to intercept," Hadley mused. "How would you know which way to go when you're digging?"

"I've seen lots of animals pinpoint burrowing prey. Maybe we could train dogs or badgers or something to point our men in the right direction."

"Interesting idea," said Vayle.

Everyone nodded.

"Something else that might help with this," said Vayle, "is some tensile strength to the wall's rubble core. Remember what Skeet taught us about the mortar we use – that it's only strong with compression. That's why the wall collapses when a big cavity is made underneath. It gets pulled apart, not pushed together. But what if we could combine stone and large tree trunks placed inside the wall? Enough wood might be able to hold the stones up over a cavity."

"Wood rots," said Lorrimer.

"It would be strong well beyond our lifetime. It's the most practical option. Any kind of metal would set the weapons production back. I think layered tree trunks, perhaps with all their branches, would provide decades of strength. Over time, walls could be rebuilt."

Nobody was entirely comfortable with the idea of whole trees decaying inside their precious wall, but they could not fault Vayle's reasoning, so it was added.

"If we have more stone to work with," said Lorrimer, "I'm for flanking towers with curtain walls."

"Round towers," Hadley added. "They might take longer to build, but if we are going to put the moat on the inside, we'll need to strengthen the wall, and round towers are harder to undermine."

"How about overhanging turrets then?" Vayle said. "They use less stone. We could use the extra to thicken the wall or the talus."

Hadley scratched out and scribbled as the ideas flowed.

"One central watch tower," said Lorrimer. "High, very high, say two hundred or three hundred feet, and small watchtowers with fire beacons on the six visible hills."

"Instead of wasting all that stone on such a high tower," said Peashot, "why don't we just stand you on top of the keep? But what's the point, anyway, of making it so high if we have towers on the hills?"

"Those watch towers can be ambushed, and if there's low cloud, we might not be able to see them from the city."

"But then your high tower will also be useless if it's got its head lost in the clouds."

"Fine, then let's have a few circular platforms lower down on the tower so it is both a high and a low ... what do you call a place where you look for stuff?"

"Vantage point," said Vayle.

Hadley added the note.

"How about we move our catapults to the outer wall?" Lorrimer said, leaning forward and looking like he was really starting to enjoy himself. "Can't see why we didn't do that last time."

"We didn't do it last time," said Vayle, "because our wall was too thin to be manned. It's also a bad idea to put catapults on a wall that isn't strong and heavily defended, because if the enemy takes the wall, they just turn the catapults around and we get attacked with our own weapons."

"Oh. Didn't think of that."

"We can do it now though," said Aedan, "seeing as we've used the extra stone to thicken it. Let's also create a slow zone over the approaching ground. The land around the walls is very flat, but it could be spoiled with mounds, ditches, and stakes pointing away from the city. It would be impossible to run across a field like that without stumbling and getting impaled, and it would slow the approach of assault towers. The slower their approach, the more time they give us to bombard them."

"How far out would the slow zone need to start?" asked Hadley.

"Our sling catapults have a range of about three hundred and fifty yards, maybe four hundred with a good height – no, what was the word, Vayle?"

"Elevation."

"How about embankments?" Peashot asked, clearly pleased at remembering something from the classes.

"We're going to be doing a lot of digging already," said Hadley. "Let's put that in the post critical stage."

He sketched a rough overall design, compiling the ideas and labelling the stages, one to four. They all looked at the result, feeling rather pleased about it, all except Aedan.

"Something bothering you?" Lorrimer asked.

"I was just wondering about how many catapults we would need to build to cover all approaches. I was wondering if we could design a smaller supporting catapult, something that could be taken apart, carried off and reassembled quickly. That way we could set up hundreds of them where the attack falls."

"How about," said Peashot, sitting up with a jolt of confidence as he detected a subject he understood well, "how about we soak the rocks for the catapults in blue or white stain so they are harder to spot against the sky?"

They laughed. It was just the sort of trick Peashot would come up with.

"That could work," said Aedan. "Let's ask if we can test it. But have you noticed how rocks often plug and stop when they hit soil? Here's another idea – curved taluses and catapults that fire big discs directly down the walls the same way that you roll a wheel down a bank." He waited for them to get the picture. "The problem is that a boulder stops regardless of whether or not it has hit anything of the enemy's. If we had massive, heavy discs rolling across the battle field, they would have many opportunities to hit something."

"I like the idea of the rolling discs," said Vayle, "but I'm not sure how good it would be for the mortar in the walls if we are going to be using them to direct every shot. How about firing them onto the battle field the way you roll a wheel from above your shoulder." He cut a disc of paper, perched it on his shoulder and wrapped his hand over the top, then slowly illustrated the motion of throwing and spinning it so that it bit into the ground and rolled forward.

"What's happening here?" Skeet demanded, marching up. "Disintegrating into games are we?"

"No, sir," said Vayle. "Aedan had an idea to use discs instead of boulders in the catapults. I was trying to show how a disc could be hurled with spin so that it runs when it lands."

Skeet's brow furrowed with contemplation. "It's not a bad idea. We have more than enough giant pines to spare and we could build saws to cut, but a disc is not stable – it will just tip and fall."

"Yes," said Aedan, "but even if it only travels for fifty yards along the ground, that's fifty times better than a rock. We could also give it a broader reach if we put a spikey axle through it."

Skeet nodded. "The release is going to be the tricky bit," he said, mimicking the throwing action. "This will not be so easily achieved with an unthinking machine. But it's a blazing good idea." He drifted into his own thoughts, moving his wrist and studying movements. Finally he nodded. "What else have you designed?"

Hadley showed him the rough sketch of their plans.

Skeet asked one or two questions, but appeared satisfied with the responses.

"Your stages are faulty," he said when they were finished. "Your plans would leave us exposed for longer than we can afford, but your rolling discs and some of the "wrong" things you've done, like trees in the wall and putting a moat on the inside to double as a reservoir – interesting, problematic but interesting. Wait here." He snatched Hadley's rough sheet of paper and strode from the room, stopping in the doorway to address the class. "You would do well to listen to this group's ideas, especially Aedan's new concept. This is the sort of thinking we need."

Aedan tried to hide his smile. None of the other groups approached his; each was clearly more intent on their own designs, but some attention was being directed his way.

Over the past days, he had pointedly ignored Malik's escalating attempts to provoke another outburst. It looked like the pale antagonist was at it again. Several of the boys were now glancing between Aedan and a sheet of paper that Malik was busy with, their amusement growing. After a few moments the page was held up for the class to see. It was a crude stick drawing. "Aedan" and "enemy soldiers" were written under the respective figures. The meaning did not take long to sink in. The figure of Aedan was removing a cowl from his head, and the enemy soldiers were running in fright. Boys burst out laughing. Cayde and Warton clapped Malik on the back.

Aedan kept to his seat, but his breath came fast and his eyes were hot. None of the boys in his group were smiling. Peashot dug through his sleeves in vain – he had not yet replaced his favourite weapon.

Hadley stood with an abruptness that caused his chair to skid backwards and fall over. "Coming?" he asked. Without waiting for an answer, he turned and headed for the back of the room.

Peashot kicked his chair aside and ran to catch up. Lacking a projectile, he launched himself past Hadley and over the table at a very surprised Malik, hitting him square in the chest and knocking him to the ground. Cayde aimed a kick at Peashot's side, and while poised on one leg, he made a soft target for Hadley's shoulder and went down easily, crashing into desks and chairs.

Lorrimer swung at Warton, missed, and hit Kian instead. While Lorrimer was apologising, Warton replied with a punch to the stomach that almost broke the tall boy in half. Warton proceeded to kick Lorrimer on the ground and that was more than Kian could take. He grabbed Warton's foot, hoisted it in the air and held it until the bigger boy slipped and fell to the ground with a thud.

Vayle stood at the edge with an air of philosophical abstraction as Malik and Peashot scuffled around on the floor trading blows, and Hadley and Cayde wrestled for supremacy, knocking down chairs, tables and careless boys in their struggle.

"Order!" Skeet shouted, bringing his cane down on a desk with a crack that brought all activity to a quivering stop.

"Explain yourselves!"

Peashot scrambled to his feet, snatched the drawing from Malik's desk and handed it to Skeet. The war-master studied it. "Your work, Malik?"

"No, sir."

"And yet the handwriting is clearly yours. All you brawlers line up outside. Every one of you. Now!"

The shrieks of wind and the meaty smacks of the cane made the boys in the class wince. Each combatant received two. Malik got another two for lying and two more for attempting to undermine a fellow student. His face wore a mixture of shock and rage as he hobbled back with small steps, his eyes stabbing in all directions. Aedan looked away.

Skeet marched back inside. "Marshals fighting amongst themselves is something this city cannot afford," he said. "Next time it will be more than a caning. Am I clear?"

The class mumbled that he was.

"Good. You are dismissed. Group three, stay behind."

Aedan's group remained on their chairs – at least Aedan and Vayle did. The others were half on and half off, looking none too comfortable.

Skeet's voice was firm. "Loyalty I like. I am glad to find it among you. That is why you were given only two. The stupidity of rage-inspired fighting I do not like. That is why you were given two. Now that's enough of this. I have arranged for you to meet with the academy's resource group this afternoon during the lunch break. I want you to explain your ideas to them. This is a privilege no junior students have ever been given, so do not embarrass me."

During field surgery the boys were subdued. The girls soon learned about the brawl. Aedan saw Malik busy sketching again, and as the class ended, there were giggles. Malik left a circle of girls crowding over the sheet of paper he had given them. As he walked by, he angled towards Aedan, brushing his shoulder as he passed. Aedan wanted to hit him. He wanted to run and hide from everyone who knew him.

He noticed Liru walking up to the group. She took the page from a tall girl called Ilona whose long hair fell to her shoulders in soft, golden curls, and whose eyes caused most boys' voices to falter. Liru glanced at the page, looked at the girls, and tore it up.

"Savage!" Ilona snapped.

"Yet you are the ones causing injury."

"Oh you always have an answer for everything, don't you?" Ilona swirled around and strode away, golden curls flowing out behind and fawners swarming around her.

Liru grinned as she approached Aedan.

"Never mind them," she said. "There's not a good wife among them. If you heard the way that Ilona talks when there's nobody to impress, you would rub manure in your hair just to make sure she would not take an interest in you."

"Look at me Liru. Do you really think I need the manure?"

"Yes."

Dejected as he was feeling, Aedan couldn't help but smile at Liru's directness.

"I was thinking of making a drawing of Malik," she said. "He will be standing on a field of battle, taking off his helm and showing his pale skin. The soldiers around will be dropping their weapons and offering him medicine."

Aedan laughed.

"Sit with me," she said, leading him to a bench in the sun. "There are a lot of rumours surrounding you. Some of the girls enjoy rumours but I prefer straight questions and answers. So I want to know what led you to marshals' training."

Aedan pulled off his shoes, sat back and closed his eyes, remembering his childhood ambitions and the tragedy that had led him to where he was. He began to tell her of his early interest in ranging through a forest that was meant to be forbidden, his love of reading, especially stories of war, valour, sacrifice and heroism, and then of the Lekran raid that had cut through his beloved hometown and taken his closest friend.

"At first I wanted to be a great soldier and commander only for the adventure of it all. I thought I would be good with strategy, and that felt like enough of a reason. But when ... when they took her, it became different. I want to bring justice to them like they have never known. I'm going to bring the sky down on that filthy island."

"I hope you make them suffer."

"I don't really want to bring pain," he said. "I want to bring justice and stop the slave trade."

"I think you will succeed. There is fire in your heart. But maybe you should not try to deny your anger. I would happily bring them as much pain as they brought me. I would cover those islands with Lekran blood."

Aedan was struck by Liru's comfort with such violent sentiments – how different she was to Kalry. "How have they hurt you?" he asked.

"They took my sister." Her face betrayed no emotion, but her voice clinked with daggers.

"Oh, I had no idea. I'm sorry."

"The Lekran raids are why we left Narralaz. My father is wealthy. He knew many important families in Castath, and he was able to purchase citizenship here."

"So then, you are at the academy for a similar reason to me?"

"To answer that, I would have to reveal what we are being trained for."

"Sorry, I didn't mean –"

"I know," she said with a soft smile. Aedan wondered how such a small and delicate creature with such mild eyes could conceal such edged thoughts.

A jolt passed through him and he flinched as a look of horror crossed his face. "I'm meant to be at that meeting. I'm dead!" Without another word he bolted from the bench and flew down the corridors towards the central hall.

"Ah, here he is."

About a hundred pairs of eyes were directed at Aedan as he stumbled, panting, through the back doors of the auditorium. His first glimpse of the roomy interior was enough to tell him that this was unlike any of the classrooms or lecture halls. From the carpeted floor, plush yellowwood panelling swept up the high walls and blended into a wide vaulted ceiling. Around the perimeter of the auditorium, hundreds of brass lamps shone against the portraits of fierce-looking past masters, probably now all dead. On the stage stood Master Skeet, looking very much alive and far fiercer than any of the portraits. Aedan trotted down an aisle between rows of tiered velvet seats to the carpeted stage. He took his place beside the other four boys who were giving him less-than-friendly looks.

"We have already covered the general defence structure," Skeet said. "You have arrived just in time to explain the idea behind your catapult."

Skeet's words were loud enough for everyone to hear.

The message in his eyes was for Aedan only. It read, "You impudent gnat! When this is over I'm going to put *you* in a catapult and fire it down a mineshaft!" He smiled as he stepped aside.

Aedan was still breathing hard, so his explanation was less than persuasive, but after a while he saw interest sparking in a few eyes. Then the objections began, and they were not voiced gently.

"It is not a practical idea," rumbled a big man in the front who spilled over his chair like a lounging bullfrog. "The labour required to build suitable wheels would be excessive."

"That is why he used the word disc and not wheel," Skeet replied in a tone that made Aedan wonder if there was bad blood between these two. "Sections of giant pines would be simple enough to cut if we rig a water-driven saw. They would cost us little and we could build up a large supply very quickly."

The big man said nothing. Aedan took it as a rude form of assent and looked away. There was something about the man's eyes he did not like.

"Would this require the building of new catapults?" a smaller voice called from the back. "Do we have the manpower for that?"

Skeet replied again. "Modifications to existing catapults might allow them to cast either discs or traditional projectiles. But this would need to be tested."

A few more questions were put and answered. The chief war councillors gathered at the front to confer, and after much discussion, the large boorish man spoke up. "Generally we find that catapults are of minimal use against the smaller mobile targets of the attacking force, but this is an idea that might change things. We would like to see if it works in practice – though I doubt it – so we will commission a team to consult with you and construct a prototype, a modification of existing weapons if possible. Some have shown an interest in the unconventional ideas that emerged earlier and would like these boys to sit in at the next defence council. As we will be in the presence of the prince and other royalty, I recommend some tightening up of manners." He swung his bulbous head towards Aedan. "And formal attire."

All stares converged on Aedan's bare feet. If toes could blush, his would have lit the hall.

"We meet tonight at the palace. The royal guard will collect you at the academy entrance in four hours. If you do not know how to behave among royalty, you have four hours to learn."

Chapter 26

"The palace – woohoo! My family will never believe this!"

Lorrimer was hopping along the corridor in some wild, gangling parody of a victory dance. The others laughed as they followed.

"Are you going to get dressed this time, Aedan," Vayle asked, "or are you considering going naked?"

"What is it with you and shoes anyway?" said Hadley. "It's like you actually enjoy the feeling of sand and soil between your toes."

"Don't you?"

"No. It's not civilised. How can you like it?"

"Back in the Mistyvales I had a friend who explained it with a poem. '*The hug of grass and the kiss of dew are greetings spoiled by the shoe.*' I changed her girly section about kissing to '*the squish of worms*' which made the rhyme not work, but definitely improved the poem. Anyway, the point we agreed on was that walking barefoot is like letting the ground hug your feet, and shoes should only be worn when absolutely necessary."

"Sounds like a nice girl," said Lorrimer. "Did you ever get kissed by her?"

Aedan's throat clenched and he couldn't answer. Behind him a furious whispering broke out in which he heard the words "stupid clod", "dead", and "forgot". He wondered how long the wound would take to close over. He sank onto his chair as he entered the dorm. A hand placed on his shoulder in passing was almost enough to make him cry, but he breathed, gathered himself, and pulled out his books. It would be best to lose himself while memorising a few more details on defensive strategies. He could not afford to indulge misery, to live in the past and stumble through life facing backwards.

During the afternoon, they washed thoroughly and dressed in their best, cleanest clothes, then strolled across the lawns and waited at the main gate for the guards that would escort them to the keep.

"They say the princess is a stunner," said Peashot.

"They also say she's eighteen and twice as tall as you," Vayle replied.

"I meant the younger one."

"The younger one is a boy."

"Oh. Well then I meant the older one. Five years is not so much, and anyway, I'll grow."

"Yes, I'm sure she thinks daily of a delinquent midget apprentice growing up to claim her hand ahead of all the nobles and princes of the realm. What could any of them possibly give that you don't have, except titles, land, wealth and all that. You don't have any of those things lying around, do you?"

"You're an idiot, Vayle. What does delinquent mean?"

"It means you. If anybody asks you to describe yourself, that's the word you want."

"Thanks. Idiot."

"My pleasure. Allisian *is* pretty though, but I've heard that the prince chops off the heads of men who stare at his sister."

Peashot snorted.

"Here comes the guard," said Hadley. "I think you'd better drop the princess talk."

The prince's guard was a group of seven tall soldiers wearing full parade armour. Plumed helms waved and red capes billowed as they marched down the road, each step ringing out with a clash of steel.

They drew up at the heavy iron gate outside the academy where the captain of the guard summoned the five boys by name and scrutinised them. His eyes indicated just the right amount of professional disapproval.

"You are to be escorted to the keep. Remain between the head and the rearguard." With that, he and two flanking soldiers turned and began to march back towards the keep. The boys scuttled after them, not so much in fear of being left behind as of being stamped on by the rearguard crashing at their heels.

The procession drew more than a few curious faces as it marched between groups of gossips and idlers, strolling parties and couples – all enjoying the lingering afternoon rays that streamed down the west-facing roads.

The walls of the keep rose before the boys, dark and stern. As they approached, the gates swung open and heavily armed sentries stood aside to allow the procession through.

The courtyard was bigger than they had expected. An assortment of soldiers and servants hurried about, finishing their duties for the day, or beginning their duties for the night, or possibly just looking busy to avoid being given additional duties.

The palace stood at the end of the courtyard, and though they had all gazed up at it through the gate, it appeared far bigger now. The building rose perhaps a hundred and fifty feet above them. Aedan noticed how the lowest doors were all eight feet above the ground with stairs leading up to them – stairs that could theoretically be destroyed when under threat. But where the stairs should have been made from wood, these were of polished granite. Clearly there was a conflict of values here.

The apprentices were handed over to a royal porter whose face hung from his skull like drooping clay and whose eyes registered neither welcome nor hostility. In fact, if it were not for the treachery of blinking eyelids, the unfocussed gaze might have belonged to a corpse. Aedan had heard about this kind of thing. Many important servants considered an appearance of bored efficiency void of interest or powers of observation to be safest. With grave indifference, the porter led them up the stairs and into an airy vestibule of the keep.

The windows here should have been no more than angled slits allowing arrows to be shot out in almost any direction and light to enter from almost none. But again, the design ideals had apparently been flung away and much larger windows cut into the stone walls.

The boys were led past guards, through a hall and up a wide marble stairway bordered with alabaster statues – all resplendent in royal robes. They climbed five storeys before the porter turned. He led them into a wide passage so lavishly decorated it made Aedan feel uncomfortable. The windows faced west, admitting bright shafts of bronzed light that glowed off the opposing wall.

They passed several grand archways and large rooms before stopping outside a decorated oak door at the end of the passage where the dead-faced porter knocked.

The spy-latch was opened. An eye inspected them, a bolt slid, and the door was swung open.

They filed into a spacious room, richly carpeted and decorated with all manner of maps, sketches of weapons, and diagrams of fortresses. On the western and southern walls were large windows – a strangely unwarlike feature for a room dedicated to the purpose of war strategy, but the commanding view gave it some justification. Light from the windows fell on two dozen men sitting at a long table that ran the length of the room. Aedan recognised some of the faces – Osric, Skeet, and Balfore the dandified mayor who was still festooned with chains and rings.

Aedan knew he was meant to bow to the prince, but because nobody in the room was dressed in any sort of royal outfit and all heads were crownless, he had no idea whom to acknowledge.

"Bow to your prince, boys," said Skeet.

Aedan glanced desperately across at Peashot for some clue, but the smaller boy shrugged. In a kind of disorganised arrangement, they all bowed, each aiming in a different direction. Vayle, at the back, was the only one to get it right. The room fell silent.

"Boys, do you intend to humiliate me?" Skeet said. "Here is your prince. Do you not recognise him?"

"Sorry, sir," Hadley replied. "Sorry, Your Highness. We have only ever seen you from the backs of crowds. We would only recognise you by those big prince clothes and the crown."

Though Hadley did not exactly say it, there was in fact nothing remarkable about Prince Burkhart, except for a general appearance of softness. A neatly arranged crop of mousy hair framed a round face with round cheeks, eyes that held more humour than command, and a surprisingly red nose looking as if it had been struck by a heavy bottle, or the contents. Aedan wondered if that was perhaps the young ruler's means of escaping the strains of leadership.

The prince laughed, stepping out from the others and dissolving the tension in the room. "That's alright. I have no love of big clothes or heavy metal hats. I suppose I look rather like the squire of one of these gentlemen here, all of whom probably appear a lot more commanding than I."

"Yes, sir. I mean no, sir – Your Highness."

Prince Burkhart clapped his hands and laughed again. "Quite right. Your candour would make you abysmal in matters of court policy where none of us may say what we really think. But let's get to the reason for your presence here. You came up with some interesting ideas in that last design of yours. While we are not convinced that they would work, we admire the boldness – something that qualified strategists will tend to place beneath caution, perhaps to the detriment of their plans. Even if your thoughts do no more than shake us from rutted thinking, it will be well worth the exercise. The ideas of thirteen- and fourteen-year-old boys have never been heard in this room before, but the present exigency calls for unusual measures and creative approaches.

"The internal moat, the rolling discs, and the dye – crafty one that – are all fresh ideas, and those are most welcome here. The dyes we will certainly attempt as it will cost us little. The angle of the sun will probably play a strong role in their success. The moat does give us some interesting possibilities. An external moat would need to be at full depth all the way round before a siege begins. There might not be time for that in our case. But if it is behind a protective wall, it could be partitioned off, drained and deepened in a section where tunnelling is taking place, then flooded again in preparation for the tunnel's arrival.

"The rolling discs are interesting – especially on the downward slopes where they could roll at speed for a mile or more. On the level, however, we feel that they would not travel any great distance before collapsing and might not be that difficult to avoid. We will still build the prototype and see what happens. Soaked in oil and set alight they would prove devastating if they could reach an enemy camp.

"As you can see, we place a high value on original concepts. So now that you know what we think of your ideas, we would like you to see if you can spot the flaws in ours. Before you look at the plans, I want to make two things clear. Firstly, if you speak of any of these things outside this room, you will all be built into the foundations of the outer wall." He smiled, but his brows were raised in a way that assured the boys this was not a joke. "Secondly, there is to be no polite deference. If you observe a flaw, you speak of it. You have been brought here because of your original perspectives. It is your duty to voice them. Now, let's get to it."

Five chairs stood open at the centre of the long table and the boys were invited to take their places before the large map unfurled there.

As Aedan settled into a plush velvet chair, he decided that he liked this prince. Burkhart struck him as an open and upfront man, someone with whom he would always know his ground. He shifted the chair up and focussed on the map, eager to say something that might win the prince's approval.

The drawing was complicated and the annotations numerous, but the work was so neat that things became quickly clear.

Trying to concentrate under the weighty eyes of the city's war council was not easy. Lorrimer, if he was absorbing anything, gave no evidence of it and fidgeted constantly. Aedan was the first to speak.

"Is this a tunnel?" he asked, pointing to lines that led from the outer wall to a small fortified hill.

"Yes," Burkhart replied, hovering over the map. "Leaving that hill to an enemy is not an option as it gives an excellent prospect for catapulting the city. It is a ghastly shortfall of the original city plan. Fortifying and holding the hill is a necessity. It will also give us an excellent means of guarding our own eastern wall, forcing an enemy to take the sloping ground on the northern, western and southern aspects. Do you see a problem?"

"Wouldn't they suspect a tunnel? And if they drew a line between the two structures and looked for the way plants grow differently after the soil has been disturbed, especially if it's dug from the top, then wouldn't they be able to sink a shaft and enter our own tunnel, entering both the city and hill fortress?"

"That is why there are very heavy iron doors on either side," said the prince. "Passwords would be required to get in."

Aedan nodded and tried to hide his frown.

"Speak, young man. You dislike the idea? You have a better one?"

"Well, I was just thinking that if the tunnel was breached, the hill fortress would not last as long without supplies and reinforcements. I was wondering if we could use the first tunnel as a trap and dig a second one in secret, one that maybe wanders off to the side before coming back to the fortress, so they would never guess where to dig."

Osric and Skeet exchanged a quiet grin. The reactions in the room ranged from amusement to shock. Some of the men had pages in front of them and began drawing.

Osric spoke up. "If a tunnel entry were attempted, there would most certainly be senior officers in the party. We could have the decoy tunnel enter the city and open into a large hall that has no exits except in the roof – a prison. False doors and racks of equipment could be installed to allay suspicion. When they have gathered a good force in the hall and begin hacking at the false doors, granite slabs could be dropped in place, sealing the tunnel as effectively as the wall. We would have a fine catch of useful prisoners."

The idea caught fire and a dozen discussions broke out. The prince smiled and turned to the boys. "What else?"

Peashot indicated a spot outside the north wall. "This is where I would build catapults if I were attacking. It's the most level and it would be out of range of the hill fortress. It would make a good camp too. Why don't we use it as a dump site for the next few years?"

The prince threw his head back and laughed.

The rest of the meeting progressed with the same informal tone and Burkhart continued to speak to the boys more as a brother than as royalty.

But something had begun to gnaw at Aedan's ease. Would he and his friends really be allowed to leave the castle, carrying secrets of such weight after being warned with no more than a wagging finger? He had read of tunnels that had been kept secret by holding the diggers on site until the work was done and then thanking and murdering them. But as he watched Burkhart exchanging a joke with Skeet, he did not think this prince would be capable of even blackening someone's eye. He was all laughter and good will, though he did not appear to be all concentration. The man flounced about the room, exchanging a joke here and a story there. He would get distracted by something outside the window, then suddenly remember himself and rush back to the map with a furrowed brow, urging everyone to focus themselves.

The fresh perspectives had unlocked a whole cascade of ideas, and old warlords brimmed with new plans. The urgency of the situation rendered many of the traditional, time-consuming methods inappropriate. So tradition was relinquishing ground to innovation.

The meeting was not quite done when everyone's attention was drawn away from the maps and plans. Something very unusual was happening in the sky. Men clustered at the windows as clouds began to weave themselves into peculiar arrangements. It almost looked as though they were alive. The room grew very quiet.

"I wish to see this from the turret," said Burkhart. "Anyone who desires to join me is welcome." He rushed to the back of the room and sprang up a circular stairway. Osric and Skeet followed, but the rest stayed at the windows. Aedan looked unenthusiastically at the remaining company and headed for the stairs, followed by the other apprentices.

The turret had an outer walkway large enough to accommodate them easily. The only trouble was that the battlement was high, even the lowered crenels. Aedan was on his toes and Peashot had to climb up and rest on his belly and elbows.

Out to the west, the plains were still awash in the last rays of a sinking sun, but as the clouds started to gather over the Pellamine Mountains, the impossible happened.

The solid thunderheads peeled away, their tops seemingly torn off by some mighty wind. And where there should have been the pale blue of afternoon, stars appeared with astonishing brightness and gleamed through the deep dark sapphire of night.

The wind died down and silence took hold of the earth and sky.

Aedan was gripping the stone wall so hard his fingers had lost their colour. Lorrimer whined softly. In the street below, citizens crouched against the walls. Dogs scampered this way and that, not knowing where to run until they shrank and cowered in alleys. Flocks of birds descended on roofs, huddling and making themselves small.

All watched.

All waited.

The stillness burst apart with a roar. It was a sound like thunder, only deeper, bigger and fuller, like a voice, yet unlike any earthly voice. It was as if the sky itself had spoken. The rumblings shook the stones of the palace as if it were no more than a mound of bark and leaves. Everyone clutched the walls and Lorrimer shrank down into a corner. Peashot fell from his perch and stayed on the ground.

Everything fell silent again, but it was a silence that waited. To speak would have been wrong for a reason none could have explained but all understood.

The cloud lit up and a bolt of lightning fell onto the Pellamines. But just as Aedan had once seen it do over Nymliss, the shaft of light did not flicker and vanish; it latched and began to glow, seeming to pour fiery gold into the depths of the granite mountain.

As quickly as it had appeared, the golden bolt was gone. A deep boom rolled over the city, causing the land to shudder once more. Before the rumblings had died away, the wind picked up again and that deep silence was ended. Clouds broke into fragments, scattering, as the rift in the sky closed and stars were covered over by the pale hues of late afternoon.

It was some time before the prince recovered himself enough to unlatch his hands from the battlements and walk silently back down the stairs. The others followed, but Aedan hung back. His face was pale and his voice was full of jumps and jolts as he called Hadley, "Did you hear something in that first peal of thunder?"

"What do you mean?"

Aedan began to reply, but then changed his mind. "Never mind," he said. "We'd better get down there." He led the way, but soon wished he hadn't because he was trembling so violently he had to match feet on every step like a small child or an old man. Eventually they reached the council room.

"Well," the prince was saying, "I must confess that I had doubted the rangers' reports, but there's no doubting what we've just witnessed. Is there anyone who can venture an explanation?"

Blank looks faced him, many still tinged with fear.

"There is one man who might be able to offer an explanation," said Balfore.

"Ah, him. Yes. I suppose I would have to listen to the answer in 'the original Gellerac'. I am well aware of the theories Culver put forward, and I will not pretend to be impressed by them. Today's event will certainly send him right back to his archives. But for now we need to appease the masses quickly and simply. I know there is little love in this room for diviners, but perhaps they are worth hearing on the matter."

"They'll have explanations, no doubt," grumbled Osric. "But how can we endorse them? Do any of us believe the answer to what we just saw is going to be found while poking through the entrails of a goat? As if the beast ate the explanation to the mystery? What just happened was something, something …"

"Real?" Skeet offered.

"Exactly!" Osric slapped the varnished wood before him with his open hand. The table shuddered to its gums as if struck by a logger's axe. "These diviners thrive on mystery because as long as there's no evidence they can't be challenged. Our people deserve something better in answer to what we just saw."

The Prince smiled. "Your straight talk would make you an awful politician, Osric – and no, I do not mean that as a compliment." There were a few polite chuckles. "The collective thoughts of the masses are volatile and need to be managed carefully. If diviners are a means of appeasement, then they work for the good of all."

Osric shook his head. "How can we, at the same time, appease the masses with walls we trust and religious guidance we don't – that we actually deem untrue?"

"Ah, Osric. You are fixed on this idea of absolute truth, but do we possess it? And even if we did, would people want it? How many of our people worship a lump of metal that's been shaped a bit, or some invented deity? In every sense, these are created gods, even down to their supposed instructions and blessings. If you were able to point people to a real god, I suspect a lot of them would prefer their own creations – easier to control, less likely to make demands. No, Osric, our people wouldn't love you if you addressed them with this unsubtle candour."

Osric said nothing, but Aedan knew that he did not agree. The prince was looking for what was expedient while Osric wanted what was right.

Burkhart turned to the group. "I shall have to make some announcement to allay concerns, else we'll have a week of panic, looting and slothfulness. Let us resume tomorrow."

Pages were collected and maps rolled up as the men gathered their things and began to head for the door. Aedan saw Osric leave and was about to follow him when the prince stepped in his way.

"I'd like you and your friends to wait behind," Burkhart said.

Aedan paled. His fears rushed back. In the books he had read, it always started with being asked to remain behind.

Chapter 27

When the room had emptied, the prince spoke with a voice that held none of its earlier cheerfulness. "Before you leave," he said, "Ganavant, the first councillor, my right hand man, would like to speak with you." As he turned to go, his soft cheeks attempted a parting smile, but his eyes avoided theirs.

Ganavant lumbered forward. He was not the tallest of men, yet he carried an impression of bewildering largeness – thick limbs, belly like a wheat sack, flabby neck, and swollen head with huge, bulging eyes. His stare was heavy and direct, and he wore no smile. Aedan remembered him now – the rude and strangely disturbing man from the meeting at the academy. This councillor had made his presence felt during the recent meeting too. Those unsettling eyes had slid from one person to the next, never vacant, always calculating.

He addressed them now in a voice that had a dark, flabby resonance.

"As you may have guessed," he began, "walking out of here after what you have seen on the table today is not a right you can claim. I have made some arrangements. Jorla awaits us."

Peashot mouthed the word "Who?" to which four pairs of shoulders were raised. Aedan was worried now. The prince, he thought, might not be capable of brutal measures, but this gurgling bullfrog of a councillor was something else.

They made their way down one level, then took a corridor that led them past a series of small galleries and halls. In one of them, Aedan thought he glimpsed the girls from their field surgery class, the young queen's envoys, seated at a long table bedecked with silver cutlery, fine crystal, and strange foods that were not immediately recognisable.

"Was that a bath of seaweed on the counter?" Peashot whispered.

"Silence!" Ganavant bawled in his deep chesty voice.

They reached a stairway and descended several flights until a service door discharged them into a large courtyard. The two guards saluted the councillor who made no response. Ganavant led the way across polished flagstones to a plain, squat building where sentries scurried to unlock a heavy gate. Inside, the room was bare except for a dark flight of stairs descending into the ground.

Aedan held his breath and Peashot lifted his shirt over his nose. The smell of putrefaction and filth was thick enough to make them cough, and it grew worse as they began to descend. At the third landing Ganavant lifted a torch from an iron ring and walked ahead of them down a low corridor that became more putrid with each step. Defiant squeaks and the patter of unseen paws filled the air while little bodies brushed and tails slithered across the boys' ankles. Lorrimer seemed to be going wild as he frantically dodged and kicked out into the darting, nipping shadows. For once, Aedan was relieved to be wearing shoes.

He noticed that low doors were passing by and started hearing faint moans in response to the group's footfall.

The dungeons – they were in the royal dungeons!

Every horror story of wrongful imprisonment and slow death came back to him as they walked further into the darkness. With every step his dread increased, and he tried to ready his mind for a desperate escape. Ganavant was not going to trick him into a cell while standing at the entrance.

They stopped before a wooden door stained by centuries of dank air and slow rot. Ganavant pushed it open and led them inside where he held his torch against a larger one mounted on the wall. The light was not generous, nor clean. The flames shed an unwholesome red glare as they bobbed and danced with demented ecstasy.

Aedan hovered at the entrance before following the others in. As the room lit up, he felt his legs weaken. He turned to the door just in time to see it slam.

"Planning on leaving so soon?" said Ganavant. "You have yet to meet your host. Boys meet Jorla."

What was left of Jorla filled several buckets, covered some of the floor, and sagged from a number of hooks and spikes. When Aedan looked back at Ganavant, it was with horror.

"Jorla," the councillor continued without emotion, "was entrusted with secrets that had the potential to endanger our entire city. He betrayed us. For the safety of all, it was necessary that he reveal the extent of his betrayal. The only way to ensure he was holding nothing back was through torture. His remains will not be buried but fed to pigs. Such is the punishment for high treason." He turned his bulging eyes on them. "Do I need to harbour any concern that you might leak what you have been shown?"

The assurances of silence could not have been more earnest.

"You are never to speak of these plans to anyone but the members of the war council. You do not even speak amongst yourselves, for you can be overheard. Remember that anyone you tell will be subject to the same punishment. Do you apprehend your position?"

Five trembling voices answered that they did indeed.

Ganavant led them back through the passage, up the stairs and out into daylight.

A large unit of soldiers waited outside. Ganavant nodded to the captain and left without another word.

The boys walked between the soldiers in a kind of stupor as they were led around the side of the palace. They had to traverse the gardens to reach the gate. On the way, they were spotted by a group of women dressed with all the magnificence of royal taste. A strikingly tall and graceful woman stepped away from the group. As she approached, there was more than one gasp.

"It's her," Vayle whispered. "It's Princess Allisian!"

Five young hearts almost leapt from their moorings as she smiled and beckoned them to approach. Unlike her elder brother, she was not afraid to wear the garments of royalty – she stood wrapped in deep blue fabrics, layered and delicate as the wings of a giant butterfly, and crowning her dark locks was a circlet of gold.

When they reached her, they bowed, this time without any confusion.

"I am Allisian," she said "and you must be the exceptional young apprentices I have heard so much about?"

"We are apprentices," Hadley said, when it appeared she was waiting for an answer, "but I'm not sure we are exceptional. We were just asked here to ..." He froze. Aedan looked at him with horror as Ganavant's words and the images from the dungeon hung before them again.

"Yes?"

"Nothing, Your Highness. We are just apprentices – that's all."

Her brows knitted, as if she were slightly hurt, and she studied Hadley with thoughtful blue eyes that Aedan suddenly realised could be spellbinding. He fixed his gaze on the floor.

"I know you were at the war council," she said. "You are not required to keep secrets from me. Surely you know that? Won't you tell me one of your ideas – ideas so interesting that they have caused apprentices to be brought to the palace?"

Heads dropped, toes squirmed within shoes, Lorrimer tugged at his ear.

"I'm sorry, Your Highness," Hadley said at last. "We promised that we would not talk about those things to anyone but the war council."

"You can't possibly think that I was excluded from that circle. Come now. What I ask is not unreasonable. Would you offend me?"

The boys writhed. Aedan wondered how annoyed Hadley was that he had been left to do the talking.

"We don't want to offend you, Highness, but we would be sent to the dungeon if we were to mention those things, even to each other. I'm sorry."

"Look at me, all of you," she said, and now her voice held a note that transformed the butterfly into something more like a dragonfly. "Is that your final answer?"

Each of the boys nodded and apologised.

She pouted, and then smiled. "I see you are boys of rigid principles. Very well, I'll not be offended. In fact, I think I like you the better for it. Let us be friends."

Aedan wasn't really sure if it was a question or an instruction. Apparently the others were equally uncertain. Not knowing what to do with it, they said nothing and looked embarrassed.

"What is your name?" she asked, straightening, rising to her full height and addressing the only boy now on her level.

"Lo – Lorrimer, Ma'am – Miss – Your Highness, sorry."

She smiled and Lorrimer blushed, fidgeted again with his ear and managed to show a few teeth through a misshapen, quivering grin.

"Highness is unfortunately a good description of me," she said. "I am unhappily taller than most of the men in this city, but I'm glad to see that you will probably overtake me. Lorrimer, you shall have to learn to dance!"

With a wink, she turned and left, a butterfly again, gliding back over the lawn to the other ladies, while Peashot and Hadley whispered a few envious taunts at the full-blushing Lorrimer.

Aedan thought he saw her making a sign to the captain of the guard. Most of the soldiers turned and left. Only two remained to escort them back to the academy. He understood with a horrible chill that they had just been tested, and that the large group of soldiers had been waiting to carry them into detainment. All was not as it seemed at this palace. He was only too eager to leave.

He began to wonder about Prince Burkhart – whether his first impression had been entirely accurate. The prince had shown them nothing but warmth and laughter, but it must have been by his instruction that Ganavant had threatened them and Allisian had tested them. Apparently, the prince was a man who preferred to be seen as a cheery leader spilling sunlight while having other hands do his darker work. His argument with Osric came back to Aedan's mind. He remembered the prince's lack of respect for truth, and it began to seem a far more worrying thing than it had at the time.

He decided to keep the thoughts to himself. Revealing them would prove dangerous – and there was something else on his mind.

As he lay awake, long into the night, he still shook beneath the remembered power of the storm.

The others had heard only thunder, but Aedan had heard more – a voice, and it had spoken. Deep as the shuddering growl of a waterfall, yet clearer than the ring of crystal – the voice had spoken his name.

Chapter 28

The days were growing warmer. Changing seasons did nothing to dim the memory of the storm, but as the weeks passed, Aedan began to wonder if he had truly heard a voice or if his imagination, awakened by the impossible sights, had lent a hand. Yet, when he drifted towards scepticism, there was a strange discomfort, a whisper at the back of his thoughts that he could not entirely hush. It insisted that not only had the voice been real, but that he would hear it again – and it caused his chest to hammer out the rhythm of emotions he couldn't even begin to understand.

Aedan went as often as he could to see his mother who was looking more settled and had begun assisting at a nearby scrivener's office. She was always delighted and proud to see her growing son. Harriet compensated for that by being even more bull-headed and domineering than before. She had given birth, and her young child did not seem to have tired her or diminished her enthusiasm for interfering in Aedan's life.

There was still no news of Clauman. Aedan's doubts about his father's character refused to wane. It was those doubts that held him fast whenever he considered making enquiries. He decided it would be safest to wait for news, though he hoped it would not be too long a wait.

On his free days, he would often find himself wandering alone in a forest or sitting atop a windy hill. Sometimes he waited on a plain while heavy clouds drove in from the west and the old familiar song of the rainbird filled the air with anticipation and his heart with memories of the Mistyvales.

First, the wind would rumble in the distance like an approaching river, then he would see grass bend, pressed by a great invisible hand. The dull rumble would rise in pitch to a swishing, lashing exultation, causing stalks to lie flat against the ground while the tougher branches of shrubs held themselves up and shrieked their defiance in the gusts. Then the first drops, cold and heavy, would plummet from the sky and burst on the ground. Aedan could not have held the smile in if he'd tried. He would pull his oilskin over his head and let the deluge press down and wash over him until the drops spent themselves, thinned, resolved into a fine haze and painted a rainbow across a dripping sky.

On these solitary outings, he always carried the leather case with the design of the oak sapling and the toadstool, and though he often took it out and stared at it, he couldn't muster the courage to look inside.

Often, he turned towards the west, towards Lekrau, and reminded himself of his purpose. Yet there were moments when he considered the enormity of what opposed him, when he wondered if he was not being completely unrealistic, and he wondered – even if he could bring justice to Lekrau, would it truly bring him peace?

But he dreaded that lost feeling of purposeless existence. Any purpose, he thought, was better than none, and what better, more noble purpose could he possibly find than – as Osric had put it – felling the oppressor? To this end, Aedan trained harder than any of them. When the others moaned about a particularly strenuous challenge, he saw it as an opportunity to increase his strength, and increase it he did. His injuries, while they still gave him a little stiffness after a heavy day, no longer held him back. Often he would be the first to complete the courses Dun and Wildemar set. If any kind of woodsmanship was involved, none of the others were even close.

The boys now jogged regularly to the tree-mantled hills and exercised the various ranging skills they were learning. Using ropes for safety, they climbed many of the rocky faces, scaled the city walls, and traversed sections of forest without touching the ground. In good weather they swam across the dam once a week, in bad weather twice. The daily routine had grown more demanding, but they now managed it, if not quite effortlessly, at least without that cloying exhaustion. Even those who had additional literacy classes were beginning to get a hold on things.

The sessions with Dun always included duels as individuals, in pairs, and in groups. Sometimes they fought with weapons but often without. Dun taught them many ways to defeat opponents using crafty, sudden movements, and always using whatever the environment offered. At first he made them fight at half speed to nurture the habit of thinking. Repeatedly, he would stop a fight and ask why someone had not swung the rope lying at his feet, kicked the sand in which he stood, or pushed over the line of barrels instead of treating them with timid respect. "Think boys, think! I cannot do it for you."

They began to move more quickly, to hit harder and with fluid ease, and above all, to think. Aedan's imaginative love of strategy was finding an interesting outlet. Since his humiliation during the first challenge, he had never again engaged in any form of combat without thinking it through, and he was finding that he could not only match the others, but better them. He came up with the strangest ideas and seemed to draw them from some inexhaustible supply.

Once, when facing Warton with blunted training spear and shield, he slipped off his boots, drawing odd looks, then lobbed his spear high into the air so that it arced just beneath the ceiling and fell towards his opponent. Warton followed the trajectory, along with everyone else, snorted at the stupidity of the decision and stepped forward, allowing the spear to drop behind him. He watched it clatter to the floor and looked around just in time to catch Aedan's shoulder full in the chest. Bare feet had enabled a soundless charge while everyone was looking at the ceiling. Warton was rammed and borne to ground.

The tricks were never repeated, and they worked more often than not.

Hadley was the strongest and best balanced, Peashot the slipperiest. Second to Aedan, Peashot was the one everyone most dreaded fighting. Malik often fought dirty, ignoring the limits that had been imposed. Many of the boys let it pass, too intimidated to object, but nobody in Aedan's dorm cared a whit for Malik's high standing. They took great pleasure repaying each dirty blow with another until he reined himself in.

One morning, Dun told them of a regiment that had escaped an enemy prison without tools or weapons, and been unable to survive the journey home. He vowed he would allow no such incompetence within the ranks of marshals, so the boys began learning how to make tools and weapons from what their garments and nature provided. They began with a class in which they used sharp rocks to cut slings from the material of their shirts, though for the exercise they didn't actually use their own shirts – scrap cloth was provided.

They practiced with their slings and with better-made leather versions until they were able to hit a rabbit-sized target at twenty paces with reasonable consistency. Some who had not used slings before, proved dangerous at first. Mistiming their releases, they launched stones in any and every direction, even backwards. There was more than one injury before the skill was mastered.

From there they moved on to batons, clubs, and quarterstaves. Wildemar took them through the forests where they found and prepared their own quarterstaves from the trees – oak, blackthorn or hawthorn were his favoured woods. In Castath, the quarterstaves were normally harvested by coppicing – cutting a tree low to its base, resulting in straight or slightly curved shoots. But this resource was denied the apprentices, and the subsequent hunt for straight branches did much to develop their eyes.

Wildemar showed them how to heat-bend wood directly over a fire. By wedging one end of the heated staff in a forked tree and leaning against the other, they were able to straighten even a very crooked branch.

Spears were next. When it came to bows, however, it was time for the specialists. Everyone knew how to find a hopeful-looking branch and string it, but as Dun had stressed, in some terrains a man could wait a week for a long shot at a buck, and a poor bow could mean his own starvation.

"It's time for you to see a true bowyer at work –"

Peashot raised his hand. "A what?"

"A bowyer is a bow maker. For the first time, I have managed to convince Torval, the most sought-after bowyer in Castath – perhaps in all of Thirna – to give you a demonstration. It will be … difficult for him." He sounded hesitant, like someone struggling with delicate information. Aedan wondered what Dun was not telling them.

"I will not be there," Dun resumed, "Master Wildemar will take you – so I'm warning you now. Don't give Torval cause to grieve his decision."

———

Streets were still dark and empty but for a few carts – farmers trundling goods in to market, store-owners setting up for the morning's business and travellers stealing a march on the day. Wildemar, with the apprentices surging behind him, crossed the city to a large workshop alongside the main timber yard. The workshop was airy and quiet. Dozens of workbenches cluttered with tools awaited the bowyers who were just beginning to drift in and take their places. Peashot kept to the front, eager eyes consuming every detail.

The smells of sap, resin and wood shavings were alluring; some of the sweet woods like maple were almost appetising. For Aedan it brought back memories of forts and tree houses, and of one unforgettable autumn when everyone at Badgerfields got involved building the new hay barn in the west field. With a sigh he drew himself back into the present.

Wildemar led them to a work bench at the end of the building, where a man was seated, waiting. This would have to be the legendary Torval. He was an elderly man who Aedan decided was unmarried, for no wife would have allowed him out in such mismatched, tatty clothes. He had a narrow rim of grey hair, a heavy bulging brow, huge gorilla arms, and a surprisingly meek expression. Aedan was at first surprised, then shocked. Archery's great Torval actually looked afraid. The boys recognised his kind immediately – the kind that would be eaten alive if put in charge of a classroom – and their confidence surged forward to dominate the space vacated by his. Fortunately, Wildemar remained with the group.

Cayde asked in his biggest voice if Torval had been a military archer. Torval's eyes dropped and he shook his head. Wildemar stuttered and mumbled and wasn't sure where to look. The response left everyone puzzled.

After a lengthy and awkward silence, in which Wildemar waited for Torval to assume command and Torval quietly studied a spot between his mismatched shoes, Wildemar coughed and proceeded to rush through an unprepared introduction. He presented the two most commonly used bows in Castath — longbows that were plain, tall and sturdy; and flatbows with powerful broad limbs that were thinned along the belly. He then fetched something from a rack that did not look like a bow at all. The short limbs were curled in on each other like the legs of a dead spider.

"This is one our bowyers have been experimenting with," he explained. "Lekrau was the first nation to start it. A small composite of different woods. See the belly? Strips of deer horn, stronger in compression. On the back — sinew, stronger in tension."

He surprised everyone when he strung it — a tricky business that required half sitting on the bow — by bending the limbs what looked to be the wrong way, against the original arc. The result was a tight little bow that vaguely resembled some of the recurved flatbows, though the curves were far deeper.

"Impressive power, these little weapons, but they tend to break easily, too easily. Crack, snap, gone. Don't think we have the glue right yet. Helped us improve our other bows though." He pulled down a strongly arched wooden bow from a long rack. "Sinew-backed," he said, pointing to the semi-transparent layer. "Increases draw weight and makes the recoil faster, much faster. Improves the lifespan too. Someone want to try it?"

Peashot sprang from the group before the question was out. The length and weight of draw were too much for him, but he succeeded in plugging an arrow very near the centre of the target.

Torval's face lit up with surprise and pleasure.

"Screaming fine shot!" said Wildemar. "Didn't expect someone your size to manage it. Here, try the composite. Might suit you better."

Peashot's eyes were glowing as he took the little bow. He sighted before drawing, pulled the string and pushed forward into the handle.

Crack!

The bow split and the arrow spun away and clattered to ground.

"Oh," said Wildemar. "Uh, sorry Torval. Very sorry."

Torval retrieved the bow gently from Peashot, holding it as someone might cradle a child. Some of the boys laughed. Torval winced at the sound and turned away to hide his broken creation behind a rack of saws and files.

Wildemar was equally uncomfortable, looking like he wanted to dart off and hide at the end of a high branch until the embarrassment had worn off. Fingers worked and face twitched, but he managed to gather himself and began tossing out little pips of information on the bow-making process, beginning with wood selection.

Yew, elm and hickory he considered ideal, if they could be found, while other woods like maple, walnut and fruit trees like plum, apple or mulberry would also produce good bows. He showed them how to test any wood by bending a thin branch and watching whether it snapped back into place or returned with more of a ponderous lethargy. Torval sat without looking up, nodding occasionally.

Aedan was beginning to wonder what the legendary bowyer was going to contribute to the class when Wildemar's store of information ran empty and he looked across at Torval and asked if he would demonstrate the full construction of a survival bow – a hunting flatbow if possible – from branch to weapon in a single day.

Torval mumbled something to Wildemar who relayed the message, a request for a volunteer. Peashot jumped forward. Torval, without explaining what he was doing, measured the reach of Peashot's arm with a marked cord, doubled this and added a few inches.

Then he rose to his feet.

The boys went very quiet, and Aedan understood why the man could never have been in the military.

Torval kept his eyes down as he began to move away, struggling for each step. His legs were bent – not just a little bandy, but completely deformed, as if they had been strapped around a barrel through his childhood and forced to set in wide looping arches. As powerful and capable as his arms were, so misshapen and useless were his legs. He had to throw his weight from side to side, weaving forward in a tottering, stumping gait.

The initial silence was broken by something worse. Malik started it – a cold sniggering amusement that was taken up by his friends and bootlickers. Wildemar called for silence, but he could not undo the insult that continued to ring in everyone's ears. Though he had taken no part in it, Aedan still felt ashamed.

When the crippled bowyer made his tottering way back, he did not raise his head. Though he had the strength in his arms to thrash the lot of them with a few strokes of the young maple trunk he now carried, he sat down quietly and began to work.

The trunk was about four inches in diameter. He sawed it to the length he had just measured and split it down the middle. Choosing the side free of knots, he used a drawknife to strip off the bark and cambium along the back until it showed a single, undamaged growth ring, then he began to tiller the limbs.

The heavy-armed bowyer hunched over his work, lost – or perhaps taking shelter – in the rhythm of the drawknife. It fell to Wildemar to explain what was taking place.

"Usually," he said, "Torval would dry the wood very slowly, tiller little bits off in stages, especially with longbows. Drying hardens wood. Tillering is thinning the limbs. Balancing them is important. Very important. Can take years. But what he's demonstrating is a hasty bow for a survival situation. The bow will be weaker, might crack slightly from forced drying. Should still deliver a good shot though."

After chipping out the rough shape of limbs and handle with a small axe, deliberately avoiding the back of the bow – the side facing the target – he placed the stave over a bed of coals and left it to dry.

Vayle raised his hand.

"Yes?" said Wildemar.

"How likely are we to be carrying axes, drawknives and all these other tools if we are in a survival situation?"

Wildemar looked at Torval. The boys looked at Torval. Torval looked at his shoes.

"Do – uh, do you – uh, think," asked Wildemar, the high branch calling him again, "that you could possibly show them with – without using specialised tools? Maybe only a small hunting knife? And still finish in a day? Possibly?"

The bowyer did not raise his eyes. He lurched and stumped over to the coals, picked up the stave and placed it in a corner.

Then he left the room.

Wildemar twitched, eyes darting everywhere except at the boys' inquiring faces.

Nobody knew what to do.

It had obviously been too bold a request. Peashot glared at Vayle.

Then Torval walked back into the room with a second bough swinging under his arm, this one about two inches thick. In his other hand was a small rock. Without a word, he took up a stick instead of his measuring cord, motioned for Peashot to step forward, repeated the measurements, and marked the bough.

His voice barely over a whisper, he turned to Wildemar. "Would you like me to use one of their knives?" he asked.

Before Wildemar had a chance to reply, Peashot slipped his knife out the sheath and handed it over.

From behind him, Aedan heard someone make a scathing comment – the monkey bow maker about to embarrass himself. He felt a sudden pang. Why would Torval risk it? He could simply say it was not possible and nobody would think any less of him. But by subjecting himself to absurd challenges like this, he was inviting further ridicule. How was he going to make a flatbow in a single day without tools? There was a reason why little knives were not used to chop branches or split firewood.

By this time the workshop had filled with bowyers, and the general noise of sawing, chopping, and filing provided a blanket for murmured conversation. Wildemar noticed of course, but did not interfere.

Aedan listened to what was developing.

It was a bet.

Malik, never short of money, was offering three to one that the bow would not be completed by sunset, or that it would break.

Cayde was writing down names and amounts.

"Northboy?" Malik whispered. "Frightened to bet against me?"

Aedan glanced back at the quiet craftsman hunched over his work. He looked old, beaten-down, friendless. The way he studied the wood with such hopeful intensity, as if he had nothing in the world apart from his craft, tugged at Aedan. He suddenly wanted the quietly courageous man to succeed in front of these sneering boys, wanted it dreadfully.

"Thought so, beggar-boy," said Malik, misreading the silence.

Aedan swung back at him. "Ten coppers says he does it."

Malik's eyes narrowed. "You actually have ten huddies?"

"You have two chims and six?"

A smirk stole over Malik's face.

Cayde filled in the bet.

Aedan had never owned ten copper huddies in his life. At this point he had only one – maybe, somewhere, possibly under his bed or behind his desk. If he lost the wager, it would mean asking

Osric for help, and that would not go well. Osric's opinions on gambling were nothing short of volcanic. If Osric refused to help ... Aedan's surge of boldness began to melt into a sticky worry.

What had he done? If the bow failed, there would be a noose around his neck, and he had just given Malik the rope. But he could not back out now.

He turned to watch the bowyer with an interest that quickly became feverish.

"What was that about?" Hadley asked.

"I bet ... a few coppers?"

"That he would fail?"

"That he would succeed?"

"What! How much?"

Aedan hesitated. "Ten."

"You bet ten huddies that he would finish! Are you mad? He was slow *with* tools. How is he even going to cut through the wood to begin with? It will take him two weeks to whittle out the basic shape." Hadley raised and dropped his hands while staring at Aedan and shaking his head.

Aedan writhed. He had no reply. They both turned to watch the bowyer, who, as yet, had not made any progress.

Torval's brows were pinched together, an expression of bear-like simplicity, as he peered from the knife to the bough and back again.

Aedan groaned, wishing again that he had not been such a fool.

After what seemed an age of short-sighted squinting, Torval reached for the knife, held it in one hand, and picked up a rock in the other. Using the knife edge as a broad chisel, he tapped on the back with the rock, cutting an angled incision into the wood all the way round as a beaver works through a tree trunk. It was slower than a saw but quicker than Aedan had expected. It allowed him the slightest tingle of desperate hope.

Wildemar, having calmed his nervous fidgets again, explained that this wood was mulberry, not as hard as maple but very supple, and a lot easier to work with – an important consideration given the lack of tools.

When the section was cut, Torval knocked the blade into the end of the beam. By hammering the back of the projecting tip and pulling on the handle, he managed to work his way down, prying the sections of wood apart until he reached the area marked as the handle. He then chiselled the long flap of wood off and repeated the procedure on the other side. The rough layout of the bow was clear now.

Then he did something Aedan would not have thought of. After sharpening the knife on the stone, he knocked the tip into a short sturdy branch, and used the resulting tool as a kind of rough drawknife. With the handle in one hand and the attached branch in the other, he was able to pull the blade along the length of the wood, slicing off long shavings that fluttered to the ground.

This was clearly something that had not been seen before in the workshop because a few of the other bowyers left their benches and drifted over to witness the unusual operation. One of them tapped Hadley on the shoulder, wanting to know why Torval was not using tools. Hadley explained, and more than one of the men nodded his surprise and approval at the old man's creativity. Once happy with the shape, Torval set the bow over the coals to dry.

"Do you want me to make the string too?" he asked Wildemar, in a quiet voice.

Aedan held his breath. He had forgotten about this part.

Before Wildemar could answer, Malik spoke up in his aloof tones, now oiled with false courtesy. "Master Wildemar, we would really appreciate being shown the whole process."

The request had nothing to do with understanding the process. All the boys knew it. In the rush of whispered complaints from those who had bet against Malik, the bowyer lurched away and returned with an enormous thorny leaf. Aedan had seen these leaves on a type of large succulent plant growing in the area.

Torval used his rock to bash the heavy leaf into wet fleshy fibres which he then separated and hung up to dry beside the stave, just as lunch was served.

Seeing how quickly the hours had slipped away caused Aedan's stomach to knot. He could swallow only a few bites of flatbread dipped in his potato-and-leek soup. His appetite wasn't improved by the slight pang he felt whenever he glanced at the far corner where Torval, separate from the groups of younger craftsmen, was hunkered down over his meal alone.

The wooden bowls were gathered up, and everyone hurried back to their places.

After turning the bow that was suspended over the coals and leaving it to bake a while longer, Torval collected the now-dry leaf fibres and separated them into strands, hanging them over the bench in front of him.

Beginning with three strands, he knotted them together at the ends, then started the tedious process of reverse-twisting, in which one strand is twisted and then looped over the other two in the reversed direction. His fingers moved slowly at first, but then they sped up until he had done almost two feet. One of the strands was growing short. He took another from the bench, twisted it into the first and continued as before, adding to the strands one at a time as needed. Within an hour, the string was complete – a tight pale-green weave that looked surprisingly neat and strong.

He coiled and placed it on the table, then collected the stave. It had lost much of its weight while drying, Wildemar explained, and would be a lot harder.

Torval sharpened the knife again and began to tiller the limbs from the belly-side, carefully weakening them until he was able to bend the bow over his knee. The limbs were broad, too broad for a handle, so he trimmed the centre section until it was a comfortable fit for a small hand, then chiselled out a rough arrow shelf.

The apprentices were drawing into two groups – one excited and daring to hope, the other still cynical yet not as confident anymore as they saw the bow materialize under the edge of the little knife. This time, when the bowyer pushed himself onto his bent legs and hobbled to the fire, there were no whispers of mocking laughter.

He held one of the limbs above the flames as if slow-roasting it. The boys had seen this when straightening quarterstaves. Torval kept touching the wood, and when it was too hot for his finger to remain on the surface, he slipped the end of the stave into a gap between bricks and bent it, holding it in place until it cooled. He looked down the length, heated and bent it again, and examined it with a grunt of satisfaction.

Aedan could see from where he was that a mild crook in the wood had been completely removed. The string would now track down the middle.

Torval then repeated the heat-bending process, this time giving the bow a gentle recurve, pointing the ends of the limbs away from the archer.

"Much better recoil," Wildemar explained.

Tension in the room grew as the sun passed its zenith and began the downward journey. Lively chatter became loud and Wildemar was compelled to hush the apprentices several times.

But now the other bowyers in the room had got wind of the bet and seemed to have arranged some bets of their own. One by one, they gathered around, ringing the old man as he settled at his bench to carve notches at the tips of the limbs.

"Need to make a natural tillering stick," he mumbled to Wildemar, and stepped through the wall of onlookers to a pile of timber where he rummaged around and withdrew a stout, forked branch. He brought it back and nailed it vertically into his workbench, then used the knife and rock to chip half-a-dozen grooves across the branch, starting about six inches below the fork and going down about two and half feet. Wildemar, after conferring with Torval, explained to the class that the bowyer had set up the branch to mimic a standing sapling or a stick wedged into the ground.

Torval placed the bow's handle in the fork, pulled the string down a few times, and hooked it into the first groove.

Aedan cringed with horror.

The curvature of the bow was so uneven that the whole thing was lopsided. It looked ridiculous. He heard sniggers from behind. Words drifted out – pathetic, crooked, can't shoot that, not a real bow ...

Using a piece of charcoal, Torval marked the rigid sections of both limbs, took the bow down and began thinning the belly in those areas with his same branch-and-handle drawknife. The next time he set the bow on the tillering stick it looked much better. Aedan released his breath.

After several stages of this, the bow was bending evenly and smoothly, but the wood itself was far from smooth. With a rough sandstone rock, he began to file the jagged sections until there were no protruding splinters.

He motioned to Wildemar who leaned in, and after a few hushed words, the master relayed the information.

"Better results if you make a paste of blackberries or some other dye. White wood can be conspicuous for hunting. Fur twisted into the string will help silence it too, reduce the chance of your quarry flinching before the arrow covers the distance."

Aedan wished they would spend less time on these useful tips and just get on with it. The afternoon rays were slanting ominously when Torval started on the arrow, beginning with a slightly bent stick which he straightened over the fire. He bound a sharp stone to the tip and glued it in place using heated pine resin mixed with a little charcoal dust. Wildemar mentioned a few other simple glues that could be made from various saps or pounded from bulbs.

Torval sliced a nock in the back end of the arrow and faint grooves a little forward. Into these grooves he fixed three trimmed feathers using more pine resin and a fine thread from the original string fibres. It was surprising just how neat and precise the great sausage fingers could be.

His face was intent as he mumbled again, pointing and motioning with his hands. Wildemar turned and explained that the feathers selected were from the same side of the bird, producing arrow rotation.

Aedan blew out his breath noisily and stamped. This time-wasting obsession with trifling details was pushing him, and all those who had betted with him, to exasperation. They glanced constantly out the window. The sun appeared to have lost its grip in the sky and begun plummeting to earth. Aedan had never seen it drop this fast.

"Wait till you make your own arrows," Wildemar said with a feral grin. "Bet or no bet, shoddy fletching – you may as well forget the bow and throw a stick."

By this stage there was not a craftsman to be found at his bench. The entire workshop had gathered around, those at the back standing on chairs. The atmosphere was like the boiling hubbub preceding a fight or race. It seemed everyone was in on the wager.

Torval was squinting and fiddling with some little thread behind the feathers. He frowned, obviously dissatisfied. Then he pulled the thread off, tossed it away and began afresh with another. Aedan dropped his head in his hands. There were several exclamations of dismay, not all of them from the boys.

The crimson sun fell lower and lower. They could actually see it move as it began to fall behind the roofs outside, but Torval was lost in his world, apparently unaware of any need for haste as he carefully rewound the thread.

Then he tied it off, nodded, and placed the arrow on the bench.

Aedan looked up with a start. It was done! The last gleam of red was fading from the wall.

He turned to Malik and pushed out his chin.

"That was the easy part," Malik said with a tone that was almost sympathetic. "It has to shoot. It breaks, you lose."

All talk was shushed as the bowyer looked up at Peashot and nodded. Peashot stepped forward, taking the bow.

The bowyer's attention was complete, his eyes young and eager. Aedan dreaded another snap, dreaded what it would do to the big man. He dreaded it even more than the difficulty he himself would face.

Malik and Cayde moved to the front. They would want to see if anything cracked or failed.

Aedan was breathing fast. Hope and fear wrestled in him as Peashot walked to his position and the arc of spectators gathered around. Aedan was near the front, and he saw with alarm that there was a slight hairline crack in the handle. Wildemar had said that forced drying could have that result. All he could do was hope.

Everyone held their breaths as Peashot lined up. He placed his feet, rested the arrow in the shelf, nocked it, and gripped the string. He took a deep breath, raised the bow, drew back, leaned into the handle … and hesitated.

Aedan wanted to scream for him to release. The wood creaked under the strain as the little boy steadied his aim. Every eye was wide, every mouth open.

Peashot's arm grew still. Then a noise split the breathless tension in the room as he released the string and it snapped away from his fingers.

The arrow hissed through the air, flew straight, and thudded into the target.

The room erupted in wild shouts and cheers. Torval smiled a shy smile while his fellow craftsmen gathered around, clasped his arm and thumped him on the back. Coins began to slide from hands and clinked into others.

Torval refused to accept the bow when Peashot tried to hand it over. "It was made for you," he said, handing it back along with the borrowed knife.

The small boy's confusion was all too obvious as he stuttered, "But – I – but …"

Aedan knew what the trouble was, understood the torment. He watched. When the attention shifted elsewhere, Peashot sidled around the back of Torval's workbench. With a movement so slight, so well covered as to be almost invisible, he slipped a fletching clamp from his pocket and placed it where it had been before the lunch break.

Aedan chuckled.

Peashot caught the look and scowled in return.

Before leaving, Wildemar thanked Torval for sharing his remarkable knowledge with the apprentices. The old bowyer studied his shoes, grimaced through the speech directed at him, and merely nodded when it was done.

"Wish we could have given him more than that," Aedan said to Peashot as Wildemar finished off and led the way out. They looked back and watched Torval cleaning his bench and replacing his tools with infinite care. The other craftsmen had left the building and he was alone again.

Peashot stopped, and then ran back inside. He drew up in front of the workbench where he placed his knife and sheath, nodded to the bowyer, and returned to the departing group.

The last sight they had was of the silent man smiling as he held the little knife in front of him. Words of appreciation were not close to his heart, but this was something he did understand.

——

Malik paid all his debts but one. He and Cayde insisted that Aedan had pulled out of the wager. Of course the bootlickers had witnessed it too.

Hadley was even angrier than Aedan. If it had not been for Dun's looming presence, there would have been a fight to rattle the walls and make the previous one look like a polite discussion. Peashot let his tongue loose within Matron Rosalie's field of surveillance and found himself on kitchen duty that evening. That same evening, Malik found himself eating a decomposed toad buried in his stew. Peashot was given a caning from Dun and hero's welcome from everyone back at the dorm.

Over the next five days, the boys worked with the assistance of several bowyers to imitate the demonstration they had been given, first with tools, and then with only their knives. They came to a full appreciation of Torval's skill and discovered just how many ways there were to ruin and break a sturdy piece of wood.

After they had each produced something resembling a bow, Wildemar set them loose in the forests. Not everyone had paid attention to the wood-selection process. As a result, some fine-looking bows were produced using soft, un-springy woods, from which eager arrows dribbled only a little further than a boy could spit.

Some tried to bypass the drying and tillering processes, scoffing at the talk of hand-shock. Aedan was one such. His first bow was made of such a thin branch that it would have endangered nothing more than a mouse at close range, so for his next attempt he used a much thicker branch. The first shot almost gave him concussion. The bow, still heavy with sap, delivered bone-rattling jolts, contributing nothing to accuracy and much to headaches. Annoyed, he tracked Kian down in a woody valley and got some help starting over.

Most of the early results were less than spectacular, but enough, perhaps, to maim very small, short-sighted and deaf antelope from a few paces downwind – ideally, not much wind. But over the weeks, the bows improved, and some, like Kian's and Peashot's, were weapons to be respected.

Wildemar revised the string-making technique that Torval had demonstrated, and introduced them to other natural fibres like flax and nettles. He then went onto rawhide and gut strings which required less labour but more drying time. Sinew strings were the most difficult to make. Tendons had to be dried and pounded until they separated into fibres which would be twisted together. One of the useful advantages with sinew was the way it could be soaked into strands that dried with their own natural glue.

The different kinds of strings – which could be combined to form rope – were useful for more than bows, so the apprentices spent several classes learning the techniques.

As the range and power of survival bows did not always stand up to larger prey, Wildemar demonstrated how to make many poisons – poisons which were sometimes used in war. He led the boys through the riverbeds, plains and forests where he ferreted about, saying nothing and noticing everything until he had found what he was after. He started with a large tree known as the quarter-mile tree – anything poisoned with its sap would collapse within a quarter mile – to the larvae of a spotty beetle that looked much like a toadstool on legs. When extracting and applying the poisons, Wildemar was very clear about never letting them onto the tips or edges of the arrow, for fear of the hunter scratching himself.

"Very dangerous. Very very dangerous," he chattered. "No antidote for any of these poisons except for the hermit rose. Some of them are slow though. Can take five days to drop your prey. The beetle larvae is the slowest, so only use it if you can't find anything else. It will give you many days hard tracking before you catch your meal."

"Won't the meat be poisoning of you?" Kian asked.

"No, no, not from eating. These poisons don't kill when swallowed. All the same, cut out the area where the arrow struck. Burn the meat. Might have broken skin on your lips or in your mouth. Not worth the chance. Dead marshals are no good."

After two months of this, Dun, with Wildemar fidgeting nearby, gathered the boys and banished them from the city for a week, allowing them no equipment but their knives. They had to prepare sensible, concealed shelters, make weapons, hunt, and feed themselves. Wildemar would find them and assess the survival skills. Dun would meet them on their return and assess the weapons.

Some of the boys grumbled and looked like they were about to protest.

Dun told them that the following year they would not be allowed knives, and that the next person who muttered would not be allowed clothes.

Aedan took to the hills like a gazelle set loose. He had a rough idea of where the others might go, and chose a different direction, setting a course where even Wildemar would struggle to find him. He laid a false trail up a dry rocky riverbed and then doubled back through a section of dense woodland, climbing from tree to tree. When he finally dropped to the ground there wasn't a footprint within half a mile. He scouted a little further and found an overhang that could be inconspicuously protected by bending and not breaking a branch from a nearby tree, so the leaves would not dry out and draw attention.

The plan worked better than he had expected. He placed a few snares with string twisted from nettles, and after eight or nine days he began to feel bloated with rabbit and quite lonely. Eventually he abandoned the exercise and wandered back to the city where Wildemar was only too happy to see him alive and gave him full marks for survival skills. It was a good thing because Dun drove a splinter deep into his hand while examining Aedan's crooked bow, a rough specimen that had been heated and bent so many times it looked like an overdone steak. Shot like one too.

It was disappointing. Aedan had held such bright hopes for the bow, cutting it from an oak branch swaying high in the air, and almost falling to his death in the process.

Dun frowned. "Did you manage to kill anything with this?" he asked.

"Almost," said Aedan, grinning slightly.

Chapter 29

"There's a room we need to explore."

Spoons lowered and five sets of eyes looked across at Aedan – the usual four and Kian's.

Over the past few weeks Aedan had been feeling as he had so often done back in the north, that it was time for his friends to share an adventure. He was still convinced that adventures were the only real forges of true friendship.

"What is it? Where is it?" asked Hadley.

"Will it get us in trouble?" Lorrimer whispered.

"It's down a corridor I discovered last night. There's another level under the training hall. The stairways are always locked but there's a collapsed section of the floor that hasn't been repaired and you can climb down –"

"Don't you sleep at night?" Vayle interrupted.

"Sometimes I get the adventuring fidgets at night, and it's been too hot to sleep lately. It's nice and cool down below. Anyway, as I was saying, there's this huge black door made of some kind of metal that looks so heavy I would have to use all my weight to open it a crack. Whatever is in there is going to be worth seeing, and, yes, of course it will get us in trouble – if we are stupid enough to get caught. Wouldn't be worth exploring otherwise."

"I'm out," said Lorrimer.

"In," said Hadley and Peashot.

Vayle and Kian looked at each other, unsure.

"How will we get in?" Vayle asked.

"Well, I know the door has to be opened sometimes 'cos I saw the scrape grooves on the floor had bits of grindings in them. Maybe they use it during the day when we are busy. But I know the cleaners work at night. They never lock themselves into a room when they are busy. If we can find the night when they are there I'm sure we'll be able to get a good look. Just need to keep quiet. They don't notice things very well."

"If they let cleaners in there, it can't be that much of a secret."

"The cleaners I've seen on the lower sections are different. I think they are more like curators or inspectors – don't know if they actually do any cleaning. I'm sure they know the biggest secrets out of everyone."

"If you are sure that it's open, I'll go," said Vayle, "but I'm not dragging myself all the way and risking a misbehaviour charge for a locked door."

"Fine. I'll check it tomorrow," said Aedan.

The following night they were all waiting up for him when he returned to the room.

"Locked," he said, throwing down a coil of rope and falling into bed.

The same thing happened the next night, and the next. Eventually the others stopped waiting up, which made the shock all the more when Aedan burst into the room, puffing.

"It's open!" he called through the darkness in a hoarse whisper, "and it doesn't look like there's anyone there!"

There were a series of yawns and confused questions from various points, and then some very strange words from a sleep-talking Lorrimer who began to spill a few dreaming thoughts over the edge of his slumber – something about third helpings of byoodifil schoew.

"Do you think we should wake him?" Peashot asked.

"He'll say no," Vayle reminded them.

"Better than having him complain that we left him out," said Aedan, shaking Lorrimer from his gourmet dreams and getting ready to deliver a customised version of his usual pre-adventure speech.

"Wha – were – haa – who?"

"Lorrimer. Wake up. The secret room's open. We're going. Vayle is off to fetch Kian. If you don't come you'll spend the rest of your life regretting it and wondering about what you might have found, and it will drive you crazy and make you wish you hadn't been such a coward, and all the girls who hear that you –"

"Alright! Alright! Just let me find my boots."

In the display room they didn't bother with the ramp or attempt the slippery statue Aedan had used earlier; instead they hoisted Lorrimer up on their shoulders and then climbed a short rope he lowered for them. After the hours they had spent in the training hall, this was a simple feat.

Aedan made sure everyone was properly awake before proceeding down the treacherous stairs. They all carried their dark lanterns unlit, except for Aedan who kept his trimmed low, so the group moved in near-blackness and in silence disrupted only by the brushing of cloth and the slapping of Lorrimer's big feet.

"Can't you put those things down more softly?" Peashot whispered.

"What things?" Clack, clack, clack …

"Your boots. You sound like you've got hammers strapped to your ankles. Why didn't you come barefoot? Aedan's barefoot."

"Aedan's mad. Have you tried –"

"Hush you two," said Aedan. "I think I see …"

The light peeping from under an entrance ahead suddenly burst out and flooded a section of the passage as the door swung open. Aedan snapped the shutter closed on his lantern and crouched against the wall as the others dropped down behind him.

Two cleaners with mops and buckets stepped into the passage. Aedan prepared to run as he watched their movements. While one of the men held the lamp, the other struggled with a key in the lock, dividing his concentration between what he was doing and saying.

"But like I says, Mik, them folks what lives out east is going to have a rough time if it's true. We got our walls and our army. What they got? Bunch o' wooden fences and hay forks. I'm telling you like I've told you before, you get her a nice job here in the city and she can stay with my sister until you've got enough to get married. Don't you be leaving her out there with these whispers of a Fenn invasion. You won't be able to turn the days back if it happens."

In the silence that followed, the lock in the door finally yielded with a rusty scrape and a click. The second cleaner handed over the broom he'd been holding, and to Aedan's relief, the men turned away and headed further down the passage while the conversation resumed.

"She already moved last year from Eymnoer. Slavers pretending to be merchants from Tullenroe hit the town, she says. Hit it bad. Now she says the further east, the better ..."

By this stage the talk was all echoes, too indistinct to follow. The cleaners unlocked another door in the distance, stepped inside and closed it behind them, dropping the passage into blackness. Aedan opened his lamp and moved off, the others following.

Clack, clack, clack ...

They hurried along, passing the door to the weapons and training halls, and continued until they reached a split.

"I've never been here," said Peashot.

The others echoed him and wanted to know how far the passages went.

"This is only the beginning," said Aedan. "I think there's more under the ground of the academy than above it."

He took the left turn. After fifty yards they reached another split and turned left again. Even in the dim light it was clear that this passage was different, older. The pale stone that had lined the walls had given way to coarse-grained reddish blocks that were roughly placed. The smooth flagstones were gone and they walked now on uneven blocks that had deep and sometimes wide fissures between them. It wasn't long before Lorrimer caught his toe and swooped to ground with a crunch of his lantern. It was a good thing it wasn't lit because oil gushed out over the blocks and soaked most of his shirt.

"Haven't you learned to lift your feet over uneven ground?" Peashot complained while helping Lorrimer up.

"I was keeping them low to be stealthy, so you would stop yakking about the noise."

"It didn't work."

"Quiet," Aedan hissed. "There are night staff in this section too."

They moved on. The air was colder here, the walls closer, and there was a forgotten smell of earth and damp and darkness. A few doors were set in the walls, deeply recessed. The wood was black with age, as if all colour had been leached from it during the long, silent years.

Hadley whistled quietly. "It's enormous down here. We must be near the edge of the academy by now."

"I don't think we're under the academy anymore," said Aedan. "I have a hunch some of these passages might lead as far as the city walls, maybe even beyond."

He stopped at a doorway on his right that turned out to be a very narrow corridor.

"Better light your lanterns now," he said.

Using a splint, they transferred his flame to the other wicks. When all but Lorrimer had a lantern, Aedan handed the tall boy his, then moved into the dark opening, asking Lorrimer to hold the light up behind him.

"Careful here," he whispered. "Watch the ground. It's collapsed in places. Keep your feet to the outside."

"Is he mad?" Vayle asked as Aedan scuttled away down the shaft.

"Took you a while to notice," Lorrimer mumbled.

Aedan stopped a few feet before an iron grille that barred the way.

"Well?" Hadley asked when he came to a stop.

Aedan leaned to the side so Hadley could see, and pointed ahead at the floor, or rather, he pointed to where the floor should have been. A black void swallowed the ground. There was nothing to step on. No way to proceed.

"But we can't –"

Aedan had braced his back against one wall and his feet against the other and started edging his way down through the hole into the darkness beneath. Hadley leaned forward as far as he dared and held out his lamp. It was twenty feet down to another tiny passage, only that the lower one had a floor. He made no comment, simply copied Aedan. Lorrimer and Vayle had a different reaction. They exchanged thoughts freely and several words drifted down, mostly colourful variants of idiotic, irresponsible and insane.

It was a while before Lorrimer, breathing hard, lamp handle clasped in his teeth and spit dribbling off his chin, touched the ground. Aedan noticed Lorrimer's oil-soaked shirt eager inches from the flame.

"How is this supposed to be fun?" Lorrimer growled.

"This way," Aedan replied, grabbing his lantern and moving off in the direction they had been going when the grille above had blocked the way.

They came to an ancient wooden door, partly eaten by time. It was not locked and Aedan pushed it open with a feeble creak. After looking left and right he whispered, "There's nobody here. Come on."

He led the way down another blocky passage, this one unexpectedly wide and high. It almost felt like stepping outdoors until the gathering lanterns provided enough light to reveal the ceiling and far wall. The paving stones showed evidence of recent heavy use – they were dirty, scraped and well-trodden rather than dusty. The boys set out again, passing a number of archways on both sides, and finally turned into a huge alcove that ended before a giant door.

Aedan had not exaggerated. The black double door was as wide and high as the passage itself. Obviously it held something important. The metal looked thick enough to scoff at battering rams. A man could pick any tool and spend a month hacking at panels like these without success. This was a door nobody could force.

And it was open, just a crack.

Aedan put his ear to the crack and listened.

"What can you hear?" Lorrimer whispered, pressing forward.

"You. What do you expect? Go breathe somewhere else."

"Oh, uh … right."

They waited.

"I think it's empty," Aedan said. "Whoever was in here must have forgotten to lock. This is even better than I'd hoped."

"Could have gone to fetch something," Vayle pointed out.

"Been gone a long time for that. I don't think anyone is coming back tonight. Here, help me with the door."

Hadley added his weight, and the two of them heaved the great door back enough to allow them in.

Their lanterns illuminated a large room whose high walls were shelved and hung with what looked like woodwork tools, but some of them were strange indeed.

"Funny place to put a carpentry workshop," Aedan said.

Vayle was inspecting the shelves. "I don't think these belong to carpenters. These are shipwright's tools."

"Shipwrights? Who builds boats underground?"

Vayle wasn't listening. He was walking to the end of the workshop, but now the others saw that it wasn't the end; there was no wall here and a lot of hollow darkness lay beyond. Following

Vayle, they passed under a great arch and, after a few paces, came to a standstill on a balcony. Surrounding them were giant swinging platforms suspended from levered beams, and wide ramps that led down, far down. As they hastily snapped open the shutters on their lanterns, greedy for more light, none could hold back the gasps.

The space was cavernous. The ceiling rose high overhead, but the floor dropped away even further, at least a hundred feet. And before them, looking as out of place as a beached whale, and far more intimidating, was a ship of such gigantic proportions that it completely dominated everything else. Even with all their lanterns open, the far end of the hull extended away into a thick, dusty gloom.

Aedan stared. He had never been to the coast and had only seen small boats on rivers and lakes. This monstrous vessel that reached almost up to the balcony was beyond anything he had imagined.

He noticed now that the assembly was not complete. The entire structure was surrounded by braces, scaffolds and supports. A large section towards the middle consisted of little more than skeletal braces, but the forward portion looked finished, and it was simply terrifying. No grand figurehead graced the prow; instead, a thirty-foot trunk-like ram tipped with black metal thrust out from the keel. He had read of such things but never seen them in their stark and vicious horror.

High above it, ballistae and catapults were fixed on the broad deck, and the bulwarks looked as solid as the battlements on a castle wall.

This was no ship. It was a fortress.

But admiration of the immense craft, and the pride he felt for his city's strength turned to confusion.

"Why do we have a dry dock in Castath, hundreds of miles from the sea?" he said. "And why build a ship underground? How would we get it out? Vayle – your father is a shipping merchant. Do you know?"

"It's not being built," said Vayle. "Look at the beams. Most are damaged, all have seen weather. The keel is shattered. This ship is a wreck that is being rebuilt."

"What for?"

"To study it, I would think. That's probably why it's here – to make sure it isn't discovered and destroyed along with all its secrets. Look at the hull – it's not like our ships at all. See the three sharp angles going from the deck to the keel instead of the gentle curve we use. Hard chined I think it's called – allows the boat to carry more weight and reach higher speeds. The ram looks hinged – clever. A punctured ship won't pull this one down even if they don't separate. And can you see the lines of portholes running along the hull. Rowers. Must have been a few hundred. Sail and oar. This thing would have been fast and it's as big as a mountain … Wait …"

Vayle put a finger to his lips as he often did when deep in thought. "I know this ship. We heard rumours of it down in Port Breklee about five years ago. I was just a child, but I remember it now. They called it a monster of the ocean. My father was convinced it never existed, but this must be it. The *Vreimdrak*, I think. Supposed to be the most devastating warship ever built. This would have been the king of the seas. Only the sea itself would have been able to sink it. Must have got caught on a lee shore."

"The rowers …" Aedan began, his voice changed. "Would they have been sailors or …"

"Slaves," said Vayle.

Aedan was quiet. His face was twitching. "What nation built this ship?"

"What nation? Who do you think? Only one nation can build ships like this. Lekrau."

Aedan pushed away from the railing and turned his back, all his admiration soured to hatred and disgust.

His lamplight fell on several racks of piled shields, spears, crossbows, javelins for the ballistae, oil-pots for catapults and much more, obviously collected from the wreck. He dropped his lamp, marched up to the weapons and snatched a spear. Then he sprinted back at the railing and flung it with all his strength. The spear shot out through the murky light, flew over the prow, and plugged into the foredeck with a sharp crack of splintering wood.

Five heads spun at him.

"If anyone finds out you did that …" Lorrimer began, but Aedan grabbed his lamp and stormed down one of the many ramps.

The great bows arched and loomed over him, dark and cruel. He snarled back, and when his feet reached the ground he began walking down the length of the hull, his solitary light casting hard shadows that stalked and weaved through the open belly of the beast.

Though he had known Lekrau commanded the seas, a few dozen men and a few flimsy river boats were all he had glimpsed of the nation. The monster that now towered over him seemed to laugh, ridiculing his insignificant anger.

He considered setting it alight.

Then he realised this would probably be in Lekrau's favour. So he walked and seethed and studied the ship. One day ... one day he would send ships like this to the bottom of the sea; one day there would be vengeance. At the stern he noticed something peculiar about the rudder mechanism – revealed by incomplete panelling. He studied it until he understood every aspect of its functioning and then filed the knowledge away in his mind.

It took him a long time to complete a circuit. When he finally made it back to the bows, the others were there. Kian and Vayle were looking at seams, Hadley was inspecting the ram while Peashot walked on top, and Lorrimer was hovering half way down to the construction floor, constantly turning his head with nervous twitches back to the gallery as if he expected to be caught at any moment.

"The stem has to be plumb because of the ram," Vayle was saying, "Raked would have been too weak. But see how it flares overhead to those bluff bows. That way they could fill the forward deck with a whole army of soldiers, catapults or whatever they wanted."

Aedan didn't recognise half the words in Vayle's explanation from either of the languages he knew, so he walked over to Hadley.

"See this, Aedan. The tip of the ram doesn't end in a point like a spear. It couldn't be any blunter. Almost looks like it was put on the wrong way. Obviously the idea was to smash planking instead of just puncturing it. Probably to make a bigger hole."

"Bronze?"

"Looks like it. No rust."

"What – is – that?" Peashot pointed and then rushed back to the ladder he had propped up against the ram – it was a good eight feet off the ground owing to the presence of a keel. He slid down and ran away from the ship to something that had been hidden in shadow. The others followed. Lorrimer remained at his sentry post.

As the other lamps arrived, the grotesque shape swelled out from the darkness. Aedan stepped back and bumped into Kian. Dark bronze teeth cast fierce shadows on the wall, and the heavy jaws looked built to crush stone pillars. It was simply colossal, made on the same daunting scale as the ship.

"What is it?" Peashot repeated, reaching out and stopping a foot short before retreating. Aedan understood why. There was something about the contraption that reminded him of an unpredictable, growling animal. It was poised to snap shut, and this metal fiend would slice through anything – wood, stone, iron, boy – it would not differentiate. Those six-inch teeth were over two inches thick at the base, but they ended in knife tips.

"It is being built like a trap," said Kian, still rubbing his nose. "See there's a thick twisty steel part by the inside."

"Can't be a trap." Hadley pointed at the length of the jaw. "It would close six feet up. Miss any animal. Miss most men's heads."

"Unless they were hanging," said Peashot. "What! Why are you looking at me like that? These people are cruel. Why wouldn't they do something bloodthirsty, like a double execution?"

"Too much trouble," said Hadley. "And it's way too powerfully built. It must have had another purpose. Maybe it was mounted against the sides of the ship and used to snap shut at other boats."

Vayle shook his head. "Don't think that would be too successful. Maybe they had a way of throwing it at another ship's mast. But that still seems clumsy."

"Whatever it is doing," said Kian, "this is being the most frightening weapon on the academy."

Everyone agreed.

They were all hovering, but nobody touched it. They made a respectful retreat and drifted back under the bows of the ship, five small points of light in a giant's cavern, insignificant as glow-worms faintly illuminating the head of the monster itself.

"Hey! Hey!" It was Lorrimer, doing his best to shout in a whisper. "I think someone's coming!"

Aedan dashed up the ramp past Lorrimer and arrived at the top just in time to see a slice of light vanish. He heard a heavy metallic clank that travelled past and then swam back at him from all angles in deep, lost echoes.

"We've been closed in!" Lorrimer cried, his whisper forgotten.

"Quick!" Aedan called, "if we don't get his attention now, we might be here for a week, without water."

It would be a death sentence.

He rushed across the balcony and into the workshop, grabbed a hammer and was about to pound on the door and give himself up to punishment and infamy when he noticed a low table beside him ... and had an idea.

"Lanterns out. Under the table, now!" he whispered as loudly as he dared. They raised no argument, and while they were puffing at wicks and scuttling out of sight, he ran to the nearest cabinet of standing shelves, braced his foot against the wall and pulled it over.

The noise was thunderous. Chisels clinked, braces rattled, anvils thumped, saws twanged, nails tinkled, and all of this was swallowed and regurgitated with a monstrous boom from the cavern beyond. Aedan dived under the table and waited.

Nothing.

A sharp pain caused him to look at his hand. With a start, he remembered his lantern. He couldn't put it out – they would need a light soon if this was to work, so he closed the shutters, hid it behind him, and hoped for the best.

He could hear Lorrimer beginning to make a soft whimpering sound.

Still nothing.

If the locks didn't turn soon he would have to start hammering.

Silence.

This was as long as he could afford to wait.

He crawled out just as an iron bolt shot loose and the great door yawned open with a whoosh.

A short, round man stepped into the workshop, a staff held up over his head. "First one of you I see I'm going to squash into a bloody pulp ..."

Aedan swallowed and ducked back under cover.

"I'm going to pluck your little ratty whiskers and swing you by your tails until the walls are painted."

There was the faintest breath of relief from several points under the table. As the man lugged his weight past them to the overturned rack, Aedan slipped from under his hiding and stalked out through the open door. The others were close on his heels and almost as quiet.

Then Lorrimer made the short dash. Clack, clack, clack ...

He was at the door when there was a shout, "Oi, what was that? Beck, that you?"

Aedan lifted the shutter on his lantern and they sprinted out into the passage, back past the archways. Aedan was counting – one, two, three, four, five, there! He swung the shutter closed when he saw the opening to the narrow corridor.

From the darkness, he looked back as the heavy curator lumbered into the passage. The man began to turn around, peering this way and that, but the boys were too far away now to be found by his lantern. Eventually, he shook his head and returned to tidy the mess and hunt rats.

The boys passed through the door and crept down the narrow passage.

"You don't expect us to climb back up, do you?" Vayle whispered.

"Well, yes," said Aedan. "There wasn't anything up there sturdy enough to tie a rope onto. But I'll lower the rope for the lanterns when I get up. Just can't take your weight."

"He wants us to climb this!" It was Lorrimer. He was not happy.

"I'm going to," said Peashot. "Always thought I could climb better than you."

"Huh? I didn't say I couldn't. Probably do it in half your time."

The climb up was a lot more difficult than the descent had been, but Aedan slid up the blocks as if he were being pushed by invisible hands. Hadley said it was lizard blood. Lorrimer said it was bare feet and he could do that too but the stone was colder than he liked.

By the time they had negotiated the delicate section where the floor was part-crumbled and where mistakes would probably result in broken legs or death, they were scratched and dusty and all steamed up from the exertion. They made the walk back in silence, stopping once to let a night guard amble sleepily round the bend ahead of them, but otherwise they were undisturbed.

Aedan reminded the others about the trigger steps on the way out, and then almost forgot them himself. He had to do a hasty double stretch at the last moment as he remembered.

When they had said goodbye to Kian, they crept back into the dorm and closed the door. It was only Hadley who felt the need to wash himself off. The others were content to dust their clothes and drop into bed.

"That," said Vayle in distant tones, "was about the most spectacular thing I've ever seen. Aedan, I'm very glad I went, and I have made up my mind that I will never go on any of your mad adventures again. Ever."

"Speak for yourself," said Peashot. "That was more fun than tenderising Master Rodwell."

Lorrimer said something incoherent, barely audible over Hadley's splashing.

"What he say?" Peashot asked.

"It was probably a complaint," said Vayle.

"Well, whatever he says, he learned how to walk quietly. Didn't make a sound on the way back."

Just then a horrible scraping noise filled the room as Lorrimer's throat or nose began to sing that most ancient song of exhausted slumber.

Aedan lay awake long into the night. The cruel shapes and vast proportions of that ship were settling in his mind. It was a destroyer of lives, of hopes, and in this it represented the entire slave trade. Even in death the ship was terrifying. He had glimpsed something of how it must feel to be under the chains of the slave-lords. Even if for only a single slave, those chains needed to be smashed. The slave-lords too.

Just before he dropped off to sleep a small part of him yawned and wished that he had set fire to the timbers.

Chapter 30

The next morning, Dun stopped them when they tried to leave the dining hall after breakfast. "To the academy gates," he said.

Skeet was waiting for them, glaring. As always, he seemed annoyed at something or other, though the sky was young and bright and the birdsong full. The boys hurried into line, falling silent as the glare passed over them.

Aedan tried not to fidget and managed to work up a look of bored unconcern. Had the curator reported the incident?

"You're going to find this a little different to the bowyers' workshop," Skeet said. "The next few days will leave your ears ringing and your fingers jangling."

"Swords!" The whispered word ran up and down the line, bringing forth twenty sets of gleaming teeth. Aedan's fears dissolved into the bright morning.

Skeet returned no eager smile. "Usually we keep this until your second year," he said. "But two weeks ago we had an update on weapons production in Greel. It seems that Fennlor is stepping up their preparations. Their smithies are opening an hour earlier and running an hour later. We cannot afford to lag behind so we have decided to keep our forges hot day and night. Though you won't be given time to fully master the art of working with steel, you need to be able to at least hammer out a basic weapon. If the Fenn begin their assault before you are old enough to be deployed on the field then you will likely find yourselves with the bowyers or the smiths."

He ran a critical, disapproving eye over them.

"The border threat has given our weapons manufacturing a much-needed kick. If you misbehave, you too will receive a kick that will send you all the way back to the academy. If you behave, you will learn how to make a sword."

The grins reappeared. Skeet rolled his eyes, signalled for them to follow and marched away.

The group wound through the streets to a section near the north wall where there were several warehouses and workshops. Outside a particularly smoky building, Skeet turned back and raised his voice over the general clangour of industry filling the area.

"We split the process into stages, beginning here – the bloomery."

He led them into a hot, smoky chamber, where despite good ventilation, the air was dry and sharp.

"Here, iron is extracted from ore by burning with charcoal. Smelting, not melting. The porous blooms that emerge are hammered to get rid of the slag, giving us pure wrought iron. Depending on where it is mined, ore can have different qualities. There are some interesting stocks reserved for special blades."

He moved across to another set of furnaces. The boys at the front had to shield their faces as they looked into the flames.

"In order to produce steel, the smelted iron is brought here where it is heated, again with charcoal, and kept at a higher temperature for a long time, sometimes for days, depending on what grade of steel is needed. This is a tricky process. Too much of the charcoal essence in the metal and the steel is brittle; not enough and it's soft as iron."

They left the bloomery and the boys jogged to keep up as Skeet marched along a sooty road towards a steady pounding din. It was not necessary for him to explain that they were approaching a smithy. He did, however, mention that it would be unwise to refer to the swordsmiths within as blacksmiths.

Again, several coal forges kept the large chamber at a sweaty heat. The room was packed. Not a bench stood empty, not a forge was cold. If Skeet's earlier words hadn't convinced the boys, one look into this room was enough to make it clear – this was a city preparing for war.

About fifty men worked at various stations – swordsmiths and their attendant strikers. Before the visitors entered, they stood in the wide doorway and Skeet shouted, "As you can see, steel weapons are not melted and moulded. Bronze weapons are, but they are weak by comparison. Steel that is moulded is far too brittle for weapons, so forges and hammers are used to draw the blades out."

He led them inside and began explaining the process, but there was a problem. What the boys heard was, "Over here is the *clang!* and if you *clang!* carefully you'll notice *clang! bang!* Can you all see it?"

He was met with twenty blank stares. "Sorry Master Skeet," Hadley said. *Clang!* "Can we see what?"

"Weren't you listening? I said this is the *clang! bang! bang!*"

More blank stares

Skeet was growing red. He turned a dangerous eye on the nearest striker, raised his voice and tried again, "The *cling! bang!* Oh for mercy's sake!" He whipped around and bellowed with such force that every hammer froze on its descent. "The next one of you mangy curs who uses his hammer while I'm talking is going to swallow it!"

The response was impressive. Hammers were cautiously laid down. Apart from the rumble from the forges, the space was filled with a respectful silence. Aedan guessed that Skeet was known here and that he held an intimidating rank.

"Now, as I said, here is where the steel is heated and hammered into the right dimensions. He pointed to a steel ingot the size of a fist. "This," he said, "is a sword hatchling, fresh from the bloomery. Depending on the price offered, it is either beaten directly into shape or subjected to processes that can include combining with other grades of steel or iron, twisting, and folding – all of which result in superior properties."

He drew his own sword and held it out.

"See the interwoven pattern on the steel that looks like the work of a thousand woodborers? This sword was a combination of four ingots that were hammered into rectangular billets, forge-welded, twisted into tight coils, flattened, folded ten times and wrapped around a softer core before being lengthened. It was a technique developed by Magnus over there, who is our chief swordsmith for good reason."

This was said for all to hear and Skeet inclined his head to the white-headed, sinewy man who bowed in acknowledgment.

"The swordsmiths are always experimenting, trying and testing new ideas. But this makes for expensive weapons. The quicker and cheaper option of hammering out a single ingot produces a useable but inferior blade that is heavily dependent on the charcoal infusion process, which if you remember, is a tricky one, often unreliable."

He moved to another bench where he used the tongs to pick up a longer piece.

"This ingot has been partially extended. If you look carefully, you'll –"

"Eeeeyooww!"

All eyes turned on Lorrimer who was furiously shaking his oversized hand and hopping over the steel block he had just flung on the ground.

"Did you think I was using the tongs to keep my fingers clean?" Skeet asked.

Lorrimer recovered himself, blushed with a heat to shame the forges, and apologised profusely. The swordsmiths and strikers were grinning at him. Skeet ignored him and carried on.

"Here, you'll see that two metals have been combined – a hard steel and a softer iron on the inside."

"Master Skeet," Vayle asked. "Why use a softer metal? Doesn't that make it weaker?"

"Fired clay is harder than wet, but which shatters when dropped? If you make a sword too rigid it will break on impact."

He moved over to where a blade had been drawn out to its full length. It was straight, double-edged, and partially fullered. He held it up and pointed first to the stumpy section at the back.

"The tang," he said, "is far more important than you would think. Get this part wrong and the handling will be horrendous. The fuller," he indicated the partly formed groove running down the middle, "reduces the overall weight without taking from the strength." He put the blade down and turned to another that was glowing in the nearest forge.

"Once the blade has reached its basic shape, it is put through several stages of heat treatment that takes two forms – annealing and tempering – differentiated by how the heated metal is cooled. Annealing is a slow cooling, making the blade softer and more flexible, while tempering ..." he drew their attention to one of the smiths who had removed a red hot blade from the forge and now submerged it in a quenching tank, producing a short, angry hiss of steam, "tempering hardens the blade, allowing for a sharp edge.

Heat treating is an art that has a big influence on the final strength."

The clanging resumed as they followed Skeet through a partial division and into an adjacent workshop. This one was just as noisy, though less percussive. Skeet made his explanations from the door.

"The grinders are the craftsmen who shape, sharpen, and eventually polish the blades so that they don't look like beaten fire-irons. The rough grinding takes place before the tempering while the steel is still soft from annealing, and the final sharpening and polishing afterwards when the edges have been hardened. So the blades and some of the swordsmiths move between these workshops. There are loyal chains of craftsmen running through the process. Each chain has its own particular methods, arrangements, and even a few secrets."

Inside were a number of men working at grinding wheels and many more at tables, scraping away with stones and files. Others polished. The boys were still feasting their eyes on the emerging blades when Skeet clapped his hands and shooed them out.

They followed a courier hefting a thickly wrapped bundle of sharp steel up a flight of stairs to the next workshop, the cutlers. Here, hilts were produced to match the size and weight of each blade. Some were plain, like the standard military arming sword of which several were to be seen at every bench. Others were of a far higher breed – mostly the swords of officers and wealthy clients.

"A poor cutler," Skeet told them, "can ruin a good blade in a number of ways, balance being the first of these. A cutler must, before anything else, be a swordsman."

As if to establish the point, one of the men at a bench nearby stood and executed a sequence of sweeping cuts and thrusts with the sword he had just completed. Satisfied, he placed it in a tray and started on another.

"The scabbard-makers produce standard scabbards for the standard-issue blades, but custom blades must take another journey. Once the scabbards are done, the blades are cleaned, oiled and ready. Right!" he said, with a note of animation. "Classes are suspended. This is where you will be for a little over a week. One day in each of the workshops, and three days making your own sword. When you are done, you will swap weapons and test their strength and handling. If you don't want to be deaf by the end of it all, stuff something in your ears."

The smiles reappeared, even bigger than before.

Aedan could see the sword he was going to make. It would be magnificent. It would be legendary, a blade by which epic battles would be won. He would call it *The Avenger*, or *The Bane of Lekrau*, and it would pass down the generations, hoarded in the vaults of kings and coveted by all ...

The glittering eyes around him revealed that he was not the only one with such ambitions. And rightly so. How difficult could a bit of hammering and grinding be?

"I'll challenge you one shift of clean-up duty," Aedan whispered to Peashot. "Best sword wins."

"Deal. You'll lose."

"You'll both lose," said Hadley. "Just you wait and see what I have in mind."

"Also me," said Kian. "I'm hating clean-up."

Soon everyone was in and the winner would have no clean-up duties for a long time.

Over the next week, they were tutored through the details of the process, and then each was given a steel ingot and a place at a forge. They were guided but not assisted in producing their own blades. When the blades cracked, which happened to more than one, they had to be forge-welded – heated and hammered together – and beaten out to length again. Every night the boys returned to the academy with grimy faces, blistered hands, dry eyes, and ringing ears.

On his second day, Aedan decided that the heat of the room would be better endured without shoes. He discovered that of all environments he had ever known, none offered nearly as many sharp objects on which to step, not to mention the showers of sparks that anointed his feet from time to time.

When he returned from the forge that evening, he approached the gate alone, barefoot, hobbling, and filthy beyond recognition. He was, of course, denied entrance, the guard thinking him a street urchin trying his luck. One of the clerks had to be summoned to verify Aedan's identity.

After his dismal failure with bows, he had chosen to heed what Skeet had said about a soft inner core. Warton too. It made for longer hours of hammering and some late nights, but they pushed on and completed their blades. For Aedan it wasn't about impressing anyone – he had a little scheme in mind, a little payback for Malik who would want to win the contest no less than the rest of them and who would certainly cheat.

Apart from Aedan and Warton, the boys all ignored advice and made their blades long, resulting in trickier labour and flimsier weapons. Nevertheless, they were proud and competitive as they hammered, ground, polished and finally hilted their creations. Each was truly awful in its own special way. But the boys were quite pleased with themselves, feeling that the art of sword-making was not as difficult as they had expected.

Skeet didn't say anything. Instead he gathered them in the enclosed marshals' courtyard and presented them with shields strapped to fir branches. They were told to swap swords so that no one held his own, and deliver ten good blows to the shields.

Aedan could see Malik and Cayde whispering. He called across all the others.

"Hey, Malik! You brave enough to swap with me?"

Everyone looked.

Malik's lips pressed tightly shut. Aedan guessed that he had been instructing Cayde to take his sword and hit as gently as possible. Aedan would do quite the opposite.

"Yep," said Peashot. "He's scared."

"Give it!" Malik snapped, taking his sword back from Cayde and making the swap with Aedan. He could not voice a warning to treat his blade gently now that everyone was watching, but the warning was in his eyes.

Aedan read it, and smiled. He was going to hit those shields as hard as his arms would allow, knowing full well that Malik would do the same.

Hadley was first, as usual. Then the others followed. The swords that did not bend shattered. When Aedan stepped up, he swung hard enough to slice through the shield, the branch and the stone underneath, but the single-ingot blade snapped clean off at the hilt on impact.

Malik, with cold fury in his eyes was next. He hacked and hammered until he was puffing. Skeet had to stop him, informing him that he was only supposed to execute ten cuts. Aedan's sword had a few nicks and the blade was bent from when Malik had purposely hit against the flat.

Aedan took it back and returned Malik's hilt – the rest of the sword having skittered away somewhere down the courtyard.

"You'll pay for this," Malik hissed.

"Nobody would pay for this," Aedan said, glancing at the stump of metal. Several boys laughed as Malik stalked away.

The testing continued. Only Warton's held its shape, though not its edge, but as all the boys had felt when trying it, the balance was so far forward it may as well have been an axe.

Then Skeet brought out a whole range of poorly made swords – from bad steel composition to misguided hilt design. He explained the flaws while demonstrating the results. They bent and broke in a number of interesting ways, and the apprentices were allowed to feel a little better.

Then Skeet drew his own sword and delivered a blinding slash, producing a deep cut in the shield and no visible damage to the blade.

"Being able to recognise a poor weapon," he said, "is as important as choosing a good one. In a sense they are the same thing. Thanks to this exercise, you should all have an intimate acquaintance with many construction defects. Now you are going to get back into the smithy during the night shift and each of you will produce at least one blade that we can add to our armoury. This time you will keep them short."

They returned to the heat and smoke and din of hammers for another week. In that time Aedan, Warton and Hadley produced not one but two serviceable weapons each, impressing the swordsmiths whose advice they had depended on.

When all the boys were done, they were allowed to mend their first blades and keep them as reminders of the need to respect the skills of a master at his craft.

Warton took the prize. Aedan came a close second – everyone had seen how heavily his sword had been punished. He didn't really mind the clean-up duty, taking pleasure in the knowledge that it would hurt Malik a hundred times more.

In spite of the unanimous vote, there was a good deal of grumbling about Warton's overfed, bloated blade. They decided to honour it with two awards – one for the strongest sword, one for the year's most interesting farming invention.

Once the rest of the blades were mended, there were dozens of mock battles to be seen in the passages at night, and one or two minor injuries. During these battles, each dorm considered itself Thirna and the rival dorms were mostly Fennlor and sometimes Lekrau.

The boys were all mightily pleased with their work, not so much because it was good, but because it was theirs. They had actually made their own swords!

It was late one night and the others had all fallen asleep when Aedan placed his on top of the bookshelf and stepped back to better appreciate the overall shape. Light from his lantern played over the uneven metal giving it that chunky look, the look of ditch water on a restless day.

But there was something else he had seen before that looked like this. He racked his brain for a moment, hoping for some terrible and daunting image, until all the little pocks and dimples from a thousand uneven hammer strikes brought an image to mind. Aedan winced. It was Harriet's oldest pot – dented with battering and hard use, and equally dull and sooty.

He pushed the image away with a shudder and decided not to dwell too much on the appearance of his new blade. This was a warrior's weapon, not some decoration for a statesman's office. What did it matter if it was a bit rugged, lacked shine, wasn't exactly straight …

He decided, after a little contemplation, not to name it. Perhaps the next one.

As he crawled into bed, he almost failed to notice the deep shudder that ran through the floor and caused the faintest slipping of dust from the walls around him. It was brief, stilled again before he gave it any attention, as if something in the earth had cleared its throat to speak and then drawn back into silence.

It was just a feather of a thought, a hint of doubt. Was there more for Castath to fear, something entirely unconnected with the plans of hostile nations? But the shudder had been too subtle and the exhaustion too great. Before he knew it, he was asleep and the thought lost.

Chapter 31

Rodwell's persistent droning bounced off Aedan's ears causing little damage. Like the rest of the boys, he had never celebrated the classes in law. But now, after the thrill of sword-making, these monotonous strings of wordy terminology held doses of boredom that were surely fatal.

Aedan turned away and let his thoughts drift out the window.

It was midmorning of a sizzling day plucked from the middle of the sun and dropped into a lingering summer. Green lawns sprawled in the golden blaze; a few students sprawled where the lawns crept under the shade of oak and plane. Birds dropped out of the sky and collapsed on leafy branches where they wheezed and panted and fell asleep; spiders ignored the flies stretched out in their webs, and all the world dreamed.

Nudged by a sleepy conscience, Aedan wrenched himself into the classroom just in time to hear Rodwell say something about eleven exclusion clauses to bad-debt penalties in merchant commerce. He uttered a tortured groan and collapsed back into blissful thoughts that fled the academy, dived into the river where they splashed around until cool, and then sat down dripping in the shade on a grassy rise. It had become one of the boys' favourite pastimes to watch from their little hill as work progressed on the grounds laid out for the much-awaited autumn festival.

The screech of chairs told Aedan that the class was over. He had survived with minimal injury and decided to apply the same technique through the rest of the day. But something long-awaited was soon to change this.

It was the beginning of Dun's evening class, and Aedan was the only one who remained where he was after the announcement. He hadn't been listening.

"Did he say we can handle them?" he asked Peashot. But Peashot was already halfway to one of the racks, reaching for a sword that was too long for him by a yard. That was all the answer Aedan needed. He snapped fully awake and headed for a line of weird leaf-bladed monstrosities.

Dun allowed the apprentices one whole class to move freely through the weapons hall where, at last, they were permitted to handle and study whatever beckoned. After the days spent making his own sword, Aedan looked through the weapons in an entirely new way, searching for weaknesses, estimating strength, and remarking on balance.

His appreciation for good blades had only grown. Around him the gleaming eyes and expressions of awe were telling. The primary fascination was, of course, with the longswords and greatswords – massive weapons that the boys pretended to lift without effort, while arms shook in their sleeves and necks were webbed with bulging veins.

Dun watched all of this with wry amusement.

The following morning, he spoke to them.

"You heard about the increased weapons production in Greel," he said. "Unfortunately it has grown worse than that. Three weeks ago one of our rangers happened on a camp of six men in the forest south of the river. The ranger was spotted and barely got away. We haven't been able to find his attackers who we suspect were Fenn scouts – skilful ones too. The thing that really concerns us is that the ranger is convinced they were trying to capture, not kill him."

Dun paused to allow the boys to reach the conclusion themselves. "It's information they were after," he said. "Now, considering the depth of inside knowledge you are given, we can no longer afford to let you out into the wilds with only hunting weapons. It's time that you learned to handle the blades you have been making. Follow me."

The boys jostled each other as Dun led them from the weapons hall into the training hall and had them sit in front of a strange new addition to the furnishings – a pig carcass. The carcass was bound in leather and steel armour, and beside it was a rack with a dozen swords. They ranged from short, stout weapons no longer than a forearm to curving single-edged blades, and finally to the towering greatsword.

"I think you can guess what we are going to do here," Dun said, "and what you will be having for lunch." He walked over to the rack. "Let's begin with edge cuts."

He drew a very short double-edged, leaf-bladed sword, hacked at the unguarded carcass, then at the leather armour and finally at the steel plate-armour. Damage was minimal. The falchion, with its heavy head and slightly curved edge was far more impressive. The standard military-issue straight-edged arming sword and the longsword, though more imposing weapons, produced less damage. A basket-hilted broadsword was no better. The curved sabre and cutlass surprised them all by slicing through the leather easily and creating an even deeper dent in the steel plate than the falchion had done.

Eager smiles showed as Dun took up the greatsword which stood almost as tall as he did. He brought it down with a shriek of wind and it gave the carcass a resounding thump, but unlike the curved blades, it was not able to slice through steel or leather.

"Now before you all sink into clouds of disappointment," Dun said, "remember that a war hammer will not pierce armour either, but it will fell an enemy. Cutting is not everything, but it is important. What have we learned from this?"

"Curved blades cut better," the boys replied.

"And thinner blades," added Vayle. "The sabre cut deeper than the falchion."

"True," said Dun, "though that also has to do with the increased blade speed of a longer weapon. Anyone know why the curved blade slices more easily?"

They thought about this for a moment before one of the boys from Warton's dorm offered a reply. "If you sit on stones that are all the same height it doesn't hurt, but if some of them are higher, it does. I think it's the same with the blade where only the high parts are pressing hard and they sink in more easily."

"That's an interesting way to describe force distribution. Another reason is that a curved blade will tend to slide over the surface and not just press as a straight sword does. A sliding blade will always cut more easily. Anyone who has worked in the kitchen will have seen this. Does everyone understand the principles?"

They did, or at least pretended to.

He moved to the other side of the rack and took up the smallest sword again. This time he stabbed. The results were even more disappointing. The shorter blades made deep punctures in both types of armour. The longer blades bent in ways that the boys had not thought possible, leaving far shallower punctures. The longsword actually bent so far that it retained its skew form and the greatsword bowed and bounced Dun away from the steel plating, revealing only a vague impression in the armour.

"Conclusions?" said Dun.

There were several responses:

"Longer blades bend."

"Shorter blades are sturdier for thrusting."

"Never underestimate short swords."

"Long swords are stupid."

Dun held up his hand. "Longer swords are not stupid," he said. "What crucial aspect have we not dealt with here?"

"Reach," said Aedan.

"Exactly. What good will your little falchion be if you can't get close enough to use it? Remember that in combat it is often the one who causes the *first* damage who wins. It is seldom necessary to cut an enemy up for firewood. A thrust to the eye or chop into the shoulder will put an end to most resistance."

He picked up the curved sabre and held it out straight. "What is the difficulty with thrusts here?"

"The point is not where you expect it to be, unless you are used to that sword," said Peashot.

"And that's a very important thing to remember. If you are watching the tip, you'll adjust naturally, but if it's dark or you're rushed, you could miss your target by a long way. When thrusting at chinks in armour or at eyes, it could render your efforts largely useless."

"Master Dun," Peashot interrupted, "is that why there are some swords back in the weapons hall that have a curved edge and a flat back with a point that looks like a sting."

"Well spotted," said Dun. He went to retrieve one of these swords and held it up. "Two protruding, curved edges would have made it too heavy at this length, so the design is a compromise. The front edge is given a curve by means of an outward bulge, but the point is dead ahead. Sickle swords also try to achieve the compromise, but as far as I'm concerned, the farmers can have them."

To end the demonstration, he took up a spear, held it at the back of the shaft, and rammed it through the steel armour and deep into the carcass where he let it rest. The wooden shaft bobbed slowly in the air.

"And the disadvantage of a spear?"

"It's only really dangerous at the tip," Hadley said. "If an enemy gets past that, it's just a stick."

Dun nodded. "Same problem if the tip gets sliced off. Now do you begin to see why there is no such thing as a supreme weapon? Respect them all for their particular strength."

The following day, the boys were presented with their first training weapons – swords, daggers, shields, spears, bows and quarterstaves. "You will begin with wooden and covered blades," Dun said. "They are shorter and lighter than full blades so that you don't develop bad habits while trying to adjust for excessive size and weight. Remember, these are only for training. From now on, during any outing that requires you to leave the safety of the Castath surrounds, you will carry sharpened steel."

Each apprentice was given two swords – one of straight wood, and one of curved iron bound in tough leather. Dun showed some of the ways they might be carried – by belt, baldric, or mounted across the back. Different applications called for different mountings and he pointed out the disadvantages to each. Both a baldric and a hip attachment could be cumbersome to movement, catching, even tripping the wearer, whereas a sword on the back was conveniently out of the way but was much more difficult to draw in an emergency and exposed an armpit that would seldom be covered by armour. Dun showed how, if this particular mounting sagged, locating and retrieving the weapon could be troublesome, and how, with a full scabbard, a long sword could only be pulled half way out before the arm was fully extended. There were modified scabbards that compensated with slits or by enclosing only part of the blade, but they created other problems.

"Generally," he said, "back mountings are recommended for short blades or very long blades that would be clumsy at the hip and could not be drawn there either."

When he had finished with scabbards, he folded his arms and put on a stern expression. "After this class, you are always to be with training sword, or quarterstaff, or bow and quiver, so that you can get comfortable with them. Even at night, some weapon is to be immediately within reach. Expect to be tested in this. Anyone who has to scratch around in the darkness to find his weapon will do circuits until morning."

It was Vayle's confidence that tripped him up. Instead of doing like the others and keeping his wooden sword under his pillow, he placed it under the bed where it wouldn't cause him discomfort.

At the wild, clanging alarm, they sprang from bed, wooden weapons clutched, while Vayle knelt in the darkness, bumped his head on the timber frame, groped around, knocked the sword deeper under the bed, and had to crawl after it on his belly. He looked quite spent when he finally stood before a sad-faced clerk who said nothing and merely pointed to the door. By morning Vayle was too tired to even hear the jibes. The training blade slept under his pillow from then on.

Dun taught the sword in a way that was far less spectacular than had been hoped. The training began with long, heavy mops. The boys were made to traverse a course of short upturned logs with the woolly-headed weapons, executing basic thrusts and cuts at each step. It was a week before their balance compensation was good enough to allow them to finish the course.

After mopping out the hall, they retired the mops and progressed to training swords. As they began working on forms and rudimentary sequences, there was no dimming of the weapons-master's obsession with balance. The number of times they heard the word "feet" was beyond counting.

"Foundations and flow," Dun called in his almost sing-song tones while he walked between them, assessing their efforts. "Feet first, then swing. Where do you want to go – where do you want to swing? Place your feet accordingly. If the blade's weight carries you and forces you to step, your footing was wrong. Lorrimer, that was awful! With your height you can't afford desperate footing. If you topple around like that, you are fighting your own clumsiness as well as your enemy, and you give him a hundred openings. Good, Hadley. There's nothing wrong with a deep step as long as you remain in control of yourself. Ha! What have we always said about moving over uneven ground, Kian? If you can't afford to look, then slide your feet. Don't just slap them down and hope for the best. Breathe, Aedan, breathe! I can see the redness of your face from here. Attack him Kian, he's too tired to oppose you. Go, go, don't let him recover!"

Kian drove forward with his encased iron sword, and sure enough, Aedan's exhaustion caused him to fold under the attack and stumble as he backed away.

Dun called them together. "A heavier weapon will naturally lead you to tighten up, especially when you are swinging hard. If you don't force yourself to breathe you will be weakened with every heartbeat. On the battlefield, it is often exhaustion that defeats rather than a lack of skill. Don't forget that." He fixed Aedan with a stare then turned to speak to the rest of them,

"From the reports we are getting, it looks as if your first real battle may take place long before your training is done. I guarantee that you will be frightened. You will find yourselves with tense muscles and shallow breathing. Fear makes you think little and swing like a mad logger. It will exhaust you rapidly, and on the battlefield, exhaustion is more dangerous than disarming. If you want to survive, you need to consciously resist these reactions."

The attention in the class after this was absolute.

Once he had covered the basics of technique, Dun devoted several classes to un-teaching the bad ideas some of them had picked up during the performances of touring adventurers, as they called themselves. They were troubadours who would tell their stories and demonstrate their skills against challengers. It was clear that some of the boys had these performances in mind the way they were hopping and spinning like dancers.

Dun asked Warton to attempt a spinning swipe. As the boy pivoted, Dun moved in and stopped Warton's arm with the wooden blade. "Never voluntarily show an opponent your back in a fight," he said. "Spins like this might help to unleash a ripping swing, and against a poor opponent they will help you look dashing, but any decent swordsman will step in and lop off your arm as it comes around.

"The same goes for these leaping heroic slashes. When one foot leaves the ground, you are unable to change direction or resist force, which is why we step quickly and deliberately. But with two feet off the ground, you have no control whatsoever until you land and steady yourself."

Again he demonstrated. Warton leapt into the air and swung down. Dun stepped in, parried the blow, and rammed with his shoulder. It threw Warton into a backward, stumbling recovery which ended when he toppled over a sand bag. The point was made.

Dun continued to lay a solid foundation of practical techniques suited to the mayhem of warfare rather than the controlled arenas of performance.

Once the basics had been grasped, other trainers were invited to build on Dun's foundation and illustrate the techniques used by the surrounding nations. Many of these trainers were senior marshals who had been posted in other lands. It was during these sessions that the boys noticed the respect shown to Dun. On several occasions, he engaged in full armoured bouts against these men, and it became clear that Dun was not a trainer because he was incapable of more. They found a new respect for the demanding master whose cheery cries shattered the silence every morning.

Dun made sure that skills were not honed in isolation and earlier practices forgotten, so every lesson ended with disarming and hand to hand challenges.

The new exercises produced many aches as the muscles in backs, shoulders and freshly calloused hands – right and left, for Dun insisted they train with both – were pushed to new levels of strength. Aedan now understood why swordsmen had fingers like owl talons.

The injuries were not plentiful, but a few concussions, cracked ribs, broken fingers and strained muscles were to be expected. Anyone who received an interesting injury became the topic for the day in Mistress Gilda's class.

Once they had gained a level of proficiency with the sword, Dun added shields, demonstrating some crafty ways of using them as weapons. He re-introduced quarterstaves and spears to the routine, progressing to more advanced techniques.

In addition, several types of bows were discussed along with a number of different methods for shooting them. The most difficult was that intended for speed, in which the archer would hold at least three and up to twelve arrows between the fingers of his string hand, and fire them in rapid succession. The technique was known as the porcupine because of the resemblance to quills. A particularly famous archer was on hand to demonstrate. The boys gaped at his rate of fire. Out in the open, he could put eight or nine arrows in the air before the first hit the ground. It was said that there were Lekran archers who could do more.

With this technique there was no reaching into a quiver for the next arrow, because they were already in his hand. Nocking only one of the arrows and pulling the string back without dropping the others was the challenge. It was a demanding method that required months of practice before anything like a success could be detected. In their cluttered, clumsy fingers, the shafts often slipped. The boys spent a lot of their time flinching and ducking as arrows edged off strings during release and whipped around their heads, while the rest of the shafts escaped to drip and drizzle at their feet. They had never seen Dun laugh with such abandon.

Peashot struggled as much as everyone else, but showed a fanatical determination. He had watched the demonstration with trembling awe, the rapid twangs of the string clearly plucking a note that resonated in his heart. The loss of the peashooter, for a time at least, was forgotten. He trained constantly, skipping classes and even practicing in his dorm, firing away against the wall until he was threatened with death and burial, in reverse order.

———

On the academic side, the language classes were proving to be the most taxing as well as the most rewarding. Learning new words and interesting expressions was the rewarding part. The rest was worse than Dun's circuits.

Orunean had the most muddled prepositions – you were *at* work, but *in* home and *on* class. Tenses were not defined by verbs, requiring constant use of adverbs of time. Then there were the idioms – and Orunean was infested with them – that crashed heedless through all rules of grammar with meanings that simply had to be memorised. Some were explainable – to buy a flecked horse meant to invest in something that was going to change, associated with the fact that grey flecks tend to diminish with time. But often the meanings were lost. Not even Giddard knew why switching gloves meant avoiding the question.

They now had two foreign languages – Orunean and Fenn. The latter was considered a priority due to the current threat. Fenn, while simpler in tenses, had come with the curse of noun genders. Peashot's frustration grew daily.

"It's to do with an old division of labour," Aedan said, explaining what Peashot had slept through in one of the classes. "It's not about things being boy or girl, it's about which gender was responsible for them. That's all that 'av' and 'el' show you."

"And no," said Liru, pre-empting the obvious retort, "you cannot just leave them all off."

Aedan resumed. "Fenn women do most of the cooking, so kitchenware is mostly female, and men look after the livestock, so the animals are mostly male. Except goats, chickens and donkeys – I'm not sure why they are different."

"So all cattle are male, even the females?"

"Unless you specify that it's a cow – in that case it's female."

"So then … females are cows! Maybe they aren't so stupid. Ouch!"

"You did not know that cows kick?" Liru said, her face betraying not even a hint of humour.

"What bothers me more," said Aedan, "is that the language has no plurals. I know you work them out by the context, but imagine the watchman: 'Help, help! The wall is being overrun by a soldier!' That might not get the right response."

"It would be better," said Liru, "than Peashot asking a father for his youngest cow's hand in marriage."

Apprentices were required to learn ten new words every day and to use the growing vocabulary in practical exercises, one of which was mealtime conversation. Those found speaking Thirnish were denied the next meal. Sitting in detached silence was also forbidden.

Of those who had never before used Orunean, Vayle was learning the fastest. As he finished his midday meal, he delivered an opinion, "*Ret ce lonti.*" Food taste pretty.

All nodded except Peashot. He wanted to voice a counter opinion, but lacked the vocabulary.

Hadley excused himself. "*Hak ver utto,*" he managed. Must go latrine.

Peashot caught the word and announced with satisfaction as he pushed his plate away, "*Ret ce utto.*"

The laughter was unfortunately enough to draw Matron Rosalie's attention and Peashot was rewarded with washing-up duty.

Another subject had been introduced. In a sense it was another language. It was known as signal spotting, and dealt with the reading and interpreting of clues from body language through to unintended messages contained in people's words. Once Giddard had covered the basics, he took the class to a judicial hearing where they silently observed the accused and took notes. On their return to the academy, Giddard asked for observations.

"Guilty!" they chimed.

"Perhaps," he said. "But that's not an observation. Which of the patterns we discussed were you able to detect?"

Hadley went first. "He gave too much irrelevant and untestable detail about when he arrived – sun, weather, carriages, his personal plans for the evening."

"That is true," said Giddard.

"And he didn't mention seeing the ruby even though it would have been obvious to anyone."

"Excellent point. So we have both aspects of an amended testimony – padding with the irrelevant, and excluding the relevant. The first could mean nothing, but the second is an attempt to appear ignorant of an opportunity. What else?"

"His smile was shaky."

"Yes, Bede, but that might be the effect of nervousness. What more about his smile?"

"Well he wasn't smiling with his eyes, only his mouth."

"Good. That is more telling. Remember how we said that a forced smile tends to leave the skin around eyes unchanged. Eyes tell the truth more than mouths. Malik?"

"I watched facial expressions when the attention was not on him. His eyes were down, he was frowning, and his fingers were never still."

"That is a good observation. Those unguarded expressions can betray a lot; in this case we strongly suspect guilt. Bear in mind, though, that they are much more reliable when we consider them against a baseline of the subject's normal behaviour. Some people just have nervous eyes or busy fingers. Who do we all know who …"

"Master Wildemar!" they replied as one.

Giddard grinned and put a finger to his lips before continuing. "So don't make final judgements using signals. None of them can send a man to prison, but they can serve to awaken suspicions and give you a warning of danger. Even in the middle of a fight."

"Master Giddard," Aedan said. "Can you give us an example?"

"Certainly. Did you notice when the prisoner wasn't looking down how his eyes kept darting to a point in the Balcony above us? Under the circumstances, it could well have indicated the presence of an ally. During a treacherous negotiation, confrontation, or even physical conflict, an ally's eyes are often sought as a kind of security. It can help you know who is backing whom. But as a more direct answer to your question, someone sneaking up behind you is often betrayed by his ally's eyes in front of you. I must warn you, though, not to be gullible. There are some who will fake this darting of eyes to turn you around. Move so as to cover both possibilities."

"Is it something we should be able to fake?"

"Absolutely. Even to the point of tossing a dagger to your non-existent partner – that would turn almost anyone around. In tournaments and challenges of honour it would be considered poor form, but when the fate of your nation is at stake, you need to make use of any means possible, and I guarantee that the field will be even."

The autumn trials were approaching when they would be examined in all subjects, but there was something far more immediate, and far more compelling, something that was spreading a feverish excitement through the whole city – the countdown to the autumn festival had ended.

In spite of deep worries about the location, for the festival grounds were outside the city walls, the prince made it clear that safety would be guaranteed. Patrols would be tripled and soldiers would be posted in a wide circle around the area. The heralds delivered Burkhart's assurances: There was no imminent danger and the celebrations would be better than ever. Aedan knew Burkhart was lying on the first count, but the glimpses he had stolen of the grounds suggested that the second part was true.

On the eve of the festival, as twilight gathered and called the birds to roost and the crickets to song, the little group of friends sat on top of the rise and surveyed the bright expanse beneath them. Green fields were ringed by stalls festooned with colourful streamers and country bunting. Labourers and stall-owners finished up their preparations and drifted to fires where music and laughter and the smell of food rose together in irresistible harmony to sweeten the breeze.

"This," said Aedan, taking a deep breath, "is going to be a festival to remember!"

Chapter 32

"Hurry *up*! How long does it take you louts to get ready?"

Peashot was hovering outside the room, alternately plucking his bow, springing in the air, and pounding the door.

For once, Hadley was not out front. He was fussing with his hair before a brass mirror – something he had taken up whenever there was a possibility of meeting the girls. But whatever air of class he contributed to the group was offset by Aedan and Peashot who invariably appeared in rumpled clothes and broom-bristle hair. Eventually everyone was ready and they rushed down the corridor and surged out of the academy.

The weeks of preparation had come to an end. Town bells rang and trumpets blared. Children ran through the streets selling ribbons – blue, green, red and white. All but the poorest and surliest bought. Each colour represented a team in which were storytellers, bards, dancers, cooks, athletes and men-at-arms. The competitions were friendly – or were intended to be – and at the closing celebration, always held on the central field, the winning team would dine with the prince. It was even whispered that the princess would be there this year.

Since throwing Warton onto his back in the class scuffle, Kian had found his dorm companions less than inviting company, so he joined Aedan's group.

Dun had not set aside the rule about bearing arms at all times, so they had each chosen what they were most comfortable with. Aedan and Lorrimer swirled quarterstaves. Hadley and Vayle carried the iron swords – but neither was entirely confident with the mounting. Hadley used the baldric, so his was swinging about his knees and getting tangled in the legs of those who bustled alongside, while Vayle's was strapped loosely and comfortably on his back where it could be easily drawn by almost anyone but him. Kian and Peashot had small bows slung over their backs and soft quivers of blunted arrows. Peashot also had a sling stuffed up his sleeve. Aedan had no doubt it would be put to use before the day was up.

They did feel more than a little foolish as they moved through the crowd with their painfully visible training weapons. If anything, it made them seem smaller and younger.

After falling in with the mass of people that squeezed into a tight plug at the gate and hurried away on the other side, they broke free and sprinted to the festival grounds, ducking and swerving between slower groups.

Tents, tables and stands lined grassy walkways, and in the centre of it all was the main field where the year's most spectacular and unforgettable events would take place. Several smaller arenas and stages were scattered about where single combatants would wear each other down to the delight of spectators – both the rowdy and the swooning variety – and bards and minstrels would hold audiences in their spells and draw tears and laughter and hopefully no vegetables.

The boys wandered between the stalls and the growing throngs of people, but as they had little money and at least two meals to purchase, theirs was the lot of admiring and wishing and moving on.

The main event, the feat of arms, was what they and most others were there for. But that would only take place much later, so they ambled around behind the tents, found a discarded barrel of spoiled apples and began their own feat of arms.

Soon another group of boys spotted the fun. Rules were set, teams chosen, and before long there was a small war of running boys, exploding apples, and a fine haze that smelled vaguely of cider. The game had reached a furious intensity when one of the festival officials detected juvenile fun and put a stop to it. Nobody ever told who crowned the man's receding head with a particularly ripe apple.

After that they scattered, but Aedan, his blood stirred, was on the lookout. The original six of them sat down on a grassy bank that gave a fine view of the tents beneath. All but Aedan and

Hadley sprawled out to bask in the sun and grin at the memory of the official's slimy hat.

After a while Aedan broke the spell. "That could be something," he said. "Look down there. See that bloke who's trying to call the girl behind the tent?"

They all sat up to witness the little drama unfolding. A young man with floppy hair, wilting posture and clutching hands was stealing glances around the edge of a stall and beckoning a younger woman. His movements, Aedan thought, were as twitchy as one of those pygmy antelope's.

The reason for the twitchiness soon became apparent. The girl's brawny father looked protective and threatening even from this distance. He was busy setting up the shelves inside his tent, and his daughter was torn between her duty and her heart. Soon, though, the father was obliged to make a trip to collect something, and as soon as he was out of sight, the girl was moving around the tent.

The boys were moving too.

Hadley was ahead, leading them in an inconspicuous flanking path to the front of the tent. The girl and her timorous young man were behind the rear wall, the morning sun betraying them with clear-cast shadows on the taut fabric.

"Count of three," Hadley mouthed. "One, two ..."

On three, all six boys wrenched the cloth up and shouted at the tops of their voices.

The tender embrace came to a sudden end. The young man shrieked and flung the girl from him as he made good his escape. He fled into the side of a wagon with a sharp "Oof!" and a forward flop of his plumed hair. The hair got in his eyes but he resumed his flight nonetheless, swerving and tottering until he had his vision back.

Peashot's laughter was so overpowering that he dropped to the ground hugging his belly as the spasms shook him. The others were equally helpless. The girl, however, showed herself to be far from helpless when she snatched up a broom and proceeded to wallop them from the tent.

"You little pile of blatherswabs! Snogsbrollies! Grudderbungs!"

At this point the young man, realising what had happened, made a dashing and heroic return. But now the girl wanted nothing to do with a man who had tossed her aside in his fright.

Accordingly, she applied the broom to his twitching frame. The boys roared with laughter and that drew the attention back to them. They stumbled away, clutching their sides while trying to dodge the yelling assailant. By the time they reached the top of their grassy bank, they were utterly drained, and dropped down with gasps of contentment. Little ripples of chuckling continued to wash over them.

"Can you imagine what he would have done if it had been at night, and lonely?" said Peashot. "He would have squeezed down a mole tunnel to escape."

"Or climbed a moonbeam," said Lorrimer.

"Where'd you get that? You haven't been reading poetry, have you?"

"Maybe."

"Ugh."

"Anybody know what a snogsbrollie is?" Aedan asked. "Is that one of your southern words?"

"Not southern," said Hadley. "I would know if it was from here. I think she's from out west. She had a whole collection of strange words. Vayle, don't you know?"

"Those weren't the kinds of words I tried to learn, but I think a snogsbrollie is what ends up on your handkerchief when you have a bad cold."

Aedan laughed. "Good thing she was looking at Hadley when she said it."

"Well a grudderbung is worse, and she definitely aimed that one at you."

"It was worth it."

They spent a good while longer congratulating themselves on their little success.

Hadley was the first to recover his thoughtful composure and he sat up to survey the grounds. "Hey, that's the bossy official who chased us away. What's he doing now?"

The others looked up to see the official shaking his head and pointing an old couple away from their prime location on the main walkway. They had obviously arrived early and set up their little table in a good spot, but now they were being chased off and directed to a gap in the last tier of food stalls. The old man was waving his arms in frustration and the woman's face was in her hands. None of it moved the official who thrust his chin forward in what was clearly a threatening glare as he pointed.

Another group was standing nearby with a cart full of tables, pots, and tent materials. As the old couple began to relocate, the official drifted across to the larger group. The movement was subtle, almost imperceptible, but Aedan spotted the purse change hands.

"It was a bribe!" he said. "They just bribed that pig-headed official to chase away the ones that got there first."

"What's a bribe?" asked Kian.

"When you give money to someone to make them do something wrong."

"Oh. We are calling it taking of the coin for conscience. But aren't officials meant to be stopping of this?"

"S'posed to."

Aedan was watching the old couple as they struggled to drag their table over to the indicated space. His face was going red and it had nothing to do with the sun.

Something snapped in him and he leapt to his feet and ran down the bank. When he reached the scene, he asked the couple if he could help with the carrying. Before they had finished expressing their gratitude, the other boys had gathered around. Between them they carried the two heavy pots and several crates of ingredients. The old lady was trying to smile but kept hiding her face. Before they were done, names had been exchanged and the couple had introduced themselves as Coren and Enna.

"You are very kind," Coren said when they had finished transporting the goods. "Not many youngsters take the initiative to help us more … uh … wise and mature ones," he said with a wink to his wife.

She attempted a frail smile but turned away and this time was unable to conceal the waterworks. It was clear that there was more on her mind than a change in location.

Coren explained. "We got to that spot early because we need to sell a lot of stew if we are to keep our little cottage. This was our last chance. We have very wealthy in-laws, but they would sooner throw money down a well than give it to us. They see poverty as a disease only made worse by charity." He looked around. "From back here we might sell half a pot a day – nobody will notice our table among all these tents. We need to sell at least two pots a day or we'll be without a roof by the end of the month."

"The official was bribed," Aedan said.

"I expected so, but there's nothing we can do now. Fighting with the officials will only get us thrown out. Still, we are very grateful for your help."

Aedan stepped back, taking in the single table dwarfed by the surrounding tents and banners. A thoughtful look crept over him.

"Kian," he said. "Your father here today?"

"Of course. He is doing building on tents and stands all over. There is lots of fixing work wanting for carpenters here."

"Any chance you could borrow a hammer and maybe a saw?"

"Let me ask. I'll be back in a flush."

"Flash," said Vayle.

"Oh, thanks." Kian sped away as Aedan paced and cradled his chin. He wasn't sure if the chin-cradling helped him think, but he had often seen William doing it when trying to solve some problem, and it had always looked so grand.

"Got an idea, Aedan?" asked Hadley.

Aedan emerged from his thoughts. "Remember those scraps of material around the back where we had the apple war earlier?"

The others nodded.

"I'm sure I remember some broken crates, leftover poles and discarded rope too. If Kian finds a hammer, we can pull nails and rework the crates into a big table. If we get a saw, we can cut the poles to the right lengths and put up a frame for the cloth. Maybe we can get it bigger than the other tents here."

"How about a banner?" said Lorrimer. "I might be able to get some paint from my uncle. He hates bribes. If I tell him the story he might even paint a sign properly."

"Boys, you are very thoughtful," said Enna, who had been listening, "but I can't ask you to spend your whole day working for us. We can't pay you, you know that."

"But we can pay *you*," said Hadley. "We've all been given enough for two meals, and if you can promise us two full portions at four copper huddies each, then we'll be smiling."

Enna looked like she didn't know what to say. Coren answered. "You won't take the meals without paying will you?"

"No, sir."

"Then all I can do is assure you that these will be the best four-huddy meals of your life." He smiled at Enna who blushed at the compliment.

"Settled," said Hadley with deep gravity, as if he had just struck a trade agreement that would alter the fate of nations.

After a little while Kian skidded around the corner and almost had an accident with the saw and hammer.

"Let's go," said Aedan. "I've got a couple more ideas to make this the best fun of the day yet."

"Now that ... that is rancid!" Vayle choked, staggering away as Aedan tipped the barrel. A thick ooze of semi-liquid potatoes crawled onto the ground and lay bubbling in the sun, killing grass and poisoning the air.

"It's perfect!" said Peashot, in unfeigned admiration of the plan. "This is definitely going to be the best part of the day!"

Aedan grinned. He was looking forward to it too, but carpentry was first on the list, and the less he had to do with it, the better for all. He could build traps and slings and such, but had never got the knack for what needed to be done now. His forts had always been better at falling down than standing up, and he'd never really had enough of an interest to work out why. Kian, however, was right at home with wood and tools. After making a quick inventory of what was available, he began allotting tasks.

Aedan and Peashot cut the cloth into sections that Kian measured off; Lorrimer joined the numerous scraps of rope to make useful lengths; Hadley knocked the crates apart, preserving the nails; and Kian and Vayle cut and spliced poles until they had enough for a large frame. When all the materials were ready, they carried them to the back-row stand where Coren and Enna were setting up pots and ingredients on their little table.

The boys drew a fair amount of attention with their burdens, and even more when they began to hammer and hoist. Kian showed himself to be something of a young master as he managed his team. All his quiet reserve was forgotten; even Hadley jumped at the lash of his tongue.

The frame went up. It towered over the neighbouring stalls. Ropes were used to secure it in place with stakes cut from branches. Thinner twines were used to haul cloth over the frame and secure it in place, and two poles that stood out front had cords threaded over their tops so that a banner could be hoisted. After deciding what the banner should say, Lorrimer ran off with the cloth to beg his uncle's help.

Kian and Hadley arranged the planks that had been salvaged from the crates. They nailed together a huge table that ran the length of the stall, and two long flanking benches. Kian examined

the tarnished wood with a critical eye and a
needed a cloth covering, so Aedan and Peas
scrounge for more. When they came back wit
stretched and secured it, wrapping even the su|
result looked impressively clean and neat.

Lorrimer returned an hour later with a b
dazzling blue. Using the cords, they hoisted the sign to the top of
the posts and stood back to admire the result. *Ennas Ecselent
Stews* flapped grandly over the large tent.

Aedan frowned. It didn't look quite right. He remembered that
Lorrimer had been illiterate, and wondered how much this uncle
knew about the letters he had painted. As he looked around he
spotted a few amused smiles, but nobody said anything so he let it
go.

The building had taken until early afternoon, and now a deep
lull of contentment settled on them as they admired their work.

"Kian, I am impressed," said Aedan. "This is a fine stall.
Makes all the others around look almost shoddy."

Kian beamed.

Enna hugged them and Coren gripped their forearms and gave
them each a large hollowed barley loaf filled to the brim with
stew.

The loaves had been freshly baked a few stalls away and the
aroma of the bread was compelling, but it was insipid against
Enna's stew. The vapours drifting out of her large copper pot were
nothing short of entrancing. Mutton, sweet potato, onions, celery,
mushrooms, rosemary, thyme, pinches of this and that, and
something secret in a bronze gourd that never left her side had
blended into a meal that defied description.

The boys had been quick to hand over their coins – despite
Coren's protests – so they could begin filling their mouths. Even
Peashot was unable to speak until the last crumb was gone and he
sat back to lick his fingers with a look of complete satisfaction.

"That was the best meal I've ever had!" he said, and for once
Lorrimer was deprived of leftovers.

The rest agreed and showered the old lady with compliments.

When everyone was done, Aedan suggested that Enna make
the second pot of stew. "I think it will sell," he told her with an
enigmatic grin as he led the way to the next objective in the plan.

It took a while to round up the boys from the apple war, but
when they had found enough of them, they explained what had

...ed, what they had done, and what they planned. The boys ...ed their teeth at the outrage, stared with fascination at the new ...anner which could be seen from a good distance, and shrieked with laughter at the plan.

Aedan led them to the fetid potatoes and the new boys were not disappointed with the force of the aroma. Aedan and Hadley agreed that it would not be wise for them – the builders of Enna's tent – to hang around while this particular operation was in progress, so they drifted off to a tiered grandstand from where they could watch.

Two boys went to the back of the intruding tent that now stood in Enna's original spot. They hoisted the flap and made enough noise to draw the furious attentions of the manager and all three cooks, while four boys leaned in the front and dumped little smelly handfuls into the pots.

"They did that perfectly," said Peashot with a hint of disappointment, no doubt, at being excluded.

The results were not immediate, but they were impressive. Cooks started arguing and pointing as they wrinkled their noses. The manager raised his voice over theirs and restored order as a customer arrived and seated himself at the table. He only took one bite.

He didn't swallow.

The manager should have given the man his money back because the shouting that ensued carried well over the showground and warned off a number of would-be patrons. The front row position now worked against the stall and many of the hungry drifted away from the yells of "rotten" and "poison" and several other deeply felt expressions, to the bright blue sign.

Over the course of the afternoon, parents were begged to take boys to the stall that had food "better than golden honey cakes", as Peashot had put it; labourers came to inspect the work of the young marshal apprentices who had used their tools and paint, and here they encountered trails of persuasive vapours and found themselves instantly hungry; and curious strollers altered course to see who Enna was and found a busy table and satisfied expressions. So for the remainder of the day there was a queue outside the stall. Coren had to make more than one trip to buy additional ingredients with the money that was flowing in.

The boys, after promising to return later, decided to explore the rest of the fairgrounds. As they moved off, Aedan stopped and pointed.

"Who's that?" he asked.

Down the line of tents, partly hidden by a stack of barrels, stood a tall man wearing a low grey hat that concealed his face.

Nobody could identify him before he slipped behind a tent.

"I'm sure I saw him before," Aedan said. "Almost looked like he was watching us."

The others weren't deeply interested. There were much more compelling things on their minds.

But the man's behaviour worried Aedan. What possible reason would anyone have for watching them from the shadows? The absence of an obvious answer bothered him more than a suspicion even of robbery. Could the stranger be a Fenn spy? But that was hardly possible considering the large number of patrolling soldiers.

He turned it over in his mind for a while and decided, in spite of the plentiful distractions calling for his attention, to remain alert.

Chapter 33

Their earlier wanderings had covered just a portion of the grounds. They now took themselves on an exploration of the lanes, arenas, tents and stands on the far side. From spices to farming tools, brass and clay trinkets to porcelain statuettes, magical charms to weapons – where festival security officials presided in number – it seemed that anything that money could buy was on display.

There was far more than the city's usual variety, for travelling merchants were even more plentiful than the local ones. They brought with them strange articles that wealthy landowners and nobles found irresistible – partly because they were foreign, but mostly because they were expensive and therefore essential trophies, however useless they might otherwise be.

Aedan overheard a richly dressed woman being told that the speckled stone in her hand was worth three silver chims. That was enough to buy a good wheelbarrow. For a stone? He wondered if the merchant would fill a bag with chunks of dolerite along the road and sell the grey rocks for the same price again in the region where he'd found the speckled ones. The merchant's wares had no hold on the boys and they moved along.

There was a gloomy booth across the lane attended by a man in midnight-amethyst robes adorned with the strangest symbols. Here were all manner of magical garments, charms, weapons, and potions in little glass vials of every colour imaginable. There were potions to make people smarter, stronger, younger, healthier, more attractive, shorter or taller. Peashot and Lorrimer remained long at the shelf, staring at the last two bottles.

"Does the magic work?" Lorrimer asked the wizard-storekeeper.

Before he could reply, Hadley barged in. "Of course it works. But all the potions do the same magic – they make money disappear. Come on, you woolheads." He gave them a shove, ignoring the wrath building on the wizard's brow, and they progressed through to a livelier part of the grounds.

The next stall almost coaxed everyone's dinner money from them. Here, all things honey were on delectable display. It wasn't just the cakes. A whole range of delights winked at them from the table – honey brittle in the shapes of horseshoes, keys and spoons; honey frosted over plums and apples; honey-and-oatmeal biscuits; and blends of honey with cream and crushed nuts served in little water bowls.

The smoke of grilled sausages drifted from another quarter and reminded the boys that they would still need to buy supper. They wrenched themselves away, casting longing looks behind them, and pushed on.

All except Lorrimer.

He tried bravely, but after a dozen steps, came to a stop with a broken whimpering sound. Then he turned and rushed back to the honey store where he flung down his remaining coins and scooped up a pile of sweet and gluey things that he carried away in hands, pockets and mouth.

"How can you be that hungry?" Peashot asked. "We just ate."

Lorrimer tried to reply, but nobody could understand the sticky sounds. After two attempts he gave up and resigned himself to a quiet ecstasy of chewing.

Besides merchants, the festival's incoming tide had brought a flood of minstrels, actors, raconteurs, magicians and acrobats. The boys found them now as they entered a broad grassy walkway between large tents. On either side were stages where various actors performed. Some were roving troupes with large wagons that served as home, change rooms, and stage. A few cloth screens had been put up to keep bystanders from seeing the performances from the lane, and three copper huddies was the standard entry charge. Aedan noticed that there were officials keeping watch on all the players and raconteurs.

It was one thing for people to whisper to each other of signs in the sky, of dark times, of the approach of fearful things from the eastern mountains – and Aedan regularly heard snatches of such talk from passing groups – but it had become known recently that anyone who spoke those ideas from a platform was quickly and forcefully silenced. Soldiers waited nearby, and they would be ready with gags and chains.

"Politics," Vayle said, when Aedan remarked on it. "Remember how careful the prince was about getting only one explanation of the storm to the heralds? I think that storm and the rumours of terrible things stirring in DinEilan concern him more than he'll admit. We know he's petrified of what fear can do if it spreads in the people. He likes to keep a very tight lid on ideas he doesn't want."

"And I wish you'd keep a lid on your talk about that meeting," Aedan replied.

"What are you being saying about a meeting?" Kian asked.

"Nothing!" the other five replied in unison.

Strains of various kinds of singing and music grew in the air as they entered Song Lane. Their group began to stretch out. Peashot was growing bored and restless. He pushed ahead to the beckoning arena, while Aedan hung back, walking slower and slower as the strands of melody and story-songs began to catch in his chest and tug in ways that were sweetness and ache at the same time. It was when he reached a large green tent that he could go no further. He stopped before the sign that read, *The Lilt and Lore of Silrin.*

"Aedan, hurry up!" Peashot yelled back. "This is the most boring part of the fair. The games are up ahead."

Aedan looked up with unfocussed eyes, as if he had just been pulled from an afternoon nap. "I think I'm going to go in here for a bit."

"But it's going to cost you your supper money," Peashot said, returning to talk a bit of sense into his deluded friend.

"I know. I still want to."

"But this stuff is as boring as law class, and anyway, why do you care about Silrin – it's some wild part of northern Thirna where the people are a bunch of – Oi!"

Hadley grinned at Peashot, ready to cuff him again. "That's where Aedan's from, cabbage-head."

Peashot's eyes cooled. "Oh, yes. Something misty?"

"Mistyvales," Aedan said. "Look, why don't you all carry on. I'll find you in the stands later."

They agreed and hurried away together like a raft freed from a dragging anchor, while Aedan parted with three of his remaining four coins and went into the tent.

He found a seat on one of the benches just as a thickset, middle-aged man climbed onto the stage alongside a woman, presumably his wife, who beamed red and round as a summer cherry. Three sons and a daughter sat on the platform holding various instruments. Among the flutes, fiddles, drums and shakers, Aedan spotted an eilo – four fretted strings over a lyre-like body. He hadn't seen one of those since leaving his home. About a dozen listeners had seated themselves, and began to quieten down as the man coughed for silence.

Without any introduction, he nodded to his wife who began to pick on the eilo. The tones were haunting with a depth that struck Aedan before he had a chance to steel himself. To some listeners, the sound may have been only pleasing or alluring; to Aedan, it was as if the secrets of his beloved home had been slipped into the notes and coaxed into the air.

The children took up their parts with a sensitivity that was no less astonishing. A few in the audience released little gasps of appreciation at the simple yet delicately woven lines of melody and harmony. But the audience fell into a complete hush when the father began to speak in his untamed accent. Aedan smiled as he recognised the northern rillom – a story with a frail strand of wispy poetic rhythm and occasionally rhyme that emerged and broke and re-formed as it pleased. He closed his eyes and listened.

"It was a black and disturbed night high upon the inland hills where the summer days are patient but the winter snows lie deep. A pup too young to know its way now slipped the watchful eye and lost itself chasing shadows upon the moor. Without lamp or coat, his young mistress dashed out in frantic search, but in her haste she missed the way and became lost herself.

"A girl alone in those frozen woods, long she cannot last, and soon she saw her folly plain and knew her fate was come. But then a great rugged shape grew from the darkness and she found herself before the gaze of a wild forest bear. Trembling she stood and wept in her arms, waiting for the teeth and claws to gouge and tear, while the beast looked down, hesitating now. At last it moved, but not to devour. It drew her near, curled upon the ground and warmed the child against the wind and the storm-filled night.

"When morning came they walked to the town, and the people came to see. But as she drew near, leaning on the bear, they began to shout, "Witch! Wood-spirit! Ghost of our daughter!" With clubs and arrows they chased girl and bear from their home, and from hers.

"One day, when a full three years had passed, a townsman found a bear cub in the forest deep. Home he bore the starved young whelp unable to run it was so weak. The townsfolk gathered around to marvel at the soft fur and tender eyes. Then they all fell quiet as a young woman stood among them with tattered garments and soiled hair. As they stepped away she pointed at the cub, and with trembling voice she cried, 'Now do you not see? The compassion you feel for your enemy's child once moved her heart for me. The only witching I ever knew, was that which this cub has done to you.'"

While listening, Aedan had felt as though he were among his spellbound friends in the Mistyvales town hall where they had first heard the story from a travelling raconteur. Their faces appeared again – Thomas horrified, Dara indignant, and the soft hazel eyes beside him had looked … sad.

The musically blanketed tale now rose into a song so moving that Aedan had to drop his head and hide the feelings coursing through him. There was no one here that knew him, so he allowed himself to feel and remember much of what he had locked away.

As the songs continued to flow, old adventures played out in his thoughts, and for a little while he lived again in the Mistyvales and spoke with old friends now lost. It caused him to wonder about his father – and hope.

When the music was over and crowd had applauded and begun to move, Aedan lingered until the room was quiet. The bench moved as someone sat beside him. He took his head out from his hands and saw the cherry-cheeked lady smiling by his side.

"You are northern, aren't you?" she asked.

"Yes Ma'am. The Mistyvales," Aedan said, though his accent said it for him. "Thank you for giving me a breath of the north again."

She smiled. "We are Bregan and Velrie. Wherever you find us, you will also find welcome at the door of our wagon."

Aedan was worried he would be drawn into a long discussion, but she only planted a kiss on his head and left him to his thoughts as the family slipped out the back to rest before the next performance. When Aedan emerged from the tent, he felt refreshed. Though old aches and losses had been uncovered, they had reminded him why he carried a staff strapped to his back.

He took a quiet stroll to gather himself before searching for his friends. On his way, he stopped to watch groups of men competing to catch and pen pigs – one of which bit a man's foot and caused a terrible commotion. There were children playing foxes and hounds – a more interesting game of catch where two foxes could take on a hound. A robed priest stood before a large silver idol of Urmullas, the deity of fortune, and announced that the storm was a portent of coming prosperity – he covered this with a reluctance that was explained when Aedan glimpsed soldiers idling nearby. But the priest became far more animated when he explained how *personal* prosperity could be assured only by making an offering to this deity whose offering box stood at his elbow.

A riddler was challenging a small group, "I have a dozen arms to each of yours, a hundred spears for each arm and a ..."

"Thorn tree," Aedan called, then ducked and ran when he saw the look on the riddler's face. He'd heard that one from a riddler in the north.

Peashot spotted him from a long way off, and the group reassembled.

There was nothing happening in the arena while it was being cleared of acrobatics equipment in preparation for the feat of arms – the central event of the afternoon. They decided to take a walk down a noisy lane, and soon they were weaving their way between throngs of idlers. A small boy ran past and bumped into Hadley. Without a word, Peashot flew off in pursuit. When the others caught up, Peashot had the smaller boy on the ground and was prying something from his hand.

"Here you go," he said to Hadley, tossing him his purse. "Hold onto it better next time." Peashot stood and the little thief slipped away between the people like a skink.

"How did you know?" Hadley asked.

"Just knew," said Peashot.

"You have a good eye for pickpockets."

Peashot didn't reply.

At the end of the lane, they came across an enormous tent where men, woman and children whirled in folk dances and where Lorrimer was spotted by a group of girls from the academy. The boys tried to duck away, but the girls matched them for speed and caught them easily in the congested lane. Liru flew up, her raven hair streaming behind her, eyes filled with laughter.

"Oh you poor young men," she teased. "What grave danger is this at your heels that you run so?"

They shuffled and looked at the ground.

"Partners are always scarce for us girls. Would you really be such beasts that you would make us struggle on our own? Lorrimer, I see you slinking away. There is a very pretty third-year student with us who has been complaining constantly about short partners, and I understand that you want to learn to dance?" She winked.

Lorrimer darted a look at Aedan who made no effort to hide the grin.

Liru was finished talking. She snatched Aedan's hand in a grip that invited no debate and led him back to the tent. The other girls giggled and did likewise with the rest of the boys – all except Peashot who had somehow disappeared.

Aedan found it a lot more enjoyable than he had expected, especially when Lorrimer introduced a comic aspect by attempting more challenging steps – to the alarm of his neighbours. He persevered with a determined set of jaw that reminded the boys all too clearly of Princess Allisian's parting words.

Aedan had heard some of these reels in the Mistyvales. One in particular caught his ear. It was a harvesters' song that all knew and sang as they danced.

Ring out
Bells of the town
And sing out
Dells and the downs
For heavy are the sheaf and tun
Full with a summer's sun

Bursting
Are barrels and the workers
Thirsting
(But none for the shirkers)
Rest for the labour's done
And ease from the winter won

After they had completed several rounds, they were breathing hard and laughing at the numerous missteps and near-collisions. Then a blast of trumpets echoed across the grounds. Crowds came to a standstill as dances and conversations stopped.

"Feat of arms!" they cried, and began streaming from all parts of the festival towards the huge stands surrounding the main arena.

Hadley led the now-larger group across the lane, under the stands and through a little gap between supports that he had found earlier, thereby avoiding the crush of people squeezing into the designated entrances. Following Hadley's lead, they climbed up between the seating boards to the top of the stand where they were able to fit all ten of them along a bench. Peashot was waiting, clearly trying not to look like he had missed out.

The stands filled up. Almost everyone wore streamers of one of the four colours.

"Why don't you have colours?" It was Delwyn, the tall, blonde girl who had danced with Lorrimer. "Here," she said, and handed out green strips of cloth which they tied around their heads.

"So we're all green team?" asked Hadley.

"All except Liru," she said.

Liru gasped, pulled the red ribbon from her head and stared at it with exaggerated horror, then tossed it away, snatched a green one from Delwyn and bound it in place with such an air of mock relief that everyone laughed. Aedan marvelled at how confident she had grown.

"I love watching from high up like this," she said.

"Me too," said Peashot. "It's like walking across the bridge over Regent Street where you can see the whole city market underneath you, and there are lots of nice piles of goat and horse dung that … some *other* children drop on those ratty, bribe-collecting hygiene inspectors that the whole city hates."

Liru chuckled. "I have been doing that for years."

"So you're one of us! I've never been able to hit the chief inspector though. He's really been –"

"I meant watching from the bridge."

Peashot's face drained. "Uh, yes, I meant that too. What I was trying to say was that I couldn't get a good view of him. Sometimes when I use 'hit' like that I actually mean 'see'."

The silence was rigid. Aedan squirmed for Peashot.

Liru turned back after a while. "I got him once," she said and grinned, jabbing Peashot in the ribs.

Aedan laughed. "I warned you about her sense of humour," he said.

The stands filled up around the huge arena as slanting rays of the afternoon sun cast spectators' shadows halfway across the field. Another brassy peal of trumpets brought the excited crowd to a gradual hush. Through a large speaker-horn, a golden-robed official announced the rules, as well as the winnings. Princess Allisian would indeed partner the winning knight at the feast. Aedan glanced over at Lorrimer – the tall boy did not cheer.

Another blast of trumpets, and the gates opened. Four teams of fully armed knights strode with crashing steps onto the field. There was no official rank of knight in Castath. It was an honorary title given to competitors who were chosen from among soldiers and citizens.

At a gesture from the announcer, they saluted the royal tier, then took up their positions at the four quarters of the field where four flags stood – blue, green, red and white. Knights could engage in any manner they chose. The winning team was the one whose flag was the last standing, the winning knight the one who showed the greatest courage.

Allisian herself, dazzling in a silken gown, dropped the gold ribbon. It had begun.

The white team was the first to sally out. Four of their ten knights began stamping towards the red flag, raising swords, maces and flails – all blunted, but all still deadly. The green team saw the weakened white base and sent six of their knights to take it. But as the white team approached the full company of reds, they swerved aside and charged the now-weakened green base.

A ruse.

Crowds began to cheer and stamp, and then a harsher din broke through the applause as green and white smashed into each other with weapons swinging and shields denting.

Red and blue looked to have a mutual understanding of preserving their numbers; a single knight from each strode forward and engaged in combat. When one fell he was replaced. Green and white supporters booed this timid and conservative approach as their own teams whittled each other down at an alarming rate.

The white flag dropped first.

The green flag stood, but it was held by only a single tottering defender. A small contingent was sent from red to attack him, but as they left, all but one of the blues rushed at the red base. The reds spotted the attack and together they retreated to their flag where, in a clatter of desperate fighting, all fell, including the flag.

It was down to the single green and blue knight. The green was exhausted, swaying in his armour as he staggered forward. He was able to preserve his dignity by landing a few prods with his sword on his opponent's shield before the huge sweep of a mace knocked him off his feet.

Blue took the win, but the green soldier was considered to have been the most valiant, having taken part in three separate confrontations in which he had demolished four opponents.

Several men had to be carried off the field on stretchers. A few dark stains showed on the cloth when the stretchers returned for more.

A whole range of contests followed – single combat, archery, wrestling, and another team event in which armed knights had to carry a ripe melon from across the field while their opponents attempted to smash it. The crowd roared with laughter when a melon was damaged near the finish and the frustrated carrier smashed it over his antagonist's helm, felling the man with the most unexpected of weapons.

While looking to the side, a movement behind the stands caught Aedan's eye. He turned to see the same tall man with the hat that kept his face in shadow. It gave him the first tingling of fear. But the next time he looked around, the man was gone.

As the sky darkened, fires and lanterns were lit, and teams of acrobatic dancers ran onto the field and began to perform. They leapt over each other, built pyramids with their bodies, balanced on horses while throwing flaming torches to each other across the arena, and walked fearlessly along ropes high above the ground. The final applause that rolled from the audience expressed equal parts congratulation and relief.

It was with an air of satisfied fatigue that the group of friends clumped down from the stands and gathered on the walkway. The boys insisted that the girls accompany them to Enna's for supper, and told them with no little pride how they had spent their morning. Aedan grinned as he passed the tent where they had added their own creative ingredients – it was empty.

Letting his eye latch on a sign – jewellery made from seashells – Aedan stole a casual glance behind him. It was the same man with the grey hat and shaded face, still fifty paces behind. The uncertainty was making him uncomfortable. It was time to solve the riddle.

"I'll catch up," he told Hadley, and turned down a side alley. Once around the corner, he ran in a big loop, emerging onto the main walkway behind the stalker who was now entering the alley, following in Aedan's tracks. Aedan darted after him, keeping one turn behind and peering carefully around the corners.

But this stalker appeared to have a nose for such tricks. At the third corner, Aedan peered around to see the man looking straight at him. He caught his breath – it was his father. A peculiar mixture of hope and uncertainty rushed through his veins. He realised just how much he had wanted this reunion. Tarnished as the relationship had been, the good times came back now and glowed in the silence that hung between them. He stepped out into the alley.

"I heard rumours that you'd entered the academy," his father said.

Aedan smiled. But the answering sneer on his father's face showed this to have been a mistake.

"Oh, smug are you? Want to show that you're better than me now? Is that why you ran off to their snooty lectures and mounds of books?"

"No," Aedan replied, suddenly confused. "No. It wasn't like that. It was when Harriet wanted to … actually it was because of what happened back in the Mistyvales – the slavers – and about taking revenge for her … and being strong enough to stop any bullies … and General Osric –"

"And nothing about me! Yes, I understand all too well. A dead girl and some general are more important to you than your own father. And Harriet! You'd actually stoop to taking that woman's advice!" Clauman's voice had risen; he was working himself into a shuddering rage.

"No, it's ... You don't understand. Harriet –"

"Oh I don't understand, do I? Is that it?" He was striding towards Aedan now, jaw clenched. He closed the distance with big steps. "It's your turncoat mother and that fool of a meddler that have been putting these ideas into your head. With a bit of fancy learning you think you've risen above me, don't you? Don't you?" He was shouting now, spit flying, eyes bulging as his rage snapped free of the last restraints. "You think you don't need to respect me anymore because you can read and scribble! Don't you? Let's see about that ..."

Aedan wanted to run but he was locked in a paralysis like that of deep sleep. He could see it all clearly and slowly. His father seized him by the neck and hoisted him off his feet while striking so hard with the other hand that Aedan barely remained conscious. Skin was burning and ears ringing when he was dropped.

"Filthy little traitor! Treacherous, milk-blooded coward! I always suspected she would teach you to despise me. You both deserved every thrashing you got and more."

Aedan wanted to say that it was not true, that he had missed his father, that he had wanted to see him – and indeed he had. But now the words curdled in him. A deep cauldron of hissing anger heaved its contents out, turning his eyes and his thoughts dark, though he was still unable to move.

Clauman took a handful of Aedan's hair in a shaking fist.

"Now," he said, barely in control of himself, "let me warn you not to interfere with matters that do not concern children. The stall you ruined earlier today was one of my sideline investments. You stole from me. Tonight my boys will collect what was stolen." Then he brought his face right down to Aedan's. "If you meddle with my operations, the discipline you have needed in the past will be like mist compared to the hailstorm I'll set on you."

Aedan stared back from a whirl of screaming, stamping fear and rage. "You ... a criminal?" he finally managed between gritted teeth.

Clauman stood and waited a long time before answering. "All that knowledge and still blind?" He looked around before continuing. "When I lived in Tullenroe, I was a better forester than any of them, but the challenge was not enough and neither was the money. I remained a forester by day, but by night I made use of the trained senses and quiet feet to become something else.

I became a legend. I left all that behind when I moved to the Mistyvales – only a fool works the small village he lives in – but here my reputation is just beginning to take root again. No window, no safe defied me, and no doddering lawman ever had any idea. Not even your mother knew – thinking herself so clever with all her books. The reason I can trust you to hold your tongue is because the knowledge would destroy your future quicker than mine. Interfere with my plans again and you will know what it is to be sorry."

He picked up his hat where it had fallen during his exertions.

"In a few weeks, things will be ready, and it will be time to fetch you back from that foolish academy. Your vacation is over. There's work for you to do, and it starts tonight – you keep yourself and your friends clear."

Chapter 34

By the time Aedan had found a water barrel and washed his face, it was late. He returned to Enna's where he found everyone had finished their meals. Lorrimer was wiping his mouth. Aedan guessed that Enna had pushed a meal at him even though he had blown his money earlier. It would have required little pushing.

"What have you been up to?" Peashot asked.

"Nothing." Aedan turned his face away from the lantern glare.

Nearby, Coren was fastening straps over a cart that held all the copper pots, pewter bowls and mugs, wash basins, cutlery and spices. Several bulging purses of coins were put into an iron box which was stowed in the cart too.

Liru and Delwyn were heading in the same direction as the elderly couple and offered to accompany them. Coren began explaining that he and Enna needed to wait for their relatives, when Malik and Ilona walked around a corner.

"Ah. Here they are," Coren said. "These are our grandchildren."

"You are brother and sister?" Hadley asked them.

"Cousins," said Ilona, with a shake of her golden hair and a winning smile. Her look turned cold as she saw Aedan.

"How did you manage to afford such a huge tent?" Ilona asked, stepping back and staring. "And a table too? And why aren't you where you set up this morning?"

Coren explained what had happened and how the boys had taken it upon themselves to build the tent.

"It was Aedan's idea," said Hadley.

"But Kian's carpentry," said Aedan, diverting the attention and hoping nobody had looked at him too closely.

Ilona turned to her grandmother, "Did you do well?" she asked.

Enna beamed as she pulled out the money bags. "We can pay the next four months, just from today's earnings," she said, tears filling her eyes.

Ilona threw her arms around her grandmother and avoided looking at Aedan.

Malik avoided looking at anyone. He took up the handles of the cart and set off towards the exit, signalling the parting of ways. Liru and Delwyn accompanied the little group as they trundled away into the night.

Aedan watched them go. Someone small peeled from the shadows and scurried ahead of the cart.

His father's words began to echo in his head. The picture hadn't been clear at first – shock had kept his mind numb – but he saw it now. And if he interfered, his life would be ruined by a father whose anger knew no bounds. It would be madness anyway. What could his little group of boys with training weapons hope to do?

All strength, all sense of purpose had been battered from him. He trailed silently behind his group of friends as they headed in the opposite direction, back to the city gates. He hoped it would be a clean robbery, that none would be hurt, especially Liru.

And then he began to feel ashamed. He knew that if it had been Kalry, a hundred fathers would not have held him back.

Once again, with her memory came purpose.

"Stop!" he said.

The others came to a halt and looked at him. He rocked slightly, staring at the ground, grimacing.

"What is it?" Hadley asked. Then he stepped closer. "Hey, how did you get these bruises?"

Aedan ignored the questions, took a breath, and looked up. "Follow me," he said.

He made a turn and then another so that they were walking back towards the other half of the party.

"Aedan, where are we going?" Hadley asked.

Aedan stopped and turned around, and for the first time, they all saw the bruises. "I think they are going to be robbed. I'm going back. It is going to be rough so don't come if you don't want to get hurt." Then he turned and set off at a run. Without a word, all five followed.

The screams made the search easy. They stepped into a shadowy section of the festival ground's outer lane and saw, a little way ahead in the bright moonlight, a large gang surrounding the party of six. Aedan counted the assailants – twelve.

Malik lay still on the ground beside one of the thieves who was moaning and clutching his head. The other boys jeered and shoved the girls, dodging out of the way of kicks and swipes. One of the boys laughed as Liru's fist skimmed his throat. He stopped laughing when she took advantage of his inattention and hoofed him in the groin. He struck her so hard that she fell back against the cart and dropped to the ground.

Peashot and Hadley started forward, but Aedan gripped their arms and held them back.

"Wait!" he said.

Peashot listened, but Hadley dragged him forward and then turned at him like a mad dog on a frail leash. He did not like being told what he could not do.

"Just trust me, Hadley. I also want to charge in, but that won't work here. We'll have no chance. Shift the disadvantage – remember? Let me think."

Reluctantly they hung back as Aedan tried desperately to clear his mind and hatch some strategy.

The gang tightened its circle.

"You and those dirty little friends of yours be making our boss angry today," one of the gangsters taunted.

Aedan grimaced at the memories recalled by the thuggish tones. He could almost see the Anvil in front of him again, dipping and lurching with his taunts.

"The boss, he says only take the money, but it looks to us like you'll be needing a mighty big lesson in manners."

Aedan's head buzzed with anger but he forced himself to concentrate. This was a large gang of much older boys and some grown men. If he and his friends simply charged in, they would accomplish nothing. Anger is a poor strategist, Dun had constantly told them.

Aedan glanced around, taking in everything that could be used to their advantage.

Moonlight flooded the scene, but he and his friends stood hidden in the shadow of a large oak. The gang stood between the last line of tents and a wall on the right. This wall was more like a tier, the higher ground above it being flush with the top; a ramp behind Aedan led to the higher level. On the left side of the alley, opposite the gang, there was an opening in the line of tents, no more than a narrow passage – it was probably this passage the gang had used to hide in. The ground beneath his feet was gravelly, and if he moved forward, he would lose the cover of shadow.

An idea grew in his mind. The gang would have to be thinned in stages.

"Peashot, Kian," he whispered, "get up the ramp behind us, and when you are above them, hit them with whatever you can – rocks, slings, even blunt arrows if there is nothing else. Aim for the head, don't stop even when we are among them. Just try not to hit us."

The two boys slipped away.

"Lorrimer, Vayle, go back round the tents and wait in that passage opposite them. Some of the gang will probably try to go through there to get behind Hadley and me when they hear us. Vayle, go ahead and crouch to trip them. Lorrimer, use your staff on their heads as they fall."

They nodded and glided off.

"Hadley, we drop however many are sent to get rid of Peashot and Kian. Take a handful of gravel for the eyes, then use your training sword like a club."

Aedan unslung his quarterstaff and removed the strap. The wild rush in his veins was causing his fingers to fumble and his hands to shake. This would not be like one of Dun's exercises. These opponents would not hold back. They would strike with the intention to harm, perhaps kill.

He tried to stop the shaking, but couldn't.

Hadley wriggled his leather-clad training sword free. Then they both scooped a handful of gravel, moved apart so they wouldn't strike each other, and took positions just inside the shadow where they would be able to see without being seen.

They waited. Aedan was breathing like he had just run a mile. Fear and excitement tightened him up, gumming his thoughts until he looked at the staff in his hand and suddenly realised he had forgotten everything he'd been taught on how to use it. He hoped, in a kind of dizzy panic, that some of the techniques might come back, otherwise he'd just have to swing and chop and hope for the best.

For an instant, he wondered if he would freeze before the charge, like he had done before his father. But there was no reminder of his father in any of the gang members that lurked ahead of him, and no echo of that crippling fear.

"Good luck," said Hadley. Aedan was somewhat comforted to hear that not even Hadley could disguise the trembling in his voice.

"Good luck," he replied.

Two rocks flew out from the upper level. One of the bandits went down with a sigh and another screamed and reeled away, clutching his nose. The next two rocks were partly deflected, surprise having been lost. There was some shouting and four of the gang separated from the group and started running towards the ramp. They drew knives and clubs, but showed no sign that they had seen the boys waiting in the thick shadow of the oak.

Aedan crouched.

Heavy boots thudded closer.

Forty yards, twenty …

He took a deep breath.

Ten, five …

Aedan and Hadley flung their handfuls of gravel. The first two gangsters broke into howls of pain and skidded to a halt, hands over their eyes. The next two had only a heartbeat to prepare as they ran into a quarterstaff wedged into the ground and a small sword swung powerfully at knee height. They both dropped. Blows fell thick and heavy on the backs of heads and any fingers that got in the way.

One of the gangsters was a hulking bull of a man. He recovered himself sufficiently to grab the staff, wrestle it away with a roar, and deliver a glancing blow to Aedan's shoulder that was still enough to knock him down. But Hadley, finished with his two, circled behind and unleashed a furious swing at the big man's head, producing a groan and a heavy thud as the body collapsed.

Aedan, panting and trembling, picked himself up from the ground and retrieved his staff. He looked back at the cart. The gang still kept their prisoners at bay while cursing the two boys throwing rocks.

It was not easy to concentrate, but he pulled his thoughts together and counted.

Only five! Where were the others?

He crouched and spun around, looking for a surprise attack. From a distance, he heard two thumps of falling bodies and a few woody-sounding whacks. The noises came from the direction of the passage. Someone began to shout and threaten in strained tones that betrayed a struggle. Another three whacks brought silence.

Six of them against five gangsters, Aedan thought, assuming Vayle and Lorrimer were still on their feet. He decided to move quickly, before anyone thought to use the prisoners as hostages. He also wanted the thugs to face away from the wall, giving Peashot and Kian targets that would not dodge.

With Hadley beside him, he ran along the tented side of the road, calling Lorrimer and Vayle as he neared. They jumped out into the open.

"It's a bunch of children!" The biggest of the gang jeered, drawing a long, cruel blade. "With toy weapons."

It was the last thing he said. The distraction had worked. Peashot's expertly aimed rock bounced off the side of his head and he crumpled. Kian's glanced from another's shoulder.

One of the remaining four turned and grabbed Ilona by the hair. Aedan flew at him, Hadley and the others following. This was the part where the tricks were done and the advantage was lost. The man holding Ilona reached for a short, curving blade like a claw.

Aedan could not afford to wrestle with that blade; he had to make a clean strike. But his arm was numb from the blow he had taken on his shoulder, and as he swung the staff round, it escaped his grip and skittered away. There was no time to run after it now.

Without breaking stride, he sped over the last few yards and leapt into the air – something Dun had forbidden – aiming his elbow at the much taller gangster's head. The distance closed as he soared, swung ... and missed. The man's head had moved. An airborne attack had made adjustment impossible. The momentum carried Aedan into the wall where he thudded against the stones and dropped to a crouch. Ilona's captor looked at him and smiled as he put the blade to her throat.

"Call them off or I'll be painting everything red."

It was what Aedan had feared. With a hostage they could dictate anything they pleased. He opened his mouth to speak when he noticed something in Ilona's hand. She raised her arm and Aedan caught the glint of a blade just before she jabbed it into her attacker's thigh. He screamed and dropped his hands to the injured limb. Ilona ducked away, but she caught her foot on something hidden in the long grass, and fell. The man drew her knife from his leg with a shudder, raised his own to throw at her, and then dropped in a heap as a rock collided with his head.

Peashot looked down with a savage smile.

Aedan's attention was pulled away as someone yelled. He turned to see Hadley struggling on the ground under a boy larger and heavier than him. The boy was clawing, spitting and biting like a rabid dog. Teeth marks in Hadley's neck began to well with blood. The clawing became more frantic and then, gradually, the arms wilted and fell limp. Hadley released his hold on the boy's neck and both of them slumped back and lay still.

Only one of the gang remained standing, knife poised. Lorrimer and Vayle were circling him. Vayle hobbled noticeably as he thrust and swung Aedan's staff, his training sword still tucked away on his back. He was clearly too weak to step in and commit himself, and it seemed that Lorrimer was too timid.

Aedan had been moving to assist Hadley, but he changed direction. He grabbed Hadley's fallen sword, ran at the thug, drew his attention with a yell, and hurled the sword at him.

The man jumped aside and faced Aedan, forgetting the other two for only an instant.

Vayle's staff descended on his head, followed by Lorrimer's and then Vayle's again. He sagged like a collapsed tent.

"Quickly," Aedan shouted, as he rushed back to Hadley who looked unnaturally still. "Tie them up. Cut ropes from the stalls."

Hadley was breathing in shallow gasps, there was a lot of blood on his face, and one eye looked wrong. Ilona left Malik propped against the cart wheel and rushed over. Aedan caught his breath as he saw the red film over the lower part of her neck.

"You're hurt."

"It's not deep," she said. "He only cut the skin." She began to look over Hadley, prodding with the greatest of care, and soon found the painful area between his ribs. She lifted his shirt to reveal an ugly-looking gash.

Aedan thought his friend was done for and turned away with a groan.

"Don't worry, Aedan," Ilona said. "It didn't reach the lungs. No bubbles in the wound. No coughing blood. You just need to help me put on a bandage for now."

"You sure?"

"I'm sure." She smiled.

"How is Liru?" he asked, looking to where Delwyn was nursing her.

"Broken arm, I think. Maybe shoulder too. She was hit very hard. And they enjoyed it." Her eyes spilled over, and Aedan's fists clenched. "What kind of people do that?" she said.

"People that belong in prison or worse."

She finished with the bandages and looked up. "Thank you, Aedan. I know it was you. We've all heard about your ways with strategy."

Aedan turned his eyes down, embarrassed.

"I have been horrible to you for a bad reason," she continued. "When you and Peashot took the last places in that endurance trial, it was Malik's best friend who lost out. Malik thought you had an unfair advantage. He hated you for it and because he's my cousin, so did I. But that friend couldn't have done what you did here, and he would never have done what you did for my grandparents. I'm glad now that you beat him, just don't tell Malik I said that. Malik spent a year training him. He's still bitter about it."

Malik's hatred suddenly made sense as the history drew into focus. But then everything in Aedan's mind went into a wild blur as the dazzling girl leaned forward and kissed him on the forehead.

Peashot and Kian jumped down. Kian's face was half bloodied by a deep scratch. A rock had been returned to him with a powerful arm. As they joined the others and helped to cut ropes, one of the gangsters began staggering to his feet. Peashot rushed at him with a wild scream and planted a knee in the man's face. The gangster fell and so did Peashot, clutching his knee and shouting a string of words that would have put any of the thugs to shame.

The tramp of boots announced a regiment of soldiers. They had heard the noise and come to inspect. Coren, who was still recovering from the shock, gave them the details. The whole gang was chained and removed to the city prison.

All but one.

Aedan noticed with a rush of dismay that the man who had wrestled his staff from him was not in the final number. That man would tell Clauman what had happened.

Hadley spent three weeks in a dangerous fever and the vision in his right eye was blurry for months afterwards. Mistress Gilda said he was very lucky to still have the eye at all. Vayle had been stabbed in his leg. He limped for weeks. Liru and Malik both had broken bones which had to be set, and the rest of the group escaped with bruises and cuts. The gang was jailed with no chance of release for many years.

News of the rescue spread through the academy, drawing a bewildering amount of attention. Envious classmates were thoroughly impressed with the injuries the boys now sported, particularly Hadley's and Malik's.

Peashot was mad that he had gained nothing more than a bruised knee.

The group told and retold the story, expanding a detail here and there, until it sounded like they had conquered an army of ogres. They remembered clearly what moves they had done, and the explaining was always accompanied by swinging arms and explosive noises – with a good measure of argument over who hit whom and when. They had the decency, however, to forget that after the encounter Lorrimer had found himself a quiet spot and indulged in a brief cry.

The whole business was something at which the girls might have rolled their eyes and raised their noses, dismissing it all as boyish imaginings. But Ilona and Liru, two of their own, had been present. So, instead, they fussed over the conquerors, Hadley in particular, calling them brave and honourable until the boys who had missed out became quite miserable and sick of it all.

Malik never once commented on the fight. He fell completely silent whenever the topic was raised. His taunting of Aedan came to an end.

It wasn't intended as an insult when Aedan said it. He was just rolling along with the banter as the class joked about what they remembered or had heard, and his tongue slipped its leash in the excitement. Someone asked if any of them had seen Malik do anything. Aedan replied, "Yes. He did a perfect copy of the possum technique, only that he got so carried away with playing dead that he fell asleep." Aedan hadn't meant for everyone to hear it, but his words happened to find a lull in other conversations. The whole class heard and most of them laughed. Malik said nothing and stared at the floor, but Vayle raised both eyebrows at Aedan, and let out a soft whistle of disapproval.

Aedan knew he'd overstepped, but there was no chance he was going to apologise to someone who had treated him so badly, and it was about time that Malik learned to take the ribbings like they all did.

The masters were all very pleased with the boys, and Matron Rosalie scolded them for being reckless. They managed to find favour with her again when they arranged for Enna to prepare a stew in the hostel kitchen. Enna was immediately given a job and Peashot an appetite.

Dun used the encounter with the gang as an exercise in strategy. He recreated the environment in the training hall where many variations were discussed and played out.

The general feeling was one of pride, but it was one in which Aedan could only partly share. Both Peashot and Hadley asked him about the bruises he had sustained before the fight, and how he had known the attack would happen, but he wouldn't talk of it, and they let him be.

One evening, Aedan crept out of bed, opened a secret cubby in his desk and withdrew a tattered page. He clutched it and made his way to the kitchens where coals would still be glowing in the oven.

For a long time he stood with the folded page in his hand, thinking, remembering. He counted the beatings – three in the north, one on the journey, one that Harriet had interrupted, and the last one. Something had changed, broken in him during that last beating. Though it was one of the mildest, it had been different. Before, he had been thrashed for something he had done, but the last time it had seemed he was being thrashed for who he was.

In him, there had been a secret longing to reunite with his father, and it had been chased away, bleeding. Clauman would not be collecting him from the academy to work with him. There would be no father-and-son togetherness.

Never again.

That bubbling cauldron of remembered injuries and fermented hate slid forward from the dark inner chamber and began to tip again.

He could not use his fists, but there was a better weapon. From now on he would know his father no more. Clauman would be a stranger to him. Aedan would be deaf to his words and blind to his face. His father was dead.

He looked at the page, considered opening and reading it one last time, then decided against it. He knew what it said, every word. None of it meant anything to him now. With a flick of the wrist, he spun it into the coals. It perched there for some time before beginning to blacken and smoulder. Finally it burst into flames.

To watch it flake and crumble hurt more than he had expected, but he did not try to rescue the page. He stayed until it had disintegrated, and wondered if little Dara would understand, for it was she who had written out the words with such care.

In the weeks that followed, Aedan took to long periods of brooding. Part of him wanted to wander out and chance upon his father that he might unleash his bitterness and completely ignore the man in the most obvious way possible, but another part of him was afraid.

His father had warned him that revenge would be severe if he meddled with the robbery. And he had meddled. It was difficult to know if the threat was real, and it hung over him like an axe suspended from the roof beams by a ragged string.

Chapter 35

"Aedan, must you get mud *all* over the floor?"

Hadley was the only one in the dorm with any notion of orderliness. His notion was unanimously disregarded.

"Just sharing," Aedan mumbled as he passed Hadley's section on the way to the little washing cubicle.

He got a lot of mud off, and a lot remained. This was fairly normal. On the way back he left samples of deep brown and wild ochre with every step.

The others were in bed. He passed their alcoves one by one and noted the familiar scenes. Hadley looked down at the mud stains and shook his head; Vayle was lost in a book, probably some abstract and philosophical tosh like the meaning of meaning, far beneath the notice of any normal boy; Lorrimer was crouched over a page, lips and pen moving together, obviously composing another poem; and Peashot was lying on his back adding a gravestone to his collection scratched in the wall.

"You miss curfew every rest day," Peashot noted, his voice carrying round the log partition as Aedan dropped onto his bed. "How come you don't have any charges?"

"Who says they know?"

"Well how do you get back through the gates?"

"I don't. I climb the wall."

"Are you mad? It's high enough to break both your legs if you fall – and the grips are tiny."

"Been good for my climbing."

"Slipping won't."

Aedan grunted.

"You're not still taking the shortcut back through the law wing are you?"

"Of course."

"Didn't you hear what happened to Kian and Warton? They got caught by that Iver everyone's been warning us about. When he finished with them Warton was actually crying – least, that's what Cayde said. Those older law students are bad news and this Iver is a champion street brawler."

"So? Why should that scare me?"

"He's at least nineteen, and huge. What are you? Thirteen?"

"Almost fourteen."

"Your birthday is next year. You're thirteen."

"My age makes no difference. I'm not walking around just because they want it to themselves. Slipping through the law-wing boulevard cuts off a quarter of a mile. Anyway, these flabby law students would have to catch me first."

Peashot made a rude sound. "One day you're going to get snagged. You're always snooping around anywhere that's forbidden or dangerous. Where'd you go today? Some wild and lonely spot again?"

"The oak and hawthorn section of the forest."

"You mean the dark and eerie section."

"I don't think it's eerie, and don't give me the Fenn-scout lecture. I always take sword, knife and bow, and anyway, the scouts would have no reason to go into those areas."

"Master Dun would skin you if he found out you were wandering there alone. But you're probably right. No scout with half a brain would go into that area. I've only seen it from the hill. Don't even know how you get in past the brambles. Sometimes I think you're like one of those tracker mongooses – still half wild."

"He's more than half wild," Vayle observed, his voice floating down the room. "Have you seen the way he moves when we're in the forests? Doesn't make me think of a mongoose. More like a marsh eel in muddy water. I heard that not even Wildemar could find him during the last survival challenge. Probably found another one of those inaccessible spots. If you ask me, I'd say he goes there to sing."

Aedan shook his head. "Vayle thinks I can't sing," he explained.

"I wouldn't put it quite like that," Vayle said. "It's just that you sing worse than anyone I've ever heard before."

Aedan threw a wet sock over the partition with just enough weight to travel two cubicles and land in Vayle's. It produced a suitable reaction of disgust.

"You always take that leather case that you hang around your neck," said Peashot. "You guard that thing like it's full of gold and rubies. Aren't you ever going to tell us what's inside?"

"Touch it and I'll kill you."

Peashot chuckled. "So what's the real reason for your gloomy wandering?" he asked. "Why do you like those kinds of places?"

"Why do you always draw gravestones?"

Peashot didn't answer.

"Maybe it's the quiet," Aedan resumed. "Lets me think, or maybe it's the opposite of normal thinking, more like untangling. I'm comfortable in those spots."

"Suits your mood lately – somewhere between angry and sulky. You've been different since the festival."

Aedan didn't want to explain.

Hadley walked up and leaned against the rough log partition. "It's not Liru's influence, is it?"

"What do you mean?" Aedan asked, bristling.

"She *is* Mardrae." Hadley was the only one in the group who hadn't warmed to Liru. It was rooted in the one unfortunate trait he shared with Malik – a distrust of those from far-off nations.

"So?"

"Well, doesn't it bother you? There's foreign and there's foreign. Kian's alright – Orunean folk aren't much different to us, but these Mardrae are *very* foreign. You don't think she could be changing you?"

"You say Mardrae like it's a disease, like any change she caused would be bad."

"Some people here think it is. Many people, actually. They say if her father wasn't rich, they wouldn't have let her into the academy."

"And you think they shouldn't have."

"No. I don't really care. Just saying that she's maybe bringing you down with her foreign ways of thinking."

Aedan was getting annoyed, partly because of the prying, partly because of the way Liru was being discussed. "She has nothing to do with that," he said, more abruptly than he'd intended. "It's something else on my mind ... something ... different. But even if she is foreign, life is tough for her in

Castath. I'm not going to make it worse by keeping away like every other bigot."

But as he thought about it, he realised it was not generosity behind his loyalty, as his words implied. It was that he cherished her company. Liru never made him feel ashamed. He drew as much from her friendship as she from his.

"Well, whatever," said Hadley. "I thought I'd just mention that she's very foreign and strange – and stern. Weirdly stern. Maybe someone more lively would be good company now."

Aedan clamped his teeth. So what if she was different? It was time to change the subject. "Well, it's not like Peashot's been any brighter since he twisted his stupid ankle," he said.

Vayle made an explosive sound from his alcove, but said nothing more.

"And anyway," Aedan continued, "with all the time you spend with Rillette, soon you are going to start agreeing with all that talk about storms bringing monsters and death and the end of the world."

"Rillette's not stupid, and how do you know that the talk isn't true?"

"I passed through DinEilan, remember. That's where all the rumours point. I never saw anything like what the people are saying."

Aedan wasn't entirely sure he believed his own words, but it felt a lot safer to mock strange claims than support them. As a cynic he couldn't be pulled down; a cynic was already down.

"Well," said Hadley, "I think we are heading for some eerie changes. A few weeks back, this group of people from a hamlet called Eastridge saw something fly overhead that was too big for a bird – and no, it wasn't a cloud. Whatever's happening, it's coming closer."

"Is this the point when you usually put your arm around Rillette?" Aedan asked.

Peashot laughed.

Hadley grinned and took it with his usual good humour.

"Oh Hadley," Peashot squeaked in his most Rillette-like voice, "You make me feel so safe the way you pretend to believe all my rubbish so you can hold me in those enormous muscly arms with your sleeves rolled so high and your chin stuck out fearlessly at the dragons and ghouls and – Ouch!"

Hadley landed a few more good blows that stopped the mockery, but he was unable to silence the laughter.

"She's never mentioned anything about dragons or ghouls," he said, trying in vain to present a serious defence to his laughing opponents. "The other stuff is real. Even Lorrimer agrees."

"What do you mean 'even Lorrimer'?" Peashot cried. "He still believes in that nursery rhyme about foot-biter faeries. That's why he always puts his boots on when he has to make a dark trip to the privy." There was no retort from Lorrimer. "What's he doing?"

"What do you think?" Hadley said. His eyes rolled with the words, but then they focussed and glinted with that familiar headlong enthusiasm. "You two hold him down. I'll snatch the page." Hadley had been trying without success to get Lorrimer to read one of his many poems – the first thing to which he had turned his fledgling literacy skills – and Hadley was not one to be put off for long.

Aedan and Peashot sauntered past. Lorrimer ignored them until they spun and pounced. By the time he had fought them off, Hadley held the page. It took all three of them to keep the tall boy down while Hadley read in snatches. Aedan managed a peek at the writing, curious as to why Hadley was struggling over the simpler words. The problem was visible at a glance.

Oe daffidilz ar disgusting worts comperd too yoo
Peepil ar blind and schupid if thay cant see its troo
Evrything els has grown uglee now eevin food
Eevin wen its muttin schoo
Beecoz nun of theez ar az pritty az yoo

Peashot had begun to snigger at the first line, Aedan at the second, and by the time the poem was finished, Hadley could read no more. The laughter was so loud that several boys appeared at the door wanting to know its meaning. Hadley was about to read for all, but Aedan seized the page and gave it back to Lorrimer. The look on Lorrimer's face had told him that the joke had gone far enough.

"Just something Lorrimer wrote," Hadley informed the visitors. "It was very good."

"Ah," said Kian. "Who is he being in love with this month?"

That sent another wave of laughter through the room.

When they had the dorm to themselves again, Peashot began singing softly, "Oh the daffodil, such a disgusting wart ..."

"I've changed my mind about something," Vayle announced over the chuckles. "I think it's only fair to Lorrimer that the truth of Peashot's sprained ankle be known."

The singing stopped.

Curious heads appeared from the alcoves. All except Peashot's.

"Come on," said Hadley. "Enough suspense. Tell us."

"Hadley, if you could push time along the way you push everything else, you'd be an old man before the month is up."

Hadley tapped his foot. The others grinned.

"It begins not in the training hall, as you all assume, but in Mistress Gilda's class. Those prize quills of hers became too much of a temptation to our friend and I saw him filch one and slip it into his pocket. I think you can imagine that it would have been too long, so he must have pushed it through the material at the bottom of the pocket to keep anything from sticking out the top.

"It should have worked, but I noticed that in the next class while Dun was speaking, Peashot began gripping the left side of his trousers and getting into the strangest positions. I think the quill had begun to slip down behind his leg. That was when Dun caught him fidgeting, and yelled, setting him off on the blue circuit."

Vayle paused for effect.

Peashot had not emerged.

"Well, guess what happens when there is a quill with two sharp ends held against the back of your leg and you bend your knee to run?"

Another pause. Lights were beginning to show in the listeners' faces.

"Everyone else was so focussed on his sprained-ankle lie that they didn't see the little patches of blood higher up. He skewered himself."

Lorrimer's laughter outdid the rest of them this time. When the fit passed it would start up again. He lay on his back, knees drawn up, feet pounding the mattress. Peashot, surly in his corner, was unable to do anything but wait.

"And the best part," Vayle sputtered, "is that he now has a fat cast on a perfectly good ankle and has to hobble around for two weeks and then attend reconditioning classes with Sister Edith for another two. Winter will be here by the time he's able to stop faking the limp."

This time, twice the number of boys jostled at the door begging to know the reason for the mirth rocking the building. But the little secret remained within the dorm. Only Kian would be told, but later.

Lorrimer was so tickled that after the oil lamps had been snuffed he continued to chortle to himself, and that's when it happened.

"Hic! Oh no ..."

There was a brief silence.

"Hic! Ouch! Blast, that was sore."

"Lorrimer, that you again?"

Silence.

"Hic!"

"Yep. It's Lorrimer. Again."

Someone snorted.

"These blasted hiccups. If I could throttle them and smash them against the – hic! – ouch! – wall ... You know how embarrassing it was at the dance. Shut up. It's not funny!"

Silence.

"Hic!"

It was too much. There was a thump as Peashot actually rolled off his bed with hilarity.

An assortment of remedies began to roll out from the various points in the dorm:

"Balance on your head while counting backwards from a hundred."

"No. Hiccups are already backwards. You have to be upright and counting forwards, but it only works if you are standing in a tub of rotten sheep intestines – the smell chases the hiccups away."

"Fill your mouth with water and block your nose – you'll be too frightened to hiccup. Of course, if you still do, it's going to be bad."

"Inhale the smoke of a burning goat hoof. Has to be left fore. Just do it outside please."

"I tried all those," Lorrimer complained. "Almost drowned with the water one. The sheep intestines made – hic! – my boots stink for the rest of the summer."

There was a brief pause.

"You mean you didn't take your boots off first?"

"And stand in that stinking tub barefoot? No – hic! – way!"

Another pause.

"Are those the same boots that are lying somewhere near your bed?"

"Y – hic! – ow! – yes."

The bellows and complaints that filled the air were enough to draw the night guard.

"Silence!" he barked from the door. "The next sound I hear will have to be explained before the disciplinary committee ..."

Chapter 36

All subjects passed. Student promoted to second year.

Not all the results listed were exemplary, especially not foreign relations, but Aedan was satisfied. He folded the report and sped back across the lawn, through the passages and into his dorm. He got no further than the entrance. The others were gathered around Lorrimer who was crumpled on the floor, face in his hands, crying.

"He failed," Peashot whispered, and the excitement of the morning dissolved. They would all be entering their second year after the break, all except Lorrimer who would be put back with the new group of first-year apprentices. They watched him in silence. Hadley turned away and marched to the door.

"Don't let him out till I get back," he said.

He was gone a long time, and when he returned, he closed the door before speaking.

"Master Giddard says it was only in languages and history where you failed, both difficult subjects for someone who has only just learned to read. He said, because of your behaviour, he would let you try those subjects again in two weeks." Hadley looked around at the others. "So we have two weeks to get Lorrimer ready. If we take turns someone can be here all the time."

They began immediately by collecting Lorrimer's books from the various points in the room where he had flung them, and tried to brighten him up. Lorrimer was never quick to a mood, but when one took him it carried him deep, and he had a long way to climb from his desolation.

Peashot insisted on having the first shift. Aedan wondered how much good it would do – Peashot, though sharper perhaps than any of them except Vayle, had lounged through those classes and stuffed most of his knowledge in right at the end. Aedan suspected his little friend had scraped over the bar tightly enough to leave skin behind, but he held his tongue and booked a later slot. A walk to the stables, he decided, would be just the thing to pass the time.

Wildemar had recently begun their horsemanship training. They had mucked out, fed, groomed, and learned how and when to shoe. It was only after several weeks that they had been allowed to tack and ride, and by this time they were quite familiar with the animals.

The master was a stickler for horsey terminology and pounced on anyone who used the word "horse" for an animal under fourteen-and-a-half hands. The animals that had been assigned to the boys were most certainly ponies. Aedan's was a young chestnut gelding that showed itself a ready worker with a gentle temperament. All the ponies they rode were small enough for boys to mount without assistance, though some of the boys looked every bit as uncomfortable as Aedan had once. But he was a little taller now, and his pony was a hand shorter than old Bluster, so he was among the more proficient riders.

They had gone through the basics of the strides and then learned to dismount, run alongside, and spring into the saddle again while the pony was trotting. There had been a few accidents, but nothing serious. With the growing confidence in horsemanship, Aedan had begun to spend snatches of free time at the stables where he had recently made an interesting discovery.

It was still mid-morning, and the whitewashed stable walls were dazzling in the young light.

Aedan heard them before he saw them – Osric and Skeet were engaged in what might have sounded like a dangerous argument, but he knew Osric well enough to recognise the tone of earnestness rather than anger.

"Royal carriage or not, seeing any fine horse tied to an overgrown, dandified cart heats my blood."

"But what is a fine horse?" Skeet retorted. "No marshal will ruthrek. These animals are three parts fire and one part mischief. They offered us twenty gold carak for this little beast. I would be robbing them at twenty carak less."

"What could you have against him? He's the most perfectly formed colt I've seen in years."

"Nothing. Nothing at all. Except that he sank his perfectly formed teeth into my arm, twice, and put his perfectly formed hoof through the door, and none of the grooms want to go anywhere near him."

"Well if you let him bite your arm twice then ... Oi! Aedan, back away, he's more dangerous than he –"

The jet-black colt was straining his neck and twisting his head in a blissful trance as the boy scratched inside his ear.

"– looks. Or maybe he isn't."

Aedan had been visiting the colt for the past few weeks, winning its trust with carrots and apples and anything else he could beg off Enna who was always happy to oblige. Though he had never been the best rider at Badgerfields, he had always been comfortable around the animals, especially the difficult ones. Winning their affection had never failed to give him extraordinary pleasure.

Osric and Skeet watched the interaction between the two. The colt was cheeky, no mistake, but it showed no malice. It almost looked as if it were making a fuss over someone it had been missing as it nuzzled Aedan's neck, mouthed and licked his ear, then tried to dig in his pockets where the smell of apple lingered.

"Put a halter on him and lead him into the field," said Osric, folding his arms and leaning against the fence. Skeet looked worried, but Aedan obeyed, eventually – the colt fighting the halter as if it were the object of some new game. He led the tall animal out into the field and tied up the lead rope so it would not catch under the hooves, then let go.

The colt looked around briefly, tossed its head and shot away at a speed that shamed every other occupant of the paddock. It galloped in a wide circle, bucking and kicking and spraying out clods of earth – a young whirlwind of unleashed horse. After another two or three laps it charged up to Aedan and came to a skidding stop just in front of him.

He gave it a good scratch on its tufty forehead whorl and then walked across to a nearby pony and brushed its mane. The colt had been following and pricked its ears at this display of rival affection. Ears went flat, teeth appeared, and the long neck stretched out and delivered a solid nip to unsuspecting hindquarters. The pony squealed and raced away to the music of laughter from the fence. When Aedan returned, Osric spoke.

"Skeet has agreed that if you take responsibility for the colt he'll end the negotiations with the royal stabler and sell him to me instead. He'll be yours if you want him."

Aedan gaped. He knew how rare these horses were and he had some idea of the breed's uncanny intelligence and legendary speed. Also the sheer impossibility of training them. But a ruthrek, if it could be trained, would be worth more than a small house. Perhaps even a large one. He thanked Osric with all the warmth of his excitement and proceeded to thank Skeet too until the colt got tired of being ignored and nipped his shoulder, sending him diving away with a yell of pain.

Skeet laughed all the way back to the main buildings.

For the next few days, Aedan read everything he could on the training of horses. Though the academy's trainer was wholly unwilling to take on the responsibility, he said he would be prepared to assist – in a limited capacity.

Initial results were utterly discouraging. To the colt, everything was a game. The lunging cord was a rope for tug of war, and the training switch something to be attacked rather than avoided. Bridling him was like trying to bridle the north wind during a hailstorm, and by the time Aedan finally managed to get the girth strap fastened, the saddle had been bucked off and trampled a hundred times. The leather was gouged and torn, but he could not afford a replacement. For the time being, it made little difference – the purpose of this exercise was to get the horse used to the feeling of carrying a weighted saddle.

Along with his roguishness, the colt's intelligence was becoming quickly apparent. He avoided many of the stupid things that other horses did, like windsucking, incessant head-tossing, and kicking his stall to tatters during storms – he only kicked when tired of being cooped up.

Within days, he took charge of the fields. All of them. Fences were only another game, and he hopped them back and forth for the sheer pleasure of it. He even crossed over to the academy grounds, wandered into a classroom, and scattered the occupants while he rearranged a few desks. He would suffer none but his to handle him, so Aedan had to be called to fetch the renegade colt. The episode landed Aedan with the job of raising the fences.

One morning, Aedan was busy being dragged around the paddock when he spotted Liru and Delwyn sitting on the fence near the stables, faces split with smiles and shoulders bobbing. He dropped the lunging rope and walked over. The colt, now interested in whatever Aedan was doing, trotted across too, dragging the rope between his hooves and watching so as to avoid stepping on it – very un-horse-like.

He gave Delwyn a brief inspection, but Liru fascinated him. Her arm was still in a cast and sling, but there was something else about her that piqued his interest. He brought his nose up against her forehead and took a few long, deep breaths, then tried to get his lips around the hair which, though finer, was as dark as his, gleaming with a hint of blue in the sunlight. Aedan saw what was happening and intervened quickly.

"I think you should tie your hair back," he said. "I'm still working on his manners."

The girls both tied their hair in buns while pouring out compliments for the sleek animal.

"What is his name?" Liru asked.

"I was thinking of something that would describe him and the best I could come up with was Midnight Hurricane – he looks like midnight and acts like a hurricane, but it's too long."

Liru pursed her lips and looked at the colt. "Why do you not use the letters from that and shorten it to Murn?"

Aedan tried it out. "Murn, yes, I like that. What do you think Delwyn?"

"It's a lot better than the names I've heard the janitors calling him," she laughed. "Oh, and the girl who tried to stroke him and got picked up by the hair."

Aedan gave the colt a dirty look. "Sometimes I think he deserves a name like Keepwellaway – painted all over him in stark white."

"Do you think he would stand still and let anyone paint him?" Liru asked.

"No. It will have to be Murn."

"Where is Lorrimer?" she asked. "I have seen the rest of you, but it is like he is hiding in his room."

"In a way, he is. He didn't make it through the exams. Hadley got permission for him to redo the ones he failed, so he's going to be locked away for a while. We're all taking turns helping him with history and languages."

"Why did you not tell me?" she asked, annoyed. "I can help."

"I don't think it would do any good. If you remember, we had to learn *two* foreign languages this year. A few of us have a decent hold on Orunean but, Fenn, the one we could use help with, you wouldn't be able to offer anything. It's really difficult."

"*Naci lar greila mranta hlon stessa!*" she snapped.

Delwyn laughed and Aedan smiled uncertainly.

"Loosely translated," Delwyn explained, "it means, 'You blithering self-assured males.' Liru is almost fluent in Fenn. She seems to have an ear for languages. She's better than me even though I have a two-year start on her."

"Oh."

"And by this," said Liru, "I hope that you mean, 'Sorry for making stupid assumptions and not asking your help for a mutual friend.'"

"Well, isn't that what 'Oh' translates to in Fenn?"

"Loosely. Now will you tell him to meet me at the tables under the plane trees or do I need to risk punishment by finding him in his dorm?"

Aedan unclipped the lunging rope, climbed through the fence and sped away. Murn cantered beside him until he reached the now-higher fence where he stopped, looked, and tossed his head. Then he headed for an adjacent field, sprang the lower fence and set about persecuting the other horses.

Lorrimer was gushing with appreciation when he came out to meet Liru, but she swept the thanks away and set to work immediately, determining his level of proficiency and engaging him in the kinds of basic discussions that would be examined.

Delwyn also asked for a turn, but Lorrimer's blushes were accompanied by a complete lack of concentration. When discussing it with Aedan, she decided it might be best if she left the instruction to the others.

Over the next few days, Lorrimer was given all the attention he could endure. He was up early and studied late, absorbing as much as he was able.

Aedan, when he was off duty, continued to spend his time skidding around the paddocks, clutching the end of a lead rope. ʻ ʻu and Delwyn joined him often. They spent several afternoons ʻng to train Murn, the girls providing commentary and laughter. Aedan was beginning to understand Skeet's original reluctance, but Murn was also beginning to see a determination in his young master that could possibly rival his own. They were gaining almost no ground in training – it generally being unclear who was in charge – but they were forging a fascinating bond that was becoming the talk of those who remained on campus during the recess.

The big day arrived, and with the good wishes and back-claps of the five boys and two girls, Lorrimer headed for his re-examination.

The whole group waited on the lawn, fidgeting, pacing, making comments that nobody heard. Peashot was the worst affected. He began throwing stones with uncharacteristically bad aim, then paced, lay down, paced, climbed and fell from a tree, and finally took himself for a walk. He was back to check perhaps before Lorrimer had even begun his exams. The rest tried to make small talk, but it all seemed too small in comparison to the answer they awaited. It was the longest morning of the year; in Peashot's estimation, about two-and-a-half weeks.

Finally Lorrimer emerged, looking haggard. All eyes fastened on his, all asking the same question. He strode quietly towards them, put on a shy smile and nodded.

The lawn erupted in whoops and cheers and congratulations. They all clapped his back, Liru hugged him and Delwyn planted a kiss on his cheek that produced a dramatic change of colour. The princess, it appeared, was losing her hold.

The girls arranged a party at Liru's house. Her wealthy parents had a mansion large enough to accommodate them all. Another four of her friends would be there, so there would be dancing partners for all.

"And this time you will dance," Liru informed Peashot. The small boy was so happy over Lorrimer's success – which he saw as largely due to his own coaching – that he was prepared to suffer a dance or two.

"As long as I don't have to dance with someone taller than me."

"Well I'm shorter than you, so you can dance with me."

Peashot considered this, stood next to her, and had Aedan measure to confirm the assertion, then nodded his approval.

The party was an explosion of colour and music, and Mardrae hospitality left them all somewhat overwhelmed. Liru's father, a dark-skinned man with strong arms and piercing eyes, spoke to them individually, expressing his pleasure at being able to host them. He knew the names of everyone who had been involved in the fight, and before leaving them to their celebrations, thanked them for defending, among others, his daughter. Even Hadley, though he remained aloof, seemed impressed by the man.

There was more food than they had ever seen at a private party – and it was all for them. Using a basic sign language Wildemar had taught, Peashot tried to convey cryptic instructions to Lorrimer about stealing some food. He was furious when Liru raised her hands and signed, "Wait ... wait ... go!" just as the butler turned his back.

Lorrimer acted like he had never seen a sight as beautiful as that heavily laden table. Until Delwyn entered the room – tall, graceful, smiling gently – and then he almost forgot to eat at all.

Peashot found that, with Liru showing him the steps and matching his stroppiness with steel of her own, dancing was actually not so bad. Lorrimer had clearly been practising. He was now able to execute a few of the more complicated moves with a surprising level of control over his gangly legs. Delwyn was enchanted.

No one felt inclined to sleep when the musicians left. The whole group took pillows and blankets and went up onto the roof where they watched stars and told stories and jokes that got progressively thinner. But the foggier the brains and the worse the jokes, the more the laughter. When the sun rose, it warmed them enough to nudge the whole party down to the dorms where they slept until lunch.

It was then that Aedan met Liru's mother. Even from across the room, he saw the pain of loss etched into her face. Deep gullies divided her brows and shadows lurked beneath hollow eyes. It was a slaver attack, many years ago, in which her eldest daughter had been taken – he had not forgotten what Liru had told him – but in the mother's eyes the grief was still fresh.

"Already I am in your debt, Aedan," she said, "and more of you I will not ask. But my Liru has told me that we share wounds from the slavers, and word of your growing skill, it has reached my ears from many mouths. I want you to know that if it ever happens that you are able to strike against the flesh of Lekrau, you will be acting not only for yourself and for Thirna, but for Mardraél too. You will strike for the thousands who have lost and the thousands who fear to lose the ones that they love. Though I have no place to ask it, if you ever find my Yulla for me, you will have the rights of a son in my house. She was the gentlest of souls. The last thing I heard from them as they dragged her away, it was that I should not worry for she would be sold to a respectable brothel."

Though her eyes had looked drained of every last tear, they flooded again. She turned and hurried from the room.

Aedan slipped away and climbed the stairs to the roof where he sat and gazed out over the rooftops and the distant plains, sombre and still under a deep and endless sky.

"Did she upset you?" It was Hadley.

Peashot and Liru arrived too. They sat down beside Aedan, looking out over the western grassland to the Pellamine ridge.

"Yes," said Aedan. "But it was a good reminder." His eyes searched the vast space for a while before he continued. "One day I am going to find Kalry's grave, and I'll plant flowers on it – blue rainbells, those were her favourite. If I can, I'll find Liru's sister, and then …" he took a deep breath, "then I'm going to give Lekrau something to fear."

"I know you are," said Peashot. "Just don't think you're going alone."

Chapter 37

It had become known as the Lakeside Terror. Unlike most of the rumours circulating through Castath, this one seemed to have a measure of credibility. Though there were no confirmed sightings of the creature itself, many had seen the remains of men and livestock – and the remains told much. The bodies had been torn and mostly devoured, the discarded bones were crushed, and the ground was covered by prints too big for anything inhabiting those areas. Then two foresters reported hearing trees fall where no loggers had been at work. The sounds preceding both falls had been the loud cracks of strained timber giving way, as if the trees had been pushed over.

For the apprentices, this was of no small interest and it completely overshadowed the talk reaching them from other areas. The reason was simple – part of the year's training would send them in the direction of Lake Vallendal and its rumoured Terror.

The academy reopened after the recess and Aedan began his second year with a level of determination none of the masters had seen before. Turning fourteen didn't make him as tall as he wanted, but it certainly helped to raise his self-confidence. The classes were more difficult, the material more extensive, and the new languages, Vinthian and Sulese, were challenging, but he ate through it all like fire in the brushwood.

Several more incursion reports only served to raise his sense of urgency. The Fenn scouting forays were escalating both in frequency and size, and to the west, a Lekran raid near Port

Breklee had shaken the locals badly. Over thirty families were taken from an undefended inland town only weeks after their soldiers had been reassigned to fortify patrols around Castath.

Aedan was growing convinced that he would be called to action well before his training was done. As he saw the walls rising up around the city and listened to the ringing of steel from forges that did not sleep, he knew that war was no longer a question of *if*, but *when*.

Dun introduced them to the heavier weaponry – war hammers, maces, and flails. As before, he spent a lot of time on footwork and balance, ensuring that missed swings did not turn the apprentices around and expose their backs. He spent no less time on breathing, as heavy weapons tended to result in clamped lungs and rapid exhaustion.

They began to work with siege weapons too – catapults, ballistae, battering rams and even assault towers – studying the use as well as the construction and inherent weaknesses of various designs.

While most of the boys thought primarily of the Fenn, Aedan imagined a Lekran soldier in front of him every time he lifted a mace, and a Lekran ship whenever he aimed the ballista.

There were many practical exercises now. The boys regularly accompanied rangers, senior apprentices and marshals on scouting expeditions. During these, they were heavily armed and took every precaution, always searching for potential Fenn ambushes and never approaching from an exposed position. When spring arrived, the undergrowth became thicker and they had to show even greater care.

Everyone knew what Dun was about to announce as he stepped in front of them at an unusually early breakfast. It was the long awaited expedition to Drumly, the great city that stood on the banks of Lake Vallendal. They had been talking and dreaming about it for weeks. It wasn't clear which held the most excitement – the lure of Drumly, the three-month suspension of normal classes, or the growing legend of the Lakeside Terror.

"Two saddlebags each," Dun said without preamble. "You are to wear your hauberks at all times and carry sword, bow, quiver of thirty arrows, and at least one knife. I expect to see you saddled and ready to move out in an hour."

Those who hadn't finished their porridge gulped it down like water as the rest clambered over the benches and rushed away to pack.

"Last one packed and saddled cleans pots tonight," Hadley shouted from the far end of the dorm.

Nobody replied, but the sounds of packing and the clinks, scrapes and clatter of weapons being strapped on became a lot more frantic. Peashot was the first out. His bags were spilling over and weapons projected at odd angles as if they had been poured over him. Aedan was next out. He looked no better but didn't care. There were few things he hated as deeply as scouring pots. Before they reached the end of the corridor, they heard the others jingling behind them.

It was dark, but they knew the grounds well enough to be able to nose their way down to the paddock fence without lanterns, and from there it was easy. They could hear the other apprentices running and shouting to each other behind them. It sounded like someone was lost and the others were laughing at him.

Hadley caught up to Aedan and Peashot before they reached the dim lantern-light of the stables and shoved them both out of the way as he charged towards his pony. It worked against him. His pony reared and began turning circles, making saddling a near impossibility. Vayle and Lorrimer ran in together. By the time they began saddling, Peashot was finished. But then he noticed he'd somehow managed to reverse the bridle and had to take it off and try again.

Nobody was entirely sure who lost. It was between Hadley and Lorrimer. So they voted and Hadley was given scouring duty and a long face.

The other boys weren't far behind and soon all were mounted and ready. Dun appeared on a large and powerfully-built roan mare and called for silence.

"It's a seven day journey. We will make camp together but you will travel in groups of four separated by a hundred yards. You will stay in these groups for the duration of this outing and be responsible for each other. If you have personal disputes, leave them behind unless you want a dispute with the cane. One marshal and one ranger will travel with each group. Learn everything you can from them." He squinted at a piece of paper. "Groups are as follows: Bede, Kian, Hadley, Cayde. Next: Warton, Malik, Lorrimer, Aedan ..."

Aedan winced. None of the others in his group seemed pleased about it either. They moved to the side and were joined by a tall marshal in a long grey cloak who introduced himself as Cedric. He had all the refinements of a courtier, and everything about him was neat and clipped. Beside him was a ranger who looked as if he had slept under a bush. There were leaves tangled in his knotty hair and several tones of earth staining a cloak that might originally have been any colour. He didn't introduce himself, didn't even make eye contact, but Cedric informed them that his name was Haywood.

Dun made a final count, moved to the front of the group and led the way from the academy, past the guards and into the waking streets of Castath. There was a short stop at the main gates and then they were out of the city. At the second intersection, they took the northeast road to Drumly and separated into their groups as Dun had instructed.

Aedan found something dreamy about the experience of being on a walking horse early in the morning. It was like sitting on a branch high in the air as the wind quietly rocks it this way and that. The silence was restful, even a little mysterious, and he felt no need to disturb it with questions.

As the day grew lighter, wooded hills began to appear ahead of them.

"Master Cedric," Lorrimer said. "Why are we travelling in split groups?"

Malik and Warton laughed, and even Aedan grinned. This had been explained more than once, but Lorrimer had apparently managed to daydream through all the explanations.

"Just call me Cedric," the marshal replied. "No need for 'Master'. The reason for the split travelling is because of the terrain ahead of us. Those tree-clad hills provide excellent placements for archers. If we travel in a single group, one volley from a few dozen bows could finish us all. But when split up, enemy scouts would only be able to attack one group and, in so doing, give away their position to the rest of us. A split force is a very unappealing target."

"Do you think we'll see Fenn scouts?"

"Not likely, but if you mean 'Will we be seen by Fenn scouts?' then I'd have to say, probably yes. Where we'll be travelling, it's not that difficult to watch while remaining unseen.

It goes both ways, though. We have many of our own people watching all over Fennlor. Surely you've been taught about that."

"A little," said Lorrimer. "But it seems much more real out here."

He wasn't the only one feeling that. Aedan's eyes were now fixed on the hills. He noticed that Malik's and Warton's were too.

By midday, they had left the plains. The road began to weave between gentle slopes covered in natural forest. In most places it kept to whatever open ground there was, but often it was swallowed by trees. They continued to talk, but quietly, their eyes questioning every shadow, searching out any hint of movement. Haywood remained as aloof as he had shown himself at first. He rode slightly ahead, ignoring their conversation for that of the forest.

It was late afternoon when he drew to a halt, his attention fixed on the road ahead. The groups in front of them stopped as well.

"What is it?" Lorrimer asked.

"Listen," said Aedan.

The drumming of hooves grew louder and they saw a lone rider take the corner. He came to a stop when Dun raised his hand and blocked the way. After a brief conversation, Dun whipped around in his saddle and made a gesture the marshals caught and passed down to the last group. Even the apprentices knew that signal. Speed.

They set off as the rider, who was dressed like an official courier, passed them in the other direction. When the horses looked tired enough to drop, Dun allowed them to walk for a mile or two and then pushed ahead again. They slowed the pace as the light faded, but Dun kept them moving until it was too dark to see the road.

Because the groups maintained their separation, there was no way to ask what had caused this sudden change. Lorrimer was sure it was a rescue. Warton and Malik thought a Fenn base had been captured. Aedan couldn't choose from the dozens of possibilities that surged into his mind.

When they made camp, Dun called the marshals and rangers to him for a brief conference. Then he walked over and addressed the boys.

"We rest until midnight," he said. "When the half-moon rises, we set out. The horses will be tired but we have no choice. If we push hard, we may just reach Drumly on the third day."

The boys were silent. There was no need to ask the question.

"It's another sighting of their so-called Terror," Dun said. "This time it was a forester that was killed and mostly eaten."

"And we are riding towards it?" Vayle asked.

Dun put his hands on his hips. "We believe it is the work of a specialised group of Fenn spies. We think they learned about local rumours and are mimicking those rumours, fabricating evidence for the legend, convincing people that there is a real monster. The talk of this so called Lakeside Terror has now taken such deep root that it is keeping local watchmen out of the forests. I think you can guess why the Fenn would want that."

"To stage an invasion," said Malik.

"Exactly. In those forests they could build and hide enough catapults to flatten the walls of Drumly in a matter of hours."

"But that won't happen for months if not years," Malik said. "Why are we rushing?"

"The sightings of this Terror are rare. So far nobody has been able to track it. Partly because the evidence is always too old and mostly, I believe, because they are looking for the wrong kinds of tracks. The rider told me that the spoor at this latest sighting is fresh. It is my hope to get there before it rains. I am going to raise a small regiment at Drumly and go hunting. It's high time to expose this subterfuge and get their foresters and rangers back where they belong."

There were no fires that night and no cooking – which suited Hadley just fine. Dried meat and biscuits weren't entirely satisfying, but nothing to complain about for boys who had missed lunch and were hungry enough to eat their saddles. They would be up in only a few hours, so they wasted no time spreading blankets on the ground and rolling up.

After getting up twice to find and brush acorns out from under him, Aedan finally began to slip away, just as he heard his name being whispered.

"Huh?" he replied.

"Do you think Dun is right?" It was Lorrimer. "He hasn't even considered that this Terror could be real. What if we are riding straight towards something much worse than Fenn spies? When you went through DinEilan, can you say for sure that there was nothing … out of the ordinary?"

Aedan thought of the curious three-toed prints and the deep, bellowing call that not even his father had been able to identify, and of the experience at Kultûhm that still gave him nightmares. He always shied away from saying it openly, but there was something frightening about DinEilan, something unnatural – and Drumly was not far from its outskirts.

"There were some things that we couldn't explain," Aedan whispered. "But everyone's imagination goes wild in that region. I'm sure Dun is right. I need to sleep."

But Lorrimer had planted something in his mind that interfered with sleep in no small way.

At midnight they rose, saddled, and set out again in the pale light that, under the thicker branches, was hardly light at all. On the third day of travelling in this manner, they entered the area where the Fenn were suspected to be working. Dun made them ride with their bows strung and held at the ready, quivers open.

Aedan was only too eager to comply. They had been allowed to choose new weapons at the beginning of the year, and for mounted archery, he had selected an unusual three-quarter length flatbow made from mountain juniper. It was broader than his old hickory riding bow, and with a sinew backing, the draw weight was greater and the recoil deadly. He was longing to put it to the test.

Most of the rangers and marshals, Aedan noticed, kept an arrow on the string. The talk came to an end. Everyone watched the forest on either side of the road.

It was early afternoon when a distant cracking of branches caused Haywood to rein in and face a high bank to their left, drawing and sighting down his arrow between the trees. The others did likewise. After a few tense breaths there was another crack, closer, louder. The horses began to sidestep and back away.

With a sudden eruption of snapping and crunching, a large speckled forest deer burst out through a section of dense foliage, charged down the bank, leaped over the road not ten feet away, and disappeared into the trees on the right.

In his fright, Lorrimer had released his arrow. It still quivered in the mossy trunk of a dead hawthorn. "Wow, that was –" he began, but Haywood cut him off with a sharp hiss.

The ranger's eyes were still fixed on the bank where the deer had emerged. As Lorrimer understood, he pulled another arrow from his quiver with such haste that he fumbled, dropped it, and barely managed to catch it against his saddle.

Aedan had ignored the deer and, like Haywood, had not taken his eyes from the bank. Whatever had frightened that deer was intimidating enough to make the threat of their party insignificant. The deer had barely noticed them. Another two groups cantered up from front and back. Cedric whispered what he had seen and twelve more arrowheads swung towards the top of the bank.

It was little more than a suggestion, but Aedan knew he wasn't the only one to have noticed it. The sound was so deep it was barely audible. It was like the distant thud of a falling boulder. He was almost sure the leaves trembled. They waited for a long time.

The rest of the groups joined them and took up similar defensive postures when they were filled in, but they neither saw nor heard anything more. Haywood and another ranger dismounted and ran fifty paces to either side of the bank where they crawled to the top. When they returned, they shook their heads.

"Permission to search in the forest?" Haywood asked Dun. Aedan was half surprised that the silent ranger was actually capable of speech.

The stocky master scratched his chin in thought. "It interests me," he said at last, "but I suspect it's nothing. I don't think the Fenn would bother working this far out. If we dig around here too long, we may lose our chance to find real evidence at that last attack site. We must get there before it rains. Groups, separate as before."

With that he rode to the front and they resumed their journey, but now nobody watched the trees on the right.

There was a visible relaxing of shoulders as they descended a long hill and finally broke out onto a wide grassy strip that fronted Drumly. It was only after they had travelled some distance into the groups of people at work that Aedan stopped looking behind him and began to turn his attention to their destination.

Drumly didn't sprawl like Castath. It was as well-proportioned and neatly built as a child's model castle. The walls were high, and sturdy towers rose behind it. With its many spires, each trailing pennants long and multi-coloured, it looked as if the travellers had arrived in time for a festival. On either side, walls and towers extended into the water of Lake Vallendal, obviously protecting the famous harbour, the source of Drumly's wealth. The local fleet traded with fishing and farming villages all the way up the east coast, and a large harbour at the north end of the Lake allowed the Orunean trade to flourish.

But there was a very big difference between this Drumly and the one that graced so many paintings and sketches. In front of the picturesque main wall, a second wall was beginning to rise from the ground. It was already twenty feet high. Engineers, stone masons and common labourers swarmed over it while soldiers stood guard. Like Castath, this was a city under threat, a city fortifying itself against the dreaded tide of flesh and steel.

Dun presented the necessary documents at two checkpoints before reaching the main gate. Here, he left his horse with the guards who knew him, and hurried away to the military headquarters.

Entering Drumly was a different kind of experience to entering Castath. There was a large courtyard behind the main gate which opened into streets that were narrower but neater and cleaner than Castath's, lined by buildings that were taller – three storeys on average. The people seemed less rowdy, better dressed and more refined. Aedan was surprised to recognise some of the clothes as Orunean – lace shirts, billowing skirts and feathered hats. He hadn't seen these since the last trader's market he had visited at Crossroads.

They dropped their bags in a small guest dormitory not far from the harbour. The day was spent, but a glimmer of sunlight still lingered, so Cedric led them all down a neatly cobbled street to the harbour. It was the first time Aedan had seen a harbour, and without a doubt, the sense to make its report in the loudest voice was the sense of smell. While walking along the wharf where quiet waters lapped against the piers and boats swayed and creaked at their moorings, he caught the look on several faces as a particularly thick pocket of late afternoon air unloaded its breath on them. Peashot covered his mouth and tried to conceal his laughter from the supervising marshals. Drumly's beauty, it seemed, came at a price.

In their groups, they climbed the stairs of a lighthouse to the lantern room and walked out onto the balcony. Here they leaned against the iron railing and stared. Lake Vallendal was even bigger than they had imagined. Distant ships were specks drifting with the wind, gradually sinking into the shadows of a bronze horizon. It seemed impossible that they could cross such an expanse.

"I would attack from the water," said Lorrimer. "Much easier access to the city."

"You would have to build ships on the lake shore in order to do it," said Malik with a snort. "It takes years to build a navy."

"Could build rafts – that's quick."

"You know how easy it is to sink rafts with catapults? They move too slowly on still water. Rafts are for rivers."

"Well then I'd wait for a windy day."

"Lorrimer, how ignorant are you? Have you learned nothing of sail? Rafts don't have keels so they can't beat into the wind. If you wait until you have a wind that blows into the harbour, you'll have to launch your rafts somewhere along this coast, paddle into the wind and then across it, which is just as difficult, and when you're finally able to sail in for the assault, your troops will be cold, wet and exhausted. Then the catapults will still get most of them. Have you seen how many catapults face the lake?"

They looked now. Every tower was crowned with at least five – and there were many towers. With their height, the range would be impressive. Aedan knew it wouldn't just be rocks. Oil and fire would rain down in abundance. He understood little of sail but decided that Malik, though less than polite with his views, was probably correct. A harbour attack was not likely unless the Fenn stole all the fishing vessels along the coast beforehand.

A familiar voice struck them from somewhere down below.

"There he is," said Warton, pointing.

It was growing dark, but small as he was from this height, Dun was hard to miss. The way his arms were moving, he did not look happy. They hurried down just as he finished speaking to the assembled boys.

"What did we miss?" Aedan asked Peashot.

"The local commander refused to let any of his men go out tonight. Not even the foresters. No one is going to show us the attack site until morning."

"I'm not complaining. Don't think I can ride another yard today. All I want to do now is sleep."

"You obviously haven't heard who's here. You'd better clean yourself up. We're dining in the governor's second hall and we have company."

Chapter 38

"So why did you not follow it?" Liru's eyes were bigger than usual. Ilona, Rillette – the tall ginger-haired girl that still held Hadley's interest – and Beatrice – the small mousy one at the table – were spellbound.

"Dun was in a hurry," said Warton.

"You sure your Master Dun wasn't just scared?" Ilona asked with a knowing smile. "Anything that could frighten a deer so that it didn't even notice you must have got him thinking."

"Dun wouldn't have been scared," said Malik with a hint of pride for his weapons master and a tone of scolding for his cousin. "He just doesn't want to lose the chance to uncover spies."

"So is he going to head out and hunt for them tomorrow?"

"Actually," said Aedan, "I have a feeling we are all heading out with him tomorrow. Why do you think they joined our groups like this? And look at the way Dun is talking with your guardian. What's her name?"

"Mistress Kern," Ilona said with a sigh that held no affection.

"She looks tough," said Lorrimer.

"Does she frighten you, Ladderboy?" Ilona asked with mock sincerity.

Malik and Warton grinned.

"Seems to be frightening that forester," said Aedan, indicating.

"It looks like he had a fight with his wife," Liru said. "That face is more unhappy than scared."

"Well," Ilona mused, "if he's married to someone like Mistress Kern, it would be both."

The girls nodded. Aedan wouldn't have thought them friends back at Castath, but they had apparently drawn together under the shadow of this common enemy.

Lorrimer was done with all the talk. Food was calling his name. He took up his plate and joined a queue. The others followed. The hall's oak tables were arranged around a longer central table that was loaded with steaming fish, duck, sausages, potatoes, and trays of breads, cheese, preserves and fruit. Over a coal pit alongside, haunches of venison sizzled and dripped, filling the hall with an aroma that almost had Lorrimer whimpering. He took something of everything and ended up with more than any mortal could devour in one sitting. Aedan was curious about the fish, but the smoke of roasting venison drifted across to him and the fish lost its appeal.

They got back to their table and Malik was the first to speak. "If you lot are going with us tomorrow," he said, "I hope you know how to keep the noise down on the trail."

All four girls raised their eyebrows.

"So you think you're more capable than us outdoors, do you?" Ilona asked.

"Would you even try to challenge that?"

She fixed an icy look on her cousin. Aedan was very glad not to be on the receiving end. It was surprising how such pretty eyes could look so dangerous.

"Let's have a little challenge," she said. "When these two foresters leave, you follow one, we'll follow the other. The winners are the ones who find out where their man lives without being seen."

"What's to stop us from lying?"

"Nothing will stop you from lying, Malik. The others in your group aren't as good at it, so we'll ask them."

"Speak for yourself."

Ilona glared. It wasn't hatred that passed between them, more like the species of contempt found acceptable between some close relatives. Aedan pretended not to notice and gave his attention to the meal.

A group of musicians entered the hall, took their seats and began filling the air with the magic of flute and fiddle and something that looked like an oversized lyre. The range of melodies was impressive. Obviously the songs had been collected from various points all along Vallendal's shore.

When the meal was over, Dun made a brief announcement — there was no curfew but they should expect to be woken before sunrise and were to travel in the groups they were now sitting in.

"Looks like the foresters are leaving," said Warton. "Ladies, do you want to choose one?"

"Think we need some advantage, do you?" Ilona snapped.

"Yes," said Malik.

She sneered at him. "We'll take the smaller one. The other, the grumpy one, will be easier to track, and if we choose him you'll bring it up later." With that she stood, and the other girls with her.

They acted it well, seeming to pay no attention to the forester that they were pursuing out of the building. Warton took the lead as the boys got up and followed the other man. There were more groups starting to leave, so they blended in well.

When they got outside, it was different. The girls were standing nearby in conversation. One of them would be watching the retreating forester and would give the signal as soon as he took a corner. The boys were about to adopt a similar tactic when they saw how fast their man was walking away.

"He was supposed to be grumpy and slow," said Warton. "If we let him get too far ahead at that pace, we'll lose him after one turn."

So they pretended to take a walk in the same direction. The forester was clearly in a hurry. He chose a street leading to the harbour, and when he reached the wharf, he turned left and headed along the water's edge. The boys had to run to catch up. They stopped at the corner overlooking the docks and peered around.

"He's running!" Aedan exclaimed.

"They hurried after him at a brisk walk, weaving from one side to the other, avoiding lamps."

"We're going to lose him," said Warton. "We need to run. Lorrimer, please try to keep your feet quiet."

The wharf had several boathouses that constantly blocked the view of their quarry whose pace seemed to be increasing. He was now a very small and indistinct shadow.

"No need to run anymore," said Aedan. "He's reached the wall. Can't go anywhere after that, and it's going to look strange if we run up to him. Let's walk from here."

They slowed and gradually closed the remaining two hundred yards.

"Can anyone see him?" Lorrimer asked.

"Can't you?" said Malik. "In the shadow of the wall."

Aedan squinted but saw nothing. As they approached, it began to look more and more like nothing.

"Where, Malik?" he asked.

Malik ignored him and increased his pace, walking ahead of the others. They reached the wall – there was no forester.

Warton turned around a few times, then kicked the stonework. "Is he a ghost? How does anyone get through a wall?"

"He must have spotted us," Aedan said.

"Great!" Malik sighed. "Nice work you lot, especially Lorrimer Thunderfoot over there. So what are we going to tell the girls?"

"The truth?" Lorrimer ventured and dropped his eyes at the look Malik gave him.

"Hey!" Aedan was inspecting the stones. "It looks like this section of the wall could be climbed."

Aedan was already off the ground but Lorrimer and then Malik called him back. Malik had the most to say. "Get down from there you uncivilised northerner. If you get caught climbing the city wall at night during these times, you'll put us all in jail. Anyway, why would a forester climb the wall? He must have slipped away into one of these buildings or maybe onto a boat. That water is dark as ink."

They spent a while looking here and there without much hope before giving it up and returning to the dorm where they crawled into their beds. The others were already fast asleep. The mystery might have kept them up longer if they hadn't been so tired.

The room was filled with lantern light when Aedan felt himself being shaken from his dreams.

"If you want breakfast, you'd better hurry," said Lorrimer.

They were the last to leave.

At the dining hall, the tables were the same and the girls were already seated, steaming bowls of porridge before them. Aedan and Lorrimer filled their bowls from one of three large copper pots on the food table, spooned out cream and honey, and then collected the last two mugs of steaming goat's milk before joining the others.

"So?" Ilona asked, her voice charged with a confidence that told the boys what they feared.

Malik looked at his bowl.

"He got away," Warton mumbled.

Ilona said nothing for a while, just smiled. "Ours lives eight blocks to the west in a little apartment on the fourth floor. He had no idea that he was being followed."

"Well yours wasn't running," Warton complained.

"Running?" Liru asked. "Why would a man run home? Did he see you?"

"I don't think he saw us," said Aedan. "Must have had some other reason. There he is now. It doesn't look like he slept much."

"Serves him right for making us lose," said Warton.

"It looks like he feels bad about it too," said Liru. "He seems even more unhappy than last night. Maybe he *is* married to Mistress Kern."

It was a large party that rode out through the main gate, but even though day had broken, it was impossible to see more than thirty yards in any direction. Drumly was known for foggy mornings, and this was proving to be one of its finest. The miserable looking senior forester rode up front with Master Dun and Mistress Kern, both of whom appeared undaunted by the weather. The rest of the queen's envoys that had accompanied the girls from Castath were apparently giving this outing a miss, and perhaps for good reason. Aedan had no doubt that Dun was going to do all he could to turn the fascinating mystery of the Lakeside Terror into a lecture.

They rode about five miles east, crossed a stone bridge, then took a narrow farm track that cut inland between the hills. After another two miles, the trees disappeared as they passed into a shallow basin that, by the almost-sweet yet still-pungent smell of cow flops, was used to graze cattle.

Here they met a mounted group of about ten foresters and forty soldiers.

"We're not taking any risks," Aedan overheard the senior forester explain to Dun. "If you and these students are hurt on our watch, we'll have to answer to Castath for it."

The escort formed a shield around them and in this way they continued to ride into the fog. Aedan was growing bored and began to look around. His eyes fell on the forester to his right. The man's clothes were mostly of a dark green, similar to the material he remembered seeing in his father's wardrobe. The cloth was old and soiled, but what caught his attention was a dark stain on the back of the jerkin around a small tear. It almost looked like the forester had recently been hit by an arrow. It was when he noticed something similar on the leather chest piece of one of the soldiers that his dreamy mind awoke. Clues began to slip into place and suddenly his stomach was in his throat.

"Warton," he called, under his breath.

Warton looked over with an unfriendly expression. He had been talking to Ilona.

"Have you noticed the damage on the clothes of our escorts?"

"Why would I care about that?"

"It looks like they've been attacked."

"Well they look fine to me."

"What if they were killed and the men wearing their clothes are the ones that killed them?"

Warton took a breath to answer and then held it as he looked at Aedan.

"Ask Ilona if they were told about the killings in this area. How many from Drumly have disappeared?"

Warton turned around and passed the question on. The answer came back quickly. "She said about a dozen foresters have been taken and maybe forty-five soldiers over the past year."

Aedan tried to keep his voice low and steady. "Without being obvious about it, look around you and count."

After a few glances around him, Warton turned back to Aedan and his face was pale.

Liru moved her pony up alongside Aedan. "What is it?" she asked.

Aedan explained what he had just said to Warton, and then he interrupted himself as he realised something. "It was guilt. That's why our forester looked so upset. I'll bet that the Fenn spies caught someone he loves and are forcing him to give them information. That's where he went last night. He *did* climb the wall. He probably went to warn the spies about Dun. That's why the soldiers met us outside the city – because they were never inside it. We are being escorted by our enemy."

Liru's face showed no emotion. Her voice was less controlled. "I think you are right. But what are they waiting for?"

"Probably leading us to their main force before they turn on us."

"Aedan, you need to tell Dun."

"I will, but you start spreading the word. Try to make it look like a joke. Tell them to laugh and pass it on."

She nodded and turned to Warton and Ilona as Aedan broke ranks and cantered to the front.

"Aedan!" Dun said, "What are you doing out of formation? Get back."

"Sir, there's something very important –"

"Did you not hear your master?" Mistress Kern snapped, her voice icy.

The forester who was riding alongside was looking at Aedan as well now. Whatever he said would be heard by many pairs of ears. At the point of giving it up, he had an idea.

"Sir, it's Lorrimer. He keeps saying *stevlos* over and over. I think it's the illness returned. Please take a look at him."

Stevlos was the Vinthian word for trap, and Lorrimer had never had a recurring illness.

Dun looked at Aedan without saying anything, but there was no doubt that the message had been received. "Very well," he said, "I'll take a look." He told the forester to lead on and directed his horse to the side of the column where he brought it to a stop and asked Aedan in a weary tone to tell him more.

While gesticulating as if describing belly aches, Aedan dropped the facts in between references to an illness that he described in detail whenever a soldier passed by. Hadley had just finished telling Vayle a joke and they laughed as they rode past, though their faces showed little amusement.

"That's the news being passed forward, Sir."

Dun nodded. "I thought something was odd when the soldiers met us out here. I wish you'd told me about the forester last night, but we can discuss that later. Right now we need to have a look at Lorrimer before he infects everyone with his sickness."

The soldier passing by looked across at Dun and turned his horse a little further away from the column. Dun rode up to Lorrimer, tested his pulse, prodded his belly and gave a few words of medical advice which Aedan guessed had something to do with not fumbling his arrows. Then the weapons master nodded to Aedan and rode back to the front of the column.

"What did he say? Aedan asked.

"String our bows, pass on the message, and get ready."

Chapter 39

The fog was causing droplets to form on everything. Bowstrings would not do well in this weather and any soldier would know. Fortunately the escort seemed mostly concerned with the trees that were just beginning to show on either side. It was a brief lifting of the fog that allowed them to see the forest closing in as the basin constricted to a funnel up ahead. Aedan had no doubt that the ambush point was approaching.

He planted one end of his bow in a stirrup, pushed the handle out and pulled the other end down. He wished now that he had chosen a bow with a lighter draw weight. At last he managed to slip the loop into the string grooves. He was surprised to see that Liru was ready. Her hands were clearly skilled at a good deal more than tying bandages.

Dun was going to use hand signals to coordinate an attack on the escort, but as the fog thickened, Aedan lost sight of Dun altogether. The message would have to be passed down, or maybe everyone would just have to copy those in front of them. It was going to be a mess.

They rode on, the tension increasing as they glanced at each other, their eyes all asking the same question: "How long?"

Trees on each side were now probably within bowshot. Dun should have given the signal and everyone knew it.

Aedan dropped back to where Cedric rode at the tail of the column. "Something is wrong," he said. "He's waiting too long."

"Dun knows how to judge an encounter better than any of us," said Cedric. "He must have a reason."

"What if he's unable to give the signal? He was riding up front with Kern and the forester. If the forester is false, maybe she is too. Maybe when he told her what was happening, she slipped a dagger under his ribs and maybe there are soldiers riding behind them so no one can see?"

Cedric strained his eyes against the fog. "I'll go and check," he said. "If you hear any shouting at all, even if you can't understand it, take it as an order to attack. Spread the word. Fast."

The marshal rode ahead into the whiteness. Aedan returned to his position and, in a voice shaking with nervous strain, gave the new instruction to those around him. He hoped it would reach everyone in time.

"I think we should get arrows on strings," Malik whispered.

Aedan nodded. The others saw them and copied.

"Keep together," Aedan said, raising his voice just enough for the group to hear. "Remember how they have been torturing and killing. Whatever happens we can't surrender. We escape or we fight. If they capture us, we die." He could see that the others understood all too well.

"Aedan," Liru said. "Good luck."

"Good luck, Liru."

The trees were less than forty paces away when there was a furious yell from somewhere up front. Aedan felt every muscle tense and his tongue wanted to freeze in his mouth, but he yelled or rather shrieked the word they had been waiting for all this time.

"Attack!"

Several more voices took up the cry. All along the column, bows sprang up, arched, and released as strings thumped. It was a disorganised volley. Several arrows struck home and a few of the imposters fell. The rest, taken by surprise, let out shouts that were very clearly in Fenn, and galloped out of range, pursued by arrows.

Some of them managed to send a few arrows of their own back. Aedan saw a ranger jolt and shudder beside him as a shaft sank into his neck. He choked once, then fell from his horse.

"Reverse column!" It sounded like Cedric's voice. "Back to Drumly!"

They spun around and were about to urge their mounts forward when a line of horsemen appeared in front of them. The retreat was cut off.

This time Aedan didn't wait for instructions. "The forest!" he yelled. "Follow me." He turned to the side and galloped away, up the slope of the basin to the trees. It wasn't that he wanted to be in charge; it was simply that hesitation would have meant death.

He could hear the others behind him, but when he reached the top of the bank, he glanced over his shoulder and was surprised to see that only his group had followed. He could hear noises – shouting and galloping and the occasional slap of a bowstring – but it was too foggy to see anything. Three soldiers appeared from the mist about seventy yards behind, then another two after them. They were about to reach the bank.

Aedan wheeled and drew to a stop. "Shoot!" he yelled, nocking and drawing an arrow. His aim was a little off, but the shot was close enough, catching a soldier in the leg. Around him another seven arrows zipped away, one after the other. Two more pursuers were hit. One fell and the rest swerved into the cover of mist.

Before the men reappeared, Aedan urged his pony into the trees and immediately turned to the left, cantering just inside the tree line, keeping an eye on anything that might be revealed in the basin.

"We need to get back to Drumly and alert the troops," he said to the others.

"And leave the rest of them behind?" Warton exclaimed, riding alongside.

"We need help, Warton. You know it's the right decision to go back. If everyone stays to fight, the news might never get back. What if there are two hundred Fenn out here?"

There was a brief pause. "Well how are we going to find our way back? In this fog we'll just get lost."

"If we keep the clearing on our left and then do the same with the road, eventually we'll get to the lake. Then all we have to do is ride along the water's edge and we'll get to the city."

"Enough talk," said Malik. "We need to be fast and quiet." He moved to the front.

Aedan looked at the others. Rillette and Bernice were trembling, their faces white. Lorrimer was glancing all around him with jittery movements that suggested he was not seeing much. At least the others seemed to be less shaken.

As he turned around, Aedan's eye snagged on a section of the forest exposed through a narrow rift in the fog. Something was out of place – a movement – but it had been at the very edge of his glance and he wasn't sure what he had seen. The motion of the horse made it difficult. He stood in the stirrups and bent his knees with the stride to keep his head level, then looked again. Far away, hidden by layers of crisscrossing branches and passing trunks, he thought he saw leaves move as if a tree was leaning – which made no sense on this windless morning. But it was so far away that it was difficult to be sure. Then the fog closed in again and it was gone. He didn't want to risk saying anything for fear of being ridiculed, but he was beginning to wonder if there was more to worry about in this forest than men.

He urged his pony forward to catch up. The undergrowth became thicker and they had to slow to a walk. Leaves were heavy with damp, and branches hung low, drenching heads and shoulders as the party moved under them, After a mile the ground became uneven, and their path was repeatedly crossed by shallow gullies and large rocks.

Shouts cut through the mist on the left. The language was Fenn. There were answering shouts from behind, and then someone called from directly ahead. Malik reined in.

"What do we do now?" Rillette moaned.

"Deeper into the forest," said Aedan. "We'll have to go around."

"But we'll get lost. I don't care what your Master Dun said. The stories I heard about this creature seemed real to me."

"The only Lakeside Terror that ever existed," Malik scoffed, "is this gang of Fenn spies. Let's go." He urged his pony to the right, heading away from the basin and into a darker section of the forest. Fallen sticks produced muffled crunches, but the dampness of the morning had softened the ground, and the progress was relatively quiet.

They had travelled about two hundred paces when Aedan whispered for Malik to stop.

"What is it?" Malik asked.

"I think I heard a noise like a hoof stomping."

"Direction?"

"I'm not sure. Let's get in between those rocks. That will hide us from most angles while we listen." They moved carefully over into the shelter. Thick pine fronds helped to conceal them further.

They waited and listened. The next time, everyone heard it. Two stomps and a snort.

Further away, a branch broke. It was not the thin snap of a twig, but a deep throaty crack that echoed between the pillars of trunks. It was a sound that told of considerable strength.

A man spoke. He was too far away for the words to be clear, but the intonation was Fenn. It seemed like a question or a challenge.

For a long time there was silence, but it came to an end as horses began to stamp and snort. It was obvious that they had sensed something dangerous and their riders were not heeding the warning.

Then there was a sound that none had expected. It was a growl, but deeper than anything Aedan had ever heard. A man screamed and several more began yelling, their voices shrill and terrified. Crashing undergrowth and drumming hooves began to fill the air. The sounds grew louder until it seemed as if the horses were going to gallop right over the rocks. Half a dozen riders clad in forest colours shot past the gap.

Then the ground began to tremble. *Ba-da-duum, ba-da-duum* ... They could feel it more than hear it, and it grew nearer and nearer. Aedan was already frightened – he knew of no animal that could shake the earth like that – but then something passed in front of the gap, and he went completely numb.

It was too quick a glimpse to make out details, but there was no missing the size. It was easily twice the height of a horse, three or four times as long, and obviously many times heavier. But its movement, apart from the dull thudding, was nearly silent, and the speed was simply staggering. It was a flash of dark fur, a tearing of wind, and then it was gone.

Rillette gave a muffled shriek and Lorrimer dropped both bow and arrow.

The yells and the pounding receded into the darkness of the trees and silence gradually returned. They listened but there was nothing more than the distant call of a lark and the dripping of water from pine needles around them.

"What ... what ..." Ilona gasped, unable to find more words.

"That must be it," Rillette whimpered.

This time nobody opposed her.

Aedan was battling to comprehend what he had just seen. He edged out from the pines, glanced about him, and looked at the ground. The debris of old branches and leaves made prints difficult to spot, but he saw depressions that could have been left by hooves, and then something that looked like a paw print, only that it was bigger than the lid of a barrel. There was no creature in Thirna that should be able to leave a print like that, and this one had not been faked. As he watched, he saw pine needles unbending inside it and water oozing into the lowest part of the depression.

"We need to get away from here," he whispered, "as fast as possible!" He led the way out from their shelter and picked a section of the forest where the undergrowth was sparse, allowing them to canter. Everyone kept looking back, dreading the sight of a towering shape or the shivering of trees as something brushed against their trunks. After a few miles, Aedan was beginning to think he might have the direction wrong. In this fog it would be easy to travel in a large circle and head right back to everything they were fleeing.

They pushed on for another mile when the trees ahead began to thin. As they drew nearer, they saw that it was only a narrow break ahead of them, like a road.

"This is the road we took," said Liru. "I remember that silver birch tree with the broken limb. The lake is to the right."

"Let's get onto the road then," said Lorrimer. "We need to get out of this forest."

"I'd rather keep to the trees as long as possible," said Aedan. "There's a chance some of the Fenn have come back this way to set up another ambush."

"Aedan's right," said Ilona. "Most of them probably won't know about that creature we just saw. Their only concern will be to prevent any of us getting to Drumly. They would definitely block the road."

They retreated and, once over a ridge, trotted another two miles through denser undergrowth until the trees thinned again. This time it was a broad grassy expanse that appeared ahead of them. The lake would be hidden by the mist, but everyone was sure it was straight ahead. They hurried down a bank and broke into a canter. There was still a chance here of turning circles in the fog, but the gradual downward slope was enough to guide them to the lapping water.

There was no need to tell anyone to turn left. Malik and Warton rode up front. This time Aedan brought up the rear. His worry now was that their ponies' hooves would draw any Fenn that might have been stationed out here. He was not wrong. The noise of his own pony masked the sounds of pursuit. But there was no mistaking the purr of an arrow that flew over his head from behind.

"Malik!" he yelled. "Faster. They are behind us!"

The cautious canter became a gallop. They had to stay near to the water's edge in order to keep their direction, but that did not make for the best ground. There were channels to be jumped and buildings to be avoided. As yet, they had reached no fences, and Aedan hoped furiously that they wouldn't. The ground was uneven and his pony landed badly after the second jump. Both Aedan's feet slipped out the stirrups and he slumped forward, almost falling over the pony's head. He lost some ground while regaining his seat and stirrups. Keeping a bow in hand was making this difficult.

That reminded him that he already had an arrow clamped in the same hand as the bow. Steadying himself, he turned in his saddle and sent a wild shot into the fog behind him. As he released it, he wished that he had looked first. A group of riders was just beginning to appear a little to the left of where he had aimed.

Another arrow hissed over him. Shooting from a moving horse was difficult, but sooner or later something was bound to hit. Sure enough, a third arrow sped past Aedan and sank into Lorrimer's arm just beneath the short sleeve of the hauberk. He screamed and dropped his bow for the last time, then put his head down and urged his pony to greater speed. The ground dropped away.

"River!" Malik shouted.

They slowed just enough for the ponies to crash through the water that was above their knees, then they charged up the far bank and set off at a gallop again.

Liru and Ilona both turned in their saddles and released arrows. There was a cry from behind. Malik spun around and tried to shoot, but Rillette was in his way.

"There's Drumly," Warton yelled from the front, but he had turned to shout at a bad time. His pony stumbled in a ditch hidden by long grass and he vaulted from the saddle, turned over in the air, and hit the ground on his back. It was clear by the looseness of his tumbling body that he had been knocked unconscious. Aedan hauled in his reins and leapt to the ground.

"Don't stop!" he yelled to the others as he noticed some of them slowing. "Get word to Drumly! Go!"

There was no time to drag Warton's heavy frame onto the saddle, so he whipped his pony's hindquarters with his bow, sending it dashing away. He had seen a low hedge nearby and he dragged Warton by the arm over the grass as the earth began to pound. A small figure appeared silently alongside him and took Warton's other arm. They sped over the grass, behind the hedge, and dropped down as hooves tore up the grass beside them and vanished into the mist.

"Liru?" Aedan said. "I told you to get to the city."

"And I chose to ignore you. I saw a building in the mist about a hundred yards back. We should take him there."

They each wrapped one of Warton's arms over their shoulders and half carried, half dragged him down the slope. Liru was right. It was a large mill on the shore of the lake. They climbed the stairs and tried the double doors. They were locked. Knocking produced no response.

"Here," said Liru. She let go of Warton's arm, picked up an axe from a nearby woodpile and swung it at the centre of the doors. Aedan considered offering to help, but he had a feeling this would not be taken well. In any case, Liru seemed to be quite capable. The way she managed the axe revealed that she was considerably stronger than she looked. On the third swing, the lock gave way. They dragged Warton inside and closed the doors behind them.

"We need to barricade this," Aedan said. His eyes scanned the dark interior. It was a wide but shallow room where he imagined farmers would deliver sacks of grain to be milled. He couldn't see anything to use as a barricade, but several pots gave him the next best thing. He piled them up in front of the doors until they balanced in a four-foot-high column. At least no one would be able to enter unnoticed.

Liru hadn't stayed to help. "Aedan, leave the door," she called from somewhere deeper in the building. "I've got an idea."

Aedan grabbed Warton's arm and gave it a tug just as the large boy woke up.

"Hey! Let go of me." He swung at Aedan, skimming his chin.

"Steady, Warton. It's me. Liru is here too. Keep your voice down. We don't know how far away those Fenn spies are."

Warton hung for a moment in a blank stare and then recognition displaced the vacancy in his eyes. He staggered to his feet and, after a few groggy steps, found he was able to walk.

They moved into a large, dark room where three millstones stood idle amid a white dusting of flour. The sluice to the water channel outside was obviously closed because the axle of the waterwheel that passed through the wall was still, along with all the gears and shafts that would turn the heavy stones. In spite of this, the room was not quiet – the tumbling of water from the millpond outside was almost loud enough to cover their footsteps.

Leaving the room, they entered a large storage area filled with sacks where Liru was uncoiling a rope ladder and lowering it through a trapdoor.

"Loading bay," she said. "There are rowboats underneath us. It must be how they transport the flour into the city, and it is how we are going to get into the city." She stepped onto the rope ladder and climbed down through the trapdoor.

Aedan turned to Warton. "Your head clear enough for this?" he asked.

"I'm fine," said Warton.

They looked down. Liru was settling into a large, flat-bottomed rowboat moored at the base of the rope ladder. Warton gripped the ropes on the sides, stepped onto the rungs, and began lowering himself. Aedan wished he would hurry. The whole ladder was shaking. Warton was beginning to freeze up.

"Warton, this is not the time to go blank. They could be here any moment. Try to –"

A loud crash of pottery echoed up from the far end of the building.

Chapter 40

"Warton!" Aedan whispered. "Move it!"

Warton looked back, uncomprehending. Clearly he was not as lucid as Aedan had thought.

"Liru," Aedan called down. "Get into the water and push the boat out the way. We're jumping."

As soon as he saw the path was clear, he drew his sword, aimed at the ropes above Warton, and swung for all he was worth. The edge was keen and it sliced through the coarse fibres, dropping the incredulous Warton down through the air and into the water with a loud splash. Aedan sheathed his sword and followed, crashing into the dark water just as Warton surfaced.

The large boy looked fully aware now, and ready for a fight, but there was no time to apologise. They hurried over to the rowboat that Liru was holding as the sound of voices reached them. It was a near thing. The boat was just sliding out from under the loading floor and into the lake when footsteps began to thump on the boards.

Four soldiers looked down through the trapdoor. One of them lowered himself and dropped into the waist-high water. It didn't take him long to spot the rowboat escaping into the fog.

He shouted to his companions and splashed across to another boat moored nearby. Three more soldiers dropped into the water and scrambled on board while the first began to row. The others unslung their bows and took aim. Arrows zipped away as they surged forward in pursuit.

In the darkest shadows, behind a large structural beam, three heads rose from the water.

"Let's move," said Aedan.

Climbing the beams to the trapdoor was difficult, but easier than it would have been to wade through the water and scramble up the muddy bank of the lake.

Aedan was the first back on the loading floor. He turned to help Liru and then Warton who, though clear-headed, seemed to be in considerable pain. They sloshed over the planks, through the building and into the entrance room where they stopped dead.

A fifth soldier was here, his back to them, sword held ready. Standing in the doorway, with leaves still clinging to his hair and clothes, was Haywood the ranger. He held a short sword and a knife. The two men were clearly sizing each other up.

It was the soldier who moved first. He stepped forward with a short, powerful swing at neck height. Haywood deflected the blow with the short sword and tried to slip in with his knife, but the soldier reversed his swing and nicked Haywood's ear.

The three apprentices yelled and drew their swords together. Haywood had already seen them, but the soldier had not, and he spun around. Haywood darted in and knocked the man on the head with the back of his knife. It wasn't enough. The soldier turned and almost ran his blade through Haywood, but the ranger deflected the thrust, and struck again and again until the sword dropped to the ground and the soldier fell.

"Don't kill him," Haywood said. "He must talk, and we must get away from here. There is something nearby that is not man or horse."

The others exchanged nervous glances.

"Did you see it?" Aedan asked.

"Heard it," said Haywood. "It's heavy. Broke a footbridge after I crossed over. That was a few miles back and I think I left it behind, but in this fog there's no knowing for sure."

Aedan looked out from the open doorway. It revealed little more than grass and mist. If it weren't for the Fenn spies that were bound to return, Aedan might have opted to wait until the weather cleared.

"Let's go," Haywood said. "Next Fenn party that searches this mill could be twenty men strong."

He threw the unconscious spy over his shoulder and led the way outside. They discovered six horses tugging at reins that were fastened to a hitching rail.

"They weren't this nervous before," said Haywood, looking around. "Quickly now."

Aedan felt his skin prickle as his eyes began to dart all over. He was caught between the urge to escape and the need to know where the threat was.

Haywood approached his horse and it calmed slightly at its master's presence. The others dashed across to the remaining horses and did what they could to bring three of them under control, but their own fear, betrayed by constant terrified glances, undermined their efforts. They knew that as soon as the reins were untied, the horses would take off. Haywood's was the only one that was manageable.

"Mount," the ranger said. "I'll untie and throw you the reins."

There was a heavy splash not too far away.

"Was that from the soldiers at the lake?" Liru asked.

"I don't think so," said Aedan. "Wrong direction. I can't see the river that we crossed, but I'm sure that's where the sound came from." He gripped the leather pommel and leapt off the ground, half pulling himself up into the saddle. Having to manage the horse without reins distracted him for an instant, but the deep thud was just loud enough to catch his attention.

He glanced at Liru. She was also in the saddle now, and the way she was looking out into the mist told him that she had heard it too.

"Hurry, Warton!" Aedan called.

A slight break in the fog showed him something he hadn't expected – an enormous hayrick about a hundred yards away. His mind lurched, disorientated.

"I don't remember riding past a hayrick," he said, suddenly unsure about his sense of direction. Was the river behind him? Which way was danger and which way was safety?

The ranger had been walking across to the hitching rail, but he went completely rigid, dropped the spy he was carrying, and followed Aedan's eyes just as the fog closed in again.

"They don't make hayricks here," he whispered, pulling the bow from over his shoulder. "Get back to the mill! At least there you have a chance."

But nobody moved – they were frozen in their saddles – and then it was too late.

There was a deep, unearthly growl and everything began to shake with a dull pounding. The ranger's hand flew to his quiver and he started shooting arrow after arrow into the fog as he backed away. His horse pulled the reins from him and bolted.

The remaining horses reared as one. It was too much for the wooden hitching rail. The beam snapped, reins came free, and the horses shot away with screams and snorts.

Aedan tried to look back at Haywood, but he almost lost his seat and had to grip the mane in order to right himself. He reached twice for the reins that were alternately slapping against the horse's flanks and skidding along the ground. If they got caught under a hoof, it would be equally bad for horse and rider.

There was a shout from somewhere far behind, a thump like a falling rock, and a shriek of pain. Then the pounding resumed and it did not seem to be fading with distance. Realisation struck like a hammer.

"It's following us!" Aedan screamed.

The horses were already galloping for their lives. Aedan gripped the saddle and leaned forward, trying again to snatch his reins as they twisted like mad snakes. Finally he caught them, but they gave him no control seeing as they ran along the left of the horse's head. He attempted to flick one side over the ears but at this speed it was hopeless, and if he fell …

A slight thinning of the fog revealed walls and spires. Apparently these horses had once belonged to the city stables and they knew the way to safety. They sped by the perimeter turrets, along the moat in front of the new outer wall, and dashed between sentries to the main gate. It was only here that Aedan realised the sounds of pursuit were gone.

The horses didn't stop until they reached the portcullis where they almost collided with a large mounted regiment heading out. It took several guards to get the panicking beasts under control and make it safe for the riders to dismount.

Aedan leapt from the saddle and ran to the front of the departing regiment. He noticed that each soldier was wearing a red band around his helm. He guessed the reason was to be able to identify the imposters. Whoever commanded this regiment was thinking clearly.

"Sir," he called out, addressing the captain at the front of the column.

The man looked at him.

"Sir, we've just come from the mill. There's a large animal in the fog that attacked us. I think our ranger is hurt and there are four Fenn spies that are probably in the building. There's another one that should be lying somewhere outside. We took their horses."

The captain's look had changed at the mention of a hostile animal, but he controlled it. He turned to his soldiers, ordered them to ready their spears and led a charge down to the mill.

Aedan waited just outside the gate with Warton and Liru for some time before part of the regiment returned. The red-banded soldiers were carrying the Fenn imposters, and Haywood.

When they reached the guards, they lowered Haywood with gentle hands. There was a lot of blood. His left arm was bent in strange ways and there was a red froth coming from his mouth.

"Crushed," said Liru softly. "I've seen this before."

"Can ..." Warton looked away before trying again. "Can he survive that?"

"It looks bad," she said, "but these rangers are tough. Maybe."

The soldiers that had brought Haywood and the Fenn captives or corpses in didn't seem to have been unsettled much. Aedan guessed that the rumble of approaching horses had caused the animal to retreat into the forest.

"Look," said Liru, pointing into the courtyard behind the main gate. "Our group."

They hurried over to where four of their original number stood in a huddle.

"You made it!" Ilona and Rillette cried together, and Ilona actually embraced Liru. Malik gripped Warton by the arm.

"Where's Lorrimer?" Aedan asked, suddenly worried.

"They took him to the infirmary," Ilona replied. "He'll be fine."

The courtyard was filling with all manner of people who wanted the news. Officers were beginning to chase the crowds off to make space for soldiers that were tramping in and forming patrol squads.

"I want a better view," said Aedan. He pushed his way over to a long flight of stairs that reached the allure of the main wall. The others followed, and the guard on duty, after hearing who they were, let them pass.

They spread out behind the battlements and looked away into the fog for a long time. It was clearing slightly, but little was visible beyond two hundred yards.

"There," said Malik, pointing directly ahead. A very large group that must have emerged from the trees was moving down to the main gate.

"That looks like everyone," said Ilona. "I wonder how they managed to stay together."

The mystery was soon cleared up. They met Cedric in the courtyard below, amidst a general commotion.

"I'm sorry I couldn't stay with you," he said. "Did Lorrimer fall?"

"Arrow in the arm," Malik replied. "He's just resting at the infirmary."

"That is a great relief." Cedric mopped his brow with a wet sleeve. "How did you manage to escape? We lost you right at the beginning."

"We broke to the east," said Malik. "Went through the forest to the lake and then along the water to the city."

The marshal nodded. "Impressive."

"Did you all break west?" Aedan asked.

"Yes, and after that we didn't see a single spy. I think they decided that, once we were prepared, we were too big a number to take on. I suspect they saw you heading in the other direction and put all their efforts into finding you. If it hadn't been for this fog, you would have had no chance."

"A regiment has been sent out to hunt them," said Aedan. "Think they'll have a chance?"

"Doubt it." They may find one or two, but nobody enjoys hunting in the fog. Too easy to run into your enemy."

"What happened to Dun?" Warton asked. "Why didn't he give the signal?"

"Poison dart. I think it was the forester's work. It's not deadly – they would have wanted him alive – but I expect he's going to sleep for most of the day."

"There's one more thing," said Aedan. "We saw … something in the forest and again down by the lake. It was big and left prints that –"

"Aedan, there's no Lakeside Terror. We came across the Fenn camp and found the moulds they have been using to make those prints. They had tools there to mimic the work of giant fangs and claws, large hammers to crush bones, even ropes and pulleys for hauling trees down. It was ingenious, but Dun was right. All a very clever hoax."

"But Cedric, we actually saw something."

"In this fog? How clearly could you see it?"

"It was just a flash, but I'm not making it up."

"I didn't say you were, but patches in the fog can take on strange shapes."

"It left a print. I could see pine needles uncurling inside it. And it attacked us later and got Haywood."

Cedric looked at him for a time, then at the others in the group. "There is no Lakeside Terror," he said. "And if you spread a story that says otherwise, you will either find yourselves ridiculed or in serious trouble. I hope there is nothing foggy in my meaning."

Aedan wanted to argue, but after a brief inner battle, he looked away. "No, Sir. I think we understand you very well."

Cedric frowned. "I hate speaking like this," he said, "but I'm also under orders. Getting regular patrols back into this forest is a crucial step for the defence of this region." He sighed, then turned and left.

"I'm pretty sure he believes us," Ilona said.

"Believes us about what?" Malik asked. "Didn't you hear him? That kind of talk is going to lead to trouble. Aedan, I hope you are planning on keeping your tongue still."

"I'll say what I want, Malik. I know what I saw."

"No you don't. None of us saw anything but a shadow in the fog, and if you say otherwise, you're on your own." He walked away and everyone but Liru followed him.

Warton stopped, glanced at Aedan, then Liru, and hesitated for an instant before turning around again and leaving.

"Is that his way of saying thank you?" Liru asked.

"It's more than I expected. You should have seen what he was like a year ago. Warton's not comfortable with things like thank you and sorry, and he probably doesn't want to look weak in front of Ilona, as if he needed us. He'll probably look out for you from now on, though – in his own way. He's not all bad. It's Malik who annoys me, as usual. I thought he was changing but he's still the same two-faced weasel."

"Malik is scared," Liru said. "Cedric was not bluffing and Malik knows it. He has a lot of the politician in him. He will act as if he did not see anything. If you speak of it, Malik will make you look superstitious and frightened."

"I know," said Aedan, "and we all understand the reason for Cedric's orders. It just makes me wonder how many more people have been told to keep quiet."

"What I am wondering is why the Fenn would remain in the same forest with that animal."

Aedan considered the question. "Maybe it wanders a lot, maybe for months at a time, and it only just came back to this area. Maybe the Fenn heard the rumours but never actually believed it was real until today."

"That sounds like a good theory, but it is wrong because there is no Lakeside Terror, remember?" Liru was starting to shiver. "I'm going to the dining hall. I am wet and cold and if there is no fire, I am going to light the curtains and blame it on you while I warm myself."

Aedan sighed. "The sad thing is that everyone would probably believe you."

The group avoided talking openly about the creature they had seen, but they fielded a host of questions concerning their movements – apparently the other groups had endured a rather boring trip through the forest after the first volley of arrows. Malik and Warton did most of the talking, but when someone asked Malik if he had considered turning possum again, he went completely silent and left the table shortly afterwards.

Dun recovered during the afternoon and was brimming with his usual energy by evening. The following day he gave the apprentices the updates. Only seven of the Fenn spies had been caught and, no doubt, interrogated. Nine had been found dead on the battlefield. The treacherous forester was never seen again. Inquiries revealed that his family had been missing for a fortnight, and they too were never found.

After the first foggy morning, the rest of the week was hot and dry. The shallow film of moisture that had coated everything was lost in a day, and by the end of the week, the woods were dry as tinder. On the rangers' recommendation, the governor ordered that the forest be set alight.

The official reason was to clear the undergrowth and lessen the number of hiding places. Aedan was fairly certain that the more immediate purpose was to drive an unwelcome denizen from the area and hopefully back to DinEilan. Most of the trees survived the blaze, but the dry undergrowth with its collection of dead sticks and leaves was ready to burn, and burn it did. Crimson flames and a wall of smoke advanced through the forest and far into the distance for three days before rain brought it all to an end.

There were no more sightings of the Lakeside Terror, either real or engineered. Patrols were sent out on regular sweeps of the forest to keep it clear. They uncovered the charred remains of a few more Fenn camps, but there were no signs that any foreigners had remained in the area.

For the next two and a half months, the apprentices learned all they could of Drumly – from its culture and commerce to the strength of its walls and the range of its catapults, which they were permitted to test under strict supervision.

Sailors taught them the essentials of oar and wind, and took them to some of the east shore villages where farmers were ready with sacks of grain, barrels of preserves and bales of wool. To Aedan, the hills behind these villages looked as fertile and verdant as the northern countryside, and they gave him a twinge of longing.

But he found himself looking down into the lake as much as over it. The limpid water revealed rock shelves that dropped away into sapphire depths where enormous carp glided over waving water ferns that looked just like trees swaying in the wind. More than once, the boys begged permission to jump overboard and splash around in the water, but Aedan always dived under the surface and drifted over this submerged world, his imagination leading him as he sensed the thrill that a bird must feel at being able to defy the pull of the earth and simply glide.

There was one place near the shore, an inviting cove, where they were not permitted to swim. The sailors called it the Dragon's Maw. Even from half a mile out they could see the vortex of swirling water. It was thought that an underground river escaped the lake at this point. The Maw was said to be responsible for the loss of several fishing vessels that had been lured by the sheltered aspect and deep water during stormy nights. The secluded cove with its inviting grassy shore suddenly took on an entirely new character. Everyone was only too happy to see it dwindle over the stern rail.

One of the sailing trips ended at a low island where Dun led the way over sharp black rocks to an ancient wreck. Most of the ship had collapsed and disintegrated, but the basic form of its hull and the solid ironwood keel told of a large, well-built vessel. Aedan guessed what Dun was going to say – the wreck was thought to have belonged to the lost Gellerac fleet that once dominated the waters of the lake. They walked around the dry, flaked timbers for a while, silent, imagining the lives that had surrounded it.

Dun and Kern, along with the other senior marshals and queen's envoys, divided themselves among the groups and used every opportunity to broaden the apprentices' knowledge. Aedan found that as his knowledge of the lakeside populace grew, so did his appreciation for this part of Thirna.

The three months came to an end. There wasn't a single apprentice that hadn't fallen in love with the quaint streets, busy harbour and magnificent lake, but fond as they had become of Drumly, they were ready to go home. As they rode out the main gate, with the spires and pennants now behind them, everyone was looking forward to seeing Castath again.

Though Aedan had heard nothing about the creature he had seen, he didn't fail to notice that the marshals and rangers now carried long spears in addition to their other weapons. The trip, however, was peaceful.

Haywood had survived – they were all relieved to see it – but he had not been left unscathed. One arm hung limp and shrivelled in a sling, completely useless, and he sat hunched in his saddle looking weak and broken. This return trip would likely be his last official commission. On the first morning, Aedan rode up alongside and thanked the ranger for his selfless bravery. Haywood only nodded and turned his eyes back to the forest.

Shouts rose up from the front group as their city came into view. If it hadn't been for the busy roads, the boys would have raced each other to the gate. When they arrived back at the academy, it was still early and they were given the day off. At the lunch break, Lorrimer took the first opportunity to talk about the creature to anyone who would listen. When it leaked, Malik took the first opportunity to openly contradict Lorrimer and mock him. Aedan looked up to see Warton frowning at Malik's words, but they both knew that if they sided with Lorrimer, the news would spread and it would be worse for all of them.

Aedan pulled his friend aside afterwards. "Lorrimer, don't you remember the way Ganavant threatened us after that meeting at the palace. It's the same here. They don't want this talk spreading."

Lorrimer wasn't really listening. He threw a book against the wall with his uninjured arm. "I told the truth and Malik made them laugh at me. I thought we had become friends."

"That's just Malik. Back here, he's got more people watching again. He doesn't want them thinking we are his friends. We're not his class. Anyway, by making everyone laugh at you, he actually helped you – not intentionally, though. If people believed what you said, the trouble would start. You'd get another invitation to the palace – the dark, underground part – and this time you might not get out again."

Lorrimer was silent for a while, but eventually he nodded. "I'll keep it to myself from now. But Aedan, what was it? Today I went through all the charts in the library that have all the animals known in Thirna. Nothing matched. You grew up in forests. Surely you have some idea of what it could have been."

Aedan shook his head. "It was something from a dream, and that's where it's going to stay. At least I hope it stays there." He frowned.

"What is it?"

Aedan scratched his head. "I keep getting this feeling we'll be sent even further east before too long, maybe even into DinEilan. I'm sure that's where this animal came from. And whatever it is, I don't think it's the worst thing out there – not even close."

Chapter 41

After a few quiet weeks at the academy, the boys began a series of shorter outings that took them to various locations in the area. They also went to see investigations and arrests within and around the city where they could observe the grey-cloaked marshals exercising some of the skills that had made them legendary. The real work of the grey marshals – the watching of surrounding nations and pre-empting of danger – was something the young apprentices would not observe for many years.

It was during one of the local patrol outings that Aedan decided to ask a favour.

Over the past weeks, suspicion had been growing to a horrible certainty. His father's threat was turning out to be real. Twice he had caught glimpses of coordinated movement around him. The first time, he had doubled back, sprinted at his supposed follower and dodged past. The second time, he had walked right into the trap. Men rose up from dirty corners ahead, and flooded in from behind. They almost caught his feet as he scrambled up a blocky wall and escaped over the roofs. It had been very close.

He was patrolling the same area now with two marshals when the sensation of being tailed crept up on him. After glancing behind, he asked the marshals if they would help him. They agreed and took another route, while Aedan headed on, shadows closing around him.

He appeared at the top of an alleyway a short while later, bolting like a rabbit, with a pack of half-a-dozen club-wielding men close behind. The pursuers were gaining on him. He put on a burst of speed, took the corner, dashed past the two heavily-armed marshals, and turned around to watch the collision.

The gang might as well have tried to run through the city gate – closed. With iron-capped quarterstaves, the marshals struck clubs from numbed hands with beguiling ease. Aedan marvelled. The blows fell with speed and precision, making short work of the six men who were summarily arrested and packed away behind bars for a long respite from their labours.

The gang would provide no information, but Aedan was fairly certain it was his father trying to bring him in. His teeth ground as he considered what he would have done to the man.

While walking back from the prison, a comment Liru had recently made came to mind. It wasn't the first time it had returned to haunt him. She had said that the hate that sometimes looked out of his eyes was worrying her, that it would not be good for him.

But who was *she* to criticise? Of all people, she should have been the one to understand. He tried to push her words from his mind.

In order to improve their communication skills, the boys dined out four nights a week with families that were native speakers of Orunean, Fenn, Vinthian and Sulese. There were many such families associated with the academy. At these dinners, the apprentices spoke only the language of the hosts, learned their manners, grew familiar with the national foods which they learned to prepare, and paid attention to the more subtle aspects such as humour.

Every second class of each subject was now presented in a foreign language. Environment, Aedan was beginning to understand, was foundational to their training, and it underpinned a great deal more than language studies.

They were required not only to learn from but to live in a wide range of environments.

The first was the wild, where they continued to develop their survival skills – trapping, fishing, hunting and, when necessary, scavenging for food. Locusts, slugs, worms, and even certain roots were among the last choices. They were taught to recognise the rocks like flint and chert, sharp and hard enough to strike a spark from steel; then Wildemar took away their steel and taught them to make fire with wood, friction and blisters.

The next environment was a little easier. Each boy had to study at least two trades, common jobs that would be found in any town or city, jobs where it would be possible to find employment and slip into the working ranks of any society. They were allowed to apprentice to farmers, butchers, masons, blacksmiths, tailors, cobblers and several more.

Aedan chose livestock farm labour and carpentry. He showed himself a natural hand with the animals, and within weeks, proved himself the most useless carpenter's apprentice in all of Castath. Whether it was a lack of patience or just the wrong kind of head for angles and planes, he produced consistently un-sellable work. His chairs never balanced until he'd sawn so much from one leg and then another that the seat was half way to the ground. His tables were never flat, the wobbly joins never flush. Even Kian, whose positive enthusiasm knew no clouds, seemed to despair of Aedan's prospects. For Aedan, the smells and feel of woodwork were nostalgic, and he did not regret his choice, though he stood alone in this.

The training environment that followed was something unexpected. For many, it proved to be the most trying aspect of their preparation. They were clothed in rags and sent, for three weeks, to work beside the poorest and lowest – fullers, street cleaners, lime-burners, gong farmers, and worst of all, the tanners whose days were spent in the heavy fumes rising from concoctions of urine, dung-water and animal skins that slowly rotted until the hair could be removed and leather produced. The boys would then spend their evenings in the worst alleys where their sleeping bays had been arranged and paid for by the academy – the streets were territorial and newcomers were not smiled on if they did not show the proper monetary respect to the alley-lords.

The programme had been running for years and the boys were expected and tolerated as the outsiders they were. Here they discovered a world that many of them had happily consigned to ignorance. For those from wealthy families, the shock was beyond words.

It was not just the matter of hygiene. On the narrow back roads of the Seeps, the veneer of civil society was missing. The brutality of selfishness and the rule of might wore no genteel cloak and stood behind no formal niceties. Here, in full view, was that which was swept under the carpets of the rich.

Aedan's worries about his father's thugs subsided a little after a few days. Perhaps, he thought, they had lost interest in him. Still, he found it difficult to sleep and jolted awake at every sound.

Like the rest of the apprentices, he was distressed by the roughness of street ways when there was no "law" or "money" walking past, but soon he began to notice kindness and generosity too, though there was little to be generous with. Old men gave their bread to a sick friend; a woman defended another's baby from a drunk; children without parents took care of their siblings, shouldering responsibilities no child should have.

At first, Aedan was not accepted into any of the surprisingly close-knit spheres. But one evening he gained the friendship of two old men, Garald and Hayes, when he stood up to a young, truncheon-swinging thief who wanted their small meal. After a long, hushed discussion the men called Aedan over to sit with them instead of "retreating so lonesome-like".

There was no trouble finding a topic of conversation, for they were deep in the streams of rumour that continued to flow in from the eastern towns. The ideas on which they wanted Aedan's opinion made Rillete's seem tame – and it was not only talk from the east.

"These be strange times," Garald said in a raspy voice, cracked with wear and age. "Since that unnatural storm with its lightning strike looking like gold and fire pouring into the earth, there's something changed here. At nights, sometimes I'm feeling things in the ground under these old bones. Shakes and shiverings that don't belong in rock. You mark my words, boy. There's something been disturbed under this city. You be sure to tell them folks back at the 'cademy."

When the three weeks were up, the ragged apprentices made their way back to the academy. A few of them were in bad shape. Seeing as the programme was under Kollis's supervision, they complained bitterly to him about the exercise. Kollis let them speak. After several had told their stories, he explained.

"There are few things that can be properly understood without experience. If you learned weapons from a book, how useful do you think you would be?"

There were a few murmured replies – not very useful.

"Understanding a society means understanding the whole society, not just the part that dresses well. As marshals, you will need to understand a city's structure from one end of the social ladder to the other. Circumstances on an operation might require you to adapt, to hide for long times where you had not expected to, or to seek information where you would rather not.

"But more importantly, the exercise was to move you to empathy and broaden your understanding of what it is to be human."

Much as he struggled to accept anything from Kollis, Aedan had to admit that there was sense here. The experience had not been the most enjoyable, but it had brought a new depth to what he saw when he looked out over the city. For the first time, some of the apprentices were beginning to understand the plight of the lower classes, not as an idea, but as hunger and thirst.

Peashot remained silent and morose through all of it. Aedan had once visited him in his alley. The little foxy-eyed boy had grunted at the attempts to spark conversation and remained facing the wall, hacking and scratching gravestones into the bricks with his knife. His mood lingered through the following week when Kollis began a series of classes on religion.

Kollis's introduction was a relatively cynical description of the old faith – the belief in the Ancient, the creator who was said to be before all and above all. He then moved on with far greater enthusiasm to the rich tapestry of faiths now accessible – Eclonism, Telresh, Chorism, Shendra, and several more.

Peashot raised his hand and said without emotion that he thought all religion was stupid and wanted to know how a tapestry of lies was a good thing.

Kollis, trying to control his voice, asked how anyone could dare make such a statement.

Peashot replied that he was surprised anyone could do otherwise. In the argument that followed, he managed to offend almost everyone in the room with his forthright and tactless evaluations of their beliefs.

Kollis, while he believed in many obscure things, did not believe in the cane. Before the class was done, Peashot succeeded in converting him.

As the apprentices were required to take partners to the dinners and learn how to conduct themselves in different cultures, they saw the girls from the medical class regularly. Delwyn caused something of a stir when she partnered Lorrimer for the first time, but it was Ilona who made them stumble and stutter and knot their tongues when asking her to partner them. She was growing prettier by the day. The boys were all noticing, and not just the boys from their class. Heads were turning wherever she went. It gave Aedan an oddly protective feeling. He had wanted to walk with her several times, but the words always got stuck when she smiled at him – and she had begun smiling at him often.

By the end of the year, Murn had grown so big that Aedan had to stand on the fence to saddle him. His coal coat rippled with eager young muscle, and though he still had the slender form of a growing horse, he was already the most impressive occupant of the stables. The only other person who dared enter the paddock with Aedan was Liru, so Aedan asked if she would be prepared to take the lead rope on his first attempt to ride.

He waited until midday when Murn was normally a shade less spirited, tacked him, gave the lead rope to Liru, and climbed gingerly up, up, and onto the saddle. Murn bent his neck around and gave Aedan a good inspection. His ears flicked slightly and he looked back at Liru.

Aedan gulped.

But these were two people Murn liked, so he allowed himself to be guided in a circle, his long steps requiring Liru to move very fast to avoid having her heels trod on.

The plan fell apart when Murn caught the scent of something that belonged to him in one of Liru's pockets. She had been nervous to begin with, and when the huge muzzle pushed against her and began to dig, her self-confidence fled. Murn discovered the pocket; his efforts doubled and Liru sped up until she was running for the fence. Aedan had to endure a high speed trot. It ended at the gate with an abrupt halt that spat him from the saddle and dropped him a long, long way down to the ground.

Murn seemed confused and nosed him until he got up laughing and rubbing his bruised hip.

"You've got something edible in your pocket haven't you?" he said to Liru.

Liru found the carrot and looked very embarrassed. Murn eased her embarrassment by snatching it away and making it disappear.

Things began to improve, but very slowly. It wasn't that Murn was a slow learner; it was that he was still very much a young storm of an animal, a very big, fast and powerful storm. Aedan knew he was not rider enough for such a horse. Not yet.

Lorrimer had worked hard on his literacy. His lantern usually burned as long as Aedan's, and the two of them often studied after the rest of the dorm had sunk into darkness. As the examinations approached, his dedication infected all around him, except Aedan who was already driven, and Vayle who had no need to be – information apparently attached itself to this boy's mind like burrs to expensive clothing.

The new languages, Sulese in particular, provided some good entertainment owing to its unusual structure. It was a vastly different language to any of the others learned thus far. Towards the end of the year, Giddard presented them with a collection of Sulese memorabilia and commentaries. Loosely translated, some of them would have read:

"The grass sparkled with dew droppings."

Warton, I am not sure if that is intended as a beautiful or a horrible image.

"I was tort to extinguish riyt from rong."

Bede, apparently not.

"Sulese are always inviting you to go for dinner to get murdered."

Kian, it would seem from this that Sulese are enthusiastically hospitable, transparent of motive, and not very good at committing murder. All are grave errors.

"Sulese food on heads with never eat hats."

Cayde, Sulese order word important very is. It must learn you.

The year's final practical assessment took them on a one month journey to Harronville. Here they were required to assess the level of war-readiness and obtain information and instructions using each of the four languages they had been taught. On their return they were to complete a series of tests which included making weapons, hunting for food, building shelters, tracking and covering tracks, memorising a map, and finally – the aspect on which the assessment hinged – present a full report translated into all of the foreign languages studied and an accurately drawn map indicating their movements. Aedan was put in a group with Hadley, Kian and Cayde.

They travelled with a ranger and a guard of six soldiers. Harronville was not a city; it was more of a large village between forested hills. For defence it had only stockades of sharpened tree trunks, but the locals had dug a moat and embankments that would slow an attack hopefully long enough for aid to arrive from Castath. Huge signal pyres, of course, stood ready.

Aedan was both impressed and concerned by the preparations he saw. Though the spiked wall told of immense labour by few, in the back of his mind was a hard reality. The Fenn army was not a rabble of bandits that would be thwarted by a wooden stockade; it was a colossal and efficient machine of destruction and these defences would be torn apart within three hours. But even if the defences could hold for three days, he knew that Burkhart would not risk his city by sending aid. Harronville, if attacked, would make its stand alone, and it would fall alone.

The others agreed with his observations. Though their report was anything but reassuring, their assessments were considered excellent.

And with this, their second year was complete.

———

Aedan's dedication had yielded impressive results. It was no secret that he was doing well. By the beginning of his third year, his reputation was beginning to glow a little, but nothing like his flushed cheeks when the most dazzling pair of eyes began locking with his. Those few held glances had given him a new perspective on things. Previously, the academy had been an august monument to invaluable knowledge founded on ancient and immovable rock. Now all that was a cloudy insignificance floating in a dizzy orbit around an epicentre that was Ilona ...

Everything had been redefined, and everything had grown beautiful. Birds sang of this budding love, and flowers grew only to be plucked for her – though he hadn't the nerve to do any more than pluck them, and so he left a colourful trail of discarded petals wherever he walked. He found himself thinking of her, imagining shining moments like her adoring laughter in response to one of his many witty remarks. Her ringing voice would cause the robins to faint and topple from their branches and butterflies to explode with happiness – joyful little puffs that would sprinkle the air with a soft haze as she leaned forward and –

"Aedan!"

The vision vanished with a sudden ethereal rip. He found himself sitting near the front of a tense and silent class. Skeet looked dangerous. He always looked dangerous, but this time the danger was focussed.

"When one of my students grins like a lovesick gargoyle at the calculations required to balance fulcrum shear with lever-arm length, I am moved to suspicion. Were you paying attention at all?"

"Yes ... uh, yes ... Master Skeet," Aedan stammered.

"Good, then you can complete the design of our improvised catapult." He handed Aedan the chalk and walked to the back of the class.

Aedan shuffled to the board, sensing the weight of forty eyes on his back. The rough catapult design had been sketched, the materials listed, but all of them were poor choices.

"Why don't we just use steel for the axle?" he asked, and immediately wished he had not spoken the thought as the class erupted in laughter. The poor materials were probably the whole point of the exercise.

He looked back at the sketch, stared with deepening incomprehension, made some burbling noises and turned red. After an age of infamy, Skeet sent him to his chair with an icy warning.

This episode was quite out of character for Aedan. His friends could get no straight answer from him, but the mystery was solved quickly enough. Later that day, a few of the boys were seated on the tiered benches that faced one of the twenty-foot crindo boards. Six of their classmates had just finished a game and were dragging the enormous pieces back to their starting arrangement before leaving. Aedan and his friends remained, drinking in the last of the afternoon before their evening training session. Ilona and three of her friends settled down across from them on the other side of the board.

Aedan found himself laughing the loudest, interjecting the most often, and glancing constantly over to the other side of the crindo square. At one point, his glance was rewarded. His face flushed. He heard only bits of the next joke and burst into uproarious laughter a beat before Vayle arrived at the punch line. There were a few curious glances. Peashot frowned openly, but

Hadley had followed Aedan's darting eyes and was now nursing a half grin.

The air cooled and began to nip. The girls left, all but Ilona, who remained on the bench, writing something on a sheet of paper. Soon Lorrimer declared it was time to head in. The boys rose and turned towards their wing. Hadley stood in Aedan's way.

"You think she's sitting there by herself because she likes the cold? She doesn't talk to Warton much anymore and I've seen you two exchanging looks."

Aedan was too surprised by Hadley's words and too terrified by their glorious implication to react.

"Go talk to her," Hadley said.

"No! Hadley, no! I – I can't!"

"Fine. Then I'm going to tell her that you would rather be early for Dun than spend time with her." He turned to Ilona, but Aedan caught his arm in a ferocious grip.

"I can't Hadley!" His voice was a frantic whisper. "It doesn't just work like that. I have to think about things, get it all sorted out first. You know what I mean."

"I know exactly what you mean - it's the same as Lorrimer standing all morning at the jumping platform over the dam. Remember how we helped him?"

"No Hadley, don't do it! Please don't –"

"Hey Ilona," Hadley called. "We're heading in. Do you mind taking care of Aedan for a bit? See that he's safe and all that?"

Ilona looked up from her writing and laughed. Aedan's vision swam. Sparrows and crickets burst into chorus and a few stars fell from the sky. She patted the bench beside her and glanced at him.

The bench was twenty yards away. He wished it were twenty miles. Oh help. He looked up, tried to swallow, but the dryness caught in his throat and he almost gagged as Ilona smiled. He staggered forward through something between a fog of bliss and a gauntlet of terror, knees all but collapsing as he dropped down beside her. A glance revealed that Hadley had gone.

Ilona shifted in her seat, put her elbow on the backrest and faced him. A confident grin toyed with the edges of her mouth. "I wrote you something," she said, reaching forward and slipping a folded note into Aedan's shirt pocket. "Don't read it until lights are out and everyone else is asleep. It's our secret."

She stood and Aedan did likewise, lifting his heels a little to reduce the disparity in height.

"You don't need to be frightened," she said, smiling.

"I'm n-not," he managed with a voice that quivered its way out between rattling teeth.

Ilona laughed, twirled around, and sprang away with graceful strides. "Our secret, remember," she called back over her shoulder.

Aedan was still too overcome with volcanic emotions to be angry with himself over a lack of self-possession. Anyway, he must have done rather well considering she smiled and laughed and gave him a letter.

A letter!

His pocket caught fire as he remembered. He snatched the folded page out, but then remembered what she had said – only once lights were out – and reverently put it back. Then he set off at a moderate sprint, leaping over benches and tables and skidding across dew-wet grass until he caught up with the others. The murderous thoughts he had raised against Hadley were as distant a reality as last winter's snow.

"Why you dawdling?" he nagged. "We'll be late."

"What's stinging your rump?" said Peashot. "We're almost an hour early. And why were you talking to Ilona anyway?"

Aedan did his best to parry the question, but Hadley, exhibiting his habitual discreetness, announced the answer to all. The name of Ilona was soon being bounced around in the air like a ball in some game. Aedan could do no more than grin and blush.

The ragging carried on until lights were out, and then for a while in the darkness until everyone was exhausted. When Aedan was convinced that the others were asleep, he unshuttered his dark lantern and withdrew the letter.

Oh, the fire that coursed through his veins as he saw his name in that most perfect script – the script that had flowed from that most perfect hand.

The letter began. *Dear Aedan.*

His smile reached across his face and the thudding in his chest was surely enough to wake the others, but a quick glance assured him that none had stirred.

Dear, she had called him dear. He clutched the page and his eyes rushed on.

There's something I've been meaning to say to you for some time.

Here it was then. He curled his toes and tucked into the pillow.

You're such a silly boy.

Aedan frowned, read it again. There it was, just like before. *Silly boy.* His mouth was slightly twisted as he pushed on.

You say such awkward things sometimes, but Rillette says all boys are like that at first. So maybe we should spend some time talking when we don't have all our friends looking at us and making it uncomfortable. Would you like to walk with me when it's my turn to do the delivery and collection at the beginning of next week? I know you are training during the first hours, but I'm sure you can think of a way to get out of it.

Meet me outside the marble archway at sunrise. Don't let me down. I'm depending on you.

There were three kisses above the name of Ilona, and Aedan almost dropped the lantern. He made a desperate grab for it, singing his fingers on the hot cover. After nursing the burns for a while he settled back down and read the letter seven or eight times over. When he could say it all by heart, except the peppery bits, he blew out the lantern and turned in for the night. It wasn't long before the lantern was relit and he was gloating over his prize once more. In such a manner he whittled away the hours.

The week that stood between him and this great appointment passed in a delirium of emotional overload and physical exhaustion, sleep being a near impossibility. Yet it did not make him bad-tempered. Instead, he found it the most natural thing to be amiable to everyone, responding even to rudeness with a deep, benign smile. He discovered himself to be the most magnanimous creature in the whole world, simply overstocked with goodness that could not be held in.

When he considered his plan for escaping classes, there was the gentlest tug of conscience, but it was easily soothed and put away. He had wanted for a long time to stand beside her, and tomorrow she would need him.

Some things were more important than others.

It was late when sleep arrived. It carried him into a wasteland of poorly designed, broken catapults where he battled great monsters with his bare hands, holding them back from a softly crying Ilona whose eyes were locked on his fearless kicks and mighty punches; and when the monsters were sent running, she flew into his arms and wept over his wounds, breathless with admiration and undying love.

When he awoke, it was dark. He smiled, stretched, and began preparations for the morning's escape.

Chapter 42

"I think he's sick." The voice was Peashot's.

Dun looked at Aedan – sweaty, his sheets soaked, skin icy. He was obviously fevered.

The empty water jar was tucked well away under the bed.

Dun excused him from the morning session. Under the worried glances and encouraging words, Aedan was made to burn with a real fever – guilt.

As soon as the corridors were quiet, he slipped out and stole through the dim light towards the archway. It looked like he was the only one here, but as he passed under the shadow of the marble edifice, a shape sprang out from the darkness. He gave a muffled shout and leapt back, dropping into a fighting stance.

Ilona walked forward, hands on her hips, laughing.

It was not the greeting he had anticipated. No clinging or weeping. It put him somewhat off balance. He tried to wipe the scare from his face and managed a silly grin as Ilona nudged him with her shoulder, nodded to the guard who didn't even look at Aedan, and led the way from the academy into the waking streets. She held two baskets which Aedan offered to carry.

"Usually Rillette makes these trips with me," she said, "but she's hurt her foot. I could have asked one of the other girls, but I decided it would be nicer to go with you."

Aedan was surprised. He was risking big trouble for this outing and he had expected something more serious – suspicious watchers and dark alleys at the very least. But as he glanced across at the graceful and slender form, the streamers of soft golden hair flowing behind a flawless profile – long forehead, fine nose, delicate chin – and those huge emerald eyes, he decided any punishment would be a small thing. How did a girl get to be so … so utterly perfect? And how did he get to be walking beside her?

Desperate to engage in some kind of conversation, but unsure how to begin, he was relieved when she broke the silence.

"I hear you have done well recently. Top of the class they say. How did you manage it?"

For the next mile, Aedan basked in the pleasure of telling a beautiful girl all about himself. Conversation, it seemed, wasn't so difficult after all. He began with his methods of study and led quickly onto his techniques in weapons, infusing as much false modesty as he could bear. He placed before her some of his deepest secrets, and some of his friends' secrets too, and was about to get started with a new design he'd been considering for a war machine when they arrived at the apothecary's store.

Ilona put a finger to her lips, cutting Aedan off in mid flow, asked him to wait out of sight, and walked inside. When she returned, the baskets were heaped with bottles. They were considerably heavier and Aedan saw an opportunity to demonstrate some of his strength – something he had been compelled to mention a little earlier, so he insisted again on carrying both. Ilona made no argument; it left her free to twirl and dance beside him, causing her bright red kirtle to swish around her ankles. She drew more than a little attention, especially from the boys and young men, but it didn't seem to worry her.

Aedan took up the conversation where they, or rather he, had left off. The now-heavy baskets and a problem he was experiencing with his shoe – the half-inch paper lifts he'd wedged under his heels to bring him nearer to Ilona's height were causing the left shoe to slip off with each step – made the description of the war machine challenging. Nevertheless, as he finished off, he felt he had provided a fairly compelling picture, especially with the design's culmination – the ground-breaking secondary torsional spring system.

For the past fifty paces or so, Ilona had been gazing up at a steep angle, obviously trying to get an idea of the machine's size by comparing it to buildings. It was time to know her opinion. Aedan took a deep breath. "Well," he said, pulse racing, "what do you think?"

Ilona was quiet for a spell, considering. Then she turned to him with a dreamy look. "Aren't these such pretty houses?"

Aedan had been ready to field a range of questions, but that one slipped him. He had to do a bit of mental scrambling before he was able to reply. "Uh ... the houses? Well ... yes, I suppose they are."

"Now that's where I'd like to live," she said, and for the next half-mile she enthused about cherry-wood floors, satin curtains, gold-edged porcelain vases and the kind of high company that could be found in those surrounds. Aedan's disappointment did not last long. He soon forgot about the war machine and gazed at Ilona with the deepest interest, captivated by the movement of her eyes and mouth, and hearing not a word.

They "conversed" in this manner down the affluent High Street. Aedan was beginning to feel more comfortable. Things were going along nicely.

As they turned a corner, the invisible arms of the bakery reached through the breeze and took hold of them. Ilona suddenly lost interest in cherry wood and satin.

"Let's drop in at Corey's," she said. "I'm starved."

They walked through the doors just in time to see a heap of barley loaves totter out from the kitchen and collapse into a large basket, revealing a young man, slightly flushed, holding a tray. He had carefully arranged flaxen hair, quick eyes, and a feathery peach-fuzz moustache that was impossibly dark, far darker than his hair. It was almost as if he had used some kind of boot polish. Aedan looked down to the boots, and when he looked up again, he was grinning.

No sooner had Moustache-boy's eyes fallen on Ilona than they detected Aedan, and the look of delight shrivelled into something nearer hate. It was a kind of hungry hate. Aedan recognised it immediately – he had seen it more than once on the morning's walk. In his companion's company, he was finding much opportunity to study the face of envy.

"Hello there, Lynford," Ilona said with a flash of perfect teeth and tilt of her head.

Lynford's smile found him again just as his father, the renowned Corey, entered the room.

"Ilona!" he called in a deep voice drawn from the vast chasms of an even deeper belly. "The Rose of Castath, as my blushing son here so rightly calls you. And Aedan. What a delight to see two of my most loyal together."

The moustache flinched at the last word and the smile beneath it shrivelled again.

"What are the latest Fenn rumours down at the academy?" the baker asked.

It was Aedan's turn to flinch as the mention of the academy woke his conscience which delivered a good bite. Fortunately Ilona took up the conversation and, after passing on the gossip, ordered two small cheese-coated loaves while the boys exchange dangerous looks. A wave of customers poured into the bakery, bringing an end to their chat. Aedan paid for the loaves and they made their way out, but not before Ilona turned and gave the miserable baker's son a parting smile.

Aedan tensed. He knew exactly what route to take the conversation. It would require subtlety and tact. He could see the way forward.

"Can't say I think much of Lynford," he began as they got onto the road. "Looks like he must spend half the morning fixing his hair. And his moustache is painted – any girl who kissed him would get a moustache herself. And ... and he'll probably end up fat like his father." He glanced at Ilona, hopeful.

She laughed at him over her loaf. "Is that jealousy speaking?"

Aedan tried to deny the charge. He bumbled and stuttered until Ilona plugged his mouth with a hunk of bread. Aedan, his hands occupied by the baskets, could do nothing but chew.

"There," Ilona said. "If you aren't going to be honest with me then don't talk."

Aedan tried to look as contrite as bulging chipmunk-cheeks would allow.

"Don't worry," said Ilona, reading his pinched brows. "I'm not cross with you, silly boy."

She stopped walking, looked at Aedan as if considering something, then led him to the whitewashed door of a modest apartment. She knocked. After a while the door was opened by a short woman with striking, angular features drawn into tired lines.

"Hello, Mum," Ilona said, leaning forward to kiss her surprised mother. Then she dashed into the house, calling something over her shoulder about entertaining Aedan for a bit while she fetched a hat.

The woman turned her sad look on Aedan and smiled faintly.

"Come in, then. Have a seat," she said, and led him to a small kitchen table. Aedan, knowing all about Malik's family wealth, was surprised at the modesty of the home. But then he remembered what Coren had said about his in-laws – obviously Malik's parents – having no interest in charity even among their own relatives. Ilona's mother sat down facing him. "So you're the one who saved my daughter a while back." She took Aedan's hand in both of hers and smiled at him. "I'm very grateful, Aedan. We are all very grateful. Ilona speaks of you often."

Aedan snatched at the words and buried them in his personal vault of treasures. He smiled and Ilona's mother continued.

"Look after her down at the campus, Aedan. She's not as tough as she seems. Six years later and I still hear her weeping at night for the father that walked out. There's a tender heart under that shell."

He could not have been more deeply moved.

Ilona danced back into the room. Aedan noticed a loose floral bonnet thing strapped to her head. He didn't see how it would help with sun, rain or wind, but the light material made her eyes appear even more arresting, and he gawped in mute approval. She kissed her mother again and led the way back onto the road. Aedan said a clumsy goodbye. As he stepped out, he realised that he still didn't know the little woman's name. Mum certainly wouldn't do. Although ... perhaps one day ... The thought gave him a sudden flush of exultant joy and a deep smile spread over his face.

"Why are you smiling like that?" Ilona asked.

"Me? Uh – oh, haha, no, it's ... it's nothing. At least, well not nothing, umm, just not really, you know, explainable, or like that ..." He swallowed, choked, and after a bout of coughing in which he finally lost his shoe and had to go back for it, hoping Ilona had not noticed the paper lifts, he managed to calm himself down and recover his breath.

Ilona was watching him, her head tilted slightly, a curious expression lurking under the dappled shade of the bonnet. "You're blushing." she said.

If he hadn't been blushing before, he did so now, challenging her for the title of Rose of Castath.

They wended their way through the crowds to the arching bridge that overlooked Regent Street's open market. Here they leaned on the stone railing and watched for a while. Aedan, his hands free at last, nibbled at his loaf, but his stomach was too full of flutters to accept much.

The scene beneath them was almost like a large colourful river, a great living painting that formed but never settled. Dabs of earthy tones – farmers and labourers mostly, in their rough trews and tunics – drifted in and settled behind the booths and tables, while glittering ripples of patrons from higher ranks, coloured with an array of vibrant surcoats, cloaks and gowns, eddied around each other and attached themselves to the booths for a time before being drawn away back into the current.

The growing waterfall of voices was spiced with the soft bubbling of pigeons and the tireless honk-and-screech of a frustrated donkey tethered a maddening five yards from a crate of cabbages. From further off, where the livestock were permitted, grunts, squeals, bleats and gentle lowing drew customers more effectively than any banner could have done.

"See the man with the red hat and tunic?" Ilona said, pointing down into the crowd. When Aedan had located him, she continued. "He's the richest landowner in the city. He owns more than a dozen inns. His son is at the academy in the law wing. On his sixteenth birthday, his father gave him a carriage with copper-tinted velvet seats and a team of six horses." A dreamy look crossed her face and Aedan had the strangest empty feeling. He was in her company, but somehow not.

On the walk back he tried to start a conversation around things in which they shared some knowledge – Mistress Gilda, the academy, and as a final bid, Rillete's injured foot – but it was like striking sparks into a puddle. Ilona's thoughts were clearly elsewhere, and Aedan tried every angle without success. By the time they reached the academy, he was spent.

Outside the gate, Ilona stopped him.

"Aedan," she said. "Do you think I'm beautiful?" She arched her brows and smiled playfully.

A wave of delight rushed over him – no wonder she had been so quiet. It was all he could do to keep up with the torrent of adjectives that poured forth. "I think you're the most ..." it began, and ran through an assortment of wonderful things, some of which he wasn't too sure about, but it felt so good to say them that he couldn't stop until he ran out of breath.

She laughed, and rewarded him with a smile that almost had him stepping forward with arms outstretched, but she danced away through the academy gate.

"Thank you, Aedan," she said, when he caught up. "It's nice having someone I can depend on." She took the baskets, then looked into his eyes and let the moment linger. As Aedan gazed, the bleak homeward walk and the rich boy and Lynford were forgotten.

Then she was gone.

If he could have made the morning last forever, he would have, yet the sigh he breathed was as much one of regret as exhaustion. It wasn't just the lack of sleep, though that contributed. He felt utterly drained. Thoughts of her nagged at his worn-out mind, keeping it from rest, like the smell of those cabbages was doing for the donkey.

After Ilona was well away, he pulled the annoying paper lifts from his shoes and took a roundabout route to his dorm. He had planned to slip in unnoticed, but it was not to be – Murn had prepared something special.

The dark ruthrek had continued to grow at an alarming rate. Muscle now coiled through powerful limbs and chest in a way that caused people to stare. It also kept them at a distance while staring because Murn was not a horse to gaze back with vacant cow-eyes. He was intelligent and restless and tended to play with anyone who came within range. It normally resulted in screams. With his increasing strength, he had discovered, only a few hours earlier, that he could jump the raised outer fence.

As Aedan made his furtive way behind hedges and walls, he began to sense that something was amiss. Nobody was lounging on the lawns. Instead, tight clusters of jabbering students were gathered in and around the buildings. Taking a corner, Aedan almost ran into one of the groundsmen who recognised him and delivered a fuming summary of the day.

Apparently, after clearing the fence, Murn had thundered up from the paddocks and made circuit of the grounds, confiscating and devouring all manner of interesting meals that would probably give him colic later. After scattering the students, even sending one or two up the trees, he made a light lunch of some rare boutique plant that had held tenure within the forbidden central precinct for two hundred years. When he was chased off, he left hoof-sized craters in the manicured lawn as a testament to his visit. He had last been seen rolling in a clover patch – part of a decorative section of the chancellor's boulevard.

Aedan snatched the halter from the shaking groundsman and raced off to find his unruly beast.

When Murn was safely stabled, Aedan was made to feel the full weight of the various desecrations. He had to labour through the night to raise the fence yet again. Kian got wind of it and helped. He ensured that the barrier was not just high but also robust. It would need to withstand experimental prods from a horse that now looked capable of charging through a stone parapet. After testing the beams Aedan had nailed in place, Kian pronounced them useless, pulled them down, and made Aedan hold while he bound and dovetailed with the precision of an artist.

Long into the night the echoes of the lonely hammer fluttered through empty acres of darkened lawns and hooded trees, lingering in the porticos and colonnades now shadow-filled and mysterious. Roosting doves cocked their heads and puzzled over these odd creatures toiling, talking and sometimes laughing in the soft glow of their lantern.

By the time the last fence was raised, the eastern skyline had begun to change moods, and the sleepy boys ambled off to a well-earned breakfast.

As soon as the meal was over, Dun called Aedan aside. He wanted the full story. He had seen him running after Murn – he knew the fever had been a hoax. Aedan hadn't slept for a while. He was too drained to construct any story but the truth, and it toppled out.

Dun laughed before assigning three weeks of that most dreaded latrine duty. It was a cunning punishment. No matter how much Aedan washed he was unable to rid himself of the smell, real or imagined, that hummed around him like flies. His friends helped things along by continually sniffing the air and frowning.

The result was that he kept as far away from Ilona as possible, but the weeks passed until there was only one sleep left.

Aedan woke long before sunrise. Unable to get back to sleep, he stared into the darkness and marvelled at how he had found a glittering diamond where everyone else had seen a stone.

Or maybe not everyone, but most had seen a stone.

Or maybe not most, but at least some had failed to notice her …

Still, none of that mattered really. What was important was that the two of them had found each other and they were devoted to each other – at least, he was. That much was certain.

He let out a huff and stared at the ceiling. There was a certain symmetry lacking.

Tomorrow he would have to resolve this, move things along. This was not a girl to lose, and – the next thought made him grip the pillow with some violence – there were one or two rivals.

Or maybe not just one or two …

———

"Are we talking about the same Ilona?" said Peashot as they ambled across the lawn.

What do you mean?" Aedan asked.

"Kindest and sweetest, you said. Have you seen the way she treats me? Flat out ignores me if I say anything to her. Kind and sweet people are kind and sweet to everyone, not just the people they like."

"Maybe you just haven't got to know her yet," said Aedan.

"Maybe *you* haven't. You're too drunk on your feelings to actually do any real thinking."

"I've been thinking about her for a month and she is the most wonderful –"

"Yes, yes, I got it all the first time. But tell me honestly – would you really think she was that wonderful if she wasn't so pretty?"

"How can you ask that? People aren't like tools you can take apart and study in order to understand them. She's not the easiest person to get to know, I'll admit that. But then gold is not the easiest treasure to collect. Her mother told me a bit about her painful background, and maybe that gives her some sharp edges, but I'm looking past all that to the wonderful person that she really is."

It was a fine speech. Aedan felt pleased with how he'd put it across. It had even steadied his own confidence.

"Well I can't comment on her background, but I can say that she treats me and Lorrimer like vermin."

Aedan decided he would have to talk to her about this some time, but for now it was not too much to accept that she didn't get on with everyone. He didn't. Neither did Peashot. For someone with a sharp mind, it was only natural that she should be quick with her tongue. She had once referred to Lorrimer as a bat-eared pole, but in jest. Everyone had laughed, even Lorrimer, though he was quiet for a long time afterwards.

They turned down one of the leafy walkways and Aedan's eyes fastened onto something under a nearby tree. All thoughts of Peashot – who was instantly forgiven – and bat-eared poles vanished with a pop, leaving only a soft vision of flowing golden locks and glittering emerald eyes. He excused himself and bounded to her like a puppy to its master.

"Hi Ilona," he began.

She smiled and he immediately forgot what he was going to say. There were two older boys and several girls in the group. He had all their attention.

"Nice … um … weather?"

It was one of those days when the curtains were drawn across the heavens and someone had left all the doors open.

She looked uncomfortable. Everyone else smiled.

Aedan wasn't exactly sure whether it was him or her or the crowd, but he wasn't getting that have-a-seat-why-don't-you feeling. He considered sitting anyway, but another look around the group put an end to the idea, so he made an excuse and went for a long blustery walk, explaining to himself that this was how things went, and that he couldn't expect to be at her side all the time, that she needed her own space too …

He kicked a pile of leaves into the wind, thinking what rotten weather they were having.

The next day, after class, Ilona called him over and asked if he would have lunch with her, seeing as her group was split apart for a while by differing schedules. He leapt at the invitation without even pretending to consider. Later, he found her waiting for him at a little table in the shade – and was it little! The table was delightfully small and Aedan blessed it under his breath as he sat down.

"You've been distant for a while," she said.

"I …" He stopped. He wasn't sure he wanted to tell her about being punished, it would make him look younger and smaller, and he certainly didn't want her knowing what form the punishment had taken. "I had to do some extra work for Dun, so I …"

"You silly boy! You forget I have a cousin who doesn't mind telling me about your reeking punishment duty."

"Oh … um …"

"He really doesn't like you," she said, "or Liru. Sometimes Malik actually frightens me the way he holds a grudge. But please don't think I'm like that. I've got lots of other friends, so why would I be cross with you if you were kept away?"

A slight furrow sank into Aedan's brow. He wasn't sure how being cross came into it. He had hoped that she would speak of missing him, not being cross with him.

"Don't be disappointed with yourself," she said, "I can't expect you to be perfect."

Now *he* was starting to get cross.

"Oh, there's something else I should tell you," she continued. "It's not really a good idea for you to join my usual group. I don't think you'll fit in very well. Let's just spend time together like this, when it's only you and me. What do you say?"

As she leaned forward on her elbows and raised one of those arched eyebrows at him, the wild churning that took hold of his insides displaced whatever else he was feeling and everything he was thinking. For the remainder of lunch they talked, perhaps not easily, but at least amicably, and with frequent lingering looks, eyes locking and darting away to the music of deep sighs.

She loved him.

Boys could not pass the table without turning and gaping. They simply bled envy. How could they not? Ilona was one who leapt from a crowd.

It was the most exciting meal Aedan had ever eaten, and he didn't taste a single mouthful. That was perhaps what enabled him to swallow the waxy rind of the cheese and a charcoal crust of burned-rye. Now that he considered it, he could recall some uninspiring flavours that had reminded him strongly of Harriet's cooking, and which had been accompanied by quizzical looks from Ilona.

For a week they met and shared lunches. To Aedan, the rest of the world was forgotten – a pale, unexciting thing out there on the edges of this numbing, exhausting perfection. They talked in the way toddlers might throw playthings around the room. There was seldom any catching of an idea and sharing it. When the lunches were over, individual opinions lay scattered about in a delicious jumble only ever one layer deep.

If Aedan had allowed himself to be searchingly honest, which he did not, he would have realised that there was a voice, somewhere between his belly and his brain, that was telling him the most absurd thing – he was lonely in her company. No matter how small the table, or how she leaned forward and drowned him with her smile, they were far, far apart. But this, indeed, was absurd.

Then her friends returned and Aedan tried to join their group. He had somehow thought that what Ilona had said about staying away from the group had been a passing thought, obliterated by their closeness. Apparently it was not.

She greeted him with a flicker of a frown and turned away to resume her conversation when he sat. From then on he may as well have been a dead log quietly rotting beside her. It was as if she hadn't even noticed his arrival. In order to cover his awkwardness, he tried to join the conversations of the others in the group, and they certainly noticed him. They made him feel like a horsefly. He could not remember being so uncomfortable or unwelcome since that evening at the marshals trials. His hand kept going to the hair over his left ear, pulling it down, covering that patch in which others found such interest. Afterwards he stamped his way back to class, kicking leaves again like someone visiting vengeance on a sworn foe.

It was a lonely week that followed. He avoided Peashot's I-told-you-so presence and spent a lot of time hanging on the paddock fences, watching Murn go through his restless antics, wishing he could have been a horse without the cares and woes of the broken-hearted.

"You come here often, don't you?"

Aedan jumped. It was Ilona. She placed her elbows and chin on the rail, only inches from Aedan, then turned and gave him a long, tender look.

Surely she adored him.

How could anyone that beautiful who made him feel like this not imply devotion when she looked at him?

"I like it here," he said. "Always feel welcome." It was a risk, but he wanted to see what she would say.

She turned to the paddock where Murn cropped, tossed and stomped a few yards away, glistening in the sun. "I like this horse," she said. "What's its name?"

Aedan sighed. "Murn. Short for Midnight Hurricane. Liru helped me name him."

Ilona pulled a face. "That will have to change," she said, half to herself. "Can you ride him yet?"

"No. Won't be riding him for a long time. He's still too difficult to handle."

"So shouldn't you sell him?"

"I'd like to train him. We're covering ground slowly."

"I think you are wasting your time," she said. "That horse is going to need an experienced trainer. You'll never manage to tame such a huge animal. Maybe we can make a deal that's better for both of us. I've finally managed to convince my aunt to buy me a horse – though it was really Malik who did the convincing. He's probably the only one that she listens to. I have a friend who says I can keep my horse at his father's stable. If you sell this Murn, you can visit with me. We can go often. We'll get to be together lots." She turned on a gleaming smile and Aedan's chest shuddered.

Then that niggling voice managed to get a few words through the fog of his thoughts, something to the effect that he didn't want to sell Murn. And another voice wanted to know who the mysterious friend was.

"Who is this friend of yours?"

"There's no need for that look. You've nothing to worry about. He's only a friend."

It was indirect and only just implied, but it was there. She was suggesting, perhaps even inviting Aedan to be more than just a friend. He gulped. Gosh she was beautiful!

"So I'll get my aunt to settle a price with you then. I've no interest in such matters. Thinking up a name is where my energy will go."

The words were taking time to sink in, but slowly Aedan was digesting her meaning. "I ... I ..."

"Yes Aedan?"

"I don't really want to sell him."

"What?" Her voice sounded almost sharp.

"Murn was a gift to me from Osric. I've got no right to sell him."

"Oh, don't be so starchy. He won't mind. You'll see."

"It would be wrong, Ilona. I can't."

"You didn't have a problem with wrong before when you skipped classes to walk me through town." Her tone had now definitely changed.

Aedan stared. The soft edges of this vision beside him were settling into some hard lines.

"Why can't she buy you another horse?" Aedan tried in a placating voice. "There are lots of others to choose from."

Stormy shapes were gathering over those delicate brows.

"Fine!" she snapped. "Be like that!" She turned to leave.

Aedan was stunned by the quick anger in her eyes, but there was more to come. She stopped and spun around. The next words struck like hailstones.

"Do you know what it cost me to be seen with someone my friends call a northern peasant?" she said. "And do you think they have forgotten about your scar? Do you know what I put aside? The richest boys in the academy want my company. After all I've given up, after all the time we spent together, I thought you would be more of a friend than this!"

Aedan was too shocked to realise he had thought the same. She whirled and strode away, leaving him dumbstruck. A bit of coldness was one thing, but he had never foreseen hostility, or what now felt like treachery, and it had sunk into the flesh of his bared heart.

She hated him, and he was beginning to return the feeling. Could she really be so callous as to think that he owed her for her interest in him?

He spent the next hour throwing and breaking anything that wouldn't get him into too much trouble. Liru spied him from a distance and came over. After getting the story, she offered, with a deadpan face, to cut Ilona's hair off and turn it into a fly swatter.

"Stupid, manipulating brat," she said. "I pity the fool who marries her."

"I thought she liked me. We had such nice times together. You should have seen the way she looked at me."

"And you should see the way that she looks at all the other boys stumbling around her. She is a spider, Aedan. One web catches many. Have you not noticed? She wants you all to belong to her, but she will never belong to any of you. The sooner you get away the better."

"Do you think I'll ever find anyone who actually wants me, scar and all?"

"Probably not."

Aedan looked up, taken aback, just as she landed a solid punch on his shoulder.

"Your scar is settling well now," she said, "and the longer hair, it mostly covers the damage. A person would have to look carefully to notice it. In time you will find her, the right one. You will see. But we have a proverb that, in your language, will say, 'a man too soon is a man deprived'. It sounds blunt in Thirnish. It rhymes in Mardrae. It is the last line of a poem telling us how we must enjoy our youth, not wish to escape it early. Let her go, Aedan. You have much time and better things to spend it on."

Aedan smiled. "You know," he said, "you can be rather wise sometimes."

"Meaning that at other times I am a fool?"

He glanced at her. He was faster, surely. It was time to find out. "Yes," he said, and ran, darting around trees, between idling students who yelled for him to grow up, and twice over tables, all with his nimble pursuer streaking after him. The chase ended at the entrance to the marshals' wing where Aedan darted in and Liru could pursue no further.

Given a few more days of reflection, Aedan allowed himself to recognise that what Peashot and Liru had said of Ilona was probably true. When Ilona tried another angle on Murn, most of the mist had cleared from his vision. Ilona's fiery eruption cleared the rest.

Much as Aedan pitied her for her difficult childhood, he had to disagree with her mother's assessment. That tender heart was well provided with tools and armour, and it had no qualms about using them to its own advantage.

Eventually Ilona found another horse and the anger left her. She became friendly with Aedan again, smiling and charming him with lingering glances as if nothing had happened. But Aedan's swimmy eyes had been opened like those of the pup that yawns and settles down for the first and last time on an ant nest.

He had thought it impossible that beneath an appearance so lovely there could be anything disagreeable. It was a lesson that would not soon be forgotten. Peashot had been right. Aedan's blindness had been in exact proportion to her looks.

Stepping back from the hazy sentimental marshes, he had intended to straighten his thoughts out by climbing deep into his studies, but what really did the job was far better. If Liru could have foreseen what her advice would inspire, she might never have uttered it.

Chapter 43

The first of them began like this. One of the boys would ask the master to come to his desk and explain something on a page. As soon as the master's back was turned to a portion of the class, a plum-sized lead weight would be tossed silently from one boy to another across the room. They never tried it with Wildemar – nothing escaped his notice, and he was far too edgy, apt to swing around at any instant – but the other masters were considered fair game. The apprentices had been engaged with this for a week when Skeet happened to spin around just as Cayde lobbed the weight across to Lorrimer.

"You!" Skeet bellowed.

When uttered with just the right tone, this is the universal name for any boy. Accordingly, all heads snapped towards the angry master. Including Lorrimer's. The weight took him just above the ear with a soft thunk and laid him out flat.

Though it provided some amusement, it was too tame for Aedan. He hatched another idea from their exercises in balance and stealth. For this particular challenge, Rodwell was chosen, as he was given to lengthy explanations while drawing out complex political pyramids and relational tensions, and during these explanations he would not turn from the chalkboard until he was done.

Aedan asked him for more background on a particularly complex issue – limited autonomy of remotely governed cities under circumstances that could recommend breaching those limits, a situation that Castath and its prince could soon face. Rodwell was delighted by the breadth of the question. He would have done better to be suspicious, especially considering Aedan's generally muted interest in the subject. Rodwell turned to the board with gusty purpose, drawing and pointing to various diagrams of governance structures while unloading in his shrill, excited tones.

Behind him, silent as ghosts, the boys rose from their seats which had already been pushed back for the purpose, drifted down the class, and filed out the door. Twenty pairs of eyes appeared over the outer windows just in time to see Rodwell turn around with a concluding flourish of his finger.

He stood, finger raised. He looked, blinked, looked again and glanced around as if to assure himself he was in the right place. When he began stumping down the room and bending his portly frame to search under the desks, it was too much for the boys who could hold the snorts and squeals back no longer. Not even the liberal caning could entirely silence them.

During the year, a junior master by the name of Braddoc had begun taking some of the history classes. This strange young man made it his prime object to overcome an all-too-obvious nervousness by being impressive and intimidating. Whenever a boy asked a question, he would stride up to the desk and lean his hands on it while he answered, making the boy look up at a steep angle. If anyone asked a question that struck him as foolish he would rush over, slam his fist on a page, and bark something like, "Open your ears and let the information in the first time!"

Peashot managed to get some iron shavings from the floor of the smithy and hid them in his book. Then he paid attention during the class until he could put together a question that would be sure to induce wrath.

It worked.

Braddoc flew up to him, slammed his fist on the thin pages covering the razor sharp iron shavings and, with a shriek of pain, swore like no master had ever done within the halls of learning. Peashot might have got away with lesser punishment had he not asked if that was Sulese and could Master Braddoc please spell it out for him because he needed to learn some more words.

Aedan's natural restlessness was finding some outlet in the pranks and schemes. But he still pined for the forests and overgrown hills of the Mistyvales and the many animals that had been as neighbours. A short walk had always put him among deer, wild hogs and foxes.

In Castath he found mostly rats.

So when he discovered a mildly poisonous grass snake trying to escape by climbing the corner between two walls, he caught and bagged it, intending to play with it later. The medical class took forever and Mistress Gilda put him on display again to demonstrate how scars continue to heal over years. From where she was exhibiting him, he glimpsed the lithe green shape pour out from a corner of his bag and slide into the assortment of models, skeletons and instruments. For an instant he worried, remembering how she had last expressed her feelings on serpents. But the mortification she was once again causing him quickly reversed that feeling, and he saw something beautiful, something poetically complete in the circumstance.

The loss of the snake was soon eased when he found a giant goblin spider. It was a hairy monster of a thing nearly as big as a dinner plate. It looked capable of preying on small dogs. He managed to catch it by tossing his shirt and knocking it to the ground where Peashot dropped a water pail on top. They kept it in their dorm, named it Killer, and fed it bugs and worms, taking the lid off only to display it to awed visitors.

Then one morning they woke up and the lid was on the ground and the pail empty.

They searched everywhere – under pillows, between sheets, inside shoes, though it would have more than filled a shoe – always expecting a hairy predator to leap out at them. The argument about who forgot to replace the lid lasted all day. For the next week they slept fitfully, jolting awake in the darkness to frantically brush off the memory of an eight-legged nightmare crawling under a shirt or chewing on an ear.

The distractions had shown Aedan that something was missing. Nothing in the predictable routine was meeting his appetite for adventure – his love of discovering things while letting his imagination lead. While focussing on his studies, he had put his nightly explorations of the academy on hold. It was time to take them up again. The place was full of secrets. Forbidden corridors led to rooms that simply had to be investigated. The only place he dared not venture was the barred passage at the bottom of the collapsing stairs. He did not question Dun's warning about prison.

On these nightly forays, Hadley and Peashot were the only ones who agreed, on occasion, to accompany him. The others were kept in their beds by the fear of Dun's cane or of the academy ghosts that were well known to drift down the dark hallways and attack any wandering student. Of course, it was always the same students who saw them and who gained considerable popularity by speaking of these harrowing encounters.

One night, after Lorrimer had made a series of spooked objections, Aedan wanted to know what it was about bed sheets that would keep anyone safe, and if Lorrimer was so well protected by them, why not wrap himself up and come along. Then all the other ghosts might see this new giant apparition and float away screaming. Lorrimer told him to shut up and go to sleep, saying those who looked for trouble always found it. The second part sounded acceptable to Aedan and he slipped out, Peashot in tow.

"You scared?" whispered Peashot.

"Nope."

"Oh. Uh, me neither." Peashot kept close, twice stepping on Aedan's heels as they padded down the dark corridor. He began whispering again. "All those ghost stories are such nonsense. Don't know who would believe them. I completely don't. Not even for a moment. Never even – Wait!" He grabbed Aedan's arm. "What was that sound?"

"Don't know. Can't hear anything over your constant talking."

"Oh. Sorry. Just letting off steam. I get really irritated with all those made up stories. None of them true. All made up … All of them …"

For all his reckless – even fearless – trouble-hunting, Peashot, like Lorrimer, was hopelessly given over to superstition.

Tonight was the night for Aedan's most defiant adventure so far. There was a sign on the outer wall of the main buildings that forbade climbing. It was as good as an invitation. The fangs of terrifying gargoyles would provide excellent grips, and the shoulders and noble heads of imposing statues seemed to have been made for a climber's boots.

"You know we'll be in the rat cells if they catch us?" Peashot whispered.

"No different to the time we slipped into the seniors' museum."

"Yes it is. At least there we could hide. How are we going to hide on these walls?"

"You tucking tail?"

"You're not the one with three charges and a final warning. One sniff of trouble and –"

"Shhh!"

They slipped off the open corridor, hurried over the lawn and crouched behind a large green soapstone carving of Olemris – a robed man missing most of his hair and part of his nose, hand outstretched, delivering a forceful lecture to the geraniums. The boys quieted their breathing. A lone student tottered along behind the colonnade, leaning forward as if the books under his arm had transferred their weight to his head.

"Probably fell asleep in one of the libraries," said Aedan.

"At least he knows how to get the best use from them."

They waited until the grounds were deserted, then Aedan led the way to a tall arch. He had spent days studying the possibilities. The dean's alcove provided the most interesting challenge. It was a deeply featured arching frame that led up to the knobbly face of the second floor.

After wiping his hands on his trousers, Aedan placed his fingers in one of several long vertical grooves, leaned back against his arms and worked his feet up the opposing surface of the groove, so that arms pulled while legs pushed, creating a kind of reverse clamping effect. By shifting one hand and one foot at a time, he worked his way up the pillar of the alcove until he reached the first gargoyle. He was puffing hard when he clutched at a feature, which turned out to be a wart-encrusted nose, and pulled himself up to a small ledge where he could rest.

Peashot took a while longer to scale the pillar. When he reached for the gargoyle there was something of desperation in the way he snatched.

The climbing from then on was easier, but the height made up for that.

When they reached the fourth floor they pulled themselves over a railing and onto a little balcony where they sat puffing and grinning at the view – in the light of a half-moon the spectacle was enchanting.

"I've always wanted to know what's in here," Aedan said, turning around and pressing his forehead against a glass pane. "These balcony doors are bigger than the museum's."

"Did you bring a candle?"

"Candle, flint, steel, char cloth, all of it. But we'll have to be careful to hood the flame. The guards would see it from the far end of the campus."

"I'll hood. You light."

The plan was not the best they had ever made. The candle produced a lot more light than Peashot was able to hood, even before he got distracted by the interior of the room and burned his thumb. With a muffled exclamation of pain, he pulled his hands away revealing a bright flame – to a guard who had been puzzling over the dull glow.

"Thieves!" the voice rang out from far beneath.

"Don't worry, it will take them ages to reach us," said Aedan. "They will have to climb four storeys worth of stairs –"

"Shoot!" the guard yelled.

Even the dim candlelight was enough for the boys to see each other's faces pale. The balcony door turned out to be less solid than it had appeared. They kicked it open and dived inside, arrows plugging into the doorframe and wooden ceiling boards. The candle dropped but was not extinguished. Aedan picked it up, looked around, and groaned. It was the biggest, most important-looking office he had ever found, which meant more trouble than he had yet managed to harvest – and were those exam papers?

He had seen enough. The inner door was wooden but felt like iron. It took several swings with a marble bust to break the lock. As stone and wood sprinkled the floor, Aedan understood that there would be no saving them if they were caught. A raucous chatter of heavy boots was growing, echoing up a nearby stairwell.

The boys heaved the door open and fled.

Fit and balanced from years of training, they darted at a giddy speed over the polished floors from one long corridor to the next, skidding around corners and vaulting down stairwells. They ran until their breathing was ragged. The darkness was only slightly relieved by moonlight spilling in through the windows. It made navigation tricky, but they were fairly certain that they were now on the opposite side of the academy, though exactly what this section was, they weren't sure. Not even Aedan had been here.

"It might be best if we split up on the way back," he said. "They will be looking for two."

Peashot agreed.

It was in the subsequent maze of passages that Aedan's sense of direction betrayed him. When he got out into the open, the moon had vanished behind cloud. He found what seemed to be the outside of his dorm. The wall looked right, the window looked right, and though he didn't remember the entry being such a squeeze, he climbed through and dropped to the boards inside. There was a light burning, which was strange. Peashot was probably telling the story.

He rounded the bend and stopped with a sharp intake of breath.

The layout was completely different – no line of desks, no alcoves, no Peashot. There were only three sections to this room. The wall-lamps were brass, the furniture delicate and painted white, the books plentiful, and the occupants awake. Three young men and three young women lounged on the carpet with several bottles between them. Both the wine and the mixed company in dorms were expulsion offenses. The alarm in their faces said as much. But the alarm was giving way to something else.

Aedan backed towards the wall. He had to get away from here. Away from them. The young men were beginning to move, and a hardness in one of their faces was tolling an alarm that Aedan knew he dared not ignore. He took another step back and was just about to turn and scramble out the window when the hard-faced one stood. He was a large man with heavy arms, heavy brows, and eyes that were now dark with anger. Fists clenched and face seething, he strode forward.

In just that glimpse, Aedan saw the terror that had stained his younger days. Though he fought it, he could not keep the talons from sinking in. With sickening realisation, he felt every muscle go slack and his legs dropped him to the floor. It was the same thing he saw in his father, the same monster. It had owned him before and it owned him still. It towered, pressed against the roof and walls, and Aedan felt the last of his strength flee from under its giant presence.

His thoughts were slow, but their muddy stickiness was not enough to block the dismay. He had told himself that this weakness was conquered at the festival during the gang fight, but in an instant of realisation, he understood that he would have crumpled had his father been there. And somehow, this man was his father in a different form. Maybe it was the size, maybe the raw hostility. Whatever it was, it had convinced that broken part of his mind which now betrayed him again and paralysed every muscle.

The young man leaned down and gripped Aedan around the neck.

"Name?" he said.

Aedan was too shaken to think. His tongue was all but dead in his mouth, but he managed to mumble his name in a trembling whisper.

"Really? The apprentice marshal who supposedly took on a gang of thieves?" He laughed – a hard, cracking sound full of blades and stones. Ridicule and contempt. "Your spine is as hollow as chicken bones!" The other men and two of the women laughed as well. One woman looked distraught, but made no attempt to interfere.

"You're also the one who's been trespassing on our boulevard, aren't you? Yes, I recognise you now. I've been wanting to collar your insolent little neck for a long time, and here you are. Finally snooped right under the watchman's heel. What are you doing here?"

Aedan managed to stutter out something about getting lost and using the wrong window.

The young man stared down at him for a long time. He grabbed the hair behind Aedan's head and turned his face up. "My name is Iver," he said. "And you are going to pay for your intrusion here. Don't try speaking of the girls or the wine. We'll have a version of the story that will keep us in the clear and muddy your name for good."

He peered into Aedan's face for a long time before speaking.

"I would greatly enjoy exposing you." He raised his fist and Aedan cringed, seeing not the man, but the dark, infinite terror, the sickening nightmares from his childhood. Iver smiled. "But I have a more profitable idea," he said. "You are going to work for me. Tomorrow, an hour after dark, you will knock at the window and wait for instructions. Fail to appear and I think you understand what I can do to you."

Aedan understood all too well. The worst of it was that Iver understood *him*. Clauman had shaped this handle on his son, and Iver had discovered it a perfect fit.

Peashot was waiting at the dorm, still grinning. Aedan mumbled something about being too exhausted for chatter, and crawled into bed, wishing he could explain, hoping Peashot would understand, knowing he wouldn't.

His thoughts were black. As much as he wanted to avoid admitting it, what Iver had said was true. His spine had a secret hollowness to it. His father had done something to him, broken something in him that could be easily overlooked. He himself had been able to overlook it for years. But overlooking it had not made it go away.

It was like a missing support in a bridge. He could take weight as easily as anyone, until that damaged section was tested, and then he buckled no matter how he tried to brace himself and fight against it. As the helplessness swelled in him, so did the hate for his father. *He* was the cause of this.

For the next few days, Aedan wholeheartedly disobeyed Iver's last instruction and kept clear of any area where the barbaric senior might discover him. He had no intention to fawn, and was certainly not going to report to someone like that. He spent his breaks in a secluded garden, telling the others that he needed a bit of time to think. It lasted for a week. Then, one day, he looked up at the sound of footsteps to see the dreaded face.

Aedan leapt up and raised his fists, but as Iver marched forward his presence caused all Aedan's poisoned memories of his father to swell into a choking cloud. But before his knees gave way, he heard a muffled shriek at the back of his thoughts. "Escape!"

He spun around only to be faced with a stone wall, but the stones were large and provided easy grips. With the sight of Iver no longer filling his vision, his mind cleared a little.

He gripped the stones in front of him, and as he pulled himself up, he felt strength explode into his limbs. It was like running on all fours the way he scuttled up the wall. There was a second storey window over to the left, not too far above him, its shutters open. He altered direction and aimed for it now that he was out of reach from the ground.

He sensed movement and heard a furious voice below him, but he blocked them out.

Haste led him to commit unwisely to a sloping edge. His fingers slipped away and then a foot as he swung out from the wall. He almost fell, but grabbed at a sharp edge and pulled himself back. It was only a few feet to the windowsill. He found some deep grips, gained the projecting window ledge, and hauled his weight up and over, dropping into a class full of students apparently writing an exam.

The supervising master looked too surprised by this intrusion to speak. Aedan didn't give him a chance to get his tongue working. He rushed for the door at the far side of the room and bolted through it. Whether Iver had followed or not, he wasn't sure. He didn't think so, but dared not wait to find out, so he fled down the corridor, descended the first stairway, and took the second branching passage. He kept running until he reached the marshals' quarter. At least here he would be safe from any student from another quadrant. Not even someone as brazen as Iver would risk the punishment that was guaranteed for anyone found crossing the marshals' threshold.

The dorm was empty. He sat on his bed, covered his eyes and tried to stop shaking. By the time his breath had recovered, so had his thoughts. He remembered now that Iver had not been alone. Malik and Cayde had followed. There could be little doubt that Malik and Iver had talked. Perhaps they were even friends.

Aedan began to consider his options. He couldn't risk being surprised again – hiding in an enclosed garden had been a foolish move. He needed to be in the open; he needed to preserve distance. Running was not the most valiant strategy, but even wolves circled and kept their distance until the time was right. Anything was better than allowing Iver to rush at him where friends could see. What choice did he have?

A sudden flood of helpless anger took hold of him. He grabbed his old wooden training sword and hurled it across the room, smashing at least one lantern. He didn't bother to look where it ended up. What had he done to deserve this? Why, after all these years, was its grip on him so complete? Kalry had once told him that he would be able to beat this thing. She had said that it was a big forest that would take a long time to clear, but how long?

Though Aedan managed to keep his distance from Iver, it brought him no peace. He lived in constant fear of being exposed. The days grew bitter indeed.

He spied on his tormentor out of necessity and discovered that he already had a personal slave, a small first-year student from the officers' quadrant. Iver, it appeared, was a thirsty man who did not want to run the risk of sneaking his own wine into the buildings.

Once, Aedan saw him beating the young boy. He could have reported it or at least yelled. Instead he ducked out of sight and ran away, trembling at the memories that had risen up, hating himself with every step.

The next day he found the boy and spoke to him, asking why he didn't just keep away.

"I've heard about you," the boy scoffed. 'What right have you got to talk? Aren't you the coward?"

The combined fear and rage that took hold of Aedan led him to a place he despised with his whole being, but he did not hold back. He didn't know why. It was easier to yell and threaten and shove, like letting go, drifting with a fierce current. In that one decision to give in to his deep hungry urge, the current dragged him a long way down. He told himself that the next time he would stand against it more easily, but he wondered. The shame that he felt afterwards only added to a flood of self-loathing in which he was already half-drowned.

What did it matter? What did he care anymore? If they were beginning to talk, wouldn't it spread to everyone he knew?

Though his friends grew deeply concerned, Aedan would not speak of it. They urged him to just confront Iver, offering to back him up. But they did not understand. How could he explain this? Even when he visited his mother, he avoided answering questions about his darkening mood. Explaining would mean revealing what he would not have anyone know. So he withdrew into a cold inner silence that was rank with bitter thoughts.

In his dreams he took his revenge. Not against Iver, but against the one who had started it all.

Clauman would approach him, eager, repentant. "Aedan, my son," he would say, "I've been looking all over for you. I need to talk with you, to say sorry and –"

Aedan would turn his back and walk away, ignoring his father's hurt voice, swallowing the acrid draught of hate. It rushed through his veins, a surging fever of power. Yet it never strengthened him. When he woke in the morning, all that lingered was the sour memory of what he had done in his dream world.

But instead of curbing his need to wander and discover, his misery drove him to recklessness and to something he would never otherwise have considered, or dared. It was time to find out why that forbidden corridor would send a student to jail.

Chapter

This time Aedan told no one. When they were all asleep, he stole from the room, dragged one of the statues in the display hall to the central feature, climbed up to the platform and descended the stairs.

Once in the cold subterranean darkness, he partly unshuttered his lantern so that only a sliver of light escaped. In the past, he had always turned left. Now he looked to the right, beyond the chain, down the narrow passage. Dun's warning rose up again. This was not like ignoring a sign that told him to keep off the grass. There was something down there that was not just forbidden but secret.

He thought about it. What did he care if the consequences were bad? Iver was turning his life to bile. What was trouble with the rules in comparison? But that was only if he were caught, and he did not intend to be caught.

He dropped down and crawled under the chain. With his head so close to the ground, he could see that the dust had been disturbed. People had passed here recently. He rose and started forward, padding cat-like on the balls of his feet, pointing the open end of the lantern down the passage. It cast the faintest yellow glow a few yards ahead to the boundary where light wrestled with shadow. With the wick trimmed to allow only the smallest flame and the forward shutter open but a crack, it did little more than soften the darkness, but it was more than enough. Aedan had no fear of the dark. It wasn't a consequence of courage. He had simply never had cause to fear it. Instead, he had often found security where he could not be seen, where he could hide and keep watch.

A sound brushed his ear, light as the touch of a moth, yet he was able to feel it in the ground. When he held his breath and listened there was nothing.

He continued forward as the corridor plummeted down a long flight of stairs so precipitous that he almost had to use his hands. The surfaces were narrow and the drops deep. He was all too aware that if his balance should carry him forward, there would be no recovery. A misstep here would hurt, for a long time. The bottom, if there was one, remained lost, far below in darkness.

He tested every surface before committing his weight, so progress was slow. It was almost an hour before he reached the level ground in front of an oak door, dry, split and papery with age. The door was slightly ajar so he pulled it open with a soft creak and cast the lantern light into what appeared to be a store room, though, by the looks of it, one that had been forgotten for a very long time.

The large room was filled with heaped sacks, ropes, rusted tools, and mildewed harnesses so old that even the mildew had died and trickled to the ground forming little heaps of grey powder. It was an odd assortment and certainly a strange place to keep all these things, for the room appeared to terminate the passage. No doors lead out from here. The stone walls were unbroken except by the door through which he had entered. Why anyone had built such an interminable stairway only to provide access to a pointless store room escaped Aedan, yet here it was. Perhaps marshals were poor architects after all. But the thought did not rest well. He was missing something and he knew it.

Another brush of sound.

It was like the air had shuddered. It came from everywhere and nowhere, as if the earth itself were sighing and the floor and walls whispered of it. What had Garald said? Shakes and shiverings that don't belong in rock … Aedan waited a long time, but there was nothing more.

Disappointed with this dull end to the night's exploration, he leaned against a pile of sacks that crumbled and produced a powdery cascade behind him. The dust and decay drew him back into his own thoughts and the ruin his life had become. As he let his mind drift back through the years, flailing for something, anything that would give a flicker of relief, he remembered what was so close that he had almost forgotten it. Reaching beneath his shirt, he pulled out the little leather case, now old and worn. He looked at it for a long time, considering. Then with a suddenness to counter the years of hesitation, he made the decision.

It was time.

He crossed back to the entrance. The sagging door ground over dusty flagstones as he pushed it closed. There was a corner at the far end of the room where he could tuck himself down between two piles of sacks, and after placing the lantern there, he sat and lifted the cord over his head. He held the little case in his palm where the light fell. Since Thomas had given it to him he had carried it, fearing to look inside, fearing the pain it would cause. But after the past weeks, he no longer cared about the pain.

Kalry was not here to take his arm anymore, but her words were here, and he suddenly needed them again. He untied the rawhide binding and, with a deep breath, slid the cover off to reveal a small walkabout diary painted with flowers, birds and beasts, all surprisingly well-proportioned for the creations of a young girl. The handwriting was as familiar as his own. It caused his breath to catch. Though the pages were tiny, there was a good deal in them owing to thin and probably expensive paper and very small handwriting. He remembered how she had found that writing small was the only way to keep the letters neat. She had objected, however, to anyone calling her normal script messy. She insisted, with a half grin, that it was a good thing if the letters wanted to be a little different every time. Aedan smiled at the memory. After a brief pause, he began to read.

Dear diary

I hope you don't mind, but I've decided not to write to you again. That's why I'm starting a new diary today, and it's the last time I'll write dear diary unless you write me something back (which of course we know you won't).

I'm not too sure who to write to. I was thinking about writing to the Ancient, but I'm worried about bothering him with silly things. Tulia said it would be wrong. Daddy said I would be wasting ink. He said there are many gods who didn't care about Mommy when she was sick and don't care about us now. But it was that angry and quick way of speaking he uses when he's just saying things because he wants to and not because he knows they are true. Emroy who was listening in as usual came up to me later and said if there is a god then why can't he see it, and then he gave one of those smiles like the sheriff does when he's thinking about something, and walked off as if he just said something cleverer than the sheriff himself.

I wanted to tell him he can't see his own head and that doesn't mean he doesn't have one. Aedan said in his case it did. I don't feel wicked for laughing because Emroy can be a real bully even when I try to be nice to him. Anyway what he said gave me an idea.

If I thought like him, Emroy I mean not Aedan, I would always lose at hide and seek because I would always be saying there's no one there when I don't see them and I'd always give up too soon. If you want to be any good at it you need to look all over and search for trampled grass and footprints and startled birds and all those kinds of things that Aedan is always showing me. I got to wondering if maybe the Ancient is like that too. Maybe he wants to hide like he wants us to look for him instead of him just appearing in the middle of the field and saying, Here I am! Because maybe then we'd just say, You're in my field, go away.

So maybe he lets the people find him who really want to find him. I remember the one time I got lost in the fir woods on the south side of the town. It was Aedan's father who found me and when he found me he even let me hug him and cry against his shoulder. But when I go to visit Aedan at his house his father is really rude and he sometimes doesn't even say hello because at those times he's not looking for me.

That reminds me about something else. Today Aedan and I went questing for the castle of the silver dwarf. Aedan was so good at finding tracks in the forest even when they weren't really there. But when he didn't know I could see him he got this deep, sad look in his face. I've seen it before and I also saw bruises that he didn't want to talk about. First I thought it was Emroy, but I overheard Dorothy saying something to Tulia that makes me wonder if his father is hurting him. Then I remembered that time I accidentally saw him hiding in the corner at his house when his father was standing in front of him and breathing like he'd been exercising. I still can't believe it. I don't want to believe it. I would give up all my collections and story books, even the ones I wrote, if I could just make it stop. I wish he was my real brother. Then he could come and live here and be safe.

Aedan's vision was too blurred to see the page. He closed his eyes and his shoulders shook silently for a while. He knew that Kalry had meant what she had written and he knew how valuable those story books had been to her. When he had reined himself in, he rubbed his eyes and started the next entry.

Dear Aedan

Seeing as my diary didn't write to me I'm going to write to you but if I catch you reading it I'll tell Dorothy that you stole those four slices of cake that made you sick on William's birthday. When I'm dead and buried you can read it all, but only you. Don't tell Emroy about the part where I thought your missing head joke was funny.

I want to write about something that I've been feeling a lot lately and today it was particulilly (I'm sure I spelled that wrong) clear.

I went walking really early in the morning, you know when stars are yawning and closing their eyes, and flowers and grass begin to stretch before the wind gets up from the valley and starts them dancing, and birds are worried about flying into things so they sit in their trees and chatter to each other telling stories about what they dreamed and what they plan to do with the day, and while I was standing there in the middle of the west field I heard something even more beautiful than the chorus of the birds.

I think the best way to describe it is by calling it a song, and almost everything can feel it. I can't hear it with my ears, it's more inside and it makes me tremble like it's trying to wake me up and I'm saying, But I am awake, and it's smiling (I think this song can smile) and saying, No you're not, because you're not singing. It seemed as young as the dew that was making my toes cold, but at the same time I knew that it was older than memory itself. (I borrowed that line from one of your mum's books.)

It made me think of that poem by Theol where he mentions the echoes of the Ancient, but that sounds too cold. To me this was like the song of the Ancient. I think I'll call it that.

I think it's a song that's always been there, but it's like it's getting louder now, like something magnificent and spetakular (that one doesn't look right either) is going to happen. It made something spetak wonderful happen in me. I was ready to burst with excitement so I ran right over to the old tulip tree and hugged it, and I think it laughed. Thomas saw me and he certainly laughed. I'm not mad with him anymore. I probably would have laughed if I'd seen him hugging a tree.

I want to tell you about all of this soon. I know we have a lot of make-believe things like the dwarf and the wandering willow and the fox with the golden tail but this is different. It's as real as rain but I think it can be ignored completely.

I hope you know about it too. It's lonely for me when we can't share things.

This time the tears poured down his face and he made no attempt to check them. How he missed her. He remembered her telling him about the song, and remembered how she had been disappointed in his subdued enthusiasm.

He began to wonder about the storm that had revealed itself over Castath, if what she described was a more subtle form of what he had experienced when he had heard his name wrapped in thunder. It really had felt like he was being woken, though somehow that stirring, that excitement, had faded. In its place were cold chains and a cauldron spilling fumes of hatred that had pulled him back into a heavy sleep.

A sharp click pierced the silence. Aedan blew out the flame and pushed himself against the wall between the mounds of sacks. The floor shook under a heavy grinding. He was momentarily confused when a shaft of light fell across the floor from the wrong side of the room. Then he understood – a door was opening in the stone wall. Aedan ground his teeth. He should have guessed it.

From where he was hiding, only the wooden door was visible, so the two voices that reached him were faceless.

"I understand that well enough, but we must humour him. He has the respect of many thinking people occupying influential positions. If he were to be silenced too directly, it would breed suspicion." The voice was familiar, but Aedan could not yet place it.

"But what he proposes will only excite ideas that could lead to unrest. His theories are going to spread like poison. You have to admit, with the increasing reports of inexplicable sightings in the east, and now these tremors that even we have felt, he will have the ears of the whole city. His ideas have a credible tone. He could ruin everything you have been working towards."

This thick throaty voice Aedan recognised immediately. It was Ganavant, the prince's big bullfrog of a councillor. The other voice, then, was Burkhart's.

"I am well aware of that, and I am glad that we are the first to be shown beyond the vaults. How he managed to open them I'll never understand. Kings have been defied by those locks for five hundred years." The stone door ground closed. Burkhart's voice was almost dreamy when he spoke again. "I still can't quite accept what my eyes told me ... It might have been a long way down, but there was no doubt – it moved! With supporting evidence like this, he could put an end to all my plans."

"That is why it must not be seen by anyone ever again. You often say that truth is not necessarily the best thing to throw at the masses. If people see what we just saw, it would cause panic like we have never imagined. It might even send them fleeing towards Fennlor, perhaps even the DinEilan of their wild stories rather than remaining here. We must close the vaults again and seal this door immediately."

"Yes, yes, Ganavant. You clutter the air with the obvious. This room will certainly be blocked off with enough stone to bury whatever is down there for good, but the dilemma of plugging the old windbag remains. How is he to be silenced without raising widespread questions?"

There was a brief pause.

"Allow him the quest," Ganavant said. "Let him go and search for answers, but let it work for us too. Accidents can happen, especially in a place unanimously rumoured to be under a curse. Men could be paid to go along and witness that his theories were shown groundless shortly before he and those loyal to him met their unfortunate ends. What if –"

"You speak of such things in the open! Your tongue is growing loose, Ganavant. You risk attaching soil to my name!"

"Forgive me, Highness." Despite the apology, the councillor's voice did not sound remorseful. It seemed to Aedan only a matter of form. This councillor was not the bowing and scraping type. Aedan imagined him to listen to reprimands while smiling inside, calculating.

The wooden door grated over the dirty stones as they pulled it open and the two men walked out of the room, but the light did not recede.

"What is it?" Burkhart asked.

"Did you not leave the door ajar?"

Aedan tensed. Fool!

"I do not clearly recall," said the prince, his voice betraying his annoyance.

"With your permission, I would like to make a quick search inside." The light grew stronger and the door creaked again. Aedan held his breath and drew his feet as tightly against him as he could. Overhearing such talk, even if he only partly understood it, would not be punished by cane but by iron, the very sharp iron of an executioner's axe.

Heavy steps re-entered the room.

"I do not believe I gave my permission," Burkhart snapped, his voice edged now, even dangerous. "I wonder if you are forgetting your place, Ganavant."

"Sorry, Highness." Again, there was no sorrow in the apology.

"Let us be gone."

The light withdrew and Aedan was left in darkness. He tried to understand what he had heard, that the prince and his councillor were conspiring to assassinate an innocent man – Culver, by the description.

And what lay behind that door that it should be sealed away forever?

He decided to wait in case anyone else emerged, but after what felt like hours, he could wait no more. He struck the flint until he raised a flame and lit his lantern, then crept out to inspect the wall.

The concealed door had closed, leaving no trace of its whereabouts. He was sure there would be a way to open it by pressing on a stone or several stones, but he was also sure that there would be traps that could swallow him if he pressed the wrong ones. Holding the lantern close to the surface, he thought he could make out a slight shine on two of them, perhaps from the oily deposits left from years of being pressed. But then this could be a trick whereby the wrong stones were touched and the right ones pressed through a garment.

He was considering anchoring himself with a rope to guard against an opening floor trap when the same sharp click cut through the wall. He blew out the lantern again and dived behind a stack of perished leather harnesses as the door opened. From his vantage point, he was able to steal a glimpse. His jaw dropped. What he was looking at was nothing like the store room.

It was a large chamber and as imposing as a royal vestibule. The walls were covered with intricate murals that looked like maps of a city, but even in that glimpse, it was clear to him that these maps described something far bigger than Castath. Surely this was the entrance to a forgotten realm, an underground kingdom.

The otherworldly feeling was strengthened by a curious light pouring through the doorway. It was not the glow of lanterns, but something brighter, warmer, and alive. It was as if red gold had been heated until it flowed over the ground and bathed the room with a shifting radiance. Every fibre of Aedan's adventurous soul strained forward.

Then the view was blocked as someone passed through the doorway. It was Culver, no mistake.

The tall chancellor entered the store room and leaned his weight against the stone door, but before it closed, there was another of those earth-born sounds, only now it was a roar – a hundred times louder and much clearer. Aedan almost leapt to his feet. As the door closed, the sound was cut off, leaving only a faint tremor in the air. That door, Aedan realised, led to the source of these disturbances and the answer to the mystery.

He had to crouch and wait until the light had disappeared, but when it was dark again, he looked up and saw the robed, grey-haired figure striding away.

He turned back to the door. Tonight would be his last chance to discover what lay beyond it, what had lain undisturbed for five hundred years and was now to be hidden for good. He checked the ropes, but they were impossibly old, crumbling at his touch. He would have to fetch another if he wanted an anchor capable of providing any security. There were several in the training hall that he could borrow. He headed off in that direction, his lantern unlit, staying well behind the Chancellor.

Climbing that mountain of stairs in the darkness was far from comfortable. This time he did use his hands. When he reached the top, the robed man was gone. Aedan felt his way along the narrow passage, under the chain, past the collapsing stairs, down the broad passage, through the weapons hall and finally into the training hall. He knew the dimensions of the space so well after the years of exercises that he did not need a light.

He rummaged about until he located a coil of rope, then counted his paces back through the doors, across the weapons hall

– only bumping against one stone pillar – and into the broad passage again. Safe now from observation, he lit the lantern, ran the rest of the way and approached the forbidden corridor. He had put one foot under the chain when his dim light revealed what he had not expected, not so soon. Three uniformed soldiers were blocking the way.

"Halt," the foremost shouted, and started forward.

Aedan knew that they would not let him walk free. The soldiers were too far away to see his face, so he turned and ran. The man chasing him was no mean athlete. Heavy steps were drawing nearer.

After only a few paces Aedan reached the stairs and had to slow down as he climbed to avoid the traps. Behind him the distance closed rapidly. He would not have enough of a lead to climb down from the central feature.

A metallic clank was followed by a scrape of rock, a yell, and a whoosh of air. The yell became a scream that ended in a cavernous splash.

Aedan looked behind him. A large portion of the stairway had hinged open, dropping the soldier into dark waters beneath. He hoped the man would not drown. Then it occurred to him that he was holding a rope, and that keeping it would only incriminate him. He slipped a quick loop around a pillar and dropped the end into the water. When he felt it tighten, he shinned up the rest of the stairs, replaced the cover, climbed down using the outraged statue, returned it to its place, and crept back to his bed. Nobody stirred.

He lay awake until morning, curiosity scratching at the edges of his mind, whining, demanding, keeping slumber well away. Too many questions. What was down there that could drive a whole city to panic? What had Culver discovered about the storms? Was there truly something to fear – and beneath the very streets of Castath?

"Jump! Get off your beds, you lazy oxen!"

This time he really did jump, and grazed his fist against a beam. He hoped Dun hadn't noticed.

Chapter 45

"We are looking for Aedan."

The soldiers were from one of the special divisions that wore the white tunics over their chain mail, setting them apart for royal duties only. There was no hiding from these elite troops, not even in the marshals' quarter.

Kollis pointed.

"Come with us please," the senior officer said.

Aedan's pale face spoke eloquently. He stood and followed the soldiers out the classroom. They gave him no explanation and were silent in response to his questions.

They knew.

He considered running, but against such men he would have little chance. They led him down the stairs which had been pulled up and reset during the night. The landing at the bottom was filled with carts of stone and mortar being wheeled towards the store room. Aedan understood now why the morning training session had taken place in the display room.

He tried to think of some way to justify himself, how he might bargain for a softer penalty. They continued on down the broad passage, through the weapons hall and into a section of the buildings Aedan had never been allowed to enter. They passed two doors and stopped outside the third where they knocked.

The door was opened by another soldier and they entered a large office. Not an inch of any wall was visible. Packed bookshelves reached from corner to corner. The biggest desk Aedan had ever seen filled a good portion of the room. He began to tremble as he saw Prince Burkhart, Ganavant, and Culver whose private office he assumed this was.

"What's the matter Aedan," asked the prince, smiling. "You look rather shaken."

"N – n – nothing Your Highness," Aedan said, trying to keep his knees locked.

Burkhart laughed easily. "I suppose this *was* a somewhat disturbing way to bring you down here. Let me put your mind at rest. We need your assistance on a matter of great importance."

Aedan relaxed slightly at the prince's easy tones, but he noticed that Ganavant was fixing him with a relentless stare. Aedan kept his attention on the prince.

"We need to send a party out to Kultûhm to investigate something. It has come to my attention that you actually entered this fortress. That would make you and your travelling companions the only living experts on the place. We can find nobody else alive who has set foot there."

Aedan was not surprised at this. He wanted to point out that he had seen no more of the place than the entrance courtyard, but he did not yet trust his voice, and Ganavant was still looking at him with those bulging, fly-hunting eyes.

"So I have assembled a group," Burkhart continued, "to accompany Culver and his assistant. Mistress Gilda tells me that you are familiar with a dark-skinned foreign girl who can act as a nurse?"

"Liru? – she would have called her Lee'runda."

"Yes, that was the one that was … recommended. She will accompany you. You leave at first light tomorrow. Do you have any questions?"

It sank in. This was not about being asked for information. He was actually being ordered to return to that dreaded place, that stronghold of unsleeping watchfulness and death. If they knew he had been there then they would know the account. They would know that the ground even within the fortress was treacherous. Last time, he had barely escaped with his life. How did they expect him to slip the noose again?

Over the past four years, Kultûhm had haunted the worst of his nightmares. His only comfort on waking had been that he would never see the place again. Now they wanted to send him back.

Aedan's jaw fell and his face greyed.

"I think I can guess your worries," Burkhart said. "You are wondering, with the months lost on the journey, if you will pass the year."

Aedan had been wondering if he would survive the year.

"Culver," Burkhart indicated the robed chancellor standing on his left, "holds the academy's high seat. He is the most learned man I know. I hereby task him with the matter of your continued education. You shall not fail the year on account of your service."

The austere man gave a stiff nod.

Aedan, in spite of his fears was embarrassed – the prince might as well have asked the chancellor to do Aedan's laundry.

"Right then," said Burkhart, "I shall be on my way. I wish you all luck. Culver, may you find the answers you seek."

The prince smiled as he left, but Aedan followed him with his eyes and, just before the door, saw the slackening of the unguarded face, as if drained by inner conflict. Ganavant's parting glance, however, was little short of a smirk. Both worried him.

"Be ready by dawn," Culver said. He did not even look at Aedan as he gathered sheets of paper from his laden wheatfield of a desk. "Meet us at the stables with your belongings packed. Saddlebags only. Dun has been briefed and will provide you with equipment and light weapons. I expect you to be punctual. Captain Senbert and his men will be waiting for us at the city gates."

Aedan spent the rest of the day in a flurry of preparation. Dun provided a sleeping roll, weatherproof cloak, and a small hunting knife, but no more weapons, not even a sling or bow. Aedan was surprised that he was to be so lightly armed, especially in the context of the Fenn crisis. It looked more like being disarmed. When he asked, Dun's answer was quick and stiff – the knife would be sufficient for the purposes of a guide; soldiers would deal with any threats. It sounded like Dun was repeating what he had been told rather than actually answering. Aedan sensed that argument would be futile.

There was much excitement among Aedan's friends, and he was assailed with many questions he could not answer. But underneath all the well-wishing, a horrible fear was beginning to gnaw at him. If ever he had needed advice, it was now, but he was not sure whom he could trust other than Osric. Reaching Osric would require leaving the academy during class hours. He could sneak out – it wouldn't be the first time – but he decided under the circumstances to play by the rules and ask permission.

Dun refused him. Like before, his response was unusually quick, as if he had been primed, so Aedan asked Skeet and was allowed out.

He found Osric at his house, preparing a gruesome dinner that contained turnip, potato and partridge, and that had somehow been transformed into axle grease – a sticky, opaque black mass that glared up from the bottom of the pot like the dead eye of some giant fish. It smelled even worse than it looked. Aedan refused so much as a sample taste.

Osric stormed and bothered about second-rate ingredients and partridges not fit for cockroaches until Aedan was able to contain his frustration no longer.

"I've been sent to Kultûhm," he blurted.

Osric dropped the spoon into the poisonous concoction with a thick plop. "Culver's quest?"

"Yes, but it's not what you think. I overheard something last night and I'm worried that we are being sent to our graves."

He told Osric about the conversation he had overheard in the store room, how Dun had armed him with nothing but a midget knife that would be questionable protection against a block of cheese, and how nobody of importance was being included. "Liru and I are both disposable. Culver and his assistant are the only two of any real standing and the rest will be common soldiers. I think they are hoping that the fortress will be our end and if it isn't, the soldiers will probably have orders to finish the job."

"Hmm." Osric sat down, causing the chair to screech with the strain, and folded his arms. "I very much doubt the soldiers would actually take you as far as the fortress if they have been given such orders. Our soldiers can be a superstitious lot, and Kultûhm is a name that some even fear to speak. They will probably travel a few days out, cut some throats, wait three months and return with a well-honed story. Soldiers who have accepted orders to commit murder would not think twice about rearranging the orders to save themselves trouble and danger."

"Wouldn't they be worried the prince would learn the truth if he investigated?"

"I think we both know that the prince's first concern right now is not with truth. Any soldiers given the orders you suspect would know it too. As long as the result and the story are expedient, Burkhart would probably be satisfied. Of late he has not been toasted for his integrity."

Aedan let his head drop forward onto the table with a thump. "How did I land myself with this?"

"I suspect that the prince does not actually want you dead, but it is well known in our circles that you were at Kultûhm, and if he did not send you along it would raise questions. It is also necessary for a nurse to accompany the party considering the possible dangers. He probably felt that this foreign girl was the one he could most afford to lose. Did he look happy about the arrangement to you?"

"I think he was trying to. Trying really hard. But he looked like he was going to be sick when he walked out."

"I would have thought so. He wants to be a good man, but there are things he wants more. I doubt he enjoyed making that decision, and he'll be partly relieved when you all return."

"What do you mean – 'when we all return'? How is that likely?"

"Because I shall see that it happens."

Aedan prepared to ask a string of questions, but the general held up his hand.

"Yes, I know the prince would intervene if he thought I intended to join the party, but in two days I'm heading out with a small patrol for a routine inspection of some of the outlying posts. Seeing as I decide where to patrol, I'm going to head east, and when I find your trail and then your camp, I'll join the quest and assume command, having a strong desire to see the fortress for myself. I have often wanted to assess it as a prospective outpost."

"Will Burkhart not arrest you on your return?"

"I'll send another officer to do the rounds. No duties will be left unattended. But even if they were, the prince would be bold to move against me. I have a unique position here – I answer to the king, to the crown in Tullenroe. I am really just on loan to Castath."

Aedan considered what Osric had said. "What if they make a move before you get there?"

"That is going to be your challenge – making sure that they don't. They will not risk thinning the party until they have travelled well beyond the last of the hamlets. That would take five days on horseback going quick and steady, but it could be done in fewer. It is vital that you slow the pace somehow."

He got up, fetched a small leather pouch from a cupboard and handed it over. "Ground frogweed. Five or six pinches of this will leave a horse very unhappy for a day or two. Won't get much more than a stiff walk and an evil wind."

Aedan took the bag and smelled the contents. It reminded him of silage. There would be no difficulty getting a horse to swallow this.

"I'll try to send a message to Culver," Osric resumed, "but chances are he's worked it out already. If you need to communicate without the soldiers understanding, use Sulese. There are only a handful of them that know it, and they are all posted outside the city. Act as if you are practicing languages. Next best would be Fenn."

Some of the weight had lifted from Aedan's mind, but much remained. Without thinking about it, he buried his head in his hands while the thoughts tumbled. Gradually he became aware of Osric's voice. "I'm sorry," he said. "Could you repeat that?"

"I said there's something else, isn't there? You have the look of a beaten animal, a look that nobody gets overnight. Giddard tells me you have started acting strangely this year. You pay no attention in classes, you keep apart from your friends, and you're either lost in your own thoughts or snappish."

"It's nothing."

Osric regarded him. "Neither of us believes that," he said.

"It's my concern. I really don't want to talk about it. There's nothing you can do. Nothing anyone can do."

"Look, if it …"

"Osric, please. I mean it. I'm grateful that you want to assist, but you can't. And thank you for being willing to help us with this quest or sham of a quest or whatever it is."

Osric's granite features remained fixed as he searched Aedan's face for answers, but Aedan was locked down, tight as a hatch in a gale. Finally the general sat back, "It will be my pleasure," he said. "Now you can repay me by cooking up something that a man can swallow without pain while we go through as many contingencies as the time will allow, beginning with the possibility that no murderous orders have been given. That the prince considered Ganavant's suggestion, we know, but whether he actually gave the order is not certain."

By morning he was the first at the stables, or at least he thought he was until Liru spoke from the shadows.

"You know what this is really about?"

Aedan managed not to jump. "What do you mean?"

"If it were the important quest they say it is, why am I here? I know why you are here – you have been to this Kultûhm – but why me? There are many nurses with more experience. It cannot be the honourable opportunity for training they say, because then they would not have chosen a foreigner. I believe that I was chosen because they would not care much if I did not make it back." Her voice was heavy and cold as the morning.

"Liru I'm sorry –"

"Do not try to make me feel better," she cut in. "I want facts." She stepped out from the shadow. Her face was rigid.

"I have only suspicions."

She inclined her head.

"You've heard that Culver had his own ideas about the storm over Castath? That he thought there might be cause for real concern, not just a bad winter or something?"

"No."

"It's not well known. I've had to piece it together. He found something underneath the city that he thinks might be related – I don't know what, but apparently it's very worrying. He also found a description that matched the unnatural storms in some ancient archive. It led him to believe the answers will be found at Kultûhm."

"That doesn't answer my question."

"Easy Liru. I'm getting there. Biting me won't help either of us."

She looked back without softening. He had never been on the other side of her annoyance, and he was not enjoying it.

"I think," he continued, "that Culver has been sent on this trip believing that he will find answers, but the real purpose is to silence him."

"And witnesses will not return," she finished for him.

Aedan nodded. "I think so. But I have a plan. I spoke to Osric and …" He trailed off.

Liru wasn't listening. She folded her arms and stared into the thinning darkness. "I believed that I had escaped from tyranny when I came here, but now I see your people can be as wicked as Lekrans."

Aedan felt the words strike him. He wanted to react, but what could he say? "Look, it's just a hunch. Maybe there's another explanation." But not even he believed that.

She turned and walked into her pony's stall, hung her lantern, and began to tack.

Before the others arrived, Aedan made arrangements to have Murn looked after by a stable boy who had overcome some of his fear of the horse, admiration driving him.

As he turned away, something caught his eye – a figure slipping behind a tree. In an instant the suspicion took shape. He dropped his saddle and ran out through the dim light, reaching the tree just as Malik's hard visage appeared on the other side.

Aedan walked around and faced him. "Why are you here?" he asked.

"What makes you think my being here has anything to do with you?" Malik sneered.

"I know it does."

Malik raised his eyebrows, then leaned against the tree and relaxed. "I'm not supposed to say anything, but who would you tell anyway?"

"Tell what?"

He looked at Aedan for a while, clearly enjoying his control of the situation. "It was my father who dropped a few words about who would go on this headless quest."

"Was it not enough to … to point that bully my way?"

"Iver was not enough," Malik said, his voice rising. "You and your savage have done more to insult me than anyone else. I'm no spineless worm that can bend and ignore it. I remember it all and how you taught your friends to do the same. Then there was the festival." Malik's face was growing red, something Aedan had never seen before. "You told the story as if you succeeded where I failed."

"But I only told what happened, and you were unconscious so how would you know?"

"Because I know *you*." Malik was breathing hard. "I finally saw, thanks to Iver. You're a worm, a little shaking worm who climbs walls to get away from a real fight. For years I was fooled like everyone else, but it was Iver who told me and then showed me the truth. You could never have done what you said you did.

You talked yourself big at *my* expense! And then you called me a possum – in front of *my* friends! Do you have any idea how far that travelled?" He paused, breathing hard. "Do you know why I was unconscious at the festival? Because I tried to defend the others against the whole gang. I didn't have my friends to back me up and I never had any chance, but I went at them anyway. And you – you called me a possum! You polished your boots with *my* name!"

The last words were shouted in a voice that was hoarse with passion. It was the first time he had shown emotion like this; it actually looked as if there were tears in his eyes. Aedan was too stunned to reply.

Malik gradually recovered himself and stepped forward. "I never thought you belonged in marshal training, but I was prepared to look the other way and let you be. Then when you insulted me, you showed me that any respect I gave you would be thrown away. You never belonged here, North-boy. You should have left. *You* brought this on yourself and her. You'll be gone for three months, and Culver's not going to trouble himself with your studies like you were promised – I saw to that as well – so you'll fail the year for sure, both of you. But that only matters if you return, and I don't think the odds favour you. You want my advice? If you reach Kultûhm alive, keep heading north and don't stop until you're back where you belong."

He turned and strode away, leaving Aedan to sort through his feelings – anger, embarrassment and even a measure of guilt – as he returned to the stables.

Culver arrived with the large hairy man Aedan remembered from the final interview of the entrance examinations. Aedan tried to ask a question, but the chancellor strode past and spoke without breaking step. "You will deal with my assistant, Fergal." His tone was as dismissive as his words.

Malik had spoken the truth then – at least that part was true. Even if they made it back from this corrupted quest, he and Liru would be failed. At the very least, the year was being stolen from them, and along with it, their friends. He should have broken Malik's nose.

The bulky assistant offered Aedan a kind smile beneath a glowing nose. "We'll speak along the way," he said from within a black forest of beard, and lumbered off to find his horse. Aedan made no effort to conceal his dismay. He remembered now that he had seen the man more recently – with a mop!

"Aren't you a cleaner?" he asked, coming up to him.

The man looked at him, quiet humour in his eyes. He was obviously in no hurry to answer. Aedan began to wonder if this servant was hard of hearing.

"I do clean, yes, among other things," Fergal said. "Are you above being taught by a cleaner?"

Aedan was not in a good mood, and lessons were the least of his concerns. He wanted to say something cutting but he realised that this poor fellow was not his enemy, and the lessons would probably make no difference in the end anyway. "No," he said, and left to finish saddling his pony.

A light wintery drizzle had come out to soak the first day of their quest. All had their hoods up, all but Fergal whose mass of black hair acted like a thatch roof. He seemed quite content with the miserable weather.

At the city gates, the party was met by a unit of a dozen soldiers and several pack-mules loaded with bags – grains, beans and other supplies for the journey. The soldiers were wearing leather armour suitable for travelling. They carried an assortment of weapons, all a lot bigger than cheese knives.

They were also cloaked and hooded so their faces were mostly hidden, but the eyes that Aedan saw were shifty and hard. These were not boys; there was no buzz of innocent enthusiasm here. He looked ahead at Liru, so small on her little pony, and he felt a thorn of worry begin to work at him. To the side, he glimpsed a soldier smiling at her. The man's look gave him more cause to shiver than the wind that now struck through the opening gates.

He thought of how he and his friends had contributed to the design of the city's defences, to the safety of its people, and wondered how things had come to this. Could the prince he served really be sending him to die for some political convenience?

He looked out at the sheets of drizzle. The men would not want to camp in the open tonight. They would push for one of the villages at a trot. He would have to slow them tomorrow. He blessed Osric quietly for the frogweed. Where was it now? He had put it under his bed so that it wouldn't be found among his packed things during the night by a suspicious Dun. He turned around with a gasp and felt through the saddlebags with mounting panic, almost spilling his clothes on the muddy road.

He had left it.

Chapter 46

Building on the outer wall was supposed to commence at first light every day, but there were no hands to be seen as the party approached the network of scaffolds and ramps. After passing a large mound of rock and stone, Aedan caught sight of a group of builders. They were huddled against the leeward shelter of the now-twelve-foot wall, trying to kindle a fire. Captain Senbert shouted at them, but a sudden watery squall turned everything white and swept his words away, apparently along with any resolve to interfere. He put his head down and urged his horse forward, leaving the builders to themselves.

The road lay empty, apart from a few unfortunates who hurried through the mud to or from the city. As soon as the party had descended the slope, the captain spurred his horse to a trot. Aedan glanced to his right as they passed Borr and Harriet's home. His mother would be there. Thinking of her made him feel like turning his pony from this hateful procession and dashing away. But she could not protect him. Who could, if the prince had in fact ordered his death? Osric, perhaps, but even that was uncertain.

The morning aged without changing, unable to outgrow its mood. It remained swamped in a dusky darkness, thick with drizzle and worried by restless wind. The belts of rain would often bring visibility down to a few yards, but in the breaks when the clouds gathered for the next squall, the travellers were permitted brief glimpses of the surrounds. Buildings began to thin out until there were only scattered farmsteads on the plains. Here, barns and homes crouched and dripped while smudges of blue smoke were pulled from their chimneys by the gusts. Only the bravest of the farmers could be spied in their fields; the rest were clearly content to bow out and let the weather do its work.

The horses had been alternately trotting and walking for a few hours when the Captain called a halt and dismounted along with a sergeant.

Aedan looked around. They were in a shallow depression – no buildings or people were visible. More to the point, their party was visible to none. With a rush of fear he wondered if this could be it. Sounds would not carry, graves could be easily dug in the softened earth, tracks would wash away in the rain. He urged his horse forward and stopped beside Liru.

"We need to talk," he said.

"What good will talking do, Aedan? I have made peace with my fate. Let me be."

"It's not your fate. Are you going to make no effort to escape any of this?"

"And then what would happen to my parents if I escape your prince. He will turn on them. I will not let that happen."

"But Liru –"

"Enough Aedan. Leave me." With that she urged her horse away.

The sergeant called out that they would stop briefly. The party dismounted. Aedan headed for the trees. On his way back, one of the soldiers stepped in front of him with a loose-lipped smirk.

"Not much luck with the girl, huh? Saw her give you the hoof. Bit dark for my usual taste, but definitely growing on me. I like a bit of pluck."

Aedan stared back, furious but helpless.

The soldier laughed and made a mock chop at Aedan's neck with an imaginary sword. "Look at me like that too often and I'll cut you down to size, little marshal."

The captain had been within earshot, but he merely turned away. He carried his head as if his neck was tired, shoulders drawn in; he looked wilted. On the few occasions when Aedan had seen his face, it had reflected turmoil.

The day continued as gloomily as it had begun. Sodden and cold, they pressed on until, in the failing light, they came to the gates of Morren. Once the horses were stabled, their riders hurried indoors where they warmed themselves before the hearth while stamping in pools of water that gathered at their feet.

The inn, named *The Rabbit's Burrow*, was a warm and cheery place, though decidedly more rustic than anything Aedan had seen in Castath. Reeds covered the clay floor, and smoky rushlights mounted against the walls put out a moody glow that barely reached the centre of the room. Under better circumstances Aedan would have found the place almost magical.

The regulars looked, for the most part, to be farmers, labourers and craftsmen – the carpenter and blacksmith were easily identified by wood shavings and soot. Between them they set up a buzz and hum of relaxed conversation. Aedan caught a few strands – caterpillars in the cabbages, a new hay wagon big enough to carry a house and that necessitated widening of all gates, predictions of rain and complaints about last month's predictions. There was talk of the latest eerie sighting at Eastridge – trees that had been devoured by something in the night – and then a story that spilled the banks of gentle murmuring.

Apparently one of the dairy cows had tried to jump a fence and only made it half way, landed on the beam, and slid forward until her forelegs reached the ground. There she remained, half on and half off until the labourers could wrestle her free. One of the men proceeded to re-enact the performance by suspending himself over the back of a chair, buttocks hoisted, legs in the air kicking uselessly. His companions were helpless with laughter.

Aedan smiled, as much at the storytellers as at their tale. Though he had grown to love Castath and the academy, he missed these quiet country ways.

A whistle and lyre were produced and two musicians, young, eager and more than a little nervous, took their places in the corner and began to pour out a medley of folksongs. The notes did not always agree, but the result was nevertheless a pleasant ambience, like the bubbling of a quiet brook.

The innkeeper was a small man with bulging cheeks and a white downy beard under grey downy hair. With a carrot plugging his mouth it would have taken little imagination to see that this was indeed his burrow. He was as polite and attentive as a grandfather hosting his nephew's birthday party.

His wife, however, was a different prospect altogether. She was a big woman with a hard face and sharp ears. At any hint of disorder, she would march through from the kitchen to raise her eyebrows as a herder raises his staff, or as a stone mason raises his hammer. The locals sensed the weight of those brows and simmered down when she appeared, but the soldiers paid her little attention. As the evening progressed, they became louder, their talk cruder, their looks meaner. Locals began to grow quiet and started leaving, a few without finishing their meals. It was as Aedan had suspected. These soldiers were of the wrong kind.

Unfortunately, the eager, bowing innkeeper could not oppose anyone's wish, so the ale flowed more freely than it ought to have done. The serving girls knew to retreat from the company of drinking soldiers, especially this kind, and the innkeeper was left to manage his own disaster.

Aedan had hoped to speak to Culver – he *needed* to speak to him, and urgently – but the chancellor and his assistant took their meals to a small table that would not accommodate a third. Aedan found another small table. Liru, instead of joining him, sat by herself until the soldier that had been watching her earlier joined her. She left him without a word and took the chair opposite Aedan. Roars of laughter rose from the soldiers who had been watching the performance. Even the captain, whose mood had been softened by a bottle of wine, was enjoying the spectacle. The rejected soldier's smile, however, was tight as a scar. Liru remained silent and ate little, though the duck pie was perfect – thick pastry and soft meat swimming in a spicy gravy.

Fergal lingered to see that Aedan and Liru found their rooms. When he turned to leave, Aedan asked if he might have a word. Fergal replied, in a voice that carried a long way, that there would be much time for talk during the journey and that whatever he had to say could wait a few days. Aedan opened his mouth to say that there might not *be* a few days. But Fergal held up a hand and spoke one Sulese word, almost like a salutation, then lumbered away, his broad shape filling the passage from wall to wall.

Vlegalyo'du. That was not a salutation. Aedan went to his room and racked his brain to dig up the meaning. It was familiar. If he had brought his books he could have found it quickly. Something told him that there was an importance attached to the word – Fergal's eyes had been intent when speaking it, as if driving some meaning home. Aedan paced, he leaned with his head against the wall and drummed his fingers, whispering the word to himself over and over. A creak distracted him, and he listened. Suddenly he forgot about the creak as his face lit up.

Listen – that's what it meant. Although it should have been *vlegalyo*. Trust a cleaner to make such a basic error.

But he began to wonder if there was more to it. Then, from an almost forgotten class he remembered the modifier *'du* signified people, in this case it would be people who listen. Listeners.

The creak from earlier now took on a meaning, and Aedan remembered that the body of soldiers in the common room had appeared a little thin. Fergal had given a warning that they were being listened to. That's why he had spoken so loudly of there being no need for haste. He must have been assuring an eavesdropper that he was not suspicious of anything.

Which meant that he was.

So Fergal and Culver also suspected treachery. Osric, then, had succeeded in getting a warning through. Aedan felt relieved in part, but wondered what the old scholar and his large assistant would be able to do. A compelling lecture would be of little help.

Liru would be no help.

Aedan was unable to sleep. The carousing of the soldiers was enough to keep anyone awake. He hoped Liru had barricaded her door. By the time the inn fell silent, he was still gazing up at the ceiling. The heavens that had already delivered more than a week's quota of drizzle now showed themselves capable of far greater things as they truly opened up. Through the pounding of heavy drops, he could not even hear his own steps when he got up from the bed and walked to the window. The drowning noise gave him an idea, not a comfortable one, but one that he would be fool to discard.

Getting out the window was the easy part; climbing down the wall under a small waterfall from the roof was something else. He had never climbed under such conditions and did not find it enjoyable. Holding the slippery surfaces was far less of a problem than actually seeing them, and breathing was more difficult still. When he reached the ground, he collapsed into a frothing pool and gasped for air until he had recovered. Even if there had been a light outside, the rain was so thick that it would have sheltered him completely, so he ran around the building to the stables, nearly tripping over the low rim of the well and ending his plans with a long, dark fall.

As he covered the last few yards before the stables, he was surprised by a faint yellow glow emerging through the rain. He guessed too late that Captain Senbert had probably mounted a guard. Unable to stop in time, he skidded under the eaves and looked up to see a soldier at the far corner of the building holding a lamp.

"Who walks there?"

Aedan hopped over the low door of the nearest stall. It was dark, but he sensed movement near him. Without waiting to discover what it was, he darted to the partition between stalls, sprang over it, and dropped into the straw on the other side. The light grew brighter and then filled the stall he had just left. A door creaked open, heavy steps advanced.

A sharp thud was followed by a grunt of pain and something collapsed onto the ground.

This was proving to be a lot more activity than he had hoped to find down here. He started planning a retreat when he heard a girl's voice.

"Aedan?"

It was Liru. He rose and looked across the dividing wall to see her poised over the fallen soldier, shovel held like an axe.

"What are you doing down here?" he asked.

"I do not trust a door lock when there are drunk soldiers around, especially soldiers like these. I hoped the captain would stop them drinking, but he drank more than any of them, getting them to huddle round while he told jokes that made them laugh the way vile men laugh at vile jokes. I came here to sleep. I did not think they would set a guard. I have been standing behind the door in case I had to defend myself. I almost crushed your head when you jumped in. What are you doing here?"

"I don't know if I should tell you."

"Why not?"

"You might try to stop me."

She looked at him without expression for a moment. "I think I spoke from bitterness earlier," she said. "Tell me what you have planned and I will hear you. If I do not agree I promise not to stand in your way."

Aedan climbed the wall back into the first stall, checked that the soldier was asleep, and tied him up properly. Then he moved to a stall further away where they would not be overheard, though the heavy rain really made the precaution unnecessary. Aedan told the whole story – from the overheard conversation under the academy to his encounter with Malik. He then explained what Osric had planned and how they needed to slow the progress.

With embarrassment he recalled how he'd forgotten the frogweed under his bed.

"Do you think Malik really has that much influence, and that much hate?" Liru asked.

"Influence – I think he might have managed to get Culver not to teach us, but I don't think he arranged for me to be here. I was going already. I'm not sure about you either. Maybe he was just trying to claim those as his own victories. I don't think he knows about the plot either. Why would he bother about making us fail if he knew we'd be murdered? As to hate – he's a lying, insulting, self-absorbed snob who can mock others but if you joke with him it's a mortal offense, and he hates deeper than most people love. In spite of that, I don't think he's a murderer … but … remember that Orunean proverb, *Carrun nos, darrim brak.*

"This year a cub, next year a tiger," Liru translated.

"Hadley once called him a rat. I thought that was a good description back then, but I'm beginning to think he could turn out more dangerous."

"To me he is still a rat, no matter how big he gets. But there is something else I must ask you. General Osric – I know him only by name, everyone does, even in Mardraél. Will he extend his protection to me and my family when we get back? All the rumours of him reveal a very frightening man."

"Osric is just as frightening as his reputation says," Aedan replied with a hint of a smile. "I think he even dwarfs his reputation. He is a fierce man but never cruel. If anything, it's cruel people that need to fear him. The one thing that really brings out the lion in him is injustice. He'll take care of you, trust me."

Liru nodded. "I will trust you."

Then Aedan explained what Fergal had said and Liru immediately translated the word and guessed the meaning.

"So he doesn't want us to look like we are suspicious or making plans?" she said.

"I suppose so."

"But we need to be concerned. We covered a great distance today, a very great distance for these conditions."

"That's why I'm here," said Aedan. "It's time to steal some horses."

Liru nodded. "The rain will cover sounds and tracks. Where do you plan to take them?"

"On the way here I saw a wood to the south. If we tie them up there, they won't be found quickly. The whole party would have to search for them before going on. It should win us a day or two. The only problem will be finding the way. It's no fun getting lost on a night like this."

"I'll join you."

"Are you sure?"

"I am always sure, even when I am wrong. Mardrae heritage. Now let's go. Two horses each?"

The rain blanketed the sounds of hooves when they left the stables and walked slowly down the road, feeling rather than seeing the way. After they had gone what felt like a mile, Aedan turned up the bank and faced south as he remembered it. He felt the wind hard on his right side. That would help. If he kept it there, he might be able to stay on a southerly course.

They travelled a long way through the grass. He was growing certain that they were off target when the wind began to dip and the whistling of branches grew ahead of them. The weather was robbed of its fierceness by the trees, but this sheltering created a different problem, for the gloomy hint of light was reduced to nothing. They had to walk with an arm outstretched and ears alert, tugging the unwilling horses behind them. It made for very slow progress. After a few hundred paces Aedan decided it was far enough. He was starting to worry about getting back before morning. If their rooms were found empty, there would be trouble.

The return trip was aided by a few lights that glimmered through sheets of rain from time to time.

It was on the way back that things went wrong. Morren was one of the least fortified towns. Aedan had not expected there to be watchmen who patrolled at night. He and Liru were sloshing their way up the road when the downpour thinned, exposing the buildings – and a sentry. The man's slouching posture went rigid; he peered under a raised hand and shouted a challenge. Aedan grabbed Liru's arm and ran up the road, past the inn.

"Intruders!" they heard. "Intruders!" The sentry was keeping up, hollering like a madman.

They slipped behind an empty wagon on the side of the road. Aedan felt around for a stone. He found one just in time, aimed up the road, and threw. The sentry approached the wagon, but when he heard the splash, he raced on, continuing his pursuit.

Aedan tried to draw Liru in the other direction, but she was kneeling and apparently plucking weeds – strong smelling ones too.

"Liru!" he hissed, "What are you doing? We must go now!"

She pocketed what she had dug up, and they ran back to the inn, but now lights were appearing in some of the windows. They darted around to the side, narrowly missing the yellow glare that spilled out as the front door opened.

"We mustn't be seen coming in," Aedan whispered. "Can you climb? My room is on the third floor. The one with the open window."

Liru answered by gripping the beams and pulling herself up. With her dark hair and dark coat she was nearly invisible, a patch of shadow edging its way up. The drenched surfaces made for slow going, but the beams were rough-hewn and still provided reasonable purchase. Aedan stood below. Catching her from a third story fall would injure them both, but might save her life, so he waited until she was in.

He sprang off the ground and clambered with lizard-like haste – voices were growing louder. Someone with a lantern was approaching from around the corner, betrayed by the swinging shadow of the wall and the swelling brightness. Aedan clapped his arms over the sill and almost fell as his foot popped off a smooth beam. He felt hands under his shoulders and it was enough to help him, none too elegantly, through the window.

"Close it!" he gasped, hitting the floor in a panting heap.

Liru grabbed the shutter and swung it closed as boots splashed around the corner below them.

"You stay here," Aedan said, "I'll take your room. That way if anyone tries to bother you I'll know first, and I'll make a noise."

They were awoken early. Horse thieves had visited them during the night. Senbert was livid. He ate his breakfast with a frown while giving orders to find the missing horses quickly. Aedan and Liru were instructed to accompany two of the soldiers and search the northern farmsteads. Aedan breathed a sigh of relief. A scattered hunt like the one being organised would mean that the day would be lost, even if one of the search parties found the horses early.

It had worked, and he and Liru had not been discovered.

During the night, he had squeezed every last drop of water from his clothes before hanging them just inside the window, then he had gone for an early walk with Liru in the drizzle. Soldiers had seen them at the well. Anyone noticing the dampness of their clothes would have no suspicions. They had considered everything.

A voice interrupted his thoughts. "Where did you get that red mud on your boots? I don't remember seeing red mud hereabouts."

Aedan gulped under Senbert's inspection.

"Must have been from one of the stops yesterday."

"It looks fresh."

Aedan wasn't sure what to say. Senbert narrowed his eyes and was about to speak again when a young farmer galloped up and hailed them.

"You men lost some horses?" he asked.

"What do you know of it?" asked the captain, transferring his suspicious look to the farmer.

"I went to check on my snares this morning. Heard a horse in the woods and discovered four of them tied to trees less than a half mile in. I'll show you the way if you can leave now."

Within an hour, the horses were recovered and the party was on its way again. The captain set a pace that did not accord with a long journey. Aedan's fears were growing into certainty.

Travelling like this, they would be leaving the outlying hamlets by the end of the fourth day, and if that happened, he doubted he would see the fifth. Osric would arrive in time to avenge him, but that was no comfort. Liru had a fixed calmness about her, but it was not like her earlier resignation. He wondered if she had some plan.

That day Aedan was sure they must have covered more than fifty miles. By the time it grew dark, there was only a small homestead in sight. The farmer, more likely out of fear than generosity, offered his hay barn for lodging. Aedan and Liru were watched closely this time. When they tried to step away from the barn to talk, Senbert called them back. It was hopeless.

The following day they moved out early, the horses striding as swiftly as before and eating up the miles at a frightening rate. Aedan was beginning to realise he would not get another convenient opportunity. The next attempt to slow the pace would have to happen soon, no matter how big the risk.

Chapter 47

The hamlet of Eastridge was a scattered arrangement. Two dozen houses were spread across a broad glen, reaching all the way up a gentle slope to the prominent ridge. One of the homes was near the road. Its crooked walls were capped with a mossy thatch that was dark with age and rot and hung almost to the ground. It made the house seem like a suspicious old man drawn up under his drooping hat, protective of his solitude, hostile to strangers. Within the building, Aedan thought, there was quite possibly just such an old man.

The only indication of life in the whole settlement was the gabbling from the goose house around the back and the smoke that billowed out of a chimney a little ways ahead. The chimney, he thought with relief, appeared to belong to a small inn.

He noticed some of the soldiers pointing in the direction of the goose house and muttering. They would pay it a visit before leaving here. He was not surprised. The coarse morals of these men had begun to speak more loudly than their uniforms. They were not soldiers, at least not at heart. They would only serve and show discipline that was personally convenient.

As he rode, this preoccupation with the soldiers took the edge off his observations, and he did not pay enough attention to the stillness of the hamlet – its eerie lifelessness.

The inn had once had a sign declaring it to be the *Never Hasty*, an apt name for a place so far removed from the main thoroughfares, but whether by mischief or chance, a good portion of the sign had been broken off, and all that remained was the word "sty".

The *sty*, then, was a small inn, and might have been called neat if clean.

But it was not.

The burly innkeeper, whose scalp was thinly decorated with dark, oily strands of hair, and whose mouth was just as thinly decorated with dark teeth, did not appear to have bathed for most of his adult life. A glance around the parlour suggested that he treated his inn with the same philosophy. Spilled and dropped food lay unmolested on the floor, and tables hid under generous coats of greasy smears.

Even the soldiers looked uncomfortable. The captain glanced out at the darkening drizzle, and when he turned back, he was scowling.

"Lodging and meals for one night," he said. "Party of eighteen."

The innkeeper was clearly unaccustomed to visitors. His unfriendly eyes grew white with surprise and he shook his head. "Closed," he said. Aedan was amused to see that his hands were shaking. These rural folk would seldom have seen such a large detachment of soldiers.

"Your establishment is empty and we are here on the prince's business," Senbert returned, "so you are now open."

The innkeeper's worry mounted. "No staff. No food," he said in clipped, almost foreign tones – clearly he was a reticent sort – and held up his hands, but the captain was not to be turned.

"You two," Senbert said to Aedan and Liru. "Get into the kitchen and make sure there is something to eat tonight."

The kitchen was everything Aedan had feared. Most pots still contained the grimy, mouldy leftovers of whatever they had last cooked. All had a coating of ashy remains at the bottom that required the attentions of hammer and chisel. Aedan, after all his cooking for Osric, knew what to do. He set about cleaning, and chopping potatoes, carrots and cabbage, while the innkeeper, who had not bothered to give his name or ask theirs, was out back catching chickens.

Aedan was sure they were alone, but he remembered Fergal's warning, so he suggested that they practice some Sulese. Liru caught his meaning and agreed. His use of the language was halting. It translated to:

"We very trouble. Tomorrow we ride. No more people around."

Liru's was only slightly better: "I do plan. Tomorrow we rest, not ride."

"Plan?" Aedan asked.

"Better you forgetful – no – ignorant."

"Rest? Why – uh – boss soldier agree rest?"

"Nice place," she said with a smile, indicating the inn. She would tell him no more.

The chicken broth was not the best meal he had ever prepared, but for cold, tired travellers, the smells were irresistible. In spite of Liru's odd taste in herbs, they eventually reached an agreement. There were no thanks offered from the soldiers, but neither were there any complaints.

Culver and Fergal hurried through their meals and retired directly. Aedan wondered about the look Fergal had given him when his bowl had been set on the table. It was as if the twinkling eyes were saying something from within the dark forest of hair and beard, but he had no idea what. Liru, strangely enough, was not worried tonight about the soldiers. She retired early too.

Aedan struggled to fall asleep. Something was going dreadfully wrong with his innards. At first he thought it might be a fever from the day spent in the cold, but then, as his stomach rebelled and muscles began to seize, he recognised the symptoms of poisoning. In spite of his cleaning, something in one of those pots had managed to ruin the meal. There would be no sleep for him.

He groaned and rolled and emptied his belly into the chamber pot several times. By morning he was a wreck. It was light when his door crashed open. Senbert stood wobbling in the frame, clutching his midriff, head slick from sweat. He opened his mouth to speak, but his eyes took in the chamber pot and Aedan's shattered state.

"So it wasn't you then," he said. "Should never have trusted the kitchen in this filthy ..." A groan of pain interrupted his words and he staggered away, leaving the door open.

Aedan remained in his bed for the rest of the day. He heard some raised voices but they were almost watery, like they belonged to a kind of half-suspended dream. The sun travelled across the room and warmed him when it reached the old, smelly straw of his pallet. The poison began to work its way from his body and he felt clarity returning to his thoughts. Rest, he told himself.

He wondered how Liru was coping. Then something that had puzzled him came back to mind – the awful herb she had added, a herb she said she had picked. That sour milk smell – it was the weed she had found the previous night.

Liru had poisoned the broth!

Then he remembered Fergal's look of recognition and his quick retreat. He and Culver had probably gone to purge themselves as soon as the show of eating was over. Liru too. Why had he been left to suffer? Then he recalled Senbert at his door and understood. After that confrontation over the muddy boots, suspicion would naturally have fallen on him.

By evening he was on his feet, but shaky. He went down to the kitchen. There was no more cooking being done. Sorry-looking soldiers appeared briefly in the common room but nothing was taken from the food stores, not even wine. They nibbled on bread from their packs and retired early. Aedan ventured down again later, but finding nobody around, puffed his way up the stairs that shook as much as his limbs, and dug out some hard biscuits from his saddlebags. It was a poor meal, but perhaps all his stomach could endure. That night he slept soundly, and come the next morning, most of his discomfort was gone. He was woken by the sergeant banging on his door and telling him to be ready within the hour.

At the stables there was a commotion around Fergal. Despite Culver's annoyance and shouted injunctions – so intimidating that even the soldiers stood back – the heavy assistant was unable to stay on top of the horse. Apparently he *had* been poisoned and had not yet recovered from the effects. As soon as he was hoisted up the one side he began to flow down the other until the soldiers gave up and let him slide and drop on the ground like a discarded bag of sand.

"Leave him," the captain said. "He is not critical to the quest. If he is not able to ride he should return to the city."

"Without him," said Culver, "I will be sorely disadvantaged. We shall have to wait until he has recovered. In the meantime, I want you and your soldiers to make a full inspection of this hamlet. There is something strange afoot here."

"We will not wait another moment!" snapped Senbert. "I can already feel the prince breathing down my neck. His orders were direct and made no mention of inspections. I want to get this over with as quickly as possible."

Aedan exchanged a look with Liru. Get it over with?

He doubted any of the soldiers had noted that detail, but he and Liru had certainly noted the way their captain spoke to the chancellor – nobody addressed Culver with that tone. Senbert, however, hardly appeared to be himself. He was nearly frantic with whatever worries assailed him, and did not back down. He yelled at the sergeant who bellowed at the soldiers, and the party moved out.

It was the fifth day. Aedan had hoped to speak to Liru or Culver, but it was as though the soldiers had been instructed to keep them apart. The hamlet was as silent and empty as on their arrival. He looked around, wondering at this. At the very least he would have expected to see a few doors slamming in acknowledgement of their presence, but there was neither sound nor movement as they left. What did Culver suspect?

By mid-afternoon they were beyond the last traces of civilisation and were now cutting through the grassland. The light was softened by a thin veil of cloud, but otherwise the day was clear and still. They climbed to the top of a gentle rise and Captain Senbert took a very long time as he surveyed the land.

Aedan watched him. Was he looking for something more permanent than a night's lodging? An alder-clad dale about a half mile to the north caught the captain's attention. He pointed and led the way down the slope.

Aedan considered calling to Liru and making a break from the soldiers. But the academy ponies would stand no chance against these hardy steeds.

He felt drops start to trickle down his forehead as they chose the campsite. Liru walked her pony beside his while they watched the soldiers dismount. He had a wild idea, but before he could say anything to Liru, the sergeant took his horse's bridle firmly and waited for him to dismount and unpack. Carrying his saddlebags and bedroll, he made for a tree some distance from the centre of the clearing where he dropped his things and sat. Liru sat down beside him. She stared at the ground as if she were about to strike it.

"What are we to do?" she asked. "First the prince, then Culver and his servant, now Osric has failed us."

"Osric has not failed us. We are still here."

"For how long? I see murder in these men's eyes."

Aedan could not disagree. He cast his gaze around, trying to appear bored. "How fast can you run?" he asked.

She looked up. "Considering what they all ate two nights ago, I might be able to outrun them. How about you?"

"I'm still aching," Aedan said, not making any effort to hide the annoyance he felt at not being warned, "but I made sure I ate a lot on the way here. I'll be able to get up this slope behind us faster than any of these armoured soldiers. I think it will be too steep and crumbly for some of them to climb at all. If we can reach the top of the hill we can drop into the valley on the other side. It has many rocks and crevices, many places to hide. Finding us there at night will not be easy."

"Very well. Should we run from here or try to walk first and hope they don't notice?"

Aedan looked around again. "The captain is missing. Now is a good time. We'll get up and walk slowly until we are called back, then we run." He stopped talking as a young soldier with pocked skin and a mean eye approached from the side and tossed down an armload of firewood.

"Seems that you are sitting in my place," he said and dropped heavily beside Aedan, filling the air with a reek of old sweat. "And it looks like you have some of my stuff too." He drew Aedan's little knife and held it up. "Yes, I remember this knife. I'm going to make you apologise for taking it."

Other footsteps drew closer and Aedan recognised the loose-lipped soldier who had spoken to him on the first day – Rork, the men called him. He was a large, powerful man, and apparently a notable swordsman. He sat so near to Liru that he was leaning against her. She tried to move but he gripped her neck and held her in place.

"They took our spot," said the first soldier. "And this thieving boy took my knife, see?" Hold him while I search for more of my things. Rork leaned over and gripped Aedan's neck while the first pushed struggling arms aside and dug through one pocket after another. The search revealed a few pebbles, some coins which were immediately recognised as stolen, and nothing else but the one thing that was nearly everything to Aedan.

"What's this?" the soldier said, holding up the little leather case with the emblem of a sapling and a toadstool. "This has paper in it. Ah yes, I remember, I use it for starting fires. We can use a page now."

Aedan screamed and struggled like a wild animal but the men were too strong for him. His kicking and writhing did no more than draw laughter. Both men now held him with strong fingers.

At the edge of his vision something flashed. The soldier who had sat so close to Liru had given her access to his dagger. In a burst of movement, she drew it, plunged it into his leg and darted from his grasp. The howl caused the other soldier to drop his guard. It was a momentary distraction but it was all Aedan needed to plant an elbow in the man's nose and slip away. It tore him to leave the diary behind, but he knew there was no way he could wrestle it free and still make good his escape.

He flew up the slope, springing from root to root where the soil was too soft, and darting through the undergrowth like a ferret. The uproar behind him was immediate. A mistake now would cost him his last chance at freedom.

He caught up to Liru and sped past her to lead the way, choosing the quickest path, reading the ground as effortlessly as he might read the words of a story. Here he was at home in a way that none of his peers would ever be. Liru mimicked how he moved from root to root, leapt upwards from the stems of trees, and spread his weight over crumbling soil when there were no better holds.

The heavy churning of boots began to drop behind. Calls became shorter as the men found their lungs burning. Aedan was just beginning to think he could stop to catch his breath when an arrow cut through the air and crunched into the bark of a tree near his head.

He moved behind a screen of thick bushes and continued climbing. He was feeling the effects of the poison now, but he pushed on, leading Liru to just beneath the crest of the hill. The last twenty feet would leave them exposed, but as another arrow plugged into the soil near him, he realised that staying put was no option.

"We need … to make a dash … over the top," he managed between breaths.

Liru nodded. She was panting too.

Aedan kept his head down and led the way through the long grass. As they reached level ground, he broke into a full sprint over the exposed hilltop, Liru at his heels. But he had not made it halfway across when three mounted soldiers appeared on their right and cantered to intercept them.

The distance closed. They were so near to freedom, but he knew they would not make it.

Then he recognised the sound of a familiar voice calling his name. He looked up at the huge soldier whose eighteen-hand-high charger stamped and ground to a halt before him. Aedan's wild eyes settled just enough for him to recognise the man. He sank down in the grass, rolled onto his back, and gave way to the exhaustion.

Liru's terrified eyes appeared above him. He grinned and pointed at the soldier. "General ... Osric," he gasped.

Fergal and a tall, middle-aged woman in military uniform now joined the first three horsemen and dismounted. The woman showed impressive balance as she sprang from the saddle. The placement of her feet was precise; there was no tottering step. Her eyes were quick and they caught Aedan staring – slender figures and long copper hair were hardly common sights within a military regiment. He wondered what kind of woman this was.

"Wait here with Fergal and Tyne," Osric ordered, and rode towards the centre of the hilltop with his two uniformed companions. Aedan had never before seen Osric fully armed. It was a frightening spectacle. He would have dwarfed standard weapons, so he bore bigger weapons which he dwarfed anyway and carried with the greatest of ease. His two companions, though not nearly as large as the general, were no less fierce or stern. Aedan now recognised them as Merter, a ranger-captain, and the renowned Commander Thormar. It was a high ranking trio, and for any soldier, a terrifying one.

Aedan saw a ragged group of pursuers crest the hilltop and stumble to a confused halt as they saw the three mounted officers.

"Fall in!" bellowed the commander.

Exhausted as they were, they scurried over and lined up. The rest of the soldiers did the same as they arrived. Captain Senbert was the last to appear, and he rushed to take a position at the head of his men. Osric left the commander in charge and walked his horse back to where the others waited.

Liru stepped close to Aedan. "You never said he was *that* big."

Osric dismounted with a thump they all felt.

"Are you hurt?" he asked.

Aedan shook his head.

"Liru?" The general dropped to a knee, and even then he was taller by several inches. She appeared confused. It was the first time Aedan had seen her fumbling for words.

"Sir, no. Thank you, sir. No, I am not hurt."

"You have nothing to fear from me," he said in a voice that, even now, rasped and growled.

"I'm not afraid," she said. "It's just that I did not expect you to know my name, or care what happened to me."

He regarded her. "After how you have been treated, I am not surprised. Nevertheless, my concern is sincere, and if any man here attempts to harm you, I shall hang him from the nearest branch. It is shameful that you were not given a woman for company so I have brought someone very special to escort you. You will have learned of Tyne, daughter of Vellian, during your studies."

The tall lady offered Liru a kind smile.

A strange croak came from Liru's mouth. She blinked and coughed and tried again. "Thank you." It was hardly more than a squeak. For once, her complete self-possession was crumbling.

Aedan guessed it was the unexpected kindness in the wake of such prolonged dread. He stepped back and gestured for Osric to hug her. The big general's face registered a combination of confusion and panic. Aedan tried again, but by now the moment was past and Liru's display of emotion was gone as quickly as it had appeared, a summer cloudburst, over in a blink.

Osric got to his feet. "Now, much as I would like to bind that lot and send them directly to the barrack prison, we are going to need them very soon. There is trouble in these hills that will find us and I'm afraid we now urgently require numbers. Even soldiers like these will understand the need to unite against a common enemy. Commander Thormar is explaining the situation to the men. I'll do the same with you, but first we need to find a defensible position. If you are camped in the comfortable and hopelessly exposed dale ahead of us you will need to collect your horses and equipment with some haste."

"Osric, there's one thing that I need to ask you now," said Aedan.

Osric raised an eyebrow.

"The soldier with the scarred face, that one, fourth in line, emptied my pockets and took Kalry's diary."

Osric turned and roared across the hilltop, "Commander!"

Thormar turned around and the whole line of soldiers flinched.

"Send me the fourth in line, now!"

Thormar snapped an order at the soldier who saluted and ran towards Osric. He came to attention somewhat further away than was customary. His face was pale, hands shaking; he looked ready to faint. Osric closed the distance with two giant strides. His voice was not loud, and it was all the more frightening for it.

"Do I need to ask questions, or are you going to come out with it?"

The soldier swallowed. "I took some of the boy's things, sir. I was only toying with him though. I'll give them back as soon as we get down to the campsite."

"Good. Because, as a soldier, thieving from those entrusted to your care is a hanging offense."

The soldier's knees were shaking. He knew.

Osric lowered his large head until his eyes hovered in front of a pair that were blinking rapidly. "Don't give me so much as a hint of doubt about you," he growled, taking his time over the words, letting them bore in.

The soldier was leaning away, almost falling over. "Yes, sir – I mean no, sir. Thank you, sir."

Osric dismissed him with a thrust of his chin and the man scampered away. He remained looking at the line before Thormar, frowning. Aedan was close enough to hear him mutter to Culver who had come alongside, "I recognise most of those soldiers. They will give us trouble before the end."

Culver nodded his grey head.

"Now," Osric said to the others. "Let us inspect the lay of the land and find a better position. We have much to do. This night, I'm afraid, will be a desperate one."

Chapter 48

It was the first time Aedan had watched Osric at work as a field general. In Castath, the man had always appeared too big, too stern, too calculating, and far too intimidating, but here he belonged. Here, he was to those behind him what a reef is to a small island in a tempest. The peril of their situation rose like dark water and broke against his unmoving form, then reached the others only as a deflected spray. The colossal depth and gravity of his confidence, and the breadth of his planning, however urgent the situation, formed a shelter behind which the soldiers clustered.

But though the disorder of mindless fear was held at bay, the urgency was felt by all. No observer would have missed the frantic haste of preparations in the dwindling light. Rushing past each other, they hoisted and lugged boulders to a stone wall that grew beneath a rocky overhang.

It was the ranger captain who had found the broad hollow in the rock. Though it was a vast improvement on their previous camp, it was no fortress. It had one strategic advantage – the hollow sank into a wall of a narrow valley, so the entrance could only be stormed from across the riverbed over an uneven, rocky approach.

Once the wall had reached a height of three feet, the horses were tethered at the back near the supplies. The men set about arming themselves and filling their tight stomachs as best they could – Osric insisted on it. The preparations had been exhausting, and they would need their strength before the night was done.

Osric dropped a heavy sack at Aedan's feet. "For you and Liru," he said. "You mentioned that Dun had not armed you properly."

With a sigh of relief, Aedan pulled out shields, helmets, plated hauberks, bracers, gloves, blades and bows. He wondered if he might need to help Liru, but she strapped on the armour and checked her weapons as comfortably as a cook arranging kitchenware.

Aedan had been given a short sword, a midsized shield that could be buckled to an arm, freeing both hands, a long dagger, a knife, and a choice of crossbow or bow. He opted for the bow. Loading a crossbow under pressure was not something he enjoyed. The daggers were like needles, the sword a razor, and it suddenly struck him that this was to be the first time he would fight with sharp tips and edges. These were not training weapons; they would do a lot more than bruise the enemy. He dropped the sword back into its scabbard with a frown and sat on the cold floor, head in hands.

The last time he had travelled through this area, some four years back, he had formed a purpose – to stand against tyrants. Tonight he would do just that. He should be brimming with fire. But all he felt was the desperate hope that his weakness would not announce itself. Not with Liru, Osric and Culver to see – and soldiers who would spread the word to every occupant of the barracks.

Osric called him. Liru was there, waiting.

"You two should know more than the outlines," Osric said. "After you left the town, Fergal remained under the pretence of illness. As soon as you were gone, he located the innkeeper – a Fenn spy – bound him and made a tour of the hamlet. It was not just the condition of the inn that had kindled his and Culver's suspicions. Perhaps you noticed it – there was only one chimney putting out smoke on the day of your arrival, a cold day. He found what they had expected. All the homes were empty, their occupants' bodies hacked and hidden in shallow graves. Under interrogation, the spy revealed that it was the work of Fenn war scouts who had made Eastridge a base for their operations. The worst hornet's nest we've ever found. You were very lucky to arrive when the scouts were engaged out to the west. Even as we left the hamlet, we saw a large party returning."

"How are they not on your tail then?" Aedan asked.

"They were. Merter's bow gave them cause to stay well back. I suspect they are waiting for the rest of their number to gather and prepare for a full assault. These men are ruthless but they are not hasty or foolish. They will attack in strength. It will be their intention to kill us to a man, and I fear, to a woman, in order to preserve their secret."

"Will the innkeeper not give away our numbers and weak condition? We were food poisoned," he added in response to raised brows. He avoided looking at Liru.

"Ah. I thought the men appeared worn for only a few days out. But no, the information will not have been passed on. The innkeeper was party to capital crimes. He was sentenced and hanged." Osric showed no emotion and Aedan glimpsed how vast was the difference between this war-hardened general and himself. He could not even stand up to a corrupt student. His eyes dropped to the floor.

"Aedan," said Osric, "there were women and children buried behind those homes, even babies. These men will show no mercy, not even to Liru. If they defeat us tonight, more innocents will die brutal deaths in other towns. The arm of justice punishes and it protects. Holding it back suspends both punishment and protection. If you find it difficult to swing your blade, think of all those who stand behind you."

Aedan understood it well, but Osric had misread the doubt in his eyes. Conscience was not where his worry lay. It was better, though, to let the misunderstanding remain. Much better. Osric could not know. Neither could Liru. He tried to steel his resolve and turned to her. "Are you going to be able to defend yourself?" he asked.

"That depends on what I face." She drew the slender sword that Osric had brought her. "This is a good weapon," she said, holding it out and catching the pale gleam of a dying sky on its blade. "But the greatest advantage I have is that I will be underestimated."

"How do you feel about killing?"

"I would willingly kill men who slaughtered families, as General Osric said. But I do not fight for your prince. He has betrayed me and it will not be forgotten."

"He's not *my* prince," Aedan said, his voice rising with his temper. "You keep calling him my prince as if I have some part in this betrayal."

"Then who is your leader?" she retorted, her own voice rising on a tide of anger and fear. "Who are your people? What are you even training for?"

Aedan opened his mouth twice but no words came out. He turned away from her and moved to an empty section of broken rocks where he sat, stood, pulled his hair, sat again and bit his fist until the dusk began to pool in the back of the cave and hid him from view.

Osric had spent the afternoon preparing for many contingencies. He now went over final instructions with the soldiers, making sure each man knew how to act. The ill-discipline that had characterised the men up until now was gone, smoke in the wind. They stood straight, attention fixed on their general. It was more than respect. Osric, as frightening as he was, represented survival. Their shallow breathing and wild eyes revealed how few of them had been tried in battle. And the odds tonight would be bad, even for experienced campaigners.

Merter, the ranger-captain, returned. He slipped into the cave like a panther. Aedan had been watching him over the afternoon and was no longer surprised that he was known as Captain Murder. It seemed he was only pretending to be civilised, and that he was barely accustomed to the society of others. He peered around him with the complete focus and deadly intensity of a hunting cat, and though he was not a big man, his prowling movements told of uncanny strength.

Aedan overheard his report to Osric. "I counted forty," he said, "but there could be as many as fifty. They are well-armed, all mounted. They will reach us soon. Their armour is mostly plated leather but they carry heavy weapons. Here are two I picked up." He held out a deep leaf-bladed sword and a large mace. Aedan wondered if the previous owners had even seen their attacker. Osric felt and tested the weapons, asked a few more questions about the armour and other weapons, and passed them on to Thormar who examined them and handed them along to the rest.

Aedan dried his palms again. He and Liru waited on the far left of the cave, in a slight recess. Merter and Tyne stood in front of them; to the right were Osric and six soldiers; and further down, Thormar commanded the remaining men. Tyne and Liru made a very careful inspection of the captured Fenn armour.

Aedan spotted the thieving soldier, known to him now as Holt, standing nearby. Holt had returned Aedan's belongings, and even made a gift of his own dagger in apology. After Osric's reprimand, he had looked genuinely sorry, as well as heartily frightened for his skin, and had promised he would do what he could to look after Aedan and Liru in the battle.

Aedan had seen this kind of change before. Some men could be so pliable under the influence of leadership that they all but mimicked the leader's character. It was quite a change from Senbert to Osric, and Aedan was not complaining. Holt looked over now and saluted. Aedan returned the gesture.

The other soldier, the one Liru had stabbed, had made no apology. The wound appeared not to be troubling him much, and Aedan had even caught him grinning at Liru. He wished now that they had spoken of it to Osric, but he knew the soldier would claim he had only intended to be friendly. He would accept a reprimand and then haunt them with his eyes. Such men were as slippery as eels and just as poisonous.

Osric was completing his final inspection and stopped before Aedan and Liru. He spoke quietly. "It is best that I do not stand near you as I shall probably be targeted. Merter and Tyne will try to shield the attack, but it is possible that men will pass them. Liru, if you have not yet told Aedan how far your training reaches, now is the time. He will need to know how to work with you."

"How do you know about my training?" she asked. "I thought only our order knew of it."

"All on the war council know."

"And I will not be tried or punished for speaking of it?"

"Not under these circumstances, not to Aedan. You'd best not speak of your final purpose, mind you, only your weapons training."

Aedan couldn't help feeling a little offended that secrets were being kept from him. Liru's abrupt and snappy manner wasn't helping either.

She drew him away from listening ears and explained. "We are taught many of the same weapons as you – I think you will have guessed that already – but using different styles. With the sword, our technique involves much movement. It is almost like dancing. We try to move out of the line of effective strikes. We only block when desperate, otherwise we dodge, deflect and counter-attack, almost always with the point and often for the hands and arms – even gauntlets have chinks. Think of a bird attacking one of those giant spiders."

"It sounds like it would be best if I took the initial attack and you 'pecked' from the sides."

"That is one of the ways it is meant to work."

"With your style of fighting, what are your weaknesses?"

"I will tire quickly if I have to keep up that kind of movement, the uneven ground here might work against me, and I am light, so even with a shield a direct hit will stun me or knock me down."

Aedan considered. "We can deal with one of those problems by clearing the ground of rocks," he said, and they set to work.

Soldiers checked the preparations for the last time and took their positions, then Osric called for silence and the waiting began.

The last traces of day vanished from the sky, and night fell. A half-moon hidden by clouds gave a dull, pale light that made shadows indistinct and shapes unclear. The view from the cave mouth revealed a boulder-strewn valley, and on the far side of the river, a sheer rock wall. It meant that the cave could not be attacked from a distance or from cover. Even archers would need to show themselves before being able to release a single arrow.

Aedan searched the shadows between boulders. Sometimes he thought he saw movement. Once, he was sure there were shapes crawling over the whole riverbed, but then all was still for so long that he decided he must have imagined them. Water gurgled, insects screeched, a pair of wood pigeons cooed a ghostly duet nearby. The grip of Aedan's sword was now so damp he was sure it would fly from his hand at the first swing, but he dared not release the handle to dry it.

There was a sound, a single click as a pebble dropped down onto the ledge in front of the cave. Dimly, mostly in silhouette, he saw Osric pointing up. Loose pebbles and coarse sand had been strewn on the crest of the rock wall. Movement above the cave was now betrayed. Osric made a looping hand signal and two soldiers readied themselves beside the horses. Another pebble dropped on the far side. Then a gentle hiss of sand spoke from several points along the newly built wall and more pebbles dropped.

One of the attack strategies Osric had foreseen was that ropes might be used to lower men with ready crossbows. The position invited it. A few dozen alder saplings would provide good anchors; Aedan imagined them being inspected now. In his mind, he could see ten or twenty men loading crossbows and tying onto the ends of ropes while others anchored themselves to the saplings and prepared to lower their companions down the short face.

It was the second shower of sand that Osric had waited for, and now it came. All the way across the outer ledge, sand drizzled and pebbles bounced. The sound was barely above the murmur of the stream, but for men who knew what it signified, it was a clarion call. Aedan was finding it difficult to breathe.

Osric made a downward motion with his arms. Two men swatted the team of horses. The animals surged forward, drawing ropes that led out the back of the cave. There was a deep crack that echoed from above, then a heavy rumble filled the air and shook the ground.

Earlier, it had demanded the strength of several horses to pull the colossal alder trunk into position, and much chopping to clear it of branches so that it would roll.

And now it rolled.

The saplings that might have stopped its progress had been partially cut so as to appear strong when tested, but not strong enough to withstand such a force.

Warning shouts were followed by the cracking of many small trees and the screams of men that grew and grew and suddenly burst on their ears as bodies dropped past the opening and thudded into the rocky ledge. A shower of debris was followed by a deep rush as the great trunk hurtled past the defenders and crashed on the rocks, scattering everyone with a shower of stones, chips of wood, and dust. A few more bodies came down with the log, but not one of them moved.

Horses reared, and soldiers were forced to subdue their steeds or be trampled. Osric gave a quiet order, and three men darted out to collect weapons. As expected, there were many crossbows. Most were broken, but half a dozen still worked – these were reloaded and placed ready.

Then all fell silent again.

Aedan estimated that between fifteen and twenty-five men had fallen, leaving enough still to mount a strong attack. Dust clouds drifted through the cave. There were some muffled coughs.

They waited.

As the air gradually cleared, Aedan studied the shadows between boulders again.

Horses snorted.

He could hear Liru's rapid and shallow breathing, and then realised his was the same. He tried to force himself to take long, deep breaths and relax his limbs, remembering all too well Dun's warning about rapid exhaustion. Yet, try as he might, it seemed impossible to calm himself.

Again he could see dozens of points of movement – it was as if the boulders themselves were crawling. There was a sharp clicking of pebbles to the left. He saw the movement. It was the ground behind the large rock Osric had expected they would use. He had balanced a few stones so that they would topple if the ground there was disturbed. Several similar traps had been rigged further down and one of these now also spoke. The archers knew where their targets would appear. They took aim.

Silence.

Aedan wanted to scream. He dreaded the charge, but he could not endure much more of this waiting.

When it happened, there was no battle cry. Behind a cloud of whistling arrows, shapes swarmed out from the two screens of rock and bounded across the riverbed towards the cave. Aedan knew the entrance would be black to the attackers, giving them nothing to aim at. It was no surprise then that only one of their arrows found a shield, one a horse, and the rest clattered against rock.

The Thirnish bows twanged and six Fenn attackers collapsed. These Thirnish soldiers were not quick enough with the bow to nock and aim again in the time remaining, but the half-dozen crossbows were raised and shot, bringing down another four. Then the wave struck. The attackers were big men who swung heavy maces and large swords with ease. A dozen of them crashed into the defences.

Osric had instructed the soldiers to stab for the eyes because men stumbling into darkness would not likely cover their faces and would not see the points of spears or swords thrust from the shadows. It worked. About half of the attackers went down without even striking their opponents, but the remaining Fenn gained a foothold and began to lay about them with devastating blows.

The Thirnish began to fall.

Aedan saw Osric throw his sword like a knife, skewering a Fenn soldier who had knocked Senbert to his knees and was about to bring a mace down on his head. The man crumpled with Osric's sword through him and Senbert sprang back to his feet.

An attacker saw Osric weaponless and turned on him, swinging a heavy sword. Osric swatted the blade aside with the shield strapped to his arm, stepped forward, and delivered a blow with his gauntleted fist that did the work of a hammer. Before the man dropped, Osric grabbed him by the throat and belt and hurled him into another two attackers, knocking them both off their feet. Senbert's blade finished them. Osric unhooked his giant mace and smashed into the next enemy soldier that caught his eye.

Two men fell on Merter and Tyne. Aedan was not surprised to see Merter's feral speed and skill – the attackers found themselves with an uncaged animal at their throats – but it was Tyne who held his attention. She fought as Liru had described – dancing, darting and slipping through defences with movements so quick and elusive that her opponent may as well have been duelling a shadow. Aedan had never seen anything like it in his training, never imagined that such grace could be so deadly. He felt an immediate respect for this tall woman.

"Aedan!" Liru screamed. "Your right!"

He spun around to see that one of the Fenn had broken through and was striding towards him, snarling and lifting his mace.

Aedan faltered.

Without any warning, the memories took hold. The image of his father bore down on him. Unreasoning rage and crushing violence. Inescapable, unopposable. All fell silent but for a rising scream of dread.

His limbs collapsed, dropping him and his sword to the ground. The whimper that escaped his throat was a sickening admission of naked helplessness. It was the whimper of a child, a voice of numb terror, of a spirit utterly crushed and taught to cower.

The mace reached the back of its arc and began the fatal swing. A dim shape clouded his vision as Liru stepped in front of him and took the blow on her shield. It lifted her off her feet and cast her through the air. She struck the wall and slid to the floor where she remained motionless.

The mace rose again. Aedan was frozen. He could neither speak nor move. He saw a hand close around the shaft and another hand grip the Fenn's throat. It was Holt who had intervened, but it was clear that he had lost his weapons.

The attacker twisted around and the two men struggled back and forth until Holt lost his footing and went to ground under a weight far greater than his own. He was outmatched. A big hand closed around his throat. He struggled and kicked, his movements becoming weaker and slower.

Aedan knew his countryman was dying. He knew he had to do something, but his body would not respond. His terror only mounted as Holt's life ebbed.

A soft tread drew his attention to the side as Tyne rushed up and thrust the point of her sword through the assailant's temple. Holt drew a great breath of air and slowly crawled from under the body of his dead enemy.

Tyne looked down at Aedan wordlessly. It was too dark to read her expression but the detached posture spoke her disdain clearly enough. She turned her back on him and went to Liru's still form.

As quickly as it had begun, the clangour of battle died out. The last attacker had fallen. Heavy breathing, the moans of the wounded, and someone's wet, foamy coughing replaced the screams and the crash of metal.

The defenders set about gathering their wounded and looking for survivors among the bodies. Only four of the Thirnish had been lost and another three were wounded. The Fenn losses, however, were considerable – forty-one were dead, most of them crushed by the alder trunk. Eight were seriously, if not mortally, wounded.

After Merter had scouted the area and was certain that the threat had passed, fires were lit and the injured properly tended. The stench of battle was heavy in the cave, making it a grim camp, but Osric was not prepared to expose the party to the arrows of possible stragglers.

Aedan recovered sufficiently to get to his feet. Liru had not moved. Tyne and Fergal were crouched beside her. They did not look at Aedan. He wanted to ask, he wanted to help, but the hot glow of his shame was enough to tell him that he did not belong there. Tyne had seen him, he knew it, and she would not forget. He looked up and caught Holt's eye, but the man turned away.

Aedan's face contorted in a spasm of self-loathing. He recoiled from the light of the fires, and headed across the riverbed. He knew he was exposing himself to a rogue archer. He didn't care. An arrow now would be a mercy. He walked downstream to where none from the cave would be able to see him. Here he sat on a boulder until the cold bit into his legs, and he let it.

Liru lay dying or crippled because of him. He had watched, unmoving, just watched while Holt had almost died mere feet away. He would never forget the look of those eyes turned towards him in frantic appeal. Holt's dagger had been in Aedan's belt, and there it had remained.

Even now, the strength in his arms was barely enough to raise his hand, but earlier it had been as if his arms were not his, as if they were the dead limbs of a corpse. He could still see them as they had flopped on the ground, useless. And the paralysis had only fed his terror.

He looked down the valley, tracing the waters that fled the scene.

Should he do the same?

What hope had he of being a marshal? Whatever courage and strength he possessed were treacherous. Maybe a prince's treachery was what he deserved.

He began to shiver and realised how cold he was. Then he cursed himself for the thought. How could he think of his own comfort after what he had done to his friends?

He did not warm himself by the fire when he returned. Osric came to check on him, asking if he had any wounds. The bitterness of Aedan's thoughts leaked poison into the tone of his answers. He hated himself the more when Osric left looking confused and snubbed.

Aedan remained in a dark corner, shivering and hoping that Liru would not die in the night.

Chapter 49

A little before first light, Merter and a few soldiers crept from the cave and scouted until they were sure none of the Fenn remained. Osric relocated them to a broad valley. Here, the injured rested for three days while the dead were buried. The Fenn were too many to be buried, so they were heaped onto a pyre near the cave and burned, the flames giving off black smoke and a thick stench.

Aedan watched it all with only the dullest interest.

Liru woke but she was in great pain. Twice, Aedan tried to speak to her, but her answers were curt. As much as he wanted to apologise, he could not bring himself to drop his shield in the face of bared teeth and baleful eyes. Instead he talked around the thing he needed to say, asking about her injuries and commenting on the proposed plans – plans in which he no longer had any interest.

If Tyne had given space, he might have been able to unload the thoughts that ate him like acid. But she hovered and glared as if he were contaminating her patient. After a few moments she would chase him off, saying that he was disturbing Liru's recovery.

Liru never asked him to stay.

Aedan felt eyes on him as he moved through the camp, and often heard laughter in his wake. No mention of his embarrassment was made in his presence, but he almost wished that it would be, just to have it out and over with. Instead, the words and the looks buzzed and darted around him like a cloud of midges.

Holt now shunned him. Aedan was not surprised. After some contemplation, he decided to return Holt's dagger, and did so with a shamefaced apology. The man snatched the dagger and walked away while Aedan was still speaking. Hanging there in mid-sentence, the anger and embarrassment that rose almost forced tears from his eyes. He needed to get away.

Without letting anyone know, he headed out, aiming vaguely for a hilltop a few miles distant. A blanket of moth-eaten cloud scudded beneath the sun, and branches pitched in the disturbed air. He walked in distracted loops, taking a long time to reach the place. After fighting through the last of the undergrowth and climbing the rocky brow, he discovered it much to his liking – isolated and bare.

He had asked himself too many questions over the past days, and found no answers. So now he sat and watched the land below while a cold, snow-born wind tumbled down from the heights, buffeted past him and raked through the stands of trees and grassy planes, making them ripple like the coat of some great beast. It could not improve his mood, but for a time it helped him forget, and feel nothing.

The sound of breaking sticks and heavy breathing drew his attention to the slope he had recently climbed. His curiosity gave way to annoyance when he saw Fergal's broad form lumbering upwards. Aedan hoped intensely that the final scramble would be too much, but the oversized cleaner was as determined as he was unwanted. Without invitation the man dropped himself down on the rock. Here he panted and blew with a grimace that revealed just how much the ascent had hurt.

When he could talk, he chose not to and, instead, dug through a pouch and found a letter which he began to read silently. Aedan wondered what kind of man would choose to invade another person's privacy in order to exercise his own.

He had paid little attention to this servant or whatever he was, and looked across at him now. At first Aedan had thought him relatively young, but the way he behaved around men of rank had made him seem very old. It wasn't a question of respect given or returned as much as a steady patience, the kind of patience that suggests a greater knowledge of others than they have of themselves, that suggests great experience, great age. But there was something about the way he stretched his arms and grinned at the sunrise or watched with amusement when one of the soldiers was about to put his lips to an overheated tin mug – these and many other almost childlike ways made him seem very young.

Part of the difficulty in fixing an age was his hiddenness. He had the appearance of being overgrown in all ways – great falls of charcoal hair lay in thick mats reaching down to his shoulders; his eyes were mostly shadowed under wild hedges of thorny eyebrows; and when he spoke, Aedan remembered, it was only a disturbance somewhere deep within that dark beard that revealed the presence of a mouth. But there was no disturbance now. The silence appeared not to bother this large hairy man in the least.

Aedan, however, was growing uncomfortable and was about to move off when Fergal coughed.

"This is the bit," he said, "listen to this: 'Never have I known such courage or resourcefulness under the most trying circumstances. If you were to take that one heart and divide it among a dozen men, they would be a dozen to be reckoned with.'"

"Are you trying to mock me?" Aedan cried, standing.

Fergal returned the letter to the pouch. "The letter was written by my brother," he said. "He was describing a boy who for the love of his young friend, leapt down a gorge two hundred feet deep in a final desperate attempt to save her. I would not have believed such a tale from any other source. My brother saw it with his own eyes and even made a part of the jump himself."

Aedan was unable to speak, so violent were the emotions boiling within his chest, so Fergal continued.

"My brother is Nulty, and he tells me that he knew you well. Do you remember him?"

Aedan nodded.

"And do you remember the day of which he wrote?"

Aedan nodded again.

"Then sit, please. I would speak with you." He waited until Aedan had settled down again and recovered. "Nulty also wrote of what he termed a dread association. He made enquiries after your departure and what he learned convinced him that your father had been beating you and your mother. The thing that gave birth to his suspicions was the way you responded when a nobleman, Dresbourn, prepared to thrash you."

Aedan was silent. He wished he did not have to see it all again in such detail. He remembered the gasps as people covered their mouths, staring in morbid fascination at his disgrace. Some had shaken their heads. Some had even laughed. None had understood.

"Why can I stand up to anyone in training?" he blurted. "Why could I fight that gang at the autumn festival but I can't hold my ground when someone reminds me of how my father used to charge at me?"

"Perhaps because when those patterns were formed, your only possible defence was to cower. That part of your mind has locked onto the idea that there is no other way to survive your father's rage. I imagine the same response is triggered when someone reminds you of him – appearance, or more likely, behaviour. Something in you believes it is him and takes you back to those first encounters."

Aedan considered this. The thugs charging towards him at the festival when he'd waited in the oak shadow had not even seen him. They were not bearing down on him with that dominating, focussed and wrathful intent. The situation had been nothing like the encounters with his father. The same was true of all the other times he had been able to hold his ground. Fergal's explanation made sense, but it brought no consolation. "Even if I understand it," Aedan said, "what use am I to anyone like this?"

"Use is a poor word, a small word. You are of great *worth* to many just as you are. But that is not to say you should expect to keep this wound."

"But how can I get rid of something that's buried where I can't find it?"

Fergal was silent and turned his gaze to the sky. Birds chattered, grassy swathes whispered to each other, clouds drifted, but Fergal remained still. Aedan was beginning to suspect that this was no mere dreaminess, no lost internal meandering. Those twinkling eyes were far too sharp. This man had something in common with those that burst into song at the dinner table or ask ludicrously personal questions in public – people's expectations of him seemed to have little influence on his behaviour. His quirk, however, was neither loud nor indiscrete. He simply felt no discomfort about bringing a conversation to a juddering halt while he had a deep and careful think.

Aedan decided to wait him out, and wait he did. It was a long time before Fergal spoke again.

"Many have overcome their fears," he said "– of battle, of heights, of loss, of society even, but these recoveries are seldom quick. Different wounds require different remedies, and yours – while not unheard of – appears to have uncommonly deep roots, no doubt due to the fact that the seed was planted in childhood. Unearthing those roots may take some work. A chat with Osric might be instructive. I think you'll find he understands the condition better than you'd expect."

Aedan sighed. "I'm not sure I want to face him or any of the others again," he said. "They think me a coward, maybe even a traitor."

"If I were you, I'd not be too concerned with the opinions of soldiers who might have been our murderers. I have spoken to the others. Osric is not disappointed in you. He is no less your friend now than before, though *you* might try to be a little less withdrawn. His confidence often deserts him in the area of relationships. If you don't make an effort to accept his bumbling attempts at kindness you will both end up feeling you are not good enough for the other. I'll not stand by such idiocy. Your bitterness will not aid you, and it will end up punishing those who care about you."

Aedan blushed. This cleaner was certainly perceptive.

"What about Liru?" he said. "She and Tyne hate me."

"I spoke with them too. Tyne's anger is understandable, though it is short-sighted in her – she knows how you and your friends once intervened on Liru's behalf. Liru's anger is emotional. She feels abandoned. It is because of how much she depended on you that she now feels as she does."

Aedan was surprised and felt a slight warmth. "Will I be able to win her trust again?" he asked.

Fergal chuckled. "If you are asking a man to predict the current of a woman's emotions, you are asking in vain. But I will say that you should try."

"Tyne won't even let me talk to Liru now."

"When were *you* ever kept where others placed you? From your first night at the academy you've been leaving footprints where they do not belong."

Aedan stared at him. "How do you know about that?" Then he remembered the size of the man they had disturbed and the mass of hair. Recognition lit his eyes.

"Remember now?" Fergal said.

"That was you?"

"It was."

"Oh. Kian noticed that you had ink dripping from your hand. Did we make you spill something?"

"And ruin a manuscript I'd been working on since morning."

"Uh – sorry. Did you tell anyone?"

"No. Neither did I tell anyone about the time you broke into the chancellor's office and used a three-century-old marble bust to open the door."

"How did you know that?"

"I know now."

Aedan ground his teeth, squirming with embarrassment at being found out so easily. "Are you going to put me in the rat cells or prison?"

"I never liked that particular bust. The sculptor must have made his impression from a death mask because it gave all of us the jitters. Unfortunately nobody had the authority to remove such an important likeness of a former chancellor. Your little adventure, it turns out, had a happy result, but you will understand if you are not thanked for your efforts."

Aedan managed a smile.

"No Aedan. I have no intention to see you incarcerated. In spite of this dread association with your father, you are still the most courageous and resourceful apprentice the academy has seen – if you are prepared to accept a cleaner's opinion."

It was the most encouraging thing he had been told in years, but in what Fergal had just said, there was a thorn. His apprenticeship, his training, his prince …

"You are quiet," said Fergal. "Are you perhaps wondering about the sense in returning to – shall we say – a precarious loyalty?"

"Yes," Aedan admitted. "But that brings up something I need to ask. If you knew about the conspiracy against us, why didn't you help slow the party down?"

"We had plans, but you and Liru moved before us. The poisoned broth was an excellent idea though."

"So you know," pursued Aedan, "that your master has been sent here to die, perhaps you too?"

"We suspected it, but your overhearing that conversation between our prince and the first councillor was very useful."

"Did Osric tell you it was me?"

"No."

"Then how did you … Oh, you didn't know, did you?"

"Again, I know now. But I had little doubt – who else would have been down there?"

"Fine. Guilty. But let's get back to the question of home. What happens after the quest? Can we go back, and if we do, for what purpose?"

Fergal thought long about this. "Going back will not be without peril. I'll not pretend to you that ensuring our safety will be a simple matter, but perhaps we shall think of something. As to purpose, well, we have a long journey ahead and much time to consider that from many angles."

"Maybe some unpleasant angles too," said Aedan. "There is a good chance we'll get to do a lot of our travelling in the bellies of wolves or some other sharp-toothed creatures. Panther almost got my mother last time. Even if we make it past them, there's the fortress itself. You know what happened to us when we entered?"

"I do."

"So how are we meant to get in?"

"With great care and delicate planning. There are many secrets to that fortress; Culver and I happen to know a few. You'll see – we have more in mind than tiptoeing through the front gates."

"But there's no other way in."

"Ah, there we have a topic for our first lesson. Can you detect the problem with what you just said?"

Aedan ran through the words a few times and then smiled. "I should have added 'that I know of.'"

"Just so. You tried to establish a fact from a lack of evidence. Unless the inquiry has been so exhaustive as to explore every possibility, the lack of evidence should never be used to ground a statement of fact. Unlikelihood certainly, but no more. A prematurely assumed fact blocks further inquiry."

"Can you give me an example?"

"The sea north of Lorfen is endless."

"But isn't it? Haven't ships travelled for a month in that direction and found nothing?"

"Indeed. But the very fact that there was still water to the north when they turned back means that the exploration was incomplete. Who can say that they would not have sighted a great landmass one day on? Another is this: There are no spies in the academy."

"Are there?" Aedan asked with shock.

"I hope not. But it would be unwise to assume not. Where easier for a spy to hide than in a place where no one believes a spy could exist? People never look beyond an assumed fact. One more: Lekrans have nothing worth respecting."

Aedan stiffened. "That's not a good topic for me."

"But it is a necessary one. Prejudice creates blindness; it is too busy hating to think. No matter how justified it might feel, prejudice will shackle you."

"But they –"

"Aedan. Use reason, not emotion. Have you made an exhaustive search of the whole population of Lekrau and found nothing worth respecting?"

Aedan's eyes were hard. "I take your point, but please could we discuss something else."

As they made their way back to the camp, Fergal illustrated the same principle by detailing several political and military defeats, and Aedan began to see how dangerous this little flaw in reasoning could be.

When they arrived at the camp, Aedan helped Osric with the meal. He understood now that there was no anger in the general's eyes, only concern. Though it was unpleasant to be in the company of those who had seen him shamed, he bore it. Fergal had given him just a thread of hope to which he clung with slowly recovering tenacity.

Tyne called him aside. "Aedan," she said in a voice that was as steady as the commander's. The eyes that Aedan had been avoiding held him, and he did not look away. He realised now that the intensity of her look was perhaps better understood as sincerity.

"I was not aware of your background," she said. "You have my apologies. The only thing I can find against your behaviour is that you should have warned Liru about your malady. She had a right to know because it was your responsibility to defend her. But I am not angry with you, and I'd be glad if you would count me as a friend." She put her hand on his shoulder, gave a gentle squeeze, then turned and walked to the fire, allowing Aedan the chance to speak to Liru alone.

Liru did not greet him when he sat. He fiddled with a twig he had broken off a sapling, peeling the bark away, exposing the pale wood.

"Liru, I'm sorry. I should have told you. I thought that in a battle it might be different. It's just very embarrassing to talk about. I've actually never talked about it. I hoped it wouldn't happen."

"You are right, Aedan. You should have told me."

"Are you angry with me?"

"Yes."

"I suppose I deserve it. Thank you for stepping in front of me. It was brave of you. I hope you don't regret it."

"I regret it with every aching breath."

"You would rather have me dead?"

"I am happy that you are alive and unhappy that I had to save you."

Aedan shuffled. "Well, I'm glad that you are feeling strong enough to speak your mind," he mumbled.

"I am Mardrae. Even dead Mardrae will speak their minds. Now go away. You are giving me a headache."

Aedan slunk back to his fire. Liru was angry and would stay that way for a long time, but at least she would talk to him. That was something. Tyne went back to her, leaving Aedan and Osric alone.

They had not spoken openly since the battle. Neither seemed to know how to begin. When they did overcome their silence they spoke at the same time. Both stopped and insisted the other proceed, pressing with equal vehemence. It was Osric who got frustrated first.

"Have you eaten?" he asked with a huff of exasperation.

Aedan looked surprised by the question. "Oh. Yes, I ate a little earlier. But I'm not that hungry."

"Not enough exercise today?"

"No, it's not that."

"Oh, of course," Osric mumbled. "Did you see the spoor outside the camp this morning? There are deer for the taking. Maybe you should head out with Merter. It might help to … to get back into the motions again."

Aedan stripped off the last of the bark from his twig, threw the shreds onto the coals where they twisted up and shrivelled before being consumed. "Maybe," he said.

Osric rubbed his stubbly beard. "Perhaps I should also give you some specific training, simulate some charges. I think Dun might not put enough into the practical aspect, the real situations."

Aedan threw the bare twig into the fire so hard that it produced a shower of sparks and sent a few coals tumbling. He glared at the pale wood. Moisture fizzed to the surface until there was none left, and then the flames had their way with the lifeless wood.

He hated this – the questions, the advice, the examination. Was he to be stripped and grilled before everyone who had seen his humiliation? The darkness beyond the camp called to him, the loneliness where he could hide, where the inhabitants of the forest would not try to mend him. They would not pierce him with their eyes or their words. They did not care.

That was the thought that stopped him from walking away. He looked at Osric and saw the honest concern, the generous hope behind his awkward and confused expression as he clearly wondered what he had said wrong.

"It's not Dun," Aedan said. "It's not familiarity or practice. You can't get me used to it because I would know it's not real. If it was real it would be like trying to catch five-ton boulders rolled off the top of the city wall."

Osric sighed and leaned forward, looking into the coals. "Aedan, I know it seems that way to you, but I don't think it's as hopeless as that. I've worked with these kinds of freeze reactions before and helped soldiers past them. Given time, I am convinced that you will master your response."

"How much time?"

"It would take a while, possibly even a few years. You'd need to overcome it in stages – incremental confrontations. Covering it over and trying to pretend it doesn't exist is what I presume you've been doing, and that's like ignoring termites in the walls. You'd have to be deliberate about it. I've seen men whose nerves were shattered from nightmarish experiences, and many of them were able to hold spears and stand their ground again."

"But not all of them?"

"You are young and too full of fire to subside beneath it. A full battle was the wrong place for you. We'll find a way to get you past it, a step at a time, though, in reality, this will probably have to wait until we get back to Castath."

Aedan said nothing. He didn't need to point out that getting back to Castath might depend on his ability to stand his ground.

Osric's eyes remained on the fire when he spoke again. "Is this damage why you never talk about your father?"

"There's another reason."

"Crime?"

Aedan was silent.

"It would go poorly for him if we were to meet," Osric said.

Aedan shifted and glanced up. "He may have hurt me, but he stood up for me too. He was the one who taught me to track and hunt and move through the woods. He taught me better than Wildemar could ever hope to. I have lots of good memories of those days."

After saying this, he wondered why he had. Why shield his father? He wanted to repay him. Yet somehow he felt the strangest need to defend when somebody else took up the attack.

"Any son should have those good memories," Osric rumbled. "But no son should have the other memories he left you. I would very much like to give him some of what he gave you."

Aedan looked away. He remembered the beatings. He remembered them well. Sometimes he still felt the creeping pain of bruises. But as he imagined his father under Osric's blows, there was an old sadness that welled up in him. He shook his head and turned to Osric.

"I hate him, I hate him, I hate him! I'll never forgive. Even in his grave I'll hate him. I hate him for how he ruined me and my mother, and if I ever see him again he'll be dead to me. But I don't want to see him beaten – I don't know why."

Osric sat long in silence, the corners of his mouth pulling down and his fists clutching. When he answered, his voice was strangely thick. "I chose differently," he said.

Chapter 50

By the end of the week, they were ready to travel. Of the fourteen soldiers they had set out with, ten remained alive and eight were fit for service – though many of these had light wounds. The two with more serious wounds were sent back to Eastridge to rest and await reinforcements.

The party travelled slowly on account of the convalescents, taking all of three weeks to reach the foothills of the DinEilan Mountains. It was the first time Aedan had seen snow on the peaks. A month earlier the slopes and some of the hills would have been under a cold sheet of white, but now the season was shifting and the lingering caps and pockets of snow receding. As the land rose up around the travellers, it also began to change its character.

Gone were the gentle hues of beech and lime; ridges grew hooded and ravines thick with the more sombre shade of blackthorn, fir and elm. Herds of deer flecked the slopes – speckled bounders and the noble errak, tall as horses with horns like spears. The grass that now dominated was soft and furry from a distance, but tough as wire underfoot. Though it could be bent into a comfortable bed, each blade was like a miniature reed ending in a needle tip. It became increasingly difficult to find suitable grazing, something Aedan remembered from his first journey here.

The company was large enough to keep wolves at a distance, but the lonely howl, that most haunting of songs, was often to be heard on the night air.

Fergal conducted his lessons with Aedan and Liru while they rode. They were astounded by the man's knowledge – he seemed to know more about any subject than any of the masters at the academy. They began to think he knew more than several put together. It was no wonder Culver had claimed him as a personal assistant. Whatever disappointment Aedan had experienced at being passed on to a mere clerk for tuition evaporated rapidly. Fergal showed himself fluent in each of the foreign languages Aedan and Liru had studied, and it soon became clear that he spoke a great many more. Occasionally he would even use illustrations from works in what he termed lost languages – languages no longer spoken, whose sounds were no longer known and had to be guessed when reading the words that lingered in clay tablets and fragile parchments.

Fergal set challenges that had to be solved using many fields of knowledge – languages, culture, politics, strategy, and of course, history.

He also began to coach them in something new – intentional observation – the habit of constantly noting and interpreting details. This was something Aedan was familiar with from the origins game he used to play at the Mistyvales, though he had never applied the technique broadly. He decided to test Fergal.

"Can you describe the first inn we stayed at?" he asked.

"You'll have to be a lot more specific than that," Fergal said, "or I'll be talking all day."

"Alright. Describe the cook."

"The cook," Fergal mumbled, "Hmm ..."

Aedan smiled, preparing for a small triumph over his new master.

"I won't bore you with the details that were of no aid," Fergal began, "but I will mention a few that were of interest. She was the mother of the tallest serving girl –"

"How –" Aedan attempted to interrupt.

"The initial resemblance was minimal until one noticed them in profile – they share a unique forward bridge of the nose and deeply sunken chin. But if the resemblance was not enough, the mother removed all doubt by her behaviour. At first I thought her sallies from the kitchen to be random or brought on by rowdiness, but she looked too purposeful for the former and the latter link was inconsistent. I soon realised that she was overseeing every time her daughter made her rounds between the soldiers. Another thing that presented itself as interesting was that on her first appearance she walked evenly, and every time she appeared after that, she limped."

"Ah," Liru said. "A weapon strapped to her leg. It would make sense if she was worried about her daughter."

"I assumed just that and made sure to avoid looking at the daughter. As a result, I spent a fair amount of time examining my table – oiled pine – on which I read a dozen names and learned that Alburn will always love Fern, though I fear the giddy letters indicate powers at work other than affection."

"Yes," laughed Aedan. "He was probably being beaten over the head by the cook with her brass spoon while he scratched her table."

Fergal grinned. "Good. You noticed her spoon was brass, and it did have some dents in it. She held it in her right hand and she was left handed – it was her writing that gave that away."

"Was her left hand against the supposedly injured leg?" Aedan asked.

"Very good. It was indeed. The next thing she revealed was the existence of a back door to the kitchen when she appeared at one point with hair blown loose and spots of rain on her shoulders. I could carry on, but I think you get the idea and hopefully see the usefulness of observation. Now Aedan, seeing as I have answered your question, what do you remember of her husband?"

"Uh … He was really small, and he had a beard, and … a white shirt, no brown, no, well he had a shirt."

"Green." said Fergal.

"Well it was dirty, so you have to admit that brown is partly right."

"It was not dirty. I have seldom observed a neater or cleaner chap in my life. Brown, I'm afraid, remains wrong."

Liru was even worse.

Fergal began drilling them, asking them regularly what they had noticed about a clearing recently traversed or about an interaction between soldiers. Aedan found it difficult to pay attention to his surroundings while listening to Fergal's instruction, but he improved over the weeks. Liru, after growing deliberate about it, showed herself to be something of a sponge for details.

Once Fergal was satisfied that they were on the right track, he had them study one soldier at a time without staring, observing each for potential threats and weaknesses. They learned that one was concealing something beneath his saddle, another was nursing a sore head, a third was uneasy about the soldier behind him. Aedan was also uneasy about him. It was Rork, that leering eel who still mocked with his eyes. As casual as he seemed, he never let his coat fall over the handle of his sword and showed by his reactions that he took in a lot more of his environment than his lazy eyes suggested. Aedan marked him as dangerous.

Any curiosity on the part of the soldiers was left unsatisfied, as none of the discussions were held in Thirnish. Orunean, the most common second language, was also avoided. Instead, they used Fenn, Vinthian and Sulese. Fergal began teaching them some basic words in two more languages – Lekran, to Aedan's disgust, and Mardrae, to Liru's delight. She was unable to hide her surprise and joy when she discovered her new master to be fluent in the language of her childhood. Soon they were singing songs, telling jokes and reciting poems together. Fergal was considerate enough to explain it all to Aedan.

These would be Aedan's fifth and sixth foreign tongues. Lekran was compulsory, but for the sixth language, the students were given a few choices. He had been wavering between Krunish and Mardrae and leaning towards the latter, so he did not object.

He was determined to catch up to Liru as fast as he could, so every night he wrote down the new words and phrases and practiced until he spoke them in his dreams. Mardrae was a fascinating language full of rich vowel tones and soft consonants. It almost sounded dreamy.

Instead of the languages becoming jumbled, he found it easier to learn and store each subsequent one, though the boundaries were not impenetrable. There were times when a Sulese word, for example, would try to pass itself off as a native in a Vinthian sentence. Fergal was sharper than any border inspector and caught the little imposters every time. Nevertheless, he declared himself to be impressed with the effort and progress of his students.

Aedan's application to Lekran, however, was another matter. He felt as though the words polluted his mind and he let them trickle out as fast as they reached him.

One day, during a spell between questions, Aedan changed the topic to something that had been gnawing at him for a long time.

"What's under the academy?" he asked.

Fergal directed a long look at him. "I gave my word not to speak of it. Anyway, you would have difficulty believing me."

"Now you are setting my curiosity alight."

"Good. Curiosity is an excellent fuel. You will find out what is down there, but not through me."

"How? There's no longer an entrance."

"Did we not cover this in your first lesson? No entrance you say?"

Aedan considered for a moment. "Are you saying there's another entrance?"

"I am not saying that, neither could I say it even if I knew it to be true. I am addressing a flaw in your reasoning – a fact constructed from the material of ignorance, a brick made of air."

"And that is all the satisfaction you are going to give me on this?"

"Very good Aedan. You are making fine progress."

Aedan huffed for a while, but soon thought of another question. "This one you might not like," he said, "but I need to know."

"I'm listening."

"Are you teaching us because Malik's father – or mother – told Culver not to?"

Fergal looked up at the clouds, apparently dreaming. When he turned around to Aedan there was a hint of amusement in his face. "Then this is why you were so surly to begin with."

Aedan dropped his eyes.

"Yes, I suspected your little pre-departure conference with Malik might have run along those lines. It is true that his mother has great influence, and also true that such a demand was made, but even if it had not been, Culver would not have taught you. You will learn to forgive him once you understand him. The chancellor is a man who keeps himself apart. He is someone very few people understand, but perhaps you will learn something of him before we return."

It still sounded like academic snobbery to Aedan, but he didn't really care. Fergal was proving to be the best tutor he had ever known. Liru said the same. If Malik had known this assistant better, he would have included him in the veto against teaching.

Camp was usually made during early afternoon, allowing time for the two apprentices to train with weapons. They never trained within view of the soldiers, and leather sleeves kept the noise of weapons down. Even Aedan was sworn to secrecy as he began to work with Liru.

Osric and Tyne acted as their instructors. Though he had known Osric for many years, Aedan had never actually trained with him. The oversized general was not capable of shifting as quickly as his smaller opponents, but the depth of each movement easily made up for this, and the speed of his arms was devastating. The blade would move so quickly and with such weight that he could parry and cut before anyone realised the offensive had shifted.

Tyne, though she was taller than most women, drifted over the grass as lightly as a summer breeze. She slipped around lunges and darted in with a fluid grace that sometimes even put Osric on the retreat. Aedan and Liru watched with dropping jaws. It was poetry.

Aedan had begun to like Tyne as he had grown to understand her. She was not the domineering, starchy woman he had first thought. She could command if needed, and she was strong, no mistake. But behind it all was a shy lady who smiled with the most endearing dimples, coloured slightly when complimented, and who was always quick to soothe any bruise. Whatever ill will she had borne Aedan was long gone, and she laughed with him as freely as with the others.

Once, as he watched her stepping and leaping around Osric, her long copper braid sweeping behind her and a half smile always tugging at her mouth, he leaned over to Liru and whispered, "They make good dancing partners."

He would say nothing when Osric and Tyne demanded to know what all the whispering was about. It was not the last such comment that passed between the youngsters. Aedan had never seen the general smile so often – and there was no doubt as to the cause. Sword-sparring was usually marked by glittering steel and ringing strikes; Tyne's bouts with Osric were marked by glittering eyes and ringing laughter.

The teaching and training covered unarmed combat, knives, swords, clubs, and quarterstaves. They alternated partners, fought in pairs, and then all fought Osric. Then they fought Osric with one hand tied behind his back. Then Tyne suggested they tie his arms and legs, put a bag over his head and give him Aedan's cheese knife to hold between his boots.

Thormar, the steady, silent commander was always to be seen around the camp, thick white smoke curling up from his pipe, and his heavy glance bringing instant order to any disturbance. His constant presence allowed Osric to move around freely.

Merter would hunt on most days. When Aedan was able to get off he would join him, slipping easily into the patient silence of the trail. Merter tolerated nobody else near him, saying the rest of them breathed through trumpets and stamped on every branch the ground had to offer.

One afternoon, following a gruelling weapons session, Aedan was stretching out in front of the camp fire, watching a deer haunch sizzle while beans and maize simmered in half-a-dozen blackened pots. He was cooking a roll of stick bread – dough wrapped around a stick – which he would stuff with beans and strips of meat. The idea was to pack it away for tomorrow's lunch, but the steam rising from the bread was tickling his nose, and he was beginning to doubt quite seriously that the bread would survive the evening.

His contemplations were interrupted when Thormar sat down beside him, his ever-present pipe belching spicy clouds. Aedan was too intimidated to cough. He'd seen this big commander smashing his way through the Fenn attack, producing almost as much devastation as the general.

"Osric tells me you are from the Mistyvales," Thormar said.

"Yes, sir."

"I'd prefer you to drop the 'sir' unless it's in front of the soldiers."

"Yes ..." Aedan caught himself in time.

"I remember the Mistyvales dimly. How well did you know Glenting?"

"I only visited there once when my father went to buy a mule."

"Would that have been at old Ainsley's stable? By the river, just under the mill?"

"Yes, how did you know?"

"Glenting was my home ... is my home. You know what it's like being northern – there's that song, something about how the blood seems ever to sing in our veins of going home."

Aedan smiled. He had heard the song and knew the longing, but in his case returning would be more complicated. "Do you think you will go back?" he asked.

"I have another three years to complete in the army and then I'll be discharged, free to stay or leave. What would you do?"

Aedan began to answer and then realised he had no idea what to say. As he thought of faithful Thomas and Dara, the other memories rushed back – the slander and accusations, the way in which he would perhaps even now be remembered. Perhaps charges had been laid against him.

"Ah, you have some attachment in Castath," said Thormar, elbowing him. "A young lass that holds you back?"

"Oh ... no, it's not like that. It's just that, well, we didn't leave the north well. There were some lies spread about me. Going back might not be a good idea."

"Now that's a serious matter ..." Thormar drew and released a small cloud that drifted towards the fire where the updraft whisked it up into the air. "I've always found it better to face lies than turn from them," he said, gazing into the flames, "like keeping my enemy in front of me. I'll tell you what, young Aedan, when you decide to head back home, if I can, I'll make the journey with you. A good word from a retired commander will go a long way – no sheriff would question my word – and I'm more than happy to add my knuckles into the bargain if they are needed."

"Thank you," Aedan said. "That means a lot to me." The man's generosity warmed him as much as the fire. He only wished that his problems in the Mistyvales could be solved that simply. "But what will you do if you go back to Glenting?" he asked.

"Ah, now you inquire after something that touches near to my heart. How much do you know about the making of pipes?"

As darkness gathered around the camp, settling at a respectful distance from the fire, Thormar expounded on the different shapes of bowl, shank and stem, the characteristics of briar root, cherry wood, maple, and clay. His voice became wistful as he told of his plans to build a small workshop at the end of a quiet street where his cabin could overlook the river, and where he could smoke an evening pipe on the veranda while dangling a lazy hook in the water. Aedan found himself wanting to swallow the hook and clutch the dream for himself. He had not thought much of a peaceful life. Other purposes had driven him. But the commander's plan sounded good, very good, except perhaps for the smoke.

Later that night after he had retired, he spent an hour trying not to smell or think of the meat-and-bean bread roll in his saddlebag. Then he finally surrendered, wolfed it down, and rolled into his blanket again with a broad smile and no remorse.

Before his thoughts grew sleepy, the vision of Thormar's peaceful retirement glowed in his mind's eye. Surely that was the end for which he too strove. Surely it was the only sense behind all the armies and weapons and spilled blood of the nation – not battle and victory, but the peace that lay on the far side, calling so patiently and so softly as to even be forgotten by those who won it. Before sleep took him, he promised himself he would not forget.

Aedan was beginning to feel slightly easier in the camp, but there was one change that was for the worse. The nearer they drew to the dreaded fortress, the longer the soldiers' hushed evening discussions became – discussions that would fall silent at the approach of anyone outside their number. Aedan managed to catch the occasional drift of speech. They were telling stories of Kultûhm, rumours of ghosts, giants, ogres and goblins. It seemed that the fortress had a claim on every legendary horror.

But the stories that would have brought laughter back within the city walls were having a different effect here. Some of the tales he had read himself: "every man that entered was lost", "sounds that cause the earth to shake and birds to fall from the sky", "black vapour like a spray of night". The last, he suspected to be from his own account, suitably embellished.

And it was not just the stories. The land, too, was growing stranger. Stands of giant trees began to reappear, more now than Aedan remembered. They loomed over the hills like ancient watchmen – many of them dead, but some very much alive. The feeling of being watched was heightened during the dim, mist-cloaked mornings which played all manner of tricks on the senses.

It was a little after first light when a trembling soldier reported seeing the shudder of distant leaves on a wooded hillside, as if some large beast was moving beneath the canopy, but Merter knew of no such beast inhabiting this area. He wanted to separate from the party and investigate, but Osric was not prepared to have anyone else lead their company through the drifting fog, so the sighting was left unexplained. But it was not forgotten.

Later, after the mist had cleared and the sun began to warm the ground, they headed towards what looked like a broad tree and turned out to be a colossal bush. Under the shade, they found, leering back at them with dark bulbous eyes, a statue that Merter assumed was some kind of boundary marker. It was a carving of the most monstrous locust, bigger than a man, made from such materials and finished with such precision that the creature looked real. Startlingly real. Normally the statues of kings or mythical guardians were used, but a locust of this size was no less impressive – or intimidating, seeing as locusts were considered portents of devastation.

The more superstitious believed that boundary markers could be imbued with dark powers. Clearly the soldiers were of this persuasion. None felt like resting anymore, and they moved on.

Aedan could sense the radiating fear. He was sure the only thing that preserved order was the weight of Osric's presence. The general's eye was quick and his discipline firm. The awe in which the soldiers held him kept them in their place, especially after the way he had led them against the Fenn war scouts with losses of less than one for each of the enemy's ten. True to his values, he not only kept the company disciplined, but immaculately neat at all times. Camp hygiene was better than that of a moderately priced inn. Uniforms were cleaned, shoes polished, beards trimmed, and no man was permitted to smell worse than his horse. None dared test Osric in this, so the party looked almost parade-ready, both in appearance and discipline.

But it was not lost on Aedan that between Osric, Merter, Thormar and Tyne, one was always on watch and the others slept fully armed.

That evening, as Aedan was stretching out by the fire, Osric told him in Sulese to wait a while and then move to the other side of the fire, away from the soldiers. That was when Aedan began to notice the silent tension between soldiers and officers. The following night, he and Liru were told to sleep with their weapons in hand under their blankets. The knot in his stomach made it difficult to rest; stars were dimming by the time exhaustion overcame him.

There was little talk in the camp when day broke, and they travelled in silence. There would be one more camp before they reached the fortress. Aedan disrupted the stillness to ask, in Fenn, what Culver was planning to do when they arrived. Fergal gave a long answer in a language Aedan had never heard. When asked for a translation, he said that it meant "patience is acquired through exercise".

By mid-morning, that dreaded round tower appeared over the distant hills, as dark and watchful as he remembered. Aedan was unable to eat anything more than a few raisins. It was afternoon when they crested the final ridge.

No one spoke.

Aedan remembered well the plain that now lay beneath them, and the rock-walled hill in the centre. On top of the rise, dominating it, Kultûhm waited, challenging them, daring them to approach. Aedan saw it as he had before – vast, lonely, and dreadful.

But if he was stilled by the sight, the others were turned to stone. There was something deeply unsettling about the fortress, in no way lessened by the intervening years. It was as though Kultûhm returned the stares of its watchers.

Osric finally broke the spell and led them down to the bank of a river. They made camp under the swaying locks of grey willows, but it was a restless camp that became increasingly uneasy as darkness settled. Heads were constantly turning in the direction of the fortress, often with sharp movements as if in response to something sensed or imagined.

A camp of frightened soldiers held far less comfort for Aedan than the surrounds. So, as he had often done over the past few days, he used a skin to collect the entrails of the deer Merter had killed, and carried them out into the night.

He could hear the soft tread of the paws that soon followed him, but made no effort to run. He skirted the hill and placed his burden on the ground, then retreated to a solitary rowan tree and pulled himself up onto a smooth-skinned branch.

He did not have long to wait. The old grey wolf looped past him and then around the meat. It circled twice more, sniffed, and crept forward. Even when the meal was under its nose, it stood long and tested the air for danger. Aedan climbed down from the branch and seated himself against the trunk. The wolf looked at him, but over the past days it had grown accustomed to this curious bringer of gifts. The meat was fresh and soon overcame the animal's fear.

As it ate, Aedan heard a soft tread nearby. He guessed it would be Tyne. Merter would have been quieter; everyone else in the camp would have been crunching leaves and branches from half a mile back. The wolf looked up and retreated a few yards as Tyne drifted in from the darkness and sat beside Aedan. After a while the wolf crept back to his meal.

"So this is where you go at night," Tyne whispered.

"I remember him," Aedan said. "The white patch over the side of his face made him stand out. This old wolf once led the pack, once terrified me. It was while we were fleeing his pack that we entered the fortress."

They watched the old animal, hunched with age, devouring the meat with hungry gulps as his nervous eyes darted around him.

"You would think," Aedan said, "that I'd feel good about this – I've grown while he, my old enemy, has shrunk. Yet all I feel is a terrible ache. I pity him, that he has been called by age to surrender his strength."

"Old words for one so young."

"From a song. I always hated that song, hated all sad songs. I thought they made happy people miserable. Now I think I understand them better. Bards write them because they can't hold them back. Sadness has got to flow out or it gets stuck and turns bitter."

Tyne sighed. "I believe you are right," she said quietly.

Aedan looked at her. "Why did you and Osric not marry? I see it in the way you smile when you bring him his food, in the way he steps beside you at the first hint of danger."

Tyne shifted. "And I thought you a child," she said. Then she was quiet for a long time.

Aedan waited. Talking with Fergal had taught him to do that.

"Perhaps," she said, "it's like with your bards. There is deep sadness that we both carry. Love opens the gate to the deepest hurt."

"That sounds wrong to me," Aedan grumbled, partly to himself.

"Maybe when you've known a little more of what it is to lose those you love, you'll think better of me, better of Osric."

Aedan decided to let her assumption be. He wondered what the loss had been with Tyne. He stared out into the moonlight a long time before he remembered a northern fable. "Have you heard the story of the two lands?" he asked.

"No. But I'd like to."

"It's a rillom, but I'm not going to get the flow or the rhyming parts right. As well as I can remember, the tale goes like this. There were once two lands where great battles were fought. After they had ended, both lands had corpses scattered all over. When the clouds approached, the first land said, 'Leave me. If you pour water onto me, you will spread the poison of these corpses all over and disturb the little peace I have left,' and it drove the clouds off. The other land took a deep breath and let the waters wash over it, gradually draining the filth away. After twenty years, the first land had become a desert and the skeletons were the only things to be seen. The second land was renewed. Not even the bones could be found."

"So the rain is love?"

"I think that's what it means."

Tyne was silent, then she shifted her feet as if to rise.

"Don't go," Aedan said. "I won't talk about that anymore." He heard her pause then settle slowly back, and realised that he had unwittingly cracked a very hard shell. He did not want to chase her away. She reminded him strangely of his mother. Under the warlike ways, she was just as soft, just as loving, and just as much in need of love.

As was he.

The moon hung over the mountains and silhouetted the lone grey wolf with silver fire. The white patch on its head was smeared a little towards the bottom, tribute to a good meal.

As a breeze trickled over the grass and pressed through the leaves, an owl hooted above them, a soft and hollow tone over the thin rustling. Beyond the wolf, the ground flowed away into hills upon hills, rising slowly in breathless awe of the shadowy mountains. Aedan's blood thrilled at the lonely beauty, the haunting perfection. It was a sight he hoped he would be able to recall for the rest of his days.

When the wolf had finished his meal and loped out into the night, they began to make their way back to camp.

A distant yell of terror froze them to the ground, but when they realised that it had come from the camp they sprang up and ran as fast as the darkness would allow. Aedan knew Tyne was trying to draw ahead but he wouldn't let her. The orange light of the fire grew until they rushed into the open circle, blades flashing.

Everyone was staring at the fortress and one of the soldiers was pointing with a hand that shook like an unfastened sail in a heavy wind.

"What is it?" Tyne asked.

The soldier answered without turning to her. "It moved!" he said, his voice thin. "The fortress is moving! I saw one of the towers change shape."

"Could it not have fallen? The fortress is very old."

"No sound," he said. "And it moved slow and careful like. The way a person moves his arm. The way living things move."

The campsite was silent for a long time. Osric reminded the sentries to watch all quarters, no matter how compelling the stir.

"Too many stories?" Tyne asked.

Osric drew her back to the fire, away from the soldiers before replying. "I don't want to say it to them, but something has moved up there more than once this evening. Merter saw it too."

After a brief consultation with Merter, Osric decided to douse the fire.

Culver seemed unperturbed by the commotion. He had returned to a scroll covered with strange, thickly packed symbols, the moonlight being strong enough for him to read. Aedan was impressed. The man certainly had unshakable self-command. It seemed nothing could touch him, not even fear. Fergal, however, stood beside them.

"What do you think," Tyne asked him.

"I think it very uncharacteristic behaviour for stone," he said. "But beyond that I am as bewildered as you."

"Culver too?"

"Him too."

"Let us not contribute to their fears," Osric said. "Appetite or not, we must demonstrate confidence or every man here will have deserted by morning."

He cut a slice of venison and the others followed his example, though they ate with their stomachs in their throats and their eyes continually wandering to the dark mass on the hill.

After they had eaten, Culver handed a scroll to Fergal who left the camp and climbed the side of a grassy rise. When he reached a flat rock, he sat and began to study the parchment, glancing up repeatedly at the dark structures ahead of him. After a while Aedan found the camp stifling again. He followed his tutor and stood nearby. The symbols on the scroll conveyed nothing to him. But when he lifted his eyes to the hulking shapes on the plain below, and beyond them to the deep silence within moon-frosted walls and shadowed spires, he understood a message more chilling than sleet.

"Are those the instructions for getting in?" he asked.

Fergal released a deep breath. "Riddles, I'm afraid, not instructions. Misinterpreted to our doom."

That was enough to put an end to Aedan's interruptions. He peered out into the night, watching to see the movement the others had reported earlier, and hoping not to. The uneventful monotony finally lulled him, and he decided to head back to the camp and his blanket.

Osric's fears were confirmed. It was starlight when he roused the camp. Six of the soldiers were gone with a portion of the food stores. Osric had seen them slip away, but had decided against challenging them. "Mortal fear," he explained, "can make a certain kind of soldier more a liability than an aid. I do not want to have to worry about daggers in our backs while facing Kultûhm. The immediate problem, though, is that we may now be in danger of wolves. Not so, Merter?"

"Possible. It's a big pack. Ten of us might seem more inviting than sixteen. The deserters run a greater risk. Perhaps they will draw the pack off, but I think not. The last time I saw the wolves, they were moving north. On their return they will reach us first."

"We must hurry," said Osric. "By first light we need to be across the plain. Tie up anything that jingles or gleams. Quickly now."

Chapter 51

The moon had set. It was by starlight that Merter picked the way over the dew-laden grass. To the left, the dark presence of the fortress could be felt more clearly than it could be seen, causing heads to turn in that direction repeatedly. Fortunately the ground was level with few obstructions or surprises. The remains of siege engines, army wagons and their fallen horses had long since disintegrated. Gentle mounds were all that remained from the disastrous final siege of Kultûhm. The fortress had never been conquered. It stood empty because it had been abandoned.

The statues that had looked enormous from a distance now defied belief. Features were not clear in the darkness, but the huge portions of sky where stars were blotted out left no doubt as to the size of these stone monoliths. It said something that the besieging army had not pulled any of them down.

Despite the measures taken to move silently, each fall of hooves or creak of saddles was like the clanging of a bell in that undisturbed and silent place. To Aedan, their passing there seemed like a coarse violation of some deep rest. He was quite sure he did not want to wake whatever it was that rested.

They kept to the outer ring of the plain, counting off the statues as they passed them. When they reached the fifth, they stopped. Culver and Fergal approached the base – a massive stone platform with a broad stairway that reached from end to end. They spoke in low tones before calling for the others.

Culver stood wrapped in thought as Fergal explained. "There are two smaller statues on either side of the giant's right foot," he said. "The one that lies must have its right arm rotated until it points to the sky, the one that tells the truth must have its left rotated until it points to the fortress."

There was silence.

"You do know which is which?" asked Osric.

"Not yet," said Fergal.

"Can we guess?"

"If we get it right, a door opens somewhere. If we get it wrong, the levers jam and the door is sealed. I also suspect there will be something more serious, like a hail of pig-sized rocks. These statues are more than they appear."

"So we must wait for light?"

"Just a little should be enough. Already I think the statues are a touch less inky."

As if in response to Fergal's observation, a barbet chattered nearby. Culver sent Merter and Senbert up the stairs to the giant's foot, the heel of which reached to their shoulders. The two smaller statues were man-sized.

After brushing away a thick carpet of dead moss and inspecting the shoulder joints, Merter called for help. "These joints will not turn easily. Dust, rain and time have done a lot. It will take more than two of us."

Osric and Tyne joined them.

They waited for the light to grow, for the details of the statues to emerge. The two stone forms may have looked alike in shadow, but as the morning crept in, they were seen to be markedly different. The one on the left was of a man with an open, smiling face. One hand was at his side and the other was held out in a gesture of welcome. The statue on the right was of a hunched woman, hook-nosed and ragged. Everything about her was vulgar from her crooked bearing to the snarl which twisted her face into a grotesque mask. Both her arms were held out in front of her, bent fingers splayed. There was no welcome here.

Culver and Fergal climbed the stairs and halted before the statues, locked in thought. After a silent contemplation, they returned to the base of the stairs and stared up at the giant that towered over a hundred and fifty feet above them. A few centuries of weather had left stains, fractures and even craters in the stone. Broken pieces lay at the base, tangled in deep grass. But the size of the statue was so great that the damage did not obscure the overall form.

This was not just an oversized man – the heavy-boned limbs, swollen hands, piggy little eyes and cavernous mouth were unmistakable. This was a true giant of legend. Yet he was smiling – not a wicked, hungry smile, but kind and respectful. Though he had the obvious strength to shatter a tower, his open-handed gesture was one of peace. Aedan almost felt kindly towards this simple, benign creature.

All waited in tense silence as the two scholars discussed what they saw, comparing the giant with the man and woman. It was clear to Aedan that the woman was the one at odds with the others. Her manner and actions falsely represented the situation. He was not surprised when she was declared to be the liar, solving the riddle. While the others prepared to shift the arms, he decided to walk around to the back of the giant statue.

Something bothered him. It had been too easy. Any puzzle deserved to be seen from a few angles. Skeet had often encouraged him to nurture his desire to look at things in a way others had not considered. Climbing onto the roof for a better view, Kalry had once called it. A walk would give him a different perspective here.

The stone foundation was considerable, and it took some time to reach the other side. When he did, he looked up, and what he saw caused him to halt in mid stride.

"Wait!" he yelled, slipping in the dewy grass as he sprinted back to the others. He glanced up, fearing a dreadful hail of rocks. "Fergal, wait! Wait! It's wrong! It's the other way round."

Everyone stared at Aedan as he scrambled around the corner. The men who were straining at the arms stopped.

Culver glared, but Aedan persisted. "The giant has a huge spiked club tucked into his belt, held against his back. Nobody would carry a club like that unless they were trying to hide it briefly. The woman is telling the truth – the giant is not to be trusted. It's the man who is lying."

Nobody spoke as they comprehended how close they had come to tragedy, and in the stillness they now heard a sound that caused the blood to drain from every face – a long, searching howl.

"They are on the north side of the fortress," Merter said in reply to the questioning glances. "The wind carries towards them. They may not know of us yet, but I wouldn't give it long. They will be here soon."

Fergal turned to Aedan. "Are you sure of what you saw?"

"Yes. I could see the spikes pressing into the giant's back. It looks uncomfortable."

Fergal exchanged a look with Culver who nodded. "Do as he says," Fergal called. "Lift the man's right arm up and turn the woman's left arm back."

They set to work, but the rigid joints defied them still. Another howl filled the air, louder, closer. Osric and Thormar joined in. Even the two scholars climbed the stairs and added their weight to the effort.

"There!" cried Liru, who was standing watch nearby.

A stream of grey and white fur coursed around the western slopes of the central hill. At first it looked as if the wolves would run past, but then they stopped, noses to the ground.

"The scent of horsemeat," said Merter. "It won't be long before they see us." He threw his weight against the stone arm, heaving and shaking with the effort.

Tyne stopped him. She drew a long, slender dagger and drove it into the joint, wriggling the blade along and dislodging a shower of natural cement and dust; then she did the same in a few more places around the joint. Osric understood and followed her example on the other statue.

"They've seen us," Liru called.

The plain was large and the pack still a few miles distant, but they moved with bewildering speed.

"Together!" said Osric. The men heaved and the woman's arm ground slowly back until it pointed to the fortress. The man's arm had further to go, but after two concerted shoves, it pointed to the sky.

Nothing happened.

All eyes turned to Culver and Fergal. They were looking around. Liru, standing at the base of the other foot ran towards them but as she reached halfway she screamed and tripped, falling hard on the stone.

"What happened?" asked Tyne, rushing up.

"I don't know. It was like the flagstones gave way under me."

Culver and Fergal were there in an instant, walking back in the direction she had come. The stone was grooved, hiding any cracks in the floor, so nobody was expecting it when the surface on which Fergal stood gave way and he began to descend on a long ramp that was flush with the flagstones on one end and tilted downwards into the earth at the other. He turned around, pressed on the rising edge of the ground with his hands and pulled himself up again. The stone ramp lifted as he took his weight from it.

"It's counterweighted," he said. "Get the horses and mules. The slope should be gradual enough to take them down. Merter, light a torch. It will be black as a dungeon down there. Aedan, bring his horse."

Aedan was surprised to see how Fergal took charge without even consulting Culver. Obviously he was given many responsibilities and was required to act as speaker in these non-academic settings.

As he ran back down the stairs to the horses, Aedan glanced across the plain and almost lost his footing. The wolves were close enough now that the wind could be seen rippling their coats as they surged over the grass, pulling the ground beneath them, ears flattened, eyes eager.

He seized the horses' reins and led the unwilling animals, clattering and snorting, up the stairs. They knew something was amiss. Merter had already descended, lit a torch, and found a way to secure the ramp in a downward position.

The horses did not descend willingly. Some had to be pulled down. The danger of hurrying beasts that were stamping and rearing was not lost on anyone, but the approaching tide presented a far greater danger. The area cleared until only Osric, Thormar and Aedan stood at the lip of the ramp, shoving the last stubborn horse, while Tyne hauled the reins from below.

Then the sea of fur reached them.

Growling and yapping filled the air as a mass of bodies, about fifty strong, swirled around the base of the statue and began leaping up the stairs. Their natural caution had diminished with the size of the party. Osric and Thormar drew their swords while Aedan tried to shove the horse without putting himself in the line of a kick.

"You two," Osric shouted. "Get down below. I'll cover."

"Ramp's blocked," said Thormar, holding his ground.

Two snarling wolves crept towards Osric. They lurched and snapped simultaneously. His sword sliced into the neck of one, but the other sank its teeth into his leg. Thormar's boot thudded home and launched the animal over the heads of its fellows while his sword swept across a line of approaching muzzles. The wolves backed away a little, but showed no intention of running. They began to circle.

Aedan saw there would be no winning this fight. The horse was frantic now as it kicked and plunged, blocking the ramp. Those hooves were as dangerous as the jaws grinning around him. With a sudden inspiration, he drew his short sword, yelled for Tyne to get out of the way, and stabbed the horse in the rump. It twitched, screamed, and rushed down.

"Clear," he yelled. "Let's go!"

No further invitation was needed. All three leaped onto the ramp and backed into the comparative darkness below. They hurried off the slope and Merter released the latch, but the ramp did not lift as it should have. A glance made it clear why not. Several wolves were creeping down, cautious, but not timid.

"Everyone lift, now!" Osric called, ducking under the stone slab and heaving upwards. All those who were not obstructed by horses joined in and the stone began to rise. The weight suddenly increased and it dipped again. A forest of muzzles appeared at the edges, wrinkled and snarling.

"More hands!" Osric grunted.

Culver, Liru and Tyne joined the effort and gradually the slab rose again. One of the muzzles was pinched in the shrinking gap and there was a yelp of pain.

"Aedan, Liru," said Osric, "it's too high now for you to reach. Find something to use as a brace."

They scurried about in the shadows, pushing between restless horses to search the walls and corners, but there was nothing. On the way back Aedan nearly had his head removed by a panicking mare that kicked out behind her, striking another horse in the ribs with a loud smack. It was so close that Aedan felt the rush of wind on his face and smelled hoof. By the time he returned empty-handed, the ramp had risen and become part of the ceiling.

"Wolves love to circle their prey," said Merter. "Once enough of them had got off the ramp to do so, it rose by itself. I don't think they will push it down again. No animal likes the feel of unstable ground. Every wolf that tips the ramp will scramble off at the sensation."

They did not have to wait long for the slab to dip. There was a frantic clicking and scratching of claws, and the little wedges of light disappeared again. Fergal was sure that there would be some lever to reset the positions of the arms and secure the slab, but it could not be found.

Osric made no secret of his concern. "I don't like leaving this to chance," he said. "Uncertainty ahead and danger behind make a poor prospect."

"And a wound on your thigh," said Tyne. "Would you like me to take a look at that?"

"It's nothing," said Osric, "Teeth barely pierced the skin."

He spoke too quickly. Aedan noticed, and wondered why Osric looked like he was blushing. Then he understood that a wound on the thigh would require removing his trousers to have it tended. He grinned at the big general's embarrassment.

Tyne raised her eyes from the bloody patch on his leg and was about to argue when she caught herself, and there was no mistaking the blush this time.

After oiling and lighting branch-and-cloth torches that had been made at the last camp, they prepared to leave the chamber. There were two exits. One was a narrow stairwell leading up, apparently through the giant's leg to what Fergal suspected was a network of tunnels within the statue. The other was a broad slope leading down.

The downward incline was steep, but not too steep for horses, and the ceiling was high enough for a mounted rider. It was as if the tunnel had been made with that in mind.

Their torches were not the best. They produced as much smoke as light, arguably more, but it was enough to reveal the precision with which the stone masons had built this tunnel. The blocks met perfectly – no fringes of mortar had been used to compensate for inaccurate measurements. There were neither dripping leaks nor powdery cracks, but the passing of time was clearly displayed in an orange fungus that spread out over the walls. Its shapes, down to the minutest details, were such perfect imitations of the branches of a tree that it seemed to be a painting. Aedan found the air surprisingly fresh. He guessed that there was a through-draft, not enough to cause the flames above his torch to flap and toss, but enough to continuously change the air over the centuries.

They travelled in single file and in silence – apart from the clopping of hooves which filled the long passage with a series of multiplying echoes and sounded like the tread of a hundred horses or more. After covering about half a mile, they reached an upward slope that led into another chamber, this one far larger. Here were racks of weapons and mounted torches. Osric found a sealed pot of tar which he opened. The seal was good, but much of the tar had hardened. The gummy centre was barely enough to supply half a dozen of the torches.

After consulting with Culver, Fergal spoke up. "We will need to leave the horses here," he said. "It is our hope to reach the archives as quickly and silently as possible. At least two must remain with the animals."

Captain Senbert and Holt, the only remaining soldiers, volunteered quickly, and at a look from Osric, Thormar said he would support them. He would be more than capable of preventing any cowardly desertion tricks. He came over to Aedan and Liru, leaned forward and put a big, calloused hand on each of their shoulders.

"You be careful, now. Young eyes and ears are sharp. Make good use of them and keep those library-dwellers safe." He angled his head towards the two academics with a grin. "If it was certain that you'd be safe here, I'd request for you to be left with us, but there are no certainties in this place. Staying with the group is probably best."

Aedan gripped the Commander's forearm. "We'll be back," he said.

"I know you will." Thormar hid it well, but in the clenching of his teeth, the truth was plain. He was deeply worried for them.

Fergal and Culver turned away from the broad passage that sloped upward and, instead, took a narrow stairway, tightly coiled and steep. Aedan noticed how Osric had to turn his shoulders to prevent them from scraping, and he thought kindly of his own small stature as he passed through the narrow opening.

It was a long climb – very long. Breathing became heavy, especially from the front. After more turns than Aedan could count, they finally reached a doorway. The stairs continued upwards, but Culver led them out into a large room, similar to the one they had left beneath them. Fergal remained to drop a white pebble at the entrance to the stairs.

"If we need to make a hasty retreat," he said, "we don't want to be arguing over directions."

They passed through a series of passages and doorways, marking each turn with a pebble, and found their way into a different section of the buildings where the passages were wider and the ceilings higher.

A heavy gate, rusted off its hinges, gave them access to a cavernous hall, well over a stone's throw across and almost as much in height. It was clear that it had once been richly adorned, but now silk tapestries hung in grey rags and thick brown carpets promised to bury any shoe in dust. A fire pit nearby held a few mounds of powder that would never burn.

Down the centre of the hall, there was a long table, partly collapsed and riddled with decay. At its far end, another table at right angles to the first, stood on a dais. It could only be the royal table. Being made of more delicate wood, this one had been eaten away to a crumbling ruin. The chairs here had all collapsed except one. In the light of the burning torches, pure, untarnished gold shone from under this chair's layer of dust, and Aedan knew that they were the first to enter this place since its abandonment. That metal would not have been left behind.

He wondered what else might be lying around.

But theirs was a quest for knowledge, and neither Culver nor Fergal gave the precious metal a second glance.

Along the hall, windows looked out over a large courtyard. The light outside was still weak, the chilly blue-grey shadows of a day awaiting sunrise. They peered out, searching for anyone or anything hostile. Apart from the unnaturally large arms of the creeper that hung from the central tower, the only signs of life were streaks of pigeon dung on the walls. But even these looked to be old stains of long-abandoned roosts, stains that no weather could remove.

"There's something unnatural here," said Osric. "I can't name it, but something is wrong with this place."

"No birds," said Merter, bringing gradual realisation to the others. "Very strange for abandoned buildings. They make perfect rookeries."

Culver led them away from the hall, through an arched passage, into a wide foyer. A grand staircase with marble steps and brass rails led up, presumably to the royal chambers. On the other side, there was a colossal oak door, now rotten and splintered and held together by its iron bracings like a pile of leaves in a gardener's arms.

"This is the part that concerns us," said Fergal. "We need to reach the central tower on the other side of a courtyard just beyond this door. It requires exposing ourselves. We will need to move quickly and silently."

"This door will not open silently," said Osric.

"Can we not get out through a window?" Aedan asked.

Fergal held his palms on either side of his belly, indicating his size. "The windows that would admit such dimensions are only to be found five storeys up."

Osric turned to the door. "We'll need to lift it before opening," he said, taking hold of a prominent horizontal bar. Merter and Fergal took places beside him, and counting down, they heaved and drew the door back. It did not scrape along the floor, but the hinges sent out a screech that shook the building to its foundations and echoed off all the cold stone and rusted iron in the fortress. They stood in shock for a moment, looking out into the empty courtyard as the sounds fluttered and died away.

Culver seemed the least affected. His expression was unreadable as he stepped through the doorway, led them down the stairs and across the flagstones. The courtyard was enclosed on all sides. Beyond the surrounding roofs, rose a daunting forest of buildings and towers. Near the middle of the courtyard, rusted manacles were fixed to the ground, suggesting that the royal entertainers had catered for savage appetites.

Immediately to the left was a stable and, to the right, a larger building that looked as if it might be a small armoury, perhaps dedicated to the tournaments – or tortures – that had taken place here. Aedan tried to peer through the open door, eager to catch a glimpse of ancient tools and weapons, but the interior was too dark. He realised with discomfort that anything within would be able to see him clearly.

Here and there were scattered possessions that seemed to have been dropped in flight – a barely recognisable shoe, a rusted spear, a shattered vase, an overturned cart, some ragged shreds of what might once have been cloth ... and a crown!

It was dirty and stained, but that didn't keep the torch light flaring in the many-jewelled gold surface. One central stone glowed so richly it was as if it had a light of its own – a brilliant fiery radiance that became smoky and bronzed towards the edges. He had never imagined a jewel like this. Beside it, the other stones and even the gold looked like the cheap quartz and tin of children's trinkets.

The dancing light in the stone called to him, drew him in. It was easy to picture how this could change his fortunes. He would not need to depend on Osric for his fees or on Borr and Harriet for his mother's lodging. Malik would no longer be able to look down on him; and he would have the resources to put Iver in his place and even to deal with his father. He would buy his freedom. He would have standing in society. Even men like Dresbourn would be forced to respect him …

"Aedan!" Fergal called.

Aedan realised he had stopped and been left behind.

"There will be plenty of that, but knowledge is our treasure. You should also know that the spoils of a commissioned quest belong by rights to the prince."

Aedan tore his eyes away from the dazzling gem and trailed after the group, feelings rioting in his chest.

Why should they have to tell the prince? Was it necessary to be truthful to a liar? Wasn't it only fair to deceive one who had deceived them?

When he caught up, Liru glanced at him, her dark eyes clear and sharp.

"You are thinking about taking it and keeping quiet?" she said.

"No."

She stopped, turned around and faced him.

"Maybe," Aedan said. "I don't know. Why do we owe the prince anything?" They resumed walking.

Liru spoke softly, "For me, it does not matter. My house is already very rich. For you, I think you would become poorer."

"Poorer? Have you lost your mind?"

"Poorer because you would give away your honesty. You would have to lie."

"But the prince lied to me."

"And so you would become like him."

Her words struck like one of Hadley's blows with the quarterstaff. He recognised the greed clawing inside him, pleading to have its way, begging him to justify taking the crown. Burkhart, too, would have had some means of justifying his actions.

Aedan walked on in silence, embarrassed and angry.

Enclosing the far side of the courtyard was a wall with a gate standing open, and a gallery where royals had most probably been entertained. To the right of the gallery was a flight of stairs that led them to a broad arched bridge. They kept low as they crossed the bridge, pushing aside some heavy fronds of ivy that dangled from a branch of the giant creeper.

Aedan glanced up at this twisting plant with its pillar-like arms that reached out over the city. The intricate shapes that its tendrils formed in the air and against the stone wall were unlike any he had seen before. They almost looked like symbols. He wondered if this creeper shared a secret with the pearlnut tree at Badgerfields, though it did not give him the same feeling. Instead of putting his ear to the thorny bark, he resolved to keep his distance at all costs.

Fergal stopped at a wide landing before double doors that were almost a foot thick and stood slightly ajar. These doors led into the enormous round tower that could be seen from leagues around. It was easily as wide as the main buildings of the keep and several times as high. While the men worked at opening the door enough to allow them in, Aedan approached the wall and looked out into the silent maze of streets.

As with the giant statues, everything here was constructed on an imposing scale. All the buildings were large and impressive, none standing under three stories, and some, like the towers, rising to great heights. The result was that the streets remained shadowy.

In these shadows were many dark objects that lined the roads. They almost looked like broken tree trunks. In one place he thought he recognised the white spidery lines of a skeleton, though he was not sure if he was seeing that with his eyes or his memories – the graveyard images from his first visit to Kultûhm kept fluttering through his mind. One thing that was not caused by memory or imagination was the smell. He noticed Merter was also sniffing the air and looking around.

"That is not the smell of abandoned stone," he said.

"Could it be wolf droppings?" Aedan asked.

"I don't think so."

"Reminds me of a rat's nest."

Merter did not answer but moved away from the door and peered down into the shadows of the deserted road.

The door shifted with a slight creak and the others slipped inside. Merter took a careful look around before following.

Culver and Fergal led the way down a broad ramp to a wide stone door. They looked, prodded, shoved and conferred. Fergal broke the silence. "We feared as much. There's a secret to opening this door that we do not possess. We will need to use a smaller entrance. Unfortunately, the only way to reach it is by climbing ten floors up to the council room – very deep floors I might add – and then descending again using a narrow turret staircase that links the counsel room and archive room."

They turned onto a wide spiral stairway and began to climb.

After one turn, Aedan stopped. The noise of feet ahead of him made it difficult to hear anything, but for a moment there had been just a hint of sound.

"What is it?" Merter asked, coming back.

"I'm not sure. It sounded almost like – like shouting."

They waited for the noisy steps of the others to move ahead, but when they listened again, all was silent. While catching up to the others, Aedan noticed with concern that a river could not have left a clearer trail across the dusty floor. With a track like this they would not be able to hide if it became necessary. Fergal need not have bothered with the pebbles.

At the tenth floor, they reached a passage that led past several chambers. At the end of the passage was the council room.

The large room was semicircular, the curved side being the outer wall of the round tower. The many windows gave ample light and made the space airy. Aedan looked around. A few leather maps had hung from the walls, but these were now largely decomposed, eaten by insects or torn by wind that moved freely through the broken shutters. Ornamental weapons were mounted on walls – spears, axes and swords, mostly rusted to frailty, except, as Aedan was fascinated to see, a few bronze weapons that had developed that pale, sea-green corrosion, beneath which he knew they would still be strong.

He walked around a large central table and approached one of the windows, looked out, and caught his breath. Not even Burkhart's council room commanded a view like this, and he was not even half way up the great tower. Ahead of him, Lake Vallendal was more like a sea reaching far out into Thirna, its western shore well beyond the reach of any eye. To the north, somewhere in the distance, was his home. But he knew, as the thought reached him, that the Mistyvales was his home no more.

He leaned out into the window, resting his torso on the deep windowsill, and looked south. The mountains of the DinEilan range were as majestic as ever, but the giants on the plain were now well beneath him. He could also see the tops of the fortress walls and marvelled at their width. Along their surfaces – more like roads than allures – were occasional mounds of wood and iron that he assumed to be the remains of catapults or carts. The breadth of the walls would have allowed these to move and pass each other with room to spare.

Far below, the labyrinth of streets unfolded. Kultûhm was not just some mountain retreat. It was a fair-sized city. Getting lost among the buildings would be easy. Looking across to the main gate, he saw the front courtyard. It was a good distance away, but his memories of it were still near.

Harsh sounds of something being struck brought Aedan back into the room. Osric, Culver and Fergal had moved around the central table and were standing before a door. The heavy oak was braced with rusty but tenacious iron, and it held fast against the kicks directed at it.

"We need the key," said Osric.

"This lock would not turn," said Fergal, "key or not."

Osric was not listening. "There, that's a key that should fit." He strode across to a snarling statue of polished granite, a violent-looking man standing with feet splayed and arms akimbo. "It will take all of us to lift it. Come along."

They gathered around and took their places.

"Don't you start getting used to this," Fergal said to Aedan, bringing a few puzzled looks.

They tried swinging gently at first, but that produced nothing more than dust. Then they took a run-up and hit the door with enough force to burst the unseen hinges. The whole structure collapsed forward with a whoosh of air and a clatter that echoed down the spiral stairway.

Merter was at the windows immediately, searching for movement, listening for any hint of sound. Aedan did the same on the other side of the room.

"Nothing," Merter said after a while, but he looked uneasy. He walked across to Aedan and peered out the neighbouring window. "We are moving too noisily," he growled. "And we are leaving tracks that a common soldier could follow."

Aedan kept glancing behind him as he moved towards the dark stairwell. He did not like having his back to the open door by which they had entered. He waited with Merter at the top of the stairs until the sound of descending feet had died away. They listened, but all was silent.

"That crown would not have remained in the courtyard if the stories about this place were all imagined," Merter said. "Keep alert, boy. Our luck may not hold much longer."

Chapter 52

It was a long and slow descent, and Aedan found it increasingly difficult to draw breath. The air in here had not been circulated. It was the forgotten air of another time held captive to grow thick with damp and with the smells of decayed wood and little forests of silent fungi.

At the bottom of the stairwell there was another door, this one of iron. But though the door was strong, the hinges had rusted to a papery softness and one heave from Osric's shoulder was enough to push it down. As the light of torches flooded the space, the whole party gasped.

It was not the little archive chamber they had expected, but a great hall, larger even than the banquet hall that they had first entered. Many columns and arches supported a high ceiling, but more striking than the fine architecture and remarkable size were the reflections. Everything here was covered in clean tiles that sparkled and reflected the torches like dew on a spring morning. Light porcelain – some white, some sky-blue – made it feel as though the chamber's roof was open to the air above.

Oil lamps and sealed oil jars were discovered and put to work, providing far better illumination. The many lamps were mounted against golden reflectors which cast a soft dreamy light through the whole chamber.

As the light grew, the far wall was revealed. It was covered with paintings that were so masterfully done they seemed almost to move – boughs dipped, grass swayed, chests breathed, and eyes looked out and watched as closely as they themselves were watched. There was writing on sections of the wall too, but none that Aedan could read. These were runes he had never seen before, but they were as exquisite as the paintings.

Culver was standing before the wall, his narrowed eyes consuming the details. Aedan wondered what the esteemed chancellor could see that escaped the rest of them, but he dared not interrupt. This was now the great learned man's place and he suspected that anyone who bothered him would be sorry indeed.

"Culver," Fergal mumbled absently while running his eyes over the shelves. "As soon as you're done with your gawping, be so good as to make your way over here."

Aedan and Liru stared.

A hundred little details suddenly fell into place and Aedan saw what had been in front of him all this time. "Culver is *your* assistant!"

Fergal drew himself out of his thoughts and glanced up at them. "Exposed then, are we?" he said with a touch of humour in his voice. "I doubted we'd be able to keep the ruse going on a journey like this. Yes, quite so. He takes the recognition and, along with it, all the attendant administration and formal duties. That way I can devote myself to the business of knowledge. A far better arrangement. If you speak of it you will find yourselves chained to re-shelving trollies in some forgotten library for the remainder of your days."

Aedan doubted the threat was sincere – no one would believe them even if they did speak of it – but decided, nevertheless, to heed the warning.

Culver joined them, his superior manner gone, thrown off like a discarded cloak. For the first time that any of them had seen, he looked at them and actually smiled. It was almost shy, even apologetic. In that instant Aedan understood that the cold, imperious air had been no more than an act. No wonder he had seemed so inhuman.

Humming to himself, Culver turned and fell in beside his master, sorting through racks of clay tablets. These tablets must have filled a thousand shelves which projected out from the walls and lined several alcoves.

A thought dropped into Aedan's mind. Could it then have been Fergal whom Giddard had once referred to as the powerful supporter, someone other than Osric who had seen great potential in him? It was an interesting idea. Maybe one day he would ask

Fergal himself. Setting the thought aside, he walked over to a shelf of clay tablets.

As before, he was unable to read the symbols. The shapes were not really pictures, but there was something more representative about them than simple lettering. He remembered now that he had once seen writing like this. The image returned to him – an engraved pillar beside that aged stone bridge in the north of DinEilan.

He studied one of the tablets, trying to find a repeated symbol. The search took him all the way to the end before he found a recurrence – an orb with wavy lines cutting through the right-hand arc. But a closer inspection revealed it to be slightly different to the first – rounder, with an extra wavy line. It did not seem possible for these to be letters of an alphabet; there were too many. Were they words, or maybe ideas? He compared the two symbols again. Conditions in the lake – choppy and choppier? Or partial cloud cover and more complete cover? He wondered how many of these symbols there were and how anyone could remember all of them.

"It's Gellerac," Fergal said, without taking his eyes from the tablets he was shuffling. "It was the language of the first literate inhabitants and the greatest innovators our land has known. The language sounds as coarse as rocks falling down a gully, but the words have great depth. Perhaps that's why the scribes so loved to press their thoughts into clay."

Aedan had no idea how Fergal could speak Thirnish and read Gellerac at the same time, but it was clear that the task was presenting little difficulty.

"Here," said Culver. "First sighting of the Darat."

"I have the details of the second siege, and here the third, so the timeline moves from right to left. Hopefully. Otherwise this could take a year."

They moved to the far left and began to search tablets.

"Inauguration of King Vrothk,"

"The three year drought."

"Encounter with the Orunesh."

"Various building projects, commissioning of the twelve statues."

"Ah, here's something. Unnatural storms."

The two men began to work through the shelf of tablets, placing the relevant ones on a marble desk.

Talk came to an end; time passed in a respectful hush, punctuated only by the clinking of clay. Merter hovered near the entrance and disappeared up the stairs every now and then.

After what must have been several hours, Tyne set about preparing a light meal from provisions she had brought. Neither Fergal nor Culver showed any interest.

Aedan was growing monumentally bored. He decided no harm could come from a better investigation of the chamber, so he took a lamp and headed over to inspect the giant paintings. At first, what he saw looked like a beautiful storm front, but then he began to look more closely. The sky was split between night and day, and from rich-looking clouds, a spear of lightning drove downward, solid, fuller than the usual spidery bolts from thunderheads.

It was not any storm; it was *the* storm. The same that had caused rumours to flood Thirna. The same that had shaken Castath and provided substance for years of superstition and rumour. The same from which he had once heard his name spoken.

Looking at the image that rose before him was, in a way, like looking at the storm itself. Something of its power was here too.

At the base of the lightning, a slight flaw caught his attention. It was the point at which the bolt met the earth, where enormous trees grew. The image was broken here by a section of unpainted, lumpy plaster. It looked like a hasty patch-up. Aedan touched it and the plaster crumbled away, revealing a fist-sized hole. He looked around to make sure that Fergal hadn't noticed. Inside the cavity something glinted.

Aedan brought his eye as close as he could without spoiling the light. It was a large ring. He put his fingers through it and pulled, gradually applying more pressure until a long brass cylinder slid out with a quiet scrape.

He was turning it in his hands, wondering if it held some secret, when the ground shuddered. There was a deep grinding and a soft cracking of mortar. Aedan paled and tried to shove the brass cylinder back, but it wouldn't go. Then he had to scramble away as the wall in front of him began to sweep outwards along the ground with the ponderousness of great mass. It was a barn-sized swivelling door, and he had released the draw-weight.

Everyone in the room looked up and dropped what they were doing as the wall pivoted. Once the door was fully open, the grinding and the movement stopped, leaving the dust to settle. All stared into the blackness beyond.

"Your doing, Aedan?" Fergal asked.

"Sorry. I didn't know anything like this would happen." He held up the brass cylinder with a sheepish look.

Fergal did not seem in the least upset. He grabbed a lamp and headed for the doorway, the others following.

This room was as dark as the first was bright, but the deep echoes told them that it was a lot bigger. Fergal walked down an aisle between large shelves and what appeared to be statues. His lamp revealed the strangest shapes. By the time the rest had collected lamps and followed, he was only a small glowing orb surrounded by colossal objects that loomed between the heavy pillars.

"Oh, it's a museum," said Tyne as she walked with Aedan into the dark cavern. The air was cold and heavy, carrying the smell of aged bones and hides. Stuffed animals lined the shelves and stood on the ground, coated in films of dust and sheets of cobwebs. A few were so decayed that patches of skin had been completely eaten away and shed hair lay beneath them in dusty heaps. There was something odd about them though. Aedan held his lamp in front of a creature he'd taken for a kind of bush pig. Apart from its size it did not resemble a pig at all. Every feature was a perfect copy of a shrew.

Then he found a pair of tatty moths. Though there was almost nothing left of their wings, it was clear that they had been as big as crows.

"I don't think it's a museum," he whispered to Tyne, the strangeness of the place seeming to demand silence. "They can't be stuffed animals – they're too big. Must be models."

"Really detailed models," Tyne whispered back as she brushed over the feathers of a dove wing as long as her arm.

They began to recognise more creatures enlarged to startling, even grotesque proportions – ants, spiders, beetles, centipedes, bees, mice and hedgehogs. The bees were larger than a man's head and the hedgehogs taller than sheep. Some were a little more than two or three times normal size; others were much more. Aedan would have expected a greater degree of consistency in the models. But as he studied the detail on the hedgehog and saw the decomposition of skin, and the bone and sinew showing through, an uncomfortable thought took hold.

Though he was not too sure about the beetles, it began to look as if the rest of the animals had been actual living creatures. He found two pygmy antelope the size of horses, and a pair of geese that might have snapped the ridge-beam of a roof on alighting, but it appeared that there was nothing bigger. Aedan felt a slight disappointment. These colossal bugs and rodents were all well and good for the girls and academics, but he wanted to see something that had the interest factor of death and terror. Like a giant wolf.

Fergal was examining one of the ants.

"Look at this," Merter called from several aisles away.

It took some walking and weaving between shelves and displays to find him. He was shining his lamp on an impossibly large snake skin that reached away into the darkness.

"I don't even want to imagine the size of the snake that wore this," said Tyne. "It must have been two feet thick. Or more."

Fergal looked puzzled. "All these animals are in pairs," he said, "and their full bodies are here. Where are the dead snakes?"

"Perhaps this was all they could retrieve," said Osric.

"Perhaps," said Fergal, "but it's unlike the Gellerac. They dearly loved symmetry."

"There's a draft," said Merter. "There must be another opening on the far side." He moved off to investigate.

Aedan took another direction. He was set on finding something more impressive. He walked as fast as he could, ignoring the bones that filled the ten-foot shelves around him. More boring little bones. What he needed ...

As he turned the corner, a pair of immense eyes glared down at him. He fell to a crouch and almost dropped his lamp, barely managing to stifle a yell of fright.

The animal's head was something that not even Osric's arms could have encircled. It had a body the size of a prize bull's and half that again. Lips were pulled back in a snarl, revealing canines longer than butchers' knives. It waited, immobile.

Aedan rose slowly from his crouch. Part of him remained convinced that this beast was as alive as he was. He stalked around to the side and relaxed a little now that he was no longer under those jaws. This animal was well preserved. It had the features and lines of a fox, but the monster that stood in front of him could not have been called by that name. A more careful inspection showed him that the proportions were different – the chest deeper, shoulders wider, jaws heavier and eyes narrower. It was an enormously powerful-looking creature.

It was not just power though. Something else lurked in that expression, even though the features were lifeless and the eyes had been replaced with translucent stones. It wasn't the first time he had seen it in this museum. Could it be … intelligence?

His light reflected off something behind the animal and its mate. He walked around and held up the lamp. It revealed a fully assembled skeleton of ancient bones still encrusted with clinging rock. He knew nothing against which he could compare the creature, except perhaps a house. Whatever it had been, it had been big. Those jaws could have accommodated both foxes. His imagination took hold and he found his thoughts drifting, painting scenes from an age when such beasts walked the land. An expression of growing wonder crossed his face as he stared up at the skeleton before him and looked back into a forgotten past.

A muffled shriek interrupted him. He spun around to see Tyne with a hand to her mouth, staring up at the fox, and Osric grinning beside her.

Aedan turned back to the skeleton and decided to get closer. He had to step around a long line of crates loaded with empty sacks. The sacks had crumbled over the centuries and produced a shower of fine dust beneath and around them. That and the gloom almost caused Aedan to miss and trip over the object at his feet, but the light caught it just in time.

"Here's something the girls will like," he laughed. "Ever seen a giant frog?"

Tyne and Osric approached.

"It's a bit dark and grimy down there," said Tyne. "Pick it up and put it on one of these crates so we can brush it off and get a decent look."

Aedan had not expected such an enthusiastic response. He bent to the job with a will. Big frogs were irresistible, always had been, and this one looked like it would have ignored flies and lived on ducks. He worked his fingers under the body and lifted, tensing and shaking with the strain. The smooth-skinned body escaped his grip and dropped the half inch he had been able to raise it. Aedan fell over and sat hard on the dusty floor. "It must be made of lead," he said. "It's as heavy –"

The frog's eyes opened, and Aedan realised in one horrible instant that this was no frog. Each lemon-sized eye covered a large section of what he had assumed to be a body. But it was not a body, it was only a head. He suddenly guessed the meaning of the shed snakeskin.

A strong hand grasped his collar and pulled him to his feet.

"Everybody out, now," Osric barked. "Back to the stairs. Don't run."

Nobody disobeyed when the general gave a flat order. Aedan glimpsed lights moving from various points in the chamber.

Ahead of him, Fergal dropped the beetle he had been inspecting and hurried towards the door. On the way through the archive room, however, he did manage to pocket a hasty handful of tablets before being ushered up the stairs.

"What is it?" he asked.

The word "snake" was enough to give wings to his flight. Aedan chanced a backward look before leaving the room but saw nothing. He knew, though, that they might need all the distance they could put between themselves and that serpent. Osric led the way, lamp in one hand, sword in the other. Aedan waited until second-last and Merter brought up the rear, climbing the stairs with a sword pointing behind him.

Contrary to traditional design, these stairs rose anti-clockwise, giving the right-handed swordsman the advantage on the way up, presumably because the archive had been considered the more difficult chamber to infiltrate, and attack from above more likely.

And so it turned out.

Aedan had climbed about half way when there was shouting, the clash of metal, and screams of pain. A sword, still attached to a hand, came sliding down the stairs. Aedan recognised the weapon; it was the standard army issue – a three foot double-edged blade and a single-handed grip with a short, straight guard. Clearly too short. After a brief halt they resumed the upward rush.

The clash of steel rose again as Aedan burst from the stairs into the council room where he saw Osric pushing back three of the soldiers who had deserted during the previous night. They kept their distance before Osric's huge sword. Aedan noticed that one of them held the jewelled crown. A fourth soldier stood behind them cursing and clutching his shortened arm that now ended in a bloody stump.

"Surprised to see us?" said the young, confident soldier who held the crown. "Place didn't look so bad in daylight. When we saw how you got in, we decided to collect our share of the loot. You would be fools to get in our way."

Osric stepped aside and pointed. "Down the stairs," he said. "You are welcome to all that you find down there."

The soldiers eyed him.

"So you think *me* a fool, old man?" said the wild-eyed youngster. "I can smell the trap in your breath. One of you is coming with us so we don't get locked down there."

"We are leaving *now!*" said Osric, moving away from the stairway entrance and leading the group around the side of the large central table, but the soldiers ran around the other side and placed themselves in the doorway, blocking the escape.

"We saw the wolf get hold of you, General," the young soldier said. "We know you won't last in a fight. The boy is a coward who shrinks like a beaten dog and the girl's a featherweight. Looks like the odds are in our favour. Your ranger isn't even interested. All we require is an escort. Then we go our own way."

Merter was indeed distracted. He was looking out the window, holding the edges and creeping along as if following some movement and staying just out of sight.

"We have made too much noise," he said. He spoke quietly but the chill in his voice hushed everyone.

That was when Aedan heard a sound he remembered well, a deep scraping, like the pouring of sand.

"What is it?" Osric asked, keeping his eyes on the soldiers.

"Only saw a shadow," Merter replied, his voice rasping with strange emotion, "but it was big. Close the door."

It was not the ranger captain's rank that caused the soldiers to obey; it was the paleness of his face. They swung the big iron doors of the main entrance closed, one of them scraping along the tiled floor with a shrill whine, and dropped an iron cross-beam into the brackets. All the surfaces were rusted, but the metal was thick enough to still possess formidable strength.

Osric and Merter ran back to the stairwell they had just climbed. They raised the door they had smashed down earlier, leaning it back into its frame. It would not stop anything, but it would give warning if moved.

"Spread out along the wall," Osric said, striding to a position in the middle of the wall between the doors. "Multiple angles."

Aedan pulled two solid bronze spears from their mountings and, despite what Osric had said about spreading out, crouched beside Liru.

The young soldier did not like how he was losing control of the situation. "Are you putting on a little show for us?" he asked. "Trying to get us distracted?"

Thump.

He turned around and looked at the braced double door of the main entrance.

Thump.

"Rork, is that you?" he called.

No reply.

He leaned against the door with a mocking smile. "This thing is solid iron. You can knock all you want but unless you tell me – "

Crash!

The young soldier flew across the room and collided with the table, breaking two of the decayed legs and collapsing in a heap of dust and splinters. The crown he had been holding slipped from his grasp, tumbled along the ground and disappeared through a gap in the smaller doorframe. They could hear it bouncing down the stairwell to the archive room.

The soldier was too dizzy to notice the crown's disappearance. He raised himself on his elbows and looked back. The iron door was dented in.

Aedan could not understand how any creature could have done this, even to corroded iron.

There was another crash. The door dented further and a hinge burst from the wall. The soldiers began to move away. Their young leader scrambled from the pile of timber and staggered to his feet.

The next impact thrust one of the doors across the room and swung the other inward to collide against the wall with a shattering of rock and plaster.

The dust concealed whatever it was that now filled the opening. Before the air cleared, there was a scream and an explosive hiss. A jet of dark, sticky vapour swelled into a black cloud, foul as carrion, flooding the room with night.

Chapter 53

In the sudden darkness, only dim, misty shapes told the whereabouts of people. Something impossibly large filled the doorway, and it began to move forward. At first Aedan thought the snake had escaped through the hole at the back of the museum in order to meet them head on, but size ruled this out. The creature before them was something on a different scale altogether.

A yellow eye as big as a shield appeared through a narrow break in the fog. The ink-black pupil flicked around the room, showing a precision that took in every occupant. That enormous eye, full of deep cunning, reduced a warrior to a mouse, nothing more.

An outline revealed the young soldier standing in the middle of the room. He produced a soft, shaking moan and turned to run. In near silence, the colossal shadowy form moved with horrifying speed. There was a crunch of jaws snapping shut and a swirling of clouds as the shape glided back to the doorway. Through the rift, they saw an arm projecting from a lipless jawline, twitching slightly as the creature sank into the mist again, leaving no one any the wiser as to what it was. Aedan, beneath his horror, had a vague impression that only part of its body was in the room. Yet what was in the room was surely bigger than any animal he had ever seen.

One of the other troopers on the far side of the room crawled up against the wall and the shadows near him thickened.

It was then that Culver saw his chance. Ignoring Osric's instruction to remain still, he jumped up into the window behind him. The wall was deep and the window presented a temporary refuge.

Had the shutter frame held together, he might have made it, but the wood cracked, his weight pulled him away, and he swung back into the room. Before he could recover, something in the mist had changed. A silent darkness rushed towards him and his final scream was cut short with a sickening crunch.

Culver was no more.

Liru hid her face. She should not have done so. The movement betrayed her presence, and the shadows darkened in front of her.

Aedan, crouching alongside, slowly raised the two spears between them, grounding the shafts in the corner between floor and wall. The weapons rattled in his hands, but he kept them pointing to where the mist looked most solid.

From hidden nostrils, the beast's breath drew and pushed over them, cold and vile as poison.

Air blowing in from the windows thinned the black fog slightly, revealing those crouched on the near side of the room, and a great glowing eye hanging in the air, the pupil studying Aedan and Liru.

Barely moving from his crouched position against the wall, Osric threw a spear. But the beast turned its head at the motion, and the spear that should have plunged into its eye must have struck hard skin. They all heard it clatter to the ground.

The eye vanished, but like a trap released, the black shadows bolted towards Osric, a movement that might have crushed every bone and smeared him against the opposite wall, but he ducked just enough to escape the full weight. Still, it knocked him to the ground, and he skidded over the floor to the far wall where he lay in a heap of broken wood. Tyne cried out and moved impulsively to help him. Again, it drew the beast.

She froze, but it was too late. This time Aedan saw a corner of the jaws – they held teeth the size of tusks. The lower jaw dropped, shivering, as if muscles were bunching.

"No," he whispered, "Not Tyne. Please not Tyne."

There was a roar of fury and Aedan glanced up just in time to see Osric on his feet again, tearing a huge double-bladed axe from the wall.

Osric was not one to repeat a mistake. This time he waited for the head to turn. Then he hurled the axe with enough force to smash through a wall, and this time it must have struck the large eye square on. The reaction was volcanic.

There was another hissing scream that caused everyone to slam their hands against their ears and cringe. The air was filled anew with black mist as the entire room was shaken by a series of wild collisions. It was as if a giant had taken hold of a tree trunk, thrust it into the room and begun smashing blindly. Chips of wood and stone flew about, tinkling like hail.

The beast's power was staggering. Had they not been tucked into the corners, every person would have been crushed.

The hissing and thumping that shook the ground gradually receded. When the air cleared, the smell remained. Everything was coated in slime. The table had been reduced to chips and powder, statues and ornaments were toppled and shattered, and huge stones had been wrenched from the mortar around the doorway as if they were no more than pebbles in mud. The entrance had been doubled in size.

They got to their feet, rubbing their eyes and swaying. Osric remained on the ground. He looked only barely conscious. He had not quite escaped the thrashings.

Merter called for silence.

Everyone listened.

The retreating sounds were still fading, then they ended abruptly. It was just a hint, but it was unmistakable – a distant clatter, much like what might be produced by an axe falling on tiles.

Merter ran to the window and thrust his head out. "Nothing," he said. "It's still in the building."

A deep scraping rush echoed up from the enlarged entrance.

"Back to the archive room!" Merter shouted. "Down the stairwell. Go, go, go!"

He and Tyne grabbed Osric by the arms and dragged his heavy body across the floor to the narrow stairwell opening across the room from the main entrance. This time the soldiers understood all too well and dashed ahead. Aedan and Fergal brought up the rear, spears pointed backwards, tips shuddering.

As they turned towards the arched stone doorway, the light in the room behind them darkened. Aedan pushed Fergal through and dived after him as something struck against the frame, releasing a cloud of dust. Clearly, the beast's head was too large to pass through, but the next instant heavy stones were falling all around Aedan, one bruising his thigh and another narrowly missing his head. With a shout of pain, he twisted around and stared at the monstrous shape moving through the billows of dust, striking, twisting, plunging, only inches from his boots. It was actually digging through the stone wall, enlarging the entrance.

He scrambled to his feet and tried to leap down the stairs, but something held him fast. Spinning around, he saw that part of his cloak had been trapped under a large rock. He knew he should unhook the cloak, but before he could do so, the frame shuddered and this time something living brushed his shoulder. It drove him to a panic. He pulled and strained to tear the cloak free, half shouting, half crying, as he imagined the beast gathering for another lunge.

A hand grasped his arm and pulled. The cloak tore off at the clasp, and he and Fergal lurched forward, tumbling down several stairs ahead of a terrific explosion of stone and dust.

Fergal pulled him to his feet and they edged down into the blackness of the stairwell – all torches having been lost above. They soon caught up with the others.

"There's another way out of the archive room," Fergal shouted over the hammering of falling rock. "Don't wait here. When the boulders start to roll down the stairs, they won't stop until they reach the bottom."

They continued on through the darkness, increasing the pace when a load of apple-sized rocks came tumbling past, striking against legs and ankles.

"Hurry," said Fergal, as an ominous pounding began to fill the space. "How far are we Merter?"

"About half way."

The thumping behind them grew with every bound – it could only be a falling boulder.

"We're not going to make it," Fergal shouted. "Everyone press up against the inside wall."

There was no time for explanations. Aedan did as he was told.

It was no longer thumping but smashing its way down the stairs towards them. A boulder large enough to do that could kill them all. Aedan turned his face away and held his breath. There was a shuddering impact just to the side and something rushed past his head, the wind pulling at his hair; then a scrape and a grunt of pain below him, a few more collisions, a scream, and the sound faded.

"Fergal?" he asked.

"Just a scratch," Fergal said, then raised his voice, "Who was hurt?"

"One of the soldiers," Merter's voice echoed up. "Sounds like a broken arm."

There was no need for further instructions. They were moving again, as fast as the darkness would allow. After a few steps, Aedan missed his footing and stumbled forward, striking the outer wall. He realised that the falling boulder must have made some large cavities in the stairs.

The sounds of digging had grown muffled, but it was obvious that the creature's efforts had not diminished in the least. Soon, the echoes of heavy tumbling objects reached them again. This time it sounded like there were many boulders.

"How far, Merter?" Fergal called.

"We're here."

Fergal and Aedan took the last few stairs as the light grew, then they stumbled into the archive room still bright with oil lamps.

"Move!" Fergal shouted. "Away from the door."

He pulled Aedan and Liru to the side and the others darted out of the way as three rocks, one almost as high as a man's waist, rushed through the opening, smashing into the shelves on the far side of the room.

The soldiers were too shaken to speak, and they stared, trembling. Even the injuries were ignored. Nobody looked for the crown which would be somewhere under the rubble.

Merter and Aedan had their eyes on the cavernous museum door on the far side of the chamber, but the snake had not emerged.

"What *was* that thing up there?" Tyne asked, her voice shrill.

Nobody knew.

Fergal hurried away. "There are five alcoves in this wall," he said. "In one of them a hidden exit was planned, but I don't know if it was completed. Perhaps it is concealed by a shelf, or worked into the floor. I'll take the one nearest the museum, the rest of you take the others. Merter, please keep an eye on the museum. There's no telling where the snake could be now."

Aedan entered an alcove and Liru took the one alongside. He began by pulling a large rug off the floor and inspecting the paving stones for any kind of groove that might indicate a trapdoor, but the grouting between blocks was solid.

Boulders continued to tumble down the stairs. He suspected that eventually that giant beast would be able to dig its way to them. He also knew that if the snake had not been properly roused earlier, this din was likely to finish the job.

He tried to concentrate. The walls were next, but packed shelves covered them. He began clearing, placing the armloads of tablets on the floor as gently as his haste would allow. From one of the other alcoves there was a tinkling crash of shattering clay. Someone, clearly, had decided that it was time for sacrifices to be made. Aedan stepped back and looked over. It was Tyne.

"Nothing here," she said, and marched into another alcove.

Fergal's indignant face showed itself briefly.

"Here," called Liru. "I think I have it."

Aedan dropped the tablets he was holding with a clatter and darted across, the others close behind. Liru was pointing to a brass lever.

"Wait! Don't touch it yet," Fergal cried, pounding into the alcove. He looked at the lever and darted from wall to wall, examining the joins. When he noticed the steel bars in the corners he nodded.

"Well?" said Tyne, her impatience in no way concealed. "Are we going to open this door or not?"

"It's not a door," Fergal replied. "Everyone, collect your lamps and get in here."

Osric was conscious but stunned, and had to be supported. It was only the soldiers who hung back with distrustful expressions.

"Suit yourselves," Fergal said, and pulled the lever.

Nothing happened.

"You're right," said Tyne. "Definitely not a door. I'm going to try another alcove."

"Patience, dear. Counterweights can have delays."

"Well right now, a delay –"

The floor shuddered and dropped, causing everyone to reach out for a support. The walls began to slide up behind the standing shelves, as the ground beneath them sank. In front of them, the floor of the archive room rose, slowly closing off the entrance.

The soldiers were still watching from the archive room. Something caused all three to look towards the museum. As if stung, they spun away and shot across the floor, screaming, fighting each other to get ahead. They dived through the shrinking gap between the archive floor and the ceiling of the cubicle, tumbling onto the heads and shoulders of the rest of the party. One landed on Osric. Tyne gripped his collar and flung him off none too gently. But neither he nor the other two had eyes for anything other than the disappearing entrance.

Then they were enclosed. It was rock on all sides.

"Fergal," Tyne said, "Is this cubicle hanging from chains?"

"Most likely."

"But they would be made of iron or steel, and everything iron in this place is rusted ..."

"Rust works its way in from the outer surface. As with the main door of the archive room, heavy chain links will still have a good deal of strength in the core."

"Are you sure about that?"

Fergal shifted. He was about to reply when there was a sharp clink of metal above them. The floor trembled and brought all conversation to an end. Everyone was holding onto something.

Another opening appeared where the first had been, dark and cold, rising up from the ground until it swallowed the entire wall. For a long time they descended in breathless silence until a rocky floor reached the level of their feet. They all lost their balance as the moving platform jolted and came to rest with a cavernous boom that echoed out around them as if they were in the belly of a mountain – and perhaps they were.

They had been carried deep under Kultûhm, into a place they hadn't known existed.

Fergal led the way onto a landing. The others followed, holding the oil lamps out, shielding their eyes and peering into the darkness beyond.

The cubicle that had lowered them was enclosed on three sides by a hollowed stone pillar. Above the ceiling of this moving cubicle, they could now see the four steel bars were fastened to chains that reached far up beyond the glow of their lamps. Aedan guessed that they ran over a giant pulley and attached to a counterweight somewhere, but was at a loss as to how it all worked. He wondered why the platform had not shot up like a startled pheasant the moment they stepped off, but then realised a simple latch would solve that problem.

As his eyes adjusted, he saw a number of carriage-sized stone blocks all around. It looked as if they had been intended as counterweights, with chains and braces lying nearby. The skill in engineering that these people had possessed was like nothing he had ever seen in Castath, and all of this had been built almost a thousand years ago.

The sound of running water drew his attention to a channel nearby. Beside it was a deep pit, and beyond that the stark white curves of a partly assembled skeleton. It was even bigger than the specimen he had seen in the museum, and altogether different in form. It looked like it had been some type of giant lizard – flat, broad and ugly. The teeth were almost as long as he was tall. Looking at it gave him an icy feeling.

"Where are we?" Tyne asked.

Fergal looked around at the hulking shapes of unfinished stone machines, the tools, the aged bones, the channels of dark water, and the great pillars of rock that stood around them like the legs of titans and reached far up to a roof only betrayed by faint, jagged contours.

"I have never learned of this place," he said. "I doubt that any living man has. If the cavity was natural to begin with, it has been vastly altered – those abandoned tools suggest that much work was still in progress."

"Fergal, please," Tyne interrupted, glancing up from Osric who was breathing hard and shivering, "that might be interesting but –"

"Which means that there is bound to be a workers' exit."

"Can't we just use another one of these moving platforms – they do go up, don't they?"

"It looks, I'm afraid to say, that they don't go anywhere. As far as the light reveals, ours seems to be the only one that was finished. We will, most probably, have to walk out, but first we need to get our bearings."

"With what reference? Not even Merter could have kept a bearing down that stairwell."

Fergal picked up a discarded rib the size of a spear and began to draw in a dusty bowl. "The archive room had a door in the wall that would be opposite us if we were to look out from our alcove. It was the door we tried on our way in, about here." He drew a line. "And at that time we were walking west I believe. Merter?"

"A point to the north perhaps, but I'd settle for west."

Using that as a reference, Fergal drew in the compass lines, and beside it, a rough layout of the city.

"These blocks" – he indicated the pale shapes around them – "which I presume to be ballast blocks, are limestone, not found in a cavern of granite. It means that there has to be a large access point for this cave on one of the main city arteries, but not too near the city gate where a build-up would cause problems."

That reminded Aedan of something. "There *was* a trapdoor in the ground near the main gate," he said. "We saw it the first time we passed through."

"Troop tunnel," said Fergal. "Allowed soldiers to reach the gate quickly from the barracks. It wouldn't lead down here. The four regions in the city that have both the broad roads and space required for a mining and construction entrance are the palace, the barracks, the area beneath the market, and the south quarter." He indicated each on his rough map. "The palace is not an option for a workers' entrance. The barracks are here." He thought for a while. "I'm going to rule that out because of the Gellerac love of military efficiency – queues of miners would interfere with smooth deployment. That leaves the market and south quarter." He fell silent again.

"Wouldn't the market be too cluttered for big loads of stone?" asked Tyne.

Fergal looked at her, or at a point somewhere beyond her, and absently twisted his fingers in his beard.

"Fergal?"

"In Castalh, that would be the logical conclusion, but the Gellerac had a culture of social elitism that is difficult for us to grasp. The southern suburbs had wide streets because that was where the wealthy settled. Whoever commissioned this entrance would have had to choose between the congestion near the market and the outrage of the wealthy. I think … yes, I think I'm going to go with the market."

"You don't sound convinced."

"Quite true, Tyne, quite true."

"Well what if you're wrong?"

"Then I will be convinced it was the other way. Now …" he said, pointing back to his map, "we are currently here, except that we are a few hundred feet beneath the surface. My map, I'm sure you will appreciate, cannot represent that dimension. Which means that our most hopeful bearing would be that way." He pointed out into the darkness, roughly in line with the grinning lizard skeleton. "Osric, are you able to walk?"

"Of course!" Osric pushed himself to his feet, took a step, and crashed into the ground like a felled pine.

"We'll get him there," said Tyne. "Merter and I can manage."

"Wouldn't it be better if I –"

"No, Fergal. I am more than strong enough, and your place is with directions."

Aedan turned to Liru and lowered his voice. "Can't argue about her being strong enough, but I think what she really means by the second part is that *her* place is with Osric."

"So you've noticed too," said Liru.

"I think even the horses noticed."

Liru's typical smiles were subtle twitches that were hard to spot in broad daylight. Where she stood in shadow, she was all but invisible. Aedan wondered if there would be brightening of her expression now. It wasn't likely, considering what they had just witnessed in the council room, but it made him realise how long it had been since she had smiled at him.

He took his place in the line that formed and moved out. Maintaining a bearing was imperative, so they were careful to fix a line through three points at any given time and, when they reached the first, to pick another at the edge of their lamp range.

As they walked, they passed more of the giant counterweighted machines, some using levers like oversized seesaws, others chains, some having a part of the mechanism reaching up to the rocky ceiling, but none ready for use. There were many bridged walkways allowing passage over the channels. These channels were beginning to look like veins the way they distributed the water so evenly.

Tools – picks, shovels, chisels, sledgehammers and numerous contraptions Aedan could not identify – were lying where they had been dropped. Carts were abandoned, their stone payloads lying beneath them in neat piles where they had fallen through the corroded trays. There were three more towering skeletons and many bones still embedded in rock, but no human remains, suggesting that the cave had been successfully evacuated.

Apart from the gurgle of water, an occasional scuff of a boot on the rocky floor or the unintentional kicking of a pebble that skittered away into darkness, the cave was silent. Yet it had a sound, or at least a feeling of great depth that whispered through the emptiness.

Then the skeletons began to grow more numerous, and this time they were human. There were many, and they were all laid out in rows, occasionally overlapping. It was a peculiar arrangement, and Aedan wondered if it had to do with some Gellerac superstition. Could this be their cemetery?

"Fergal," he called. "Why were they placed like this?"

Fergal stopped and turned. He did not answer immediately, and when he did, his voice was raw.

"They weren't placed in the sense that you are thinking. These skeletons are lined up because the dung in which they were encased has decomposed." All eyes were drawn across a pale graveyard. "Kultûhm," he said, "was abandoned, but a great many did not escape."

The air no longer seemed as clean as it had. As they walked on, Aedan found his breathing becoming shallow. It was not just the *sense* of contamination. There really was something in the air that was not right.

Finally, one of the soldiers blurted out, "What is that smell?"

"Probably bats," said Tyne. "Stop breathing and it will go away." Aedan was close enough to hear her mumble, "And so will you."

Fergal again drew to a halt and everyone stopped.

"What is it?" Merter asked from under Osric's shoulder.

"I think you'd better take a look."

After setting Osric down, Merter walked to where Fergal stood. Aedan, of course, was already there.

"They look like the tree trunks we saw in the streets ..." Merter froze. "Oh no!" he whispered.

Fergal raised his lamp and Aedan did likewise. Ahead of them stretched acres of what they now understood to be tree-sized droppings, fresh droppings.

"It was what I was worried about," said Fergal. "Where else would something that big make its lair?"

Chapter 54

High up in the round tower, choking clouds swirled in the breeze. From shutterless windows, rusty afternoon light spilled across the council room, illuminating the haze and creating thick bars of curling gold. A stone shifted and then dropped, releasing another small cloud into the air.

The dust did not settle quickly, but when it did, it revealed a room that was vastly changed. Where the narrow opening to the stairwell had been, there was now what could only be described as a colossal burrow. This tunnel reached down almost fifty feet before it was utterly clogged with rocks and crumbled mortar.

Another stone came loose and bounded into the void.

The sound was hollow.

From high in the air, a richly coloured mountain barbet dropped onto the windowsill in a flurry of deep ochres and hazy blues. He was a young bird. As he cast a plucky eye over the strange shapes surrounding him, he decided he was impressed – no – satisfied with his discovery. After a few more glances here and there, he settled and began to preen himself. Between every few draws of his beak he would tilt his head to the side and babble to himself of his own growing finery and of the magnificence of his new roost. And it *was* his.

For nowhere in the building behind him or in the city beneath was there another creature to be seen.

Far below, deep in the earth, Tyne, Merter and Osric were all heaving for breath, but none called for a slackening of pace as they ran. The foul stench had passed but the memory had not. If anything, the dread had grown. Their heads turned constantly, but the only breaks to the monotony of the cave floor were the many water channels. The ground fell away slightly and the lights of their oil lamps revealed a glistening surface, dark as slate but smoother.

"Oh – water," said Fergal, stumbling to a halt in front of a wide, dark lake. "So still it almost caught me out, or in."

"Bridge to the left," said Merter.

"I don't see it."

"Trust me, Fergal. It's there."

They ran along the side to the left, and after a while, the lines of a stone bridge emerged.

"How did you see it from that far away?" Tyne demanded.

"Peripheral vision. Better perception in darkness when not looking directly –"

"Yes, yes, I know all that. But I saw nothing, I'm convinced there is a cat hiding somewhere up in your family tree."

The bridge was long and wide, spanning a body of water that was a few hundred yards across and could have been anywhere between a foot and a mile deep.

When they reached the land on the other side, they passed a cart that still held its load – and it sparkled. This time Aedan ignored it and ran on. He didn't want another confrontation with Liru. The soldiers, however, lingered, and when they caught up, their pockets were bulging. The flaps of their coats were down and nothing showed, but they were unable to conceal the glittering that escaped from their eyes.

The ground began to rise again, more steeply now. It was too much for the staggering Osric and his bearers.

"We can't slow down for them," one of the soldiers said, his voice raspy and dry.

"Good point," said Fergal. "Why don't you three run along, and we'll catch up?"

Nobody ran on. They all knew that Fergal was the only one capable of finding a way out.

"It's time we took charge here," the soldier announced, reaching for his sword. But Merter slipped across like a shadow and had his knife at the man's throat before the sword was halfway drawn.

Aedan stared. He had never seen anyone move that fast.

"Want to play?" Merter growled.

The soldier raised his hands slowly. Merter took the sword, handing it to Tyne; then in another catlike burst, he knocked the man back and snatched the weapons from his two injured comrades before they were able to mount any resistance.

"Osric," Merter said. "May I kill them?"

When the general spoke, he sounded tired and his teeth were clearly gritted against tremendous pain. "It would probably be justice, but the procedure for punishing their crimes is a little more involved. My conscience could not accept such executions, though a part of me wishes you hadn't troubled yourself to ask."

Merter's knife hovered. Everyone held their breaths and stared. Slowly, the blade descended, but it was not re-sheathed. Merter tucked it against his forearm and carried it there as they resumed the climb. The confiscated weapons were left and forgotten, but the tension was not, and it held a keener edge than any of the abandoned steel.

They had climbed only a hundred feet when Merter pointed.

"Could that be a way out?" he asked.

It was still hidden in darkness, but as they approached, the light revealed a towering wooden structure that rose to the height of the ceiling that was now only just discernible three hundred feet or more above them. The wooden beams were thick, and though they had suffered from the passage of time, they retained enough strength to hold together.

"I don't think it's a way out," said Fergal. "There's only one other thing it can be, and one way to be sure. Hide your lamps under your cloaks for a moment; try not to set yourselves alight."

They did as they were told.

"Can you see it? Above the tower?"

Aedan peered up into the darkness. The faintest point of light reflected back at them, though there was nothing to reflect.

"Looks like a sliver of daylight," said Merter.

It faded.

"Daylight would have remained," Fergal explained. "This tower was built to retrieve an earthstar. The gems absorb and radiate light for a short time. That's how the Gellerac discovered them, and entirely by accident."

"Why didn't they take it?" Aedan asked. "The tower seems to be right there?"

"It was always an official ceremony. One of many things that I imagine were interrupted. Let us be gone."

They continued up the steep slope, but a noise from behind drew Aedan's attention. He turned and stared. The uninjured soldier had remained at the tower. He was already thirty feet up the ladder, lamp swinging.

"Look," Aedan called. "He's going for the earthstar."

They stopped and faced around.

"Don't shout," said Fergal. "We can't risk the noise. He has made his choice."

They turned and left the lone soldier rising into the inky darkness behind them.

The cave narrowed and looked as if it was about to split.

Merter stopped. "Quiet," he said.

The party drew to a halt. Aedan tried to still his breathing.

"What was it?" Fergal whispered after a while.

"I thought I heard a fall of stones. It sounded far off, a long way behind the wooden scaffolding."

The sudden pounding of blood in Aedan's ears made it difficult to hear anything else.

"Put out all the lamps but Fergal's," Merter whispered.

The darkness swamped in on them.

"Now be careful with your feet. Lift them high so you don't kick a stone. Fergal, lead on."

They reached the split. There were abandoned tools and mounds of broken rock on both sides. Fergal stood in silence, looking one way then the other.

"Merter," he whispered, "What do you see?"

After a brief pause the ranger captain replied. "Left, I can see lots of edged objects, maybe tools in racks, right nothing. I think –"

This time there was no need for him to call for silence. They all heard it, a deep wash of parting water. They spun around. The lake was hidden in darkness, but the climbing soldier was a starry beacon.

Aedan hoped the climber would be seen first. He was too frightened to even recognise the selfishness of the thought. He hurried after Fergal, almost pushing him in his haste.

They took the left split, and sure enough, Fergal's pale lamplight fell on rows of shelves, part-filled with mining and construction tools. Aedan realised that it would be logical for this to be located near a main entrance. The cave narrowed further.

The ceiling dropped until it was less than a hundred feet above them.

They passed a large metal cage, jumped a water channel and stopped before a deep rectangular pit. The lamp revealed skeletons strewn across its floor, but unlike the other skeletons, these were crushed, absolutely flattened as if they had been painstakingly hammered until no ridge or mound projected upward above half an inch.

Beyond the pit was a solid rock wall.

A horrible realisation took hold of Aedan. Fergal had been wrong.

For all his brilliance, he had brought them to a dead end.

A faraway shriek of terror caused the whole party to turn back as one. In the distance, they could still see the soldier on the ladder. He was more than half way up, but something was amiss. The lamp had fallen, burst open on the beams and set the wood alight.

"Clumsy fool," Tyne muttered.

"I don't think it was clumsiness," said Merter quietly. "Watch the tower."

As the soldier clung to the ladder and managed to get his dangling feet back onto the rungs, the entire structure shook and he was nearly flung into the air. With one desperate hand he managed to retain his hold. This time he wound his arms and legs around the beams like a frightened toddler clinging to his father's leg. The flames spread quickly through the dust-dry timber. Something big shifted beneath the tower, a shadow it seemed, but it did not waver with the flames as a shadow would have done.

A crack of splitting beams echoed through the cave. The tower shuddered and leaned. Sounds of rippling fire travelled across the space, fire that cast its glare over the lake that now shimmered with countless reflections. An arching pillar of smoke stood up from the ground, weaving and leaning, but then Aedan realised that the fire had not yet reached the ground.

It could not be smoke.

He heard someone whimper nearby as all began to grasp the full size and form of the beast in whose lair they were trapped.

It had the long supple lines of a serpent, but the impossible size of a mythical dragon, and its shape was different too – broader, more lizard like, and far more powerful. The hide was an armour of scales black as midnight, interrupted only on the underside by a pattern of sickly off-white bands that looked almost like a host of grasping arms. The monster reared over a hundred feet into the air, and that was probably less than half its body.

Instead of trying to think of some way out, Aedan stared, transfixed by the sight before him, the lurid terror holding him in a vice.

Flames reached the soldier and his screams tore through the air. The dark pillar rose up behind him, no longer hidden in shadow, bright flames reflecting off its metallic hide. The soldier drew himself up, set his feet on a rung and leapt away from the inferno. He did not travel far. The animal's lunge was precise, the speed blinding, and the soldier's scream was cut off.

There was more than one breath of horror.

Aedan turned to Fergal. But Fergal was not to be seen. The light from the burning tower had rendered his lamp unnecessary, and he had moved off without anyone noticing. Aedan started back towards the cage they had passed earlier. He saw Fergal standing in the shadow, staring at a puddle of water that had formed beneath a leak above him, twirling his beard.

"Fergal?"

"Bring the others over will you, Aedan."

Aedan's mind was spinning, so he made no attempt to reason, simply ran back and passed on the message. When they arrived, Fergal ordered everyone into the cage.

"It won't work," Tyne objected, "That thing will tear through this cage like it's made of straw."

Fergal ignored her. He was pulling on a rusted chain nearby, producing some shrill screechings above him. Aedan cringed and spun to look behind him, searching the area around the fire which was now a tumbling inferno lighting the cave for half a mile in each direction and glaring off a thousand sparkling surfaces. But there was no sign of movement.

Or was there?

A ridge of dark rock stood between them and the blaze. Aedan didn't remember that ridge.

"Fergal," he called in a trembling voice. "Fergal, hurry!"

Fergal released the chain, stepped into the cage and closed the barred door with another shriek of metal. Aedan winced.

"We're in a trap," Tyne whispered. "Why are we here?"

"Patience, Tyne," Fergal said. "Nothing more we can do, and panic won't aid our cause. Like I said, counterweights can take time."

A reverberating thunder filled the air as the tower split and began to collapse. Flame-wreathed timbers hurtled to ground with a slowness conjured by distance until they plunged into the growing hill of coals.

Something snatched Aedan's attention away. There was a clatter of chains above, a violent lurch that had everyone staggering to regain their balance, and the cage lifted and began to rise into the air.

"How did you work it out?" Aedan managed, trying to mask his terror with interest.

"It was the pit with those crushed skeletons that gave it away," said Fergal. "That's where the counterweight comes to rest. The dripping water was the clue to explaining the water channels – weight equalisation. The chain I pulled must open a sluice in a channel above the cave. Water rushes into what I presume is a hollowed out limestone block until its weight is greater than ours, and we begin to rise."

Aedan was pretending to listen while his eyes searched the ground below.

Fergal continued, "The movement probably causes the sluice to close so we don't accelerate as we rise. At the top there is likely to be another set of chains to adjust the water-level in the ballast block according to the load going down. Simple, but most good designs are."

Aedan realised Fergal had stopped talking. He didn't want to reveal that he had missed every point, so he asked, "How were you able to think that out while the soldier was trying to escape?"

"I could not bear watching again. I had to turn my thoughts elsewhere."

"Fergal," said Merter, "I think silence would be wise. Look."

At first Aedan didn't see what Merter was referring to. The Fire still raged in the distance. Though the light was glaring, the dark rock and undulating surfaces still hid much in shadow. There was the lake, its waters beginning to settle, the rows of carved stone columns – a motionless army – and the dark cave floor, slate-like in the shadows. Apart from that pronounced ridge about half way along, there were no distinct features.

Then the ridge shifted.

The simultaneous flinching of every occupant caused the cage to sway and creak. Aedan looked up and wondered how deeply the rust had sunk into those chains.

He looked back. The ridge was gone.

They were now a good fifty feet in the air, and an arch of the cave ceiling began to obscure the view. The steel floor blocked the lower angle. After a few more feet they were no longer able to see anything beneath them.

"Weapons out," Osric wheezed.

Aedan understood, though he had no illusions of matching Osric's throw. The look of calculation he had seen in those yellow eyes had convinced him that such a trick could not be repeated.

They readied themselves, blades pointing out through the bars like the spines of a hedgehog, but this was an unhappily plucked hedgehog. With the soldiers disarmed and Osric unable to rise from the ground, the defence did not look reassuring.

Chains clinked and creaked. The counterweight appeared from above, passed them not far to the side and dropped away at a speed equal to their ascent. Aedan was able to glimpse the pool of water in its hollowed out centre before it disappeared from view.

With the fire light cut off, they rose into a darkness relieved only by Fergal's oil lamp. He snuffed it, and all was lost to the eye but the faintest outlines.

Creak, rattle, clink, clink, clink ...

If there was movement taking place beneath them, the growing noise of the chains masked it. Still they listened, straining their senses to the limits of that divide between the real and the imagined.

Aedan was just beginning to relax when his ears were assaulted by a hiss like the spray of a tempest. He gripped the bar in front of him just as something slammed against the base of the cage and threw it upwards. For a perilous moment, they hung in the air, the floor no longer beneath their feet, and then steel and flesh fell as one and came to a jarring halt as the chains locked taut.

But not all of them.

The cage staggered and listed over to the side as one of the ancient links broke free and the chain tumbled down onto the roof bars with a deafening clatter.

Everyone slid over the floor and came to a stop with arms and legs stuck out through the bars, wriggling, squirming to work their way back in. Aedan almost impaled himself on his sword. It slipped from his grasp, but snagged at the edge where he managed to retrieve it. Liru was less fortunate; hers flew out beyond reach and fell away.

They scrambled to their feet as best they could, braced themselves, and waited. Aedan's arm was scratched raw from the rusty metal surfaces.

The space around them constricted – more heard than seen in the darkness. Aedan caught his breath, but then guessed that the cage had entered a channel in the rock. They were nearing the exit. The angle of the cage, however, was wrong, and the edges caught on protrusions, scraping and juddering with a harsh metallic din. It was a good thing no limbs still dangled – they would have been torn off in a blink, and a scream.

The clattering did not relent until a dim light grew above them and they screeched to a halt in a large storage or loading room partly filled with stone blocks and mining equipment. Daylight, at last, poured in through windows and warehouse-sized doors.

The cage did not quite reach the level; it was still partly sunk in the channel which meant the door could only open partway. They squeezed out one at a time and climbed up onto the landing platform. Fergal and Merter remained until last.

As Fergal was stepping up, the cage shuddered and jumped several feet, launching him up in the air. Tyne and Aedan reached out and caught him as he dropped onto the edge of the platform. For a moment the three of them stood tottering. Liru darted in, gripped Fergal's cloak and pulled. It was enough to shift the balance and they staggered away from the drop.

"Hurry Merter!" Fergal shouted. "I think it's found the ballast chains."

Merter was still inside the cage. He tried the door, but it was now completely obstructed by rock.

He was trapped.

The group stared in horror as the cage lurched again. This time another chain snapped and the tilt increased. Merter grabbed hold of the bars and scaled them with wild haste. Clinging to the roof struts, he traversed until he found a bar that was partly detached at one end. He put all his weight on it and wrenched. It moved, but it would not give. He reversed his feet, lifting them and placing them against the roof to push his body downwards as he pulled on the loose bar again. His face bloomed red, veins swelled, and his whole frame shuddered with the effort, but still the bar would not yield.

Chains snapped taut again and the jolt threw Merter to the steel floor. A link burst and another chain fell slack, dipping its corner into the waiting emptiness. The cage was now beneath the level of the landing. Merter was on his feet again and up the bars, straining with frantic desperation.

"Oh," said Liru, looking away. "I can't watch this."

Aedan glanced to the side and noticed that Tyne was not there. His eye caught movement from behind and he saw her now, sprinting back from a tool rack with a sledgehammer. She rushed past them, leapt, and landed with graceful precision on a small square plate in the centre of the cage roof. Then she spun, raised the sledgehammer, and struck at the bar Merter had attempted to loosen.

The first blow glanced to the side. She gritted her teeth and swung again. This time the bar broke free and spun down onto the floor. Merter surged up through the gap and leapt onto the outer frame. He turned back, helped Tyne across and hoisted her up to waiting arms.

Then the last chain broke.

Tyne's scream was even louder than the clatter of steel as the cage, followed by the chains, dropped down the shaft, crashing from side to side as it descended. Merter, who had been standing on the cage roof, was thrown against the rock walls where he clawed in vain and fell back onto the bars.

For an instant the structure wedged in the darkness right at the very roof of the cave beneath them. Aedan felt a surge of hope, but it was snatched away. There was a creak of metal, a shrill scrape, and an eerie quiet as the iron enclosure fell away into the void.

The dread silence held them for a moment. It ended with a crash that boomed up from hollow depths.

"Could he have caught onto the rock when the cage jammed?" Aedan asked, his voice trembling.

"Merter! Merter!" Tyne screamed.

They all listened. There was no reply. Again and again they called until their throats ached, but the only sounds that reached them were the soft collapses of burning timber.

Aedan saw that Liru was crying, then he realised his own cheeks were wet.

When it was certain that Merter was lost, Fergal drew them away from the edge and helped Tyne support Osric. They hurried to the large doors and stepped out onto a broad street. Fergal glanced around, getting his bearings, then he called Aedan and pointed.

"This road bends but it will eventually take you past the palace courtyard. From there you'll recognise the way back."

"Why are you telling me this?" Aedan asked.

"You need to get word to Thormar, and you need to get Liru to safety."

"But –"

"I'll hear no argument. We will be slow, perhaps too slow. Your lingering will do us no good. In fact, the larger the group, the slimmer the hope of remaining unseen. Now go!"

Aedan set off with Liru at a run, the two injured soldiers following. They kept to the shadowed walls as much as possible, glancing around every corner before crossing roads.

Coming to a wide open space, they stopped. Something remained of a few stalls and stands, but otherwise the place was cluttered with debris. It was the old market. Aedan decided not to attempt a dash across the middle and, instead, took a course through the long shadows of the high western walls. As they completed their circuit, they looked back to see the soldiers entering the market square and running straight across, stamping and kicking their way through the disorder with enough noise to travel several blocks down the silent streets.

"Idiots!" Liru said.

They turned and ran on. Twice they had to cross the road to negotiate once-imposing statues, marks of the city's former magnificence now stretched out on their broken faces, and often they danced between skeletons.

Eventually the leaning gate to the royal courtyard came into view. They passed through it and ran across the open space. Aedan knew the crown would be gone, but he looked anyway.

They rushed through the main doors, down the sleeping banquet hall, along the series of passages still marked by Fergal's pebbles, and reached the stairwell.

"No lamp," Aedan said. "It's going to be night down there."

He looked behind him. The two soldiers had closed the distance. They were sprinting and the panic in their eyes was fresh.

"Move!" the first shouted.

With a hand on each wall, Aedan led the way down the narrow stairs. Liru's light steps and shallow breathing followed close behind. The soldiers were moving fast, too fast. It wasn't long before one of them fell, thudding and wincing until he came to a stop just behind Liru where he swore freely and struggled to regain his feet. He was lucky. Such mistakes could be fatal.

"I never saw the snake you woke," said Liru between rapid breaths. "Was it small enough to follow us here?"

"The head was as big as a saddle. I think it could get down this stairwell, but I'm sure it could eat a horse."

They burst from the darkness into the staging chamber. A torch flickered with a dark red flame and black smoke, and as he looked around, Aedan knew they should not have come here.

Chapter

"Slipped the net did you?"

It was Rork, the heavy soldier with the loose jaw and slippery, leering eyes. He flung a crossbow down, drew a very bloody sword and strode towards them.

From behind, a noise of pounding feet grew and the two soldiers burst into the room, knocking Aedan and Liru to the side and tumbling into Rork. The first clutched a bleeding head, and the second, a clotted stump of a forearm.

"Monster!" the first of them gasped. "Quick – we need weapons."

"Monster?" Rork said, raising his eyebrows, smiling slightly.

"Some kind of serpent-dragon thing. Oh yes, you just go ahead and laugh. It's real and it's as big as a whale! It swallowed Marvyn and Drake like they were rats."

"Marvyn and Drake *were* rats, and you're a gutless, spleenless, brainless liar. What really happened?" Rork shouted, spit leaping from his flabby lopsided mouth as he shoved the man in front of him.

While the soldiers bawled and cursed, Aedan looked around the room. Senbert and Holt were on the floor, gagged and bound. Aedan felt his knees weaken as he recognised Commander Thormar lying in a dark pool. There was a crossbow bolt protruding from between his shoulder blades, and it looked as if someone had been hacking at his head and torso.

Aedan turned his eyes to Rork. Only the lowest of wretches could shoot that big-hearted man in the back and then.... He tried to steady himself, to keep his anger back and his eyes from misting. Images of a lazy river and a quiet porch that would now remain empty kept tugging, goading him. Thormar had not deserved this.

These soldiers would be chased down and hanged if word ever reached Castath. Their lives would depend on making sure it never did. Thormar, Aedan realised, was only the first. As soon as the soldiers ended their argument, he and Liru would be silenced for good.

Aedan noticed Holt looking at him. When their stares locked, Holt motioned with his eyes and head down the passage. The message was clear.

Run!

Heading back to the others was not an option – the entrance to the stairwell they had just left was blocked with jostling soldiers, and the ascending ramp was an unknown. The long corridor out was the only escape. With small steps, Aedan edged away from the light, taking Liru's arm and keeping her beside him. He had learned that sudden lateral movement would be more likely to draw attention, so he backed directly away with slow steps. The black slime still clung to them, so as they neared the end of the chamber they almost dissolved into the shadows. They could now move to the side. Aedan drew Liru quietly towards the tunnel.

Five paces.

He felt the ground with his foot before each step. They could not afford to stumble.

Three paces.

The soldiers fell silent. His grip tightened on Liru's arm and he prepared to run. But the lull was brief. The voices grew again, louder than before. Aedan and Liru slipped into the darkness of the long passage.

"Shoes off," Aedan whispered.

The stone was cold, but smooth and dry. A red glow from behind was just enough to show them where the walls were. They set off at a run, swift and silent.

After a hundred paces the darkness was complete. They slowed down but kept jogging, arms held out on each side. Whispered reflections from their own pattering feet helped them sense their way between the walls.

Aedan thought they might be nearing the end when there was a terrific din of shouting. It was followed by the ominous clatter of hooves as a rider appeared behind them at the far end of the tunnel, flaming torch in hand. The light was only a spark in the distance, not enough to show Aedan the incline ahead. He and Liru both pitched forward as they reached it. They scrambled to their feet and hurried up into the chamber where the wolves had pressed them.

It was dark in here. Aedan took Liru's hand for fear of losing her. He worked his way along the dark walls until he found the narrow entrance to the stairway he had seen on their arrival.

The thrumming hooves drew nearer, shaking the dark space with echoes.

Climbing these turret-stairs – far steeper than anything they had seen in the fortress – without a light would be precarious at best, but there was no choice. Aedan went first. The stairs were narrow, even at the outer edges. Each was at least twice as high as it was wide. A fall here would be much like a fall down a ravine. Bare feet helped somewhat, but the surfaces were dusty and even bare feet could slip. They climbed at a pace that was balanced between urgency and caution.

The hooves fell silent.

They climbed on. Though his hands were encumbered by the boots he was holding, Aedan found it necessary to use both hands and feet. He whispered for Liru to do likewise. The darkness made it all too easy for them to topple over backwards. He was sure there would be exits in the rock at stages, maybe narrow passages that would enable them to loop around a pursuer, but he found none, only the interminable stairs. He was puffing hard now.

But then a doorway appeared in the outer wall. A faint radiance betrayed the narrow exit while the stairs continued on upwards. Aedan made the decision quickly. He slipped through the opening into a dimly illuminated space.

It was a long and narrow room filled with racks from floor to ceiling. Some held arrows and crossbows that were mostly disintegrated, and the rest held rocks grouped in sizes – hundreds of them. Trolleys stood beside the racks, many already loaded.

Aedan hurried to the far end of the room. It opened onto a wide corridor running left and right. Cut in the outer wall were arrow slits and, between them, slightly larger openings. The featured surface on the outside of the statue had completely hidden these. Behind the openings stood compact catapults of a design Aedan had never seen. They were eaten through with rust and cloaked with moss and ivy, but what remained of the intricate arrangements of hinges, rails and wound steel looked enormously powerful.

These towering statues did far more than provide lookouts and archery posts; they were guard towers in disguise. Aedan had no doubt that the range of the catapults overlapped that from fortress walls; it meant that a siege force would have been caught in a death zone, bombarded from both sides.

The rocks gave Aedan an idea. "Let's try and roll one of these down the stairs," he said.

They rushed back to the entrance, grabbed the closest trolley and pushed it, but the ancient wheels were rusted solid. Aedan grabbed one of the mid-sized boulders, wrenched with all his might and staggered with it in his arms to the opening. As he rolled it out onto the stairs, a large hand gripped the corner of the doorway.

The first impact of the boulder was followed by a roar of pain and anger, but Aedan didn't wait to find out what the damage was. He whirled around and yelled at Liru. "Run! Go right. Go right!"

Before he reached the end of the room he caught up to her, grabbed her arm and led her to the left. He hoped Rork hadn't seen. They rushed along the gently bending corridor, weaving between trolleys and catapults, stumbling occasionally over boulders hidden in the dusty half-light. After fifty paces they reached a turret stairwell leading up, while the passage continued to encircle the giant statue. Aedan worried that they might encounter Rork circling in the opposite direction, so they took the stairs. It led them up to another level much like the first.

They stopped and listened.

Aedan was unsure now. Could Rork have found another stairwell? Could he be on the same level, ahead of them?

The silence was broken only by the low hooting of wind through arrow slits. Then there was another sound. They both heard it – a soft metallic scrape, like the tip of a sword brushing stone, the sound a man could make if climbing a turret-stair with his sword held out in front of him. Rork had not fallen for the trick. He was right behind them.

They ran. The angle of the outer rock here was slightly different, allowing shafts of sunlight to slice across the passage. It made the obstacles even more difficult to spot. They both tripped several times. When they reached the ammunition room, identical to the one below, they stopped and looked back. This time, there was no uncertainty. Big steps pounded towards them and a tall figure flashed from the darkness whenever it cut through a shaft of light.

Aedan hurried past the racks to the doorway that opened onto the original stairwell. Up or down? There was no time to ponder. He chose up and climbed a little more than a turn before stopping.

"Quiet," he whispered.

They heard the scrape of Rork's jacket as he entered the stairway. Then he fell silent, obviously listening for his prey.

After the sudden exertion, Aedan found his head was less than steady, like water slopping around in a recently moved tub. It made his orientation on the steep, dark stairs uncertain, and for a dizzy moment he felt as if he were falling backwards.

His fingers were cold from the stone under his hands when the sound of boots reached him. Rork was moving down. When the impacts of his large boots had faded to near-silence, Aedan started climbing again. He remembered the height of the statue and wondered how much of the giant was left when he thumped his head against something above him. There was a flash of light, then darkness and pain.

"Ahh!"

"What is it?" Liru asked.

Aedan reached up and pushed. The trapdoor broke off its rusted hinges and fell away with a clang. He winced at the sound. The light revealed a movable stone block beside him. He guessed that it could be slid across to seal off the opening above, but he could not see how to shift it.

He climbed the last few stairs up through the trapdoor. As he stepped into the open air and looked out, he immediately crouched. Liru crawled out and Aedan replaced the trapdoor, hoping their pursuer would be uncertain about the direction of the sound and abandon the chase in the darkness. As Liru stood, her knees bent too, and she instinctively put a hand to the ground.

They were standing on a small circular platform, perhaps twenty feet across, obviously on top of the giant's head. A low, ivy-clad parapet surrounded them. They could now see that the statues on either side had similar platforms on top, each overlooking the green plain that rolled out a long, long way below, rich velvet in the afternoon sun. But it was not only the height that was causing them to stoop, it was the wind.

A thick bank of cloud was barrelling in from the mountain, and the gusts that swept majestic grassy waves down the hills and across the plain were almost pushing them off their feet.

Then something extraordinary began to happen, and Aedan felt a wild excitement.

"Look. Look!" he said, pointing. "It's the storm you missed last time. It's happening again!"

Liru turned and gasped.

Bright afternoon hues began to peel away above the curiously shaped bank of clouds, revealing the azure of night, and from this deep blue darkness, stars emerged until they covered half the sky. The western sun still cast its glow over the land, painting it with copper fire. The wind picked up and the clouds continued to alter shape in the strangest ways, as if they were being moulded rather than blown, and then they began to move as one, as an army charging in formation, though no army ever moved with this speed. They rushed forward until they were directly above, then they stopped.

And all fell silent.

The wind died, birds hushed, the whole land waited.

It was like a scream in the emptiness of night when the broken trapdoor slid open.

Chapter 56

A head emerged from the stairwell. Rork's half-lidded, cunning eyes fixed themselves on Liru. He was a big man, and strong. Aedan had seen him during the Fenn encounter – he had not gained his dangerous reputation for nothing.

Aedan drew his short sword and considered rushing forward while Rork was still half buried, but the man's long arm and longer sword were already clear, swishing as casually as a tomcat's tail.

"You going to stand against me you little coward?" He stepped up onto the platform, bigger than Aedan remembered – now that Osric was not nearby.

"Aedan," Liru whispered, "I lost my weapons earlier. I will not die at his hand. If you cannot fight him, I will jump."

Aedan stamped down a black upwelling of despair. He concentrated on the swords, trying to distract himself from what he knew was lurking inside. Given time away from all this, he would have mastered his weakness, or at least tried with every ounce of strength he possessed. But such time, he realised, would never be his. The injustice of it all made him want to weep. He had to choke back the misery clawing its way up his throat as he ground his teeth and held himself rigid in a guard stance.

"You defy *me*!" Rork yelled and strode forward.

In one horrible instant, the soldier was no more. All Aedan could see was his father.

They were in the old kitchen back in the Mistyvales. His mother was crouched on the ground, crying. Aedan's words still hung in the air – he had actually reprimanded his father, tried to intervene. But instead of softening with remorse, Clauman's eyes flickered wild and black, spilling rage as they fixed themselves on Aedan with a predator's intent. As he took that first stride forward and his arm drew back, something was different, and Aedan felt it in every bone. This was not discipline, it was assault. It was betrayal by the one who had been his strength. Even before the blows began to fall, his trust was violated and something broke deep in his mind, planting a fear more vivid than nightmares, more destructive than hemlock.

The giant figure advanced.

Though Aedan fought the vision with all the strength left in him, trying to clear it away as if groping at the threads of a rope-like clinging to his face, its hold on him was too strong. The image of his father loomed higher and higher.

He saw the tip of his sword fall as strength drained from his arms. His legs grew weak and he knew they were buckling.

Then a movement to his side reminded him of Liru and, dimly, he recalled that she was unarmed. He cried out as he set his knees and clamped them. For once, they held. He would not fall to the ground. Yet, try as he might, he could not make his arms answer. The sword hung limp from his wilted fingers, tip buried in the mossy stone.

He would stand before this last assault, but it would be the way a dead tree stands before a logger.

This was it then. All his life had been for nothing, for waste.

Like arrows raining down in a thick and deadly hail, sharp thoughts began to run him through with such speed that everything else turned to a nightmarish stillness.

He had failed.

Failed Kalry.

Failed Liru.

Failed Peashot, Hadley, Osric.

He had shamed himself and disgusted all who had supported him.

Perhaps it was right that it should end here. He had caused enough ruin.

Shaft after shaft pierced his mind – shafts that quivered and rang and screamed of pitiful failure and utter worthlessness. What was the point of living when he would continue to fail those who leaned on him?

Then, from within, another thought rose into the chaos of his hammering, shaking mind, a thought that stood out with icy clarity. He knew where the blame lay.

His father.

His father had planted the weakness in his bones that had caused him to wilt before Dresbourn, before Iver, before the Fenn, and now before Rork. It had meant injury not only to him, but to those he cared about. Aedan's long-brewed, potent swill of violent resentment bubbled up inside him, turning his vision black.

He would hate his father forever. Even in the grave. This hate was the one thing that couldn't be taken from him, the only thing left to him.

A faint, choking sob tugged at his ear, and a light step, Liru's final step towards the parapet. If there was another step, he did not hear it, because everything suddenly disappeared.

It was like being struck through by solid light. Heat built up in his chest until it seemed it would burn him to cinders, but instead it worked on him like the warmth of the morning sun. Power was crackling and sparking around.

Then he heard a voice that was the roar of thunder and the gurgle of a stream, a voice as old as the sky but filled with the lightness of a child's laughter.

"Aedan," it said. And in that one word there was enough to make his heart burst.

He was already on his knees, and he was glad of it. He could not understand what was happening, but he wanted to kneel before the one who spoke with this voice.

A warm, singing wind rose up and as it blew, the statue, Kultûhm, DinEilan, Vallendal – they misted and dwindled away until they were gone.

Around him was starlight. His feet touched the ground, but it was like standing on clear ice, for stars glittered far beneath him too. The singing began to build, a growing, thrilling exultation that all but seared him with its beauty.

Then it was as if a shroud made of stars was dropped. At first he could see nothing but the brilliance of pure, solid light pouring down around him. When his vision cleared a little, he found himself before a great throne. It was not just a chair – it was more like a mountain before which even the heights of DinEilan would have been dwarfed. The upper reaches rose among the stars, lost to his eyes.

Then, like an eruption of all the lightning ever to burn the skies, the throne was filled, and Aedan immediately dropped his eyes before one who was simply beyond the limits of sight or comprehension. The radiance was overwhelming.

And in that untainted light, there was no hiding. Of all the times he had found himself where he did not belong, none came anywhere close to this. Never had he fallen so far short of the requirements for entry, yet here he stood, and there was no bluff, no excuse, no argument he could make for himself that would hold up in this place.

Until now, he had always thought of himself as good and noble of heart. Yes, there had been some wrong choices, but it was an unasked-for history that had forced him into those paths. Those choices were his father's doing, his father's fault.

He was damaged, not guilty. He had loathed himself at times when seeing the warped changes taking place, but how could he blame himself? Measured against his father or any of the other tyrants he had known, it was obvious that he was on the better side of the line.

Reasoning this way, he had always felt justified. Aside from a few smudges, his soul was clean.

But now, instead of being compared against dirt, he was searched by the radiance of utter purity. He gasped at what was revealed. He stood as a hog dripping filth, a hog that had somehow slipped into the royal throne room, blinking and stinking, and realising for the first time that there was a measure as high above the ways of the sty as life is above death.

What answer could he make?

As he lowered his gaze, he saw that he was holding a deep cauldron. When he looked inside he almost vomited. He did not need to be told what it contained. It was the vile mixture of all the hatred stored and brewed for his father, the debt he had kept, that he intended to settle. It was his treasure.

"Kneel," the voice said, shaking the ground.

He tried, but the cauldron was as big as a storage vat. It prevented him from reaching his knees. Afraid to look up, he cringed, fearing that he would be told to release it, knowing he could not – would not – and dreading the wrath that would follow.

"I'm sorry," he whispered, thinking not only of his unbending knees, but of all the filth of the sty he had brought with him, and his inability to rid himself of it.

He would be thrown out. He *should* be thrown out. That would be justice. He began to turn away.

The next words were quiet, but they caused every muscle to lock and hold him in place. "If you choose, you may walk away from me, Aedan. But I will not walk away from you."

"But ... I don't understand," Aedan stammered. "Am I here to be punished?"

"You are here to be freed." The words rumbled like an avalanche, and the shudder in Aedan's chest was beyond any emotion he had ever known.

That word, kneel, echoed again in his mind. In it rang not the groans of enslavement, but the song of freedom. He knew why. It was about belonging, the right kind of belonging. It was isolation that led to enslavement. He had discovered that.

Though there was more to fear before this throne than in ten thousand of Kultûhm's giant beasts, it was not wrath that he sensed or dread that welled in him.

An invisible torrent surged from the throne, washed through him, wrapped around him. He felt as if he were a fish that had hatched and managed to survive in the muddy pool of a dry riverbed, and was now being swept up into soft, clear waters. It was unlike anything he could define. This was defining him.

And then he looked into the cauldron.

The fumes were poison, and the container stood between him and the throne. It blocked part of the life-giving flow, leaving a shielded place where bitterness still coursed through his veins and gathered in dark clots. Did he really want this?

The decision was more intimidating than any bridge- or cliff-jump, but he drew a breath, and in his mind, leapt free of the old, dark refuge.

He tried to pull the cauldron away from him, but he could not. It was as if it had grown into his skin.

"Help me!" he cried.

There was no surge of power, just the faintest tingling in his arms. He looked down and pulled again, and this time, it tore partly away from his skin. The pain was intense, and as the raw skin was exposed, he felt a sudden vulnerability, for the cauldron had been a kind of shield. But from the river that was rushing around him, he drew courage and wrenched again. The cauldron ripped free, and once he had torn it loose, he flung it down on the ground where the noxious liquid poured out and was washed away.

Finally, he was able to fall to his knees, and as he did so, the stains that covered him began to fade.

Then, from a distance, he saw his father. His fist clenched automatically and he felt something in his grip. It was a dagger. He understood at once what he needed to do, what he had never been able to do before. Looking not at his father, but towards the foot of the throne, he opened his hand and dropped the blade, releasing judgement to one higher.

As the dagger melted away, light flooded that part of him that he had kept hidden by the cauldron, kept in bitterness and shadow, and he yelled with fright at what was revealed. Crouching in that inner bastion of hate, that long-guarded place where he had so often fled and braced himself with fantasies of revenge, he saw it. It was not strength that had kept him company in that place, but a coiled, venomous thing of fear. His numbing, paralysing fear. A lying, twisted demon that now looked up at him with more hatred than he had ever known.

But the light that illuminated suddenly became solid, a pure rushing torrent. It struck the twisted shape with power both infinite and effortless, tearing it loose and flinging it out, its screams fading to nothing.

The bitterness and poison slowly washed away. It was peace, deeper and broader than the starfields around him. It was belonging. It was freedom. Kneeling before the one who could only be the Ancient had not been the cost of freedom, but the means.

For a long time he laughed and wept and laughed again, released.

Then he saw something completely unexpected, and this time he did not understand at all. It was a book, old and faded. The cover was of red leather and the design on the front was a lizard curled twice around itself. He did not like the look of it and turned away, but it was put before him again, pressed towards him. It was clear what he was expected to do, though not why. He reached out to take the book and as he touched it, the vision faded.

Stars began to wash away as hills, mountains and clouds took their place. The light thinned into a few sparks and cleared as if a huge basin had been emptied and the last drops had fallen.

Liru and Rork were staring at him.

"You are alive!" Liru said, clutching his arm. "It struck you, it held you, and you are not even burned."

Aedan could still feel something burning in his chest, but he could see no mark on his hands or clothes.

Rork was recovering himself. "Yes, you are alive," he said. "Let's see how long you manage that with steel through your belly." He had stepped a good way back, but now he came forward, cutting at the air before him and snarling.

It was the same beast, the same terror, but something was different.

Aedan watched as the sword rose over the man's head, as the foot was planted, the weight shifted, and the blade brought down with a fatal shriek.

There was a clash of steel.

He stared. The blade had not reached him. A sword had blocked it. *His* sword. Raised by *his* arm. How could he do that? How could he defy the monster?

Rork swung again, harder this time.

The blow fell like a hammer on the flat of Aedan's blade, nearly wrenching it from his numb hands. The shock stung him all the way to his elbows.

Rork bellowed and raised his sword overhead. As the large soldier towered before him, Aedan realised what was different. It was the fear. Though it was still there, it was no longer infinite and crushing, undoing him from within. That hidden traitor whispering lies into his mind was gone. And there was something else. The one who had spoken to him in the lightning dwarfed this enemy that faced him now. Dwarfed him utterly.

The enemy too was beginning to change. Though he could still see the wrathful image of his father, the shadows were falling away. Those great black wings that could blot out the sun, the claws that could tear through mountains – illusions, lies. They had been powerful ones that had taken deep root, but they were now cracking and disintegrating like paper that has encountered fire. The monster was crumbling, shrinking, revealing a man.

Rork was only a man.

A traitor and a murderer certainly, but that made him less not more. Aedan had been trained to fight such as these.

And then it struck him that Rork was making that most inexcusable of mistakes – he was underestimating his adversary and exposing himself with a wild, undefended attack.

Aedan's training rushed back, bursting into his thoughts and settling into place, ready. In that instant, icy clarity returned. He gathered himself, clamped his fingers around the handle of the sword, and lunged, thrusting at the soldier's chest.

The sword tip pierced leather armour, but barely. It produced little more than a deep scratch. From the exercises with pig carcasses, Aedan recognised the springy feel of hitting a rib. Rork leapt back, clutching his chest, seeing the patch of blood on his hand. He smiled.

Aedan wanted to yell with frustration. That had been his big chance. He'd have to work hard for the next one. This was no regular soldier he faced. Rork was a specialist swordsman, a veteran whose experience surpassed his own by a considerable margin.

"You want to fight now, do you?" Rork said. "That suits me fine." He stepped forward and unleashed a series of cuts that Aedan managed to block and deflect, but he was driven backwards.

"Aedan!" Liru cried. "He'll push us over the edge! Don't step back again!"

Aedan had no advantage or opportunity, but neither did he have a choice. He stabbed at Rork's throat. His thrust was easily parried and Rork swung the pommel across into Aedan's eye, then drove a knee into his midriff. Aedan collapsed and, by sheer force of hard-learned habit, rolled away as the point of a longsword sparked off the ground beside him. Dun had been strict. Boys who lay and groaned after an injury were punished severely enough to purge them of the habit.

Completing the turn, Aedan lunged along the ground at Rork's ankle. The steel nipped through the skin and Rork leapt back, giving Aedan the space to scramble to his feet.

He realised he would not be given another chance like the first. This was a soldier who had picked many fights and won them all. As he watched Rork take his guard, he noticed the sturdy foot placement and the ease with which he flicked the long blade from side to side. Rork favoured the double grip, it was becoming clear now. His feet were planted wide and square for powerful swinging. It was a single-minded, forward-focussed style that was slightly rigid, leaving his back rounded, shoulders and neck tight, and his eyes blind to anything that might threaten him from behind.

It gave Aedan an idea.

He remembered how Liru had been trained and how they had worked together when teamed against Osric. Without turning, he spoke.

"*Liru, kiel na aviestros le malatia ena. Keu ni ra nam.*" It was Fenn. He did not trust his Sulese at such a moment. He knew Rork spoke Orunean, but no more. Liru came up behind Aedan.

"So you think you can protect your wench, do you?" Rork jeered. "Want her to stay behind you? Let's see you manage that."

Aedan did not smile, but he could have. Rork had failed to notice Liru slip a long dagger from the sheath behind Aedan's back and conceal it in her sleeve.

The next attack was brutal. Blows fell like rocks. It was all Aedan could do to keep from being sliced in two. The man's guard was impenetrable. The length of his blade preserved a distance too great to permit any kind of counter; not that Aedan could have exploited one if it had appeared – he was staggering under the onslaught. Twice he had been too slow to recover and almost lost his arm. Two cuts, one deep, bled freely. Blood ran down onto his hand, slicking the grip.

In spite of all the training Aedan had received, this man's long-practiced skill and far greater strength were too much. Rork drove him along the edge of the platform. Aedan blocked a furious swipe. His left hand broke from the slimy grip and he stumbled to the ground. Rork stabbed and Aedan was not quick enough this time. The tip drove into his left shoulder and held him on the stone. Rork lifted the sword up over his head.

Liru was no fool. As soon as Rork had separated Aedan from her, she had trailed the big swordsman. His frontal style kept his neck tight and his attention forward, so he had no idea of the danger that stalked him. Aedan had seen her raise the blade more than once, and he knew what held her back. She had seen the force of Aedan's thrust reduced by the armour. Her attack would need to find a chink, and be pinpoint accurate. It would also need to be a surprise, which meant only one opportunity. She could not afford to squander it.

But now her eyes enlarged, her jaw locked and Aedan knew she had committed. She darted forward and drove the narrow blade deep into the exposed armpit, withdrawing it in the same instant. Rork screamed and spun towards Liru. From where he lay, Aedan reached up and thrust his sword into Rork's leg, then fell back beneath the sweep of the longsword, narrowly escaping decapitation. The blade cut through his shirt and sliced across his chest. He rolled to the side as the enraged soldier prepared for another cut. He heard Rork shout again, and saw Liru dancing away with a crimson dagger dripping, while Rork clutched his other leg.

The man staggered, but he was far from spent, and he had learned their tactic. Keeping now to the parapet, he clenched his sword in one hand. Aedan got to his feet, but he was dizzy from the injuries and struggled to keep his distance from the advancing soldier. He tripped over the pile of shoes and almost fell down the stairs while backing away. The longsword rang on the stone where he had sprawled an instant earlier. Liru darted in, but Rork swung on her too quickly and she avoided the blade by a hair, ducking beneath it and diving away.

"*Ena bruer,*" Aedan called: I tire. He was losing strength faster than Rork. He had hoped to wear the man down, but he could see that it was not going to work. They needed to do something else, and quickly.

"*Nega ra loyi. Ena lok,*" she said: Make him stand. I throw.

Aedan knew that this would leave her defenceless if she missed. But he could think of nothing better. He stopped retreating, braced his feet and took his guard. To his right, Liru stood. He knew she was estimating the turn of the dagger and measuring the distance to her target. He had seen her practicing. She could hit a small tree from that distance eight or nine times out of ten. Getting the turns right was always the tricky part. The first throw could sometimes strike on the handle or the length of the blade. As well as getting this rotation right on the first throw, she would need aim for neck or head – small targets. She was not strong enough to pierce armour.

Aedan glanced down to his left. The parapet was low – barely over his knee – and beyond that, air. Deep air. A long free, uninterrupted drop to the ground.

Rork approached, keeping to the edge. He could not afford to let Liru circle him again. He prodded fast and hard. Aedan parried, weakly, dropping to one knee. Rork grinned and drew back, preparing to run Aedan through.

Liru's action was quick, no swaying or lurching, just a sliding back of her arm and an even throw. The dagger sang as the blade flashed in the late sun, sliced through the air and cut Rork across the back of the neck.

The turn had been a fraction too slow and where he should have received the point, it was the edge that struck his skin, leaving no more than a shallow gash. The dagger glanced off. Aedan saw it spinning away over the edge, growing smaller and smaller until he lost it against the distant grass.

He staggered to his feet and braced himself. He did not see a way through this, but he would not cringe again.

"It was a good throw. You did well," he said to Liru, not caring now that Rork understood.

Liru was moving around on the platform, but Aedan could not afford to look. His eyes were fixed on the swishing longsword.

"It was a pig of a throw!" she yelled. "But this one won't miss."

Aedan and Rork both turned to glimpse something streaking towards Rork's head. He raised his hands to ward it off, stepped backwards, and caught his heel on the low parapet. With a mounting scream and swinging arms, he tipped slowly away and dropped into the emptiness beyond the platform, twisting and tumbling through the air. The cries faded, faded, and then ended abruptly.

Aedan could find little pity for this soldier who would have murdered children, though, he decided, he was feeling a lot less like a child.

Liru came up and guided him away from the edge.

"How did you find another weapon?" Aedan mumbled, remembering now that he still had a knife he could have given her.

"Hush, Aedan. You have lost too much blood. I need to get help to bring you down those stairs or you will fall."

She made him lie down, then bound the wounds with strips cut from his shirt.

"Don't attempt the stairs, you hear me?" she said.

Aedan looked at her.

"Promise me Aedan."

"Promise," he said.

She knelt down and put her hand on his good shoulder, looking at him with uncharacteristic softness. "Because if you do, I really will mix poison into the salve." She smiled in the simple, direct way he knew so well, the rare smile he had missed for so long.

He smiled back.

Then she squeezed his shoulder and left.

Aedan felt happy tears slipping down his cheeks as her footsteps receded. If his chest had not ached so, he might have laughed.

The late summer air was warm on his skin. He closed his eyes. Time passed, and he began to drift.

But before he could find sleep, something disturbed him – a sound that did not accord with Liru's return or wind in the ivy. It was a soft, drawn-out scraping, and with every breath he took, it grew louder.

Chapter 57

Long shadows stretched over the grass. They were the shadows of giant statues, silent watchmen that were even more imposing for their silence – a soldier with a spear, a robed and hooded man clutching a twisted knife, a strange lizard-like being with terrible claws and a tail, a giant with a club hidden behind his back, and many more that encircled the fortress. But it was the giant that broke the stillness. At first it might have seemed a shadow, a trick of the light, but a closer look would have revealed that a shape was moving, flowing like a dark stream of liquid rock over the statue's back. Flowing upward.

Aedan's dreamy thoughts vanished and he propped himself up on his elbows. The sound was growing louder, drawing nearer. He could almost feel it in the stone now. He decided that, in spite of Liru's warning, he had no choice but to attempt the stairs.

The numbing battle-fire had cooled, and his wounds ached as he turned over – and froze. The trapdoor was only a few feet away, yet it was too far. He would not make it.

Each lemon-sized eye glittered like a gem in the sunlight, even more radiant for the setting of leathery scales which were still coated in the museum's dust.

Aedan held his breath.

The snake glided swiftly around him, more and more of its long body being pulled up onto the platform until he was surrounded.

As slowly as he could, he rolled to his side and drew his knife – Liru had taken the sword. Then, by gradual inches, he pushed his weight up onto one knee and slid a foot out and forward. That would provide the balance he would need. The snake had stopped coiling. It was facing away, but turned and watched him now.

He remembered how Osric had aimed for the eye. This would be a much easier throw – a half turn. He rotated the knife in his fingers until he was holding it by the blade. If the snake held still during the movement of his arm he would be unlikely to miss, and the eye would be ruined.

But the snake did not hold still.

It rose up, solid as a tree trunk, and looked down at him. The knife shook in Aedan's hand, but he held onto it and fixed his attention within a ridged and featured iris, concentrating on the large, round pupil in which he and all of Kultûhm were clearly reflected. The way the head faced, the right side presented the most direct target. But as he took aim, the strangest feeling of reluctance came over him.

It was in those eyes. This was not the mere calculation of a predator. The look of intelligence he had seen or imagined in the face of the great fox – it was the same here. These creatures were not just bigger. There was more that was changed in them than size.

But while that colossal serpentine monster had chilled him with its air of ancient cunning, this animal had the look of a child – full of questions, full of awe, drinking in the world around it, gulping as fast as it can and still being flooded. And the way it was looking at him was almost the way a child … but that was impossible.

Relaxing his throwing arm, he let his eyes travel over the creature before him. This was the snake he had woken. The marks of his hands still lingered on the dusty sides of its magnificent head. Frog indeed!

How long had it slept? For dust to gather like this, it must have been years well beyond his lifetime, or many lifetimes. What was it thinking while holding his gaze?

And that was when he had the most overwhelming impression that the snake was not only thinking but speaking, or trying to speak, though it had no words.

It lowered its head, one tentative inch at a time, and approached his. Every master in the academy would have condemned what Aedan now did. He loosened his grip on the blade until it had almost dropped, and then reached out the other hand. The snake blinked, watched for some time, and began to lean forward.

It was the growing racket of footsteps from the stairs that broke the spell. The snake swung across and peered down through the trapdoor in a movement so fast that there was no doubting its strength. It turned back to Aedan, this time pausing only inches before him, then darted over the edge, its long body whisking around the platform and slipping over the parapet. Aedan crawled to where it had disappeared. He looked over to see a dark trunk gliding along the body of the giant, around its club, and down towards the plain.

"Aedan! What are you doing over there? Come back here!" It was Liru using her angry-nurse voice, one that normally produced instant obedience. But this time Aedan beckoned for her to join him. She, Senbert and Holt approached the parapet at a crouch and looked down where Aedan was pointing. From this height it looked like an earthworm or a centipede slipping through grass towards the fortress. When it reached the stone walls, it rose up, pressed itself into a corner between wall and turret, and threaded its way up as easily as a man would climb a ladder.

"What made you look for it?" Liru asked.

There was no reply. Aedan had lost consciousness.

It was the restful sounds of a camp that awoke him – crackling fire, wind-shaken leaves, quiet talk. When he smelled stew, he tried to sit up, only to groan and flop back down again. There was another fire in the camp – it was located in his shoulder – and his head felt like it had been boiled. In fact, his whole body seemed to have been subjected to some horrible torture and drained of strength.

Liru rushed over and put a hand to his forehead.

"The food is not ready yet. I'll give you a bowl when it's done. You rest now. Are you thirsty?"

"As sand," he croaked.

Liru handed him a waterskin and Aedan drank until he had to break for air. When he passed the skin back it was empty.

"Chew this," Liru said, putting something that tasted like a stick into his mouth.

"What is it?"

"Willow bark. Might help with the pain."

"By distracting me with the taste?"

Tyne came over and sat down, but did not attempt to nurse him. She appeared almost to defer to Liru. Aedan looked puzzled at this and Tyne read his expression.

"Liru knows more about the physician's arts than I do," she said. "I expect she knows more than her instructors at the academy."

"I can believe that," said Aedan, talking around the half-chewed bark and noting with amusement how Liru refused to show any bashfulness at being the subject of the discussion.

"Liru told us what you did, Aedan. Rork was a well-known fighter, and a ruthless one. None of us would have enjoyed facing him. Except Osric perhaps. We are all very impressed with you. You overcame your fear. When Osric heard what happened he looked as proud as a father."

"It was Liru who knocked Rork off the platform."

"We can all see by the injuries where his attention was focussed. Liru would never have had her chance had he not been completely fixed on you, and that could not have happened unless you were a threat to him. It was your courage that gave Liru the opportunity she needed. Both of you have earned great respect."

Aedan had lost too much blood to colour with the praise, but he did feel Tyne's words warming him. "Where are we?" he asked after a brief silence.

"About seven or eight miles from the fortress," she replied. "Osric, despite his injuries, wanted to cover more ground, but Liru has been protecting you with some ferocity. She did not think you were fit to travel any further with your loss of blood. She said that if we carried on she would remain here with you. She's a very stubborn girl."

Aedan smiled.

"It was amusing to see them glaring at each other," Tyne continued. "I don't think Osric has experienced that in a while."

"I did not wish to be insubordinate," said Liru, "but the general, he was worried about uncertainties, and it was a certainty that Aedan would not last long being bounced around on a horse's back. Among my people, it is the doctor who makes these decisions."

"Don't worry," said Tyne, "Osric is not angry. He suspected it was the right call from your first objection. If he had really believed you wrong he would have tied you to your horse and led it himself – for your own good." She rose and sniffed her coat.

"I'm going to wash this reeking slime off. Don't want it spoiling the taste of supper."

"No!" said Aedan, sitting up and collapsing again with another groan. "Don't wash it off. Nobody must wash it off. The wolves – last time it was the smell that kept them at a distance. Maybe they are afraid of it."

"But it stinks!"

"So does the belly of a wolf. After the belly it only gets worse."

"Aedan!"

"Could the slime draw the serpent?" Liru asked.

"It didn't follow us last time. But the wolves did."

Tyne sat back down again, wrinkling her nose.

"Tell me," Aedan said, trying to ignore the pounding in his head. "What happened in the staging room? How did you get past the soldiers?"

"They didn't give much trouble," Tyne mumbled.

"Oh yes they did," said Liru, interrupting as she might do to an older sister. "Fergal told me what really happened. When he and Tyne got Osric to the bottom of the stairway, they stopped at the tips of those two soldiers' swords – they'd armed themselves again, though the one had to use his left hand. Osric was barely able to stay on his feet, and when they tried to stab him, Fergal said it was as if someone had slapped a wasp nest. Tyne was everywhere at once. By the time Fergal had found a weapon there was nobody left to fight."

Tyne was far less comfortable with being discussed; she was studying some arbitrary point in the dark canopy of leaves.

"Osric was in danger you say?" Aedan asked. "Then I'm not really surprised."

Liru grinned.

Tyne glanced at them and blushed. "Ooh, you two are merciless brats!" she said.

Later, Aedan finished three helpings of a stew that tasted of beans and barley, and drained a second waterskin. Liru was delighted, saying an appetite like that was good news to any doctor.

During the second watch, Aedan's sleep became shallow. Something was disturbing him, a sound that did not belong in his dreams. His fingers closed around the knife handle. He opened his eyes without moving and listened. There it was again, a soft metallic scrape. He turned his head as quietly as he could. Tyne was on watch. Her tall outline moved gracefully on the far side of the camp. But the noise he had heard was nearer. He glanced towards the fireplace. Something seemed to be in front of the embers, a dark silhouette, but he wasn't sure if he was imagining it.

It moved.

Aedan jolted with such violence he almost lost his knife, but he did not lose his voice and shouted for all he was worth. He tried to jump to his feet and, instead, collapsed in a spasm of aches. The rest of the party was up in no time, weapons in hand, converging on the fireplace as Aedan pointed and continued shouting.

The creature stayed where it was, either unaware or supremely confident.

Aedan was prepared for a horrifying attack – an explosion of fangs and claws and a wild, thrashing escape, or a whirr of blades and screams – but he was not prepared for the voice that now spoke from within the crouching shape.

"Is there any more stew?" it asked. The voice was familiar, yet it could not be.

"Merter?" Tyne's voice trembled.

"Sorry for sneaking in. I didn't want to wake anyone after –"

That was as far as she let him get before smothering him with a weepy hug. Poor Merter was crushed with embraces, handshakes and back-claps until he looked almost panicked with claustrophobia.

The fire was rebuilt and everyone settled down to hear the explanation.

"After that cage dropped away – Oh, and thank you Tyne for getting me out, else I'd be done – I fell in stages until the structure jammed just long enough for me to catch onto the wall. It was just at the roof of the cave and I could see those giant coils directly beneath me – that creature is even bigger than I'd thought. I heard you calling but I decided that if I yelled back I'd be as likely to get the beast's attention as yours, so I moved into a corner of the rock channel and started climbing up. The walls were rough and the holds were good. The corner also made things a lot easier, but it still took most of the afternoon.

"By the time I got out, it was late and the fortress was still as a crypt. I decided not to follow the highway of prints you'd left through the dust and debris because I was afraid you might reset the locks on the entrance and I have no idea how to open them from the inside. I headed west instead, the main gate. I knew wolves would be about, and seeing as I'd lost my sword in the cave, I broke into a large house and took two bronze display swords – the steel swords were all rusted to nothing, and these are really fine weapons."

Aedan looked at the short, falchion-like blades still covered in their thin layer of pale corrosion.

"It was dark by the time I found my way out the main gate. Locating you took a while."

"How did you do it?" asked Tyne.

"Strong breeze off the mountain. I stayed downwind, ran until I smelled fire and stew, headed upwind."

Osric laughed and cut off abruptly, clutching his ribs with a grimace. "I thought you'd be peering at bent blades of grass and listening to their complaints about hooves," he said.

"Too hungry, and I'm still hungry. Will someone please –"

Osric tossed him a saddlebag. Merter dug inside until he found something edible and set to work. After a few mouthfuls he sent everyone to bed and took the watch. Tyne objected but he told her to shut up and sleep because he owed her his life. That earned him another hug after which he melted away into the surrounding darkness without even the snap of a twig or the crunch of gravel.

"I wish I could move like that," Tyne complained.

"Even mice envy him," said Osric, "I think you were right about him being part cat. Frankly, I'm not actually that surprised to see him alive and well. Probably still has several lives to go. At least with him snooping around out there we can afford some deep sleep. We'll need it. Tomorrow we must cover a good thirty miles, injuries or not. I won't risk another night this close to the fortress."

By morning, Aedan felt better than he had expected. His wounds, expertly stitched, drained, and bound, felt as if they had already started to mend.

As Aedan had predicted, the wolves were thrown into confusion by the scent, or rather, the stink of the party. After twice approaching, they abandoned this smelly quarry that they could not bring themselves to attack.

The mood in the camp was solemn for a time. More than half their number had died in Kultûhm. Once they were a safe distance from the fortress, they held a quiet memorial, each speaking in memory of those lost.

Osric's face seldom betrayed tender emotions, but Aedan knew he mourned the loss of the faithful and steady commander whose large presence and billowing pipe had become as reassuring to the party as the campfire. The tears ran freely down Tyne's cheeks as Osric recalled to them a man whose honour and loyalty had earned him respect among his friends, his troops, and even some of his enemies.

Fergal spoke of the Culver none of them had known – a shy and quiet man with a quick sense of humour and an insatiable craving for tales of adventure and romance. He told with a smile how he had often caught the great man lost in a book full of brave heroes rescuing fluttering maidens from pirates and dragons, instead of attending to more serious duties. Fergal's expression remained hidden, but his voice revealed the sadness that rested on him.

As was the custom when bodies were out of reach, the mourners placed headstones and buried articles that had belonged to the dead. Aedan thought of burying a pipe Thormar had given him but, after a brief consideration, decided against it. The pipe was inseparably linked to something the man had said, something Aedan never wanted to forget – that the only good reason for war was peace.

He let go of the pipe, allowed it to drop back in his pocket and recalled the face of the rough commander who had shown him nothing but kindness. Yes, Thormar would have understood. He would have approved.

Chapter 58

It was only after a week that they decided to discuss what had happened and what it meant. At nightfall, Captain Senbert and Holt were posted on sentry duty, while Fergal gathered the rest around the fire.

"I came here in the hope of answering a question," he began. "It was this: Did the storm over the Pellamines set in motion something that could destroy our city? Perhaps you felt the disturbances that have been taking place under Castath ever since that lightning bolt?"

"I did," said Tyne.

"I felt nothing," said Osric.

"Yes, well, you shake the earth every time you step," she said, tossing a pebble at one of his massive boots. "Of course you wouldn't notice."

Fergal moved on. "There was something in our archives that gave me cause for concern. I knew that there had been reports of strange storms at Kultûhm shortly before it was abandoned. The theory that formed in my mind was that the latched, prolonged bolt of lightning disturbed something in the ground under Kultûhm which led to earthquakes. Nobody wants to be under stone roofs or beside block towers when they are shaking and leaning. I suspected something like that, possibly combined with a release of noxious fumes through a fissure in the earth, might have been enough to drive the inhabitants from the fortress.

"So, if the very security of our own walls and buildings was about to become a threat, it was necessary to know. We had the choice to either wait and find out, hoping that the Fenn army would not be camped outside our walls at the time, or travel to the Kultûhm archives and try to glimpse our future by looking into their history. To quote Agoligh, 'History is the shadow of tomorrow.' Though it does sound so much better in the original Gellerac. My ears ache under the dead weight of these limping translations."

"Gellerac," said Osric, "sounds like a throat infection, and it was the language of a people cruel enough to be considered an infection themselves. I was forced to learn a little of it during a course in historical tactics and I think it gave me scars inside my mouth. All that snorting and scraping to get your meaning out has never seemed worth the effort to me."

"*Ghavgk krreshûgg.*"

"And yet when you produce noises like that, *you* sound like the uncultured barbarian. It's enough to make a man's tonsils bleed."

Fergal sighed and continued. "What we found in the Kultûhm archives was not exactly what I had expected. According to the records, the storms were first seen about eight hundred years ago. The Gellerac documented observing them over the mountains for some five years before they ceased completely – until now. More surprising than the storms themselves, were the strange things they found at the lightning strike points. These copses of giant trees that we have been seeing all over DinEilan are the points, and I think you can guess what else they found there. All the giant insects, rodents and worse that we discovered in that museum were collected from such points. Being a systematic people, they collected pairs. They believed that the lightning both enlarged and killed whatever it struck."

"But it didn't kill the snake," said Aedan.

"Actually, I'm not sure the lightning killed any of them. I spent my time with the creatures that had not been damaged by skinning and stuffing. I found no signs of decomposition at all. Nothing. It was like they had entered some kind of extreme hibernation that can apparently last for hundreds of years."

"You mean the others were skinned alive?" Tyne blurted.

"Alive, yes, but not conscious."

Aedan winced at the thought of those magnificent creatures being cut up in their slumber.

"Some of you might have guessed it by now – the riddle of the missing snake. Remember all the animals had been collected in pairs, yet there was only one snake. That giant beast was the second snake."

"But it was ten – twenty times the size," said Osric, "and the shape and markings were different."

"It has been alive for over eight hundred years, growing, and it would seem, changing in other ways too."

Everyone was silent, incredulous, waiting for more.

"It is my guess," Fergal resumed, "that when the first snake began to stir, the Gellerac quickly closed and sealed that storage room in the hope of suffocating it. But a correct identification would have shown why that was the worst idea. If you ignore the size, it's –"

"A yellow-eyed mole viper," said Merter. He was clearly more concerned with safety than looking respectful, because he sat with his back to the fire and the conversation, keeping his vision unspoiled by light as he searched through the surrounding shadows. "Though the proportions are changed and it has learned to spit like nothing I've ever seen."

"True," said Fergal. "Now as you can imagine, a burrowing snake, given enough time, would quite possibly be able to force a way out from what was meant to be its grave. I think we can allow ourselves the liberty of a guess as to why Kultûhm was deserted, and why it remains so. I don't think earthquakes had anything to do with it."

Again they were quiet, contemplating what Fergal had just revealed, imagining the horror that the Gellerac must have faced within their own walls.

"The snake also explains the lack of birds," said Merter.

"Quite so."

"Then the quest is concluded and the question answered?" Osric asked. "We have no need to fear Castath's walls being shaken down around our ears. Correct?"

"The question is partly answered," said Fergal, "but the evidence does not establish a negative like that. All I can say is that there is nothing here to confirm my original theory. The shakings in the earth beneath Castath remain unexplained, and whether or not they pose a threat, I have yet to determine."

"Bit of a limp conclusion if you ask me," Osric growled. "You academics are always so timid with your words. Your conclusion sounds like a different form of the question."

"And so it is, Osric," Fergal said with a chuckle. "Slightly whittled, sharper, but it is still a question. In time it will be sharp enough to impale the answer."

"Fergal," Tyne interrupted, "you said the shakings in the earth might not pose a threat, but what if that weird lightning bolt over the Pellamines created some awful creature near the city?"

"It is possible. There's little more than dry rock up on the Pellamines, but it is always unwise to assume security. Perhaps a discreet investigation would be in order. If we do find something threatening, we would need to destroy it without waking it."

"I'll see to that on our return," Osric said.

Aedan had been sitting on a question for days and he decided he wouldn't get a better time to ask it. "In the museum there were skeletons," he said, his voice betraying his excitement, "and there were others in the mine below. Massive things. Bigger than any of the animals in the museum by far. What were they?"

"I'm not entirely sure," said Fergal. "They were discovered during mining. It was the Gellerac belief that these creatures from a lost age were being returned to the land, but the storms that were returning them were killing them in the process. We know now that the storms weren't killing them, but the Gellerac learned it too late."

"So do you think it's true – that we might see monsters like that?"

"I screaming well hope not!" Tyne snapped. "Aedan, haven't you seen enough monsters already?"

Fergal laughed. "I don't know," he said, "but I do share Tyne's sentiments, and as she so eloquently put it, I also screaming well hope not. But the simple fact is that these are events for which we have no explanation. We may begin to understand aspects of it, but there is some power moving here that lies outside the frame of traditional knowledge. We may be on the cusp of the incredible, or terrible, and possibly both."

"There seems to be a lot you don't know," said Tyne. "I hope that doesn't sound rude – it's just that I expected with all that reading you scholars do, you would have more answers. Didn't think there would be so many uncertainties for your kind."

"I do not take offence at that, Tyne. In fact, I am happy that I give that impression. *Lukrûggn krarsh mrastrafthi ghevk.* Agoligh again. Loosely translated: The confession of ignorance is crucial to the pursuit of knowledge. Another way of putting it is that those who pretend to know never will – they lack the humility to learn. What we have fallen upon is something truly mysterious – not a word we scholars like to use, but a fitting one. I don't believe anyone understands what is happening or what is to come. If I had given a closed answer to each of your questions, I would not be worth listening to."

After a lull, Merter spoke, still with his back to them. "Fergal, I know that you managed to get through those locks under the academy. I know that you have some idea of what lies beneath Castath."

Everyone fell silent.

Fergal gazed long into the coals before replying. "I'll tell you what I may," he said, "but it will do little to appease your curiosity. Castath, or Athgrim's Castle, as you might recall, was built on the grassed-over ruins of a much older civilisation. There is quite a labyrinth of tunnels and caverns beneath the academy and beyond it – this is no secret – but very few know that the tunnels have been cleared of rubble and restored. What almost nobody knows is that the underground ruins go far, far deeper than these first levels. None of us knows how deep. That ancient civilisation must have preferred their chances beneath the ground to above it.

"One of the deepest rooms we have been able to access is vaguely reminiscent of a royal antechamber – with some very peculiar elements – and it ends at a stone door like a mountain on a hinge. It took some time and much reading to understand the locks, but in the end I was able to open the door – giving the credit, naturally, to Culver. Inside is a circular cavern with three more giant doors – none of which I have succeeded in unlocking – and a peculiar shaft extending down into the earth, the purpose of which also eludes me. But by lowering a pair of lamps at the end of a three hundred foot rope, we were able to observe something that I would struggle to explain even if I were permitted. It is this that has given me cause for worry, and the prince cause to seal off the entrance with sixty feet of solid stone and hard mortar."

The breathless hush that followed was turgid, even violent with curiosity. But Fergal disregarded it with practiced ease.

"You can't stop there!" Tyne burst out. "Can't you give us *some* idea of what it is?"

"I'm afraid, my dear girl, that I may not offer details. I am bound to secrecy, and in this case I believe the secrecy to be necessary. However, I'll keep observing and perhaps one day I shall find cause to break my silence."

"How will you keep observing? I thought you said it was now inaccessible."

Fergal looked over at her, his expression altogether blank. "No. I don't recall using the word inaccessible. I only said Burkhart ordered the entrance to be sealed."

"But don't they mean the … Ugh, you and your riddles." Tyne looked away, dropped her chin into her palms and glared at the fire.

Osric laughed. "Very well, Fergal," he said. "Keep your secrets. We will have to trust you as our watchman. Now, what about Aedan? Why is he unchanged?"

"It would seem that whatever struck Aedan was something different. It could not have been traditional lightning, for he survived a direct strike, nor could it have been the phenomenon that changes things, for he is unchanged."

Aedan knew this was not true. Though he hadn't grown any bigger, something else was different – he could still feel the heat in his chest and a curious tingling in his fingers and occasionally his toes; it also felt at times as if his hands and feet were surrounded by water rather than air. But he was reluctant to speak of it. After Mistress Gilda's exhibitions of his scar, he had no desire to be scrutinised again as an object of interest. That gave him a thought. He reached up and touched his left ear, then dropped his hand with a sigh. It was still only a half ear. He pulled the hair down over it as he had done times beyond counting.

"Any ideas on the second snake's unusual behaviour around Aedan?" Osric asked.

"Perhaps the confusion following a sleep of a few hundred years," said Fergal. "Merter?"

"Perhaps," the ranger said, not turning around.

Aedan was thoughtful. He could still see the snake's eyes and feel the way it had appeared to question him. At first he had considered its circling him to be a threat, but the more he thought of it, the more it began to seem like a protective gesture. He shook his head. It was ludicrous to think like this. Perhaps it was worth remembering that he had been near collapse from his wounds. Perceptions would most likely have been distorted.

After a lull, Fergal spoke again. "We need to be clear on what we say to Prince Burkhart, so I need you all to listen very well.

Firstly, he is not to know my true position as Culver's master. Secondly, it is imperative to convince him that none of us foresees any threat. The prince's objective in allowing this journey was to silence any voice that spoke of danger to the city. If we return and claim that the original suspicions were not confirmed, which is perfectly true, his objective is accomplished and he will probably be relieved that our blood is not on his hands.

"The threat of a Fenn invasion was one thing, but talk of Castath itself being unstable was too much for him. Clearly, he has plans that are threatened by the concerns I raised through Culver. I don't believe his interest is the peace of the city, in spite of his constant declarations. I am convinced something else is brewing in his political pot. Something he is prepared to defend with extreme measures. If we threaten to spread a warning of danger, I fear we will not see the end of one day in Castath."

"I hate to admit it," Osric said, "but every word strikes true as a javelin. We will need to tread very carefully upon our return. I almost repent of bringing Tyne."

"Because I'm a woman?" she asked. "Would you rather have left Liru without suitable company?"

Osric opened his mouth only to hang wordless and confused. This was a kind of battle he had never learned to fight.

Tyne grinned and lobbed a stick at Osric who snatched it from the air and tossed it back into her waiting hand. His confusion melted into a smile and Aedan wondered, as often before, what the general was waiting for.

———

Midsummer was bursting around them and, unfortunately, above them. The cloudbursts were regular and heavy, driving them often to huddle under rocky overhangs or hide in swaying woods that chattered with rain and whistled in the gusts of heavy downpours. Afterwards they would steam themselves beside huge fires if they could find enough dry wood, otherwise they shivered beside little smoky fires that produced little heat and drew much teary coughing. On a few occasions, the wood was so wet that Merter didn't even bother to attempt lighting it.

But the rain seldom lasted and it was not uncommon for a stormy morning to be followed by a golden afternoon. When riding through open sections, Aedan's eyes would often wander out across the hills, and beyond them to the spine of the DinEilan mountains, growing blue once more with hazy distance.

Yet it often seemed to him as if something of this wild land was still nearby. It was in the way the horses lifted their noses at night and began to stamp and jostle, in the way he found himself spinning around to look behind him into the darkness. He couldn't shake the feeling that the camp was being watched. It was a long time before this unease faded and he was able to relax.

Fergal took up his lessons again, and Osric and Tyne resumed their training – though Aedan had to be careful with his injuries at first. Merter also began sharing some of his woodcraft skills, taking not just Aedan, but Liru too when tracking or hunting. His first lesson was to teach her to walk quietly.

He pointed out spoor and explained the habits of creatures from mice to gazelle. Aedan was constantly impressed by how easily the ranger spotted tracks from the saddle that most rangers would only have seen from a crouch, and that were hardly visible to Liru when she put her nose to the ground – slight shifts of thin dust on the clay, blades of grass only marginally bent, a dead branch missing a corner of its bark where a hoof had trod.

Even more fascinating than the search for what and where, was the study of when. Merter showed how to determine the age of many kinds of tracks and taught the importance of understanding the environment. Dryness, he said, was often – and mistakenly – taken as a primary indication of age. But prints dried at different rates according to many factors like soil type, shade, wind, humidity and such, so that an hour-old print in one environment might look like a three-day print in another. Young trackers had often been fooled in this way and stumbled onto the camp of someone they thought to be leagues ahead of them.

It was during one of Merter's lessons that they came across the oversized bush where the stone carving of the locust had rested. The locust was gone. At first they thought they had the location wrong, but then Merter found the earthy patch still riddled with crawling things that had lost their shelter. Deep gouges in the soil led away along a vague hollowed impression of bent grass and broken stalks.

"No wonder it looked so real," Aedan said with a slight tremor as he began scanning the nearby trees.

When the rest of the party joined them, Fergal stood for a long time looking at the vacated resting place.

Aedan stepped beside him. "Do you think," he asked, "that maybe the storms that have returned after all these centuries are causing these animals to wake?"

"It's a reasonable hypothesis," Fergal replied without looking up.

"What woke the bigger snake though?"

"Maybe it was struck twice. Maybe it never entered the deep hibernation of the others, and all the handling caused it to stir while it was being laid out in the museum by the curators."

Aedan shivered. "But then how did the smaller one wake? Do you think it could have been struck recently while deep inside the museum?"

"There was a hole leading to the open, remember. If it had been raining during the storm, water could have carried the lightning below easily enough. I've heard of that kind of thing happening on farms. Let's not get fixed on the double-strike idea though. Perhaps the first snake was just a light sleeper, and perhaps the others are now all emerging from their hibernation. Something that I vaguely glimpsed when you pushed me through that doorway – and thank you for that – there was a long scar on the larger snake's head. I suspect it was the first and last cut of the skinner, and doubtless, it was this that woke the beast."

"Maybe that's what made it so hostile to people," Aedan said.

"I don't know that hostile is the right word. Basic hunger would be sufficient explanation for the animal's actions."

But Aedan could not forget the way the second snake had behaved after being woken more gently. The look in its eyes had not been animal. He wondered …

Then he remembered something from a long time back. "When we first came through DinEilan, we heard a strange call just before morning. My father said it had the pattern of a woodland fox, but it was too deep. He said there was no fox big enough for a voice like that. I think I understand now. Think I also know why it sounded lonely."

Fergal grunted. "So then there are at least five of these monsters loose in DinEilan. Two snakes, a fox, a locust, and the Lakeside Terror that once haunted Drumly – yes, I know it was more than a legend. Also, let's not forget whatever it was that uprooted trees and did away with the rangers in that first confirmed report. It might have been the animal from Drumly, but possibly not."

"Maybe the same one Merter wanted to look for when we spotted those trees moving after the Fenn attack?"

"That might have had another explanation, but maybe."

"There's something else I've been thinking about," Aedan resumed, encouraged by Fergal's patient ear. "Back at Badgerfields in the Mistyvales, there was this giant tree that grew near the manor house. Nobody knew what it was, but we called it a pearlnut. Sometimes I thought it looked a bit like a plane tree with that mottled-looking bark and those fresh green leaves, only that the bark didn't flake and each leaf was as big as a blanket, and instead of those prickly seeds, the tree produced the most delicious nuts you ever tasted ..."

Aedan reached the end of his breath without getting anywhere near his point. The last words were pushed out like the final drops from an orange squeezed dry. His face was red and he sucked an undignified breath. Placing a theory before the man he now knew to be the chancellor was unnerving him more than a little.

"The thing is," Aedan pursued, "there were no big trees nearby, but there were others like it miles out into the forest, a huge number of them, far more spread out than any of these strike-point copses – I could see them when I climbed high enough, though it was really difficult to get ..."

He shook his head and reached for his point. "It makes me think our tree was an offspring from a seed that had been carried. If that's so, then could it be possible these giant creatures could reproduce too?"

"And fill the land with the thunder of their walking?"

"Yes, or slithering."

Fergal blew out a slow breath. "I find myself caught between excitement and dread at the prospect. But tell me – these trees that you saw out in the forest, were they all the same species?"

"I – I, yes I think so. Why"

"Because it confirms a suspicion I've had. It's likely that more than one species was struck but only one of them has spread. I've been wondering about incompatibility with the environment – if some of these new species might not struggle to survive, and if it would be possible for them to adapt within days. The biggest problem is actually not adaptation but correct internal functioning. With animals, massively oversized offspring are almost never healthy and they usually die young. These creatures, it would seem, have overcome this – possibly their internal proportions are changed – but even so, the environment may not accommodate them.

"It falls outside the scope of your studies, but a diversion into the natural sciences won't harm you. Here are some examples that should illustrate the point. Take the enlarged birds – both seed and insect-eating types would now have beaks too blunt and cumbersome for their accustomed sources of food; bees would crush any flowers they attempted to visit; mosquitoes would not be able to land soft and undetected when they drop like acorns; moles' tunnels stay open in loamy soil, but if they were many times wider they would collapse – that's why sappers have to use wooden support beams.

"Consider trees for a moment. A tree with a tap root that grows to several times its normal height would need to sink its root to several times the usual depth – and most locations would not have soil deep enough. This might explain the numerous dead giant trees. There are many more examples, but these should suffice to illustrate the difficulties of survival."

"But ... the snake seems to have done it."

"Quite right. I don't say that it is impossible, only unlikely. The larger of the snakes is one that has clearly managed to make the rapid adaptation – and it appears to have done more than just adapt. The changes in its form make me wonder if we are even correct in referring to it as a snake any more ..." Fergal thought in silence for a while. "But let's put that aside for now. We were speaking of adaptation. Once the former inhabitants of Kultûhm were no more, it might have learned to take deer, or even hunt in the lake. There are some very big fish there – maybe even some horrifyingly big ones if the same lightning struck the water. It's possible that it has learned to slow its metabolism, possible that it hibernates for long periods."

"So ... do you think the pearlnut tree was the one that was able to adapt?"

"It appears likely, but much more investigation would be needed to confirm it, investigation that is not going to happen, because, as I understand, nobody goes into Nymliss."

"Uh ... that's not exactly true."

Fergal shook his head and sighed. "What else did you find in there?"

"I never went as far in as those giant trees – that would have taken days of winding through the forest, so I can't really – uh –

confirm anything, but I did once find the tip of a big skeleton. At least, I think it was a skeleton."

"So this tree of yours then is the only example we have of possible propagation. I certainly hope you are wrong. Even if only the mole vipers began to multiply – can you imagine how our world would change?"

Osric stepped up. As his heavy boot thumped down, something that had bothered Aedan for years finally dropped into place.

"It's a trap!" he exclaimed without thinking of the consequences. "Those huge bronze jaws with the giant teeth and the spring by the Lekran ship ..."

Osric and Fergal spun on him.

"How did you learn about *that*?" Osric demanded, almost in a shriek. "Not even Dun is allowed in there. Construction teams were blindfolded and carted in. Only ..."

Fergal began to laugh and dropped his head into his hands. "Ah, Osric. I think we should have known better by now, don't you? How do you think he found out? That academy is yielding its secrets to young Aedan like an overburdened plum tree tossing down its fruit."

Osric held up a finger in front of Aedan's face, his lips tight as if he was about to explode with threats and warnings. Aedan could see them gathering under the surface, wrestling for front position, getting jumbled and crowded. Eventually they combined into a soulish "Bahh!" of disgust. Osric shook his head and marched away with thumping strides, crushing the grass underfoot.

"Well could it be?" Aedan ventured.

Fergal was still grinning – at least his eyes were. "A trap you mean?"

"Yes."

"That is a most disagreeable thought. But I do see the logic of it. Our best guess back then was that it was intended for crippling rival boats somehow, but the design never seemed ideal for any application we could imagine. Though I don't think I want to know what could be caught in a trap that size, your suggestion is the simplest so far, and the simplest explanation is often the correct one. But this has reminded me of something. One of the builders once made a peculiar report – he found a spear embedded in the woodwork of the deck."

Aedan dropped his head and looked at the ground, preparing for some red-hot words, but all he heard was a thoughtful "Hmm".

They spent the next two days keeping watch for the newly awakened locust. There were a few false alarms – the large shape of a mottled crane was twice mistaken for the oversized insect as it beat its ponderous way across the sky, but nothing of the locust was seen.

After a particularly muggy day and a late-afternoon cloudburst, they were drying themselves off before the fire when Aedan remembered something he had kept losing between the cracks in his thoughts.

"Liru," he said. "You never told me how you came by another weapon. You only took the dagger. What did you throw at Rork?"

She looked away and peered into the fire, which Aedan thought odd as she was normally so direct. She replied with only a hint of embarrassment, "Your boot."

Chapter 59

"Are you ready for this?" Fergal asked.

"Yes," Aedan said. It was the right answer. It was the only answer, though he and Fergal both knew it to be wind. He looked at the palace and unthinkingly clenched his fists. When he noticed a guard looking at him, he compelled himself to relax and assume a posture more befitting a humble subject.

They had returned to Castath slowly because of injuries, so the journey had taken almost two months. Eastridge was now a military outpost. It was secure, but the presence of soldiers was a hard reminder of the cruelty that lurked beyond the mountains.

When the travellers had crested the last rise and the broad grasslands and proud city of Castath stood beneath them again, Aedan had been struck by its frailness after the mighty walls and hulking sentinels of Kultûhm. Still, the improvements to defences were considerable.

The outer walls had grown taller and there was work taking place on the nearby hill. He felt proud to have been a part of those designs. Then the pride fell and withered with a knife in its back. Betrayal. He could not shake it from his mind. He had been betrayed. Liru, Culver, Fergal – they had all served the city, and the prince had been willing to have them slaughtered to suppress an honest yet inconvenient suspicion of danger.

The only thing that kept Aedan's anger in check was his caution.

Leaving Castath was an option, but it would mean leaving those who had become family to him. He did not have the heart to start over, not again, not yet. And he still had much to learn.

The party was silent as the bustle of country roads became the familiar rumble of the city – clopping hooves, rattling wheels, the shouting of peasants, haggling of merchants, and the wild games of children. After months of quiet travel it was an overwhelming onslaught. They were approaching the city gate when they were intercepted by a jingling regiment of the special guard, silver armour and spotless white tunics flashing in the sun. The captain of the regiment summoned them to the keep, immediately.

They had expected this.

When they arrived, the whole group, enclosed in a cage of marching soldiers, was taken into the centre of the courtyard where they now waited.

Aedan glanced over at Liru. She looked as angry as he felt. This was not a reception of welcome or thanks. It was quarantine.

At a signal, the regiment marched them into the main building. This time they were shown into a windowless chamber, thickly carpeted and lavishly ornamented, where only the prince and Ganavant awaited them, each behind a large desk.

"Welcome! Welcome!" Burkhart cried, throwing his arms open as if he would embrace them, and staying behind his desk.

Ganavant did not smile.

"We have so much to discuss and I am eager to hear what you have discovered. The whole city is abuzz over your return – somehow the news of your approach arrived before you did."

It was almost a question. His eyes had a hard glint as they darted from one member of the party to the next, but nobody offered an explanation.

Aedan thought back to the conversation he had noticed between Fergal and a young courier while they were still a ways out. Cunning. The widespread curiosity would make secret murders difficult. He wondered if that would be enough.

When nobody in the group offered a reply, Burkhart resumed. "Before we get started, tell me, what has become of the rest of the party? Where are Culver and the other soldiers?"

Fergal had reverted to his passive, subordinate role. To the prince, he would be no more than a voluminous and offensively bushy clerk. It was Osric who replied.

"Culver is dead, along with Commander Thormar and all the soldiers except those sent back to Eastridge and the two you see here. We encountered many hardships along the way."

"Osric," said Ganavant, "how is it that you were among this number? The prince's commission did not include you."

"You are correct, Ganavant. It did not include me, but neither did it exclude me. My standing commission from the king in Tullenroe is to ensure the safety of the southern empire and the success of its ventures. When this venture – deemed of the highest importance by our prince – came under threat, my duty was clear. I am surprised it is not clear to you."

"Your judgements strike me as ill-considered and wasteful of resources. You are a general. A whole town had been lost and you chose to accompany a small band of travellers."

Osric never made threats. His reputation and presence were so intimidating that he did not need to. He turned now and faced Ganavant with a look that caused even the furniture to gulp.

"Truly Ganavant? Is that how they strike you? Despite the fact that Eastridge was recovered without the loss of a single soldier? Despite the fact that you are still in complete ignorance of what Culver's party faced? Despite the fact that our prince here named the quest an inquiry of the highest importance, and without my presence it would certainly have failed? Your assessment is strangely at odds with the facts, Councillor."

"You exceeded your orders," Ganavant snapped. "You interfered where you were not authorised."

Osric stepped forward, dropped his plate-sized hands on the table and leaned towards Ganavant. "Interfered?" he said, "Now why would you choose that word? Am I to understand that you had some desire to deliberately exclude the first general of the realm from this quest?"

Any other man would have backed away, but Ganavant stood where he was and looked up with toad-like detachment that could have been indifference or calculation. Aedan had never seen anyone stand up to the general before. Osric was frightening, but it was not Osric who seemed the more dangerous of the two. There was something unnatural, something disturbing about those big slithering eyes that seemed always to be measuring, just waiting for the range to be right.

"Osric," the prince said, "I concede that Ganavant has been less than cordial. I would ask that we put this behind us and move on. Will you tell me what befell the party, why so many were lost? And please, let us be seated. I have much to ask and I would have you all comfortable."

The velvet-cushioned chairs looked as delicate as sea shells with spindly flamingo legs. Aedan glanced over at Osric's, half expecting it to crumple under the bull-weight for which it was clearly not designed.

When it held together, he chanced a quick look at the prince. Burkhart was attired in his usual carefree way. He seemed almost to disdain the elegant fripperies of royalty, as if he wanted to look like a man of the people, comfortable as one of them. But his eyes were not comfortable. They would not settle anywhere, and shadows hung beneath them in spite of a nose that glowed more brightly than before. His cheeks, once pudgy, were taut. Every now and then they would jump and twitch as if spiders wriggled under the skin. This was the face of a man beset by worries, anchored to the floor of a rising sea. Still, he was working hard to appear jovial, leaning back in his chair and fixing a kindly expression on his wilted features.

After seating himself, Osric detailed the journey.

Aedan saw the events as they unfolded in his mind's eye to the rhythm of Osric's words. But something distracted him. A slight movement of Merter's head revealed that he had heard it too. The tread and scuffle of boots – many boots – in the hallway outside. More than the escort that had brought them in. The steps were quiet, but there were too many for them to remain unheard. They were soldiers. Aedan was sure of it – soldiers were not known for stealth. Ganavant showed no reaction, but the prince coughed, leaned in his chair, crossed and re-crossed his legs. He almost succeeded in drowning out the sound.

Osric's voice did not waver. He spoke on. When he reached the stage where the soldiers deserted, the prince interrupted.

"I would not have expected soldiers to desert or rebel under a general's command," he said.

"It is a point well made," Osric replied, something glinting in his eye. "But these men, I happen to know, were decommissioned and were meant to be serving time in the barrack prison for various crimes, all of them serious – insubordination, defection, striking an officer. They were not soldiers but law-breakers. How is it that they ended up under Senbert's command?"

Ganavant pointed. "Senbert," he said. "Consider yourself under arrest."

"Highness," Osric interrupted, "it seems that your councillor is unaware – a captain does not have the authority to release prisoners. The order could only have come from much higher. I would be deeply interested to learn who signed those releases."

For a moment, nobody spoke. If Ganavant was concerned, he did not show it. He actually seemed amused at Osric's tone.

"You leave this to me," said the prince. "It is best that you do not speak of the matter again. I'll investigate it myself."

"Actually," Osric said. "I should inform you that I have already written of the matter in my last report to your father."

Ganavant shifted slightly, but Burkhart leapt to his feet and shouted, "You wrote to the king! About this!"

"Naturally. It is my responsibility. I am the first general of the realm. My eyes are the king's."

Ganavant turned to the prince. "They must have intercepted the courier near the city gate," he said. "Shall I issue a recall?"

The prince nodded and Ganavant stamped over to the door. "Quick!" he yelled to the guards outside. "Put together a squad of rangers. Find today's north-bound courier. Arrest him and bring him to me. If the seals on any documents are broken I'll throw you and every one of the rangers in prison."

There was a barked "Yessir" and a clatter of receding boots.

Aedan could have cried with dismay. That had been Osric's security. Why had he spoken of it? There was no courier who could avoid a squad of rangers.

Osric turned to Ganavant. "Why did you not tell me before you did that?" he asked.

"Because you have already *interfered* enough," the councillor said, emphasising the word this time as he sat.

"It would only have been to save you the trouble and the waste of resources, which I understand to be of great concern to you."

"No waste. The rangers and your letter will be back before the day is over."

"I'm afraid that is not likely."

"General Osric, how is one courier going to avoid a team of my men. It seems your wits are not what they say. Unless you managed to find a flying horse, there is no doubt of the outcome. Did you use a flying horse?" Ganavant asked with a smirk.

"I think it was a mule cart."

"And why in the name of summer snow would my rangers not catch your mule cart?"

"Because the cart left over three months ago. I dispatched my report before leaving for Kultûhm. The package I sent earlier today contains a letter and a small gift for my niece on her birthday."

Ganavant stopped smirking. Burkhart, by the whiteness of his face, appeared to have stopped breathing.

Osric continued. "The king's personal emissary and military escort should enter our gates within the month. If he finds so much as a whiff of foul dealing, the position of first councillor might just become a dangerous one. I hope, for your sake, that there are no stains when he arrives."

The room fell silent.

Ganavant fixed his eyes on Osric. This time there was no indifference. The smile lingered, but it was sickly, and poisonous.

Prince Burkhart recovered himself with somewhat more effort. "I will be glad to welcome the royal emissary on his arrival," he stammered, and paused to cough. "I have no doubt that everything will be found to be in order. Will you excuse me for just a moment?" He walked to the door and slipped outside. The boots were much quieter this time as they withdrew, but soldiers truly were not famed for stealth.

When Burkhart returned, he was in better possession of himself and asked Osric to resume.

Osric told of the entry into the fortress, though he held back several details.

"A snake?" said the Prince. "Is that all? Surely a company of armed men could deal with a big snake. Could we not send a larger detachment to drive it off and harvest the treasures of Kultûhm?"

"It is too big. Its head would not get through the door."

Ganavant threw his quill down and glared with open disgust.

Osric ignored him. "And it is changed in more ways than size. A hundred attackers would not survive as long as it took to count them. We owe our escape more to luck than anything else. I believe this creature is the reason the fortress was abandoned and the reason it remains that way."

"That would make it almost a thousand years old," said Burkhart. "That's not natural."

"Highness, this creature is hardly natural as we understand the word."

Burkhart leaned back and kicked his feet up onto the desk, gradually regaining his boyish manner. "So, the myths have some basis. It would also mean that Culver was wrong. He believed the storms triggered earthquakes that were responsible for emptying Kultûhm. Did he learn anything of them before his demise? You — I've forgotten your name ..."

"Fergal, Highness."

"Yes, that's it. You were Culver's assistant. Can you tell us what he discovered?"

"Culver found mention of the storms, but nothing of quakes, so the link between the two was not validated. He would have agreed with General Osric's assessment of why Kultûhm stands empty."

"Did you agree with Culver's theories about the storms?"

"No, Highness. I did not." It was quite true. Culver had produced no theories about the storms.

"Are there any among you who hold to Culver's ideas?"

None of them did. Even if they had, there was a tension in the air that warned them to keep silent. It was clear that the prince had some reason for hushing this threat of disaster, a reason that could move him to extreme measures.

"Well, though the loss of Culver saddens me," the prince said with deep relief and not a hint of sadness, "it is perhaps a good thing that the inquiry has been shown inconclusive. The storms have no deeper meaning than a message from the gods. My diviners have succeeded in circulating an interpretation of peace through the city. It was a grave concern that Culver might fill people's heads with dangerous ideas, sowing fear, threatening the security of our people, the stability of our city. Such ideas can undermine our strength. They might even be considered treasonous."

The prince had not made this speech idly, and he looked around the room from one person to the next, avoiding only Osric. "Are there any among you who feel any need to pursue or spread Culver's notions, that we are facing some horrific devastation?"

None did. They had agreed not to mention the possibility of some dangerous creature slumbering on top of the Pellamines. If Burkhart even suspected them of spreading fear ...

"Good," the prince said. "Then you are free to go, but do not disappoint me. You will doubtless be asked of your journey and I want you to be loud in your rejection of Culver's theories. You have served Castath well and I commend you all for your bravery and skill. I have many ears beyond these walls and will be listening to hear how you continue to serve the city by spreading a report of peaceful assurance."

Though he wore a bright smile, the threat was obvious to everyone. Aedan knew the prince well enough to understand the full meaning. They were now puppets whose mouths were under the prince's control. A loose word, an unguarded opinion, and they would receive the attentions of grimy tools in a black dungeon.

As they left, Aedan realised with a sudden nausea how close they had walked to the edge, how treacherous their prince's preparations had been. Burkhart was all casual warmth and easy laughter, and behind this sunny curtain was a readiness to murder – perhaps not with his own hands, but Ganavant would be more than willing to perform any such task. He, Aedan guessed, was the dark arm of the prince's rule. And he would make a dangerous enemy, one who would embrace the lowest means.

Though Osric's rank was higher, Ganavant held more power in this city, for he was clearly the prince's favoured man. Ganavant was not encumbered by a conscience, which made him a tool that Burkhart could apply to any purpose, honourable or otherwise. Osric could never be such a man. It was for this very reason that he was trusted by King Elgar.

The prince drew those of supple morals to his inner circle, and he would no sooner confide in Osric than undress in public. Osric's eyes were indeed the king's eyes, and it was becoming clear that Burkhart had much to hide from them both.

Clouds were darkening the city's keep. The northern king's favour, Aedan realised, might not protect Osric long, and that meant that Osric might not be able to protect him.

Aedan now had two matters on which his careless tongue would bring about his death. During the silent walk back to the academy, he envied the scampering street children whose names the prince did not know.

Chapter 60

"Hey, look! It's the wanderer returned."

"He's got bigger."

"And uglier."

"Aedan, did you bring us gifts? Rescue any foreign princesses?"

"Did you bring one for Lorrimer? He hasn't fallen in love for weeks now."

"Shut up Peashot. You've been pining like a pigeon for Liru for three months."

"Pigeon's don't pine, Lorrimer."

"Yes, they do."

"Oh, so now you're an expert on pigeons?"

"Lorrimer knows nothing about pigeons, but he *is* the expert on pining."

In spite of his uncertainties about returning to Burkhart's city, it felt good to be among his friends again, and Aedan slipped into the routine quickly enough. Thanks to Fergal's teaching and Osric's training, he did not seem to have lost much ground. Some of the topics he had covered were slightly different, though. The examinations were only two weeks away and he nearly injured himself catching up.

The examiners were satisfied by his progress, with the usual exception of Kollis. Dun was particularly impressed, remarking that Aedan was noticeably stronger and judged his encounters with a far steadier eye. The worst result was in Lekran. Aedan's grip on the language was found to be the poorest in the class. Law was nearly as bad. Rodwell felt that Aedan was not applying himself. He was right. Aedan had lost all interest in Burkhart's leadership and the laws by which he ruled. He passed the subject, but barely. His third year was complete.

Liru, too, was promoted.

Malik did not openly display his fury, but none could miss the thorns in his eyes.

As usual, Vayle received perfect results for anything that tested his extraordinary memory, and Lorrimer endured a perfect agony of suspense followed by infinite bliss when he slipped over the bar.

Giddard asked Aedan to stay behind after the final class of the year.

The wizened master seated himself on his table and scratched the deep wrinkles around his mouth. "Since leaving for Kultûhm, you have changed in a way that I have seldom observed before. Perhaps I should say never before. Since you've been back, people have been watching and noticing. They've also been talking and I, of course, have been listening."

He dropped his hand and looked straight at Aedan.

Aedan shuffled.

"This is the first time," Giddard resumed, "that I have ever heard of a third-year student making an apology to a first-year student and then offering to teach him and his friends a few personally-devised combat tricks. I can tell you the impression it made on them was staggering. That little boy is standing taller than he's ever done. He used to be as dull as a corpse – couldn't get any participation from him. Now he participates so much I can hardly get a word in myself."

Aedan laughed. "I'm glad to hear it," he said.

"I learned from Fergal what happened to you out east," Giddard said. "I have no idea how to understand it, but I can say that the change in you is not imagined. All the masters have noticed, even Kollis, though you are not likely to hear it from him, and though I believe he attributes the change to his own efforts at improving you." Giddard's face betrayed nothing, and Aedan had the good sense not to laugh.

The party at Liru's had become a tradition. This time, due to her long absence, her parents agreed to host all of Liru's and Aedan's classmates, as well as Delwyn, of course. It was unnecessary to inform Malik that he was not welcome. Neither he nor Cayde arrived. They spent the time before the celebration inventing reasons why it would be an awful event, and casting wistful looks at their excited classmates.

When everyone had arrived and the music began, Peashot surprised Liru by knowing the steps to her favourite dances, and chatting to her in the most appalling Mardrae. She was delighted with the efforts, and her bright smile and raven hair whirled constantly across the dance floor. Though she and Peashot were inseparable, it was clear that she was as proud of Aedan as of a brother, telling the story of his fight with Rork many times over. Aedan always diverted the attention, finishing it off with the little detail on how the famed swordsman had finally been toppled.

Ilona had forgotten her dislike of Liru – for how long, none could say – and she was apparently determined to win back Aedan's affection, insisting on dancing with him more than once. But then she seemed equally intent on winning the affections of Hadley, Warton, and two or three others. She had grown even more dazzling and it was not lost on the boys. Perhaps the only person more taken with her looks was Ilona herself, and it went a long way to spoiling them. When Aedan saw how sure she was of being admired, it almost made him dislike her. But then when those eyes searched him out ...

Aedan was disappointed with himself for being so easily drawn back to the spider's web, as Liru had once put it. He fell into blackest despair when Ilona danced with Hadley, and studied her for signs of disinterest. Then she danced with Warton, and Aedan's heart dropped another foot into the earth. When Kian approached her for a dance and Aedan saw her derisive sneer, he suddenly woke as if from a drugged stupor. Peashot's comment floated back to him – kind and sweet people are kind and sweet to everyone. Ilona was nice when she wanted something. It was like a beautiful mask she put on for a purpose, and beneath it was steel.

Despite this, Aedan's eye was still lured whenever the golden hair swung across the dance floor.

The following afternoon Aedan began searching the libraries. There were five of them in the marshals' division alone. The image that had appeared in the lightning was still clear in his mind – a red leather cover with a picture of a lizard curled twice on itself. At first he thought the search would be quick as there were not many volumes bound in red leather, but after fruitlessly scouring all the libraries in his quadrant, he began to wonder.

Access to the other quadrants was not that straightforward. Security, however, was less strict in the law wing. By dressing up and assuming a preoccupied look tinctured with that pained superiority he had often noticed in the students from this wing, he was allowed to pass.

The search was fruitless. The officers' wing possessed only one library, and it did not seem anyone cared who entered. Again, the book was not to be seen.

He might have been able to pose as a law student, but he had no intention of disguising himself as a girl, so he asked Liru if she would search the libraries in the women's section. It took her a whole day, but she gave no sign of exhaustion when she returned and suggested that they try the army-owned city library in the morning. Peashot and Lorrimer got wind of the search and offered to join in. By midday they had scoured every shelf without success.

"Are you sure it was a lizard?" Lorrimer asked. "I saw one with a coiled chain."

"It was definitely a lizard," said Aedan. "I can still see it as clearly as your face."

"As unpleasant?"

"Shut up, Peashot."

The fiery-haired, trouble-hunting boy was about to step it up a notch. He opened his mouth, but whatever he was going to say was lost as he sprang in the air with a howl of pain. Liru gave him a stern look when he landed.

Aedan was not sure how to announce himself to Fergal. He wasn't even sure if it would be possible to reach his office unattended. When he got back to the academy, he gathered a pile of books from his shelf and put on a frustrated look of someone doing errands. The guards knew his face and when they saw the tell-tale errand expression, they let him pass without a question.

The knock was answered by a familiar voice. Aedan opened the door. Fergal was busy studying a map against the far wall.

"Come in, Aedan."

Aedan paused. "How did you know it was me?"

"Because everyone who has permission to knock at my door has been given clear instructions not to, on pain of death or something along those lines; because I expected it would take you three days after the conclusion of your examinations to search the libraries for the book you asked me about during our return journey; because your persistent nature and penchant for finding yourself where you do not belong were bound to lead you down here in spite of it being forbidden; and because your knock was too timid for anyone on a real errand. Then, of course, there is the reflection in the brass shield over there."

"Oh ... Uh, I really didn't mean to disturb you."

"I sincerely hope that is untrue. If you arrived here with no objective capable of disturbing me then you arrived with no objective at all, and you will have succeeded in disturbing me without purpose."

Any man is rendered more intimidating by the walls of his office and Aedan found himself considerably off balance now.

"Are you angry with me?" he asked.

"Do I look angry?"

Aedan could never tell what mood Fergal was in. He was not even sure if the man was capable of such things. Whatever emotions played through Fergal's thoughts ran as deep as water gurgling under a glacier.

"I ... don't know," said Aedan. "I can't really tell." He saw the eyes wrinkle slightly.

"Fair enough," Fergal said. "Osric the stone-faced himself accused me of being unreadable." He moved over to a bookshelf that spanned the room and drew a red volume which he handed to Aedan. On the cover was an image burned into the leather surface – a lizard wrapped twice around itself, exactly as Aedan had described the book to Fergal during the journey home.

"You hid it from me!"

"I did not. I spent some time searching, and when I found it I drew it for you. There are archives that you do not know about. Very few of us have access. Before you leave here, you need to assure me that you will look after this volume. It is an original and there are no copies."

"I will," said Aedan, barely able to contain his excitement.

"I might have sent word earlier," Fergal mused, half to himself. "Could have saved you a lot of searching, but I thought it good to hold back for two reasons. Firstly, it would cause you to become acquainted with the shelves of all the libraries you have access to and those you do not; secondly, it would be fitting punishment for disturbing me."

"But I hadn't disturbed you yet."

"Quite so. An appalling exercise of distorted ethics – punishment before crime as if making a purchase. But as it turns out, my wrath is appeased and I send you on your way with pleasant wishes and the stern warning I hope you have not forgotten."

"I haven't forgotten – I'll look after it. But how do I return it when I'm done?"

"By disturbing me again, boy. How else? Now off with you."

Aedan ran all the way back to his dorm as fast as his cumbersome pile of books would allow. It was the second time he almost triggered one of the stair traps. They had caught two inattentive daydreamers over the years. The first was Lorrimer who had been seen a moment earlier lagging behind with dreamy eyes and a tender smile. The second was also Lorrimer, and this time he took two others with him. He claimed to have been thinking about an abstract problem in trade law. No one even pretended to believe him.

When Aedan reached the dorm, he tossed his own books on the desk and settled down to discover what was hidden within the red covers.

The script was less than neat, but it was not this that caused him to frown. He worked through the first words. Some were familiar – enough to tell him that the book was written in Lekran.

He slammed the cover shut and pushed it away. After pacing the room a few times, he decided to at least find out what it was about. There was no name on the cover, but the title page made it clear. *The Customs and Rituals of Ulnoi.* If Fergal had not cautioned him against damaging the book, he would have repeatedly hurled it against the wall until it fell apart, then burned the pages and mixed the ashes with pig muck. Ulnoi was the foulest word he knew in any language. It was the north island of Lekrau, the island where his beloved Kalry had been offered to whatever filthy gods those murderers served. And he was expected to read this?

He clapped the book shut again, booted his chair across the room and stormed out.

The sun was shining outside and it annoyed him further. What was this obsession that everyone seemed to have with understanding Lekrau? Why was he constantly pushed to not just face but to study the one culture that was death to him? He felt tricked, betrayed. Forgiving and confronting his father was one thing, but this was going too far.

The rest of the day was spent in a fog of disappointment lit with the occasional flashes of anger. He could not throw the book out; neither could he return it so soon unless he wanted to hear Fergal's opinion on blinding prejudice and the need to overcome it. He pushed the volume to the back of his shelf and stacked the rest of his books in front until the red cover was hidden. Then he concerned himself with other matters and drove the book from his thoughts.

One of these matters was the arrival of the emissary from Tullenroe along with two hundred cavalry. The entrance was spectacular. Prince Burkhart and his entire retinue publically welcomed them, and – Aedan suspected – privately wished them dead. If there were any uncomfortable scenes, though, they took place behind thick walls.

———

Murn had not been saddled for months and it took a while to reacquaint him with the leather. Aedan went back to the sand bags and started over. But it was quicker this time. He worked up the courage to get on the horse's back again, at first just sitting, then walking with a lead, and then, finally, with the bridle.

Sometimes Murn took it into his head to perform, and then he was a ship in a tempest. It was a game to him; most things were. Students would come to watch Aedan aboard the dark beast. He tried valiantly to put on a good show, but mostly he looked like a desperate sailor clinging to the mast for dear life.

The few moments of trotting or walking were never long. Murn had too much energy. His antics weren't vindictive, but shaking Aedan loose was an entertaining challenge. Aedan put up some jumps which gave Murn a new purpose. It also gave Aedan several new bruises.

The mischievous ruthrek was still causing trouble with the other horses, in fact, with anyone or anything that came within range.

A dog once slipped into a neighbouring arena, yapping at the ponies' hocks. They neighed and tooted and galloped clear. The dog was having a wonderful time.

Then it spied the tall, dark horse standing alone in the middle of its paddock. The dog's hair bristled, courage poured into its veins. It stalked into clear ground, head low, shoulders rolling, eyes fixed. Then, when the distance was right, it launched into a furious, barking charge, straight for the isolated horse.

The dog left the paddock a moment later, doing at least double its initial speed. It was no longer barking but yelping, then squealing, and it's back legs looked as if they were about to run under its body and overtake the rest of the dog. Twenty feet behind and gaining fast, was half a ton of black, barrelling fate. The dog shot under the fence and kept going until its yelps faded away. Murn thundered to a stop just before the beams, looking mildly disappointed. He had enjoyed the game.

When the rest of the students returned from recess, so did Aedan's greatest source of misery – Iver. Aedan was strolling across the wintry lawns, looking nowhere in particular when he heard a deep voice behind him.

"Worm!" the senior barked.

Aedan stood where he was as the tall law student strode up to him and grasped the front of his shirt in a big fist.

"Thought you could hide forever did you?"

Aedan made no reply.

Iver smiled. "I've had an idea. I thought it would be a good for the world to know about your hollow spine so I've written up a detailed account of your break-in and how you behaved when you were caught. It makes for fascinating reading. You are going to work for me whether you like it or not. Report to my quarters tonight for instructions and if you don't show up, I'll have a hundred copies made of my little report and I'll hand them out to anyone who is interested. Can you imagine how the news would travel? A marshal with no spine. Anyone who wanted to test it out would only prove its truth. If you try to hide from me again, I'll ruin you."

When Aedan returned to his group, he was preoccupied as he sat down. No more running, no more circling, he thought.

That afternoon, Liru and Peashot, worried about Aedan, went looking for him and finally located him at the stables. It was a loud tinkling rattle that drew their attention. When it stopped, they saw Aedan straighten up and emerge from Murn's stall with a bucket. Even Murn looked puzzled and nosed over Aedan's shoulder.

"You *can* tell the difference between a cow and a stallion, right?" asked Peashot, wrinkling his nose at the bucket.

Aedan shrugged. "It's a rotten habit some horses have. When they get into the stables they foul the straw. I thought I would try something to keep it clean. Better for his hooves."

"You do this every day?"

"No. Don't think I'll try it again. It splashes."

Peashot backed away.

"Liru," Aedan said, "I've been meaning to ask you. You have access to the chemistry labs, don't you?"

"Yes."

"Do you think they would let you take a small vial of powdered madder root?"

"I'll see if I can find some. I'm sure it would be fine. What's it for?"

"Just a little experiment I was thinking about." Aedan would say no more.

It was night. Every one of Aedan's classmates was there bar Malik. They crept past the half-nosed statue of Olemris – still frowning at his herbaceous audience – past two sentries, between the giant crindo boards, and through the forbidden boulevard of the law wing. Then they took cover in the shadows while Aedan knocked on an open shutter.

Iver's heavy-browed face appeared. Aedan began handing the costly wine bottles through the window. Even he could tell that this was good stock. Iver had made it clear that a single broken bottle would be repaid with a broken arm. Aedan had treated the bottles like gold, wrapping them in his own clothes to protect them. When the last bottle was handed over, Iver said something and Aedan bowed slightly and withdrew.

"Are you going to tell us now why we are here?" Hadley asked on behalf of the waiting group.

Aedan spoke in a whisper. It only took a sentence before the entire group rushed to the window as one. They stayed low, not looking, but listening.

There was a good party going on inside. Many women's voices were mingled in the din.

Corks popped, Iver's name was cheered, and there was the sound of backslapping. The bully's voice could be heard as he told them about his new slave. There was a clinking of glass and the gurgling of wine. A toast was proposed, something about shaping the world any way they pleased. More cheers were heard and then everything grew strangely silent. There was some violent coughing.

"Wow! Kicks like a mule!"

"What year did you say this was?"

"Sort of smells like a mule too."

"I think one of the bottles was a bit corked."

"Mine tastes funny. Actually it tastes … it tastes …"

"I think I'm going to throw up!"

"Iver, what filth have you bought us?"

"Quick, she's going to be sick!"

"No! Not on the carpet!"

"If you've poisoned my Gertie …"

The small crowd of listening boys was shaking so violently with suppressed mirth that it seemed they would burst apart. They scampered and staggered around the corner where they laughed until they ached.

"Ah," Peashot sighed, stumbling up to Aedan. "If only Murn could have been here to take pride in his work. The world's first horse wine-maker. Oh – madder root – it's a red dye isn't it?"

"With a bitter taste. I had to match the colour to the original wine. I hope it didn't spoil the flavour."

The reprisal came early the next day. Aedan was alone, flicking acorns over the benches. Iver marched down to him at a pace that was nearly a run. When Aedan saw him approach, he felt his knees begin to tremble.

He whispered under his breath, "Just a man. Just a man ..." and set his jaw. The fear was there – there was no denying it – but it no longer crushed him. Though that treacherous section of his bridge was groaning, it was not collapsing as before. It was holding the weight. He had to finish this.

Iver caught Aedan by the front of the shirt and twisted it, almost lifting him off the ground.

"You want to die?" he snarled.

"I'm sorry, sir, was the wine not good?" Aedan spoke loudly. Too loudly.

"Keep your voice down, you impudent beggar."

"Why? Don't you want people to know that you've been forcing students to smuggle your wine? I thought that would make you seem strong."

"Don't play with me, worm. Remember, I have half a dozen witnesses to back up whatever story I decide to tell, and you have –"

"Twenty-eight."

Iver stared. Aedan pointed to the trees where the long line of his classmates appeared, less only Malik and Cayde. Eleven of the girls were there too, having got wind of what was happening. This was something they would not miss. The large group waved and called greetings to the senior, whom they all addressed as "Sir".

Iver let Aedan's shirt go.

"I would be more than happy to stay on as your smuggler," Aedan said. "I have really enjoyed my position. No?"

Iver spat. Aedan brushed his face off, turned and walked away.

"Come back here you snivelling cur, and I'll ..."

Aedan came back and this time the way he walked was somehow different, more purposeful.

Iver clenched his fists. But it was all too obvious that if he beat Aedan to a pulp, there would be a whole line of witnesses to testify at his expulsion hearing. And if he lost ... Aedan was looking at him in a way that was almost – almost eager.

"I'm resigning," Aedan said. "And I'm also removing the other boy from your employment. If we" – he gestured to his friends – "speak of what we saw now and last night, you face not just expulsion, but barring from all forms of legal practice in the district. I checked with my master of legal studies."

Iver looked like he was about to explode. His eyes grew black as a winter's night and his face turned pink and swelled up, but his hands stayed at his sides. Eventually he threw off some choice threats and curses, and marched back across the field to a chorus of cheering and applause.

Chapter 61

Winter had the day in a firm grip and was filling it with a wind made of ice and nails. Aedan was happy for once to be indoors, though he regretted not bringing a lantern. He was cleaning out Murn's stall which – while providing an escape from the wind – was dark as night on this gloomy morning. Telling the good straw from the soiled was not easily done by sight, and he was not prepared to lower his nose and sniff. He held his breath and thought, with a grin, of Iver, as he tossed another forkful of pungent straw to the side.

Snatches of voices slipped through the open door as they rode the gusts of cold air. Aedan looked out from the dim stable and immediately pulled back. It was the royal guard, plumes and capes being flung about them, spoiling their dignity. It made them look like perched birds when the wind catches them from behind.

Ahead of the soldiers, wrapped in thick coats, were two men Aedan would have recognised from any distance – the Prince, who walked with an unusually eager spring to his step, and Ganavant who, as always, thumped beside him like a giant bullfrog. Two more men walked on the other side of the prince, and it appeared as if he was giving them a tour of sorts by the way he pointed and talked.

Aedan had no desire to be seen by Burkhart or his councillor. He wanted to keep as far away from those men as possible. The corners of his stall were sunk in darkness, so he moved into the blackest one and waited. He just wanted them to pass on. The party appeared to have stopped nearby, judging from the voices.

Then the two strangers stepped into the doorway of Murn's stall and began to speak, keeping their voices low. Something about them struck Aedan as unusual, but when he heard the words he understood. They were speaking Vinthian. He could follow most of the conversation.

"What think you of the city so far?"

"I think she will like it. I think she will like it very much."

"Can they withstand the Fenn?"

"Let's hope so. We may not find another leader so *ralge* as this young prince."

"Let us ask if we can inspect the defences. Considering the *krulua*, it is not an inappropriate request."

Aedan had understood all the words but *ralge* and *krulua*. Burkhart's nervous manner suggested that there was some kind of foreign courtship underway. If that was the case then *ralge* probably meant desirable or something, and *krulua* courtship. He ran the new words through his mind a few times so he would be able to ask about them later.

The two men had finished talking. They were looking out at the paddocks, looking at Murn.

"That is an animal worth remembering," the nearer of the two said. They watched for a long time.

Aedan did not like the way they admired his horse. He was happy to see the last of them as the party reassembled and moved away across the lawns.

Aedan ran back to the main buildings as soon as Burkhart turned the corner and was hidden from sight.

"Finished the book already?" Fergal asked as Aedan pushed the door open.

Aedan dropped his gaze. "No. It's something else. Can we be overheard?"

"Not if you close the door."

Aedan did so and took the seat Fergal indicated. "Do you remember you once said you thought Prince Burkhart had another motivation for suppressing any rumours of danger to the city?"

"I do."

"Well, I just overheard another ... Stop laughing at me. It wasn't my fault. I was busy in the stable and they happened to have a discussion in the doorway of *my* horse's stall."

"I apologise. I'm only amused at your consistency. Let's hear what concerns you."

Aedan repeated the conversation as well as he could remember. When Fergal made no response, he offered an opinion. "It looked to me like the prince was showing off. Is there a woman he wants to impress? Some royal Vinthian he is courting?"

Fergal did not answer. "Recite the conversation again slowly," he said, taking up a quill and a blank parchment, "this time without translating it."

Aedan did so. "What does *ralge* mean?" he asked.

"Somewhere between innocent and trusting."

"Oh." Aedan saw how big a difference that made to the meaning. "And *krulua*?"

"Negotiations."

"So this has nothing to do with a romantic arrangement, then, does it?"

"That might be there too, but the discussion you overheard implies a political arrangement, such as a trade agreement or military alliance, and this would indeed be a strong reason for Burkhart to suppress rumours of danger or anything that might cast his city in a bad light."

"Who is the woman they talk about?"

"Officially, King Renka still holds the throne in Vinterus. But one of our sentinels –"

"Sentinels?"

"A delicate word for something else. You'll learn about them in time. One of our sentinels delivered a message that has not yet been circulated. It contains only unproven suspicions. Princess Irrinel is considered by many in that palace to be ambitious and black-hearted enough to murder her parents for the throne." Fergal paused. "Our sentinel suspects she has already done so and is hiding their deaths while she consolidates her position. What you overheard seems to confirm this."

"Do you think Prince Burkhart knows?"

"Whether he believes he is negotiating with Renka or Irrinel is of little consequence, because we are forbidden by our king to form any kind of alliance with Vinterus. They are a treacherous nation with a history of dishonour and underhand dealings. Burkhart, it would appear, is making free with the southern reaches of his father's kingdom as if it were his own. If I know

King Elgar, then this is news that would most certainly bring an end to Burkhart's rule here."

"Another secret that could get me hanged," Aedan groaned.

"Not hanged. That's only for public executions. Dungeon axes and swine feed-troughs are for hushing."

Aedan put his head in his palms for a while. "Can we get word to Tullenroe, to the king?" he asked.

"We would need far better proof than we now have, or stern eyes would be turned on us. We need to wait until it is clear what is happening, until it can be proven. Then we will send word."

"I would give a few toes to see the last of this prince. Being in his city is like standing in a bear trap that's been jammed with a stick. I keep wondering when the stick will break."

"Don't panic, Aedan. For the time being we are no great threat to Burkhart. He has far more troublesome things on his mind. He is not likely to think of much beyond these negotiations and the Fenn threat. We will find a way to deal with him eventually. Something will slip and we'll have our proof. Hang onto your toes for now. If things get desperate you can make Burkhart an offer."

Aedan laughed. Fergal's eyes were lost in thought while his hand dug somewhere through the wild bush of a beard, probably just as lost.

"I'll let Osric know," he said. "In fact, I think the academy high council should be told."

"May I know who they are?"

"Considering the context in which your name will be mentioned, it is a fair request. I am chairman. Sorn and Edreas – whom you do not know – along with Giddard and Balfore hold the other seats.

"Balfore, mayor of the city south?"

"Yes. We needed a man with strong political influence. He has done fine work for both the city and the academy. He would not approve of this disloyalty to the throne."

"Seeing the prince reminded me of the last time I overheard them ... and I was wondering ..."

"No, Aedan. I am not going to show you what lies beneath the academy."

"I *hate* mysteries that are forbidden. They are like meals you have to watch other people eat."

"Did I forbid you to search or explore?"

"Won't I be punished if I'm caught?"

"Of course – and I will be most surprised and a little disappointed if you see that as a closed door."

"You have a strange set of ideals, Fergal."

"Nothing to do with ideals. I consider it to be part of your training. I gave my word not to admit anyone, and I will keep that. You are training to be a marshal, and marshals are required to go where others cannot. Your explorations will not be by my enabling and will be for your advancement and ultimately for the good of Castath."

Aedan grunted and rose to his feet, but Fergal was not one to forget things.

"Have you even started on the book?"

Aedan frowned. "No."

Fergal said nothing. It struck harder than the worst of Dun's shouting. That silence gnawed at him all the way back to his dorm. He pulled the red volume out and looked at the cover. The design was as familiar now as his own hand. He sat down, opened the book and tried to read. But it had the same effect as a plate of rotten offal.

"No!" he growled, shutting it and putting it back. "Not that. Anything but that!"

He drove it out of his thoughts again, but it was like shaking a pebble to the front of his shoe – just when he thought it was gone, it would slip back and make its presence felt. The only means of getting it out was by reading the book, and he could not do that. He *would* not do that. So he nudged the pebble away and pretended and thought of other things until it slipped under his tread and made him wince and almost scream with frustration. But that was the course he had chosen and he held to it.

——

Since news of Eastridge had arrived in Castath, much had changed. Aedan had noticed on his return that there were fewer soldiers patrolling within the city. Castath had no separate police force – all internal security was managed by the military – so when garrisons had been posted in a broad arc to the east, the military presence back home was thinned.

As a compromise, marshal apprentices and student officers were assigned to patrols, assisting them from time to time in order to supplement the numbers. Even so, there was no hiding the fact that fewer eyes watched inside the walls.

A cruel counterpart to this was the growing number of naive country folk that had moved to the city from their isolated homes in the east.

The result was not unforeseeable.

Aedan and Lorrimer were paired with a group of soldiers – the very old and very young. All they managed to do was aid those they found beaten and robbed, and load up those who had fared worse. The patrols were too few to be everywhere they were needed, and spotters picked them out from a long way off.

Aedan's mood sank through the day, but it was the last scene that turned him white with anger. An old woman, her skin cut and swollen with puffy bruises and her jaw struck almost from her face, hung weeping over a dead man, presumably her aged husband. The depth of her heartache was like a solid weight that rose with her soft keening and settled on the shoulders of everyone there. The younger soldiers were constantly brushing their cheeks as they tried to help her up and lift her onto the cart, but with feeble arms she fought them off and clung to the dead man, burying her face in his neck, gently brushing his thin white hair. "Oh Sherwin, Sherwin, my Sherwin ..." she cried. The couple's rough country clothes told enough of the story.

Lorrimer stood at a distance with his back to the scene. Aedan tried to watch but kept turning away, striking at the air with his iron-sheathed quarterstaff, wishing it was not air that he was striking.

That night he visited Osric's house. The general was packing for a fortnight-long patrol in the east.

"I saw an old couple near Miller's Court today," he said, sitting down. "They were old enough to be grandparents. His neck was broken and it looked like they used a hammer on her face. What is happening to our city? We send our garrisons out to defend it and it begins to cut itself up from inside."

Osric paused, waterskin in one hand, oatmeal loaf in the other. "The irony of war," he said. "It has always been this way. We are taught to think that the battle lines separate the good from the bad, but the truth, as you are beginning to understand, is less comfortable. When we have clearer knowledge of Fenn movements, perhaps we can pull back some of the patrols. Until then the dogs will take their chances."

"Osric, what are the Fenn after? I know it's not silver. We don't have much left. It wouldn't be food because their soil is just as rich as ours. What do we have that could justify a full scale war?"

"You've done some study in trade. What gem could bring about a war if even a small deposit were found?"

"Earthstars. But we don't ..."

Osric looked at him in silence.

"We do?"

"I should not really answer that, but seeing as you have been a guest in the war council and seeing as you shared knowledge that has more than once provided vital clues, I shall tell you. But it must not be passed on. The deposit was only recently found, and it has brought great danger. We are like the poor man who has just discovered a treasure trove beneath his floor. No walls to his property, flimsy locks to his doors, and merchants who would follow him back home the moment he attempted to trade. A nation trading in these gems needs to be well fortified before entering the market, or it will simply be invaded. We can't even use the stones to buy arms or hire builders. Fortunately for us, the Fenn would not want to spread the word for fear of competition."

"Have you ever seen an earthstar."

"A few. You've seen at least two yourself at Kultûhm. Don't you remember?"

"I saw a speck of light at the top of a cave."

"You saw one up close. You wanted it."

"Oh, the gem in the crown!"

"Yes."

Aedan sat back and considered. "How did the Fenn hear about our deposit?"

"I'm not sure. Prince Burkhart has not told us. I suspect he tried to look for buyers."

"Is it as bad as that? Try to sell and the buyer becomes a thief?"

"That's about the way of it. The most hostile market I know. Horrible things to have to sell."

"Do you think news of the earthstars has reached Vinterus?"

"I truly hope not, and so should you. If our young prince has not held his tongue we may find ourselves in a two-front war, with Lekrau always hovering."

Osric finished packing his food, slung his bags over his shoulder and strode to the door. "There's something you should know," he said. "Both Holt and Captain Senbert have disappeared. I've checked prisons, patrol rosters, discharges, and even asked the officers. Nothing. It's as if the earth swallowed them. I don't think they will ever be seen again."

Aedan stared, a needle of fear slipping behind his collar.

"Keep out of Burkhart's way, Aedan. Even further out of Ganavant's."

"I always do."

Osric glared at him. "There is nobody in Castath for whom that is less true." The door slammed. It was the general's version of a warm goodbye.

Aedan lingered for a while, staring into the grain of the rough oak table as if he would find in it some answer to how people could do to others what he had seen that day. And why one nation would rise against another for a few sparkling rocks.

His thoughts produced neither answers nor solace. He had intended to fix a meal, but his appetite was charred. Instead, he trudged out through the city to the walls, climbed a rickety builders' ladder, and found his usual lonely spot between sentries where he could stare out into the heavy darkness.

A while later, big feet slapped towards him and Lorrimer lowered himself onto the stone. They watched the night in silence before Lorrimer spoke.

"Still upset?" he asked.

"Still," Aedan said.

"Me too. I thought I could handle blood, but the people we saw today, none of them were armed, and even with weapons they would have been helpless. What kind of cowards ..." he trailed off.

"Do you think," Aedan said, after a while, "that anger is wrong?"

"Don't know. Maybe it depends on how you use it."

"Or where it comes from?"

"What do you mean?" Lorrimer asked.

"Well, I used to think real men turned their anger into revenge, and that's what got them to be respected. But I tried it a few times and it didn't make me feel like a man any more than swearing or kicking the chickens. But when I saw that old woman today, the anger I felt was huge and it seemed like a right kind of anger. Does that make sense?"

"I think so. Makes sense to me. I felt like that too. So did most of the soldiers, judging by how their faces looked."

Lorrimer was quiet for a time and when he spoke again his voice was different. It was the voice of someone who has decided to release a long-held secret.

"One of my uncles used to come over when he was drunk and play this game where he would jab his knife into the table between my fingers. I could see my father was scared, but he didn't want to argue with his brother-in-law, so instead he just laughed – that thin, false kind of laugh. When he hugged me afterwards I hated it. It was like he was lying. I used to think if he cared anything he would have got angry. If you care about people and you really love them, you *should* get angry at the things that put them in danger or hurt them."

"You've also got to decide to do something," said Aedan. "I used to get angry when my father ..." he caught himself, and then, after a moment's hesitation, decided he was tired of hiding it. If Lorrimer could lay down his secrets, so could he. It was time.

"I got angry when my father beat my mother," he said. "The day I decided to stand in front of him, things got really bad for me. I thought I'd made a huge mistake at the time, but I don't anymore. I would rather be the person who steps in front of a whole gang to defend someone and gets beaten up for it than the person who watches from a safe hiding. There were times I hid, and I think the shame hurts more than the bruises would have."

A distant series of creaks interrupted him. "Listen," said Aedan. "It's the main gate. It must be Osric's patrol leaving. He loves heading out at odd hours. That way nobody knows when to expect him. I wish I was going with."

Lorrimer did not chime in with his agreement. "If they actually meet an enemy front," he said, "I wonder how many of them will make it back."

The next morning, Brenton, the stabler, shocked Aedan with stories of what was taking place near his home. Later, Aedan went to visit Garald and Hayes in the Seeps. The things they told him, he could hardly believe. It was even worse than he had thought. A reign of sickening lawlessness was spreading unchecked.

The knowledge turned inside Aedan like a bad meal. It shattered whatever was left of his assumptions about solidarity — that when war threatened, people with a common enemy stood together, princes and peasants, thespians and thieves. How, in a time like this, could men turn on their own? Apparently, to some, their own did not extend beyond their hands and feet, and they would turn on anyone and do anything that suited them.

Many who had run to the city for shelter had found all that they had dreaded, and found it here within the walls that should have protected them. Aedan remembered his first experiences — the gang that had tried to rob his father, his encounters with the Anvil whom he somewhat hoped to run into again, the gang he had spotted at work and that had tried to collar him.

And then he had an idea that sent him running.

Aedan was grim as he explained. Dun's mouth stretched into a smile that held little humour.

"Fetch the whole class," he said. "I'll collect a few of the seniors."

It took a little time to find everyone, but they were finally gathered in the weapons hall.

"It's Aedan's idea," Dun said, "and it is a blazing good one. For some of you it will be your first uncontrolled encounter with the sharp end of a blade and men who will not hold back. But I believe the time is right."

Almost all the boys had passed their sixteenth birthdays, and they were strong for their age. As Dun began to explain, the faces watching him grew angry, then firm, and then eager.

Chapter

It was afternoon in the Seeps, but already the light had fled, along with any respectable company. Some of the narrower alleyways were almost dark enough to warrant the use of lamps. But there was no lamp among the group of frightened young women that hurried between the mounds of refuse, shrieking at rats and arguing over directions in thin, frightened voices.

They came to a sudden halt as the shapes of three men filled the alley ahead of them. Gasps of horror escaped them when they spun and found that the alley behind them was now blocked too. They stood, quivering, drawing their shawls over their heads as if to hide, but it was too late.

"Pay up!" the largest and dirtiest of the men said. "Leave your money and we will let you pass."

The women were too frightened to protest. Coins clinked, some dropping on the floor as the foremost girl collected them and handed them over.

"Now will you let us pass?" she pleaded.

"I lied," he said with a laugh as filthy as the floor of the alley. "I'm not much for counting, but it looks like there's as many of you as there is of us. One each boys!" He stepped forward and put his unwashed hand around the first girl's neck. The other men closed in.

"You've done this to many girls, haven't you?" she asked.

"Many," he said with a smile of pure evil. "We all have. Pickings have been good lately."

"I thought so." This time the girl's voice was softer. It did not sound frightened, but it was heavy with sadness and it shook with swelling anger.

"You're going to give me trouble, aren't you?" the man growled, raising a club and tensing to bring it down hard.

But the swing was never completed.

The sharp tip of a dagger sprouted through his left arm. He shrieked and released his grip on her neck. The girl stepped forward and plunged another dagger into his right armpit.

With a howl of agony he dropped the club which she deftly caught and swung at his face. The blow struck with such force that it smashed several teeth from his mouth and sent them skittering into grimy shadows. A second blow knocked him off his feet and he landed solidly on his back. He lay still, breath fizzing through the bloody ooze that trickled from his mouth.

Aedan pulled the shawl and wig from his head, spat, and turned to see the other men falling under a similar wrath.

Dun had instructed the boys to avoid killing unless their lives were threatened. But this gang had a dark name; it had been given special mention. "These men are widely rumoured to be guilty of the worst crimes," Dun had said. "At even a suggestion of ruthless intent, you are to use your daggers. That is an order. Today you are fully authorised by the City of Castath to administer capital punishment for capital crimes."

Aedan had let the man take his neck because he needed to know the truth before acting. He could have stabbed for the chest, but he wanted the noose to have the final word.

The boys carried both daggers and clubs strapped against their kirtles and hidden by thin cloaks. After what the gang leader had said, Aedan was not surprised to see that every member of his team had used daggers.

One of the gang members looked to be dead, or nearly so, and the rest were either unconscious or lay gurgling and twisting in mortal agony. Hadley was still punching the man that lay beneath him, his face contorted with rage. No one interfered.

"Call the soldiers," Aedan said.

Peashot jogged down the alley and returned with a heavily armed patrol. At their head was Cameron, the polite old captain who had spoken to Aedan on the day of his arrival, almost four years back, and who well-remembered the young lad who had once asked his name at the city gate.

Aedan gave a short account. When he was finished, Cameron stepped over to the leader and planted a savage kick in the man's neck.

"Been wanting to do that for a long time. Lots of us have heard of this Mole-Alley gang – earned a hanging ten times over. They confessed to a capital crime then attempted to repeat it. Their deal's done, at last. Commander's waiting at the gallows with the judge. I can guarantee you this lot will be swinging tonight, dead or alive. Any of you hurt?"

"No," said Aedan, turning to look around. The revulsion still burned in him as he remembered the leader's depraved boast. It almost pushed him to march over and put his daggers to work again. It was the first time in months he was glad to be serving the law.

The others were silent. None of them had ever had to clean their blades before. There had been laughter in the wake of the first two encounters as the soldiers had bound the gangs of thieves and dragged them off to prison, but there was no laughter now.

"That's three gangs," said Cameron. "You boys are doing what we soldiers could never do. Even in disguise we look like soldiers, we smell like soldiers, and gangs have sharp noses."

Aedan turned to his companions. "One more?" he said.

"What do you have in mind?" asked Hadley.

Aedan was silent for a moment. "Let's team up with one of the other groups and take the Earl's-quarter gang.

"But that's a huge gang!" Lorrimer exclaimed. "One of the most powerful in the city."

"And one of the busiest. If they land in jail, everyone will hear about it. It will do more than taking a dozen smaller ones."

"I think Lorrimer's right," said Vayle. "Aren't they too big for us?"

"I doubt we'll see the whole lot, but the soldiers will have to be nearby for this one."

"How? The spotters cover at least five blocks. If soldiers are anywhere near, it will be like hunting deer and taking a brass band along for company."

Aedan's eyes took on a glazed, distant look. "I have an idea," he said, "though it's not going to be comfortable for the soldiers."

The farmer who usually delivered the feed and hay to the royal stables was nowhere to be seen on the big cart, and apparently his children were making the delivery for him. It was not uncommon; many things were out of order during this time. In spite of the crowded conditions in the city, this was not a busy street, for it was a delivery track strewn with manure and its narrowness meant that pedestrians never fared well.

Night had settled and a lantern swung near the driver, a young, nervous-looking boy. This time, Peashot did not have to act nervous – he was strung as tight as a harp. A bulging purse was secured to his belt and he tapped it constantly while his eyes scanned the road.

The cart was at the darkest point of the lane, approaching an intersection where a lone boy idled, when a wheel slipped off the axle. The girls, who had been singing songs, began to cry as they understood their isolation, and the boys tried in vain to lift the wagon and replace the wheel. Peashot and Kian hopped down, walked across to the much bigger boy, and asked if he would find some men to help. Peashot dug a silver chim out of his money bag and handed it over, promising another if help were found.

The boy was no idler but a spotter. He would report the situation in detail – a group of children making a farmer's deliveries, a few boys but no adults around, and at least one large money bag. Before long the narrow space began to reverberate with the tramping of heavy feet. About twenty strong men arrived, showing an eagerness that did not accord with the mending of a wagon wheel.

The spotter indicated Peashot and spoke quietly. A wiry man barked a few sharp orders, and two of the group ran a hundred paces down the lane where they stopped and faced away, standing guard.

This gang was cautious and well organised. One of them stood apart. He was tall and deep-striding, and the other members parted before him as he walked into a shadowy section of the road and watched. Aedan marked him. Though he gave no orders, his mere presence dominated the gang. This, surely, was the mastermind who led the city's most cunning group of outlaws. They were not murderers but they were thieves, and dauntingly successful ones.

Peashot stood atop the wagon, pointing down at the wheel. He did not want to provide an easy target for a snatch and run.

Six men came up, three on either side of the wagon, squeezing past the mules, eyeing the boxes under the seat.

"What you got in there boy?" the wiry man asked.

"Nothing," said Peashot.

"Well then you won't mind if we take them along with us."

"They are my father's."

"Not anymore. That there money bag – you'd best hand that over too."

One of the men began to climb up to the driver's seat. Peashot unhooked the money bag and slung it at the gangster's head, knocking him down and scattering coins all over the road so that they tinkled and called in sweet voices to greedy ears.

As soon as the attention was off Peashot, the three boys and seven girls dashed off the front of the cart. They demonstrated surprising agility as they ran along a beam separating the mules, and sprinted away, screaming. Even the girls dodged between the gang members with uncanny ease, passing them and making good their escape.

A large girl, who might have answered to the name of Warton, was not that light on her feet. Someone tried to stop her. Instead of screaming for help, she raised two club-like fists and punched her way free. Her assailant landed on his back with a thump and a rapidly swelling eye. Five of the children went straight, five turned into the adjoining alley.

But then they stopped and spun around.

"Scatter!" It was the tall man in the shadows whom Aedan had singled out earlier. The man was hardly visible, but his voice moved the gang like the touch of a whip.

They turned and ran towards the exits the children were blocking. These children were behaving strangely though. They seemed to be sowing seed, seed that bounced and skittered over the cobbles with hundreds of metallic tings, unlike coins – thinner, sharper.

The gangsters thundered towards them and did not slow down at the sight of this puny barricades of children, and the apparently senseless littering meant nothing to them. They made no effort to avoid the little bits of metal. This gang would rush past like wind and vanish into the shadows beyond, organised, silent and strong. But there was neither organisation nor silence in what now took place.

The little bits of metal were caltrops – sharp, four-pointed bladelike stars with one point always raised to the sky.

Howls of pain filled the air as the upward-facing blades slipped through boot soles and sank deep into flesh and bone.

Some of the blades even emerged on the other side. The shrieking thieves collapsed onto more steel points – the caltrops were everywhere now – but none of them could stand again until they had pulled the spikes from their feet.

At the same time, the wagon burst open like a termite-infested log. Soldiers threw off hay-covered panels and poured out front and sides. They cut off the third escape and worked their way forward, knocking down any thieves still on their feet.

The soldiers clanked about as if they were running with pots strapped to their boots, and this was, in fact, not far from the reality. The steel plates under their soles did make the cobbles slippery, but it saved them from the more immediate concern of a road with teeth.

No gang could put up much of a fight under the circumstances. The children kept throwing the little four pointed horrors under the feet of any gangster who was attempting to make a stand.

Aedan had not forgotten about the two who had taken up sentry positions further down the road behind him. They were still there – he could see their outlines – but then they turned and jogged away, only now there were three. He assumed the third was the leader who had slipped past.

Twenty-two men were arrested, many of them well-known members of the criminal elite. Cameron was actually laughing with delight. Most of the soldiers had seen the whole performance through spy-holes; they were grinning as they led their wincing prisoners away.

The boys took off their disguises and lit lamps while they cleared the road of caltrops.

"What gave you this idea?" Peashot asked Aedan.

"Remember when we were making our first swords – the day I went to the forge barefoot? I was a cripple and the rest of you were fine."

Peashot grinned. "Might have given you a good idea, but I'm still going to remember that as one of the stupidest things you ever did."

It took some time to clean the street and it was late when they made their way back to the academy. As they trudged homeward, the mood was lightened by the memory of thieves hobbling about and howling and sitting down, and then springing up howling again. It was a quiet group, though, with much on their minds, and the laughter was punctuated with long silences.

Aedan excused himself, saying he needed to fetch a new shirt from Osric's house, but he really just wanted to be alone for a while.

None of the boys had noticed the stealthy figures trailing them through the darkness. When Aedan split off, he drew the followers, and they closed the distance quickly.

Chapter

It was the second dull scrape he'd heard. Soft, easily ignored. There were many cats that scavenged in this part of town.

Since Malik had successfully tailed him in his first year at the academy, Aedan had been vigilant, constantly checking his surroundings. But tonight his thoughts were unusually heavy and sluggish. Another scrape, this time closer. When he turned, it was too late.

The clonk of a wooden batten rang through his skull. He sprawled forward and tried to roll to his feet, but two men were on him before he could recover himself. They took an arm each, yanked him up, and dragged him against a wall.

A third man approached with a deep stride. Aedan, in spite of his dizziness, recognised him immediately. It was the man who had called the warning, the one he'd assumed to be the mastermind. But now he began to hear the chimes of recognition from elsewhere, from before the last gang roundup, long before. Then the man stepped into a beam of light from an overhead window.

"I have tried very hard not to despise you," Clauman said, "but you are determined to earn my hatred."

Aedan did not speak. He stared at his father's tall figure with growing dread.

"Do you know what you did tonight?"

Aedan guessed in an instant. He looked down, suddenly ashamed, despite the voice of reason protesting that he should not be.

"Yes, you know don't you? With all your supposed knowledge I would have expected you to learn where my interests lay and respect them. Nearly three years ago you defied me. You overturned one of my projects and brought about the loss of many of my collectors. Then you cowered away in your little academy safe house. Tonight, you robbed me of half my best men."

"I didn't know it was your gang."

"Because you did not bother yourself to find out!" Clauman shouted, stepping forward. Aedan saw the veins swelling in his father's neck and heard the heavy breathing. But Clauman contained himself and stopped short. A calculating look came into his eyes that worried Aedan even more.

"It's time for you to pay back, and this is how you will do it. My operations thrive on information – layouts, numbers, schedules, and of course, security measures. You will find a way of providing me with those. If you betray me again, I'll turn all my attention to destroying you."

Aedan was trembling. He knew his father was no more than a man, yet his words brought back all the fears of childhood. That same demon began to claw at him again, prying his heart open and hurling mockery into the depths of his being. It told him that he was a broken, beaten pulp, and if he did not shrink away and hide he would be crushed. His legs began to tremble and he felt his back slipping against the stone wall.

"Step aside," Clauman ordered his two men. They let Aedan go, and he sagged to the ground. "Answer me," Clauman said, glaring at his son.

Aedan's mouth was dry and his voice would not come as he tried to form words.

Clauman smiled. "I understand that language. I will expect you to contact me within a week. Find something that will begin to pay back the losses you brought about." He turned and strode away, his men jogging to keep up.

Aedan saw them dwindle away. The danger was gone, but something else was gone too, something he needed. He was not sure what it was, but its absence made him realise that he had escaped nothing by his silence. He felt a sudden weight settle on him and he understood what he had lost.

Freedom.

He had faced his jailor and not even made an attempt to gain the key.

Every muscle felt like it was made of shivering lard, but he pushed himself up, filled his lungs and shouted, though it came out more like a shriek.

"No!"

The three figures stopped moving. They turned and began to walk back. There was no mistaking the way his father strode now. The arms were pushed slightly out over balled fists. Every movement betrayed a pounding, swinging fury. Clauman did not even break stride. He hit Aedan in the stomach and hammered him to the ground.

"You dare to speak to me like that? I didn't think you needed to be reminded of your place, but I am happy to do the necessary." He kicked, causing Aedan to skid back against the wall where he coughed and gasped for breath.

"Do you understand, or must I carry on?"

Aedan understood. The message was sharp and clear. But another message began to rumble in his mind. It was the message he had understood as that colossal voice had spoken his name the second time. It was a message so pure with its kindness, and so terrifying with its power, that the lies had crawled out from their hidings and melted before it.

From where Aedan sprawled in the stink and grime, he looked up between the buildings into the great depths of the night, at stars beyond the reach of the highest mountains. Someone whose voice had made even those distant stars tremble with awe knew his name.

The same warmth grew in him.

Though he still drew thin, scraping breaths of air, he pushed himself to his feet.

A weight he could not see was pressing him down, but he would not bow under it again. He looked at his father and, as he did so, a covering began to slip. He glimpsed the man behind the horror that had stalked his past. As with Rork, as with Iver, there was no monster, only a man who had behaved monstrously. And as before, it made him seem smaller, not bigger.

Clauman laughed a hard laugh. "Want to stand up to me do you?" He hit again, but this time the blows did not fall as cleanly as before. Aedan was blocking and ducking. Though there were openings for retaliation, he took none of them.

Clauman was breathing hard when his son stumbled and dropped under a furious rain of punches. But this time Aedan rolled quickly and got to his feet again.

"How about we hold him?" asked one of the gangsters, stepping up to Aedan – but he stepped too close.

It was a movement like the strike of a python. The base of Aedan's palm crunched into the thief's nose, knocking him backwards. A knee followed, driving into the groin, doubling him over, bringing his head in line for Aedan's elbow. A short swing, a solid blow. Before he knew what had happened, the man was sagging. He dropped with a soft moan.

It was one of Dun's standard sequences.

The other gangster had been approaching, but now kept his distance.

Clauman watched his son for a long time before speaking. "Why didn't you strike me?" he asked.

"I don't want to," Aedan said.

"Still a coward then."

"No. Because I forgave you. It took more courage to do that than hating you. Hating and hitting are easy."

"Call it what you want, but it seems that my blows have finally turned you into a man."

Aedan could hardly believe the words. "A man? You made me into a cowering worm! It was something very different to your treatment that got me to my feet. It's as different from the way you treated me as rain is from drought."

"So you hold back your hands and hit me with your words? Just like a woman. Just like a traitor."

"I did not betray you!" Aedan cried. "I stayed with Mother because she needed me more than you did."

Clauman swallowed. "How is …" He squeezed his eyes shut and said no more.

"She misses you," Aedan said.

Clauman's eyes opened again, but his jaw was clenched and his look hard. "She has her friends. She chose them." he said.

"She needed family."

"And I did not?!" Clauman almost screamed the question. The light from the window glistened in his eyes now. It was the first time Aedan had seen anything beyond the rigid, proud barrier – and for the first time he knew that it had been only a barrier. There was a person who hid behind it, someone who felt the same pain that he did, who had the same need for family, for acceptance.

"Even in the Mistyvales, you turned your back on me," Clauman said. "If you weren't learning languages with … with … her, languages that excluded me, then you were off to that daughter of Dresbourn's as if his family was better than ours."

"It was *you* who drove me away! At Badgerfields I was never frightened. Kalry was the sister I needed when you were too angry to be my father. She accepted me *always*."

"So I did not measure up to your standards, and that justified throwing me out?"

"Throwing you out? *You* were the one who walked out. Don't you remember?"

"I walked out on the meddling of others. Do you think I *wanted* to lose my family?" he shouted and kicked a discarded crate so hard that it flew into the wall and shattered.

Aedan's mouth opened. He had always believed that this was exactly what his father had wanted. "I thought –"

Someone opened a shutter in the wall above and stuck his head out. "Keep it down out there, will you," he called.

Clauman unhooked a short club and flung it at the window with a roar, sending the man tumbling back into his house. The shutters slammed closed. Clauman inclined his head for Aedan to continue.

"I thought you did want to leave us," Aedan said. "Why did you not come back? You knew we couldn't have found you."

Clauman's eyes dropped and searched the ground. They found a pair of big boots and suddenly he became aware of the gangster who was listening with ill-concealed interest. He straightened up and his jaw locked. "Because I cannot abide traitors."

"But I did not betray you!"

Clauman looked at him. "Even now you betray me by denying your help, your repayment." All his former hardness was returning. The father and husband who had stepped from behind his shield was gone, and the light now glinted off a face of iron.

"What you ask of me is wrong," Aedan said.

"No son of mine would dare instruct me or question my judgement." His mouth twisted. "So you cannot be my son."

He turned and walked away with the gangster who carried his sleeping companion over a shoulder.

When they had left, Aedan slid down against the wall and cried like one of the country children in the overcrowded streets who had lost his father.

Chapter 64

Most of the apprentices were still a little moody and preoccupied the next day, so when Aedan wouldn't talk about the new bruises, he was not harried. Dun cancelled their early training session and spoke to them of the previous day's work. He was thoroughly pleased with the results.

The gangs of Castath had taken a heavy knock. Twenty-three small gangs and four large ones had lost many members to the city jails, some to the gallows. News had spread and it was clear that the days of easy crime had been interrupted.

Not all the operations, though, had run without loss. One group of older marshal apprentices had been surprised by a reserve force. Two of the boys were dead and one critically wounded. The gang was rounded up during the day as a priority, and every member convicted of murder.

Law-breaking across the city lost much of its appeal. The surprises continued. Houses that should have been perfect targets for burglary were found dripping with marshals and soldiers. The city's honest folk sensed the change and began to move about with less fear.

The gibbets were full, the jails too. A heavy hand closed on the city's crime and several days passed during which nothing more than petty theft was reported. It was even rumoured that many of the shady prospectors had found honest employment.

When Osric returned from his two-week patrol, Aedan found out and went to visit. The general, Tyne and Merter sat at the table – now covered in a soft cream cloth – before a small mountain of fresh crumpets, a pot of honey, and mugs of steaming tea. The scene was made cosier by the absence of lanterns; the room was lit instead by a bright fire humming in the hearth.

Aedan grinned as he looked around. This could only be Tyne's influence. He had never seen the room so far removed from its accustomed stern character, and he had never seen its owner so comfortable.

In that moment Aedan understood that Osric was not rigid and severe because he enjoyed it – he was that way because he didn't know how to be anything else. Aedan had once wondered if the general was too set in his nature, if that was why he had never married, if there was no place for a woman, not even Tyne. But it was clear, just by looking at him, that he relished the softening she brought to his life. The way the two of them were smiling ran deeper than the warmth of a greeting.

Tyne's long hair was loose, falling gently on her shoulders and giving her an air of homeliness, of womanliness that her tight braid and uniform had muted. It was almost difficult to believe she was the same person. Osric's eyes were unable to leave her for long, even at Aedan's entrance.

Aedan ground his teeth with frustration at these wonderful, silly people. They were like starving urchins hovering before a feast, trying to convince themselves that food was not the right thing for them. Their reasons for remaining apart made no sense. Tyne had said Aedan was too young to understand, but young or old, what right did yesterday's hurt have to steal today's happiness? Only the right that was surrendered, surely.

Here were two fearsome soldiers yielding what they both longed for without a fight. He wished there was a way he could knock them from their delusion, but it was Osric who did the knocking.

"Aedan, it's good to see you again!" he boomed, reaching over and delivering a clap on the back that struck like a hoof. Merter, sitting as usual with his back to the fire, gripped Aedan's forearm warmly, and Tyne hugged him and asked after Liru.

While Aedan was being plied with tea and honey-drenched crumpets, Osric took up the conversation. "We heard about the business with the gangs while we were still out on patrol," he said. "We were just talking about it when you came in. Your idea?"

"I had to do something," Aedan said. "Men can't be permitted to behave like beasts."

"Couldn't agree more. You and your friends did a fine job. Has your mother stayed safe through all this?"

"Yes. She is safe. When I arrived in my patrol uniform she didn't recognise me at first. We had a good laugh until Harriet arrived. I wish it was Harriet who didn't recognise me. Ever. To her, I am the cause of all griefs in Thirna. The Fenn would not be threatening our borders if I had just done everything she insisted on."

They laughed, but Aedan was quiet.

"Aedan," said Tyne. "Are you alright? You look like you're heavy inside."

"I met my father," he said, after considering whether or not to mention it and deciding, as with Lorrimer, that carrying it alone was doing him no good. "It was almost like he really wanted to put our family together again, but he ended off by disowning me."

This might have been enough for Osric, but Tyne wanted to know all the details. When Aedan had finished telling the story, they were thoughtful.

"What made him beat you as a child?" she asked. "Don't answer if it's too bold a question."

"Once I tried to stop him hurting my mother when they were arguing. He said I had betrayed him. Before, on his angry days he used to just ignore me. After that he didn't ignore me anymore."

Osric looked as if he was about to smash a hole in the table. His breathing was shallow, his face flushed, and his lips tight with the effort of holding back whatever snapped and growled inside.

It was Tyne who eventually spoke. "I am glad that you were able to face him. I think it is what we were all hoping for. It's a bitter sadness, though, that he did not decide differently. Pride is the biggest thief of all. But perhaps he will yet change his mind."

Aedan might have reacted to anyone else pointing out his father's error, but there was no blame in Tyne's voice and no doubting her sincerity. He remembered how his father had recognised and condemned Dresbourn's pride years ago, yet held fast to his own.

"Perhaps," he said. He wondered if she knew how much hope stood behind the word.

———

The room was dark. Daylight was several hours away, but Aedan knew further sleep would be impossible. It was the same dream and this time it was sharper, sterner. The image of that Lekran book would appear and he would hear the word "Read", then he would wake as if he had been pushed from slumber. He knew he could ignore it, turn over and wait for daylight, but this time it was as though there was urgency in the voice. It was the same huge voice that he had twice heard. He was caught between wanting to obey it and wanting to avoid that sickening book.

The blankets were warm. He turned over and closed his eyes, but the sense of disappointment that poured over him was so deep that he sat up.

"Fine," he grumbled. "I'll do it."

Working by feel, he got up, pushed aside the books on his shelf and drew out the volume from where it was buried. Then he took his thickest blanket – for the night was cold – scraped around until he found his lantern, and crept out the door and down the passage to one of the study coves. He lit his wick from the night lamp that was mounted nearby. The disappointment had left him, he noticed, and in spite of his hatred of everything Lekran, he felt a curious peace.

Perhaps, he thought, this was not so much about getting over his hatred as it was about getting over his sensitivity. He would not be much use in a war against a nation whose culture he could not face without a wave of sickening weakness. What he was doing now was like building a resistance to poison in gradual increments. It was beginning to make sense. The time had come for him to look in the face of his enemy and not turn away. There were forms of strength that came only at a great price.

With a new feeling of purpose, he wrapped himself in his blanket, dug into the couch, and began to read.

The first chapter was entitled "Homes, Social Structure, Customs and Celebrations". The going was slow. There was much he did not understand given his poor handle on the language. He had just begun the section dealing with religion when Dun's whistle filled the passage.

He had read through the night.

Hiding the book under his shirt, he slipped back into his room before many pairs of curious eyes found him.

Strangely, he did not fall asleep during his classes. That night, during his study session, he continued where he had left off and finished the section on religion. He turned to the next section. Sacrifices. His heart began to pound as he skimmed over the words. It was as he had feared. On Ulnoi, they did not sacrifice goats or cattle.

He closed the book and closed his mind to the persistent voice. He was not yet ready for this. Would he ever be?

It took him a long time to fall asleep that night, but when he did, he dreamed immediately. He saw the chapter clearly before him – *Sacrifices* was written boldly across the page and the same voice called him to read.

In his dream he shouted, "But I can't! The pain ..."

"Courage," the voice replied.

Then he awoke.

As before, it was dark. Muttering, he tore himself away from the warm cocoon of his bed, gathered the book, blanket and lamp, and padded over the icy flagstones back to the study nook. After settling down and wrapping the blanket until there were none of those little breezy gaps, he began to read, thinking what a ridiculous, meaningless and injurious waste of hours this was. He knew he needed the toughening, understood the value of the exercise, but was beginning to doubt if this was the most effective approach. Nevertheless, he pushed his eyes along.

The words on the page made him wince, as if each one was a knife stabbing out at him. He was so desperate to fend off the meaning that he almost missed a sentence hidden within the awful details, but the further he moved from it, the more it tugged him back until he left his place and returned to the nagging line.

Vraanenim slaggo lag srette buuin.

As with much of what he was reading, he only grasped part of the idea. *Vraan* was women, *Vraanenim*, he assumed with a shiver, were the female sacrificial victims or supposed volunteers. He didn't care. *Lag* – must, *slaggo* – age, but *srette buuin* meant nothing to him.

At first the words drifted in his tired thoughts, disconnected, irrelevant. Then, like shards of magnetised iron, they began to snap together and formed an idea, an idea that sprang from the page and struck him full in depths of his sleepy mind, shattering his drowsiness.

He gasped, a sudden wheezing gasp, as if a great vat of icy water had been emptied over his head. The couch skidded back into the wall with a thump as he lurched to his feet, dropping the book and tipping the lantern so that it smashed on the floor and went out. He didn't even notice.

His eyes grew wide and his twitching mouth opened further as the thought took hold of him. Snatching up the book, he took off down the passage at a speed that set the paintings rattling in his wake. By the time the blanket had crumpled to the ground, he was out of sight.

Never had he covered the distance to Fergal's office so quickly. In his haste, he flung the covering boards right off the platform in the display room, but he was already darting down the stairs by the time they banged against the floor. Even if he had stood on one of the trigger-steps, the trap would have opened on nothing more than his dust.

"Fergal! Fergal!" he shouted as he flew along the dark corridor and whipped under the archways. He did not wait for an answer. He knocked and opened the door in one movement and came to a quivering stop in the office that apparently never slept.

"Aedan, what manner of –"

Aedan ignored him and interrupted, "Fergal, what does *srette buuin* mean? It's Lekran for a number or an age. I need to know. Now! Please!"

Fergal sat back in his large chair, aiming a severe look at the young intruder, but then the raised eyebrows settled down again. "It is neither a number, nor an age," he said, "but a ceremony that represents both. It is the entry into womanhood, which, for Lekrans happens at the age of eighteen. Now before we go any further, I insist on knowing what this is about."

Aedan was pale and looked very much like he was about to drop to the ground.

"Quin deceived us," he whispered. "Kalry is alive!"

Then he did drop to the ground and woke a little while later to see Fergal holding a bottle under his nose. His nostrils were complaining about red-hot pins.

The big man helped him into a couch, then sat back in his own chair and faced Aedan. A soft whisper of fire and a quiet pop from a burning log were all that disturbed the silence for a while. Fergal would be the last person to feel the need to fill it with words.

"Read me the section," he said, looking with disapproval at the book that showed the corner of a page sticking out where it should not be, and a small stream of oil running down the cover. Aedan did not see any of this. He found the page easily – it was the one that had been folded when the book dropped at his feet. He read the line and looked at Fergal with desperate, expectant eyes. The wait was the worst torture he had ever known.

"Fergal, please … Say something!"

Fergal glanced up from the fire. "It must be so," he said. "The man who wrote that book was both trustworthy and knowledgeable. Quin, on the other hand, has nothing to recommend him. All you told me of him suggests that an honest message would be something out of character. Perhaps it was his intention to ensure that there would be no pursuit, though Ulnoi is considered by many to be less assailable than an eyrie."

"I don't care how unassailable it is," Aedan said, standing. "I'm assailing it."

"Sit down, Aedan. I did not say there was no hope, but the difficulty is something extreme. Sit, sit. Too much haste and fire and you'll burn down the stable instead of mounting a rescue."

Aedan sat, though everything in him cried out against it. His whole mind and body were shivering with suppressed energy.

Fergal looked across into the fire, twisting little ragged ropes in his beard, and when he spoke, Aedan could not believe what he heard.

Chapter 65

"A year! You want me to prepare for a year?" he cried, jumping to his feet again.

Fergal motioned and waited again for him to sit. "Two years would be better, but as I recall, she is a little older than you. What will her age be on this coming midsummer's day?"

"Seventeen."

"That's when the sacrifices are held, so she is safe this year, but will be called upon in about a year and a half. Travel and the actual attempt to save her will take a few months, and you don't want to time it so that you arrive on the day, which takes off at least six months. You will need to be there by the beginning of winter. That gives you just under a year to prepare."

"But what if they move early, what if they get her age wrong?"

"These people are very particular over such details. They are not likely to make a mistake. That is fairly certain. But what is absolutely certain is that if *you* move early you will throw away your only chance. On the Lekran isles, Ulnoi in particular, foreigners who are not slaves are made into slaves as a matter of law. You open your mouth and say one word that holds a foreign accent, or show an ignorance of one of the many strange customs and it is all over. For both of you."

He paused to let the words sink in before continuing. "The layout of the island is not favourable for a sneak-spy-and-snatch operation. There is forest in the western reaches, but everyone lives on the east side where there is almost no cover. You will have to move in the open, through their society. I won't conceal from you that even with a year's preparation, taking a sacrificial tribute from Ulnoi will be like stealing a fish from the jaws of a bear. I will aid you, but in rebellion against the fear that I am sending you to your doom."

Aedan began to understand that he would not be leaving that night.

"I'm assuming you have paid little attention in your Lekran classes," said Fergal. Aedan avoided his look. "So you have a considerable amount of learning to do in a relatively short time. But there is another problem."

Aedan raised his eyes.

"Prince Burkhart is not likely to let you go."

"But –"

Fergal hushed him with a wave. "Which means that we will need to be careful about how we get you out of here. You will also need help on Lekrau. I recommend asking Tyne. She has been posted on one of those islands before. She is fluent in the language and knows the culture."

"Why would you help me do something that the prince would oppose?"

"Because, since Burkhart betrayed us all, my allegiance is to his father, the king, and I know that the king would approve of sending you – partly for Kalry's sake, and partly because it is time that we begin to strike back at Lekrau. For too long we have presented that nation with a soft belly, an invitation.

"The thing is, Aedan, you don't know the full truth. Reports of Lekran raids have been suppressed by Burkhart's direct orders. Many more were taken this past year than in previous years. If you are successful, we will learn much that could be used against the slavers. Burkhart sees only the immediate threat of the Fenn, and has pulled all resources from watching Lekrau. I believe that this is short-sighted and may cost us dearly. So I shall not only aid you, but see that you are commissioned – though Burkhart will probably overrule the commission if he learns of it. I'll provide whatever resources the academy can offer, and Osric will no doubt be able to supply a good deal more."

"It's starting to sound like a big operation. How will we keep it all hidden?"

"I have a few ideas," Fergal said, and turned back to the fire. Aedan knew from the rough treatment the beard was getting that something was amiss.

"What is it?" Aedan asked.

"This is not going to work …"

Aedan began to interrupt and Fergal glared him to silence from beneath the bristling eyebrows.

"This is not going to work if you simply add Lekran studies to your current programme. You have less than a year. Less than one year, Aedan. In any of your languages, have you even approached native fluency in that time?"

Aedan knew he was not required to answer.

"And it's not just the words of the language. It's the whole culture. You need to *be* Lekran – the opinions you have of national figures and their deeds, the foods you prefer and how you like them done, your favourite jokes, your attitude towards slaves and how you react to them when you see them mistreated on the road … After Krunvar, there is no nation whose ways are so unnatural to us, no nation where our habits and manners stand out so clearly."

"Quin succeeded."

"That's just it. He did not. You and Kalry found him out. What if you encounter curious children on Ulnoi?"

"I understand all of this, but what choice do I have?"

Fergal leaned towards the fire, putting his elbows on the armrests. "The only way I see that offers a reasonable chance," he said, "is a way that will cost you everything you have worked for. You will need to give up your studies and your ambitions to become a grey marshal. Your preparation will need to be full-time and the programme will take you to your limits and beyond. You will lose a year and then much of the following year in your attempt to locate and bring Kalry back. By the time you return to Castath, if you do, I doubt even I could get you back into your current position."

Aedan looked confused. "Fergal, do you really think that would give me even an instant of hesitation?"

Fergal's eyes crinkled and the beard moved, betraying the hidden smile. "An excellent reply," he said. He looked from under the hedges awhile. "I believe you will succeed, young Aedan. Tomorrow I shall speak to your masters and explain that I have appointed you as my assistant whom I will personally train. You will continue your classes with Dun, and one or two other subjects that might prove useful to you, but the rest will come to an end.

From tomorrow you will begin to learn – at frightening speed – how to be Lekran."

"Can I not begin now?"

Fergal laughed and, after brief consideration, pointed to the red volume. "Finish it by morning," he said. "We'll go through it in greater detail again when you have a better grasp of the language. Try to get at least an hour's sleep. If you thought the marshals' programme was demanding …"

Aedan was already on his feet.

"One more thing," said Fergal. "Don't tell anyone. Not yet. If these plans reach the wrong ears we could both be tried for intended desertion – you have a form of military training and this is a time of war preparation. Remember that."

———

"It tastes like raw fish entrails!"

"Quite correct. Raw fish entrails tend to do that. Now have another mouthful and try to get this one down."

Fergal was merciless. Where he had obtained the hideous grey mush, Aedan did not care to know, but the fact remained that this was a Lekran delicacy, and one that he would need to be able to devour with relish in front of watchful eyes. He made another attempt, gagged and ejected it into the bucket.

Fergal sighed. "Try to think of steak while chewing."

"I *can't*. The taste is too convincing."

"Well you'll have to find some way of getting it down. You'll need some breakfast in you."

"Don't the Lekrans eat bread?"

"Of course, but swallowing bread is a skill you already have. Now do you want to learn or not?"

Aedan gripped the bowl, held it to his lips and tipped, swallowing in great gulps and trying not to think at all. When he replaced the bowl on the table there was a moment of uncertainty as he hovered over the bucket, neck and shoulders twitching, but miraculously, it all stayed down.

"Good," said Fergal. "When Dun has finished with you, I want you back here and ready to study like never before."

Aedan jogged away on shaky legs, looking as green as the sea that was washing around inside him.

He had broken the news to his dorm before breakfast that he had been appointed as an assistant to one of the senior clerks. They had looked at him as if he had lost his mind. He'd seen surprise, confusion and sadness in their faces, and it had hurt more than expected.

During the training session, he had to answer, or rather parry, several more questions. Warton, to Aedan's surprise, was openly upset. He actually seemed angry. Even Cayde frowned. Malik was the only one who looked pleased.

Aedan wished that he could tell them everything, but Fergal's warning rang in his ears like a tower bell.

When he got back from Dun's class, the fishy dish had settled, and he braced himself for the next obstacle. Fergal unlocked a heavy door at the back of his office and pushed it. It swung open with a sigh, admitting a cool breath of air that was heavy with leather and paper and deep thought. Aedan stepped through onto a walkway overlooking the biggest library he had ever imagined. Four levels of book-filled balconies ran around the circumference, and on the vast floor beneath, stepladders and even movable staircases enabled dwarfed figures to scale the towering islands filled with honeycombs of scrolls.

"This," said Fergal, "is where the masters and approved senior students draw the knowledge that is delivered in the classes. Many of these books are uncopied originals. All of them are important. You will be spending a large portion of your time here with Lekran histories, folk-tales, plays, songs, and plenty more. The real beauty of it is that most of the volumes have been written by Lekrans. If you are to learn to behave like one of them, you need to think like one of them, which means that you must now study from their perspective, not ours."

"I thought that kind of writing was kept away from the public – censored."

"It is. But this is not a public library. You will find a lot here that will turn you red with anger; foreign opinions of us can be very offensive. You had best get over your reactions – those would give you away quickly indeed. Let me take you to your section."

They were on the highest of the balconies. Fergal led the way along a book-lined wall to a turret stairway that appeared to be made of solid brass. They descended one level and walked to the far corner. Regularly placed lamps cast a good light and Aedan was able to make out the titles and sequential numbers on spines.

"Roughly between these two pillars," Fergal said, indicating a collection of perhaps five hundred books, some of them almost as thick as the stone pillars themselves. "Did you finish the first book?"

"Yes, but there is a lot I didn't understand."

"That was to be expected. I suggest that you start with three collections of children's stories, followed by three of popular folk tales. These are things every Lekran would know, things you cannot afford to pass over. They will also help with your grasp of the language on a foundational level. There are three Lekran-to-Thirnish dictionaries. You may keep one with you, but it would be better for you to use the straight Lekran dictionary as soon as you are able. How large is your current Lekran vocabulary?"

"Maybe four hundred words and another two hundred that are vague."

"By the end of two weeks, I want you at a thousand. That's in the region of forty words a day. Write down every new word along with a phonetic, all the meanings, and space for several examples of how it can be used. You are not to avoid a single word in the children's stories or the folk tales – those are the words that form the basis of a language, words you need to fall back on without hesitation. I will aid you with pronunciation and syntax. You will spend an hour every day with Kollis and an hour with Tyne."

Fergal ignored Aedan's look of displeasure at the mention of Kollis. "From now on you will speak to all of us in Lekran only."

With this, Fergal switched seamlessly into the language and Aedan had to concentrate to follow the next words. "*Olin mjierta nau Leikrar* ... Your food will be Lekran and you will not only eat it but learn to prepare it. I have had arrangements made so that you can still take your meals in the company of your friends, though they will probably find them strange."

What Aedan heard was, "Your food will ... Lekran and ... you will not ... eat it but ... learn ... it. I ... made ... you ... meals ... of your friends ... will ... find them strange." One possible meaning of this was strange indeed.

Fergal placed his reading lantern on one of the large desks that stood against the balcony railing. "The assistant's desk in my office is now yours. I expect it to be cluttered with books before the hour is up."

He walked away and left Aedan to stare, bewildered, swaying slightly, as the enormity of what he had undertaken began to settle on him. When the giddiness passed, he took a hold of himself and attacked the shelves, skimming over titles until he found the section of children's literature. He selected a weighty volume that cracked open and released a puff of dust. The pages were dark with age, but the script was neat and easy to follow. He picked a few more collections, and after much searching, found two dictionaries, then staggered back to the office beneath the pile of books, lamp balanced on top.

Fergal insisted that Aedan interrupt him for help with pronunciations after every tenth word he wrote down. It was a language with difficult sounds requiring all manner of unfamiliar contortions of tongue and lips to form the complex vowels.

The day went slowly.

Lekran folk stories were strange, full of sea monsters that crawled up onto the shore in the forms of serpents or jelly-like masses with hundreds of creeping tentacles. The heroes, if the illustrations were to be trusted, scoffed at armour or anything else that interfered with the display of their muscles. They donned only loincloths and attacked the beasts with only spears. Most of the stories had similar themes to the ones Aedan had grown up with, but the way the themes were illustrated was alien, sometimes amusing, and often disturbing. It seemed to be a culture where strength and domination were honoured. Kindness and mercy made few appearances.

"Very good," said Fergal, when Aedan explained these observations. "You are quite right, but I advise you not to share that with your dinner hosts tonight."

Aedan looked back wordlessly. For fifth and sixth foreign languages they had not yet been required to socialise with native speakers.

"You didn't think you would be able to prepare in the comfortable isolation of study without actually meeting the people themselves?"

"But I ..." Aedan could not put the Lekran words together quickly enough and Fergal ploughed on.

"The sooner you put aside your barrier of prejudice, the better. These are good people I am sending you to. Getting to know and appreciate them will help to close the distance you would otherwise preserve between yourself and the subjects of your studies."

That was the beginning and end of the argument. Every night from then on, Aedan dined with the Lekran families that Fergal knew. There were four families. Two came from wealth, and two from more indigent circumstances. These were people who had been granted citizenship of limited rights in exchange for political favours. They were essentially traitors to their homeland, but they were natives of Lekrau and had not forgotten the customs of their people.

Aedan rotated through the families, dining as a Lekran every night of the week. The initial warmth of welcome and the self-consciousness of entertaining a stranger caused his hosts to suppress many cultural peculiarities, but soon these began to show through.

He noticed how the women's roles were more subordinate, how children never dared to interrupt, how the father determined what was funny or interesting, how this was never challenged, how nobody was ever thanked for doing what was perceived to be a duty, and a hundred other social currents that no book would have properly revealed. Yet beneath it all he perceived a comfort with the customs, or perhaps just an unwillingness to challenge them. But no matter how familiar they became, some of these social norms continued to feel wrong to him.

A number of the dishes were as strange as that first breakfast Fergal had prepared. Aedan had more than one desperate moment when getting the food down was only a shade less difficult than swallowing bricks. By sheer force of will he avoided humiliating himself. He even began to like some of the peculiar foods.

One of the more unsettling lessons he learned was never to touch the women. After Aedan took an embarrassed woman's hand in greeting, her husband drew him aside and explained that taking an unmarried woman's hand was akin to a proposal of marriage, and touching another man's wife was an insult only atoned for with blood. Aedan understood by this that a significant quantity of blood would be required. He apologised profusely and never repeated the mistake. It was a stark warning of how easily a cultural blunder could ruin everything once he was on Lekran soil.

"Fergal," Aedan began after returning from one of these dinners. "I have something I want to do and I think I can convince you, but you are not going to like it."

Chapter 66

The first spring winds rushed in from across the plain, carrying a stream of dead leaves, wheat husks and dizzy midges that tumbled past the five people sitting on the west wall. The early sun was just cresting the hill. It warmed their backs and threw long shadows out over the grassy expanse. As the parapets here had not been completed, they were able to sit side by side on the broad surface with their feet dangling.

"Thank you," Liru said, squeezing Aedan's arm. "You already know my answer."

"And mine," said Peashot as he leaned forward, puffed into the tube, and sat back with a slightly tilted head to better appreciate the yell of pain from below.

"Hadley?" said Aedan.

"I have a few questions." While he was all momentum when following his own instincts, he had shown a curious tendency to think a good deal more about others' plans.

"Ask away," said Aedan. It wasn't the first time Hadley was cross-examining his ideas.

"Firstly, why take so many? Doesn't that make it harder to move unnoticed?"

"In Thirna yes, but on the Lekran Isles it is different. The more slaves people have, the more important they are and the less they are interfered with, up to a point. Tyne has seen it herself. She was posted there for a year."

"It's just like that," she said.

"Alright. Then how did you convince this Fergal to include us? Taking two marshal apprentices and Liru out of training for the duration of the rescue is a big cost. I don't see how he can justify it for the rescue of two girls who can't really be of any help to Castath. What did you promise him?"

Aedan laughed. "I didn't offer you as a library slave if that's what you are worried about. I told him that Liru's sister would be a potential source of information valuable to Castath, and to find her we need Liru. I also said that with you and Peashot along, sabotage becomes feasible."

"Sabotage!" Peashot's face lit up.

Hadley's grinned. "Exactly what are we going to sabotage?"

"I'd like to destroy all their sacrificial temples and sink every one of their slave ships. That would be a good start."

"I'm sure you'd also like to fly."

"Even if we only sink one ship," Aedan said, this time without humour, "it will more than pay back our absence from Castath. There is a retired Captain who is going to give us some instruction on Lekran ports and ship design and how to cause the most damage with limited tools."

"That sounds reasonable. My last question, then: Will we be able to come back?"

"The orders will be official," said Aedan. "General Osric himself will sign them. But it's complicated. We are fairly sure Prince Burkhart would try to stop us if he found out. He's too short-sighted to see the advantages of something like this and too insecure to attempt anything that might anger the Lekrans. We won't directly break any laws by leaving, but we'll be slipping between them on the way out, and coming back might be complicated."

"Burkhart is a two-faced, lying, murderous coward who needs a lashing from his father," Peashot mumbled. "Liru told me what he tried to do to you two."

Everyone was quite happy to let these words hang in the air unchallenged.

"At worst," Aedan resumed, "we could be arrested on our return. I know of two soldiers who were made to disappear without any trial or official record. So it's dangerous. At best, you'll lose a year of your studies."

Peashot almost looked bored with the details. Aedan guessed he'd be making the journey with them even if he was guaranteed an execution on his return.

Hadley was done thinking. That toppling look came into his eyes. "I doubt the worst case is likely," he said. "Dropping back a year doesn't look so bad either. You're going to drop back two if you don't lose your place altogether, and Lorrimer has been skimming through by magic – he's due to fail about now. I'd go anyway, but it's nice to know I won't be alone afterwards. I'm in. Only thing that's going to annoy me now is the waiting."

"Couldn't Lorrimer come?" asked Peashot.

"His height would draw too much attention," Aedan said. "Think of how tall he'll be in another year. And Vayle wouldn't want to go. We all know how difficult it is to just get him to drop whatever he's reading and actually *do* something."

Hadley and Peashot laughed. Vayle had earned himself the reputation – he preferred contemplating plans to implementing them. He was roughly Hadley's opposite.

"Also," said Tyne, "With Liru's sister, Aedan and I will have four slaves when we reach Ulnoi. Any more could begin to make us look more important than we can afford. Unusually wealthy strangers will tend to be noticed more."

"So you think we make good slaves," said Peashot, loading another stone with a mean smirk.

"Rotten slave," said Aedan. "Good saboteur."

"What language is that?"

"Yours, blockhead. It means someone who sabotages, you know – breaks stuff. You're good at that."

"Good?" Hadley said. "Complete genius is more like it."

"So are we all agreed?" Aedan looked around.

They all agreed, except Peashot who was taking aim. Liru flicked his ear, and that brought him back. "Ouch! Yes, yes, of course I'm in, blockheads. Sorry Tyne. Didn't mean you. Ouch! Or you, Liru."

"Then remember that if a word of this gets out, it's all over. Try to get as fluent as you can in Lekran. As slaves, you will not be expected to sound like natives, but the more pairs of working ears we have, the better. Also, get used to Lekran weapons. We won't take any of our own. I hope we don't need to fight, but if we do, you don't want to discover in the moment that their blades are shorter and heavier and the crossbows have a very tricky latch. Lekrans also have some strange weapons that are in the upper racks in the weapons hall. I'll speak to Fergal. Maybe he can nudge Master Dun to teach us how to use them. Lekrau is, after all, a constant threat."

Aedan and Peashot lingered after the others had left – Aedan because Fergal did not expect him back immediately, Peashot because he never cared much what any of the masters expected from him. He hadn't been in trouble for almost a fortnight and some disturbance was due.

They talked of this and that – Fennlor, classes, Murn, Liru and Kalry, but no matter what they spoke of, it was Kalry who filled Aedan's mind, and butterflies and birds and storms crashed about in his belly.

Peashot aimed, puffed, and scooted back to savour another bark of pain. "You are different since Kultûhm," he said. "You don't walk around looking like you have a dagger up your sleeve and a score to settle. Liru says you look stronger. *I* just think it looks like you aren't taking your daily draught of poison, whatever it was."

"Close enough."

"She thinks something happened to you in the lightning. What was it?"

Aedan thought for a while. "It wasn't something," he said, "it was someone. To be plain, I'm still trying to understand it myself. I think the lightning was only a doorway, just like my dreams have been lately."

"You're not going to start blabbing like those diviners our prince has on every street corner?"

Aedan laughed. "If I do, please hit me very hard."

"With pleasure," said Peashot, clicking his knuckles. "But don't you think you could have imagined the whole experience? Shock or something?"

"If you were there you'd understand why it couldn't have been anything like that. Ever had that experience when you wake up and it's snowing in the night? Maybe you even walk out and let it land on your shoulders, but by morning it's all melted? The only person who saw the proof was you, and the only proof you can give anyone else is that you're convinced it was real. That's what it's like for me. I know I've got a strong imagination, but this was far, far beyond anything my imagination can produce."

"You're not talking it up? The way people do about things they own or places they've been?"

"I'm not talking it up or making it better than it was. I can't even get close to what it was like. It was better than anything else I know."

"Even better than Kalry?" Peashot grinned.

Aedan felt the blood rush to his face. He tried not to smile – it was hopeless. "I would have to say yes, but – it was better in a different way."

"What's she like?"

It was a question to breach a dam wall. Aedan took a deep breath. "She's what I wanted Ilona to be. She really *is* the kindest and sweetest person I know –"

"Huh!" Peashot interrupted. "So where does that put me?"

"Last. Idiot."

Peashot smirked.

"Kalry always used to make me want to be nicer to others because she made it look so good. Being kind to people made her happy. To see it was really something – and it wasn't just people. I remember that time I walked through town with Ilona and there was a donkey braying because it couldn't reach the stand of cabbages. I secretly wanted to go buy it one, but I had a feeling Ilona would have rolled her eyes at me. That's the difference. Kalry wouldn't have been able to enjoy herself *without* doing something for the hungry donkey, and she would have run down to the market with me, shared the cost, and smiled all the way home."

"Pretty?"

Aedan laughed. "Not in the same way as Ilona. Ilona's a rose or something sophisticated. Kalry's more like a wildflower – a simpler kind of beauty, but it felt more complete, more honest. When she smiled at me it was like being hugged. It wasn't just the way she looked. Her thoughts were … Let me put it this way – conversations with her were like magical journeys. There was also something about the way she spoke, like a kind of singing in her voice that brought everything she said to life – you should have seen the way babies would listen to her. Big eager eyes, spellbound. There was one thing everyone used to tease her about, it was her messy hair, but I remember it as threaded with trapped sunlight. And she had these laughing hazel eyes, more brown than green, as soft and warm as rich tilled earth baking in the sun of a spring morning –"

"Ugh. Stop! What's with all the poetry? All you had to say was yes, she's pretty. I can just see you and Lorrimer bent over the lines you've obviously been composing, sniffing and weeping and –"

Aedan lurched over and snapped a solid punch at the unguarded shoulder. It brought Peashot's mockery to an abrupt end and he leaned back, probing the damage to his freshly bitten tongue. He drew his finger out and brightened when he saw a little blood.

"I suppose I'd best get going," he said. "Classes feel weird now that you are missing. Even Malik commented on it."

"Oh? What did he say?"

"Something that earned him a gut punch."

"You don't have to fight my battles."

Peashot frowned. "What's that got to do with it? Think I would miss an opportunity like that? It was truffle pudding."

"Is that where you got the mark under your eye?"

"Pathetic, isn't it? I thought I would at least get a nice blue plum. All he could manage was this little sissy bruise. Looks like a coal smudge."

Aedan laughed. "You just don't mind pain, do you? Sometimes I'm convinced it actually makes you comfortable."

Peashot smirked.

"Well," said Aedan, "thanks for giving Malik my regards."

"Sure. I'll see you at lunch. Can't wait to smell what they put in front of you today. That grey thing you ate yesterday had us all checking under our shoes."

"Better get used to it. What do you think you're going to eat on Lekrau?"

Peashot grumbled and sauntered off.

For a while Aedan sat, letting the wind gust around and buffet his shoulders, thinking about what had happened at Kultûhm.

He was beginning to feel that his encounter with the Ancient was no mere favouring – a timely intervention by a watchful guardian. There was more to it, like he'd been equipped, though exactly how was still unclear.

He looked up over the nearby walls and spires of the knife-like Pellamine range. Then he raised his eyes to the young blue of the morning sky. As he did so, something in his chest blazed. His hands and feet prickled with that peculiar feeling, as though the air around them was no longer air, but something else. This was the fourth or fifth time it had happened since the lightning strike, and it gave him the strangest feeling that something about him was changing, being transformed in a way that his friends had not yet seen, and that not even Fergal would comprehend. He had a sudden urge to leap out from the wall. The sensation was so strong that he moved away from the edge and pressed his back against a large block of stone. Thoughts like these were dangerous.

When the tingling had gone, he drew out the little leather-encased journal. He never looked at it unless he was alone. It had a trick of drawing tears.

Now that he knew Kalry to be alive, he wasn't too sure if he should read it anymore. After a small inner battle, his scruples were defeated. He promised himself, though, that it would be the last time. There were two entries he wanted to pay a last visit. He found the first and began to read.

Remember when we found that cave in Nymliss and there was that huge claw sticking out of a pile of rocks we couldn't move? Well that day I realised that wonderful terrible incredible things were actually possible because that claw had to have belonged to a real animal big enough to eat cows or trees for breakfast. (I hope it preferred trees.) And it wasn't a pretend discovery! No matter what Emroy and my father and my tutor said when I told them. (This doesn't mean that I think pretend discoveries aren't important, it's just that a pretend discovery can't actually bite you.)

Can you imagine if we could have lived in times when enormous animals like that were alive. I know trolls and dragons and all those are made up (I think) but imagine if there were creatures just as spektackuler (I'm really going to have to ask your mum about this word) that were actually walking around and we had to run away from them unless maybe hopefully we could make friends with them.

Now this brings me back to what I wrote in my last entry, about the song that I can sense all around me. It's like the earth and the trees and the birds and the flies, no not the flies, but everything else is excited about something. Everyone would laugh at me if I said it, but I think there is some huge and ancient power breathing into the world the same way we blow on little sparks to make a fire. Remember that ecscwisit storm you told me about that happened over Nymliss that one time, and ever since then Nymliss has felt all tingly and mysterious? From what travellers are saying it sounds like those storms are also over DinEilan. Maybe they'll move over the whole world. I'm sure they are changing things.

Just imagining what could happen is already making me full of jumps and squeals. I can't even describe the feeling I have about it. How do you describe something indescribable? I read somewhere that the best word for things that are bigger than words is wonder. It's now my favourite word and I need it here, because I think the time we are living in is going to be a dawn of wonder, the beginning of something incredible, a time of mysteries and legends and heroes, just like in the old stories.

If that's what's about to happen then I'm going to be excited and scared and you are going to have to let me hold your hand. Just please don't spit in it first.

Aedan grinned at that. He wondered now for the first time if the claw had really belonged to a *dead* animal. They had prodded and tugged and wrestled to pull it free. What had really lain behind that screen of rocks – a skeleton, or something in a deep sleep?

The second entry he wanted to read had broken his heart at the time, and now called to him like the sounds of a celebration. He found the page and angled it so that the morning sun reflected off paper that was stained, thumbed, creased, and crinkled from more than one soaking. Around the edges, ink had run into little rivulets and pools now dried, but the young handwriting he knew so well was still legible.

Dear Aedan

You weren't at Badgerfields today so I played hide and seek with Thomas and Dara. I decided to hide in the forest and I went in a bit too deep. At first it was fun practising all those bird calls we've been learning and hooting into my fist like an owl (I'm getting really good now) but then I realised it was too quiet and I got muddled trying to find the way home. By the time I got out again it was dark and I was horribly frightened. I'm scared that one day I might get so lost that nobody will find me. I thought that was going to happen today.

It made me think about that story of the little boy who wandered into Nymliss and he was given up for lost by the end of the week. I think most people were just too scared to go and look for him properly.

I wouldn't have been scared if you had been there. You can find anything. I'll never forget the day you took me along a fox trail and we actually saw the fox and her cubs. I don't know how you see prints from those little scuffs in the dirt. I actually thought you were making it up until the vixen growled.

I suppose it's silly to write this in *my* diary, but I'm going to one day ask you to promise me that if I'm ever so lost in the forest that nobody even knows where to start, you will look for me until you find me. I'll draw flowers in the earth and arrange pine cones like hearts, you know, all that girly stuff you tease me about, then you'll know it's me and not some bandit's trail.

I'll have to tell you one of these days.

When you set out, please bring some of Dorothy's muffins because there's nothing to eat in most places that are any good for getting lost in, so I'll probably be starving. But don't wait for her to cook new ones, just take whatever is in the cupboard. And bring my wool jersey too, the old blue one with the holes in the elbows. It's probably going to be lying under the bed or dangling over the chair or hiding under something. Ask Tulia to dig for it.

Just so you know, I'm not asking you to do all this only because you are good at finding things. It's because when I get rescued I want it to be you. It was sort of weird when your father found me once. If I see Emroy first, I think I'll pretend not to see him and stay lost until someone else comes along. He tried to kiss me one time and when I pushed him away he raised his arm like he would hit me. I didn't tell you because I knew you would go and punch him in the face and then he would have tried to use that horrible cane on your head. He is really not a nice boy. He is not allowed to be part of my rescue!

I'm very fussy about this. It has to be you because I want to be found by someone, you know, like a princess being found by a prince. I haven't forgotten that you always made your nose go like wrinkled dead frog skin when those parts of the stories came along, but this is *my* rescue, so I get to say how it happens. If I cry, it will be because I'm happy to bursting. Just remember that. You'll spoil the magic if you ask what's wrong.

I have to go. Dinner's ready. Don't forget about the muffins.

Aedan closed the diary for the last time and slipped it back into its cover, and for the first time, there were no tears. He held it before him and looked again at the image on the case – the toadstool and the sapling. He still remembered asking her what it meant and hadn't forgotten her answer.

"Oh, Aedan! I'd spoil it all if I told you what I think it means before you've had a chance to think too. A mystery is so much more exciting than a wrapped up answer, wouldn't you say? A mystery carries on but an answer just ends."

The following day Aedan had told her that he'd thought about it, and decided it meant slow beginnings were not so bad because the sapling would outgrow the toadstool. Then he demanded her interpretation.

"Maybe," she said with one of her thoughtful, faraway smiles. "But what if it's a toadstool like the pearlnut tree? When I look, I imagine the remains of a tiny picnic under the sapling, and the hasty footprints of the silver dwarf. On the ground are little holes where his sword and arrows were pushed into the ground, just so he could be ready in case of danger. There's a concealed hatch in the side of the toadstool that has been slammed tight, and the grass is starting to move as a wicked creeper approaches, awake like the pearlnut tree, only in a dangerous way. It's a story, an adventure – and it's just beginning."

"So it is," Aedan whispered as he got to his feet and looked out to the west. Out there, far away was Lekrau, and somewhere on the northmost island, she was captive. He wished he could say something to the wind and have it carry the message to her. He raised his eyes to the sky again.

"I'm not sure if you can hear me," he said, "but I don't really think you need a storm to carry you around. And I'm not sure if I can ask you this, but I can't see that you would be angry, so would you mind telling her somehow that I'm getting ready to find her?"

There was no rumbling answer, but neither did he have that awkward feeling of having spoken to nothing.

With a deep breath, full and rich, Aedan turned around and looked at the protruding rungs of the long, shuddering ladder he had climbed in order to gain the top of the wall.

His feet and hands began tingling again, and in a sudden flood of something he could not define and dared not contain, he sprinted past the ladder and leapt off the wall. He hurtled out over an awful drop that was now inevitable. It would be a landing to crush every bone in his legs.

But whatever it was that had blazed in him earlier, now flared up again. He spread his arms and pulled down on the air as it whistled past. It caught in his fingers, almost like water.

And he slowed. Slightly, but enough.

He landed with a solid thud. Dust leapt from the ground, but his legs did not buckle. They felt strong, he felt strong, though he lacked even the beginnings of an explanation.

A stonemason had been working nearby. He was no longer working. His mouth hinged open. A chisel dropped from his grasp unnoticed and clinked into the debris of chippings and rubble.

Aedan stood up from his crouch, peering at his hands and feet with dawning astonishment. Gradually, he became aware of the stonemason and realised he was the object of the man's gaping stare, so he nodded a greeting and jogged away, a slow smile growing across his face.

He had a book to finish today. He would make it two.

END OF BOOK ONE

Author's Note

Some writers manage to work effectively in the gaps around a day job, but I've never had much success that way. I wrote for about ten years part-time, and while I scratched and tapped a good deal and learned a good deal more, I could never keep a big idea together during extended interruptions when the day job burst its banks and stole personal time. I also found that much of what I wrote in the exhausted hours around work was as flat as the way I'd felt while grinding it out.

Eventually, I realised that in order to imagine, capture and build the first part of this story, I needed uninterrupted time – and lots of it. Without the gift of time, there is no way I could have finished this book.

So I would like to thank my parents for constant, generous, trusting, uncomplaining support, without which my collected efforts would have been no better than one of Osric's stews – an under- over-done disaster of little bits and pieces glued into a sticky and unpalatable confusion, prose to be attempted only by the very brave or the closely related.

Then, much is owed to Richard Allen who did the scene sketches and fought his way through a thorny first draft in order to arrive, torn and bleeding, at the idea for the first cover. He made hundreds of corrections to the text and gave many excellent suggestions. The sketches are even better than I'd hoped; they truly open up the world of the story. Fantastic work, bro!

Many thanks to Jared Mitchell for appearing on the original cover and for the hours spent putting up with cameras as we acted out the scenes for the sketches.

To Werner Botha and Dhruva Moodley from Animmate, I deeply appreciate the professional skill and impressive work ethic you showed. The new cover has captured that scene in front of Kultûhm in a way I only dreamed possible. (The scene, if anyone is wondering, is of Aedan staring up at the fortress just before Culver's party finds the tunnel beneath the stone giant).

To the proof readers (whose feedback in many cases was too deep and detailed for me to call them beta readers), surname-alphabetically: Richard Allen, Ed Dalton, Hamilton Elliott, Adam

Fairall, Valerie Ganzevoort, Elizabeth Haber, Samantha Hawkins, Angie Hayler, William Inman, Danny Jacobs, Brad Kingon, Rob and Ally Jones, Jean MacCallum, Wendy Morgan, Brent Meyers, Bryony Nicol, Max Painter, Stephen Pohlman, Andrew Poppleton, John Poppleton, Leandra Scheepers, David Tapp, Jeff Thompson, Gary Van Lieshout, Jason Viljoen, and then my family – Shaun & Charnell, Josh & Carol-Ann, Kitta & Andy, and of course, Mom and Dad.

I cannot even begin to explain how much improvement you were responsible for – not just typos, but fixes to character, plot and artwork. I am so grateful for the time you made to read, to consider what you'd read, and then provide me with pages of comments, suggestions and reference material, all of which have made this a much, much better book than it was. You guys are amazing!

To the reader, thank you for beginning this journey with me. I really value the company of every reader and hope that you've enjoyed the story so far.

I'd love to hear from you. If you're able to write a review of this book, I'd greatly appreciate it. Every review helps pave the way to future books in the series (or, if the reviews are terrible, they will help pave the way to a different career). Either way, honest reviews are helpful to both writers and readers. If you spot any typos (bearing in mind that I use UK spelling and grammar) please mail me. I'll be more than happy to credit you on the website.

If you would like to keep up with releases, beginning with the sequel to this book, the surest way to stay in the loop is by joining the mailing list at www.jrenshaw.com. I guarantee you won't get spammed with progress updates and all that sort of thing. The email will go out only when the next book is ready.

You can find me at www.jrenshaw.com or on facebook: Jonathan Renshaw (Author), www.facebook.com/authorjrenshaw.

I hope to meet with you again in book 2, and this time you'd better bring an oilskin …

Made in the USA
San Bernardino, CA
25 November 2017